Dark Ter...

THE GOLLANCZ BOOK OF HORROR

Also available from Gollancz

Dark Terrors
Dark Terrors 2
Dark Terrors 3
Dark Terrors 4
Dark Terrors 5

Also edited by Stephen Jones
and available in paperback

Shadows over Innsmouth

Dancing with the Dark

The Conan Chronicles Volume 1:
The People of the Black Circle by Robert E. Howard

The Conan Chronicles Volume 2:
The Hour of the Dragon by Robert E. Howard

The Emperor of Dreams by Clark Ashton Smith

Dark Terrors 6

THE GOLLANCZ BOOK OF HORROR

Edited by
Stephen Jones and David Sutton

GOLLANCZ

LONDON

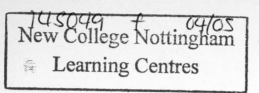
This compilation Copyright © Stephen Jones and David Sutton 2002

All rights reserved

The right of individual contributors to be
identified as the authors of this work has been
asserted by them in accordance with the
Copyright, Designs and Patents Act 1988.

This edition published in Great Britain in 2002 by

Victor Gollancz
An imprint of Orion Books Ltd
Orion House, 5 Upper St Martin's Lane, London WC2H 9EA

A CIP catalogue record for this book is available
from the British Library

ISBN 0 575 07248 2 (cased)
ISBN 0 575 07249 0 (trade paperback)

Typeset by SetSystems Ltd, Saffron Walden, Essex

Printed in Great Britain by
Clays Ltd, St Ives plc

Contents

About the Editors

Stephen Jones lives in London. He is the winner of two World Fantasy Awards, three Horror Writers Association Bram Stoker Awards and two International Horror Guild Awards, as well as being a thirteen-time recipient of the British Fantasy Award and a Hugo Award nominee. A former television producer/director and genre-movie publicist and consultant (the first three *Hellraiser* movies, *Night Life*, *Nightbreed*, *Split Second*, *Mind Ripper*, *Last Gasp*, etc.), he is the co-editor of *Horror: 100 Best Books*, *The Best Horror from Fantasy Tales*, *Gaslight & Ghosts*, *Now We Are Sick*, *H. P. Lovecraft's Book of Horror*, *The Anthology of Fantasy & the Supernatural*, *Secret City: Strange Tales of London* and *The Mammoth Book of Best New Horror*, *Dark Terrors*, *Dark Voices* and *Fantasy Tales* series. He has written *Creepshows: The Illustrated Stephen King Movie Guide*, *The Essential Monster Movie Guide*, *The Illustrated Vampire Movie Guide*, *The Illustrated Dinosaur Movie Guide*, *The Illustrated Frankenstein Movie Guide* and *The Illustrated Werewolf Movie Guide*, and compiled *The Mammoth Book of Terror*, *The Mammoth Book of Vampires*, *The Mammoth Book of Zombies*, *The Mammoth Book of Dracula*, *The Mammoth Book of Vampire Stories by Women*, *Shadows over Innsmouth*, *Dancing with the Dark*, *Dark of the Night*, *Dark Detectives*, *White of the Moon*, *Keep Out the Night*, *Exorcisms and Ecstasies* by Karl Edward Wagner, *The Vampire Stories of R. Chetwynd-Hayes*, *Phantoms and Fiends* and *Frights and Fancies* by R. Chetwynd-Hayes, *James Herbert: By Horror Haunted*, *The Conan Chronicles* by Robert E. Howard (two volumes), *The Emperor of Dreams: The Lost Worlds of Clark Ashton Smith*, *Clive Barker's A–Z of Horror*, *Clive Barker's Shadows in Eden*, *Clive Barker's The Nightbreed Chronicles* and the *Hellraiser Chronicles*. You can visit his web site at www.herebedragons.co.uk/jones

David Sutton lives in Birmingham. He has won the World Fantasy Award, The International Horror Guild Award and twelve British Fantasy Awards. Anthologies under his editorship include *New Writings in Horror & the Supernatural* (two volumes), *The Satyr's Head & Other Tales of Terror* and, jointly edited with Stephen Jones, *The Best Horror from Fantasy Tales*, *The Anthology of Fantasy & the Supernatural*, *Dark Voices: The Pan Book of Horror Stories* (five volumes) and the *Dark Terrors* series. Recent publications include *Voices from Shadow*, a non-fiction anthology celebrating the twentieth anniversary of his magazine *Shadow*; *On the Fringe for Thirty Years: A History of Horror in the British Small Press*, and the anthology *Phantoms of Venice*, all from Shadow Publishing. You can visit his web site at http://ourworld.compuserve.com/homepages/davesandra

Acknowledgements

Special thanks, as always, to our indefatigable editor, Jo Fletcher.

Introduction

Horror is changing. Once again a new generation of writers is emerging, and many of them are already firmly established as tomorrow's stars of horror fiction.

The pulp writers (those who are still with us) and the bestselling authors of the 1980s horror boom are beginning to find themselves eclipsed by newer names who are carving out solid reputations for themselves through sheer hard work and perseverance. And with most of the mainstream publishers on both sides of the Atlantic including little or no horror on their lists any more, many of these newcomers have emerged over the past decade from the so-called small press, where they have honed their skills in small-circulation magazines and limited-edition books.

As always, some of these new writers will find their careers falling by the wayside (writing is, at best, a precarious way to earn a living), but many others will survive and, hopefully, flourish in a field which has never been stronger in terms of creativity, if not commerciality.

Yet sometimes these fledgling authors still need a break. It is often all too easy to be lauded by your peers when you are all working in the same, small field of endeavour. Sometimes these writers require a forum to bring their work to a wider (and perhaps more discerning) readership.

That is where *Dark Terrors* comes in. With this bumper sixth volume we have attempted to include as many different representations of horror fiction as we can, from quiet, psychological terror to hardgore splatter; from the supernatural to science fiction; from high adventure to black comedy. The full range of horror's literary strengths are presented within these covers, conjured up by a range of writers whose careers span at least five decades.

So do not worry if you have not heard of some of our contributors before. Read their stories anyway. All the writers in this volume already come with a pedigree, and for those newer names, this will, we trust, provide an opportunity for them to present their work to a more extensive audience while they establish themselves in an often much-maligned genre.

As we have said before, we do not expect our readers to enjoy every single story in a book of this size (although, of course, it is always gratifying when they tell us that they did so). However, you will experience more than the occasional shudder while enjoying the fearsome feast laid out over the following pages, and we hope that you will discover a writer or two who was perhaps unfamiliar to you and whose work you will be inspired to seek out in the future. That is the only way in which those authors and, indeed, the horror field itself, can continue to develop and flourish.

Stephen Jones and David Sutton
April, 2002

The Retrospective

RAMSEY CAMPBELL

Trent had no idea how long he was unable to think for rage. The guard kept out of sight while she announced the unscheduled stop, and didn't reappear until the trainload of passengers had crowded onto the narrow platform. As the train dragged itself away into a tunnel simulated by elderly trees and the low March afternoon sky that was plastered with layers of darkness, she poked her head out of the rearmost window to announce that the next train should be due in an hour. The resentful mutters of the crowd only aggravated Trent's frustration. He needed a leisurely evening and, if he could manage it for a change, a night's sleep in preparation for a working breakfast. If he'd known the journey would be broken, he could have reread his paperwork instead of contemplating scenery he couldn't even remember. No doubt the next train would already be laden with commuters – he doubted it would give him space to work. His skull was beginning to feel shrivelled and hollow when it occurred to him that if he caught a later train he would both ensure himself a seat and have time to drop in on his parents. When had he last been home to see them? All at once he felt so guilty that he preferred not to look anyone in the face as he excused his slow way to the ticket office.

It was closed – a board lent it the appearance of a frame divested of a photograph – but flanked by a timetable. Stoneby to London, Stoneby to London ... There were trains on the hour, like the striking of a clock. He emerged from the short wooden passage into the somewhat less gloomy street, only to falter. Where was the sweet shop whose window used to exhibit dozens of glass-stoppered jars full of colours he could taste? Where was the toyshop fronted by a headlong model train that had never stopped for the travellers paralysed on the platform? What had happened to the bakery displaying tiered white cakes elaborate as Gothic steeples, and the bridal shop next door, where the headless figures in their pale dresses had made him think of Anne

Boleyn? Now the street was overrun with the same fast-food eateries and immature clothes shops that surrounded him whenever he left his present apartment, and he couldn't recall how much change he'd seen on his last visit, whenever that had been. He felt suddenly so desperate to be somewhere more like home that he almost didn't wait for twin green men to pipe up and usher him across the road.

The short cut was still there, in a sense. Instead of separating the toyshop from the wedding dresses, it squeezed between a window occupied by a regiment of boots and a hamburger outlet dogged by plastic cartons. Once he was in the alley the clamour of traffic relented, but the narrow passage through featureless discoloured concrete made him feel walled in by the unfamiliar. Then the concrete gave way to russet bricks and released him into a street he knew.

At least, it conformed to his memory until he looked closer. The building opposite, which had begun life as a music hall, had ceased to be a cinema. A pair of letters clung to the whitish border of the rusty iron marquee, two letters N so insecure they were on the way to being Zs. He was striving to remember if the cinema had been shut last time he'd seen it when he noticed that the boards on either side of the lobby contained posters too small for the frames. The neighbouring buildings were boarded up. As he crossed the deserted street, the posters grew legible. MEMORIES OF STONEBY, the amateurish printing said.

The two wide steps beneath the marquee were cracked and chipped and stained. The glass of the ticket booth in the middle of the marble floor was too blackened to see through. Behind the booth the doors into the auditorium stood ajar. Uncertain what the gap was showing him, he ventured to peer in.

At first the dimness yielded up no more than a strip of carpet framed by floorboards just as grubby, and then he thought someone absolutely motionless was watching him from the dark. The watcher was roped off from him – the several indistinct figures were. He assumed they represented elements of local history: there was certainly something familiar about them. That impression, and the blurred faces with their dully glinting eyes, might have transfixed him if he hadn't remembered that he was supposed to be seeing his parents. He left the echo of his footsteps dwindling in the lobby and hurried around the side of the museum.

Where the alley crossed another he turned left along the rear of the building. In the high wall to his right a series of solid wooden gates led to back yards, the third of which belonged to his old house. As a child he'd used the gate as a short cut to the cinema, clutching a coin in his fist, which had smelled of metal whenever he'd raised it to his face in the crowded restless dark. His parents had never bolted the gate until he was home again, but now the only effect of his trying the latch was to rouse a clatter of claws and the snarling of a neighbour's dog that sounded either muzzled or gagged with food, and so he made for the street his old house faced.

The sunless sky was bringing on a twilight murky as an unlit room. He could have taken the street for an aisle between two blocks of dimness so lacking in features they might have been identical. Presumably any children who lived in the terrace were home from school by now, though he couldn't see the flicker of a single television in the windows draped with dusk, while the breadwinners had yet to return. Trent picked his way over the broken upheaved slabs of the pavement, supporting himself on the roof of a lone parked car until it shifted rustily under his hand, to his parents' front gate.

The small plot of a garden was a mass of weeds that had spilled across the short path. He couldn't feel it underfoot as he tramped to the door, which was the colour of the oncoming dark. He was fumbling in his pocket and then with the catches of his briefcase when he realised he would hardly have brought his old keys with him. He rang the doorbell, or at least pressed the askew pallid button that set off a muffled rattle somewhere in the house.

For the duration of more breaths than he could recall taking, there was no response. He was about to revive the noise, though he found it somehow distressing, when he heard footsteps shuffling down the hall. Their slowness made it sound as long as it had seemed in his childhood, so that he had the odd notion that whoever opened the door would tower over him.

It was his mother, and smaller than ever – wrinkled and whitish as a figure composed of dough that had been left to collect dust, a wad of it on top of and behind her head. She wore a tweed coat over a garment he took to be a nightdress, which exposed only her prominent ankles above a pair of unmatched slippers. Her head wavered upwards as the corners of her lips did. Once all these had steadied she murmured 'Is it you, Nigel? Are you back again?'

'I thought it was past time I was.'

'It's always too long.' She shuffled in a tight circle to present her stooped back to him before calling 'Guess who it is, Walter.'

'Hess looking for a place to hide,' Trent's father responded from some depth of the house.

'No, not old red-nosed Rudolph. Someone a bit younger and a bit more English.'

'The Queen come to tea.'

'He'll never change, will he?' Trent's mother muttered and raised what was left of her voice. 'It's the boy. It's Nigel.'

'About time. Let's see what he's managed to make of himself.'

She made a gesture like a desultory grab at something in the air above her left shoulder, apparently to beckon Trent along the hall. 'Be quick with the door, there's a good boy. We don't want the chill roosting in our old bones.'

As soon as the door shut behind him he couldn't distinguish whether the stairs that narrowed the hall by half were carpeted only with dimness. He trudged after his mother past a door that seemed barely sketched on the crawling murk and, more immediately than he expected, another. His mother opened a third, beyond which was the kitchen, he recalled rather than saw. It smelled of damp he hoped was mostly tea. By straining his senses he was just able to discern his father seated in some of the dark. 'Shall we have the light on?' Trent suggested.

'Can't you see? Thought you were supposed to be the young one round here.' After a pause his father said 'Come back for bunny, have you?'

Trent couldn't recall ever having owned a rabbit, toy or otherwise, yet the question seemed capable of reviving some aspect of his child-hood. He was feeling surrounded by entirely too much darkness when his mother said 'Now, Walter, don't be teasing' and clicked the switch.

The naked dusty bulb seemed to draw the contents of the room inwards – the blackened stove and stained metal sink, the venerable shelves and cabinets and cupboards Trent's father had built, the glossy pallid walls. The old man was sunk in an armchair, the least appropriate of an assortment of seats surrounding the round table decorated with crumbs and unwashed plates. His pear-shaped variously reddish face appeared to have been given over to producing fat to merge with the rest of him. He used both shaky inflated hands to close the lapels of his faded dressing gown over his pendulous chest cobwebbed with grey hairs. 'You've got your light,' he said, 'so take your place.'

Lowering himself onto a chair that had once been straight, Trent lost sight of the entrance to the alley – of the impression that it was the only aspect of the yard the window managed to illuminate. 'Will I make you some tea?' his mother said.

She wasn't asking him to predict the future, he reassured himself. 'So long as you're both having some as well.'

'Not much else to do these days.'

'It won't be that bad really, will it?' Trent said, forcing a guilty laugh. 'Aren't you still seeing . . .'

'What are we seeing?' his father prompted with some force.

'Your friends,' Trent said, having discovered that he couldn't recall a single name. 'They can't all have moved away.'

'Nobody moves any longer.'

Trent didn't know whether to take that as a veiled rebuke. 'So what have you two been doing with yourselves lately?'

'Late's the word.'

'Nigel's here now,' Trent's mother said, perhaps relevantly, over the descending hollow drum-roll of the kettle she was filling from the tap.

More time than was reasonable seemed to have passed since he'd entered the house. He was restraining himself from glancing even surreptitiously at his watch when his father quivered an impatient hand at him. 'So what are you up to now?'

'He means your work.'

'Same as always.'

Trent hoped that would suffice until he was able to reclaim his memory from the darkness that had gathered in his skull, but his parents' stares were as blank as his mind. 'And what's that?' his mother said.

He felt as though her forgetfulness had seized him. Desperate to be reminded what his briefcase contained, he nevertheless used reaching for it as a chance to glimpse his watch. The next train was due in less than half an hour. As Trent scrabbled at the catches of the briefcase, his father said 'New buildings, isn't it? That's what you put up.'

'Plan,' Trent said, clutching the briefcase on his lap. 'I draw them.'

'Of course you do,' said his mother. 'That's what you always wanted.'

It was partly so as not to feel minimised that Trent declared 'I wouldn't want to be responsible for some of the changes in town.'

'Then don't be.'

'You won't see much else changing round here,' Trent's mother said.

'Didn't anyone object?'

'You have to let the world move on,' she said. 'Leave it to the young ones.'

Trent wasn't sure if he was included in that or only wanted to be. 'How long have we had a museum?'

His father's eyes grew so blank Trent could have fancied they weren't in use. 'Since I remember.'

'No, that's not right,' Trent objected as gently as his nerves permitted. 'It was a cinema and before that a theatre. You took me to a show there once.'

'Did we?' A glint surfaced in his mother's eyes. 'We used to like shows, didn't we, Walter? Shows and dancing. Didn't we go on all night sometimes and they wondered where we'd got to?'

Her husband shook his head once slowly, whether to enliven memories or deny their existence Trent couldn't tell. 'The show you took me to,' he insisted, 'I remember someone dancing with a stick. And there was a lady comedian, or maybe not a lady but dressed up.'

Perhaps it was the strain of excavating the recollection that made it seem both lurid and encased in darkness – the outsize figure prancing sluggishly about the stage and turning towards him a sly greasy smile as crimson as a wound, the ponderous slap on the boards of feet that sounded unshod, the onslaughts of laughter that followed comments Trent found so incomprehensible he feared they were about him, the shadow that kept swelling on whatever backdrop the performer had, an effect suggesting that the figure was about to grow yet more gigantic. Surely some or preferably most of that was a childhood nightmare rather than a memory. 'Was there some tea?' Trent blurted.

At first it seemed his mother's eyes were past seeing through their own blankness. 'In the show, do you mean?'

'Here.' When that fell short of her he said more urgently 'Now.'

'Why, you should have reminded me,' she protested and stood up. How long had she been seated opposite him? He was so anxious to remember that he didn't immediately grasp what she was doing. 'Mother, don't,' he nearly screamed, flinging himself off his chair.

'No rush. It isn't anything like ready.' She took her hand out of the kettle on the stove – he wasn't sure if he glimpsed steam trailing from her fingers as she replaced the lid. 'We haven't got much longer, have we?' she said. 'We mustn't keep you from your duties.'

'You won't do that again, will you?'

'What's that, son?'

He was dismayed to think she might already have forgotten. 'You won't put yourself in danger.'

'There's nothing we'd call that round here,' his father said.

'You'll look after each other, won't you? I really ought to catch the next train. I'll be back to see you again soon, I promise, and next time it'll be longer.'

'It will.'

His parents said that not quite in chorus, apparently competing at slowness. 'Till next time, then,' he said and shook his father's hand before hugging his mother. Both felt disconcertingly cold and unyielding, as if the appearance of each had hardened into a carapace. He gripped the handle of his briefcase while he strove to twist the rusty key in the back door. 'I'll go my old way, shall I? It's quicker.'

When nobody answered he hauled open the door, which felt unhinged. Cobwebbed weeds sprawled over the doorstep into the kitchen at once. Weedy mounds of earth or rubble had overwhelmed the yard and the path. He picked his way to the gate and with an effort turned his head, but nobody was following to close the gate: his mother was still at her post by the stove, his father was deep in the armchair. He had to use both hands to wrench the bolt out of its socket, and almost forgot to retrieve his briefcase as he stumbled into the alley. The passage was unwelcomingly dark, not least because the light from the house failed to reach it – no, because the kitchen was unlit. He dragged the gate shut and took time to engage the latch before heading for the rear of the museum.

Damp must be stiffening his limbs. He hoped it was in the air, not in his parents' house. Was it affecting his vision as well? When he slogged to the end of the alley the street appeared to be composed of little but darkness, except for the museum. The doors to the old auditorium were further ajar, and as he crossed the road Trent saw figures miming in the dimness. He hadn't time to identify their faces before panting down the alley where brick was ousted by concrete.

Figures sat in the stark restaurants and modelled clothes in windows. Otherwise the street was deserted except for a man who dashed into the station too fast for Trent to see his face. The man let fly a wordless plea and waved his briefcase as he sprinted through the booking hall. Trent had just begun to precipitate himself across the road when he heard the slam of a carriage door. He staggered ahead of his breath onto the platform in time to see the last light of a train vanish into the trees, which looked more like a tunnel than ever.

His skull felt frail with rage again. Once he regained the ability to move he stumped to glower at the timetable next to the boarded-up office. His fiercest glare was unable to change the wait into less than an hour. He marched up and down a few times, but each end of the platform met him with increasing darkness. He had to keep moving to ward off a chill stiffness. He trudged into the street and frowned about him.

The fast-food outlets didn't appeal to him, neither their impersonal refreshments nor the way all the diners faced the street as though to watch him. not that doing so lent them any animation. He couldn't even see anyone eating. Ignoring the raw red childishly sketched men, he lurched across the road into the alley.

He oughtn't to go to his parents. So instant a return might well confuse them, and just now his own mind felt more than sufficiently unfocused. The only light, however tentative, in the next street came from the museum. He crossed the roadway, which was as lightless as the low sky, and climbed the faint steps.

Was the ticket booth lit? A patch of the blackened glass had been rubbed relatively clear from within. He was fumbling for money to plant on the sill under the gap at the foot of the window when he managed to discern that the figure in the booth was made of wax. While it resembled the middle-aged woman who had occupied the booth when the building was a cinema, it ought to look years – no, decades – older. Its left grey-cardiganed arm was raised to indicate the auditorium. He was unable to judge its expression for the gloom inside the booth. Tramping to the doors, he pushed them wide.

That seemed only to darken the auditorium, but he felt the need to keep on the move before his eyes had quite adjusted. The apparently sourceless twilight put him in mind of the glow doled out by the candle that used to stand in an encrusted saucer on the table by his childhood bed. As he advanced under the enormous unseen roof, he thought he was walking on the same carpet that had led into the cinema and indeed the theatre. He was abreast of the first of the figures on either side of the aisle before he recognised them.

He'd forgotten they were sisters, the two women who had run the bakery and the adjacent bridal shop. Had they really been twins? They were playing bridesmaids in identical white ankle-length dresses – whitish, rather, and trimmed with dust. Presumably it was muslin as well as dust that gloved their hands, which were pointing with all their digits along the aisle. The dull glints of their grimy eyes appeared to spy sidelong on him. He'd taken only a few steps when he stumbled to a halt and peered about him.

The next exhibits were disconcerting enough. No doubt the toyshop owner was meant to be introducing his model railway, but he looked as if he was crouching sideways to grab whatever sought refuge in the miniature tunnel. Opposite him the sweetshop man was enticing children to his counter, which was heaped with sweets powdered grey, by performing on a sugar whistle not entirely distinguishable from his glimmering teeth. Trent hadn't time to ascertain what was odd about the children's wide round eyes, because he was growing aware of the extent of the museum.

Surely it must be a trick of the unreliable illumination, but the more he gazed around him, the further the dimness populated with unmoving figures seemed to stretch. If it actually extended so far ahead and to both sides, it would encompass at least the whole of the street that contained his parents' house. He wavered forward a couple of paces, which only encouraged figures to solidify out of that part of the murk. He swivelled as quickly as he was able and stalked out of the museum.

The echoes of his footsteps pursued him across the lobby like mocking applause. He could hear no other sound, and couldn't tell whether he was being watched from the ticket booth. He found his way down the marble steps and along the front of the museum. In a few seconds he was sidling crabwise along it in order to differentiate the alley from the unlit façade. He wandered further than he should have, and made his way back more slowly. Before long he was groping with his free hand at the wall as he ranged back and forth, but it was no use. There was no alley, just unbroken brick.

He was floundering in search of a crossroads, from which there surely had to be a route to his old house, when he realised he might as well be blind. He glanced back, praying wordlessly for any relief from the dark. There was only the glow from the museum lobby. It seemed as feeble as the candle flame had grown in the moment before it guttered into smoke, and so remote he thought his stiff limbs might be past carrying him to it. When he retreated towards it, at first he seemed not to be moving at all.

More time passed than he could grasp before he felt sure the light was closer. Later still he managed to distinguish the outstretched fingertips of his free hand. He clung to his briefcase as though it might be snatched from him. He was abreast of the lobby, and preparing to abandon its glow for the alley that led to the station, when he thought he heard a whisper from inside the museum. 'Are you looking for us?'

It was either a whisper, or so distant that it might as well be one. 'We're in here, son,' it said, and its companion added 'You'll have to come to us.'

'Mother?' It was unquestionably her voice, however faint. He almost tripped over the steps as he sent himself into the lobby. For a moment, entangled in the clapping of his footsteps on the marble, he thought he heard a large but muted sound, as of the surreptitious arrangement of a crowd. He blundered to the doors and peered into the auditorium.

Under the roof, which might well have been an extension of the low ponderous black sky, the aisle and its guardians were at least as dim as ever. Had things changed, or had he failed to notice details earlier? The bridal sisters were licking their lips, and he wasn't sure if they were dressed as bridesmaids or baked into giant tiered cakes from which they were trying to struggle free. Both of the toyshop owner's hands looked eager to seize the arrested train if it should try to reach the safety of the tunnel, and the bulging eyes of the children crowded around the man with the sugar whistle – were those sweets? Trent might have retreated if his mother's voice hadn't spoken to him. 'That's it, son. Don't leave us this time.'

'Have a thought for us. Don't start us wondering where you are again. We're past coming to find you.'

'Where are you? I can't see.'

'Just carry on straight,' his parents' voices took it in turns to murmur.

He faltered before lurching between the first exhibits. Beyond them matters could hardly be said to improve. He did his best not to see too much of the milkman holding the reins of a horse while a cow followed the cart, but the man's left eye seemed large enough for the horse, the right for the cow. Opposite him stood a rag and bone collector whose trade was apparent from the companion that hung onto his arm, and Trent was almost glad of the flickering dimness. 'How much further?' he cried in a voice that the place shrank almost to nothing.

'No more than you can walk at your age.'

Trent hung onto the impression that his father sounded closer than before and hugged his briefcase while he made his legs carry him past a policeman who'd removed his helmet to reveal a bald-ridged head as pointed as a chrysalis, a priest whose smooth face was balanced on a collar of the same paleness as and no thicker than a child's wrist, a window cleaner with scrawny legs folded like a grasshopper's, a bus conductor choked by his tie that was caught in his ticket machine while at the front of the otherwise deserted vehicle the driver displayed exactly the same would-be comical strangled face and askew swollen tongue . . . They were nightmares, Trent told himself: some he remembered having suffered as a child, and the rest he was afraid to remember in case they grew clearer. 'I still can't see you,' he all but wailed.

'Down here, son.'

Did they mean ahead? He hoped he wasn't being told to use any of the side aisles, not least because they seemed capable of demonstrating that the place was even vaster than he feared. The sights they contained were more elaborate too. Off to the right was a brass band, not marching but frozen in the act of tiptoeing towards him: though all the players had lowered their instruments, their mouths were perfectly round. In the dimness to his left, and scarcely more luminous, was a reddish bonfire surrounded by figures that wore charred masks, unless those were their faces, and beyond that was a street party where children sat at trestle tables strewn with food and grimaced in imitation of the distorted versions of their faces borne by deflating balloons they held on strings . . . Trent twisted his stiff body around in case some form of reassurance was to be found behind him, but the exit to the lobby was so distant he could have mistaken it for the last of a flame. He half closed his eyes to blot out the sights he had to pass, only to find that made the shadows of the exhibits and the darkness into which the shadows trailed loom closer, as if the dimness was on the point of being finally extinguished. He was suddenly aware that if the building had still been a theatre, the aisle would have brought him to the stage by now. 'Where are you?' he called but was afraid to raise his voice. 'Can't you speak?'

'Right here.'

His eyes sprang so wide they felt fitted into their sockets. His parents weren't just close, they were behind him. He turned with difficulty and saw why he'd strayed past them. His mother was wearing a top hat and tails and had finished twirling a cane that resembled a lengthening of one knobbly finger; his father was bulging out of a shabby flowered dress that failed to conceal several sections of a pinkish bra. They'd dressed up to cure Trent of his nightmare about the theatre perform- ance, he remembered, but they had only brought it into his waking hours. He backed away from it – from their waxen faces greyish with down, their smiles as fixed as their eyes. His legs collided with an object that folded them up, and he tottered sideways to sit helplessly on it. 'That's it, son,' his mother succeeded in murmuring.

'That's your place,' his father said with a last shifting of his lips.

Trent glared downwards and saw he was trapped by a school desk barely large enough to accommodate him. On either side of him sat motionless children as furred with grey as their desks, even their eyes. Between him and his parents a teacher in a gown and mortarboard was standing not quite still and sneering at him. 'Mr Bunnie,' Trent gasped, remembering how the teacher had always responded to being addressed by his name as though it was an insult. Then, in a moment of clarity that felt like a beacon in the dark, he realised he had some defence. 'This isn't me,' he tried to say calmly but firmly. 'This is.'

His fingers were almost too unmanageable to deal with the briefcase.

He levered at the rusty metal buttons with his thumbs until at last the catches flew open and the contents spilled across the desk. For a breath, if he had any, Trent couldn't see them in the dimness, and then he made out that they were half a dozen infantile crayon drawings of houses. 'I've done more than that,' he struggled to protest, 'I am more,' but his mouth had finished working. He managed only to raise his head, and never knew which was worse: his paralysis, or his parents' doting smiles, or the sneer that the teacher's face seemed to have widened to encompass – the sneer that had always meant that once a child was inside the school gates, his parents could no longer protect him. It might have been an eternity before the failure of the dimness or of Trent's eyes . . .

Ramsey Campbell has received more awards for horror fiction than any other writer. He has been named Grand Master by the World Horror Convention and received a Lifetime Achievement Award from the Horror Writers Association. A film of his novel *Pact of the Fathers* is in development in Spain, *The Darkest Part of the Woods* is his latest supernatural novel, and he is currently working on another, *The Overnight*. Campbell's M. R. Jamesian anthology *Meddling with Ghosts* is published by the British Library, and he has co-edited *Gathering the Bones* with Jack Dann and Dennis Etchison. S. T. Joshi's study *Ramsey Campbell and Modern Horror Fiction* is available from Liverpool University Press, while *Ramsey Campbell, Probably* is a large non-fiction collection from PS Publishing. According to the author, ' "The Retrospective" grew from the idea of the museum in an unfamiliar town. It feels to me somewhat like my tribute to Thomas Ligotti.'

We're Going Where the Sun Shines Brightly

CHRISTOPHER FOWLER

'No more fairy stories at nanny's knee it is all aboard the fairy bus for the dungeons'

Geoffrey Willans

'He's just an innocent,' said Dougie, lighting a grubby dog-end. 'You have to fall from grace before you can understand anything adult. He couldn't see that she wasn't interested in him. She was really old, thirty at least.'

'And he was still chasing her around the bar when you left?' I asked.

'Mickie will try to shag anything.' Dougie examined the end of his cigarette with distaste. 'Because he's a pathetic virgin.'

'Thirty, and she still turned him down?' I wasn't about to mention that I was also a virgin.

'She had a face like a rag and bone man's horse, and it didn't put him off. The whole thing was creepy.' Dougie swallowed smoke and had a coughing fit. 'Roll on summer holidays.'

'Roll on summer holidays.'

We were on our fag break, up near the roof of the Aldenham Bus & Coach Overhaul Works. Through the hangar doors you could see it was grey and raining.

'We'll have two weeks to get him laid then,' said Dougie, once he'd got his breath back. 'If he doesn't get a bird soon he's going to do himself a mischief.'

If he does get a bird, I remember thinking, *she's the one he'll do mischief to*. Mickie had scary energy, undirected, uncontrolled. I assumed it was because he was young; we all were.

The Aldenham Bus & Coach Overhaul Works was built on the site of an old aerodrome. The aircraft hangars that had once housed Mosquitoes and Hurricanes had been converted to contain machinery. The uneven concrete squares of the runways were empty and pockmarked by pools of iridescent water. Beyond were the wet green hedgerows that shielded the factory from the arterial road. The glory of war days still haunted the horizons of the surrounding meadows, a taunting memory of something nobler.

I was one of the youngest workers. I hated the job, the old men who smelled of roll-ups and sweat, the acrid air of filing-dust and rust, the sinus-sting of spray-paint that hung in the thick air, the machines that shuddered and punched panels from sheets of steel. The sheds churned with the thought-destroying thump of the presses, like the noise of an endless summer storm, its sound condensed and released by the high whine of pistons. Everything around me was black and brown and shades of grey, drained of any sensation other than the slam of the safety barriers and the shake of steel sheeting that vibrated through the soles of your boots.

I wasn't stupid. I didn't think that working in this place was all there was to life. I sensed – but had no way of knowing for sure – that the world beyond the factory was filled with mysteries. I had been growing increasingly restless at home. I lay on my bed, listening to the strikes and reprisals of my parents' conversation, and felt that somewhere, away from the odour of unused rooms and beeswaxed sideboards, away from the bitter tang of factory metal, there were beautiful girls who laughed and threw themselves recklessly into the arms of boys the same age as me. I wasn't going to be like Mickie, getting drunk and chasing old boilers around pubs all night. I was going to make something of myself.

I was not alone in my dreams. There were four of us; Dougie had thick square glasses and worked weekends in a hardware store, saving every penny he earned for plans he had no imagination to realise. Mickie was skinny and blond and never took off his cap, and went on about girls in a voice that cracked like someone skating on thin ice. Chris wore his hair in a perfectly greased quiff, and spoke in an attempt at a refined voice. His clothes were always perfectly ironed. He was too worried about what other people thought to ever let himself relax, and insisted on calling us 'fellas', 'Hey fellas. I've got a great idea,' as though he was in one of those youth films from the sixties that now look as though they come from another world, Planet Politeness. But of course it *was* the sixties, we were teenagers, and none of us had a clue about the corruption of time.

It was Chris's 'Hey, fellas, I've got a great idea,' that started it. His idea sounded hopeless, especially as we had only seven days to go before the start of our summer holidays. Dougie and I were on a fag break, sitting waiting for Chris, when we saw him driving toward us through the rain, and at that moment we realised dreams were possible, and our world turned into Technicolor.

Chris had heard that London Transport might be willing to sell one of their old Routemaster buses, and managed to persuade them to let him have it on the condition that we did it up, because its seats were slashed to bits and its engine was knackered. And it was my idea to have some of the blokes at the factory overhaul the engine and convert the interior into something more liveable, so that it ended up looking like a double-decker caravan, even though we kept the red exterior and the number and destination board proclaiming it to be a Number 9 heading for Piccadilly.

Suddenly we had a chance to fulfil our dreams, and there was a way to escape the troglodyte days of the English summer. We no longer had to make do with the bandstands, chip-shops and smutty-postcard racks of the South Coast. We would fix up the bus and head for the South of France, where the sky was wide, the sea was warm and the promenades were filled with the promise of sex.

We only managed to get the bus roadworthy by paying mates to work late, so that by the time we were granted our licence we were almost broke, but we were so determined to escape that nothing was going to stop us. On a drizzly Saturday morning we headed for Calais with some half-baked idea that we might even get as far as Greece before having to turn around. Mickie thought if we proved the journey was manageable to the bus company they might allow us to take fee-paying guests on charter trips, but we hadn't thought any of it through. It just seemed possible; everything is possible when you don't know the drawbacks. Opportunity can present itself to innocents just as much as it can to corrupt old men, and we had an advantage: we were the young ones.

It seemed that the sun began shining at Calais, and as the bus laboured to leave the hills of the town we saw only empty sunlit roads ahead, tarmac dappled in cool green shadows of the trees. We didn't reach Paris until dusk the following day (the bus's top speed was none too impressive), and went bouncing off to meet girls in the bars of Montmartre. We didn't get to meet girls; we attempted conversations with a few, but they couldn't – or wouldn't – understand us, and in the process we became paralytically pissed, probably due to our overexcitement at being somewhere new. The first real way you can separate yourself from your parents is by choosing who to have sex with. It's an act of rebellion, and even betrayal; that's why it's so easy to be a coward and behave badly about the whole thing.

That night we slept like the dead, sexless and still innocent, in the bus, and left for the South late the next morning, nursing beer-and-brandy hangovers. It was a beautiful journey. The roads were less crowded then, and you had time to look around. Just outside Avignon, where the distant walls of the gated city could be glimpsed, we saw a pretty young girl seated in a red MG with a steaming radiator, and stopped to help her. The car was old and the seals would be hard to repair, so I suggested that she came with us. We could phone ahead for the parts, I explained, and Chris would replace them for her on the way back. The girl, Irene, agreed so readily that I knew she had her eye on one of us, but which one? She had bobbed black hair and black eye-shadow, a short pleated skirt and white kinky boots. She was so at ease in our company that she made us look like children.

By the time we reached Marseille, I knew she fancied Chris, and that night, stopping on the road to St Tropez, I was sure she would sleep with him. Dougie was the most put out, and sulked until we took him drinking in a bar that played samba music and was filled – for some reason I now forget – with loud Brazilian girls. They laughed at everything, downing as many drinks as we did, and then picked us off like sharpshooters attacking targets.

The one I took back began to undress me while we were still in the street. We made awkward, squeaky love on one of the bench seats upstairs in the bus. She freed me from more than my parents; she freed me from England, and all of my embarrassing, desperate memories. I can't remember ever being happier. In the morning she left with her shoes in one hand and a kiss blown lazily over her shoulder.

On that first morning after my fall from innocence, everything looked different: the sky was an angry blue that hurt the eyes, the air was pungent with wild lavender and the sea was filled with whining white motorboats. As we set off towards Nice, Mickie worked out routes that avoided heavy inclines, bypassing the dramatic bulk of the Massif d'Esterel because the bus overheated easily. We avoided the fire-ravaged scrubland surrounding St Raphael and Fréjus, staying mostly to the main roads, but there was a point where the throb of the engine began to exacerbate our hangovers, so we took to a turn-off through the pines, firs, olive groves and mimosa trees looking for a spot where we could buy a beer and a baguette.

Three of us were no longer virgins. Only Mickie was left, and suddenly it looked like he was the odd one out. He grew nastier as the day progressed. It was as though we were in on a joke that he wasn't being allowed to share.

The sharp morning air felt electrically charged as we sat in a meadow waiting for the bus's radiator to calm itself. Dougie talked about what he wanted to do with his life. He had no intention of staying in a hardware store for ever, selling locks and drill bits. He wanted to go to art college and learn how to paint. He had started drawing, and had been encouraged by the sale of a picture. Mickie liked working at the depot, but saw it as a temporary job, something to do before he discovered what really interested him. I wanted to be a musician. I'd traded some time in a recording studio and was in the process of putting together a demo tape, but work always got in the way. Chris wanted to set up a business of his own in the city, something to do with owning a chain of bars. He'd worked out a business plan of sorts, and was on the lookout for investors. By the time we hit the road once more, we had sorted out the rest of our lives.

'So you don't mind what you do so long as it makes you rich.' Chris and I wound each other up whenever we discussed the future. It was that stupid argument you have about keeping your scruples once you were rich and powerful, as if you had a choice.

'I'll still have principles, obviously,' he replied, resting his arms on the great black steering wheel and taking his eyes from the road to look at me. 'If you give up what you believe in, you'll be poor anyway.'

'Nice sentiment,' Dougie agreed. 'I only hope you manage to keep it.'

'I don't want to turn into my dad,' said Mickie, 'pissed all the time and talking about the good old days, like there was some kind of magical time when he didn't behave like an arsehole.'

'If we all unite with a single political conscience, the young have enough energy to rebuild the world,' offered Irene in one of those general French statements calculated to annoy everyone. But there were riots in Paris that year, so I guess she was just expressing a widely shared viewpoint.

'You're forgetting one thing,' Dougie pointed out. 'The young lack power and money, and once they finally have them, they don't want to change the world any more, they want to keep it all for themselves. The rich get away with murder.'

Before we could move on to eradicating hunger in the Third World, Irene reminded us that she wanted to visit Grasse because she had heard they made perfumes there, and she wanted to buy some bath salts. According to Mickie's map the road was too narrow, the bends too sharp for the bus to handle, so we turned around and coasted onto a long flat road that cut between two plains studded with ochre rocks, lined with rows of dark cypresses. For a while we saw scattered farmhouses in the distance. Then there was nothing but meadowland and woods.

It was as we entered the tunnel of trees that the mood changed. The sunlight was fragmented here, and the black tarred road, frayed into earth at its edges, was shadowed in wavering green. The air cooled and for the first time I noticed birdsong, not along the road itself, but beyond it, back in the sunlight. It was my turn to drive. Chris and Irene were sitting upstairs. Mickie and Dougie had finished their card game and were staring vacantly from the windows when the engine started to noisily slip gears. The bus coasted on to the lowest point of the road and I knew it would not make the next rise. We came to a stop in the deep green shadows and I put on the handbrake.

'What's happened?' called Dougie, springing up into the driver's cabin.

'I don't know,' I admitted. 'It feels like we've gone into neutral. Take a look under the bonnet, would you?'

Chris and Irene came down from upstairs and watched as Dougie stripped off his shirt and slid beneath the bus. After a couple of minutes he emerged, wiping grease on his jeans.

'There's a small rubber grommet that holds all the gear cables together,' he explained. 'It must have perished, so that when you shifted gears it broke and the cables came loose.'

'Is it fixable?' I asked.

'If you can find me a length of flex I can tie the gear cables together temporarily. It'll be fine so long as you don't put it into "park". If I can find a truck garage in Nice I'll probably be able to find a ring of about the same diameter. Maybe I can make a temporary one.' He climbed back under the bus to take another look. The mistral tugged at the high branches above our heads. The wind in the trees made a strangely melancholy sound.

'Did it suddenly get cold?' Irene hugged her thin arms. Chris came over and wrapped a sweater around her shoulders. 'It's going to be dark soon. Look how low the sun is.'

'Nothing to worry about,' I promised cheerfully. 'If Dougie can't fix it we'll get a lift from someone.'

'Who?' asked Irene. 'We haven't passed another vehicle in at least an hour. There's no one around for miles.'

'Don't be such a worryguts,' said Mickie, swinging around on the platform pole. 'There's bound to be someone along eventually.' He cocked his head comically, but there was nothing to be heard except the rasp of crickets. Dougie's legs stuck out from under the bus. Every once in a while there was a clang of metal and he swore. Finally he emerged, smothered in thick black grease.

'I've managed to tie the cables up, but I don't know how long it will hold.'

'What did you use?' asked Chris.

'I found a packet of rubber johnnies in your bag.'

'You've been going through my stuff?'

'You haven't used many of them, have you? It said "Super Strong" on the packet. Let's hope they're right.'

A pale mist was settling across the plains like milk dispersing in water. We set off carefully, determined to change gear as little as possible. 'How can we best do that?' I asked Chris, who was driving.

'Stick to this low route, I guess. It looks flatter, but if anything comes the other way they'll have to go off-road to get around us.' Tree branches continually scraped the roof of the bus. We crawled through a number of derelict villages, past peeling stucco walls and dry fountains, and the road became even narrower.

'We could get stuck and not be able to turn around,' warned Mickie, scrutinising his map. 'This road isn't even marked.'

'What else can we do?' I asked. 'If it gets too much, we'll have to stay here the night and walk to a town in the morning.'

'You'll be lucky. There's fuck-all for miles around.'

The bus crept around a tight bend into another tunnel of trees. 'What's that up ahead?' I pointed to the side of the road. A dusty silver Mercedes saloon was badly parked there. I could make out some movement in the shadows.

'What?' Chris peered through the windscreen. 'I can't see anything.'

'Neither can I,' complained Dougie.

'You need your eyes tested. It's got English number plates.' A sticker on the boot of the car read: 'Come to HOVE'. There was a straw hat on the back window ledge, the kind Englishmen buy when they go to France in the mistaken belief that it makes them look sophisticated. I nudged Chris's arm. 'Pull over. It's our lucky day.' He pulled up the brake handle and left the motor idling.

'I'll go and talk to them.' I jumped down from the rear platform and ran on ahead. Evidently the two men inside had not heard me approaching, because they looked startled when I knocked on the window of the car. The driver, red-faced and pot-bellied, wearing a blue striped shirt that was too tight to adequately contain him, jerked his head around and studied me with unfocused eyes. His face was broken-veined and double-chinned. He collected his wits for a moment before partially lowering the electric window. The other man was grey-haired and thin, with a prominent sore-looking nose and a sharp Adam's apple, who remained hunched over the back of the passenger seat with his arms extended to the floor. A cool blast from the air-conditioned interior fanned my face.

'Yes, what is it?' he asked in English, as though answering the door to an unexpected neighbour.

I'd been about to ask him for help, but from what I saw it looked as though the situation might be reversed. The overweight man looked angry and frightened. Clearly my intrusion wasn't welcome.

'You're English,' I said stupidly, as if this made us all part of the same club. I peered across at the other man, who now raised his head. He looked ill, or drunk, or both. A livid gash across his cheek was speckling blood onto his yellow T-shirt and the seat back. Both men were in their late forties. Having caught them doing something they didn't want anyone to see, I could only ramble on with my original request for help.

'We've broken down and, well, I was hoping you might be going near a village where I could call out a mechanic, and get him to fix—'

'I don't know, hang on.' The fat man turned to his companion, who was struggling upright in the passenger seat. 'Michael, this chap wants a lift.' He gestured impatiently at the man's head.

Michael looked in the wing mirror and hastily wiped his bleeding face with an oil rag. 'No, we're not going there,' he began in some confusion. 'Fucking hell, Sam, can't you deal with it?' He turned back to me. 'Now is not a good time, kid, so piss off, will you?'

Sam, the overweight driver, shifted uncomfortably in the driving seat. 'Look, I'm sorry, we're a bit tied up and, ah, can't really help you.'

Their attitude annoyed and puzzled me. They were the ones in the brand new air-conditioned Mercedes and they couldn't even give me a lift? 'It's just that I think we'll be stuck here all night if I can't get a lift to a town,' I explained, 'because no cars have been past for—'

'What part of this conversation didn't you understand, you little prick?' shouted the sickly man suddenly. He writhed about in the seat and kicked open the car door, storming around to my side. He made a grab for my shirt, but I ducked back. As I did so, I saw that the rear passenger door was open. A large material-wrapped bundle on the back seat seemed to be slowly sliding out of the car and into the ditch at the side of the road. Something smelled bad.

The fat man manoeuvred his way out of the car and pulled his partner aside. 'For Christ's sake, he's just a kid, leave him alone.'

I stared back at the moving bundle, half in the car, half in the road. There were brown leaves and arrowhead-shaped pine needles stuck to it, and it had begun to make a low gurgling noise.

I looked back along the avenue of rustling cypress trees, but the others must have stayed on board, and it was now too dark to see even the outline of the bus.

'Go back to your vehicle, pal. There'll be someone along soon. Just forget you saw us, all right?'

'Sure, no problem.' I backed cautiously away. I didn't want trouble. These old guys looked burned out and messed up about something, and I really didn't want to know what they'd been doing. Secret cruelties occurred in lonely spots like this.

But as I turned and passed the rear of the Mercedes, I couldn't help looking back at the shifting sack, only now I saw that it was a person unballing itself from a foetal position, because a head had appeared. It was a middle-aged woman in a grey cardigan and a dark blue flower-print skirt. Her hair was the same colour as the leaves in the ditch she was heaving herself into. I realised that she was making the gurgling noise because when she looked up at me and tried to speak, blood swilled over her yellow bottom teeth and ran down her chin, forming a scarlet stalactite. She looked desperate, and determined to crawl out of the car by dragging herself forward on her elbows. 'What's wrong with her?' I couldn't stop myself from asking.

Now the fat guy, Sam, was coming at me with his thick Mont Blanc wallet open. He was pulling out 100-franc notes, separating them and counting them at the same time, the way bank tellers do. His breath was hot and sour with brandy. A blood vessel had burst in his right eye, clouding it crimson. He thrust the notes at me. 'Just take these and move on, son.' He checked himself, made a quick calculation, decided he had underbribed and added several more notes from the wallet. He held the money further out, like a child trying to feed a zoo animal that was known to bite. 'Go on, take it.'

'I don't want your money,' I said. It was his quick recalculation of the amount that disgusted me. 'What the hell have you done to her?'

'It's his wife.' Sam gestured over at his bony-faced companion. 'She drank too much.'

'What's wrong with her face?'

'He hit her.' The companion's protests were overridden. 'It was sort of – a game – that got a bit out of hand, that's all.'

I looked down at the woman as she pulled herself forward on her elbows, her rump slipping off the leather bench seat and toppling her into the ditch beside the car. It crossed my mind that if I bent down to help her, I might be overpowered by the two men. The skinny one had a screwdriver in his hand. We stood silent in an awkward stand-off as she whimpered and spat between us.

'We can take care of this ourselves, sonny.' Sam's money-hand hung half-proffered at his hip, as though he was still hoping I'd take the cash, but was also reluctant to part with it.

'Just tell me what happened. I'm not going until you do.' I kept an eye on the other one, sensing he was the more dangerous of the two. I was just a skinny kid making brave, trying not to betray my fear.

'She was fucking me about, that's what,' shouted the skinny companion. The gash on his cheek had reopened, and was dripping on his T-shirt. 'Now either you help us, or you join her.'

'We're not going to make this worse, Michael.' The overweight driver dragged a handkerchief from his pocket and mopped his sweating forehead.

'That's it, keep using my fucking name. This is all your fault, you're never man enough to see it through, I always have to finish everything you start.' He gave the crawling woman a vicious kick in the gut, and another in the head. She began whimpering more loudly, and tried to draw in her arms and knees as protection, but the amount of haemorrhaged matter she was leaving behind her as she moved suggested that her internal injuries were already serious. She was missing a sandal, and the back of her skirt was caught up in her pants. She was dying, and it was so undignified.

Michael dropped to his knees and started to do something that caused the woman to shriek. When I dared to look, I saw that he was banging a screwdriver into her ear with the flat of his hand. I gave a yell, ran forward and stood beside her, flinching with indecision as Sam opened the car boot and removed a large yellow sponge. He returned to the back seat and began wiping smears from the cream leather upholstery while Michael stamped on the end of the screwdriver with his foot.

The scene was tripped into my memory like some distant, grotesque photograph of a forgotten crime: the red-faced driver carefully wiping the seats, his stomach pushing over the belt of his trousers, studiously ignoring his screaming companion who, deranged with anger, was leaping about on something with a screwdriver sticking out of its head, a pathetic victim-thing that looked no longer human, just a squirming sack wrapped in pleated floral material. The shiny silver Mercedes still gleamed in the dying light of the day, half lost in the deep cool verdure of the arched trees. Beside its rear tyre a stream of crimson was filling the ditch beside the road.

I ran for help.

I told myself that there was nothing else I could do. I ran without looking back, into the deeper darkness of the tunnel, then out onto the brow of the road where the bus had stopped. Its engine was still running, and its headlights were now on. Irene and Chris were standing beside the boarding platform as Mickie and Dougie ran forward.

'Where the hell have you been?' asked Dougie. 'We came looking for you.'

'Just beyond the end of the road there.' I gestured back into the darkness.

'That's where we looked,' said Mickie, who clearly didn't believe me.

'I was beside the Mercedes.' I barely knew how to start explaining what I had seen, how I had hopelessly failed to intervene.

'What Mercedes? There was no car.'

'Don't talk shit, it's right there.'

'No, mate.'

'Come with me.' I grabbed at Dougie's sleeve, pulling them all forward in turn. 'Before they get away.' We walked through the tunnel of branches to the spot where I had encountered the travellers and their victim, but there was no sign of the Mercedes, and now it was too dark to find the bloody ditch.

'They must have pushed her body into the woods,' I cried. 'Help me. She could still be alive.' I was still shoving into the brambles when I felt their hands on my arms, pulling me back towards the bus and the star-filled night.

Nothing went right after that. We slept in the bus and searched the road again the next morning, but we found nothing. Chris hitched a ride to the nearest town and got the bus repaired. I argued with the others, went to the police and eventually convinced them to listen.

Two doubtful gendarmes took me back to the place where I thought I had seen the Mercedes, but we couldn't find the spot. One stretch of road looked just like the next, and after a while they stopped pretending to believe me. The rest of the holiday was a disaster. Irene angrily returned to her car without us. We went on, drunkenly rowing until the bus broke down again. This time it defied all attempts at being repaired, and we had to leave it behind. The last time I saw the big red bus it was sitting in a lay-by near a cement factory, abandoned to the corrosive air.

We took trains and a ferry home.

After the holiday, the four of us drifted apart.

Chris died of a drug overdose when he was twenty-eight. Dougie just disappeared. Only Mickie and I are still in contact, although now he prefers to be called Michael. I'm still plain Sam. I'm no longer a skinny kid; I've put on quite a bit of weight. I have to buy a lot of business lunches to keep my clients happy. Our company's deep in debt, and once the auditors start investigating, we'll all be in trouble. Michael has gone grey and looks ill. He's married to a woman he hates, and I'm having an affair with her behind his back. We drink too much. We lie too much. We're going on holiday together, driving through France.

I was seventeen when I met my degraded mirror-image. I am forty now, and hardly a day passes when I don't think of that sunset evening in the forest. I have already created the circumstances that will return me to that dark spot. I saw the man I have become, and there is not a damned thing I can do about it now. Once you fall, you never get back up.

But as the shadows of fate close in around me, how I miss the bus, the fun and laughter, the innocence that lasted until my first summer holiday.

Christopher Fowler's novels include *Roofworld*, *Rune*, *Red Bride*, *Darkest Day*, *Spanky*, *Psychoville*, *Disturbia*, *Soho Black* and *Calabash*. His short fiction has been collected in *City Jitters*, *The Bureau of Lost Souls*, *Flesh Wounds*, *Sharper Knives*, *Personal Demons*, *Uncut* and *The Devil in Me*, and he was the recipient of the 1998 British Fantasy Award for his short story 'Wageslaves'. His story 'The Master Builder' became a CBS-TV movie starring Tippi Hedren, while another, 'Left Hand Drive', won Best British Short Film. He also scripted the 1997 graphic novel *Menz Insana*, illustrated by John Bolton. He is currently working on his eighth short story collection, *Night Nerves*, has completed his tenth novel, *Full Dark House* (a Bryant & May murder mystery in which he kills off one of his detectives), and is just finishing his eleventh, *Plastic*, about a shopaholic housewife trapped in a blacked-out building. 'Some friends and I shared a nightmarish three-day journey through France in a collapsing car during a series of rainstorms,' recalls Fowler. 'Parts of the vehicle kept dropping off. I had to refill a radiator standing in a frozen stream armed only with a mini Perrier bottle. We crossed Mont Blanc with no alternator and only one working cassette we'd found in the boot, a mind-bendingly awful Cliff Richard album. At one point we got stuck behind a broken-down travelling circus on a narrow bridge, and I thought "Maybe I'm trapped in a movie". This story came from that trip.'

A Habit of Hating

JOHN BURKE

Now that I look back and assess it honestly, I've got to admit that I've always felt most intensely alive and somehow more loving when I was hating. Everything's so drab when you're just making polite conversation at a party or listening sympathetically to a friend's problems. Much more fun to be writing blistering letters to British Gas or phoning some cowering little girl on the local council. I've been almost sorry when the stupid little bureaucrats crumble and apologise.

And way back, if one had only had the chance, the guts, all the adult weight and know-how . . .

School, and all the slights they heaped on you. Dismal daily routine, dismal men who held sway. A schoolmaster plastered with dandruff who once contemptuously kicked my rather shabby satchel out of the way as he strode through the cloakroom. I'd love to go back with my adult powers and ram his face down one of the lavatory pans until he drowned or, even better, choked on his own shit. Yes, I'd still love to do that. And Tubby Blackshaw – a slimy fat bully, always trying to grope your testicles. I dreamed of being bigger and stronger, and twisting his until they came off in my hand.

You think things like that, but of course you don't really mean them, do you?

I did, though. Still do. Still hate the bastards in the past, and find plenty more as time goes by.

Last year a scrawny blonde in the office complained to the Divisional Co-ordinator that I kept looking at her in a funny sort of way. He laughed when formally questioning me about it. Of course she was a neurotic little drip, and he never for a moment thought that I'd done any such thing.

'I mean, she's hardly worth a second look, eh?'

We laughed, man to man; though he never guessed how much I

loathed him, pretentious little brown-noser who'd squelched his way up the promotional ladder.

Of course, in this instance he was right. Until then I'd hardly noticed skinny Miss Goffin. Now, although I was careful not to stare too directly, I couldn't help glancing at her in a way which sent her scuttling off down corridors towards offices she hadn't really meant to go to. Having been duly reprimanded, she wouldn't dare risk another complaint. I wondered, in an abstract way, if I could frighten her into throwing herself off the roof, but our labs and offices were a sprawl of single-storey buildings, and even if she could be willed into climbing up on a roof and jumping, she'd probably only thump down on to the grass verge and bruise her bony shoulders.

She was a scrawny little nonentity, but the effect she was having on me proved to be quite stimulating. I was healthily indignant that she should have laid that complaint against me, and found myself ready to spread that hatred over others. Kids who stamped their chewing gum on to pavements: I dreamed of making them scrape it up with their teeth and then swallow it. Women, kids and prams always blocking the pavement while they gossiped below a large clock jutting out from a department store: let it drop on their heads, chiming jubilantly as their screeching voices rasped into silence.

And then there were the things I'd like to inflict on some of my wife's repulsive friends. Just the thought of them . . .

No more than the thought, for a while.

To be fair, it wasn't just the office moron or Amanda's friends who were bringing things to the boil. Always simmering away below the surface had been the memory of Deborah's treachery.

Not that I had always hated Deborah. For a long time I neither hated nor loved. I went to bed with honey-haired Deborah in her flat a quarter of a mile from my own bedsitter, stayed the night if it suited me or walked home immediately afterwards if it suited me, along those featureless streets and comfortably into my own bed. That was the way we both wanted it: no commitments, no intensity. Or so I believed. Until she confessed that she was pregnant, and I knew she must have been cheating on me.

Because I'm sterile. Always have been.

That was one of the things that Deborah said suited her just fine, just as it suited me. No risks, no responsibilities. Yet suddenly she was all aglow at the prospect of having a baby.

'I can't expect you to understand, Tony. I really am sorry. Truly I am.'

Truly she wasn't. No way was she sorry. She was bathed in a sickly, self-satisfied radiance. It was a radiance I couldn't share, but I did find some new incitements of my own. Only now, when I knew she had been a shabby cheat all along and I could begin steadily hating her, did those grey streets take on a different light. Instead of drowsing along them, I was wide awake. My mind tingled, I was ready for something. It would show itself soon. Had to be soon. The drizzle glittered a dancing silver, the wet pavements gave off a rich, musky smell. The tatty Cherry Tree pub on the corner looked as if it had been newly repainted, and the sounds from inside were livelier than they used to be. I swaggered past and thought of Deborah and out loud called her a bitch, and laughed and hated her and laughed all the more. Discarding her and detesting her gave a new shimmering edge to everything else.

Amanda was different.

Different to start with, anyway. I did believe I loved Amanda. We were married and we were happy. Well, content, anyway. We had nothing to quarrel about. I went off each morning to the laboratory while Amanda went to sit behind the reception desk at a management consultancy, always looking smart and sounding confident in her command of the up-to-the-minute jargon of the trade.

At weekends she devoted herself to our small garden and the greenhouse. We had the neatest possible flowerbeds, and no herb or pot-plant could be featured in a colour supplement without it appearing promptly inside or outside the household. Evenings together were tranquil. We played Scrabble a lot, and backgammon. I handed over tips about plant propagation or growth inhibitors which our lab researchers had been testing, and could see her mind wander until she simply had to scurry out to the greenhouse and adjust the heating and do her umpteenth survey of the month. We watched a lot of gardening programmes on the television.

Occasionally we went to bed early, and made love quietly, and slept tranquilly afterwards. Once, after reading a paperback she had been given by one of her firm's clients, she asked me to beat her, which I tried to do lightly and methodically, until something took possession of me and I began to raise weals on her back and she howled and asked me for Christ's sake to stop. But I couldn't. Things between us had been so complacent, so ordinary. Now it was different. She had asked for it, and she was getting it.

Until she struck back. Not physically, but somehow flailing out at me with her mind. My arm was wrenched agonisingly to one side. My fingers went lifeless and I dropped the cane. Sweat broke out on my forehead.

Amanda's voice was a harsh voice I had never heard before. 'You were enjoying that. You *liked* hurting me.'

'You were the one who wanted it.' I had difficulty in steadying my breathing. 'You *asked* me to do it.'

'But you enjoyed it so much. Too much.'

She looked at me with a mixture of fear and calculation for a few evenings after that. And something was pulsating inside me, some urgent appetite which had to be satisfied.

It was fed, for starters, by my growing irritation at those silly catch-phrases which old schoolfriends consider the height of wit and secret communion.

'Remember the famous occasion when . . .' 'Famous' meaning that nobody outside their own pathetic little clique had ever heard of it or would ever find it in the least amusing.

'And old Miss Murray. The old dragon! Ugh!' Marjorie Johnson, who was married and had two teenage children, still twittered like a gauche teenager herself. 'We believed that at night, in her own room, she paced about breathing flames. One night she'd be bound to set the school on fire with her breath.'

Amanda shuddered with a terror not entirely feigned. She had always had a real fear of being burned alive, trapped in a car or in a room she couldn't get out of.

I wondered what Marjorie's special intimate fear was, and how it could be most poetically and lethally turned against her.

Afterwards, Amanda said, 'Tony, Marjorie was a bit upset, the way you looked at her.'

'What on earth are you on about?'

'She says you gave her a *look*. Gave her the creeps.'

'The woman does drivel on. Don't any of you ever grow out of those old school hang-ups and bunfights in the dorm?'

And of course there was Bunty, with that repulsive dog of hers.

'He's such a great big softie,' she drooled as the hulking great thing slouched about our lawn.

I saw Amanda's face as it crapped on her wallflowers and then knocked over an urn of fuchsias. 'It doesn't matter,' she said tightly when Bunty apologised as though any apology was an absurdity when the perpetrator of the offence was so lovable. 'Honestly, it doesn't matter a bit.'

But I felt that Amanda wouldn't complain this time if I looked or spoke in a certain way.

'From what I've heard,' I said, 'Rottweilers aren't exactly reliable. Likely to turn on their owners without warning.'

'Rubbish.' Bunty sniffed at me just as her dog might sniff before peeing on my leg. 'A lot sweeter-tempered than most human beings I know. Much more reliable. And loving.'

I pictured that hefty black and brown beloved turning on her and tearing her apart. Amanda looked at me and went very pale. But we both knew we had an unspoken compact.

A week later in the park, in front of half a dozen witnesses – and I'm sorry to say I wasn't one of them – the creature sprang on its besotted owner and sank its teeth into her right arm. By the time it was hauled off, there wasn't much of Bunty's arm that remained user-friendly.

Amanda avoided my eyes when we heard the news, but while I was pouring a drink she said, 'The way you looked at poor Bunty, *and* at that dog . . . anyone would think you'd wished it on her.'

'You weren't actually wishing her the best of British luck yourself,' I ventured. 'I don't think it could have been done without your collaboration.'

She said nothing. But she knew what I was talking about. And if she was worried, so was I. When the attack happened, I had felt her full power. No matter how she coyly tried denying it to herself, she was the one with the great gift – the true potency for doing what had to be done.

I was envious. She looked so demure and uncomplicated. But she had a gift that, once let loose, I couldn't hope to compete with.

All would be well if we stayed on the same side.

One afternoon I got home to find Amanda already there, earlier than usual, unpacking an emerald dress from a box and laying it reverently on our bed. 'I've been invited out.'

'Some office romance?' I knew it wouldn't be.

'The big boss. Several important clients coming to dinner, and at the last minute he realised they were short of one lady to make up the numbers. Could I step in at short notice – and buy myself a new dress and charge it to the firm.'

'Have a wonderful time,' I said as she left. And I meant it. I didn't begrudge her a treat of this kind, though I hoped she wouldn't move too far, too fast, onto a different level from the one we had comfortably established for ourselves.

On the music centre I was replaying, for the fourth time, that bit of
the concert pieces from Berg's *Lulu* where Lulu is carved up by Jack
the Ripper, when the front door opened and Amanda came in, tight-
lipped. She had been gone less than an hour.

I flicked the remote control to cut short the wonderful murderous
discords. 'Something wrong? One tycoon refused to sit down with
another?'

'The bastard.' Amanda was not crying, but her eyes were blinking
furiously. 'The rotten bastard.'

I had never heard her use language like that before, or speak with
such venom. Before I could make any soothing noises, or even decide
whether they would be welcome, she raged on. 'When I got there, it
turned out that one of the men wasn't going to show up, so please I
wasn't needed and please would I go home. Only of course the firm
would pay for a taxi and I can keep the dress.'

'The bastard.' I said it more quietly than she had done, but much
more decisively.

'How can they expect me to go back to that place? How can I be
expected to work there, having to see that disgusting swine swaggering
in and out every day? I don't think I can bear to be in the same
building.' She collapsed into her usual chair.

'No, I don't see how you can.' I sat opposite her, both of us in our
usual positions. 'He'll have to go, won't he?'

'Don't be silly, Tony. He's the boss.'

'And we have to remove him.'

'You can't be serious?'

I was very serious, and she knew it.

In the morning I phoned the lab to say I would be late, and
accompanied my wife to her place of work. We didn't discuss exactly
what was going to happen, because we didn't know. But we did know,
deep down, that something would.

We were there watching, concentrating, when Mr Broderick's black
Merc rolled up and he got out, leaving his chauffeur to ease it round
the block to the underground car park entrance. We didn't even know
that repairs were going on in the lift shaft. So we could hardly be held
responsible, even by ourselves, for the fact that, thirty seconds after the
main door had been held open for him by a uniformed commissionaire,
Mr Broderick had somehow stepped into the open shaft just as the lift
came down on a test run. Someone had failed to take proper safety
precautions.

Or the precautions had been mysteriously overridden.

That evening we silently watched a television programme dealing with the extirpation of garden pests.

The following Tuesday I happened to see Deborah in the street with her little boy wriggling in his pushchair. She was preparing to smile at me, even solicit my congratulations, and I could imagine the twee remarks that would come gushing out. I kept walking straight ahead, and before we drew closer she swung the pushchair perilously across the traffic towards the opposite pavement.

One day she would surely shove it straight under a bus.

Could I make her do that, simply by looking at her? Not that I'd wish any such tragedy on her, of course. It was over long ago; I had nothing to do with her any more, or she with me.

But suddenly the sun was shining, catching the weather vane on the town hall tower, and I laughed, and the day was bright with hatred – honest, invigorating hatred, good for the bloodstream and for striding out . . . and meditating.

One evening Amanda insisted that we throw a dinner party to celebrate the anniversary of two of her group graduating, or one getting married or remarried, or something equally trivial.

'And you won't give them any of your *looks*, will you?' It was only half a joke.

There were three of her friends – Marjorie, Christine and Penelope – and their husbands: the pimply one, the confident third-level quango administrator who sweated more liberally and grew noisier with each glass of wine, and the weaselly little bank manager. One thing the three men had in common: they all looked sheepish as their wives burbled on about the famous occasion when the loo had overflowed, or the utterly *ghastly* day when that dreadful girl from Shrewsbury had brought not just her dreadful father but his awful floozie blind drunk to prizegiving; and that simply frightful Emma something-or-other who had ruined the school choir's performance of chunks from *Hiawatha* because she couldn't read music but couldn't be chucked out after her father had just presented the school with a new gym.

The women's voices rose half an octave in the squawking ecstasy of reminiscence. I watched their lips twisting, pouting, gushing out banalities, and thought how lovely it would be to petrify each of those faces just as they had reached their most grotesque grimace. Like the old childhood threat about pulling faces just as the wind changed.

As usual, one of them decided it was her turn to dominate the conversation. This time it was Penelope Bibby, whose husband was the quangocrat. On a basis of nudge-nudge secrets which he had confided to her, she liked to do her own bit of nodding and winking, keen to air her knowledge about the workings of insurance companies and investment analysts being given a hard time by a Sunday business-supplement investigation.

'I mean, I ask you, some of the things these companies bury in the small prints! I mean, look at *our* policy. Do you have a smoke alarm, do you have a fire escape, do you smoke in bed, do you make love at too high a temperature?' She sniggered. 'I suppose *you* meet all the right criteria, Amanda? Still got the rope ladder? Always had it,' she confided to the rest of us, 'in the dorm. Scared stiff of being burned alive. Not that they ever pampered us with a proper fire. But Amanda insisted on keeping her rope ladder coiled up under the bed.'

Amanda had gone very pink and wasn't laughing. I knew it was true, but it wasn't one of the memories she liked to toss to and fro. I tried to turn it against the others by asking what each of them was most scared of.

All the women started babbling at once, as if proud of their lovable little fears and failings. Penelope, anxious to cover up her gaffe, was the loudest of all in her eagerness to tell us of her nightmare of a car windscreen shattering in her face while driving. 'Broken glass,' she wailed. 'My eyes, I'm so sensitive about my eyes. Can't even bear to have a doctor examining them.'

Tom Bibby said, 'Modern windscreens don't shatter like that.' The weariness in his tone made it obvious that he had told her this a dozen times before.

Christine admitted to a terror of moths and butterflies. Her husband looked embarrassed. I said breezily that he ought to take her to the butterfly farm ten miles away and shake her out of it.

Christine shuddered and glared at me.

Penelope challenged me. 'And what about you, Tony? What scares the pants off you?'

'Women,' I said. 'Only it's not so much a matter of *scaring* them off me . . .'

Penelope made a face, but the others laughed thinly, and the moments of tension were over. For the time being.

When Amanda went out to the kitchen to bring on a fruit pudding she had slaved over after reading the recipe in the back of her gardening magazine, I took some plates out to clear the table. I kissed her. She looked startled. We didn't usually get demonstrative out of bed, but I felt something reaching between us, coming to fulfilment. I welcomed the sensation, but she was trying to keep it at arm's length.

Clasping her hands round the fruit bowl as if to steady herself, she said, 'I suppose Penny really is getting a bit of a bore.'

We went back in. Neither of us looked at Penelope, who was still rattling on.

Tom Bibby was uneasy. I could tell he wanted his wife to shut up, but he wasn't going to say so in front of the rest of us.

That night Amanda and I made love more fiercely than either of us had been used to. When it was over, she panted, 'You were thinking of Penny.'

'Penelope? Good God, I've never fancied—'

'Not fancying her. I mean, you're thinking of how to . . . wipe her out. And I don't want anything to do with it.'

'You're sure of that?'

'Of course I'm sure.'

My arm was around her damp shoulders, my lips close to her left ear. 'If you don't want to, it won't work. And it already *is* working, just the way it did with your boss.'

'That was an accident.'

'One that you willed.'

She was trembling in the darkness, only it wasn't really dark. The bedroom was filled with a wonderful light. 'Tony, what's going to happen?'

'We'll have to wait and see.'

The trouble was that we didn't actually see it. All we got were garbled but colourful reports a week later.

Tom and Penelope had been at home, having a candle lit dinner. Very romantic, I'm sure. They didn't notice one of the candles burning down faster than the other until the glass candlestick cracked. Slivers of glass exploded into Penelope's face, one of them long enough and sharp enough to reach her brain.

And I wasn't even there to see it.

At the funeral we all shook hands in a silly, solemn way. The women had taken the opportunity to look very chic in their sadness. Christine was wearing a fine black veil. 'Charming,' I said. 'Just like a butterfly net.'

If she could have spat at me through the veil, I think she'd have done so.

Her husband was at my elbow. 'Haven't you done enough damage?' He snapped out that he had been stupid enough to listen to me, and had taken her to the butterfly farm. 'She's starting treatment with a psychiatrist. Going to cost me a bloody fortune.'

It was funny. Of course it had to be funny. There's no pleasure in creating horror for anybody else if you're horrified yourself. It has to be a superb joke, so private and overwhelming that you don't want to share it with anybody else.

Except with a partner who can contribute.

Late at night, in bed holding hands while Amanda kept sobbing, 'No . . . no, please no, Tony,' as if I were raping her, we found ourselves concentrating on Christine. In spite of all the girlish matiness, between them there must be old scores to settle from way, way back. So together we flooded Christine's mind with a whirl and swirl of butterflies, and when she screamed and reached out to turn the light on, we willed a squadron of moths towards the bulb.

Two days later we heard that Christine had gone away for 'a rest cure', as Marjorie half fearfully, half gloatingly, put it.

'Tony, that's enough.' Amanda flinched when I put my hand on her arm. 'It's got to stop. We're pushing them into things they're terrified of.'

'More fool them.'

One Saturday afternoon we went out for a walk. If we hadn't been together, our minds not concentrating on anything in particular, but free to interlock if triggered, things might not have worked out as they did.

On the slope above the supermarket we saw Deborah pushing her little boy uphill in his pushchair with a load of groceries in the basket. She glanced at me and looked away.

Amanda said, 'Isn't that the girl you used to . . . I mean, before we . . .'

'Yes, that's her.'

'What right has she got to have a child?'

It was the first time Amanda had ever mentioned the matter. I couldn't be sure whether it was her own resentment, or something she had telepathically picked up from me. But we both felt the tug of it, the sudden fierce brightness all round us, and something almost like a halo enfolding the pushchair.

It broke away from Deborah's grip and began running downhill, gathering speed. There was nobody close enough to stop it plunging under an artic swinging towards the delivery bay of the supermarket. Somebody somewhere began screaming. And beside me, Amanda was sobbing, 'No, I didn't mean it, I didn't, didn't . . .'

It made quite a mess, as if tins of tomatoes in the load had burst and spilled their squashed red contents into the gutter.

I tried to put an arm round Amanda, but she wrenched herself away. 'How could you make me do that?'

'I didn't make you do anything you didn't want to.'

Our evenings were no longer so tranquil. At the appointed hour we tried to turn our minds to backgammon or Scrabble, but one evening when she came up with the word MURDER she tried to make out that I had somehow controlled the order of letters. She must have known that it was her own fingers which had selected them. We didn't go on with that game, or ever start another one.

We weren't invited to meals with those of her friends who remained, and we didn't invite them to our home any more.

Looking at Amanda across the fireplace one evening, I had a chill feeling that all the joy of hating outwards had been turned inwards. Things I had detested in her friends were deeply ingrained in her, too. How could I ever have married a girl called Amanda? It was such a stupid name. I must always have hated the name Amanda without facing up to the fact. Now it grew daily more and more hateful. Her mannerisms were not just as bad as those of her nauseating clique, but worse. I had never noticed before that when we tried to sit quietly reading, she had a habit of lifting a page long before she was ready to turn it over and scratching the inner edge with a fingernail. And when at last I could bear it no longer and was taking a deep breath before complaining, she said, without looking up, 'Do you have to keep clicking your tongue against your teeth like that?'

It dawned on me, almost too late, not only that I hated her and could now feel free to hate her, but that she felt the same about me.

Who was going to make the first move?

One Saturday evening I half closed my eyes and willed her to lean forward and fall towards the fire. Like all the others, a straightforward accident. But nothing happened. When she glanced up, I could see in her eyes that she sensed what had been in my mind. Her defences were primed.

There was a high wind that night. I heard slates fall on the dustbin and the path beside the back door. On the Sunday morning, Amanda tried to persuade me to fetch a ladder and see to the slates. I said I preferred to wait until Monday and get someone in who was properly qualified for that kind of work.

'You're scared,' she said.

'I've got no head for heights. You know that.'

Yes, she knew, all right. But although she concentrated on me, there was no way that, on her own, she could will me up on to that roof. She was stronger than I, and I was growing to envy that and to hate her all the more – all her pretences of unwillingness, of being led astray by me – but never quite strong enough if I resisted. Her only chance was if she could catch me unawares.

And the same went for me and my chances.

I worked a lot of overtime in the lab, doing simple jobs which required no concentration. Every day was bright now with promise. All the lab equipment shone as if newly installed and not yet stained by use. My mind shone implacably. I was truly alive, made doubly alert by fear and my own power to inflict fear.

I couldn't destroy Amanda in anything like the way the others had been destroyed. No remote control this time, and certainly not powerful back-up from her. It had to be close and real. I had to be right there on the spot. This time I wanted to *see* it happen.

On the afternoon when I finally made up my mind, I stayed a long time in the Cherry Tree on the way home. I pretended to have had more to drink than I'd really had, blundering into the umbrella stand on the way in and chucking a batch of pages torn from a technical magazine on to the coffee table, grunting as if I had a hard evening's work ahead of me.

She hardly bothered to listen to me. She had been turning over the pages of a glossy gardening magazine, scratching each page as she did so. Even if I'd had any doubts, that would have settled it. When she went out to talk gibberish to some seedlings in the greenhouse, I waited a few moments and then followed her.

She was always relaxed in those surroundings. Too relaxed. When she saw me coming, it was too late.

I swear I didn't actually make it happen. Not physically. It was just that I looked at the gas cylinder connected to the greenhouse heater, and as I looked, it suddenly vomited flame. I was nowhere near it, honestly. But all at once the whole greenhouse was a vast glass oven. Amanda was engulfed in flame as she screamed and groped towards the door.

The only thing I actually did was turn the key outside, and then when the smell of burnt flesh was billowing through the cracks in the blistered glass, turned it back again. Then I went indoors and called the ambulance.

There was no way her rope ladder was going to get her out of that.

At the funeral, those of her friends still alive stared at me. I didn't know all of them, but somebody seemed to have passed on tales about me. None of the women went in for the usual slobbering kisses, and their husbands didn't shake my hand.

As I walked away from the graveside, I looked up at the top of the church tower. Even craning my neck at this angle made me dizzy. That must have been why I saw Amanda so clearly up there, willing me to come and join her at the parapet. And there were other shapes crowding in behind her, and some behind me and around me. A wisp of Penelope, a long wail from Marjorie, and all of them urging me to go into the stair turret and climb to the top. But there was no reason to be scared of shadows, even shadows who knew from what had been said at those dinner parties, or hinted at by Amanda during one of their hen parties, about my fear of heights. What remained of Amanda wasn't strong enough on her own to drag me up there, and those other wraiths were as pathetic dead as when they had been alive.

My feet firmly on solid ground, all I'm conscious of is this emptiness now it's all over. Now Amanda's dead, I'm looking impersonally at what I've done, yet at the same time looking at it in dismay. Because I've destroyed the only person who could have shared the joke.

Like I said, loving and hating are so close. I'd loved Amanda. Really loved her, in my own way. It was her own fault that she'd had to be killed, and the true horror is that now there's nobody left to love or hate.

Except myself.

And I don't hate myself. Well, not all that much. Not yet.

And when I do . . .

John Burke was born in Rye, Sussex, and grew up in Liverpool, where his father became a Chief Inspector of Police. He won an Atlantic Award in Literature for his first novel, *Swift Summer*, and worked in publishing, the oil business and as European Story Editor for 20th Century-Fox Productions before becoming a full-time writer. Burke has published nearly 150 books, including *The Devil's Footsteps*, *The Black Charade* and *Ladygrove* in his 'Dr Caspian' trilogy about a Victorian psychic detective. He has also written novelisations of film and TV programmes such as *The Bill*, *London's Burning*, *Dr Terror's House of Horrors* and two volumes of *The Hammer Horror Film Omnibus*. In recent years Robert Hale has published a sequence of his thrillers, including a detective-cum-horror story, *Stalking Widow*, followed in the autumn of 2002 by *The Second Strain*. A collection of his short weird tales, edited by Nicholas Royle, recently appeared under the title of *We've Been Waiting for You* in a limited edition from Ash-Tree Press in Canada. As the author explains: 'The preceding short story arose, as far as I can analyse the workings of my own weird subconscious, from a couple of minor irritations – two horsy women screeching away in an otherwise quietly sociable bar, and the sight of chewing gum being stamped into the pavement by some scruffy schoolboys – which provoked me into fairly light-hearted fantasies of how to punish them. From trivial beginnings, the idea began to turn sinister. Add up lots of petty everyday nuisances, and see how far one mind could be tipped over into a desire for quite disproportionate revenge. As with so many stories I've written, it was a matter of beginning with a glimmering of an idea derived from something quite small, and then seeing how far it would go – almost of its own accord – after a few paragraphs.'

Dead Snow

TREY R. BARKER

Tilton yelled at him.

Like the pimp had yelled at the burned woman in the tight skirt; the one with round bums dotting her cheeks like tribal scarification. Her pimp had stood next to her, his cigarette giving their faces an orange glow. ''Choo lookin' at, white bread?' he had asked. 'Wanna go at my lady? Gotta wait 'til she back to livin'.'

she said something just when we hit the ice i remember that

'Joey? Where are you?'

A wino grabbed Joey's ankle. 'Got some money?'

'You're gonna die, you know.' Tilton's voice was muffled by the snow.

'I'm already dead.' Joey ran deeper into the alley.

'Hey,' the wino called. 'How come you ain't leave no tracks?'

Joey had seen the dead, had smelled their rancid, meaty odour. Their wounds were obvious and bloody; bruised features, missing limbs, the sleepy faces of natural death. The dead had packed that tiny room, asking the old man – Joey thought of him as Reaper Bob – to save them.

'Damnit, Joey,' Tilton called. 'I'm trying to help. You don't have much time left. A few hours maybe.'

As Joey ran, a hot iron stitched his side. His chest heaved, his heart pounded. Is this what it felt like? Is this what Jennifer had felt when it began?

Except she had said her wrists tingled, that she couldn't breathe.

'Please, Jennifer,' Joey whispered. 'Where are you?'

she touched my face i remember that

An abandoned building hovered over the alley, rusted metal fire-escapes like broken arms. Its darkness engulfed him as he went in. Broken glass, boarded windows, burned beams. He had to stay away from Tilton. He had to find Jennifer.

Then he could go back to Reaper Bob.

It was a noble thing, Tilton trying to help. Tilton wanted to save his lifelong friend – 'Can Joey come out and play?' said in the soft falsetto of a young boy carrying G.I. Joe Action Figures. But Joey had answered that nobility by running. Terrified and lost without Jennifer, Joey had fled the dead room.

'Joey. Quit dicking around.' Tilton's voice so plaintive. 'Please. Let's go back.'

Joey looked through a gap in the boards. Tilton stood in the alley, streetlamp-yellow snow falling gently on his head, the wino crawling up behind him.

'We don't have time, you're going to be dead pretty quick.'

'I can't come back without Jennifer.'

'You first, then we'll deal with her.'

'She'll be dead by then.'

'She's dead—'

sat on the kerb and jabbed her palm with her finger i remember that

—already,' Tilton said. 'I don't want you to die.'

'You my mother now?' Joey peered through the boards again, saw only the wino.

'Let's go,' Tilton said.

Iron hands hauled Joey to his feet. He sputtered and when Tilton dragged him outside, Joey's feet flailed at the snow-stained pavement.

'No, it'll be too late for her. She's all I have.'

'You have me. You've always had me.'

The wino looked up from his heap. 'Money?'

'That's different,' Joey said.

'Love is love,' Tilton said.

'That's not what I meant.'

'It's what I—'

'Got some money?' The wino grabbed at Tilton and managed to tangle his hands in Tilton's feet. Tilton and Joey fell on top of the drunk. The man grunted, Tilton yelped. The three of them rolled together, Joey tangling Tilton's hands with the wino's.

'What are you doing?' Tilton said.

Joey jumped to his feet and ran.

'What the hell's the matter with you?' Tilton yelled.

'I gotta find Jennifer.'

said something but i don't remember what

I need to remember. I need to know what she said.

*

'I wish it were someone else.' How many times had I said that? A hundred? A million? Anybody else. A homeless guy or a battered wife or even an autistic kid. Anyone who didn't have a life as good as mine. Joey's beautiful green eyes were shocked every time I said it. It offended his soul.

But he hugged me. There had been lots of hugs lately. Gentle and soothing and yet somehow agitating. I did want the touch, but not gently. A soft touch is a reminder that I am Ms Kobold, cardiac patient. I'm tired of the pity. 'Hear about Jennifer?' 'She's so young.' 'Runs in her family.' 'Defective blood, I guess.'

Anybody else. I don't care who. 'I am a horrible person.'

'Only,' Joey always answered, 'if you forced somebody to have a heart attack. That would probably be horrible.'

Then I would giggle. Sometimes it was actually funny, sometimes I just wanted us to hear me laugh. His face would light up like a cheap Christmas tree. But laughing always brought pain: my thigh where they stabbed me with the catheter, my chest where it had all started. During deepest night, when I slept alone because I hardly slept, I fantasised the pain was rejection, my heart trying to spit out the stents the cardiologist had implanted.

Pressing his lips against my temple, he asked, 'How about a drive?'

I wanted to get out of the house, to get some sunshine in my head. But outside was where the world had hurt me. 'I need to rest.' Even though there had been nothing but rest since the heart attack. The first two weeks I slept. The next two I dozed in bed with our black and grey portable TV as companion. After the TV drove me insane, Joey cleaned out the corner newsstand. I had hundreds of magazines in one great pile of 'unread'. Then in a pile of 'read'. And then? Then I hated them. I threw them against the wall. Out the door. Through the open window. They reminded me I was Ms Kobold.

I didn't want to be the cardiac patient. I wanted to be Jennifer. Wife. Companion. Lover. All those things I was to Joey. But to myself I was a jogger, a swimmer, a carpenter. I called for those things when I was awake and dreamed of them when I slept. But the doctor had given me eight pages of recovery rules, beginning with total rest. 'Maybe in a few weeks,' he had said, 'I'll allow you to piss by yourself. Or go downstairs to watch TV.' And work? He had smiled as though the four-day ICU bill of one hundred and sixty-four thousand dollars wasn't a problem. 'You'll see me five or six times before you work again. And you'll probably never work like you used to.'

'Chances are,' I said to Joey, 'it'll happen again.'

'A short drive. You haven't been out since you got home from the hospital.'

Why was it so hard to understand? I had to recover. 'Honey, I'm not ready. I have to get my strength back, don't I? And I need to answer all the e-mails and letters. I've got to write thank-yous for the cards and flowers and things. And I have to take all my pills and read all the damned recipe books for low fat foods even though there wasn't much blockage and I need to learn to fucking breathe and meditate so I don't get completely stressed out so no, Joey, I'm not going for a drive, I've got too much to do.'

Then I was crying. Like I had for so much of every moment since I collapsed on the sidewalk. I cried because I hated that this had happened to me. Everyone said it wasn't my fault – 'Runs in your family' – but it was. I had worked too hard, hadn't exercised enough, hadn't relaxed enough, was born into the wrong genetic pool.

Still crying, I stood. I wanted to storm into the bathroom and slam the door. But the pain – and the dizziness from the blood-thinners – snapped me to the floor. Joey was there instantly, his face riddled with fright. 'Jennifer? Holy shit. I'm calling the ambulance.'

'No, I'm fine. Just a little dizzy. It's not another heart attack.'

His hands were on mine, his eyes on mine. He would have sat there for ever, I think. It would have been nice to try that, just sit and not worry about heart disease and bills and the rest of it.

The pain comes and goes. There is always a dull hurt, but I never know when the spikes are coming. And every time the pain interrupts us, becomes a third partner in our marriage, I am again Ms Kobold, cardiac patient. Ms Kobold's face is hard and tired, her eyes exhausted. She moves slowly, and sometimes giant rivers of pain run through her veins.

Together, we limped back to the couch. 'You're right. You're not ready to go out yet.'

I sighed. 'Crap, I'm so sorry, Joey. You shouldn't have to deal with this, you shouldn't have to—'

'Jennifer, you have nothing to apologise for. You had a heart attack, it's going to take some time to recover.' He frowned. 'God, that's so freaky to say. Breast cancer or suicide or old age or something. But heart attacks for women? I thought that was only for old guys.'

I grabbed my crotch and farted. 'Call me Geezer.'

We giggled together and I was able to imagine things were good, that heart disease wasn't hanging over us.

'I know just the thing for you, sweetie pie.' Dramatically, he produced a videotape from his coat pocket.

'Please. Not *Half a Loaf of Kung-Fu* again.'

'This is a new one. *Sergeant Kabukiman NYPD*.'

'Sounds too artistic for me,' I said. 'We might have to take it out and go with something like *Shrunken Heads*.'

Or *Shrunken Heart*, I wanted to say. But of course that wasn't a movie, that was me.

Twenty hours since the accident.

He stood in his yard, snow falling on his head though it didn't feel cold.

Twenty hours since he'd found himself looking up at the road and hearing the awful scream of metal against asphalt. Nearly a full day since he'd seen the hood and the left front quarter panel of the car peel away like flesh off bone.

He and the rest of the dead – and they were everywhere – moved quietly and mostly unseen through the living. Some were casual about their passing, but others wore their deaths like formal suits.

Joey had slipped onto the bus to get home. As it pulled away from the kerb, Tilton had come out of the alley. Seeing Joey, he had tapped his watch.

Time was running out.

The street lights around Joey's house layered a soft yellow sheen over the entire neighbourhood. It was as though some artist had dipped the entire block in streetlamp-yellow: the snow, the cars, the houses, all the colour of Jennifer's lemons.

'Jennifer,' he called when he reached the porch.

The door was locked.

His keys were still in the wrecked car, long since dragged away by a tow-truck. He threw the newspaper hard through the front window, shattering the glass, and then crawled into the house.

'Jennifer?'

He searched room to room and everything was in its place, nothing disturbed, nothing gone. But in the kitchen, he noticed a new soup bowl. White with purple flowers. Shadowed green stems held the blooms aloft. There was a matching spoon and they were tied together with purple ribbon.

'The hell we get these?'

He toyed with the spoon, stared at the bowl. Maybe Jennifer had bought them before—

Suddenly she was in his head again, panic in his throat.

He had forgotten her. Standing there, staring at the bowl, she had slipped away, disappeared as though she had never existed.

'It's happening,' he said, quickly checking the bathroom and the smaller bedroom. 'Tilton said it would.'

Twenty hours and already holes had appeared. How long would it be until he couldn't remember Jennifer at all? Until there was no face to see, no name sitting on his tongue?

And what about her? Was she forgetting him?

Be here, he willed, tears in his eyes. Please be here.

His chest was bleeding again. Tilton had packed it tightly with bandages, but still the blood flowed. How much blood-loss? Bleeding at the crash site, bleeding at Tilton's place after Tilton had hauled him from the wreckage, bleeding two or three times since then.

Joey snorted as he checked the utility room and the den. Be damned funny if he bled out before they could raise him from the dead, wouldn't it?

Almost as funny as seeing the look on the checkout boy's face at the drugstore when Tilton had plopped down fourteen boxes of gauze bandages.

Tilton had stopped the bleeding, but he couldn't stop the march. Death goose-stepped next to Joey, each second ticking off more of his and Jennifer's souls. Soon enough, there wouldn't be anything left and it wouldn't matter if he found Jennifer or not.

said something i remember that

'Jennifer, come on,' Joey called. 'Where are you?'

The house was silent. The panic in his chest grew, spread to his arms and legs, his face, like a warm disease.

The longer you're dead, Tilton had said, the more pieces get left behind.

Wasn't that already happening? Didn't certain words already sound strange in his head, like they were bullshit words, made up for no reason?

Like Jennifer. Or was it Jenilee? Or Jenna?

'It's Jennifer,' he shouted. 'She's my wife. She's my best friend.' Joey pounded the walls. 'Where are you?'

Then he knew. If she were here, she'd be in the bedroom. It was where she'd spent most of her time since the heart attack.

But what if she was? She'd been in the same crash Joey had. If she was here, she was probably in shock. Maybe dealing with the pain of a dead husband. Or maybe she had died and didn't even remember she was married.

He swallowed back the lump of fear sitting uncomfortably in his throat. Quickly, he twisted the knob and shoved the bedroom door open.

Nothing. A dark room, but he didn't hear her breathing, didn't smell her sweet odour, didn't feel the press of her in the air.

The curtain was open and through it, Joey watched the snow fall. Beneath the streetlamp light, it was yellow.

The house was empty and her name felt strange on his tongue.

There was a second.

Four and a half weeks after the first. I never told Joey. I was in the shower. Massive chest pain, though a lesser version of what I'd had on the sidewalk. Where the first had been like someone cutting out my heart with a white-hot knife, this was simply someone jabbing me with that knife. I climbed out of the shower and placed one of the nitroglycerine pills under my tongue. After it dissolved, I took a second. Vision blurry, I sat on the toilet seat and eventually the pain subsided. In fifteen minutes, I was fine. Tired, but alive.

Chances are damned good I'll have another.

I have heart disease. There is no cure. It will kill me some day. I don't want it to control me, but it does, snaking its way into every facet of our lives.

'Want some more lemonade?' Joey constantly asked.

Lemonade is safe. When we are so worried about fat and cholesterol and stress and all the things that might kill me, lemonade is safe. Obviously, non-fat. But it also takes me back to when I was a little girl. Mama used to make gallons of it when we'd go with her friends to the Midland County Zoo – 'Our carnival of animals', their radio ads blared. We'd eat sandwiches and drink lemonade and watch the animals.

I drove with Joey yesterday. I worried about it, but I had to get out. I grabbed my nitro pills and off we went. When I hit that front porch, got that winter sunlight on my face, most of my pain dissipated. Again, it was like being a little girl. I'd scrape my knee and Mama would bandage it. She'd pour me a glass of her lemonade and then cup my chin with her hand. With that touch, the world was fine. And when the sunlight cupped my face, the world was fine again. The medical bills, half paid by insurance, would figure themselves out. My lack of working – and income – would figure itself out. My constant need for pills and stress-free living would figure itself out. God alone knew how any of that would happen, but it would, the sun warming my face – cupping my face – told me so.

Joey drove and I bathed in the scenery. Trees and farms, rivers and creeks. The mountains. Mile after mile and every turn of the wheels left a bit more of the anger and pain behind. Eventually, Joey drove me to Sallee Park, on the outskirts of Denver's industrial yards, but a beautiful park anyway. Winter grass stretched out like a brown wool blanket, while the evergreens towered over traffic. And this month's art display? Metal animal sculptures. A ten-foot-tall lion, a tiger. An elephant that rose two storeys, a horse that was too small. Three dogs running. Bones of metal, skin of fabric, everything painted in primary colours. Those colours bowled me over. Everything since the attack had been muted, dulled, drab. But these sculptures were almost electric. Bright colour, digital colour, Technicolor.

We sat on a bench near a giraffe and the sun warmed us. For that slice of time, as long or as short as it might be, there were no pictures of my heart in our medical folders, there were no daily pill boxes to organise my regimen. Under this sun, on this day, everything was fine.

Joey ran across the street, disappearing back into the World, and returned with yoghurt.

'Because I can't have ice-cream,' I said quietly.

'Yoghurt's just as good.'

Joey had begun watching our diet before I was even out of the hospital. I thought the key was moderation, but Joey cut certain things out completely. I hated him a little for that because I wanted my burgers, my enchiladas and barbecue. I wanted my pre-heart attack food. More than that, I wanted my pre-heart attack life.

I stared at the yoghurt. 'I hate this.'

Joey put an arm around my shoulder. 'I know it's tough, it's tough on me, too, but—'

'Chances are,' I said.

'Yeah, chances are. That's why we do the right stuff. Change what we eat. Exercise. Take the medicine.'

'It's nine pills a day, Joey.'

'You want to live, that's what you do.'

'None of that would have saved my grandfather. Or Mama. Two and counting, Joey. I didn't tell you about the second.'

'I know, Jennifer.'

'She's in a wheelchair, Joey.'

'I know that, Jennifer.'

'She can't even remember my name half the time, Joey.'

'Jennifer, I know that, but—'

This wasn't the conversation he wanted to have. He wanted to laugh and tell bad jokes and imagine a vacation – when I was cleared to travel – and were we going to Mark's birthday party and all the other things that made up our lives.

Made up our lives *before*, I thought. Our lives are different now, informed by a heart attack and pills and exercise and anger and smouldering depression. I constantly talked about my grandfather – dead at forty-six – and about my mother – first attack at age thirty-nine, second at fifty-one, stroke two years later, nursing home at fifty-four – and about whether I was destined to die with a suffocating pain in my chest. It was becoming quite the obsession for me. *'Watch her,'* the doctor had said. *'Depression is pretty common the second or third month after a coronary event.'*

'It was pretty bad, wasn't it?' I asked for the thousandth time.

'You were unconscious for nearly an hour. They had you in the cath lab for two. Clogged artery, massive stress, over-exertion. But it's over now, Jennifer. Drugs, therapy, you're going to live a million years.'

I snorted bitterly. 'A million years of wondering when it's going to kill me.' I raised my face to the sun and closed my eyes. 'It's nice out here. Thanks for bringing me.'

'I'm good for some things.'

I squeezed his thigh. 'And what would that be . . . beyond taking out the garbage?'

'I can make a mean macaroni and cheese.'

I laughed, and even to my cynical ears, it was a sweet sound. 'A microwave chef. I love you, Joey, and I'm sorry you have to change yourself because of me.'

When he hugged me, his fierceness was surprising, almost scary. 'God, I love you, too, but never again, okay? I don't think I can take it.'

'Never again, then,' I said. 'No more heart attacks.' I looked out over the animals. Had they moved closer? Did they want to play? 'Carnival of the animals.'

'Saint-Saëns,' Joey answered.

I laughed. 'Midland County Zoo.'

Yellow folded into blue, gave way to hints of orange and green. The snow flashed off and on, as though it were electric. Electric and surrounded by cars, trucks. Everything slid on the ice. Everything slammed into telephone poles and mailboxes.

He knew the intersection – Colfax and Race – and knew the pizza place on the corner – pepperoni and goat cheese. But after that, he had no idea. It was like a sinkhole had opened in his head, an abyss that could suck down cars on desert highways or houses on beachfront property. The how and why of this moment had fallen into that sinkhole.

It was because he was dying. Tilton and Reaper Bob had warned him. Bits and pieces will slough off, they said, like sheets of ice off glaciers.

Her name was Jen-something. She was dead. She was his wife. He needed to find her. Yet all he could remember was a white soup bowl. When he looked inside that bowl for her name, he found nothing.

They were close, the dead. Block over, block up. A quick walk, up the barely lit stairway, past the second-floor landing. To the third floor and the heavy door. To the waiting-room where the pimp with the cigarette waited with the whore.

If Joey went now, he'd be in that room, his heart beating again, before his face was snow-wet. If he went, he'd be resurrected.

Simple. Quick.

Alone.

she kissed me i remember that

He remembered that over and over. It was a kiss with no beginning, no end.

He remembered her limping to the car after being thrown out. Not to drag him out, but to say something. She spoke and he wanted to tell her he loved her. But the seat had twisted and his face was pressed against the steering wheel. He held her eyes tightly.

I love you, he wanted to say. Life didn't exist until you came along.

Corny though it was, he tried to say it anyway.

She walked away and sat on the kerb and began punching her palm with her fingers.

Then Tilton had pulled Joey from the wreck, bandaged him, took him to Reaper Bob.

Joey's memory was muddy, a dirty river in flood.

'Fuck,' he said quietly. He wanted to spend his last hours finding his wife. But his fear held him as tightly as the car's seatbelt. It squeezed him until there was no air left in his lungs.

He wanted to be heroic.

But he was scared of dying.

'I love you, Jennifer,' he said quietly.

Reaper Bob was two blocks away. In fifteen minutes, he'd be alive. Then he'd find Jennifer and give her a proper burial.

It's a longer drive this time. It's snowing, and even on slushy streets, it's beautiful. The cityscape-lit snow constantly changes, one colour to another, one shape to another. In a strange way, it reminds me of our marriage. We are changing just as quickly as the falling snow. We have new diets, new exercises, new life plans.

I detest it.

Quit bitching, I think. Life is life. I'm alive so shut the hell up, Joey's tired of hearing it. Even *I'm* tired of hearing it.

So I get my nitro pills and my cell phone and we drive. I believe it helps Joey to think of me reintegrating myself back into the World. When we drive, Joey's face lights up. He's like a kid on summer vacation. It doesn't matter what happened yesterday because today is a new day, another chance to get it right. To me, today is just another chance I'll have a coronary event.

I woke up last night with the pain. Maybe I slept crooked, maybe I pulled a muscle. Possibilities both, but I knew it was coronary-event pain. Clutching the cordless phone, I went to the bathroom and put two nitro tablets under my tongue. I waited. The pain didn't get worse, but it certainly didn't get better. Another pill and I waited. The label says, 'If no relief after three doses, call 911'. I took a fourth pill, the last in a bottle of twenty sublingual pills.

I waited.

Ten minutes later, the pain was mostly gone and I threw up, my stomach as knotted as the arteries in my heart, as the thoughts in my head. And the cold, from the blood-thinners, hit me like a ton of stents.

Back in bed, I lay awake all night, waiting for the pain again.

While Joey was at work today, now working fifty and sixty hours a week, I had the nitro refilled and delivered. It costs more for delivery, but I'd rather do that on the sly than have Joey realise I've taken them all.

'Look at that,' Joey said as we drove.

We were passing the park with the animals. The snow had covered just the tops. It was like the animals were so huge the clouds covered them.

While we were both looking, the car hit a patch of black ice. We slid sideways and my heart flew into my throat. My hands grabbed the dashboard and my feet pumped brakes that weren't there.

'Hang on,' Joey yelled.

We slid sideways, banged into the kerb. The car shook like a Tonka truck being played with by some giant boy.

'God, I'm so sorry, Jennifer,' he said. His face was as white as the snow on the animals; his anxious breath steamed the windshield. 'You okay?'

My teeth rattled as badly as if I had been standing in the snow naked for days. They bit into my tongue. Warm blood flooded my mouth.

'Shit,' I yelled. I slammed a fist into the dashboard. 'I bit my tongue. For fuck's sake, it'll bleed for forty-five minutes.' Courtesy of the blood-thinners.

'Shhhhh,' Joey said. 'I'm sorry about that, I wasn't paying attention.'

Part of me wanted to scream at him, but part of me felt sorry for him. He was trying to make the best of a situation that wasn't his fault. Not the icy roads, not the sliding car, not the heart attack. He was an innocent man dragged along, like someone had chained him to the back of a moving truck.

I hugged him and kissed his cheek. 'It wasn't you. Don't worry about it.' I sucked down some blood. 'I'm fine. Let's go home.'

'No shit,' he said. 'Watch the rest of *Kabukiman* and have some hot chocolate.'

The snow was getting heavier, the streets icier. The snow wasn't beautiful any more. It didn't sparkle with street light or twinkle as it hit the ground. It was just grey and slushy, marred by dirt and tyres and footprints.

I'm tired. I've been tired since that moment on the sidewalk. And everything since that moment has made me more tired. My nitro pills shouldn't have to be refilled. Imagined conversations with Mama shouldn't be with her standing over my coffin. Joey shouldn't have to deal with my bad genes. I shouldn't have to go insane wondering when the next massive coronary event will occur.

My medical arc will include more pills, more therapy. Eventually, heart surgery of some sort. And in the end – if I make it to the end – chances are I'll be my mother.

I don't want that.

And I don't want Joey struggling to pay bills we can't really afford.

I love him and that's what I'm saying when I unbuckle my seatbelt and then twist the wheel as violently as I can. Before the car hits a parked truck and flips, I cup his face like Mama used to do to mine.

*

They use poultices.

Strips of the dead who didn't make it. Reaper Bob presses those against the wounds. Blood squeezes out of them, runs over the wounded skin of those who can still live.

The pimp and whore were gone. But Tilton was there. Relief flooded his face when Joey walked in. He snapped his phone closed and shoved it into a pocket.

'The phone,' Joey said with stark realisation. 'She called you.' It was why Tilton had been there so quickly. She hadn't been punching her palm, she'd been dialling her cell phone.

'I'm glad you're back, Joey.'

Joey began to cry. 'I can't find her. She wasn't at the house and I don't know where else to even look.'

Tilton held Joey tightly. 'We gotta worry about you.'

Joey nodded. 'We'd better do it quick, too, because my memory is getting awful spotty.'

Tilton banged on the interior door, behind which Reaper Bob worked. 'He's here. let's do it.'

When Reaper Bob appeared to take Joey inside, Joey didn't move. His guts were twisted and frozen. 'She's dead, isn't she?'

'Yeah,' Tilton said. 'But you got me.'

'Yeah.' Joey squeezed Tilton's arm. 'But I miss her.'

'I know.'

The strips of flesh were ragged, as though they'd been torn from the dead rather than cut. Reaper Bob asked Tilton to press them against Joey's wounds. Joey backed away.

'It won't hurt,' Reaper Bob said. 'They'll help you. They'll save you.'

'And Jennifer will die.'

she cupped my face

'Joey,' Tilton said. 'Please, just let him do it.'

'She grabbed the wheel. She killed herself.'

Tilton shook his head. 'It was an accident. Joey.'

'No. She wanted it to look that way . . . so the insurance will pay . . . but she was tired. She had a couple more attacks since the big one, did you know that? She tried to hide it, but she was eating those nitro pills right and left.' Hot tears stung his cheeks while Reaper Bob worked. 'She said she loved me.'

'We both do.'

'And she said something else, but I can't remember—'

Zoo, he realised.

'Holy fuck.' Joey jumped up, his body on fire. 'I know where she is.'
'Joey, no,' Tilton shouted. 'Damnit, leave her be or you'll die.'
'She's at the park, Tilton. She's with the animals.'
'What?'
Joey dashed down the steps, taking two, sometimes three, at a time.
'The last thing she said. "I miss the zoo."'

I can hear them. It's vaguely surprising; I thought I'd be dead by now.
Joey's voice, usually so sweet and tame, is edgy and jagged.
'I'm so sorry . . . I should have been there for you.'
He thinks it's his fault. He thinks I did this because of him.
'She's dead,' Tilton says. 'I'm sorry, Joey, but we've got to get you
back.'
I came here to die. My skull has a hole in it and my right arm is
broken in three places. I can't count how many breaks my left leg has.
I cough up blood and it hurts when I take a deep breath. It's probably
broken ribs puncturing my lung.
Joey falls to his knees at my side. I don't see him, my eyes have
swollen closed, but I feel him. 'We can save her. Damnit, we can save
her.'
'It's too late for her. We've got to save you.'
I want to open my eyes then. I want to yell at him. Why is he still
dead? I want to shake him and maybe slap his face five or six times.
I did this horrible thing so he'd get on with his pre-heart attack life.
To make sure he'd have life insurance money for bills, to make sure he
could go back to who he had been before our lives changed.
'You don't understand, Tilton.' He grabs my hand and kisses it. His
lips are cold and rough. 'Why are you so fucking worried about me?'
'Because I love you, dumbshit. Are you that blind? I love you and I
don't want you to die.'
That was it, wasn't it? I'd known, I think, for all of our marriage.
Tilton and his boyfriends who always looked and acted a little too
much like Joey.
'I'm dead already,' Joey says.
'I can save you.'
'Damnit, I'm not dead because I'm dead, I'm dead because Jennifer
is dead.'
No, I want to shout. No, no, *no*!
'Help me,' Joey says.
There is a long silence, but finally Tilton says, 'Fine, but you can't

carry her, you're too injured. Let me do it. You get back as fast as you can, I'll get her there.'

Joey, my love, cups my face. It's not the warm touch I spent the last ten years with. He's cold. 'I'll see you soon,' he whispers. Then he cries as he leaves me behind. He has been scared since my heart attack. He was scared for me, absolutely, but he was scared for himself, too. I came too close to death for him to come away unscathed. He saw, in my foxtrot with mortality, his own dance card being filled.

When he's gone, I hear Tilton over me. Clothes shuffle and I feel a warm stream on my chest and neck, on my face and head.

He's pissing on me and I just want to laugh. It's his foul little way of saying he won, of saying he'll have Joey and I'll have six feet of dirt in a pauper's grave.

'Fuck you,' Tilton says. 'You selfish bitch. He never loved you. He loves me. But he couldn't see it because you wouldn't get your tits out of his face.'

He zips up and walks away.

'Have a great death,' he mutters over his shoulder.

Not a great death, there is no such thing. But a fulfilled one. It's what I want and what I need to give Joey. I'm taking myself away from him, but I'm giving him himself back. No more of my medications or limitations.

I hope he understands I do this not just for myself, but because I love him.

Maybe I am a selfish bitch. Maybe I have done the wrong thing. Maybe letting Tilton bring me back from the dead would have solved my medical problems. Maybe I could have been as good as pre-heart attack.

But what can I do now?

Can I hear the snow falling? Have the streetlights turned it the same shade of yellow as Mama's lemonade?

Joey waited on the landing, next to Reaper Bob.

'It's good to be back,' Joey said.

The man nodded. 'Yeah. Nothing better than breathing living air. You know, you were dead for a good long while.'

'How long?'

'Twenty-two, twenty-three hours. I seen people dead that long don't come back at all.' He shrugged. 'Other hand, I seen them dead twice as long come back full.'

Tilton came up the stairs, a question on his face. When Joey and the black man nodded, Tilton danced a quick little jig. 'Oh, man. I am so glad. I was afraid you'd die.'

Reaper Bob grinned and clapped Joey on the back. 'I do good work. So, you get her?'

Tilton looked away uncomfortably.

'Who?' Joey asked.

'My mistake,' Reaper Bob said. 'I got him mixed up with some other cracker who was supposed to bring me his best friend's wife.'

'Speaking of wives,' Joey said. He held up his ring finger. 'The hell is this?'

'Bad joke,' Tilton said. 'You were drunk. I tried to get you to marry that prostitute works out of Kitty's.'

Joey frowned, no memory of the Kitty's pro in his head at all. 'Shit,' he said. 'I must have had a load on.'

Reaper Bob headed back inside. 'Break's over, I guess.'

Joey offered his hand. 'Thanks, man, I appreciate it.'

'No problem.'

The snow fell gently on Joey and Tilton's faces, melting over their coats.

'It's a nice night,' Joey said.

'Yeah.'

'How about some ribs?' Joey said. 'Seems like a million years since I've had any."

Tilton nodded. 'A few months, anyway.'

'Maybe after dinner we can head down to Blue's Mob, find us some loving.'

'Maybe,' Tilton said.

Trey R. Barker was born in Texas and currently lives near Chicago, Illinois, with his wife LuAnn. A musician with an affinity for African percussion and Southern blues, his past jobs have included reporter, editor, pizza cook, sandwich-maker, phone solicitor, karaoke salesman and doll assembler. Barker's short fiction, encompassing everything from fantasy to horror, science fiction to crime/mystery, traditional Westerns to poetry, has appeared in around a hundred publications. Fairwood Press recently released a chapbook of the author's Green River stories, *Where the Southern Cross the Dog*. He was also co-editor of the critically acclaimed anthology *Crime Spree* from December Girl Press. Barker also works in the theatre, where he is the International Tour Technical Director for the David Taylor Dance Theater. His written work for the stage includes an adaptation of Charles Dickens' *A Christmas Carol*, Agatha Christie's *The Mysterious Affair at Styles* and an original one-man show based on the life of Edgar Allan Poe. 'Although I tend to use quite a large amount of biography in my stories,' notes the author, 'that was not my intention here. I actually sought to write about Camille Saint-Saëns' *Carnival of the Animals*, a piece of programme music he wrote in 1886 (and wouldn't allow to be published until after his death because he thought it too "silly" for a composer of serious reputation). But as I began to discover the characters in the story, the images of the animals became less important and stray elements of biography worked their way in. By the time I was finished, I had written one of those cathartic pieces writers so often talk about but which I had never experienced before.'

The Dinosaur Hunter

STEPHEN BAXTER

It was the morning of the last day.

Joan Useb didn't know that yet, of course. As it began it seemed like any other day in Joan's life – although she herself regarded her life, and a typical day in it, as somewhat peculiar by most people's standards.

After breakfast, she emerged from her field tent under a sky that was already a washed-out blue-white.

She was surrounded by kilometres of badlands: layered rock coloured purple, red, brown, shaped into hillocks and valleys. Maybe half a kilometre from her father's field site rolled the sluggish waters of the Fort Peck reservoir, a huge artificial lake made by damming the Missouri river.

This was the setting in which she first saw the Silver Woman.

Or thought she saw her. She couldn't be sure; it was just something out of the corner of her eye, a figure standing alone.

Staring at her.

When she looked again, there was nothing there, nobody.

This was Hell Creek, Montana. Joan was thirteen years old.

As she had become aware of the state of the world beyond the cocoon in which she had grown up, Joan had had a lot of arguments with her father.

'Let me out of this box you've brought me up in,' she would say.

'I'm trying to equip you to cope with a dangerous and unpredictable future,' he would reply.

And he would tell her his story of the lily-pond. Lovelock's lily-pond, he called it.

'Suppose you have a lily that doubles in size every day. Suppose at that rate it would take fifty days to cover the pond. It starts out small, just a scrap, a few petals. When it got to the point that it covered half the pond, you might start to worry. But you know when that would be? *The forty-ninth day.*'

'Dad, can't you talk straight to me?'

'You know what's going on out there. I think the world's problems are multiplying exponentially. I think things will fall apart faster than anybody expects.'

'Dad—'

'We won't be able to tell when the forty-ninth day comes. I just want us to be somewhere safe when it does.'

She was infuriated, of course. She felt as if he was talking to her like she was a kid.

The oviraptor led her chicks through deepening snow.

The ground was rising. They were climbing a young hill, in fact a foothill of the Rockies.

The oviraptor was a small predatory dinosaur.

This little family had been saved thus far from the great extinction, where so many had died, by a chance combination of clouds and rocks and trees, of wind direction, the closeness of a pond that gave shelter from the firestorms.

But now they were in trouble.

The snow – lying over what had been tropical vegetation just days ago – wasn't thick. In fact, this time of darkness was a period of intense dryness, all over the planet. But the snow was a disaster for the mother oviraptor.

She belonged to one of the smaller raptor species: she was about the size of a chicken. Her gaudy feathers helped keep out the cold, and her hind legs were long enough for her to step out of this baffling, terrifying white stuff.

But for her four surviving chicks it was different. Just weeks old, they were too small to be able to lift their bodies out of the snow. As they struggled to follow their mother their stubby feathers were already soaked, and the snow around their bellies was sucking away their body heat. They peeped mournfully, seeking their mother's help.

In her despair and anger the mother dinosaur snapped at the snow around her. But the snow did not respond.

From a bay at the end of the reservoir, Joan followed a dry creek channel into the hills, picking her way over the rubble-littered floor. The channel had been water-cut through the sedimentary rocks here, like a slice through a cake. All the strata of sandstone and shale were horizontal, flat as the day they were laid down in vanished seas, and they were neatly displayed around her.

She had her rock hammer at her belt – a gift from her dad when she was ten years old, already proudly scuffed by many hours in the field – and she used it now to dig through the crumbling surface layers until fresh unweathered rock was exposed.

She knew the story of this land. The countless sand grains that made up the lowest layer of black shale had once been eroded by rainfall from the Rockies and washed down into a long-vanished ocean, warm and deep. The ocean bed had, in its turn, been hardened to rock, lifted back into the light by the Earth's inner heat, and eroded again, here at the arid modern surface.

Thus the substance of the world was recycled, over and over. That was an idea she had always liked.

At last, buried in the black shale, she found a hard, white lump, an irregular bit of limestone. It cracked open to reveal shining red: an ammonite shell, a spiral about as big as her fist. Carefully she chipped away at the surrounding limestone, exposing the iridescent mother-of-pearl surface. The ammonites, who had died under the dinosaur-killer comet, had been a successful group worldwide. They were related to nautiluses, but this shell was far more fantastic and elaborate than any modern specimen.

Satisfied, she tucked her hammer in her belt and, ammonite in hand, strode up the creek to find her father.

It had all started to go wrong before Joan was even born.

Earth had been long overdue for a major volcanic incident.

Beneath the island of New Guinea, magma had been stirring: molten rock, a thousand cubic kilometres of it. This great bleeding had been moving up through faults in Earth's thin outer crust, up towards the huge, ancient caldera called Rabaul, at a rate of ten metres every month. It was an astounding pace for a geological event, a testament to mighty energies.

Rabaul had erupted cataclysmically many times before. Two such eruptions had been identified by human scientists, one some fifteen hundred years earlier, the other around two thousand years before that. It would surely happen again sometime.

Or the mountain might go back to sleep.

Most people didn't think about it. It was a crowded world, with plenty of problems to worry about even more immediate than a grumbling volcano.

They had been wrong.

As Joan climbed, she rose up through the strata – and so up through time, for the younger layers of the rock overlay the old, the most basic principle of geology.

Soon the black marine shales had been replaced by dark brown sandstones. These strata had been laid down at the shore of that ancient sea: she could make out impressions of snail and clam shells. One stratum was covered in ripples, just like a sandy beach in California, but when she touched the surface she found cold dead rock, for this beach had been dry for a hundred million years.

Further up the creek she found thicker, lighter-coloured deposits, laid down by a river, probably feeding a fresh-water lake or a swamp. In the rocks here there were streaks of black – coal, made of plant material, compressed leaves and twigs, bark and flowers. She knew that if she looked hard enough she could find tiny blackened bones and teeth and vertebrae of animals, of lizards and mammals and birds, and dinosaurs.

The sun had risen higher; by the time she had reached the uppermost layer she was sweating. But the rocks here were brighter in colour, red, brown and purple. They too contained bones of birds, mammals, crocodiles – but no dinosaurs. It was the relic of a different world.

And lying sandwiched between the two worlds, new and old, was a layer of grey clay no thicker than her hand, shot through with coal. Her father called this the Cretaceous-Tertiary boundary clay.

She knew the story, of course.

The comet had been at least ten kilometres in diameter, and had hit the Earth somewhere off the coast of Mexico. The resulting explosion was ten thousand times as strong as the detonation of all mankind's nuclear weapons.

It had been a bad day to be a dinosaur in Texas.

When the dust and ash had finally rained out, it had laid down this clay, the boundary clay: a dirt that contained the ash of the lush Cretaceous forests, and millions upon millions of dinosaurs.

Oviraptors were good mothers.

Like their relatives the crocodiles, many dinosaurs had close family ties with their offspring. Oviraptors were particularly parental. Their fossilised bones were so often found in the presence of eggs, in fact, that uncomprehending human palaeontologists would later give them a name that meant *egg-hunter*.

But this oviraptor mother, struggling through the dread comet winter, could do little to protect her chicks. That gruesome fact had turned the motherhood bond into a fiery rope that squeezed her heart.

At last the oviraptor reached a steep rise. Scorched bare of vegetation, the rocky ground was slippery with frost and hard to climb. But the oviraptor gratefully hurried forward, out of the drifting snow.

Her chicks followed, shivering and bedraggled bundles of feathers, looking more like baby birds than ferocious carnivorous dinosaurs.

One of her favourite bedtime stories was about boundary clay.

That told you a lot about how she had grown up, she thought.

Her father said it was a kind of archaeologist's urban myth. It told how an archaeologist out in the field, somewhere in the world, had – painstakingly, carefully – dug out from just under the Cretaceous boundary clay what could only be a bullet, embedded in the hip-bone of a tyrannosaur.

It makes sense, George used to say to his wide-eyed daughter. *Suppose you had a time machine, and you wanted to hunt dinos.*

Like in all those sci-fi stories, she would say.

Yes. Like in the stories. But suppose you were scrupulous; suppose you didn't want to change history by killing a dinosaur that never got hunted in its original history. What would you do?

I know what you'd do, she said. *You'd go back and do your hunting where whatever you did would have made no difference at all. You'd go to the day the comet hit. You'd go to Texas.*

That's right. Everything close to the comet impact zone – by close, I mean a thousand kilometres – was crisped. Honey, on that day you could have built a klick-high barbecue of brontosaurs and it would have made no difference to future history. That's the place to go, to hunt your dinosaurs. The day the comet fell . . .

As she approached her father's field site she could hear voices, the occasional clank of hammers, blaring rock.

Many of the dig workers were amateurs, what her father called his 'Cretaceous irregulars'. They spent their summers discovering the past. They would pay for their own gas and drive into the badlands in pick-ups loaded with bags of plaster, rolls of burlap and beer. They worked long hours without pay – and often without much appreciation from those who used them.

Of course times had changed; there were a lot fewer of them now.

Her father, George, saw her coming. He hallooed and came to meet her.

He wore a disreputable broad-brimmed hat that shaded his grinning face, and a pair of shorts that, however practical, made him look unforgivably like a nerd – a dusty-kneed nerd at that. But here he was greeting her with a brisk hug. 'Hi, honey. Hot enough?' He looked politely at her ammonite, but she could tell he was too excited about some discovery of his own. 'I found a tooth . . .'

'A tooth?'

'Wait 'til you see it!'

So she followed him to his table.

A little way away, an immense bone lay on the brown dirt. Most of the field workers were working on the bone, slapping on burlap and bright white plaster. It looked like a hip bone, if she was any judge, maybe from *Tyrannosaurus rex*: no great surprise, as almost all the tyrannosaur fossils ever discovered had come from this area.

She longed to go see the vast *T. rex* bone. And besides, she hankered to join the jokey party of young workers.

. . . And there was the Silver Woman, again.

She was standing behind the field workers, watching them carefully. But they didn't seem to see her. She was short, Joan was able to see, by comparison with the workers, no more than four feet high. And she wore a kind of overall that shone bright silver.

She cast no shadow on the ground. And the shadows and highlights on her chin, her fur, her clothes looked wrong, as if cast not by the sun, but by some invisible light source.

She turned to look Joan in the eye. She had fur on her face, like a chimp.

She vanished. As simple as that, like a clumsy special effect.

Joan gasped, and felt oddly dizzy. But nobody else had reacted. Get a grip, Joan.

Anyhow, her father had reached his table and she had to pay attention.

When Rabaul had blown its top, George Useb had immediately taken his wife, his unborn child, his life, away, out of the cities, off into the archaeological field, in the interior of the continental US. He was seeking as much safety as he could find, out here in the most physically isolated part of Fortress America.

Even when his wife had upped and left, pining for city life, he had insisted on keeping Joan here with him.

Joan had spent little time in towns or cities, with people. Even now, she had been barely touched by the cataclysms that swept around the world. On the other hand, she had spent hardly any time with people her own age.

She didn't know if that was a good thing or not. How could she tell?

It was a complex time to be thirteen years old. But then, it always was.

Using tweezers – carefully, carefully – George held up a tiny scrap of something black. '*Look* at that,' he said. 'What do you think?'

She looked closely. 'Umm . . . a tooth?'

He gazed at his prize proudly. 'Joan, this isn't *just* a tooth. I think it's a *Purgatorius* tooth.'

'Say what?'

'*Purgatorius*. A dinosaur-era mammal. Found it right under the boundary clay.'

'You can tell all that from a tooth?'

'Sure. I mean, look at this thing. It's a precise piece of dental engineering, already the result of a hundred and fifty million years of evolution. It's all connected, you see. If you're a mammal you have specialised teeth so you can shear your food more rapidly – and so you can fuel a faster metabolism. But you can only have teeth like this if your mother produces milk, so you don't need to be born with your final set of teeth; the specialist tools can grow in place later. Didn't you ever wonder why you had milk teeth?'

She tried to keep interested, out of politeness. But there was something about the blackened, tiny tooth that Joan found disturbing.

Consider her ammonite shell. It had been trapped in a limestone coffin for maybe *seventy million years* – an unimaginable amount of time – and for what? Had whole lineages of ammonites flourished and died, with nobody around even to see what was going on, just so a kid like her could dig out a desk ornament? And, in another seventy million years, would her skull and kneecaps and whatever else be likewise dug up and marvelled over by uncomprehending eyes?

Maybe it was that unwelcome perspective, the pitiless depths of time, that had turned her off science. If life was so brief and meaningless, who wanted to know?

Her father, a twentieth-century rationalist stiff, hated her to talk like that. He hadn't brought her out here for her head to turn to mush, he would say.

She tried to express what she was feeling. 'Dad – what's the point?'

She compared her ammonite's robust beauty to the ugly shard of enamel in her father's tweezers. 'It's all dead and gone. Maybe the past has no use unless it's beautiful.'

He looked pained. 'Now, honey – how can you say that? A lot of people are going to care a great deal about this find of mine. You know why? Because it's a *primate*. Primate bones are hard to find, Joan – because most primates, for most of their history, have spent their lives climbing trees, and forests don't make good fossils. And *Purgatorius* here is maybe the first of the line.'

'An ancestor?'

'Honey, this little scrap could be all that's left of the most remote ancestor of you and me – and everybody alive – and the chimps and gorillas and lemurs. Not only that, she, or her family, survived the comet impact that destroyed the dinos . . .'

Joan held up her hands. 'All right, I'm impressed. What did she look like?'

'She?'

Joan thought that over. 'Yes, she.'

'Okay. Umm – what do you *think* she looked like?'

'Something like a monkey?'

'More like a rat – but much smaller, shrew-size, with a bushy tail. But *Purgatorius* was still a primate – I mean, *already* a primate. The forest is a hazardous world where you have to be able to spot which branch to jump to next, and judge your jump right, *and* grab hold of it – without fail, every time. It makes for grasping hands, sharp eyes, a large, fuel-hungry brain . . .'

Joan rubbed her nose. 'One of these days you'll find something really sexy in the boundary clay.'

He pulled a face. 'Oh, like a bullet?'

'Dad . . .'

'*Dad can I go now?* Okay. Go play with the *T. rex* bone.'

She turned and ran.

He called after her, 'But just think – *Purgatorius* might have lived like a squirrel, but she saw *T. rex* in the flesh, all five tons of flesh, in fact . . . Hey! You forgot your ammonite.'

But Joan wasn't listening.

Because outside the tent, the Silver Woman was waiting again.

This time Joan was able to walk right up to her. She looked like a chimp, an upright chimp. Her face was like a chimp's too, hairy, with flattened nostrils, and a brain pan small enough for Joan to have cupped in one hand. But she had on that shining coverall, and an array of some kind of tools at her belt.

Oddly, Joan wasn't afraid. 'Tell me who you are,' she said.

The Silver Woman didn't reply.

'What do you want?'

The Silver Woman opened her mouth with a popping sound, as if she wasn't used to speaking aloud. 'The tooth-schh,' she said at last, indistinctly.

Joan frowned. 'The tooth? The *Purgatorius* tooth? Why?'

'A . . . treash-ure.' The word took some saying.

'You want me to help you?' She tried to think it through. 'You want me to steal a damn tooth from my father and give it to you? Why should I?'

The woman shrugged, her narrow shoulders working. Joan saw how slack her skin was, as if she had no fat on her body.

'Tell me who you are,' Joan demanded again.

'You know,' the woman whispered.

And she disappeared again.

George Useb's instinct about Rabaul had been right.

The millions who had been killed during the eruption and its immediate aftermath were only the first.

The volcano's lingering legacy did most of the damage – specifically, the vast volumes of material it had injected into the upper air.

It had rained, and rained, and rained, all over the world, for weeks.

After the rain, as the sky ran dry, came the drought.

As the disaster became planet-wide, cholera, measles, typhus and dysentery epidemics broke out on a massive scale. Huge refugee flows washed back and forth. Medical and relief infrastructures were totally overwhelmed, and in many areas political administration quickly disintegrated.

Banditry and war followed. Scrappy, multi-polar conflict broke out across much of Africa, South America and Asia. The last United Nations-hosted summit conference ended in a mass assassination. And so on.

And in all this – as radiation flooded the air, as the fires burned around the planet, as the sun failed to shine – the world's ecosystem, already under pressure, began to implode.

And humans discovered conclusively at last that they were still, after all, just animals embedded in an ecosystem.

It wasn't Rabaul. That wasn't the cause. That was just the final straw.

Everything had been stretched to breaking point anyhow. It wasn't even bad luck. If it hadn't been Rabaul it would have been another volcano, or a quake or an asteroid, or some damn thing.

It was turning out to be remarkably easy for a world to end.

The oviraptor came to an opening in the loose rubble and volcanic stones. She could see nothing, but her sensitive hearing and sense of smell told her that here was a cave. She could make a nest, if she could find pine needles or dead fern fronds or other debris . . .

But the cave smelled odd: of something alive, something warm. This was no cave but a burrow. And whatever had dug it out was *here*, at the back of the little tunnel. She could sense it, a quivering mass of flesh, shivering as she was.

The chicks, climbing up behind her, smelled it too. They started to screech their hunger.

She didn't recognise the smell; evidently this burrower's upland range didn't overlap her lowland home. She had no clear idea of what it was, how big it was, how well it could defend itself. But it didn't matter: right now she had no choice.

She hurled herself forward, deep into the cave, mouth agape. Suddenly she felt better than she had done for days. She was, after all, a raptor; this was what she did.

The segnosaur fought back, as best he could.

He was actually larger than the raptor that attacked him. He had an awkward, sprawling body with wide hind feet, but his neck was long, his head small, like an ostrich's, his beak toothless, his arms short. His best weapons were his powerful hands, which were equipped with long, straight claws. These were hands designed for digging.

The segnosaur was one of the few species of dinosaur that constructed burrows. His deep, complex network of tunnels had enabled him to live out the horrific events of the extinction. Many of his kind, in fact, still survived across the continent, in mountain localities like this.

But the world still contained many hungry carnivores, and a dwindling food supply. One by one the segnosaur's kind were being hunted down, no matter how deep their caves, a final saurian population steadily wiped out by increasingly desperate predators.

And so it was now. The segnosaur actually managed to lay a hand on the oviraptor, laying open her back with a raked digging claw. But he was no match for this ferocious, expert killer.

She laid open his belly.

The segnosaur felt his guts spill on the ground he had scraped out so carefully, could feel the cold that invaded him. He lived long enough to feel the raptor chicks' small teeth bite into his liver.

By evening, most of the casuals had upped and gone.

The sky that night was huge and crammed with stars. The Milky Way, a side-on view of a giant spiral galaxy, was a highway across the night.

Joan lay on her back, gazing up, imagining the rocky Earth had vanished, the strata and their cargo of fossils and all, and that she was adrift in space.

In the twenty-first century you couldn't go anywhere to escape the traces of mankind. The lake she could hear lapping gently was artificial; all the land around here was fenced-off rangeland. A couple of centuries ago there would have been huge herds of antelope and buffalo where now only crickets chirped. But if she tried, under this huge sky, she could imagine she really had been cast back into the past, a time before people had begun to rebuild the Earth.

She wondered if *Purgatorius* would have seen the same stars. Had they swum about the sky, across sixty-five million years? Did the Galaxy itself turn, like some huge pinwheel in the night?

. . . the Silver Woman was standing over her. Joan saw she wore a necklace, strung with what looked like fossils: bits of tiny, perfect skulls, jawbones, pelvises.

Joan sat up. '*Tell me who you are.*'

'You know.'

And Joan, her scalp crawling, thought she did.

But if you're here, she thought, that means today is the forty-ninth day.

'What are you doing? Taking elephants? Hunting whales? Looking for artworks to save, books, sculptures . . .'

The Silver Woman said only, 'Tooth-shsh.'

Joan felt anger build. 'Are you a time traveller? Are you a ghost? *Are you real?* How did I *know* about you? Have you gone back into the past to set me up for this meeting? That's what time travellers do, isn't it? Have you been messing with time, messing with my life, fucking with my head?'

The Silver Woman wouldn't reply to any of this.

Joan gave in to her rage and fear. 'I won't help you steal from my father. I don't care where you're from. Get away! Get away!' And she picked up badlands rocks, big handfuls of them, and hurled them at the Silver Woman until she disappeared again.

A flaring, high above, caught her eye.

There were lights in the sky. Not stars, not planes, not satellites. Lights that flared and died. Silent, remote explosions, all around the sky's equator.

It had been hard for the mother oviraptor.

The prey species were all gone now. The last dinosaurs were destroying each other, in battles as savage as any in their long age.

At last the oviraptor's chicks, starving, had fallen on each other. The stronger three had ganged up on the weakest. And then, with a grisly logic, two had turned on one.

In the end – to her shame, her horror, violating all her mothering instincts – the oviraptor herself had devoured the last of her chicks.

And now, though she did not know it, she was the last of her kind.

But still she starved.

Now she faced something new. A biped, with bits of bone at its neck. Fur that was moonlight silver. Raising something towards her.

Something that spat light.

She couldn't have gone on much longer anyhow. It had taken all her strength just to keep upright, to keep lifting her legs out of the snow. She didn't fight, threaten, try to flee. She just stood there.

There was an instant of almost welcome heat.

Suppose I threw you back down the strata, back into time, her father had once said. *After just a hundred thousand years you'd lose that nice high forehead of yours. Your upright-walker legs would be gone after three or four million years, because you'd be spending most of your time on all fours, like the chimps. You'd grow your tail back after twenty-five million years. After thirty-five million you'd lose the last of your ape features, like your teeth: after that you'd be a monkey, child. And then you'd keep on shrinking. Forty million years deep you'd look something like a lemur. And eventually—*

Eventually, she would be a little ratty thing, peering up as dinosaurs danced under swimming stars.

There was a sound of thunder. It was as if great feet were stamping down on the fossil-laden bedrock, somewhere beyond the horizon.

Fear brushed her mind. She had bitched about her isolation. But she had always been safe with her father, here in her rocky cocoon.

The Silver Woman appeared again. She stood there, under the wheeling stars, looking at Joan.

Joan blurted, 'Take me with you.'

The Silver Woman said, 'Already enough-ghgh – of *you*.' And she vanished.

Joan got up off the ground and ran to the warm tent, an island of light amongst the pale silhouettes of the rock formations, where her father waited for her.

The stomping grew louder, as if some fiery beast was approaching.

Stephen Baxter has degrees in mathematics, from Cambridge University, and engineering, from Southampton University. He worked as a teacher of maths and physics, and in 1991 he applied to become a cosmonaut on the Mir space station. His first professionally published story appeared in 1987 and he has been a full-time author since 1995. His books have been published in many different languages, and he is a winner of the Philip K. Dick Award, the John W. Campbell Memorial Award, the British Science Fiction Association Award, Germany's Kurd Lasswitz Award and Japan's Seiun Award. He has also been nominated for several others, including the Arthur C. Clarke, the Hugo and the Locus awards. The author of more than a hundred science fiction short stories, Baxter's novel *Voyage* was dramatised for BBC Radio in 1999 and his novel *Timelike Infinity* and story 'Pilot' are both in development as feature films. His latest novel is *Evolution*, from Gollancz. 'This story is a spin-off of my research for a novel on human evolution,' he reveals. 'I remembered Ray Bradbury's famous old story 'A Sound of Thunder', in which dinosaur hunters cause a tiny change in the past that makes ripples through history. But I realised that we know there was one day where you could go back to hunt dinosaurs and make no difference at all . . .'

There Lies the Danger . . .

BASIL COPPER

I

As Joshua Arkwright sat at the typewriter in his study one bright April day he was in reflective mood. One of the world's most successful novelists, he had achieved much in his long and vigorous life. He had published over one hundred books in his lifetime, many of which had been acclaimed as classics, but now, at eighty-five, he was aware of his waning powers. It was not that he had a morbid fear of death, but he knew that he had many more fine works of fiction to give the world and, not for the first time, he regretted the inevitable approach of mortality.

He had, in fact, written a number of works which touched on the subject and he eagerly devoured medical journals which contained articles on efforts currently being made by scientists in the study of prolonging life. He had been particularly interested in recent newspaper reports on experiments being done by Professor Conrad Voss in Switzerland, which were apparently yielding remarkable results. On impulse, he had asked his secretary to contact Voss, and now he was impatiently awaiting a reply to his queries.

He was interrupted by a deferential tapping at his study door and the somewhat flushed face of Yvonne appeared.

'Professor Voss is calling. I will put him through.'

Arkwright nodded, without a flicker of emotion on his face, though his pulse was a little erratic as he picked up the telephone.

'Voss here. Many thanks for your enquiries.' The voice was low and modulated and he spoke perfect English.

'I am grateful for your call, Professor. You know my age, of course.'

There was a muffled chuckle from the other end of the wire.

'Naturally, my good sir. I keep an extensive reference library here and I have long been an admirer of your works.'

Arkwright felt a wave of gratification sweeping over him.

'And I have followed your own career with interest, Professor. My questions stem from the fact that I feel I have a good deal yet to give the world, but time is pressing and my powers – physical, of course, not imaginative – are waning. I have excellent medical advice, but it seems to me that no one has ever approached the reported success of your experiments ... I could come over if you thought there was a possibility ...'

'Certainly. And I could accommodate you in my private quarters. A social visit to all intents and purposes. And strictly no publicity.'

'Naturally, Professor. And I will have the necessary arrangements put in hand immediately. I cannot get away at once, but shall we say in a week's time? On the fifteenth, if that would be convenient for you?'

'Admirable, Mr Arkwright. If you let me know the flight time, I will have you met at the airport at Geneva.'

When Arkwright put the receiver down he sat for a long time staring out of the window, not seeing the landscaped gardens below, but with many strange thoughts whirling through his brain. But the die was cast and what could he lose? For Voss had experimented not only on animals, but on human beings, with astonishing results, if the reports in the leading British and Continental medical journals were anything to go by. He picked up the extension and asked Yvonne to come in immediately.

II

'You understand I cannot promise you immortality. That is quite beyond medical science at the present time, and perhaps for all time. But what I can promise – even at your advanced age – is another forty or fifty productive years, during which you will feel and behave like a much younger man.'

Professor Voss, a striking-looking person in his early fifties, with dark hair cut *en brosse*, sat behind a vast desk in his consulting room and spread well-manicured hands on the blotter in front of him. The sun was slowly declining behind the snow-capped mountains and casting great shadows over the town and placid lake below, while the well-regulated life of his household went smoothly on behind the grey metal door which led to the main building.

Voss hesitated as he regarded the other, his faded grey eyes sparkling behind gold-rimmed spectacles. 'You have not asked me the most important question, Mr Arkwright. Though I am sure it is at the forefront of your mind.'

Caught off balance, the prospective patient was at a momentary loss. But Voss immediately put him at his ease.

'You were going to ask me, surely, that if my treatment is so successful, why have I not experimented on myself?'

Arkwright put up his hand in protest, but the Professor cut him short, though still with an amiable smile on his face. 'But I have, my dear sir.' He indicated the rows of metal filing cabinets against the far wall. 'My experiments have been far more thorough and extensive than the world believes. And I have all the patients' birth certificates available.'

'I am impressed,' Arkwright said.

The Professor's smile widened. 'That is what they all say,' he answered gently. 'A new age is dawning, Mr Arkwright. Greatly prolonged life, renewed activity without pain or disease. Something the world has long been waiting for.'

'I must apologise if I have inadvertently . . .' his visitor began.

'There is no need for any apology. We deal in hard facts here.'

Arkwright changed the subject. 'How long will the treatment take? Your young lady secretary told me . . .'

Voss had a satisfied expression on his face now. 'The young lady, as you call her, is over sixty! She was one of my first patients, and has been an invaluable help to me over the past years.'

Arkwright sat back in his comfortable leather chair, lost for words for once.

'You asked about the length of treatment. A month or so normally, give or take a few days, depending on the patient. You have kindly supplied me with your own medical records. You are in remarkably good health for a man of your age. As to the treatment, that would be expensive, of course . . .' He paused, giving Arkwright an enquiring look.

The author brushed the hidden query aside. 'Money is of no importance,' he said curtly.

Voss gave him a slight bow. 'I thought as much. But I have to ask these questions as a matter of form.'

'Of course.'

'As you can imagine, much of the procedures and details of the equipment used are secret,' Voss continued. 'I and my medical staff have spent thousands of hours, and I myself have poured a fortune into developing the finest possible equipment, to give near-perfect results.'

He spread his hands wide on the blotter again. 'Nothing in this life is perfect, as you know,' he said disarmingly. 'But we come very close to it. Apart from the treatment mentioned, there are many injections to a formula arrived at over a good many years.'

Arkwright leaned forward in the chair. 'And the results?'

'Completely successful. I will show you some of the records here which you may peruse. Needless to say, the identities of patients will not be divulged. But I can assure you that patients I treated some fifteen years ago are alive and well and looking remarkably young for their real ages. You realise, of course, that enormous sums of money are involved. Other clinics and institutions would do anything to get hold of our formulae. That is why we have to observe absolute secrecy.'

'How will the change take place?'

'Very gradually, of course. About a year, in most cases. The hair will slowly turn black, or to its original colour. In bald patients, the hair grows naturally again. As they regress, wrinkles disappear, the skin becomes smooth and elastic and eventually a man or woman of about thirty emerges. Though I am afraid that some patients have had to change their identities and perhaps move to another town or even country. Some have abandoned old wives and taken young girls to their beds.' He shrugged. 'Regrettable, but I cannot help that.'

'Of course not. When will we start?'

'In two or three days, when you have settled down. I deal with only one patient at a time as the treatment takes up all the resources of the clinic. In the meantime I will show you to my private quarters, where an excellent dinner awaits us.'

III

Arkwright returned to England some while later, after his intensive course of treatment, still a little sceptical, despite the Professor's assurances. He had spent a considerable sum of money, but that did not bother him at all. Despite all the documentary and photographic evidence the staff at the clinic had supplied him with, he was impatient to see tangible results, though he had been assured countless times that they would be slow in coming. However, the prognosis in his case, after exhaustive medical tests, was positive.

Sure enough, over a month later Arkwright began to notice a slight darkening of the hair at the side of his head, while a certain stiffness in his limbs, which had persisted for some years, was disappearing.

Though inwardly excited, it was still too early for him to assess the progress of the treatment, but he quietly made plans to retreat to an isolated house he owned in the West Country, where the metamorphosis, if indeed it did happen, would be unnoticed by friends and colleagues.

There would be problems, he realised, if he suddenly reappeared in the world with an appearance akin to that of his own son, if he had ever had one. He would meet those contingencies in due course. So far as his literary career was concerned, his publishers had been using old publicity photographs for many years, so that would not present a problem.

And in any case, many of his old friends and colleagues had died off as the years had passed and he had no living relatives. He had not realised this sort of situation would arise, and he had to carefully think out a plan of campaign. In the meantime he revelled in returning strength and ability, and once again he was busy at his writing desk, where the rattle of his portable typewriter was heard at ever-increasing periods as various plot points came to him.

He retained his present house and staff and would keep in touch by telephone when he reached his secondary home. He had already made arrangements to have his important correspondence sent on. A month later he was installed in his new quarters, where he had a permanent housekeeper and a gardener. Later, he would move to a hotel and change quarters from time to time until the transformation was complete. Beyond that, he had nothing worked out.

After the year was up, he looked in the mirror of his hotel room on the South Coast and saw a vigorous young man of about thirty looking back at him. His new life had begun.

IV

Dr Poole, busy examining specimens under the microscope in the clinic in Lausanne, was suddenly interrupted by a sharp exclamation from Professor Voss, who was studying various documents at his desk on the other side of the laboratory.

'What is it?' he asked.

'Come and look at this.'

Poole crossed to peer over his colleague's shoulder at the national newspapers spread out before the Professor. Large headings on most of the front pages gave the startling news of the sudden death of the great

author, Joshua Arkwright, during a tennis match in Cannes. While Poole sat down at the desk to study the reports with increasing sadness, Voss crossed to the far corner of the huge room and dialled the international operator. He was engaged in a long conversation in English before putting down the receiver. He came back rubbing his hands.

'This is tragic indeed,' Poole observed.

Voss sat down in his big padded chair and said nothing for a long moment. 'Well, he had six good years, my dear Poole. In that time he penned half a dozen wonderful books, had children by two different women, and was currently engaged to a beautiful girl of eighteen.'

Poole stared at him open-mouthed.

'Not a bad record,' Voss went on, 'considering that his real age was ninety-two.'

'But what actually happened?' Poole asked. 'It gives few details here, merely listing all his achievements during his lifetime.'

Voss gave him a grim smile. 'He was playing several tennis matches under the blazing sun!'

Poole was thunderstruck. 'But surely you warned him about over-exertion?'

Voss nodded. 'Naturally. But I can understand why this happened. He was a vigorous young man in the prime of life. I have been speaking to the pathologist who carried out the autopsy. His body had been returned for burial in England, of course, as you have just read.' He stared at Poole, with a cynical expression on his face. 'His heart was absolutely withered, if I may use a non-medical term. Of course he was warned. This is something we must look at for the future.'

He gave a short, mirthless laugh. 'After all, I am myself a hundred and five years old, am I not? But I know how to behave sensibly.' He shrugged. 'The exuberance of youth! There lies the danger . . .'

Basil Copper worked as a journalist and editor of a local newspaper before becoming a full-time writer in 1970. His first story in the horror field, 'The Spider', was published in 1964 in *The Fifth Pan Book of Horror Stories*, since when his short fiction has appeared in numerous anthologies, been extensively adapted for radio, and collected in *Not after Nightfall*, *Here Be Daemons*, *From Evil's Pillow*, *And Afterward the Dark*, *Voices of Doom*, *When Footsteps Echo*, *Whispers in the Night* and, more recently, *Cold Hand on My Shoulder* from Sarob Press. Along with two non-fiction studies of the vampire and werewolf legends, his other books include the novels *The Great White Space*, *The Curse of the Fleers*, *Necropolis*, *House of the Wolf* and *The Black*

Death. He has also written more than fifty hardboiled thrillers about Los Angeles private detective Mike Faraday, and has continued the adventures of August Derleth's Sherlock Holmes-like detective Solar Pons in several volumes from Fedogan & Bremer. As Copper explains about the preceding story, 'It comes from recent TV and radio coverage on new scientific discoveries, using stem cells to extend lifespan. It was announced that injecting mice and other small rodents with the relevant cells had actually increased their longevity by fifty per cent, and they hoped to be able to do the same for human beings in due course. That was the premise, but first I started with the twist at the end. The genesis of the title comes from a piece of dialogue uttered by Boris Karloff in one of my favourite horror films, *The Black Castle*.'

Your Shadow Knows You Well

NANCY KILPATRICK

You are here by mistake. Everything is a mistake with Russell. You came to Mexico because he willed it, or so it seems to you.

This is not the type of vacation you enjoy. Russell, though, is enamoured with the exotic, the bizarre, especially the macabre. Particularly with death. You made a weak attempt to dissuade him from entering El Museo de las Momias – the nearly-missed brass sign on the building adjacent to the cemetery, the unmanned ticket booth, the unlocked door, no visitors but the two of you. 'It's like a horror movie,' you said but, as happens so often, Russell ignored you.

And now you stand in a dusty, claustrophobic room, the door to the outer world slamming shut behind you, as if annihilating all life outside – if this *was* a horror movie, the door would be locked, and you are not quite sure if it is or isn't but you cannot bring yourself to check, and you know that Russell will not.

Your eyes take long moments to adjust to the dimness. Your lungs fill with what you know to be the powdery casings of insects, and the unpleasant scent of mould. Every instinct in you screams *flee!* Almost every instinct. The voice in your head that orders you to please Russell dominates. He turns suddenly and touches the flesh of your upper arm, and all thoughts of escape vanish.

You follow him further in like the obedient dog you often envision yourself to be, beyond the entrance, into a chamber that somehow reminds you of the catacombs Russell took you to see in Paris, although here no bones are piled against the walls. Corridors stretch one after the other like the links of a chain. Each corridor leads to another room that from where you stand looks exactly like the one you are in. Surrounding you are horizontal wood and glass cases, an army of coffins, containing . . . what? You join Russell at one case and stare at the thing inside.

It is a living human being. Or so it seems to you at first. The bony body is barely clothed – the worn leather of boots, a scrap of fabric at the crotch. The face – skin taut over bone – is familiar because the features seem so common. For a moment, it occurs to you to break the glass and free this man who is trapped in a living death. But as you stare, you realise there is no movement. The eyes must be plastic, the hair a wig, the lips twisted in a scream . . . All is so lifelike. It is as if you know this person, or knew him, and yet you are certain you have never met. And he is, after all, not real.

'Great stuff!' Russell enthuses. He moves to the case to the left, and you follow on his heels. Inside is another wax form, or a manikin of some kind. It must be, for these could not really be the dried remains of what were once breathing human beings, people like yourself, ordinary people – men, women, babies even – caught up in a life that allows too many expectations and fulfils too few. A life which no one gets out of alive, as Russell is fond of joking. For you, life often feels so terrifying that you fear your own shadow, so getting out alive is the least of your worries.

You notice your shadow now. Pressed across the floor. A sombre black entity pasted into this grim environment. You contemplate the Jungian theory you studied at University when you had hopes of becoming a psychotherapist. The idea of the shadow intrigued you, opposite traits, rejected, which remain unintegrated into the personality: criminal as good man, policeman as thief. How alive and sparkling such concepts were to you ten years ago. How alien they appear to you now, distant thoughts that you cannot bring to bear on your own life and so they have become unimportant. Your shadow is disturbingly flat. It lies limp across the floor, halfway up the length of one case, as if directing you towards . . .

Russell's hand encircles your upper arm. He pulls you away. You are glad you did not need to see what your dark side finds so compelling.

Russell stops and releases you and suddenly you feel a chill, and shiver. He does not notice, absorbed in reading aloud from a book he purchased in the town of Guanajuato. He translates the Spanish in an orderly fashion, as he does everything, identifying what is in each case, providing the history, if available. As he reads, the stories build to extreme proportions in your mind, injecting a deeper chill that crackles up your spine. The 250-year-old French doctor, who died away from home, his remains exhumed like all the others here for lack of payment for perpetual care. The fatally injured pregnant woman – there, in that case! A replica of her foetus, carved out of her body.

'"*La momia más pequeño del mundo*" – the smallest mummy in the world,' Russell tells you.

What kind of place is this? Who has brought together all of these monstrous manikins? Russell's voice is loud in the emptiness, faintly echoing, excited, his delight obvious. Suddenly you are struck by the horrifying realisation that you have blocked from your consciousness until now: these are not effigies at all, but mummified bodies, as if the secrets of the preservation techniques of Lenin and Perron have been rediscovered. The dead woman is frighteningly real. So is her foetus.

'Somebody almost figured out how Lenin's been preserved,' Russell says. That you have always been in synch like this never ceases to amaze you. But there is one huge difference between you and Russell: this synchronistic connection delights him; with you, it intensifies the mind-numbing realisation that eats through your soul like a cancer, making you wonder how your spirit became locked to his.

You watch Russell race from case to case, grabbing the wooden edges, pressing his face to the glass, voice full of glee, the proverbial child in a candy store. It was his enthusiasm for life that attracted you to him in the first place. His daring contrasted with your shy, conservative nature. Because of Russell, you have been spared an ordinary life of home, career, children. You know you have seen and done things because of him that, left to your own devices and permitted to dawdle in your contained and timid little world, such extraordinary experiences would have passed you by. You have come to rely heavily on him, as if your very life depends on Russell's – he holds the oxygen; each breath you take is a gift because he shares his air. Without him, you would suffocate. That he knows this and uses physical contact to control you passes almost unnoticed now – by you, by everyone. You gave up freedom willingly at first and, after a decade together, slavery has become second nature.

There are many cases here, many mummified corpses denied eternal rest. As you scan the room, you are most disturbed by the similarities. Each body seems so ordinary, like the neighbours and grocery clerks to whom you only say 'Hello' and 'Lovely day'. Like your co-workers, whom you speak to out of necessity, to stave off the pain of isolation. These people who pass through your life so regularly, who are not your friends but are more than strangers. Your sister and brother, and your mother, all the family left that you are supposed to be close to, yet you often feel as if you do not know them. Real relationships have proven to be a burden, and when Russell entered your life, you gradually realised that you no longer needed most of them. No one else can understand your emotional bondage to Russell, not even you. Your few remaining confidantes look at you with pity, and have stopped suggesting that you leave him. You see them rarely now.

There are brief moments when you delude yourself that you and Russell share the ultimate in intimate communication, moments when his touch transports you to another realm, of safety and intensity. Times when you make love and the scent of his body fills your nostrils with a feral knowledge – two animals, paired for life. The feeling envelops you in security. And then, afterwards, while he sleeps and you watch his face with tenderness in your heart and see a vulnerability and need there that is never reflected at any other time, you believe you have attained bliss.

But most of the time you feel more alone than you could ever have imagined possible. It becomes achingly clear that what you perceive as love is one-sided. All that keeps you from ending it is the silly thought that Russell needs you, somehow, and there are days when it is a struggle to hold onto this idea. When you are in a black mood, being bitterly honest with yourself, you fear you are expendable, replaceable, and that if you disappear tomorrow, his life will go on without so much as a hiccough of sadness or regret. Annoyance, perhaps, that you have caused him to begin again the search for someone to take care of him. Excitement that the hunt can start anew.

There are days when you believe your life has absolutely no meaning.

You stare at the dead things in these cases, thinking how fortunate they are. Their pain of living has been washed away by nothingness. How you envy them. You wonder what it feels like to die, if the soul exists as you once believed it does, if the spirit ascends. Or descends. The weight of Hell's existence diminished once it became clear that you were already there.

Russell calls you to come look, and you join him before a case like the others, the case your shadow passed over. This one holds a woman, about your own age.

'This could be you,' he says cheerfully.

Her hair, or the tufts that remain, is the same colour as your own. Her eyes, the shape of her body. She is about as tall as you, and of similar weight, or so she might have been if there were more than skin and bone remaining. While not your twin, the resemblance is uncanny, enough to categorise you both as the same 'type'. What is not the same is that her flesh is charred.

'I couldn't tell you apart in a police line-up,' Russell jokes.

But you do not laugh. She is dead. You are alive. That he cannot appreciate a difference either means he is blind, or that he sees little merit to you being alive or dead.

Looking into this case is too much like looking into a mirror. Her scorched features cannot disguise the fact that reflected back at you is an individual whose life was not under her own control, a woman forced beyond a point of no return. She mirrors those elements you loathe within yourself, and you are surprised when Russell reads her history to learn that she has committed atrocious acts, acts that, on a bad day, reflect your darkest fantasies.

'"Anna Maria Negro." I'll say she's black! They burned her good,' he says. Then adds, 'Pretty ordinary name.' As if her name disappoints him. As if he does not remember that your name is Marianne. You want to suggest he say her name backwards, but sense it will only lead to unpleasantness.

Anna Maria died on your birthday, two hundred years before you were born. A remarkable coincidence, you feel. Russell does not notice this, since he does not remember your birthday unless you remind him. You do not bring the coincidence to his attention. She died at the age you are now. You fantasise that as her soul departed her body it time-travelled, seeking through the centuries a new body – your body – and that your spirits are linked. Perhaps it is the evil Anna Maria who dwells within you, who is sucking your vitality, causing you to subjugate your energy and stray from the path you were born to follow? Maybe this is why you feel such an eerie *sympatía* with the remains of this mummified woman, imprisoned in her case as you are imprisoned in your life.

You do not tell Russell your thoughts, of course, since from past experience you know he will be annoyed. At best, he will call you silly. You cannot bear his disapproval.

Quickly he becomes tired of Anna Maria and moves away, down the corridor, rounding a corner, out of range. He is bored with her as he becomes bored with you on a regular basis. You see him as a man who hides from his feelings, and also from yours. He cannot be involved with the intricacies of a true relationship. You know enough to realise that his boredom stems from an inability to allow your reality into his life. He is afraid that if he opens up to you, he will lose himself – Psychology 101. To disguise this, he pretends you are shallow. To protect him, you pretend to be so.

From the very beginning you understood his fear, felt his pain. Back then, you struggled to express yourself to him, in a gentle and delicate way, to avoid intensifying his defences. Then your frustration grew, and what escalated to shouting resulted in abandonment, and you had to work hard to bring him back to you. Now you regret your actions, all of them. If he had simply drifted away then, perhaps your soul would belong to you still. But your love of Russell – your fear of losing him, his need of you, your naïve idea that enough love would change him – all of it resulted in misguided actions which led to this indenture. Slavery by its nature demands reassurance, but Russell's reaction has always been the same: he refuses to reassure you. He cuts you off before you can tell him what truly bothers you. You cannot recall when you stopped making the effort to confront him. Or when you settled for sex as the answer to all your needs.

Now he does not care. He makes advances in your presence towards other women that you know he pursues when given a chance. You turn away from this disrespect, knowing but unknowing. You feel you have no options. You cannot tell him the hurt this behaviour evokes in you, which you know he knows since the one time long ago, when you did discuss his infidelities and made it clear. He has forgotten his vague agreement that he would cease such activity, at least in your presence, which was the most you could hope for. Forgotten, or disregarded, since by now he knows he can do as he pleases. You are there for him, will always be there. Despite everything, you know he needs you and that need inspires your devotion. Love chains you to him, and your need for him to love you back holds those chains in place. You despise yourself enough that no hate is left over for him.

You stare at this woman he has left you with. Her marble eyes stare back at you. At any moment you expect her to move, to grin maniacally, to show sharp pointed teeth, her eyes to turn blood-red, her head to spin completely around. Of course nothing like that occurs, and this lack of movement is unnerving because it is too much like the inertia that has become your norm. No wonder Russell could detect no difference between the two of you.

He has left the book on top of her case, as if daring you to read it. Her story begs to be studied, and you stare at the page of Spanish, letting the few words you understand sum up her life as they swirl through you. Your mind begins to run footage of her existence that you have produced, and the script is all too familiar. Her story is your story, the story of so many women over the world, over time: victims. Chained by love, padlocked by sex, the only intimacy. Self-victimisation takes a variety of forms, but you believe it always culminates in annihilation.

Anna Maria is like a doll you played with as a child. Suddenly you remember that toy vividly. Lifesize, or your size. She walked and talked. Her verbal repertoire was limited, but enough to create a dialogue. You wonder if Anna Maria will respond. You glance down the corridor. Russell is nowhere in sight.

'Hello,' you whisper. Your small voice, fragile as ash, drifts to you like a greeting from another age. Anna Maria says nothing. You stare at her face, willing her lips to move. And suddenly, to your half-surprise, they do.

'Say again,' you ask her, and press your ear to the glass case, waiting.

> At the heart of darkness
> blackness swirls
> leeching light
> paring back time
> sending you this message:
> Your Shadow knows you well.

'Did you say that?' you whisper.

You *said that.*

You are astonished. The poem you wrote, with your own hand, when you were young, still learning, alive with hope, eager for life. A poem about the power of the shadowy self – the part of you that you do not know, perhaps do not care to know. No one else has read that poem, not even Russell – it is the only thing you have withheld from him.

You stare at Anna Maria. Her cracked lips have moved again, you are certain. Now they curl into a definite smile. She is a long-lost friend, a mother, a lover who sees you inside and out, who can touch your heart and body without inflicting pain or demanding bondage. You are astonished at the realisation of this perfection.

'She's a witch,' a voice behind you says, and you jump. Russell stands so close. 'Says so in the book. She's got you talking to yourself. Maybe that's what you need, a lifesize doll. Someone to play with. A *playmate.*' His grin is perverse as he looks around. 'There's nobody here,' he says, and you know what he is thinking.

No! Do not let him!

'No, we can't—'

'Marianne, don't be so selfish!' he tells you severely. But you are here, with him, and you will be an accomplice.

No sooner has he said this than he orders, 'Pick one.'

'What?'

'There are plenty of bodies here. There's not even a guard. Nobody will miss it. Pick the one we take home.'

A glacier melts through your bloodstream, turning it to crimson ice water that courses through your veins, numbing you as it travels. 'I just don't think—'

'*Don't* think. You're not good at it!' Russell laughs.

Choose another!

You stare at Anna Maria, helpless.

'Pick one, or I will.'

You know that he wants you to pick Anna Maria. Clearly he wants this one sitting on your couch, upholstered with the flesh of an endangered species; joining you at the dining room table where the centrepiece is a bone he shoved into your purse at the catacombs in Paris; propped up on the toilet seat while you bathe, an arm draped languidly over the tombstone pilfered from a Boston cemetery; sleeping between you and Russell in your bed, and doing more!

Horror causes you to tremble. This is the part of Russell that terrifies you. He has forced you yet again into a no-win situation. His is a win-win: if you love him, you will pick Anna Maria. If you do not love him you will not choose, or you will choose another. And then you will be forced to deal with his displeasure, which will result in rejection. All roads lead to the same place with Russell. Regardless of what you do, he will take Anna Maria.

His hand grasps your neck at the back, beneath your hair, burning your skin, cooking the frigid waters until you boil with desire.

Please, you think silently, hoping Anna Maria will hear you. And understand. There is no escape.

No!

'Her,' you say, in a weak voice, your betraying finger shaking as you point.

'Give me your shoulder bag,' he says, and you hand it over. This case has no door, no lock. He uses the soft pigskin to try to smash the glass surrounding Anna Maria, but it will not yield.

I have warned you!

You mumble nervously, 'Maybe we should forget—'

'Shut up!' Russell snaps, and glares at you, erecting a barrier. His eyes dart, rodent-like, around the room, searching for some implement that will shatter the glass.

Do not do this!

He races down the corridor and quickly you lean towards the case to frantically whisper, 'Please, please, forgive me. It will be okay. You'll be safe with me—'

As safe as you are?

The sweet voice has turned hard. You stare at Anna Maria and see that her smile has been replaced with a severe slash. Her eyes accuse you.

She is right. You cannot defend yourself, let alone another. You step away from the case, deflated.

'This should do it!' Russell says. He hefts the metal fire extinguisher and smashes it against the case. The glass quivers. He hits it again, harder. It spiderwebs.

Stop him!

He slams the metal through the glass. It explodes, sending shards everywhere – into his face, your arms, splattering blood all over Anna Maria.

A scream rushes through a vortex of time. It is unbearable. You clasp your hands over your ears as you back away.

The silence that follows is not complete. Your heart roars in your ears. Your body longs to convulse. You begin to retch.

Russell ignores you. He reaches into the case and slowly caresses Anna Maria's shoulder, her chest, her breast. A charge runs through your body as if he is touching not her but you. He grasps Anna Maria around the waist and prepares to lift her out. 'She'll make a nice addition . . . What the—?'

Suddenly two scorched hands, more like claws, grasp his wrists. He is yanked forward. Into the case with her. On top of her, like a reluctant lover.

'Fuck! Help me! I'm stuck here. Something's caught me,' he cries as he struggles with Anna Maria.

You are shocked. Paralysed. Encased in eternal time.

Russell's words finally penetrate beyond your ears, into your mind, and your body moves forward instinctively. Your hands grab his arms to pull him away.

Then your eyes lock with Anna Maria's. An understanding that spans the ages flows from her to you.

Go!

This will be your last chance, your only chance of freedom.

'Marianne, what the *fuck* are you doing! You're useless! Pull me out of here – now!'

You release him. And step away. Back out of the room. Out the door, which is not locked after all.

'Marianne, don't leave me! Yes, go get help. But hurry back. Please!'

The words nearly touch you. You hesitate only a moment, but then close the door on his demands. You have no intention of helping him any more.

Immediately your eyes are drawn to the hot sunlight streaming from the clear sky above. White light like fire, that burns away nightmares and memories, and forms shadows. Shadows which you no longer fear.

Anna Maria Negro. A witch, the book said. Burned alive in the eighteenth century. One of nine million killed worldwide over four centuries of the Inquisition. Because she was a woman? Living alone? Owning property? Her accusers insisted she cast spells, turned men into animals, evoked demons, embraced evil. She did all of that, and more. Her story is larger, one you know intuitively. Of how strong women become weak. Of how they teach their daughters submission, silence and compliance as protection. Generation upon generation, living with a terror that mutates into something hideous and unnameable, the only solace physical touch, purchased at an impossible price. You know Anna Maria's story well. It is a woman's story. Your story. And her revenge is your own.

Your shadow, now relaxed, stretches out sensually before you on the dusty ground; long and full, possessing a life of its own. 'Hello, Anna Maria,' you say, and hear her seductive voice answer back.

Buenos dias, chiquita!

For the first time in what seems forever, you smile; you no longer feel alone. But then, an old worry nags at you. 'Russell's in good hands, isn't he? He'll be taken care of, won't he?'

Worry yourself no longer, a powerful voice replies. Then, in a sultry, enticing tone, the words darkly mesmerising as they swirl through your hungry body: *Russell will get what he deserves!*

Nancy Kilpatrick has been called 'Canada's Queen of the Undead' is a Bram Stoker Award finalist and winner of the Arthur Ellis Award. She has published more than fourteen novels, more than one hundred and fifty short stories, five collections, and has edited seven anthologies. Her books include *Sex and the Single Vampire*, *Endorphins*, *Dracula: An Eternal Love Story* (based on the stage musical), *Love Bites*, *Child of the Night*, *Near Death*, *Reborn* and *The Vampire Stories of Nancy Kilpatrick*. Under her pseudonym 'Amarantha Knight' she wrote several volumes in the erotic *The Darker Passions* series, and she is currently working on a non-fiction book about Gothic culture, which will be published by St Martin's Press in 2003. 'The museum in this story really exists,' reveals Kilpatrick. 'I visited it in Guanajuato, Mexico, during the

Day of the Dead celebrations in 1999. Most of the four hours we spent at the Museo de las Momias, my companion and I were alone with the wood and glass cases and their eerie contents. We did a website about this trip, with a page of photographs devoted to the mummies: www3.sympatico.ca/nancy. kilpatrick'

Eglantine's Time

JAY LAKE

Women had worn high-button shoes when that syringe was new. It gleamed, antique glass and brass fittings, the cylinder's arms curled like the youthful curve of Eglantine's breast, the glass barrel with the engraved volumetric scale glittering like a mirror in the desert. She imagined the huge, crude needle slipping elegantly into her body, perhaps between the scarred ridges of the soles of her feet, or beneath her tongue, within the folds of her labia. It would bring a brief, sharp excruciation that would catch her breath like the smallest of pleasures. Pain was a friend, always there for Eglantine in her withered legs and shivering muscles, most especially in the ceremonies of medicine. But friend pain had a close cousin, death, which was the province of the syringe.

'Don't touch the terminal.' Nurse Woodbourne walked on crêpe-soled shoes that made no noise at all, save for a small squeak when crossing the metal doorframe. Eglantine could never quite hear Nurse's quiet footfalls, but somehow she still knew when Nurse was coming, like an itch in her head.

Nurse slapped the metal railing. 'Look at me when I'm talking. We don't want the straps again, do we?'

Eglantine hunched tighter in the bed. She had been nowhere near the computer, and she knew better than to try to message for help anyway. There was no one to e-mail, no one left but herself since her sister-twins had been taken to Isolation one by one. She imagined Nurse's thoughts, tried to deflect the tides of irritation. 'No ma'am. I wasn't going to—'

'Wasn't doesn't, isn't won't.' Lips set thin like pressed fingers, Nurse Woodbourne grabbed Eglantine's arm with a deep pinch that would leave bruises for days. Nurse checked the pulse, putting Eglantine in her place with an iron grip and a rough exercise of authority. 'Doctor's coming at seven for an examination. The Terminal Exam. If we answer his questions the *right* way,' her voice lowered for stress, 'we'll be fine. Otherwise . . .'

Nurse glanced at the syringe, poised on a linen-clothed silver tray upon the mantel. An enormous mirror framed in intricately ornamented gold leaf hung above it, implying a place of honour that in an ordinary house might have hosted a clock or funerary urn.

After Nurse left, Eglantine picked at the flecked paint of her iron-railed bed for a while. Her greasy hair was gathered between her teeth to suck as she imagined the Terminal Exam. One way or the other, Eglantine's time in Isolation would soon be over. She would pass the Exam, surpass her sisters, and somehow set things right for the first time in her life.

Some weeks earlier Nurse Woodbourne had explained about air bubbles and embolisms. She'd brought a grey striped kitten for Eglantine to hold while the animal licked the salt sweat from her trembling fingers and stretched tiny claws into her forearms. Besides her caregivers, it was the first living thing Eglantine had touched in the long months since they'd brought her into Isolation from Crèche.

Then Nurse had drawn twenty millilitres of saline into the great glass syringe, with the slow patience of ritual and a rare smile. She introduced an air bubble, then injected the kitten. After a few moments, the animal spasmed, mewed once, then died in a spurt of urine and faeces on Eglantine's lap.

'I'll leave this on the mantel,' Nurse said, laying the syringe on the cloth-covered tray. 'It should focus our mind most instructively. This is for our own good, missy.' Nurse never called Eglantine by name.

Eventually Eglantine put the dead kitten in her bedpan, when she couldn't stand the stench any more and the fur was too matted to pet.

Doctor Brockton came in, white coat dangling open over his tweed suit. He was a big man with a roast-beef face and wild white hair who always smelled of brandy. Unlike some of the other doctors, Brockton didn't wear a stethoscope. Instead, he usually carried notebooks and little analysers to probe her nose or mouth. Today all he carried was a clipboard and a bottle labelled 'Saline'. Doctor Brockton placed the bottle on the mantel next to the syringe before turning to favour her with a yellowed smile. His voice boomed, overflowing the space of her high-ceilinged room. 'So how are we today?'

Mindful of Nurse Woodbourne hovering in the doorway, Eglantine smiled. 'Fine, Doctor.'

'Well, this is your big day.' Doctor Brockton picked up the glass syringe, toying with it. 'You've done well in Isolation. If your Terminal Examination is successful, you will be released to Training.'

If she was unsuccessful, well, the syringe had certainly focused Eglantine's attention. And the world had done her no good at all. 'No one has ever succeeded, have they?' she said, in spite of better judgement.

'Young lady,' Nurse Woodbourne began, but Doctor Brockton halted her with a wave of his hand.

'Wait, Nurse. My dear Eglantine, each Terminal Examination is unique to the subject. You will pass or fail on your strengths, into a brave new world of possibilities. If you come into your own, as we all hope, you will be a great force for good in the world. Any other outcome is just a case history. We don't want to be a case history, do we?' Eglantine realised Doctor's tone was as false as his thoughts.

'Case histories,' Eglantine whispered. Once, just before being brought to Isolation, she had been allowed to see the graves of her sister-twins in the heat-withered elm grove behind Crèche. Adelaide the eldest and bravest. Bettina, who could walk almost like an ordinary person. Clothilde – pretty but for the odours of her uncontrollable anal fistulae. Desdemona, smartest of them all. Now her, Eglantine.

I am better than my sisters, Eglantine told herself. To hell with the world, I will survive so I can redeem their deaths.

Doctor Brockton sat in a wingback chair near her bed. He pulled a stopwatch from a coat pocket and consulted his clipboard. 'Enough. What is the product of three hundred and forty-two and seventy-nine point five?'

The numbers were as natural to Eglantine as breathing. Perhaps more so. 'Twenty-seven thousand one hundred and eighty-nine,' she replied. Why did he even need to ask?

'Point eight seconds,' the doctor called. Nurse Woodbourne made a note on another clipboard.

'The cube root of twelve hundred and thirteen?'

It went on for hours, questions rattling like summer hail.

Eglantine was so tired. Her jaw was sore. Her head hurt. Pain was back, in all her joints both good and malformed. She was hot. Even Doctor Brockton had removed his coat and tie. He and Nurse Woodbourne had taken breaks for water and body stretches, but Eglantine just lay in her bed, sweating into her linen gown and becoming dizzy without even moving. The syringe glittered on the mantle like the first star in the evening sky.

Doctor Brockton leaned forward on his wingback chair. His white hair was plastered to his head. 'What colour am I thinking of?'

Colours thundered in her head. Eglantine suddenly knew, the way she knew primes. 'Mauve.' It was like discovering eyes and ears she'd never had before, opening a door she had never seen. Her senses sharpened even as she gasped.

Doctor glanced at Nurse Woodbourne.

Eglantine heard him as clearly as a shout, though he said nothing at all. 'You think I've made it,' she said. She could feel everything in the room, the lace curtains, the oxygen feeds in the wall, the dead cricket she hadn't known was under the bureau. Nurse and Doctor, as if they were laid open before her.

Nurse Woodbourne set the clipboard down on the cricket's chest of drawers and stepped forward to pat Eglantine's cheek. 'There, there,' she said in a strained mockery of tenderness, lips tense with fright.

Eglantine stared into Nurse's pale grey eyes. 'You think I'm a waste of time and effort, toxic genes regrown over and over for no purpose.' She glanced over at Doctor. 'You're thinking of the syringe and the saline, of the grey kitten. Nurse is afraid of what I might do. Doctor . . .' Eglantine gasped, the painful years of her life drawn into angry focus. 'This was all suffering, to force me to grow into my power. For the sake of this . . . this *stress*, you killed my sister-twins.'

Eglantine's mind, now bigger than the room, flooded with cascades of memory – fear, loathing, panic – from Doctor Brockton and Nurse Woodbourne. Pain, her old friend pain, washed through her, but so much she could barely think. Her crippled body felt as if it would burst its bounds, legs uncrimping with the power of her mind. She was becoming free.

The floods in her mind opened new channels, powers to match her expanding sense. Eglantine reached out with a curl of emotion, shunting much of her pain to Nurse, who collapsed choking to the floor. As Doctor Brockton jumped for the syringe, Eglantine used a newfound mental hand to smash the gilded mirror, spraying his face with splintered glass. She made sure some got in his eyes.

Walking was hard, dragging her tiny gnarled feet and trembling legs over broken glass and Nurse Woodbourne's slick vomit. Eglantine concentrated on keeping the metal door shut against the orderlies responding to the whooping alarms as she staggered to the mantel for the glass syringe.

'Case histories it is then,' she whispered to Doctor Brockton, who clutched fists to his blind, bleeding eyes.

Still standing on her strengthening legs, Eglantine leaned down towards him with the empty syringe.

When she was done, carrying the syringe for luck, Eglantine left her room and strolled towards the graves underneath the withered elms to raise the dead.

Jay Lake lives in Portland, Oregon, with his family and their books. His recent fiction appearances include *Beyond the Last Star*, *Clean Sheets*, *Frequency*, *Hour of Pain*, *Ideomancer*, *Strange Horizons* and *The Third Alternative*. In addition to reviewing short fiction for *Tangent Online*, he is a Writers of the Future Finalist. 'This story was always about the syringe,' recalls the author. 'All my life I've had a low-grade fascination with antique medical equipment, perhaps because my grandfather was a dentist back before World War II and kept that sort of stuff around the house. Old brass, cloudy glass and mysterious, grotty stains that didn't bear further investigation. And believe me, that syringe took a beating from my first readers and my regular workshop. I stuck with it, out of sheer perversity and love for that gleaming artefact of medical priesthood. As for Eglantine herself, she is named after that cousin of *The Borrowers* who was eaten by the cat. So really, this story is about my childhood memories, I suppose. Enjoy.'

The Burgers of Calais

GRAHAM MASTERTON

I never cared for northern parts and I never much cared for eastern parts neither, because I hate the cold and I don't have any time for those bluff, ruddy-faced people who live there, with their rugged plaid coats and their Timberland boots and their way of whacking you on the back when you least expect it, like whacking you on the back is supposed to be some kind of friendly gesture or something.

I don't like what goes on there, neither. Everybody behaves so cheerful and folksy, but believe me, that folksiness hides some real grisly secrets that would turn your blood to iced gazpacho.

You can guess, then, that I was distinctly unamused when I was driving back home early last October from Presque Isle, Maine, and my beloved '71 Mercury Marquis dropped her entire engine on the highway like a cow giving birth.

The only reason I had driven all the way to Presque Isle, Maine, was to lay to rest my old Army buddy Dean Brunswick III (may God forgive him for what he did in Colonel Wrightman's cigar-box). I couldn't wait to get back south, but now I found myself stuck a half-mile away from Calais, Maine, population 4,003 and one of the most northernmost, easternmost, back-whackingest towns you could ever have waking nightmares about.

Calais is locally pronounced 'CAL-us' and believe me a callus is exactly what it is – a hard, corny little spot on the right elbow of America. Especially when you have an engineless uninsured automobile and a maxed-out Visa card and only $226 in your billfold and no friends or relations back home who can afford to send you more than a cheery hello.

I left my beloved Mercury tilted up on the leafy embankment by the side of US Route 1 South and walked into town. I never cared a whole lot for walking, mainly because my weight has kind of edged up a little since I left the Army in '86, due to a pathological lack of restraint when it comes to filé gumbo and Cajun spiced chicken with lots of crunchy bits and mustard-barbecued spare ribs and Key lime pies. My landlady Rita Personage says that when she first saw me she thought that Orson Welles had risen from the dead, and I must say I do have quite a line in flappy white double-breasted sport coats, not to mention a few wide-brimmed white hats, though not all in prime condition since I lost my job with the Louisiana Restaurant Association which was a heinous political fix involving some of the shadier elements in the East Baton Rouge catering community and also possibly the fact that I was on the less balletic side of 289 pounds.

It was a piercing bright day. The sky was blue like ink and the trees were all turning gold and red and crispy brown. Calais is one of those neat New England towns with white clapboard houses and churches with spires and cheery people waving to each other as they drive up and down the streets at 2½ mph.

By the time I reached North and Main I was sweating like a cheese and severely in need of a beer. There was a *whip, whip, whoop* behind me and it was a police patrol car. I stopped and the officer put down his window. He had mirror sunglasses and a sandy moustache that looked as if he kept his nailbrush on his upper lip. And freckles. You know the type.

'Wasn't speeding, was I, officer?'

He took off his sunglasses. He didn't smile. He didn't even blink. He said, 'You look like a man with a problem, sir.'

'I know. I've been on Redu-Quick for over six months now and I haven't lost a pound.'

That really cracked him up, not. 'You in need of some assistance?' he asked me.

'Well, my car suffered a minor mechanical fault a ways back there and I was going into town to see if I could get anybody to fix it.'

'That your clapped-out saddle-bronze Marquis out on Route One?'

'That's the one. Nothing that a few minutes in the crusher couldn't solve.'

'Want to show me some ID?'

'Sure.' I handed him my driver's licence and my identity card from the restaurant association. He peered at them, and for some reason actually *sniffed* them.

'John Henry Dauphin, Choctaw Drive, East Baton Rouge. You're a long way from home, Mr Dauphin.'

'I've just buried one of my old Army buddies up in Presque Isle.'

'And you *drove* all the way up here?'

'Sure, it's only two thousand three hundred and seven miles. It's a pretty fascinating drive, if you don't have any drying paint that needs watching.'

'Louisiana Restaurant Association . . . that's who you work for?'

'That's right,' I lied. Well, he didn't have to know that I was out of a job. 'I'm a restaurant hygiene consultant. Hey – bet you never guessed that I was in the food business.'

'Okay . . . the best thing you can do is call into Lyle's Autos down at the other end of Main Street, get your vehicle towed off the highway as soon as possible. If you require a place to stay I can recommend the Calais Motor Inn.'

'Thank you. I may stay for a while. Looks like a nice town. Very . . . well-swept.'

'It is,' he said, as if he were warning me to make sure that it stayed that way. He handed back my ID and drove off at the mandatory snail's pace.

Lyle's Autos was actually run by a stocky man called Nils Guttormsen. He had a grey crewcut and a permanently surprised face, like a chipmunk going through the sound barrier backwards. He charged me a mere $65 for towing my car into his workshop, which was only slightly more than a quarter of everything I had in the world, and he estimated that he could put the engine back into it for less than $785, which was about $784 more than it was actually worth.

'How long will it take, Nils?'

'Well, John, you need it urgent?'

'Not really, Nils . . . I thought I might stick around town for a while. So – you know – why don't you take your own sweet time?'

'Okay, John. I have to get transmission parts from Bangor. I could have it ready, say Tuesday?'

'Good deal, Nils. Take longer if you want. Make it the Tuesday after next. Or even the Tuesday after that.'

'You'll be wanting a car while I'm working on yours, John.'

'Will I, Nils? No, I don't think so. I could use some exercise, believe me.'

'It's entirely up to you, John. But I've got a couple of nifty Toyotas to rent if you change your mind. They look small but there's plenty of room in them. Big enough to carry a sofa.'

'Thanks for the compliment, Nils.'

*

I hefted my battered old suitcase to the Calais Motor Inn, changing hands every few yards all the way down Main Street. Fortunately the desk accepted my Visa impression without even the hint of hysterical laughter. The Calais Motor Inn was a plain, comfortable motel, with plaid carpets and a shiny bar with tinkly music where I did justice to three bottles of chilled Molson's and a ham-and-Swiss-cheese triple-decker sandwich on rye with coleslaw and straw fried potatoes, and two helpings of cookie crunch ice-cream to keep my energy levels up.

The waitress was a pretty snubby-nose woman with cropped blonde hair and kind of a Swedish look about her.

'Had enough?' she asked me.

'Enough of what? Cookie crunch ice-cream or Calais in general?'

'My name's Velma,' she said.

'John,' I replied, and bobbed up from my leatherette seat to shake her hand.

'Just passing through, John?' she asked me.

'I don't know, Velma ... I was thinking of sticking around for a while. Where would somebody like me find themselves a job? And don't say the circus.'

'Is that what you do, John?' she asked me.

'What do you mean, Velma?'

'Make jokes about yourself before anybody gets them in?'

'Of course not. Didn't you know that all fat guys have to be funny by federal statute? No, I'm a realist. I know what my relationship is with food and I've learned to live with it.'

'You're a good-looking guy, John, you know that?'

'You can't fool me, Velma. All fat people look the same. If fat people could run faster, they'd all be bank robbers, because nobody can tell them apart.'

'Well, John, if you want a job you can try the want ads in the local paper, *The Quoddy Whirlpool.*'

'The what?'

'The bay here is called the Passamaquoddy, and out by Eastport we've got the Old Sow Whirlpool, which is the biggest whirlpool in the Western hemisphere.'

'I see. Thanks for the warning.'

'You should take a drive around the Quoddy Loop ... it's beautiful. Fishing quays, lighthouses, lakes. Some good restaurants, too.'

'My car's in the shop right now, Velma. Nothing too serious. Engine fell out.'

'You're welcome to borrow mine, John. It's only a Volkswagen but I don't hardly ever use it.'

I looked up at her and narrowed my eyes. Down in Baton Rouge the folks slide around on a snail's trail of courtesy and Southern charm, but I can't imagine any one of them offering a total stranger the use of their car, especially a total stranger who was liable to ruin the suspension just by sitting in the driver's seat.

'That's very gracious of you, Velma.'

I bought *The Quoddy Whirlpool*. If you were going into hospital for a heart bypass they could give you that paper instead of a general anaesthetic. Under 'Help Wanted' somebody was advertising for a 'talented' screen-door repair person and somebody else needed an experienced leaf-blower mechanic and somebody else was looking for a twice-weekly dog-walker for their Presa Canario. Since I happened to know that Presa Canarios stand two feet tall and weigh almost as much as I do, and that two of them notoriously ripped an innocent woman in San Francisco into bloody shreds I was not wholly motivated to apply for the last of those positions.

In the end I went to the Maine Job Service on Beech Street. A bald guy in a green zip-up hand-knitted cardigan sat behind a desk with photographs of his toothy wife on it (presumably the perpetrator of the green zip-up hand-knitted cardigan) while I had to hold my hand up all the time to stop the sun from shining in my eyes.

'So . . . what is your field of expertise, Mr Dauphin?'

'Oh, please, call me John. I'm a restaurant hygienist. I have an FSIS qualification from Baton Rouge University and nine years' experience working for the Louisiana Restaurant Association.'

'What brings you up to Calais, Maine, John?'

'I just felt it was time for a radical change of location.' I squinted at the nameplate on his desk. 'Martin.'

'I'm afraid I don't have anything available on quite your level of expertise, John. But I do have one or two catering opportunities.'

'What exact kind of catering opportunities, Martin?'

'Vittles need a cleaner . . . that's an excellent restaurant, Vittles, one of the premier eateries in town. It's situated in the Calais Motor Inn.'

'Ah.' As a guest of the Calais Motor Inn, I couldn't exactly see myself eating dinner in the restaurant and then carrying my own dishes into the kitchen and washing them up.

'Then Tony's have an opportunity for a breakfast chef.'

'Tony's?'

'Tony's Gourmet Burgers on North Street.'

'I see. What do they pay?'

'They pay more than Burger King or McDonald's. They have outlets all over Maine and New Brunswick, but they're more of a family business. More of a *quality* restaurant, if you know what I mean. I always take my own family to eat there.'

'And is that all you have?'

'I have plenty of opportunities in fishing and associated trades. Do you have any expertise with drift nets?'

'Drift nets? Are you kidding? I spent my whole childhood trawling for pilchards off the coast of Greenland.'

Martin looked across his desk at me, sitting there with my hand raised like I needed to go to the bathroom. When he spoke his voice was very biscuity and dry. 'Why don't you call round at Tony's, John? See if you like the look of it. I'll give Mr Le Renges a call, tell him you're on your way.'

'Thanks, Martin.'

Tony's Gourmet Burgers was one block away from Burger King and two blocks away from McDonald's, on a straight tree-lined street where the 4x4s rolled past at 2½ mph and everybody waved to each other and whacked each other on the back whenever they could get near enough and you felt like a hidden orchestra was going to strike up the theme to *Providence*.

All the same, Tony's was quite a handsome-looking restaurant with a brick front and brass carriage-lamps outside with flickering artificial flames. A chalkboard proudly proclaimed that this was 'the home of wholesome, hearty food, lovingly prepared in our own kitchens by people who really care'. Inside, it was fitted out with dark wood panelling and tables with green chequered cloths and gilt-framed engravings of whitetail deer, black bear and moose. It was crowded with cheery-looking families, and you certainly couldn't fault it for ambiance. Smart, but homely, with none of that wipe-clean feeling you get at McDonald's.

At the rear of the restaurant was a copper bar with an open grill, where a spotty young guy in a green apron and a tall green chef's hat was sizzling hamburgers and steaks.

A redheaded girl in a short green pleated skirt sashayed up to me and gave me a 500-watt smile, complete with teeth-braces. 'You prefer a booth or a table, sir?'

'Actually, neither. I have an appointment to see Mr Le Renges.'

'He's right in back ... why don't you follow me? What name shall I say?'

'John.'

Mr Le Renges was sitting in a blood-red leather chair with a reproduction antique table beside him, on which there was a fax machine, a silver carriage clock and a glass of seltzer. He was a bony man of forty-five or so with dyed-black collar-length hair which he had combed with something approaching genius to conceal his dead-white scalp. His nose was sharp and multi-faceted, and his eyes glittered under his overgrown eyebrows like blowflies. He wore a very white open-neck shirt with long 1970s collar-points and a tailored black three-piece suit. I had the feeling that he thought he bore more than a passing resemblance to Al Pacino.

On the panelled wall behind him hung an array of certificates from the Calais Regional Chamber of Commerce and the Maine Restaurant Guide and even one from Les Chevaliers de la Haute Cuisine Canadienne.

'Come in, John,' said Mr Le Renges, in a distinctly French-Canadian accent. 'Sit down, please ... the couch, perhaps? That chair's a little—'

'A little *little*?'

'I was thinking only of your comfort, John. You see, my policy is always to make the people who work for me feel happy and comfortable. I don't have a desk, I never have. A desk is a statement which says that I am more important than you. I am *not* more important. Everybody who works here is of equal importance, and of equal value.'

'You've been reading the McDonald's Bible. Always make your staff feel valued. Then you won't have to pay them so much.'

I could tell that Mr Le Renges didn't quite know if he liked that remark. It was the way he twitched his head, like Data in *Star Trek*. But I could also tell that he was the kind of guy who was anxious that nobody should leave him without fully comprehending what a wonderful human being he was.

He sipped some seltzer and eyed me over the rim of the glass. 'You are perhaps a little *mature* to be seeking work as a burger chef.'

'Mature? I'm positively overripe. But I've been working in the upper echelons of the restaurant trade for so long, I thought it was time that I went back to basics. Got my hands dirty, so to speak.'

'At Tony's Gourmet Burgers, John, our hygiene is second to none.'

'Of course. When I say getting my hands dirty – that's like a metaphor. Food hygiene, that's my specialty. I know everything there is to know about proper cooking times and defrosting and never picking your nose while you're making a Caesar salad.'

'What's your cooking experience, John?'

'I was a cook in the Army. Three times winner of the Fort Polk prize for culinary excellence. It made me very good at home economics. I can make a pound-and-a-half of ground beef stretch between two platoons of infantry and a heavy armoured assault force.'

'You're a funny guy, John,' said Mr Le Renges, without the slightest indication that he was amused.

'I'm fat, Tony. Funny goes with the territory.'

'I don't want you to make me laugh, John. I want you to cook burgers. And it's "Mr Le Renges" to you.'

He took me through to the kitchen, which was tiled in dark brown ceramic with stainless-steel counters. Two gawky young kids were using microwave ovens to thaw out frozen hamburger patties and frozen bacon and frozen fried chicken and frozen French fries. 'This is Chip and this is Denzil.'

'How's it going, Chip? Denzil?'

Chip and Denzil stared at me numbly and mumbled, ''kay I guess.'

'And this is Letitia.' A frowning dark-haired girl was painstakingly tearing up iceberg lettuce as if it were as difficult as lacemaking.

'Letitia's one of our *challenged* crew members,' said Mr Le Renges, resting one of his hairy tarantula hands on her shoulder. 'The state of Maine gives us special tax relief to employ the challenged, but even if they didn't I'd still want to have her here. That's the kind of guy I am, John. I've been called to do more than feed people. I've been called to enrich their lives.'

Letitia looked up at me with unfocused aquamarine eyes. She was pretty, but she had the expression of a smalltown beauty queen who has just been hit on the head by half a brick. Some instinct told me that Tony Le Renges wasn't using her only as an iceberg lettuce tearer.

'We take pride in the supreme quality of our food,' he said. Without any apparent sense of irony he opened a huge freezer at the back of the kitchen and showed me the frozen steaks and the frost-covered envelopes of pre-cooked chilli, ready for boiling in the bag. He showed me the freeze-dried vegetables and the frozen corn bread and the dehydrated lobster chowder (just add hot water). And this was in Maine, where you can practically find fresh lobsters waltzing down the street.

None of this made me weak with shock. Even the best restaurants use a considerable proportion of pre-cooked and pre-packaged food, and fast-food outlets like McDonald's and Burger King use nothing else. Even their scrambled eggs come dried and pre-scrambled in a packet.

What impressed me was how Mr Le Renges could sell this ordinary, industrialised stuff as 'wholesome, hearty food, lovingly cooked in our own kitchens by people who really care' when most of it was grudgingly thrown together in giant factories by minimum-wage shift-workers who didn't give a rat's ass.

Mr Le Renges must have had an inkling about the way my mind was working.

'You know what our secret is?' he asked me.

'If I'm going to come and cook here, Mr Le Renges, I think it might be a good idea if you told me.'

'We have the best-tasting burgers anywhere, that's our secret. McDonald's and Burger King don't even come *close*. Once you've tasted one of our burgers, you won't want anything else. Here – Kevin – pass me a burger so that John here can try it.'

'That's okay,' I told him. 'I'll take your word for it. I had a sandwich already.'

'No, John, if you're going to work here, I insist.'

'Listen, Mr Le Renges, I'm a professional food hygienist. I know what goes into burgers and that's why I never eat them. Never.'

'What are you suggesting?'

'I'm not suggesting anything. It's just that I know for a fact that a proportion of undesirable material makes its way into ground beef and I don't particularly want to eat it.'

'Undesirable material? What do you mean?'

'Well, *waste products*, if you want me to be blunt about it. Cattle are slaughtered and disembowelled so fast that it makes it inevitable that a certain amount of excrement contaminates the meat.'

'Listen, John, how do you think I compete with McDonald's and Burger King? I make my customers feel as if they're a cut above people who eat at the big fast-food chains. I make them feel as if they're discerning diners.'

'But you're serving up pretty much the same type of food.'

'Of course we are. That's what our customers are used to, that's what they like. But we make it just a little more expensive, and we serve it up like it's something really special. We give them a proper restaurant experience, that's why they come here for birthdays and special occasions.'

'But that must whack up your overheads.'

'What we lose on overheads we gain by sourcing our own foodstuffs.'

'You mean you can buy this stuff cheaper than McDonald's? How do you do that? You don't have a millionth of their buying power.'

'We use farmers' and stockbreeders' co-operatives. Little guys, that the big fast-food chains don't want to do business with. That's why our burgers taste better, and that's why they don't contain anything that you wouldn't want to eat.'

Kevin came over from the grill with a well-charred burger patty on a plate. His spots were glowing angrily from the heat. Mr Le Renges handed me a fork and said, 'There . . . try it.'

I cut a small piece off and peered at it suspiciously. 'No shit?' I asked him.

'Nothing but one thousand per cent protein, I promise you.'

I dry-swallowed, and then I put the morsel in my mouth. I chewed it slowly, trying not to think about the manure-splattered ramps of the slaughterhouses that I had visited around Baton Rouge. Mr Le Renges watched me with those glittering blowfly eyes of his and that didn't make it any more appetising, either.

But, surprisingly, the burger actually tasted pretty good. It was tender, with just the right amount of crunchiness on the outside, and it was well-seasoned with onion and salt and pepper and the tiniest touch of chilli, and there was another flavour, too, that really lifted it.

'Cumin?' I asked Mr Le Renges.

'Aha. That would be telling. But you like it, don't you?'

I cut off another piece. 'Okay, I have to confess that I do.'

Mr Le Renges whacked me on the back so that I almost choked. 'You see, John? Now you know what I was talking about when I told you that I was called to enrich people's lives. I keep small farmers in business, and at the same time I give the people of Calais a very important community venue with the best food that I can economically serve up. Well, not only Calais. I have Tony's Gourmet Burgers in Old Town and Millinocket and Waterville and I've just opened a new flagship restaurant in St Stephen, over the river in Canada.'

'Well, congratulations,' I coughed. 'When do you want me to start?'

I dreamed that I was sitting by the window of Rocco's restaurant on Drusilla Lane in Baton Rouge, eating a spicy catfish poboy with a cheese fry basket and a side of brown gravy. I had just ordered my bread pudding when the phone rang and the receptionist told me in a clogged-up voice that it was five-fifteen in the morning.

'Why are you telling me this?' I asked her.

'You asked for an alarm call, sir. Five-fifteen, and it's five-fifteen.'

I heaved myself up in bed. Outside my window it was still totally dark. It was then that I remembered that I was now the *chef de petit déjeuner* at Tony's, and I was supposed to be over on North Street at 6:00 am sharp to open up the premises and start getting the bacon griddled and the eggs shirred and the coffee percolating.

I stared at myself in the mirror. 'Why did you do this to yourself?' I asked me.

'Because you're a nitpicking perfectionist who couldn't turn a blind eye to three mouse droppings at the Cajun Queen Restaurant, that's why. And they probably weren't even mouse droppings at all. Just capers.'

'Capers schmapers.'

It was so cold outside that the deserted sidewalks shone like hammered glass. I walked to North Street where Chip had just opened up the restaurant.

'Morning, Chip.'

'Yeah.' He showed me how to switch off the alarm and switch on the lights. Then we went through to the kitchen and he showed me how to heat up the griddle and take out the frozen bacon and the frozen burgers and mix up the 'fresh squeezed' orange juice (just add water).

We had been there only ten minutes when a young mousey-haired girl with a pale face and dark circles under her eyes came through the door. 'Hi,' she said. 'I'm Anita. You must be John.'

'Hi, Anita,' I said, wiping my fingers on my green apron and shaking hands. 'How about a cup of coffee before the hordes descend on us?'

'Okay, then,' she blinked. From the expression on her face I think she must have thought I said 'whores'.

But they were hordes all right, and once they started coming through that door they didn't stop. By a quarter past seven every booth and every table was crowded with businessmen and postal workers and truckers and even the sandy-haired cop who had first flagged me down as I walked into town. I couldn't believe that these people got up so early. Not only that, they were all so *cheerful* too, like they couldn't wait to start another day's drudgery. It was all, 'Good morning, Sam! And how are you on this cold and frosty morning!' 'Good morning, Mrs Trent! See *you* wrapped up warm and toasty!' 'Hi, Rick! Great day for the race – the human race!' I mean, *please*.

They not only looked hearty and talked hearty, they ate hearty, too. For two hours solid I was sizzling bacon and flipping burgers and frying eggs and browning corned-beef hash. Anita was dashing from table to table with juice and coffee and double orders of toast, and it wasn't until 8:00 am that a sassy black girl called Oona came in to help her.

Gradually, however, the restaurant began to empty out, with more back-whacking and more cheery goodbyes, until we were left with nobody but two FedEx drivers and an old woman who looked as if she was going to take the next six months to chew her way through two slices of Canadian bacon.

It was then that one of the FedEx drivers put his hand over his mouth and spat into it. He frowned down at what he had found in his burger and showed it to his friend. Then he got up from the table and came over to the grill, his hand cupped over his mouth.

'Broken my darn tooth,' he said.

'How d'you do that?' I asked him.

'Bit into my burger and there was *this* in it.'

He held up a small black object between his finger and thumb.

I took it from him and turned it this way and that. There was no doubt about it, it was a bullet, slightly flattened by impact.

'I'm real sorry,' I said. 'Look, this is my first day here. All I can do is report it to the management and you can have your breakfast on us.'

'I'm going to have to see a darn dentist,' he complained. 'I can't abide the darn dentist. And what if I'd swallowed it? I could of got lead poisoning.'

'I'm sorry. I'll show it to the owner just as soon as he gets here.'

'This'll cost plenty, I bet you. Do you want to take a look?' Before I could stop him he stretched open his mouth and showed me a chipped front incisor and a mouthful of mushed-up hamburger.

Mr Le Renges came in at 11:00 am. Outside it was starting to get windy and his hair had flapped over to one side like a crow's wing. Before I could collar him he dived straight into his office and closed the door, presumably to spend some time rearranging his wayward locks. He came out five minutes later, briskly chafing his hands together like a man eager to get down to business.

'Well, John, how did it go?'

'Pretty good, Mr Le Renges. Place was packed out.'

'Always is. People know a good deal when they see one.'

'Only one problem. A guy found this in his burger.' I handed him the bullet. He inspected it closely, and then he shook his head.

'That didn't come from one of our burgers, John.'

'I saw him spit it out myself. He broke one of his front teeth.'

'Oldest trick in the book. Guy needs dental work, he comes into a restaurant and pretends he broke his tooth on something he ate. Gets the restaurant to stump up for his dentist's bill.'

'Well, it didn't look that way to me.'

'That's because you're not as well-versed in the wiles of dishonest customers as I am. You didn't apologise, I hope?'

'I didn't charge him for his breakfast.'

'You shouldn't have done that, John. That's practically an admission of liability. Well, let's hope the bastard doesn't try to take it any further.'

'Aren't you going to inform the health and safety people?'

'Of course not.'

'What about your suppliers?'

'You know as well as I do that all ground beef is magnetically screened for metal particles.'

'Sure. But this is a bullet and it's made of lead and lead isn't magnetic.'

'They don't *shoot* cows, John.'

'Of course not. But anything could have happened. Maybe some kid took a potshot at it when it was standing in a field, and the bullet was lodged in its muscle.'

'John, every one of our burgers is very carefully sourced from people who are really *evangelical* when it comes to quality meat. There is no way that this bullet came from one of our burgers, and I hope you're prepared to back me up and say that there was absolutely no sign of any bullet in that customer's patty when you grilled it.'

'I didn't actually *see* it, no. But—'

Mr Le Renges dropped the bullet into his wastebasket. 'Attaboy, John. You'll be back here bright and early tomorrow morning, then?'

'Early, yes. Bright? Well, maybe.'

All right, you can call me a hairsplitting go-by-the-book bureaucrat, but the way I see it, any job has to be done properly or else it's not worth getting out of bed in the morning to do it, especially if you have to get out of bed at 5:15 am. I walked back to the Calais Motor Inn looking for a bite of lunch and I ordered a fried chicken salad with iceberg lettuce, tomato, bacon bits, cheddar and mozzarella and home-made croutons, with onion strings and fried pickles on the side. But as comforting as all of this was, I couldn't stop thinking about that bullet and wondering where it had come from. I could understand why Mr Le Renges didn't want to report it to the health and safety inspectors, but why didn't he want to have a hard word with his own supplier?

Velma came up with another beer. 'You're looking serious today, John. I thought you had to be happy by law.'

'Got something on my mind, Velma, that's all.'

She sat down beside me. 'How did the job go?'

'It's an existence. I grill, therefore I am. But something happened today . . . I don't know. It's made me feel kind of uncomfortable.'

'What do you mean, John?'

'It's like having my shorts twisted, only it's inside my head. I keep trying to tug it this way and that way and it still feels not quite right.'

'Go on.'

I told her about the bullet and the way in which Mr Le Renges had insisted that he wasn't going to report it.

'Well, that happens. You do get customers who bring in a dead fly and hide it in their salad so they won't have to pay.'

'I know. But, I don't know.'

After a double portion of chocolate ice-cream with vanilla-flavoured wafers I walked back to Tony's, where the lunchtime session was just finishing. 'Mr Le Renges still here?' I asked Oona.

'He went over to St Stephen. He won't be back until six, thank God.'

'You don't like him much, do you?'

'He gives me the heeby-jeebies, if you must know.'

I went through to Mr Le Renges' office. Fortunately, he had left it unlocked. I looked in the wastebasket and the bullet was still there. I picked it out and dropped it into my pocket.

On my way back to the Calais Motor Inn a big blue pick-up truck tooted at me. It was Nils Guttormsen from Lyle's Autos, still looking surprised.

'They brought over your transmission parts from Bangor this morning, John. I should have her up and running in a couple of days.'

'That's great news, Nils. No need to break your ass.' Especially since I don't have any money to pay you yet.

I showed the bullet to Velma.

'That's truly weird, isn't it?' she said.

'You're right, Velma. It's weird, but it's not unusual for hamburger meat to be contaminated. In fact, it's more usual than unusual, which is why I never eat hamburgers.'

'I don't know if I want to hear this, John.'

'You should, Velma. See – they used to have federal inspectors in

every slaughterhouse, but the Reagan administration wanted to save
money, so they allowed the meatpacking industry to take care of its
own hygiene procedures. Streamlined Inspection System for Cattle,
that's what they call it – SIS-C.'

'I never heard of that, John.'

'Well, Velma, as an ordinary citizen you probably wouldn't have. But
the upshot was that when they had no USDA inspectors breathing
down their necks, most of the slaughterhouses doubled their line-speed,
and that meant there was much more risk of contamination. I mean, if
you can imagine a dead cow hanging up by its heels and a guy cutting
its stomach open, and then heaving out its intestines by hand, which
they still do, that's a very skilled job, and if a gutter makes one mistake
floop! everything goes everywhere, blood, guts, dirt, manure, and that
happens to one in five cows. Twenty per cent.'

'Oh my God.'

'Oh, it's worse than that, Velma. These days, with SIS-C, meatpack-
ers can get away with processing far more diseased cattle. I've seen
cows coming into the slaughterhouse with abscesses and tapeworms
and measles. The beef scraps they ship out for hamburgers are all
mixed up with manure, hair, insects, metal filings, urine and vomit.'

'You're making me feel nauseous, John. I had a hamburger for supper
last night.'

'Make it your last, Velma. It's not just the contamination, it's the
quality of the beef they use. Most of the cattle they slaughter for
hamburgers are old dairy cattle, because they're cheap and their meat
isn't too fatty. But they're full of antibiotics and they've often been
infected with *E. coli* and salmonella. You take just one hamburger, that's
not the meat from a single animal, that's mixed-up meat from dozens
or even hundreds of different cows, and it takes only one diseased cow
to contaminate thirty-two thousand pounds of ground beef.'

'That's like a horror story, John.'

'You're too right, Velma.'

'But this bullet, John. Where would this bullet come from?'

'That's what I want to know, Velma. I can't take it to the health
people because then I'd lose my job and if I lose my job I can't pay for
my automobile to be repaired and Nils Guttormsen is going to
impound it and I'll never get back to Baton Rouge unless I fucking
walk and it's two thousand three hundred and seven miles.'

'That far, hunh?'

'That far.'

'Why don't you show it to Eddie Bertilson?'

'What?'

'The bullet. Why don't you show it to Eddie Bertilson. Bertilson's Sporting Guns and Ammo, over on Orchard Street? He'll tell you where it came from.'

'You think so?'

'I know so. He knows everything about guns and ammo. He used to be married to my cousin Patricia.'

'You're a star, Velma. I'll go do that. When I come back, maybe you and I could have some dinner together and then I'll make wild energetic love to you.'

'No.'

'No?'

'I like you, John, but no.'

'Oh.'

Eddie Bertilson was one of those extreme pains-in-the-ass people who note down the tailfin numbers of military aircraft in Turkey and get themselves arrested for espionage. But I have to admit that he knew everything possible about guns and ammo and when he took a look at that bullet he knew directly what it was.

He was small and bald with dark-tinted glasses and hair growing out of his ears, and a Grateful Dead T-shirt with greasy finger-wipes on it. He screwed this jeweller's eyeglass into his socket and turned the bullet this way and that.

'Where'd you find this?' he wanted to know.

'Do I have to tell you?'

'No, you don't, because I can tell *you* where you found it. You found it amongst the memorabilia of a Vietnam vet.'

'Did I?' The gun store was small and poky and smelled of oil. There were all kinds of hunting rifles arranged in cabinets behind the counter, not to mention pictures of anything that a visitor to Calais might want to kill: woodcock, ruffed grouse, black duck, mallard, blue-wing and green-wing teal.

'This is a 7.92mm Gewehr Patrone 98 slug which was the standard ammunition of the Maschinengewehr 34 machine gun designed by Louis Stange for the German army in 1934. After the Second World War it was used by the Czechs, the French, the Israelis and the Biafrans, and a few turned up in Vietnam, stolen from the French.'

'It's a machine-gun bullet?'

'That's right,' said Eddie, dropping it back in the palm of my hand with great satisfaction at his own expertise.

'So you wouldn't use this to kill, say, a cow?'

'No. Unlikely.'

The next morning Chip and I opened the restaurant as usual and by 8:00 am we were packed to the windows. Just before nine a black panel van drew up outside and two guys in white caps and overalls climbed out. They came down the side alley to the kitchen door and knocked.

'Delivery from St Croix Meats,' said one of them. He was a stocky guy with a walrus moustache and a deep diagonal scar across his mouth, as if he had been told to shut up by somebody with a machete.

'Sure,' said Chip, and opened up the freezer for him. He and his pal brought in a dozen cardboard boxes labelled Hamburger Patties.

'Always get your hamburgers from the same company?' I asked Chip.

'St Croix, sure. Mr Le Renges is the owner.'

'Ah.' No wonder Mr Le Renges hadn't wanted to talk to his supplier about the bullet: his supplier was him. I bent my head sideways so that I could read the address. US Route 1, Robbinstown.

It was a brilliantly sunny afternoon and the woods around Calais were all golden and crimson and rusty-coloured. Velma drove us down US 1 with Frank and Nancy Sinatra singing 'Something Stupid' on the radio.

'I don't know why you're doing this, John. I mean, who cares if somebody found a bullet in their hamburger?'

'*I* care, Velma. Do you think I'm going to be able to live out the rest of my life without finding out how an American cow got hit by a Viet Cong machine gun?'

It took us almost an hour to find St Croix Meats because the building was way in back of an industrial park – a big grey rectangular place with six or seven black panel vans parked outside it and no signs anywhere. The only reason I knew that we had come to the right place was because I saw Mr Le Renges walking across the yard outside with the biggest, ugliest dog that I had ever seen in my life. I'm not a dog expert, but I suddenly realised who had been advertising in *The Quoddy Whirlpool* for somebody to walk their Presa Canario.

'What are you going to do now?' Velma asked me. There was a security guard on the gate and there was no way that a 289-pound man in a flappy white raincoat was going to be able to tippy-toe his way in without being noticed.

Just then, however, I saw the guy with the scar who had delivered our hamburgers that morning. He climbed into one of the black vans, started it up, and manoeuvred it out of the yard.

'Follow that van,' I asked Velma.

'What for, John?'

'I want to see where it goes, that's all.'

'This is not much of a date, John.'

'I'll make it up to you, I promise.'

'Dinner and wild energetic love?'

'We could skip the dinner if you're not hungry.'

We followed the van for nearly two-and-a-half hours, until it began to grow dark. I was baffled by the route it took. First of all it stopped at a small medical centre in Pembroke. Then it went to a veterinarian just outside of Mathias. It circled back towards Calais, visiting two small dairy farms, before calling last of all at the rear entrance of Calais Memorial Hospital, back in town.

It wasn't always possible for us to see what was happening, but at one of the dairy farms we saw the van drivers carrying cattle carcases out of the outbuildings, and at the Memorial Hospital we saw them pushing out large wheeled containers, rather like laundry hampers.

Velma said, 'I have to get back to work now. My shift starts at six.'

'I don't understand this, Velma,' I said. 'They were carrying dead cattle out of those farms, but USDA regulations state that cattle have to be processed no more than two hours after they've been slaughtered. After that time, bacteria multiply so much that they're almost imposs- ible to get rid of.'

'So Mr Le Renges is using rotten beef for his hamburgers?'

'Looks like it. But what else? I can understand rotten beef. Dozens of slaughterhouses use rotten beef. But why did the van call at the hospital? And the veterinarian?'

Velma stopped the car outside the motel and stared at me. 'Oh, you're not serious.'

'I have to take a look inside that meatpacking plant, Velma.'

'You're sure you haven't bitten off more than you can chew?'

'Very apt phrase, Velma.'

My energy levels were beginning to decline again so I treated myself to a fried shrimp sandwich and a couple of Molson's with a small triangular diet-sized piece of pecan pie to follow. Then I walked around to the hospital and went to the rear entrance where the van from St Croix Meats had parked. A hospital porter with greasy hair and squinty eyes and glasses was standing out back taking a smoke.

'How's it going, feller?' I asked him.

'Okay. Anything I can do for you?'

'Maybe, I've been looking for a friend of mine. Old drinking buddy from way back.'

'Oh, yeah?'

'Somebody told me he's been working around here, driving a van. Said they'd seen him here at the hospital.'

The greasy-haired porter blew smoke out of his nostrils. 'We get vans in and out of here all day.'

'This guy's got a scar, right across his mouth. You couldn't miss him.'

'Oh you mean the guy from BioGlean?'

'BioGlean?'

'Sure. They collect, like, surgical waste, and get rid of it.'

'What's that, "surgical waste"?'

'Well, you know. Somebody has their leg amputated, somebody has their arm cut off. Spleens, intestines, stuff like that. You'd be amazed how much stuff a busy hospital has to get rid of.'

'I thought they incinerated it.'

'They used to, but BioGlean kind of specialise, and I guess it's cheaper than running an incinerator night and day. They even go round auto shops and take bits of bodies out of car wrecks. You don't realise, do you, that the cops won't do it, and that the mechanics don't want to do it, so I guess somebody has to.'

He paused, and then he said, 'What's your name? Next time your buddy calls by, I'll tell him that you were looking for him.'

'Ralph Waldo Emerson. I'm staying at the Chandler House on Chandler.'

'Okay . . . Ralph Waldo Emerson. Funny, that. Name kind of rings a bell.'

I borrowed Velma's car and drove back out to Robbinstown. I parked in the shadow of a large computer warehouse. St Croix Meats was surrounded by a high fence topped with razor wire and the front yard was brightly floodlit. A uniformed security guard sat in a small booth by the gate, reading *The Quoddy Whirlpool*. With any luck, it would send him to sleep and I would be able to walk right past him.

I waited for over an hour, but there didn't seem to be any way for me to sneak inside. All the lights were on, and now and then I saw workers in hard hats and long rubber aprons walking in and out of the building. Maybe this was the time for me to give up trying to play detective and call the police.

The outside temperature was sinking deeper and deeper and I was beginning to feel cold and cramped in Velma's little Volkswagen. After a while I had to climb out and stretch my legs. I walked as near to the main gate as I could without being seen, and stood next to a skinny maple tree. I felt like an elephant trying to hide behind a lamppost. The security guard was still awake. Maybe he was reading an exciting article about the sudden drop in cod prices.

I had almost decided to call it a night when I heard a car approaching along the road behind me. I managed to hide most of me behind the tree and Mr Le Renges drove past and up to the front gate. At first I thought somebody was sitting in his Lexus with him, but then I realised it was that huge, ugly Presa Canario. It looked like a cross between a Great Dane and a hound from Hell, and it was bigger than he was. It turned its head and I saw its eyes reflected scarlet. It was like being stared at by Satan, believe me.

The security guard came out to open the gate and for a moment he and Mr Le Renges chatted to each other, their breath smoking in the frosty evening air. I thought of crouching down and trying to make my way into the slaughterhouse behind Mr Le Renges' car, but there was no chance that I could do it without being spotted.

'Everything okay, Vernon?'

'Silent like the grave, Mr Le Renges.'

'That's what I like to hear, Vernon. How's that daughter of yours, Louise? Got over her autism yet?'

'Not exactly, Mr Le Renges. Doctors say it's going to take some time.'

Mr Le Renges was still talking when one of his big black vans came burbling up the road and stopped behind his Lexus. Its driver waited patiently. After all, Mr Le Renges was the boss. I hesitated for a moment and then I sidestepped out from behind my skinny little tree and circled around the back of the van. There was a wide aluminum step below the rear doors, and two door-handles that I could cling on to.

'You are out of your cotton-picking mind,' I told me. But still, I climbed up onto the step, as easy as I could. You don't jump onto the back of a van when you're as heavy as me, not unless you want the driver to bounce up and hit his head on the roof.

Mr Le Renges seemed to go on talking for ever, but at last he gave the security guard a wave and drove forward into the yard, and the van followed him. I pressed myself close to the rear doors, in the hope that I wouldn't be quite so obtrusive, but the security guard went back into his booth and shook open his paper and didn't even glance my way.

A man in a bloodied white coat and a hard hat came out of the slaughterhouse building and opened the car door for Mr Le Renges. They spoke for a moment and then Mr Le Renges went inside the building himself. The man in the bloodied white coat opened the car's passenger door and let his enormous dog jump out. The dog salaciously sniffed at the blood before the man took hold of its leash. He went walking off with it – or, rather, the dog went walking off with him, its claws scrabbling on the blacktop.

I pushed my way in through the side door that I had seen all the cutters and gutters walking in and out of. Inside there was a long corridor with a wet tiled floor, and then an open door which led to a changing-room and a toilet. Rows of white hard hats were hanging on hooks, as well as rubber aprons and rubber boots. There was an overwhelming smell of stale blood and disinfectant.

Two booted feet were visible underneath the door of the toilet stall and clouds of cigarette smoke were rising up above it.

'Only two more hours, thank Christ,' said a disembodied voice.

'See the play-off?' I responded as I took off my raincoat and hung it up.

'Yeah, what a goddamn fiasco. They ought to can that Kershinsky.'

I put on a heavy rubber apron and just about managed to tie it up at the back. Then I sat down and tugged on a pair of boots.

'You going to watch the New Brunswick game?' asked the disembodied voice.

'I don't know. I've got a hot date that day.'

There was a pause and more smoke rose up, and then the voice said, 'Who *is* that? Is that you, Stemmens?'

I left the changing-room without answering. I squeaked back along the corridor in my rubber boots and went through to the main slaughterhouse building.

You don't even want to imagine what it was like in there. A high, echoing, brightly lit building with a production line clanking and rattling, mincers grinding and roaring, and thirty or forty cutters in aprons and hard hats boning and chopping and trimming. The noise and the stench of blood were overwhelming, and for a moment I just stood there with my hand pressed over my mouth and nose, with that fried shrimp sandwich churning in my stomach as if the shrimp were still alive.

The black vans were backed up to one end of the production line and men were heaving out the meat that they had been gleaning during the day. They were dumping it straight onto the killing floor where normally the live cattle would be stunned and killed – heaps and heaps of it, a tangle of sagging cattle and human arms and legs, along with glistening strings of intestines and globs of fat and things that looked like run-over dogs and knackered donkeys, except it was all so mixed-up and disgusting that I couldn't be sure what it all was. It was flesh, that was all that mattered. The cutters were boning it and cutting it into scraps, and the scraps were being dumped into giant stainless-steel machines and ground by giant augers into a pale-pink pulp. The pulp was seasoned with salt and pepper and dried onions and spices. Then it was mechanically pressed into patties and covered with cling-film and run through a metal-detector and frozen. All ready to be served up sizzling-hot for somebody's breakfast.

'Jesus,' I said, out loud.

'You talking to me?' said a voice right next to me. 'You talking to *me*?'

I turned around. It was Mr Le Renges. He had a look on his face like he'd just walked into a washroom door without opening it.

'What the fuck are *you* doing here?' he demanded.

'I have to cook this stuff, Mr Le Renges. I have to serve it to people. I thought I ought to find out what was in it.'

He didn't say anything at first. He looked to the left and he looked to the right, and it was like he was doing everything he could to control his temper. Eventually he sniffed sharply up his right nostril and said, 'It's all the same. Don't you get that?'

'Excuse me? What's all the same?'

'Meat, wherever it comes from. Human legs are the same as cow's legs, or pig's legs, or goat's legs. For Christ's sake, it's all protein.'

I pointed to a tiny arm protruding from the mess on the production line. 'That's a baby. That's a human baby. That's just *protein*?'

Mr Le Renges rubbed his forehead as if he couldn't understand what I was talking about. 'You ate one of your burgers. You know how good they taste.'

'Look at this stuff!' I shouted at him, and now three or four cutters turned around and began to give me less-than-friendly stares. 'This is shit! This is total and utter shit! You can't feed people on dead cattle and dead babies and amputated legs!'

'Oh yes?' he challenged me. 'And why the hell not? Do you really think this is any worse than the crap they serve up at all of the franchise restaurants? They serve up diseased dairy cows, full of worms and flukes and all kinds of shit. At least a human leg won't have *E. coli* infection. At least a stillborn baby won't be full of steroids.'

'You don't think there's any moral dimension here?' I shouted back. 'Look at this! For Christ's sake! We're talking cannibalism here!'

Mr Le Renges drew back his hair with his hand, and inadvertently exposed his bald patch. 'The major fast-food companies source their meat at the cheapest possible outlets. How do you think I compete? I don't *buy* my meat. The sources I use, they pay me to take the meat away. Hospitals, farms, auto repair shops, health clinics. They've all got excess protein they don't know what to do with. So BioGlean comes around and relieves them of everything they don't know how to get rid of, and Tony's Gourmet Burgers recycles it.'

'You're sick, Mr Le Renges.'

'Not sick, John. Not at all. Just practical. You ate human flesh in that piece of hamburger I offered you, and did you suffer any ill effects? No. Of course not. In fact I see Tony's Gourmet Burgers as the pioneers of really decent food.'

While we were talking, the production line had stopped and a small crowd of cutters and gutters had gathered around us, all carrying cleavers and boning-knives.

'You won't get any of these men to say a word against me,' said Mr Le Renges. 'They get paid twice as much as any other slaughterhouse-men in Maine; or in any other state, believe me. They don't kill anybody, ever. They simply cut up meat, whatever it is, and they do a damn fine job.'

I walked across to one of the huge stainless-steel vats in which the meat was minced into glistening pink gloop. The men began to circle closer and I was beginning to get seriously concerned that I might end up as pink gloop too.

'You realise I'm going to have to report this to the police and the USDA,' I warned Mr Le Renges, even though my voice was about two octaves above normal.

'I don't think so,' said Mr Le Renges.

'So what are you going to do? You're going to have me gutted and minced up like the rest of this stuff?'

Mr Le Renges smiled and shook his head, and it was at that moment that the slaughterman who had been taking his dog for a walk came onto the killing floor, with the hellbeast still straining at its leash.

'If any of my men were to touch you, John, that would be homicide, wouldn't it? But if Cerberus slipped its collar and went for you – what could I do? He's a very powerful dog, after all. And if I had twenty or thirty eye-witnesses to swear that you provoked him . . .'

The Presa Canario was pulling so hard at its leash that it was practically choking, and its claws were sliding on the bloody metal floor. You never saw such a hideous brindled collection of teeth and muscle in your whole life, and its eyes reflected the light as if it had been caught in a flash photograph.

'Kevin, unclip his collar,' said Mr Le Renges.

'This is not a good idea, Mr Le Renges,' I cautioned him. 'If anything happens to me, I have friends here who know where I am and what I've been doing.'

'Kevin,' Mr Le Renges repeated, unimpressed.

The slaughterman leaned forward and unclipped the Presa Canario's collar. It bounded forward, snarling, and I took a step back until my rear end was pressed against the stainless-steel vat. There was no place else to go.

'Now, *kill*!' shouted Mr Le Renges, and stiffly pointed his arm at me.

The dog lowered its head almost to the floor and bunched up its shoulder muscles. Strings of saliva swung from its jowls, and its cock suddenly appeared, red and pointed, as if it was sexually aroused by the idea of tearing my throat out.

I lifted my left arm to protect myself. I mean, I could live without a left arm, but not without a throat. It was then that I had a sudden flashback. I remembered when I was a kid, when I was thin and runty and terrified of dogs. My father had given me a packet of dog treats to take to school, so that if I was threatened by a dog I could offer it something to appease it. '*Always remember that kid. Dogs prefer food to children, every time. Food is easier to eat.*'

I reached into the vat behind me and scooped out a huge handful of pink gloop. It felt disgusting . . . soft and fatty, and it dripped. I held it towards the Presa Canario and said, 'Here, Cerberus! You feel like a snack, boy? Try some of this!'

The dog stared up at me with those red reflective eyes as if I were mad. Its black lips rolled back and it bared its teeth and snarled like a massed chorus of death-rattles.

I took a step closer, still holding out the heap of gloop, praying that the dog wouldn't take a bite at it and take off my fingers as well. But the Presa Canario lifted its head and sniffed at the meat with deep suspicion.

'*Kill*, Cerberus, you stupid mutt!' shouted Mr Le Renges.

I took another step towards it, and then another. 'Here, boy. Supper.'

The dog turned its head away. I pushed the gloop closer and closer, but it wouldn't take it, didn't even want to sniff it.

I turned to Mr Le Renges. 'There you are . . . even a dog won't eat your burgers.'

Mr Le Renges snatched the dog's leash from the slaughterman. He went up to the animal and whipped it across the snout, once, twice, three times. 'You pathetic disobedient piece of shit!'

Mistake. Big, *big* mistake. Cerberus didn't want to go near me and my handful of gloop, but it was still an attack dog. It let out a bark that was almost a roar and sprang at Mr Le Renges in utter fury. It knocked him back onto the floor and it crunched its teeth right into his hairline. He screamed and thrashed and tried to beat it off. But the beast jerked its head furiously from side to side, and with each jerk it pulled more of his face away, inch by inch. Forehead first, then his eyebrows, then his nose.

Right in front of us, with a noise like somebody trying to rip up a pillowcase, the dog exposed Mr Le Renges's bloodied, wildly popping eyes, the bubbly black holes of his nostrils, his grinning lipless teeth.

He was still screaming and gargling when three of the slaughtermen pulled the dog away. Strong as they were, even they couldn't hold it, and it twisted away from them and trotted off to the other side of the killing floor with Mr Le Renges's face dangling from its jaws like a slippery Hallowe'en mask.

I turned to the slaughtermen. They were too shocked to speak. One of them dropped his knife, and then the others did, too, and they chimed on the floor like church bells.

I stayed in Calais long enough for Nils to finish fixing my car and to make a statement to the sandy-haired police officer. The weather was beginning to grow colder and I wanted to get back to the warmth of Louisiana, not to mention the rare beef muffelettas with gravy and onion strings.

Velma lent me the money to pay for my auto repairs and the Calais Motor Inn waived all charges because they said I was so public-spirited. I was even on the front page of *The Quoddy Whirlpool*. There was a picture of the mayor whacking me on the back, under the banner headline HAMBURGER HYGIENE HERO.

Velma came out to say goodbye on the morning I left. It was crisp and cold and the leaves were rattling across the parking lot.

'Maybe I should come with you,' she said.

I shook my head. 'You got vision, Velma. You can see the thin man inside me and that's the man you like. But I'm never going to be thin, ever. The poboys call and my stomach always listens.'

The last I saw of her, she was shading her eyes against the sun, and I have to admit that I was sorry to leave her behind. I've never been back to Calais since and I doubt if I ever will. I don't even know if Tony's Gourmet Burgers is still there. If it is, though, and you're tempted to stop in and order one, remember there's always a risk that any burger you buy from Tony Le Renges *is* people.

Graham Masterton has published four new horror novels – *The Doorkeepers*, *Snowman*, *Swimmer*, *Trauma* (aka *Bonnie Winter*) – since moving to Cork, Ireland, in 1999. *Katie Maguire*, a dark thriller set in the Cork underworld, is scheduled for publication in late 2002, while a young adult fantasy, *Jessica's Angel*, is due early in 2003. 'Despite some matchless pubs,' Masterton reveals, 'Ireland is a very productive place for writers. There's something in the air, not all of which is rain.' 2002 also saw a special twenty-fifth anniversary edition of his first horror novel, *The Manitou*, and the republication of much of his backlist, including *Flesh & Blood* and a double edition of *Ritual* and *Walkers*. *Spirit* and *The Chosen Child* were also recently both published in the United States for the first time. 'I can feel a genuine resurgence of interest in horror – particularly from younger readers – but there's no doubt that today's fans expect great sophistication and very high quality. After all, they've been weaned on *The Sixth Sense* and *The Mothman Prophesies*, not *Creepy Tales* and *Hammer House of Horrors*, the way we were.' The author has continued his support of abused children while in Ireland, and he was guest of honour at the 2002 ball held by the Irish Society for the Prevention of Cruelty to Children. About the preceding story, Masterton adds: 'For those who didn't get it . . . "Tony Le Renges" is an anagram of *Soylent Green*.'

Hide and Seek

NICHOLAS ROYLE

It was a way to pass the time and keep the kids happy. Kids. When I was a kid myself I didn't like the word. I didn't like being referred to as one of 'the kids'. It seemed unrespectful, dismissive. I preferred to be one of 'the children'. When my own kids were born, I consequently referred to them always as 'the children', never 'the kids'. In fact, to qualify that, it was when the first one was born that I stuck religiously to that rule, which lasted until just after the second one came along. The second and final one, I might add. Nothing I've ever done in my life drains the energy quite like having kids. Don't get me wrong: I wouldn't go back. I wouldn't unhave them. My life has been enriched – immeasurably. Practically anyone who's had kids will tell you the same. Apart from the abusers, the loveless, the miserable. So no, I wouldn't go back, but nor would I have any more. I'm shattered as it is; plus, how could I love another one as much as I adore the two I've got? Mind you, I thought that after the birth of the first one.

Harry, our firstborn, is a handful, as naughty as he is adorable. Good as an angel one minute, absolute horror the next. Would I have him any other way? The standard answer is no. I wouldn't want him any different. The standard answer sucks, however. Doesn't take a genius to work that one out. Sure I'd have him different. I'd have him good all the time. It would make life easier, that's all. However, he's lovable the way he is and if making him any less naughty made him any less lovable, then, no, I wouldn't have him any different.

He's funny. He makes faces and strikes poses I wouldn't have thought a four-year-old capable of. He's a mimic in the making. I love him like – well, there is no like. I love him more than anything or anyone I've ever loved. Before his sister came long. Now I love her the same way I love him. I'm nuts about her. If our relationship is less developed, less complex than the relationship I have with Harry, that's only because he's got two years' head start. Our dialogue is less sophisticated, but we still talk. In fact she's talking more and more all the time. For months, while other two-year-olds were chattering away, Sophie remained silent. She'd point and she'd cry, but she didn't have much vocab. Then it started to come in a rush. Now she knows words I didn't know she knew. Every day she surprises me with another one. The longest sentence she can speak gets longer every day. She's also the most beautiful little girl you've ever seen (takes after her mum – my wife – Sally), but then they all say that.

Sometimes when I'm out with the two of them somewhere I forget that while Harry's walking beside me and holding my hand, Sophie's sitting on my shoulders, and I briefly slip into a dizzying panic. Where is she? Where have I left her? Will I ever see her again? Sure you will, she's on your shoulders, you dummy. It's like forgetting you're wearing your glasses. Don't tell me you've never done that: searched for your glasses for a good quarter of an hour, only to realise eventually they're stuck on the front of your head.

But those moments, those moments when I forget she's there and I don't know where she is, they remind me of when Harry was little. I mean really little, three months or so. When having a baby was still a novelty, when you turned round and saw him lying in his Moses basket and gave a little start because you'd forgotten, you'd forgotten you'd got a kid – or a child.

I had this fear that one day I'd look in the Moses basket and he wouldn't be there. Not that he could climb or roll out of it, he couldn't, but that he just wouldn't be there. That somehow I would have reverted to that pre-parental state. Gone backwards at speed. One minute I had a child, the next minute I didn't. It didn't make any sense, of course, but a lot of stuff goes through your head in those early months that doesn't make any sense.

I was looking after both the kids. Sally was working late, attending a meeting. Harry kept going on about Agnes, one of his little friends. He wanted her to come round. Or to go round to hers. We couldn't do that, I explained, because Agnes's parents had invited us round to theirs the other day. You have to be invited, I explained to him. You can't invite yourself.

Agnes's parents were our closest friends and they lived just two streets away. To stop Harry going on about it, I called them to invite them over. It turned out Agnes's mum, Siobhan, was at the same meeting Sally was at. They worked in the same field. So Agnes's dad, William, was looking after Agnes on his own. Looks like the tables have been turned, he joked. Our wives are out at work and we're left holding the babies.

Then he explained he was trying to finish some work of his own and needed to make the most of Siobhan's being out at the meeting. He was going to try to get Agnes into bed early. Instead, I offered to look after Agnes while he got on with his work. I'll bring her back after an hour or so, I said. Are you sure? He asked. No problem, I said. She's a very easy child.

William dropped Agnes round and she ran into the house, all excited at spending time with Harry and Sophie. William called after her, hoping for a goodbye kiss or hug before he went back home, but she was gone. I saw his crestfallen face, knew how he felt, but knew also that he'd be feeling relieved to have offloaded Agnes for a bit, so he'd be able to get some work done, or just have a break. I locked the door after him: my kids knew about not leaving the house unattended, and no doubt Agnes did too, but it didn't pay to be careless. So there I was now with three of them to keep happy at least until Sally got home. No problem, I'd said to William. No problem, I thought to myself. I loved Agnes almost like my own. Almost. There's always that almost. The love you have for your own kids is different. It's instinctive, fiercely protective. With someone else's kids it's less visceral, more of an affectionate responsibility.

Let's play hide and seek, I suggested. Yes! they all shouted, jumping up and down. Hide and seek. Hide and seek.

Who wants to hide first? I asked. Me! they chorused.

When Harry first started playing hide and seek, when he was two and a half, perhaps, or three, he'd tell you where he was going to hide. I'm going to hide under the bed, he'd say, and you'd try to explain why that wasn't really going to work. Later he would just close his eyes, believing that if he closed his eyes, not only could he not see you, but you couldn't see him either. Eventually he got the hang of it and became quite proficient at the game. He got so that you genuinely couldn't find him for two or three minutes. It was pretty much the only time, apart from when he was asleep, that you could get him to keep still and quiet for more than ten seconds. For this reason we encouraged the playing of hide and seek.

Sophie was still only learning, like Harry had been at her age. And Agnes – well, I was about to find out how good Agnes was at hide and seek.

Who's going to hide first? I asked, as if I didn't know. All three shouted 'Me!' and put their hands up, but I knew from experience that if it wasn't Harry, then it wasn't going to work. He'd go into a sulk, wouldn't play properly and everything would start to fall apart. OK, Harry first, I said, raising my arms and my voice to forestall protest. The rest of us count to ten.

Twenty, he shouted as he bounded up the stairs.

I counted loudly enough to drown out his retreat and the girls joined in. Sophie was jumping up and down with excitement. She had just learned how to jump and liked to do it as much as possible whenever there was a situation that seemed to call for it. Twenty, we concluded at the tops of our voices. Coming ready or not. Dead silence from the rest of the house. That's my boy.

Shall we look in the kitchen first, I suggested, in case he managed to sneak past us while we had our eyes shut?

The girls both nodded and I led the way into the kitchen, which smelled of onions and fried minced lamb. Still steaming on the hob was the big pan of chilli I'd made earlier for Sally and me to enjoy in front of the TV when the kids were in bed. The fridge door was a collage of art postcards, Bob the Builder yoghurt magnets and photo booth pictures of me and Sally with the kids. Over in the corner, a stereo was playing Porcupine Tree's *Lightbulb Sun* album for about the twenty-third time that day.

No sign of him here, I said. Shall we look in the dining room?

The knocked-through dining room and lounge looked like it usually did when both kids had been home for more than half an hour. Like a cyclone had ripped through the boxes, crates and cupboards filled with toys. A riot of Thomas the Tank Engine, Buzz Lightyear and Woody, Teletubbies and Barbie. Scott Tracey and Lady Penelope masks. Bob the Builder construction vehicles. Britains models and Matchbox Super-fast cars (handed down from father to son). Teddy bears, rag dolls and dozens of assorted soft toys. Full marks to the kids for having out-Chapmanned the Chapman Brothers, who would have been proud of the maelstrom of miscegenation and mutilation.

No sign of him here either, I said, checking under the coffee table and behind the settee. Shall we look upstairs?

Yes!

Upstairs we looked in Sophie's room. We'd recently taken the side off her cot. As a result she could get out of bed and wander in the night, which was marginally preferable to one of us having to go to her if she started crying. Let her come to us instead.

Harry wasn't in Sophie's room.

Sophie and Agnes had already checked out the bathroom. Next was

Harry's room. Harry had recently become keen on colouring in and cutting out and sticking down. His masterpieces covered every available inch of wall space. On the floor was a little pile of jagged scraps of paper from his most recent sesssion with the kiddie-proof scissors. I quickly looked under his bed, but could only see his plastic Ikea toy crate-on-castors that I knew was full of dressing-up gear, Batman costumes, old scarves and so on. He wasn't in the walk-in cupboard or the walnut wardrobe.

By now the girls were shouting his name, enjoying the fact that we couldn't find him. We had a quick but thorough look in my and Sally's bedroom, but he wasn't in there either, so he had to be upstairs again. The top floor held my office, another bathroom and the spare bedroom. As soon as we'd looked in all three I began seriously to wonder where he might be. It occurred to me that, although I couldn't imagine how he might have done it, there was the tiniest of possibilities that he could have slipped past us while we were in his room and nipped downstairs. So I ran downstairs and rechecked every possible hiding place. It didn't take long; I knew where they all were by now. I made my way back upstairs like a cop with a search warrant, clearing rooms as I went, mentally chalking a cross on the door, one stroke on the way in, another as I left. Back at the top of the house, I finally admitted to myself that I was anxious.

Harry was good at hide and seek, but not this good. How was it possible, in a house I knew so well, for him to vanish so completely? I forced myself to be calm and to stick to a methodological approach. He couldn't have left the house – the front and back doors were locked, as were the windows. The door to the cellar was kept bolted. The door leading to the crawlspace that was all that was left of the loft after its conversion was not locked, but it was inaccessible behind the ratty old settee in my office and neither of our children had ever shown the slightest interest in it. I looked down at Sophie and Agnes. Their eyes were wide with excitement. Sophie was jumping up and down, shouting Harry's name.

Follow me, I said, something having made me think of triple-checking his favourite hiding place. In Harry's bedroom I got down on all fours and pulled out the plastic toy crate from under his bed. There he was, in the far corner, still as a statue, scarcely breathing. His eyes met mine and he started to smile.

He crawled out and I hugged him so tightly he protested that it hurt. I'd lost my appetite for hide and seek, but naturally the kids hadn't and Sophie was insisting on hiding next. I knew if I stopped the game there'd be trouble, so we counted to twenty while she toddled off. It took us less than another twenty seconds to find her, a tell-tale giggling lump under the duvet in my and Sally's bed.

In fairness, I now had to let Agnes go off and hide despite overwhelming tiredness on my part and a growing desire to head back downstairs, open a beer and listen to the news on the radio while allowing the kids to veg out in front of Cartoon Network. I couldn't expect either William or Sally for another fifteen minutes.

. . . eighteen, nineteen, *twenty*!

The first place Harry looked was under his own bed. I think we might have heard if she'd hidden in here, I suggested, but in fact we hadn't heard anything at all. She'd managed to slip out and hide without leaving us any clues.

Let's look in Mummy and Daddy's room, Harry urged.

Sophie instantly copied what he'd said in her more condensed delivery, in which all the words ran together and could only be decoded by remembering what had been said before.

Agnes wasn't in Mummy and Daddy's room. The three of us climbed the stairs again to the top floor. Spare bedroom, bathroom, my office – all clear. Back down to the first floor. Bathroom, Sophie's room – both empty. We trooped downstairs, Harry running on ahead, wanting to be the one to find Agnes. There was no sign of her in the lounge, dining room or kitchen. Back in the hall, I noticed her shoes at the bottom of the stairs. She'd taken them off just after coming into the house.

I checked the locks on the doors and windows, then we ran back up to the first floor. I looked under each of the beds, behind all the curtains, in every cupboard. I added my voice to those of Harry and Sophie. I shouted that her Dad was due to collect her and he'd want to get straight back. It was time to come out. She'd won. (*No, I won!* Harry protested.) Come on, come on out, Agnes!

I ran up to the top floor without waiting for Harry and Sophie. I shoved the settee in the office out of the way and yanked open the door to the crawlspace, shining a light inside. Fishing tackle, rolled-up film posters, Christmas decorations, stacks of used padded envelopes, suitcases full of old clothes I couldn't bear to throw away – but no little girl, no Agnes. I looked under my desk, behind the oversize books on the bottom shelves of the bookcases, in the corner between the radio and the radiator. Running back out of my office I collided with Sophie on her way in. She fell over and started crying, but I ran on, into the spare bedroom. I ripped the sheets off the bed, hauled the TV away from the wall. In the adjoining bathroom I tore aside the shower curtain.

As I took the stairs three at a time back down to the next floor I could hear that both children were crying now. In our bedroom I emptied the laundry basket, fought my way through the dresses in Sally's wardrobe. I made myself stop and stare into the room's reflection in the full-length mirror in case that revealed any hidden detail I had somehow otherwise missed. I ran into Sophie's room and climbed up onto a chair to open the door to the linen cupboard.

I had checked everywhere, every possible hiding place, and she wasn't to be found. She'd gone.

The door bell rang. Sophie's room was just at the top of the stairs, so I could see right down to the front door. Through the frosted glass I could see that it wasn't Sally. Anyway, she would have used her keys. It was William.

Nicholas Royle is the author of four novels – *Counterparts, Saxophone Dreams, The Matter of the Heart* and *The Director's Cut* – in addition to more than a hundred short stories, which have appeared in a variety of anthologies and magazines. He has also edited eleven anthologies. He lives in west London with his wife and two children. Currently he is working on a new novel, *Straight to Video*, and a non-fiction project. After a six-year stint as a writer and editor at *Time Out*, he finally gave up the day job in the autumn of 2001 to write full-time. 'When my son was only a few weeks old, I used to have this fear that I would look down into the Moses basket or into the car seat and find that they were empty. The best horror story I can think of that plays on parental anxieties of this kind is Alex Hamilton's "The Baby-sitters", which appeared in his excellent 1966 collection *Beam of Malice*. The same Alex Hamilton compiles the annual fast-sellers chart for *The Guardian*'s books pages, which makes equally disturbing reading.'

Moving History

GEOFF NICHOLSON

I expect you're a lot like me. You're basically a sane, decent, healthy, happy human being, and yet every time you go into, say, a fast-food restaurant, you look around and you can't help thinking how much fun it would be to go on a deranged killing spree.

You can picture the pathetic, horrified faces as you brandish your powerful semi-automatic weapon and begin firing it 'indiscriminately', as they like to say, into the lumpen, lard-filled mass of humanity gathered there. You imagine bone and hair fragments being scattered through the air and landing in the deep-fat fryers with a satisfying sizzle. You see blood and brains being sprayed onto the cheerful easy-to-clean surfaces of the counters and tables, onto the floor and walls and ceiling. You imagine people panicking, and puking up the high-fat, high-sugar, highly industrialised sludge they've just crammed down their fat throats. These thoughts please you.

It's okay. We all think about this stuff. There's no shame in it. You, me, everybody, we all experience the same basic impulses. However, you and I are not quite the same. Whereas you and everybody else only think about it, I think about it and then go ahead and do it. It's just the way I am. And I don't restrict myself to fast-food restaurants. I have created bloody mayhem in other places too: shopping malls, cineplexes, water parks, Irish theme pubs; anywhere that modern, leisured man assembles, spends money and pretends to be having a good time. But fast-food restaurants are definitely where I do my best work.

And I know what you're thinking: if this guy is such a hot-shot mass murderer, how come I've never heard of him? Why aren't his exploits in every newspaper, on every news programme? How come there isn't a bulletin board and a web ring and a chat room? How come some death-metal band hasn't memorialised him in song? How come he hasn't been caught?

And the answer is simple: because until very recently I did all my mass murdering in a kink in the fabric of the space/time continuum. Hang about and I'll explain.

It started when I bought myself an old car, a classic. It was a Big Fifties Ford, a 1959 Low Line Zephyr Mark 2 – a real period piece, a gorgeous bit of moving history, according to the bloke who sold it to me, from the era when Britain was trying gamely but ineptly to produce American-looking cars. So my Zephyr was two-tone yellow and black, and it had a wide, snarly radiator grille, and it very nearly, but not quite, had fins.

It also had a three-speed gear box with an unsynchronised first gear, and the shift was on the steering column, so it was basically a complete bugger to drive, but you know, that was somehow part of the charm.

But actually, what really attracted me, the real reason I bought the thing – and I know this probably sounds a bit shallow – was the dashboard. In its heyday the car had apparently been used for rallying, so it had all sorts of extra clocks and dials mounted in a big centre console. I didn't know what most of the stuff was for. I supposed it had something to do with time trials and keeping to an average speed, because that's what rallying was all about in those days, I think, and one of the dials looked like a giant stopwatch sort of thing. It was all pretty inscrutable, but I thought it looked really cool and retro and authentically Fifties in a mad, boffinish sort of way.

So I bought the car and drove around in it and I thought I really looked the business, though I'm not one of those nutters who dresses up in Fifties clothes – I think that's just pathetic. I wasn't trying to relive somebody else's youth.

A bit of Fifties music might have been all right, but in fact I couldn't play any music at all in my car. When the mechanics put in all the extra instrumentation they'd taken out the radio. But I didn't really care about that. Because, I mean, if I'd wanted really authentic English pop music from the Fifties I'd have been forced to play Alma Cogan or Frankie Vaughan or Tommy Steele, and who the hell can live with that?

Same with food. If you wanted authentic English Fifties food and drink what would you have had? Marmite sandwiches and Horlicks? Semolina pudding and Vimto? *Please!* Authenticity has to have its limits. The Fifties was a pre-fast-food era as far as England was concerned, and the truth is, okay I admit it, I'm a fast-food junkie. Yes, yes, I realise there are many powerful and ironic contradictions here, but what are you going to do?

So as soon as I got the car I drove to my nearest corporate, multinational burger bar, anticipating a totally modern, artery-clogging burger and fries. I walked in and the urge to kill came over me, the same as usual. There are all sorts of things that bring it on. The colours of the décor, the overhead light that's bright enough to conduct an autopsy by, the sad, hideous proles stuffing their own and their children's faces with calories and cholesterol. But on this occasion my homicidal impulse was stoked by the space cadet behind the counter. His badge said he was called Gordon, and I knew right away that he deserved to die.

Okay, so life had dealt him a disappointing hand. He probably dreamed of being a metal sculptor or a designer of cool websites, rather than a burger drone, but there he was dealing with sarcastic and hostile members of the public, people like me, and I thought he really ought to learn to like it because he almost certainly wasn't going anywhere better.

'What would you like today, sir?' he said.

'Oh, let's see,' I said, sounding sarcastic and hostile, 'maybe I'd like a little Chilean sea bass, or kidneys flambé, or perhaps quail rubbed with fines herbes, or perhaps . . . now that I think about it, oh, let me see, how about a burger and fries.'

He didn't say anything, but I could tell what he was thinking, and I had the intense desire to order a number of those killingly hot, microwaved, so-called 'apple' so-called 'pies' and to shove one of them into each of his orifices. But I didn't. I took my burger and fries and went back to the car with them. At least that way I could eat while sitting in elegant and stylish surroundings.

I finished the burger and it was really unsatisfying and I was wishing I'd got another one, but I couldn't face going back and dealing with that twerp again. So I just sat there and drummed my fingers on the dashboard and I idly messed about with the instruments on the console, including the one that looked like a stopwatch, and suddenly something happened. I couldn't have told you exactly what. It was partly like blacking out but there was also something weirdly pleasant about it, as if I'd fallen asleep just for a second but that had been long enough to have a dream that I knew was really great even though I couldn't remember any of it. Then, almost immediately, the feeling had gone and I was my old self again, but then I saw that I still had a burger in my hand.

Obviously I wondered if I was going mad, but I ate the second burger, and somehow I knew that it wasn't *actually* a second burger, it was just the first one that I was eating again, or in fact for the first time. So it wasn't any more satisfying than it had been before, and that seemed significant.

Something very odd was obviously going on, but I didn't immediately think, 'Ah yes, I've travelled back in time,' because you wouldn't, would you? But I did suspect I'd come upon something to do with clocks and duration and reliving history.

So I drove home and started to experiment. The first thing I did was root around in the car's glove compartment and I found a pen and wrote the word 'Burger' on my hand, and then I turned back the stopwatch thing again. Along came that weird feeling and before I knew it my hand was clear and the pen was back in the glove compartment where it had always been. Interesting.

I did a few other things that involved melting ice cubes and burned matches and slashing the back of my hand with a razor blade; dealing with irreversible processes that magically reversed themselves when I put the clock back.

After I'd messed around for most of the evening I concluded that, baffling and improbable as it surely seemed, the old Zephyr was a kind of time machine; a very basic model, obviously. It could take you into the past, but not very far. After a great deal of trial and error I discovered that the most you could go back was fifteen minutes. And you couldn't just turn the stopwatch thing back time and time again, and keep receding. No, you could only do it once and then you had to wait for it to come back to zero before you could do it again.

The other major thing I discovered was that this form of time travel wasn't, so to speak, retroactive. I mean that if you turned the clock back by fifteen minutes and then, say, cut the head off a beloved domestic pet, then the head stayed cut off even when the clock went back to zero. But if you did it the other way round, cut the head off and then turned the clock back, the head miraculously reattached itself to the body. The system obviously had its limitations, but I didn't think I had any grounds for complaint, and I could see that it definitely had possibilities.

So the next day I went back to the same burger bar and I said to the snot boy behind the counter, 'Still no Chilean sea bass then?' And he said, 'Excuse me, sir?' so I smacked him in the mouth. I didn't do the hot apple pie thing because it would have taken far too long. Then I left the restaurant. A couple of people shouted after me, but nobody tried to stop me. So I went back to the car and waited. After a couple of minutes, as expected, the boy and his manager came out looking for me. They spotted me in the car and as they were approaching I reached for the console and turned back the stopwatch thing and that weird feeling came back, and then it was fifteen minutes earlier. (I looked at my own watch to make sure.) I was still sitting in the car. I hadn't gone into the restaurant, I hadn't hit the boy, and none of it had ever happened. So no harm done, right?

Obviously my first thought was that this discovery of mine could be a profound force for good. But then I thought about it a bit more and realised it probably wasn't going to be as profound as all that. I mean, there are real limits to how much you can improve the world in just fifteen minutes. And I realised, as everyone always does, that you have to change yourself before you can change the world. So I decided to change.

I decided that instead of being my sane, decent, healthy, happy self, I would become the sort of person who goes about committing hideous crimes involving violence and death, but only for fifteen minutes or so at a time, and then I would turn the clock back and all would be fine again: neither I nor my victims would live to regret it. Okay, it didn't make me a saint, but for entirely obvious reasons it didn't make me a criminal either. And as with all these impulses, I thought better out than in. And definitely better exorcised in a kink in the fabric of the space/time continuum rather than in the real world.

After that, I got myself a powerful semi-automatic weapon and pretty much went on a killing spree, or to be more precise, a long series of short killing sprees, each one restricted to no more than fifteen minutes.

Basically I'd go into some burger bar or pizza slum or Palookaville Fried Chicken joint, and for about a quarter of an hour I'd let rip. Basically I'd shoot the place, its staff and its customers to absolute buggery. You know the routine: blood, guts, facial wounds, mewling babies, people losing control of their sphincters; old and young, male and female, people of every race and creed united in the messy indignity of death. But only for fifteen minutes at the most.

It was a lot of fun, but you had to know what you were doing. Timing was everything. If the slaughtering took more than fifteen minutes then obviously I couldn't turn the clock back far enough to ensure that it had never happened. See what I mean? Let's say, just theoretically, I got myself into a hostage situation where I killed one person per minute for seventeen minutes and then turned the clock back; well obviously the first two victims would still be dead because they were killed outside the fifteen-minute time span that I'd recouped. And that would have been just terrible.

And in reality I never had the full fifteen minutes because within that

time I had to do the slaughtering, get from the scene of the crime back
to where the car was parked, then mess with the stopwatch thing. So I
had ten or twelve minutes of slaughtering at the max.

Inevitably I did meet the odd idiot who wanted to play the hero,
confront me and slow me down, and that was irritating at first and
potentially disastrous, but somehow I always managed to deal with it,
and eventually it became part of the process. Regardless of how well
things were going, a moment would always arrive when I had to just
walk away from the scene of mayhem and get back to the car, and if
the restaurant was full and I hadn't managed to kill them all, then
sometimes one or two of them would take it into their heads to pursue
me, and that could be the best bit of all.

By the time I got to the Zephyr the pursuers would sometimes be
only ten or fifteen yards behind, but that was enough. I'd slide behind
the wheel, and sometimes I'd wait until they were just a matter of feet
away, and then I'd turn back the stopwatch thing, and all was right with
the world again. It was subtle stuff.

Over the months I tried to ring the changes with my murder scenes.
I operated successfully in furniture stores, in opticians, in cybercafés,
railway stations, and they all had their attractions. But when the local
mall opened a spanking new food court, I knew it was what I'd been
waiting for.

If fast-food restaurants make you want to kill, then food courts make
you want to commit genocide. It's all there, everything you could
possibly want and despise. Oh the variety of loathsome food! Not just
burgers and fries, but fake American-style 'do-nuts', fake Chinese, fake
Mexican, fake cappuccino bars and French bakeries. Every possible
irritation: children's parties, plastic cutlery, unwiped tables, people
hangin' and chillin'. Is that Phil Collins being played through the tinny
speakers?

So I got my powerful semi-automatic weapon and I went in there
and I was like a kid in a sweetshop; firing at random, glass shards
cascading into the chop suey, wounded cashiers bleeding onto the
baguettes, men in nylon track-suits getting their genitalia blown off. I
could have carried on all night. But I didn't.

I stayed in control. I knew the exact moment when I had to tear
myself away and get back to the car, and I duly did. I walked out of the
food court so casually that the two security guards standing outside the
automatic doors didn't even seem to recognise me as the crazed
gunman, which was actually a disappointment. So as I walked by them
I said, 'Hey, I'm the one you want.'

Even then they seemed a bit reluctant. It probably had something to do with the gun I was brandishing. So when I got to the car I called to them and threw the gun aside so they could see I was unarmed. Then they realised that since they were supposed to be security guards they really ought to do something, so very gingerly they started to approach the Zephyr.

I leaned against the front wing. I was feeling good, and maybe I was feeling a bit cocky, but I knew that time was on my side. When the guards were about twenty feet away I opened the car door and got in, and my hand was halfway towards the stopwatch thing before I realised something was terribly out of joint. There was no stopwatch thing, no centre console, nothing.

It appeared that some bastard had broken into the car (well, not broken in *per se*, because I always left the door unlocked so I could get in quickly), and presumably he intended to steal it, but then he must have taken one look at the olde-worlde technology and realised he'd never be able to drive the thing. So as a parting shot he'd decided to do some major vandalism and he'd ripped out the centre console and taken it away with him as a souvenir. Pathetic, eh? Who can understand the banality of the criminal mind?

So I was left with a more or less conventionally equipped 1959 Low Line Zephyr Mark 2, without any rallying instrumentation. I was stuck right where I was in the present, and there was nothing I could do about it. I didn't panic. I didn't try to drive away. I just sat back and waited for what was coming to me. I started to feel a familiar and overwhelming need for a burger.

Geoff Nicholson was born in Sheffield and now spends his time commuting between homes in London and New York. The author of thirteen novels, including *Street Sleeper*, *Hunters and Gatherers*, *Everything and More*, *Footsucker*, *Bleeding London* (shortlisted for the 1997 Whitbread Fiction Award), *Flesh Guitar* and *Bedlam Burning*, he previously appeared in *Dark Terrors 4*. 'When I was a kid,' recalls Nicholson, 'my Uncle Oliver actually did, briefly, drive a big 1950s Zephyr. It was yellow and black, and (at least in my imagination) it had leopardskin seats. When he owned it, of course, it wasn't history at all, it was the very latest thing. Later he swore by Toyotas.'

Aversion Therapy

SAMANTHA LEE

He was the pain and the pain was him.

The pain of eyes gouged out with blunt knives, of baby heads smashed against walls, of women nailed to trees through amputated breasts.

His mother on her knees forced to pleasure a grinning monster while another took her from behind. Choking, weeping. Not human in their eyes. And so – not human.

They had tied him to a chair so he could watch her humiliation, screaming for them to stop, powerless to end her shame. He strained at the bonds that cut through the skin of his wrists, his heart pounding with the horror of it, his mind blurring, trying to blot it out.

Enough. Let her go. He would tell them anything.

His mother cast aside like a piece of garbage, blood pooling beneath her violated body, left with nothing but fear and nausea and memories that would forever haunt her until she blotted them out with a rusty knife drawn across her wrists, an empty bottle of meths beside her, unwashed, uncared for, in a rat-infested alley in the bombed-out remains of the city.

He awoke with a jolt, bathed in sweat, a band of light falling across his bloodshot eyes.

Outside, the sun shone down on a tranquil landscape. Through the bars of the narrow window which gave onto the exercise yard of the interrogation building he could see mountain peaks bordering a fertile valley down the centre of which a wide river wound lazily through green fields. A view peaceful as the first day of a wakening world. Like Eden had been. Before the creator's favourite child, Lucifer, son of the morning, fell from grace and, charismatic in his beauty and guile, introduced mankind to its dark side.

And let pain out of its box.

The siesta was over.

But the pain remained.

He rose from his truckle bed and observed himself in the cracked mirror, slicking back his dark hair, the agony throbbing in his temples now, travelling in bursts down the back of his neck into his spine, alerting all the exposed nerve-ends clustered there.

Just over the rise, on the other side of the gun-blasted stand of pines, in the lee of the great oak that had stood sentinel since Napoleon had swept through the valley, in a quiet white house smelling of newly baked bread and furniture polish, he imagined his mother cooking dinner, singing quietly to herself so as not to wake Anna.

As she'd sung when he had been a child.

And he, waking, would make no sound, drinking in the pure, clear tones, taking comfort from the sweetness of her voice, trying to forget the throb of the belt bruises from the latest beating that she had tried to prevent and, in failing, had taken the blows on herself.

To protect him.

Rising when the song was done, he would creep into the garden to pull the wings off flies, transferring the pain to something more vulnerable.

As he'd grown older and the beatings had become more savage, his fury and impotence had escalated, bringing with it the dissection of mice and stoats, peaking in the hounding of children smaller than himself, robbed of their innocence in secret ceremonies of his own devising, sworn to silence by the fear of more excruciating initiations to come.

Pain, a hard taskmaster.

It gripped him like a vice, leaving him no peace.

He thought of Anna, who called him the gentlest of lovers – the child big within her – stroking his hair, telling him he was the most wonderful man in the world.

Sometimes, afterwards, he would rest his head against the mound of her stomach, feel the baby quicken, and the pain would ease. For a moment. But no more than a moment.

Wounds – gaping, serrated. Stomachs torn apart, bayonet-ripped, guts spilling, slithering down to the knees, the hands grasping to stop them falling out, eyes popping, mouths agape in disbelief. Shattered kneecaps. Splintered bone protruding through charred and broken skin. Grown men calling for their mothers. To kiss it and make it better. Mothers lying in alleyways, drunken, broken.

Secrets. Memories.

Soon now they would come for him. He would need to be ready. He must be strong. Show no fear in the face of the pain.

If only this current pain would go away. It beat against the inside of his skull like the tongue of a great bell, clanging in his pulse, reverberating in his veins. Bringing tidings of the enemy at the gates. Warning of rape and pillage and looting. Of genocide and murder. Of excruciating, unthinkable, unstoppable horrors to come.

Normality so close. His mother sweeping the flagstone floor. Anna bathing her bloated body, the skin so soft, so vulnerable in the pale light of the drawn curtains.

Nothing to save the child but that wall of flesh. And flesh so fragile, so rendable.

His blood chilled at the thought, goose pimples rising against the terror of possibilities – of being unable to stave off the human degradation and the ongoing, inescapable pain.

Irony.

His mother so proud of him. A Captain in the Army – like his father before him – keeping the forces of chaos at bay.

He would survive it. *Must* survive it. For them.

And he could. Until the night, when reality retreated, and his defences were down. Then the pain really came into its own. Getting its *own* back.

At night there was no escape.

At night the pain would creep out of the darkness, chuckling obscenely, running and re-running looped memories of scenes he would rather forget. In glorious Technicolor and stereophonic sound. Then he would wake weeping, unable to shut out the bitter smell of vomit and excrement. Or hold the demons at bay.

Except with something worse.

Pain's sweet revenge.

Somewhere in the dungeons, someone began to scream: a high-pitched animal wail of terror and disbelief. Pain did that to you. Took you by surprise. Left you without defence. Unless you got there first.

A great shudder ran through his body. He turned from the windows, pressing the nails into the soft flesh of his palms to calm himself.

Time to prepare.

Slowly he slid on the uniform jacket that he had hung on the back of the chair before he had laid down to rest, buttoning it up to the neck, checking in the mirror for stray hairs on the khaki shoulders, peering for cracks in the façade of his handsome, ruined face.

There were none.

The eyes were dead, of course.

But otherwise he looked almost human.

He took a bottle from his desk drawer and swallowed a bitter mouthful of neat gin, the raw alcohol rushing to his stomach, lightening his head. Then he settled himself behind the desk and placed the military cap on his head, the shiny black brim shading the empty eyes. The soul driven from behind them. By the things he'd seen. By the things he'd done.

His mother – or somebody else's? He couldn't remember. Like the babies. Like the crucified women. Like the gouged eyes and the torn-out tongues and the screaming and the blood.

Why did he do it?

He knew why.

Not for a cause. Not because he liked it. But because he needed it to survive. To keep his own pain at bay.

Only the pain could relieve the pain.

Briefly, he checked at the tools of his trade, arranged neatly on the iron rack. The electric probes, the bastinado, the flaying knife, the pliers for ripping out nails, tearing teeth from gum. He touched each piece of equipment lovingly and a strange calm settled over him, a relief that soon it would be over, for now, at least. The pain transferred, to other nerve-endings, other flesh.

Outside in the corridor he could hear the mutterings of the guards, see through the frosted glass of the door the huddled shapes of today's suspects, their trousers already wet with the anticipation of what they could not avoid.

Their fate.

And his.

Placing his perfectly manicured hands palms down on the desktop, he took three deep breaths to calm the last vestiges of terror in his heart.

He was the pain and the pain was him.

But he was safe.

For today, at least.

'Bring in the first prisoner,' he barked.

Samantha Lee's output is as diverse as it is prolific, covering as it does fact, fiction, horror, fantasy, articles, novels, self-development and exercise books, short stories, literary criticism, TV and movie screenplays and poetry. Her numerous short stories have been featured on radio and television as well as in magazines and award-winning anthologies such as *Fantasy Tales* and *Shadows*. Of her fourteen books to date, the last three, *Amy*, *The Bogle* and *The Belltower* are part of Scholastic's best-selling Young Adult imprint Point Horror Unleashed. She is currently working on a sword & sorcery screenplay and collaborating on a graphic novel with comics illustrator and movie art director Paul Bateman. 'The idea for this story came during a film workshop given by Rutger Hauer at the Edinburgh Festival. He was explaining that the way to play a drunk is not to fall about but, *au contraire*, to try to walk straight. That's what drunks do. They're attempting to look sober. And the most effective way to play a villain is as someone quite rational. Because nobody thinks he's a bad guy. This gave me pause. And a whole new take on his masterly portrayal of the killer android in *Blade Runner*. He thinks he's the hero. As does Hannibal Lecter, a civilised, educated intellectual with the teensiest flaw in his character which he justifies by only "eating the rude". The most frightening thing about evil is that it can *always* justify itself and that, in the case of the majority of serial killers at least, it cloaks itself in the most mundane kind of normality. There but for the grace of God goes your next-door neighbour.'

The Cure

TONY RICHARDS

I thought it was her, the woman who opened the door. She was old enough, and looked right, in her flowing, floral-print clothes, with her white hair in a bun and her small, golden-rimmed spectacles. And the way she looked me up and down . . .

Her pale blue eyes seemed to take in everything at once: the crow's-feet creases of pain around my eyes and mouth. And the way that the radiation and the chemotherapy had robbed me – at thirty-two – of nearly all my hair. The fact that I no longer properly filled out my own clothes.

Her gaze lingered on my own eyes for longer than was polite. Perhaps taking in the awful fear that I saw every morning in the mirror.

I had just six weeks. If that.

Neither of us was saying anything, right at the moment. So I broke the impasse with a hasty, 'Madame Celeste?'

She gave a small, tight smile. Shook her head. And answered, 'I am her translator and assistant. Please come through. The fee is fifty pounds.'

Just an ordinary little maisonette in a quiet suburb. Just a handbill I'd had thrust between my barely willing fingers on the street. *Madame Celeste, faith-healer. Thousands of satisfied clients. Will cure all ills.*

Silly. No, amend that – quite ridiculous. But when you're thirty-two and you have just six weeks left . . . if that . . . you'll try anything.

She was younger than I was, which took me aback. In her mid-twenties, and slender, and quite pretty. Sitting on a breakfast stool in a perfectly ordinary fitted kitchen-diner, dressed in jeans and a white T-shirt and swinging her bare feet. Of what nationality? It was impossible to tell. Dark, certainly. But she could have been Latin-American, or from the Indian subcontinent, Turkish, Kurdish, or even a gypsy. Strange, how we try to pigeonhole people the moment we see them. And even stranger, these days, just how difficult that is. Human beings do not fit into neat categories quite as simply as they used to.

She glanced up at me – her irises were deep black. Flashed me a very white . . . and reassuring? . . . smile. Then turned her attention to her assistant. They ducked heads together and conversed in whispers. It was obviously a foreign tongue, but one that I could not make out. I felt nervous and awkward, so I looked around the room.

There was not so much as a small crucifix. What had I been expecting?

More than this. More than laminated surfaces and tiles and a waffle-maker.

A faith-healer? Of what faith?

'Do you have the money?' the assistant asked, bringing my head back round.

They were both looking at me now.

I handed it over.

'Please step forward, within reach. She has to touch you.'

Didn't they want me to tell them what was wrong? The cancer that had started in my liver and then spread like . . .

Like . . . ?

Like nothing else in the world spreads. No similes. No metaphors. The worst word in the English language has to be 'malignant'.

I took an awkward three steps, still feeling perfectly ridiculous. Sweat was running down my upper lip. I almost flinched when Madame Celeste reached out, suddenly remembering stories about healers in South America who plunged their hands into their patients and pulled tumours out. All that she did, though, was brush her palm across my stomach. Then her arm withdrew, she looked away.

The smile on her assistant's face grew slightly broader. And she informed me, 'You're done.'

Before the diagnosis I'd have thrown a fit. Except, before the diagnosis, I'd have thrown away the handbill, thought of anyone who kept it and visited 'Madame Celeste' as a feeble-minded dunce.

I'd not only try anything by now, though. I'd accept anything, as well. I didn't let out so much as a grunt at being cheated, since what difference did it make. They could keep the fifty. I just turned around and went home.

There was no pain at all over the next few days. By the end of the week, I realised that I had gained a little weight again, and some of my hair was coming back. And the fear in the eyes was not as terrible as it had been before. As though my eyes knew something that the rest of me did not.

X-rays and an MRI confirmed it.

'It's complete remission!' the consultant beamed, as though he'd had something to do with it. 'You must be extremely pleased.'

Did he specialise in understatement?

I went to my favourite bar and drank a lot, then realised I had someone to thank.

It was still a perfectly ordinary maisonette. Still a perfectly ordinary kitchen-diner. She was with another client, though she didn't seem to mind me standing there and watching.

I was sure I recognised him, from the hospital. A very old man in a wheelchair, with his equally old wife. Even being seated seemed a hardship to him. He was almost doubled over, his face twisted up with pain and effort. His breathing was wheezy and uneven. And how long did *this* one have? Not even my original six weeks, I imagined.

His wife's face was completely blank, as though she had already lost him.

The five notes were handed over. Madame Celeste did the exact same thing, except her palm went slightly higher up this time.

The wife obviously wanted to say something, protest, when she realised it was over. Then she noticed me, standing there by the door. And there must have been something in my expression. She simply turned the chair around, with some difficulty, and went on her way.

Madame Celeste and her assistant smiled at me, and then conferred, the same way they had last time.

'Is there something else wrong?' I was asked.

'I just . . . I had to . . .'

'Yes – we know.'

'If there's any way that I can . . .'

'It was a service that you paid for. Madame Celeste does not expect any gifts, gratuities, or thanks.'

'How can I *not* thank her?' I came back, rather astonished.

But all the assistant did was glance at her wristwatch.

'If you'll excuse us, we have another client due in a few minutes. We're extremely busy here, you know.'

I began to notice it over the next couple of weeks. I was busy as all hell myself, having returned to my office job. But the adverts and the handbills and the cards pushed through my letter box began to impinge on my consciousness, at last. Dozens of them, in the classified section of the local paper. Dozens more, letting you know of their presence by means of cards in newsagents' windows, even in phone boxes next to BUSTY BLONDE 18 YEAR OLD SEEKS FUN. Madame Celeste was far from alone.

Dozens?

There were *thousands* like her, just in my neck of the woods. God knew how many thousand right across the country. And I began thinking to myself, there's a whole new religion going on here.

Either that, or a very old one.

Life never quite returns to normal after something like I'd been through. You can do the same things as you used to, go to the same places, entertain yourself in the same ways. But there's always a brittle feeling to everything, a jaggedness that was never there before. You feel very slightly manic, deep down, and that is not pleasant. But considering the alternative . . .

It was now five and a half weeks since I'd visited Madame Celeste. In a few more days, I realised – and I smiled – I'd have been no more of this world. My sentence had been commuted. The phone had rung, and it had been the Governor on the other end. That felt good. My inner mania faded slightly.

I was due one final check-up at out-patients. I was walking from the bus stop to the hospital, a sunny day. I reached the gates.

There was the old man I'd seen in the kitchen-diner.

He was no longer in his wheelchair. He was standing perfectly upright, and seemed to have gained several pounds. His face was not so withered. It was still screwed up with pain, though.

He was crying uncontrollably, his shoulder against the gate post.

I went up to him, astonished. Asked, 'Are you all right?'

His tear-filled eyes came a slit open, and he peered at me, not seeming to recognise me at all. His mouth moved. A sound came out, but he was so choked up with crying it was just that.

So he tried again. One word. Was it 'horrible'?

His eyelids screwed up tightly, and remained like that this time.

'Do you need any help? Where's your wife?'

But all he did was shake his head, and then start crying even harder, quite forgetting I was there.

He was senile, I decided. Madame Celeste had been able to get him out of his chair, but curing his mind was beyond her.

I went on my way.

*

Six weeks exactly. I woke up. Another sunny day. Chinks of golden light pouring through my curtains.

Some of them were touching me. My left hand and shoulder. My bare chest.

I'd come wide awake but, oddly, I couldn't seem to feel them. Couldn't detect any warmth. The rays of sunlight looked . . . peculiar. They'd never appeared oppressive before. Never made me want to shy away.

I didn't seem to be breathing properly. Felt quite choked. As though the air was full of heavy dust.

Oh God, what was wrong now? I pulled on a robe, went down and made some breakfast.

The milk smelled sour, so I threw it out. But the coffee smelled sour too. And tasted of nothing.

The toast and butter seemed to have the consistency of sponge and axle-grease.

Was I coming down with the flu?

I switched on the radio. The music jarred my ears. I turned it off.

My breathing was still laboured.

Everything I tried to eat tasted of nothing. The same with drink. I couldn't listen to music at all. Sunlight left me, in every sense, cold. I watched my favourite sitcom that evening, and didn't laugh.

I woke up the next morning and my breathing was *still* laboured.

Flowers I passed by had no smell. Even young women on the tube into work aroused no interest in me.

The flu? Or even ME? Or a side-effect of the chemo? I went to my GP. Who could find nothing.

Then it started dawning on me. Had the cancer come back?

My consultant saw me again quickly enough, as concerned as I was. But I was still clear.

'You came very close to dying,' he told me. 'Sometimes there can be quite a strong psychological backlash.'

He suggested I give Prozac a try.

I tried it for a while. It did absolutely nothing. Then I threw the tablets away and tried getting very drunk instead.

It was all the badness of inebria, with none of the good. My head swam and I felt sick and I finally was, very messily, but with none of the loose happiness that usually precedes that, none of the unfettered joy or false invulnerability.

I'd never tried drugs. No, correct that, I had. Prozac. Why should anything bought on a street corner work any better?

What was the solution here? There had to be a cure for this.

I had trouble getting to sleep, and I loathed waking up because it was always the same.

My breathing? It was as though I were trying to breathe under-ground. As though I had been buried and . . .

And it had started six weeks after seeing Madame Celeste. Possibly on the exact day I had been supposed to—

Stop that! Stop that utter nonsense! You're a rational human being, and if you're actually going to start entertaining notions of some price to be paid, some Faustian hocus-pocus . . .!

But then I remembered what the old man had said, leaning against the gate post, half-drowning in his own tears. What he *might* have said.

'Horrible.'

It had just been bad, to start with. Just like feeling . . . out of sorts. But as one day overtook the next . . .

It wasn't that it got worse. It just simply didn't change.

How long now? A fortnight?

I hadn't smiled. I hadn't tasted anything, felt anything, even taken a good deep clean breath. Everything seemed bled of colour. Even during the chemo, I'd had nothing quite like that. Maybe I was going mad.

Was there *anything* that I could find enjoyment in?

I realised there might be. But even that realisation didn't make me crack a smile.

I'd been badly ill, quite visibly so. And so it had been a while.

There was this girl at work, though, who'd seemed interested in me in the past. I took her to a bar that evening, made no secret of the fact that I was trying to get her drunk.

I was not good company, and was aware of that. But maybe she took the darkness of my mood as something dangerous and exciting.

Whatever, we were back at her place just as the sun set.

And it wasn't that I couldn't. All the reflexes were still in place. It was that . . . it made me feel nothing.

Nothing except envy. Her head was thrown back, her eyelids half-closed in that fluttery way, her lips wet and parted. She was making little groans.

I was still trying to draw a proper breath, as I had been doing for two weeks now.

I simply stopped, halfway through it. Rolled off the bed and started pulling my clothes back on.

She was awfully drunk. She swore at me. Said something about it being a little late to find out I was gay.

Something hit the door, thrown hard, as I went through it.

How did that make me feel? Guess.

I had to make my way on foot, without a map, and so it took more than two hours before I found the maisonette again. Most of the windows around me were dark, up and down the ordinary street. Including hers.

I banged on the door until the older woman answered.

She was in a nightrobe, her hair askew, and looked alarmed to see me.

'What did she do to me?' I yelled.

'Would you please keep your voice down. Do you know what time it is?'

'What did that bitch *do* to me?'

'Exactly what you wanted.'

'What I—?'

'You had six weeks left. You wanted to go beyond that. So you have.'

'So I . . .'

'Not as you were before, though. Still alive or not, your time is up.'

And, for the first time since that awful morning, my mouth formed a smile. But it was suspicion and wryness only, no humour at all.

'What are you telling me? That she is Mephistopheles, and she saved my life, and now she's got my soul or something?'

The woman's head gave a tiny shake. 'No, precisely the opposite. Quite a while ago, your kind made a deal with my employer. An agreement, if you will. A covenant. You would live in this place for a period of time, worship her, and try to avoid evil. After that, you'd be looked after for the whole rest of eternity. But it's not simply that you do not believe in that these days. It's . . . you don't even *want* it. You just want to stay here. Whatever it takes. Whosoever offers it.

'Do you realise how hurtful she finds that? So many of you going back on your word, trying to cheat her with cheap tricks? Hundreds like you come here every week. And, like you, they're still around. If that's what you want, well, that's what she'll now give you.'

At that point, a younger female voice started calling out from the back, in that same peculiar language I had overheard before. The assistant turned her head and answered similarly.

I was still trying to understand what she'd just told me. Was she seriously suggesting that I'd . . .?

Broken some kind of contract? With . . .?

My confusion started turning into renewed anger.

'What *language* is that you're speaking?' I burst out, louder than ever.

She stopped then, and looked back at me pointedly.

'The language of the Covenant,' she told me. 'Aramaic.'

And she slammed the door shut in my slack, cold face.

Tony Richards is a full-time writer who lives in London with his wife. He is the author of two novels – *The Harvest Bride* (nominated for a Horror Writers Association Bram Stoker award) and *Night Feast*. His short fiction has appeared in *The Magazine of Fantasy & Science Fiction*, *Weird Tales*, *Asimov's Science Fiction*, *Alfred Hitchcock's Mystery Magazine*, *The Third Alternative* and various anthologies. Widely travelled, he often uses the places he has been as settings for his work. About the preceding story, the author reveals: 'I suppose I really wrote "The Cure" as a reaction to the death/possibly-fatal-diagnosis of a couple of people close to me last year. The story is thus therapeutic.'

Plot Twist

DAVID J. SCHOW

On the morning of the fifth day, Donny announced that he'd figured it all out. It wasn't the first time.

'Okay,' he said. 'Millions of years ago, these aliens come to Earth and find all this slowly evolving microspodia. Maybe they're, like, college students working on their thesis project. And they seed the planet with germs that eventually evolve into human society – our culture is literally a *culture*, right? Except that we're not what was intended. It was an impure formula or something. And they come back after millennia, which is like summer vacation to them, and they see their science experiment has spoiled in the dish. We're the *worst* thing that could have happened. We've blown their control baseline, their work is down the toilet and they have to declare us a cull, flush the first experiment and start over. But they take a look at us and decide, hey, maybe there's something here worth saving. Something they can use to, you know, rescue their asses from flunking. So they take this teeny sample, like one cell, and decide to test it to see if it does anything interesting. And that's why we're here.'

Vira said, 'That's above and beyond your previous bullshit, and I think I've hit my patience ceiling.'

Zach didn't say anything because he was staring forlornly at their remaining food supply – one energy bar, destined for a three-way split, one tin of Vienna sausage (eight count), and a pint of bottled water that had already been hit hard.

'I'm waiting for *your* brilliant explanation,' Donny said sourly. His real name was Demetrius, but he hated it. Vira's real name was Ellen, but she'd legally changed it. Zach was born 'Kevyn'; same general deal.

'I'm out,' said Vira, tired of the game. 'Tapped. Done. I give up.' She looked up at the reddening sunrise sky and shouted, 'Hey! Hear me? I quit. Fuck you. If there's aliens up there toying with us, then they can kiss my anal squint!'

Donny started, as though he actually thought outer space men might materialise to punish them. At least that would have brought some sort of closure.

'Don't yell,' said Zach, nailing her, still playing leader. 'That'll dry you up. Who got to the water while I was sleeping?'

Donny and Vira both denied it; the usual stalemate. Zach expected this and let it slide because he already knew he'd stolen that bonus sip himself.

'Sun's coming up,' said Donny unnecessarily. 'The only constant seems to be this man-against-nature thing.'

'You said that yesterday, too, sexist asshole,' said Vira.

'Look around you,' said Zach, pointing to each extreme of the compass. 'Desert. Road. Desert. More road. More desert. And so on. Do you see, for example, a crashed plane that we could rebuild into a cleverly composited escape vehicle? No. A glint on the horizon that would indicate a breath of civilisation? No way. A social dynamic amongst us, two men and one woman, that will lead to some sort of revelation that can save us? Uh-uh, negative.' He pointed again. 'Road. Desert. Let's get moving.'

'Why?' said Vira, watching her little patch of shade dwindle.

'Because when we moved the first time and didn't stay put, we found the food, didn't we?'

'That's the only reason?'

'We might find something else.'

She coloured with anger, or perhaps it was just the odd, vividly tilted light of dawn. 'So we can just keep going, keep doing this?'

'We last another day, we might figure something out.'

'Like the "why"?' Donny said. 'As in why-us?'

'No, all I meant was we might get back to normal, and we certainly won't do that sitting on our butts and staying in one place waiting for the supplies to run out.'

Vira snorted at the all-encompassing grandeur of the word 'supplies', pertaining to their edibles, which did not even total a snack.

'I want an answer,' said Donny. 'I want to know why.'

'That's your biggest problem, Don-O.' Zach extended his open hand to Vira, who rose tropistically, like a plant turning automatically to meet the light. 'Come on, sweetie, let's go.'

They turned their backs on the sun and began their march, in the same direction they'd been tracking since, well, for ever.

*

Most of the fourth day had been wasted on equally stupid theories.

'I've got it,' Donny said, which caused Vira to roll her eyes. It was becoming her comedic double-take reaction to anything Donny proposed. Donny was an endlessly hopeful idiot.

'Okay, like, we're characters in this movie, or a novel or something. And we can't figure out where we are or how we got here, and shit keeps happening, and we keep on keeping on, but our memories and characters keep altering when we're not looking. It's because we're fictional characters, right, except we don't know we are. And the movie studio guys keep asking for changes, or the editors at the publishing house keep saying, "What's their arc?" or "How do they grow from their experience?" And we don't know because we were just *made up* by some writer, who has no idea we're cognisant and suffering.'

'I wish there was a big, shiny-new toilet, right here in the middle of the scrub,' said Vira.

'Why?' said Donny, tired of performing his body functions in the wild.

'Because I don't know what I'd do first,' said Vira. 'Drink some water from the tank, or jam your head into the bowl and flush.'

'Children, children,' said Zach. 'Come on. We hit a spot of luck yesterday, didn't we? The food.'

'Yeah,' Donny chimed in. 'Plot twist, see? Nobody'd ever expect that we'd just find food, when we needed it. In stories, everything has to be explained; everything has to pay off.'

'Your definition of *food* and mine differ radically,' said Vira. 'I want a quart of goddamn seltzer, and then a bacon cheeseburger and a goddamn fucking chocolate malt, with a goddamn fucking cherry, and fuck you and your latest fucking lame-ass, bullshit story.'

'Yeah, great, terrific,' said Donny. 'Thanks for your boundlessly vast contribution to the resolution of our predicament. You're not helping.'

'I'm the chaos factor,' said Vira. 'I'm here precisely to fuck up all your neat little explanations.'

'And I'm the third wheel,' said Donny. 'You guys will kill me first, because you've already got a, you know, relationship.'

'Yeah, that'll get us far,' said Zach, trying for drollery and failing. It was just too hot to screw around.

They kept their bearings on the sun and tried not to deviate from the straight line inscribed on the sand by their passage. Yesterday's footprints had blown away as soon as they were out of sight. The desert was harshly Saharan – dunes tessellated by wind, with vegetation so sporadic it appeared to be an afterthought, or really sub-par set dressing. They were amazed by the appearance of a paddle cactus, just one, and even more amazed when Zach demonstrated how it could provide drinkable moisture.

'Perfect example,' Donny said. 'How did you know that?'

'I don't know,' said Zach. 'I've always known it.'

'Read it in a manual? See it on a nature documentary? Or maybe you came wired with that specific information for a reason.'

'There is no reason,' said Zach, trying to work up spit and failing at that too. His throat was arid. His brain was frying. 'I just knew it.'

'It doesn't work,' Donny said, shaking his head, sniffing at denial. 'There's gotta be a reason.'

'Reason for *what*?' Vira apparently had plenty of spit left. 'We had an accident! You are so full of shit.'

'Maybe it wasn't an accident,' said Donny. He was trying for an ominous tone, but neither Zach nor Vira cared to appreciate his dramatic sense.

By the middle of the third day, they were all sunburnt, peeling and dehydrated. They resembled lost Foreign Legionnaires, dusted to a desert tan, with wildly white Lawrence of Arabia eyes, long sleeves and makeshift burnooses keeping the solar peril from most of their desperately thirsty flesh.

'If you mention God to me one more time, I'm going to knock a few of your teeth out and you can drink your own blood,' warned Zach.

'My only point is that this strongly resembles some sort of Biblical test,' said Donny, chastened. 'This kind of stuff happens all the time in the Bible, the Koran, Taoist philosophy, native superstitions – they're all moral parables. Guys are always undergoing extreme physical hardship, and at the end there's a revelation. That's what a vision quest is.'

'A vision quest is when you starve yourself until you see hallucinations,' said Vira. 'We've been there and done that. I don't feel particularly revelated.'

'We haven't gone far enough, is all.'

'Then explain why we haven't seen a smidge of traffic on this goddamn road since we started walking. We should have seen a thousand cars by now, all headed to and from Vegas. We should have passed a dozen convenience marts and gas stations with nice, air-conditioned restrooms. And all we've got since we lost sight of our own car, which was alone on the road, is hot, hot, more hot, and about a bazillion highway stripes, all cooking on this goddamn fucking roadway that leads to fucking nowhere!'

'Alternate dimension,' said Donny.

Zach actually stopped walking to crank around and peer at Donny with disgust. '*What?*'

'Alternate dimension, co-existing simultaneously with our own reality. We got knocked out of sync. And now we're trapped in a place that's sort of like where we were – the world we came from – except there's nothing around, and nobody, and we've got to find a rift or convergence and wait for the planes to re-synchronise, and plop, we're back to normal.'

'Do you want to strangle him or should I?' said Vira.

'I liked the God explanation better,' said Zach. He was joking, but no one appreciated it just now.

'Aren't we grown-ups?' said Vira. 'Aren't we rational adults? Can we please leave all that goddamn God shit and the fucking Bible and all that outmoded tripe and corrupt thinking behind in the twentieth century, where it belongs? Shit, it was useless and stupid a couple of whole centuries earlier than that – enslaving people, giving sheep a butcher to canonise. Giving morons false hope. Pie in the sky by and by when you die. It's such exhausted, wheezy, rote crap.'

'Aren't we operating on false hope?' said Donny.

'No, Donny,' said Zach. 'We're operating on the tightrope between slim, pathetic hope and none at all. Free your mind. You're too strictured and trapped by your need to organise everything so it has a nice, neat ending – a little snap in the tail to make idiots go *woooo*. You want to know reasons, and there ain't no reasons, and you want to know something real? I'll tell you this one for free: real freedom is the complete loss of hope.'

'That's deep,' said Donny, not getting it.

Vira shielded her eyes and tried to see into the future. 'Forget cars and stop-marts,' she said. 'We haven't seen any animals. Desert animals lie low in the daytime, but we haven't seen any. Not a single bird. Not a vulture, even.'

'It's not life, but it's a living,' joked Zach.

'The sun is cooking me,' said Vira. 'Pretty soon we'll all be deep-fried to a golden-black.' She shielded her eyes to indict the glowering sphere above, which was slow-cooking them like a laggard comet. The sky was cloudless.

'If it *is* the sun,' said Donny.

Zach and Vira could not complain any more. They merely stopped, turned in unison and sighed at Donny, who would not stop. Donny, naturally, took this as a cue to elaborate.

'I mean, this east-to-west trajectory could be just an assumption on our part. We could be walking north, for all we really know. What if it's not the sun? What if it's just some errant fireball, messing with us?'

'Then we just spent another day walking in the wrong direction,' said Zach.

'What if it's not a "day"?' said Donny. He dug his wristwatch out of his pocket. He'd stowed it yesterday when the heat had begun to brand his wrist with convection. Now he noticed, for the first time, that his watch had stopped.

'Five thirty-five,' he said. 'Weird.'

Zach and Vira turned slowly (conserving energy), did not speak (conserving moisture), and glowered at Donny with an expression Donny had come to class as The Look. When people gave you The Look, they were awaiting a punchline they were sure they would dislike.

'It's when the car shut down yesterday,' he said. 'I remember because I made a mental note of it.'

'That's *it*?' said Vira. 'No dumb theory about how we're all slip-slid into the spaces between ticks of the clock?'

'Donny, when was the last time you looked at your watch before yesterday? Isn't it possible that your crappy watch just doesn't work, and has been dead all this time, and you just thought it was 5.35 when you glanced at it yesterday?' Somehow, while Donny wasn't looking, Zach had become the leader of their little expedition.

'You guys aren't listening to me,' Donny said, feeling somewhat whipped. 'The watch shut down the same time the car did.'

Vira was strapping on attitude, full-bore: 'And that's got to *mean something*, right? Spare us.'

What Donny spared them was the hurt reaction that had almost made it past his lips: *I thought you guys were my friends.* He just stared, blankly, as though channelling alien radio.

'Hey.' Zach had found something. Topic closed.

A black nylon loop was sticking out of the sand off the right shoulder of the road. When Zach pulled, he freed a small backpack that looked identical to the one Vira was already toting. They both waited, almost fatalistically, for Donny to make a point of this.

He held both hands palm-out in a placating gesture. 'I'm not saying a word, if that makes you happy.'

Inside the backpack they found two malt-flavoured energy bars, two pint bottles of water, two tins of Vienna sausage, and two bags of salty chips, and everything was nearly too hot to touch.

'That's just plain scary,' said Vira, examining the rucksack. 'It *is* like mine.'

'Oh, shit,' said Donny. 'Maybe we've done this already.'

Vira caught herself short of showing Donny a little mercy. 'Here we go,' she said in a vast sigh, hotly expelling air she couldn't afford to lose.

'We're trapped inside of some kind of Möbius strip, endlessly repeating our previous actions. Has to be. Look at the backpack. It doesn't look like Vira's – it *is* Vira's. From the last time we were here. And we don't remember because whatever purpose is behind all this hasn't been achieved. Whatever happened, last time, we blew it. And if we blow it again, we'll find another backpack just like this one.'

'Do you want a third of this or do you want to continue the lecture?' Zach had drawn his Swiss Army knife to divide one of the energy bars, but the protein goo was already so warm it practically poured apart.

'No, look at it.' Donny was flushed with fear and anger now. 'Two of everything. Only two. Why only two? Who's the odd guy out, here? Me. What the fuck happens to me?'

'Shut up, Donny!' said Vira. 'Look at the damned thing – it doesn't have my wallet, my ID, my hairbrush, tampons, or any of the other stuff in *my* backpack. It's a fucking coincidence!'

'No. Something happens. Something changes. One of us gets gone.'

'Donny, you're gonna pop a blood vessel, man.' Zach cracked one of the tins and took a ginger sip of the water packing the mini-wieners.

'And I'm not hungry,' Donny continued. 'I see that stuff, food, and I should be starving, but I'm not. We walked all day yesterday and all today and we should be ready to hog a whole buffet . . . but all I feel is that *edge* of hunger, of thirst. Just enough to keep me crazy.'

'I wholeheartedly agree about the "crazy" part,' said Vira.

'Eat anyway,' said Zach 'Save your energy for your next explanation of what the hell has happened to us.'

'Yeah, we'll be laughing about this tomorrow,' said Vira, methodically swallowing capfuls from the sports bottle of water, knowing enough not to chug, not to waste, to take it extraordinarily slow and easy.

'Anybody care for an alternate point of view?' said Zach, relishing the salt in the chips even though they made him thirsty. 'The backpack is a marker. Someone else has made this trip. And they left this stuff behind because they got out, got rescued, or didn't need it any more.'

'Yeah, maybe because they died.' Donny was still sour, and not meeting their eyes. Privately he thought Zach's proposal was too upbeat to be real, and was full of holes besides. Maybe he was just playing optimist to cheer Vira up. In a book or a TV show or a movie, it just would not track because it begged too much backstory.

'If somebody just dropped this and died, we'd've seen a body,' said Vira. She was always on Zach's side.

'Not if the sand blew over it,' said Donny.

'Jesus fuck, there's just no winning with you,' she said. 'You just *have* to be right all the time.'

That caused more long minutes to elapse in silence as they picked through their paltry booty. Donny looked out, away ... anywhere but at his two increasingly annoying friends. Vira and Zach huddled, murmuring things he could not overhear, and neither of them acknowledged his presence until he jerked them back to the real world.

'Look at that,' he said.

'What?' Zach rose to squint downroad.

Donny pointed. 'I think I see something. That way.'

'Then it's time to burn a little energy, I guess. We get lucky, we can leave the backpack in the sand for the next sucker. Sweetie?'

Vira dusted her jeans and stood up. 'Yeah. Ten-hut, let's march.' She tried to think of a sarcasm about the Yellow Brick Road and Dorothy, or the Wild Bunch, minus one, but it was just too goddamned hot.

Donny led them, appearing to scent-track. Normally he liked to walk two paces behind Zach and Vira because he enjoyed watching Vira's ass move. Perhaps if he walked with his partners to the rear, they would just disappear at some point. Plucked away. It could happen. It happened in stories, in movies.

They walked towards it, but it turned out to be nothing.

They had wasted most of the second day waiting around the car under the arc of the sun. Waiting for rescue. Waiting for answers, for trespassers, for anything outside themselves. That was when Donny had begun ticking off his handy theories.

'Okay, we're all drunk,' he said, knowing they weren't. 'We're stoned. This is really a dream. See the car? We actually crashed it and we're all dead, and this is Hell or something. Purgatory. Limbo.'

'I love that concept,' said Zach. 'Hell-or-something.'

'Water jug's empty,' said Vira. They'd stashed a gallon container in the back seat prior to departing on their road trip. One day of busy hydration had killed it. Her careful make-up had smudged, melted, run down her face and evaporated.

Zach tied a T-shirt around his head to save his scalp from getting fried. 'We just sit tight and try not to perspire,' he joked. 'Someone'll come along. *We* came along.'

'Las Vegas used to be the greatest psychological temptation in the country,' said Donny. 'Going there to gamble was an act of will, requiring a pilgrim to penetrate a sterile cordon of desert. You can't go to Vegas accidentally; you have to make the decision and then travel across a wasteland to get there. It's not like you're at a mall and think, *oh, I'll do a little gambling while I'm here, too.* And once you do the forced march, you're there and there's only one thing to do, really – what you came for. That's more strategically subtle than most ordinary people can handle. Nobody thinks about that.'

'And your point,' said Vira, 'is . . . what?'

'Just that it's interesting, don't you think?'

'I think it's fucking *hot* and I wish I wasn't here.' She fanned herself and Donny won an unexpected flash of sweat-beaded nipple, perfect as a liquor ad.

'We can't drink the water out of the radiator,' said Zach, returning from beneath the hood and wiping oil from his hands.

'Why are you even thinking like that?' said Vira. 'We're not stranded. We're on a main highway, even if it is in the middle of buttfuck-nowhere. Some hillbilly in a pick-up truck will come along. What about all the other people driving to Vegas? We didn't just wander off the map, or get lost on some country switchback. We're not going to have to wait here long enough to think about drinking the water from the radiator, or eating the goddamn car.'

'Guy did that in New Hampshire,' said Donny. 'Cut a Chevy up into little cubes and ate it. Ingested it, passed it. Guy ate a car.'

'*Shut up*, Donny!' Vira had been making a point, and resented derailment at the mercy of Donny's internal almanac. Donny was chock-full of trivia like this. He thought he was urbane. He was passably interesting at parties and good for scut errands since he always volunteered. Now Vira guessed that Donny's canine openness and availability was just a cruel trick, a dodge intended to keep him around people who could at least pretend to be interested in all the useless shit that spilled from his mouth.

Ever the mediator, Zach tried to defuse her. 'What are you getting at, Vira?'

'You guys talk as if we just drove off the edge of the Earth or something. The car just stopped, period. We're not going to have to dig a goddamn well to find drinking water because the car just stopped, and it just-stopped a couple of hours ago, and other people will come along, and we'll be inconvenienced and probably have to rent another car, or stay overnight in some shithole like Barstow, but it's an inconvenience, and Donny is running his face-hole like we've been abducted to another planet.'

'I'm not saying anything,' said Donny. 'But have you seen any more cars, for, what, five-six hours we've been here?'

'Children, children,' said Zach. 'Stop fighting or I'll turn this car right around.' That made Vira laugh. If only. Then Zach ambled towards the sprawl of flat-paddle cactus they'd pressed into service as a restroom privacy shield.

'Maybe you should piss in the empty water jug,' said Donny. 'We might have to boil our own urine and drink it.'

'I'd rather die,' said Vira. 'Hey, there's an idea – we can kill you and eat you for the moisture in your body, if you don't shut up.'

When Zach had buttoned up and returned, he had resumed his air of command and decision. 'So I guess it's down to this: do we stay, or do we start walking?'

'Stay,' said Vira. 'At least we've got the car for shade. Who knows how cold it gets at night? This is the desert, after all, and we didn't bring a lot of blankets.'

'We march,' said Donny. 'Vegas could be just over the next rise and we've been sitting here all day like the victims of some cosmic joke.'

'Sun's going down,' said Zach. 'I'm inclined to spend the night walking. We've got two flashlights, matches, a melted candy bar and half a bottle of flat soda I found under the passenger seat. We take extra clothes to cover our skin in case we get stuck another day. And we stay on the road, in case somebody comes along – that'll do us as much good as sticking by the car, hoping someone spots it.'

'It also wears us out faster,' said Vira. 'I'm not built for this nature shit. *Nature* is what you go through to get from the limo to the hotel lobby.'

'Come on, Vira,' Donny said. 'Where's your sense of adventure?'

'The only adventure I want to have right now is in a jacuzzi, with room service.'

'Ahh,' said Donny. 'Cable porn and pizza and cold, cold beer.'

'3:00 am blackjack action and free cocktails,' said Zach. 'Hot showers and cool sheets. Jesus, I have to stop; I'm getting a hard-on.'

'Yeah, Donny, you start walking and Zach and I will stay here and try to conserve moisture.' Vira smiled wickedly. At least they were bantering now, grabbing back towards something normal. But she collected her backpack from the seat, as though resigned to a hike, hoping it would turn out to be brief but worthwhile.

They walked away the hours absorbed by dusk, until the sun was gone. The road stayed flat and straight except for regular hummocks that kept the distance maddeningly out of view, diffused in heat shimmer. At the crest of each rise waited another long stretch of road, and another rise in the distance.

'Human walking speed is four to six miles per hour at a brisk and steady pace,' said Donny. His voice tended to lapse into a statistical drone. 'Figure half that, the way we're clumping along.'

'Conserving moisture,' Vira reminded him.

'The arc of the sun says we've been doing this for about four hours. That would put us between twelve and fifteen miles from the car. And I still don't see anything.'

'That's because it's dark,' said Zach. He knew what Donny was intimating. At night you could see the glow of Vegas against the sky from a hundred miles out. There was no glow.

'Yeah, and if it's dark for eight hours, say, and the sun comes up over *there*, we've got another twenty-odd miles.'

'I am *not* walking twenty miles,' said Vira. 'I've got to sit down and cool off.'

'Good idea,' said Zach. 'When it gets cold, we can walk to stay warm.'

Vira flumped heavily down in the sand, trying to kink out her legs. 'You guys notice something else?'

They both looked at her, wrestling off her athletic shoes.

'All the time we've been walking and walking? Since we started there hasn't been a single highway sign.'

The trip had been Vira's idea, another of her just-jump-in-the-car-and-go notions. Spontaneity permitted her the pretence of no encumbrances or responsibilities, which in turn allowed her the fantasy that she was still under thirty, still abrim with potential with no room for regret.

Zach grumpily acceded, mostly because he liked to gamble. A two-day pass to Vegas would allow him to flush his brain and sort out his life, which was in danger of becoming stale from too much easy despair, the snake of self-deconstruction gobbling its own tail.

Taking off on an adventure gave them the illusion of control over their lives. They weren't dead yet, nor off the map. Most of their friends, however, begged off with the usual smorgasbord of excuses – jobs, babies, commitments, obligations, all couched in placating language that broadcast its intention not to offend. It was a good method of sifting one's so-called allies: hit them with a wild-card proposition and see who bites.

'What about Donny?' said Vira.

'He'll be farting around his apartment, waiting for his phone to ring,' said Zach. 'He can spell the driving, and you know he'll volunteer half the gas, just to get out and see different scenery.'

'Remind me why he's our friend?' Vira was nude, mistrusting her vanity mirror, working search-and-destroy on perceived flaws. No tan lines. They had a variety of acquaintances, each good for one isolated conversational topic, to be accessed as needed. Donny's status held at mid-list.

Zach shook his head, feeling superior to the shortcomings of his friends. None of *them* were about to get laid right now. 'Because we both know that Donny doesn't really have anybody else. He's our holiday orphan, our warm body. Spear carrier. Cannon fodder. Come on, he's not so bad. We get stranded in the desert, we can stand back-to-back and defend your honour.'

She had turned side-saddle in the chair before the vanity, and gathered his tumescing cock into her grasp to speak to it. 'Are you suggesting the Sandwich of Love? Hm? One below and one above? You're the buns and I'm the meat?'

'No,' he said between clenched teeth, sucking a breath, coming up rock-hard.

'Good.' She stroked the beast in her hand. 'Donny's not my type anyway.'

He showed up so fast that Zach and Vira barely had time to jump out of the shower, the aura of sex still clinging to them. Vira just made it into abbreviated cutoffs and a knotted top while Zach struggled wet legs into unyielding jeans. Vira felt Donny's eyes take inventory, up-down, from her still-damp cascade of black hair, the full length of both slender legs, to her big feet. Her breasts were nicely scooped, with hard nubs declaring themselves too prominently as they blotted through the sheer material of her top. She caught Donny cutting his gaze away when she looked up. Not her type.

Donny was well-groomed but brittle, as though his look had been not so much preserved as shellacked. He had always lived moment-to-moment, hand to mouth, cheque to cheque; not so charming, when one began to add on years without progress. He had duly logged his time as a depressed philosopher, overstaying college, scooping up handy opportunities, staying slightly out of step, but thereby remaining available for any lark or diversion.

Zach emerged from the bedroom, towelling his hair and pretending like he hadn't just had sex. He was at least ten years older than Vira; what the hell was *that* about, wondered Donny. What really worried him was that he might be no further along than Zach, given another decade. A better apartment, a cleaner car, steady sex, and . . . what else? Zach had two degrees and worked for an airline company doing God knew what. He had Vira. He seemed to understand how the world worked, as though he could perceive things just out of reach by Donny's sensory apparatus. But was that progress? Donny always teased himself with the possibilities, should he finally catch up to his paternal pal; pass him, maybe. All Donny needed was the right opportunity. He had spent his entire life training to be ready when it knocked.

Their friendship was convenient, if nothing else.

'Okay, now we're far enough gone that you have to catch me up on the important stuff,' bellowed Zach from the pilot bucket of his muscle car. Air, industrial-dryer hot, blasted through the open cabin and tried to sterilise them. 'No chitchat. The good stuff. Like, are you seeing anybody?'

'Nope.' Donny tried to make it sound offhand, like *not today*, but it came out like *not ever, and you know it*.

Vira craned around, one arm over the seat, mischief in her eyes. 'Don't even *try* to convince me that nobody's looking.'

'I'm just not in a big hurry, that's all,' Donny said from the back seat.

He watched the knowing glance flicker between his two amigos. Zach had laid out the argument many times before, convinced that Donny set girlfriend standards so high that any candidate was already sabotaged. Donny would counter that his last serious relationship had wrecked him. Then Vira would swoop in a flanking manoeuvre, accusing him of inventing the former mystery girlfriend (whom Zach and Vira had neither seen nor met) in order to simplify his existence by virtue of a romantic catastrophe. Donny's perfect love was so perfect she could not be real, Vira would say. Or: so perfect that she would never have had anything to do with him in the first place. It was nothing aberrant; lots of people lived their lives exactly this way.

Zach and Vira would claim they just wanted to see their friend happy. Happier.

Donny deflected the whole topic, thinking himself humble and respectful, a gentleman. In his mind, he dared them to feel sorry for him.

They chugged super-caffeinated soda and ate up miles and listened to music. They were alone on the road when Zach smelled the gaskets burning.

None of them knew how much they would miss the car, how much they would long for it, days later.

'We have to do something unpredictable,' said Donny.

'Is this another theory?' Vira was in no mood.

The day was shading into night. They had been walking at least a week, by rough estimate and a sunrise-sunset count.

'If we were supposed to just keeping doing this, ad infinitum, then we would have tripped over some more food,' said Donny. 'What has to happen now is we need to shake up the system. Do something deterministic. Declare ourselves in a way that has nothing to do with patterns.'

'Well, I declare I'm gonna collapse here and try to sleep,' said Zach, sitting down heavily in the sand.

'You've just contradicted every other argument you've made,' said Vira, more weary than surprised.

'No, Vira,' said Zach. 'I can see it. No explanation works. Therefore, logic isn't a way out. It's the kind of answer you get to by working through all the other answers. Right, Donny?'

He shrugged. 'Except I can't suggest what to try.'

'We could walk back to the car,' said Vira. They glared at her. 'Joke,' she said, putting up her hands, surrendering. She shielded her eyes and plopped backwards onto the sand as though her spine had been extracted.

Zach encamped nearby – not cuddle-close, but near enough to look possessive – like an infantryman who has learned how to drop and sleep in full gear. Soon he was snoring softly, the sound obscured by the light wind that always seemed to kick up at sunset. Just enough to stir the sand into a genuine annoyance. Zach rolled over, cushioning his forehead on his arms, forming a little box of deeper darkness. Burying his head in the sand, thought Donny, who remained irritated that his friends had accepted the routine of their bizarre situation so readily, and without question.

Donny pulled off his boots, one-two. There was nothing else to look at except the skyline, the sand, an occasional weed, and the two sleepers. He was not tired. His heart was racing.

He weighed one boot in his hand. It was scuffed and dusty, and radiated stored heat like fresh bread from an oven. One-two.

One: holding the toe of the boot, Donny clocked Zach smartly in his occipital ditch, right where the backbone met the brain stem. Zach went limp and Vira did not stir. They were exhausted; fled to another place, chasing dreams. Donny sat on Zach's head, mashing it down into the sand until Zach stopped breathing.

Now Donny felt the surge. He had it all – correctitude, the energising thud of his heart, dilated pupils, an erection, and the exhilarative adrenalin spike of knowing he was on the right track. He was *doing* something, taking declarative action.

After all, what were friends for?

Two: there were no fist-sized rocks or round stones, so Donny used his other boot to hit Vira in the back of the head, so he would not have to look at fresh blood while he raped her. By the second time, she was bloody anyway. She might have orgasmed once, through sheer autonomic reflex. Donny pinched her nose shut and clamped her mouth until she, too, stopped breathing. As she cooled, he did her once more. It really had been a while since he'd got laid. He woke up still on top of her, neck cricked from the odd position in which he'd dozed. His weight had pushed her partially into the sand, half-interring her, but she was in no position to complain, or criticise, or judge him any more. Or feel sorry for him.

Their water bottle was down to condensation. Night was better for walking in a desert. And Donny had taken action.

He left his companions behind and soldiered onwards alone, until his bootheels wore away to nothing. If he ever found civilisation, he'd feel sorry later.

David J. Schow's *Wild Hairs* (Babbage Press), a collection of his non-fiction columns from *Fangoria* magazine, recently won the International Horror Guild Award. A contributor to several past volumes of *Dark Terrors*, he *still* lives in the Hollywood Hills, *still* works in the 'script mines', and now wonders what the cinema equivalent of blacklung might be. His authorship of *The Outer Limits Companion* has led to a brisk consultancy with Rittenhouse Archives (trading cards) and Sideshow Toys (action figures). His work for Mark Rance's production company, Three-Legged Cat, can be seen in the supplements on the new DVDs for *From Hell* and *Reservoir Dogs*. He has also contributed to several documentaries produced by Nobels Gate for Channel 4 Television, including those for *The Shawshank Redemption*, *The Wicker Man* and *Alien*. He tries not to become too confused with David J. Skal, who produced the DVD documentary *Back to the Black Lagoon*, on which he (Schow, not

Skal) appears as a 'Creature Connoisseur'. Schow is also visible interviewing cinematographers Conrad Hall and William Fraker on the DVD of the 'lost' Leslie Stevens film, *Incubus* (the one in Esperanto, starring William Shatner). His latest books include the final volume of the *Lost Bloch* trilogy (subtitled *Crimes and Punishments*); *Eye*, a new collection from Subterranean Press, and a resurrected, polished and spiffed-up reissue of his first collection, *Seeing Red*; a new collection of living dead stories entitled *Zombie Jam*, and the short novel *Rock Breaks Scissors Cut*. About 'Plot Twist', Schow notes: 'I suppose its conceptual antecedent is the Thomas Disch classic "Descending", but it's also a rumination on an unfair precondition foisted on a lot of horror fiction – the "necessity" for a twist ending, a snap in the tail. This story's concerns lie elsewhere.'

Job 37

GEMMA FILES

Speak to me
for Gods sake.
There are worse things
than death
though you and I
are not likely
to experience
any of them.
            Pat Lowther

—. . . two, three. Okay: Looks like we're go.

   This is session seventeen, research project 4.7, Freihoeven ParaPsych Department; we're interviewing subjects whose professions are associated, prospectively, with the accumulation of psychic fragments, and this particular tape will be filed under the heading of Job 37.

   Anyway, uh – how's that mike sitting? You comfortable with that?

—Yeah, it's okay, thanks. (PAUSE) So . . . what do you want to know?

—First off? Well, first off . . . why this? Pretty – odd – career to specialise in, by most people's standards.

—I guess. (PAUSE) You mean *gross*, though. Right?

—Okay, I'll be a little more specific: You own your own business – a cleaning business. And you clean up . . .

—Blood, mostly. Blood, brain-matter, decomposed flesh; sick, shit, kinda bugs feed on sick, shit, dead people. All that.

*

—How'd you decide to get into it?

—Um. (PAUSE) I've always cleaned, always been a cleaner. I never really went through any other jobs, when I was a kid – always did like janitorial work, maid service, hotel cleaning staff jobs, whatever. Because that was what I grew up around, right? My mom, her mom. They used to take me around when they were cleaning up office buildings, 'cause they couldn't pay for anybody to watch me at nights. One time when I was almost one year old I even drank some solvent 'cause I was crawling around in the supply closet while they bagged shredder waste two floors up, and my grandma wanted to call 911, but my mom was like: Hell *no*, they'll take her away from me for sure.

—Jesus. What'd she do?

—Just made me drink milk 'til I puked, made me puke again, made me keep drinking milk. She thought that'd get rid of the burning inside my mouth, and I guess she was right; I remember I was all swollen up for a week after, though. I mean, I could breathe, but I couldn't eat for shit. (PAUSE) And I *still* hate fucking milk.

—So you're working as a cleaner . . .

—Yeah. And I started my own service, right, 'cause I thought why not? I'm bonded, got a good record, so getting the licences was easy enough. So, my third or fourth appointment, when I'm just settling into it – this guy was a lawyer, and he used to drink 24/7. Never a hair out of place, but you could *smell* it on him the minute you walked in, like he slept in a bathtub fulla vodka. Now, his regular day was Thursday, but when I come in, first thing I find out is he'd shot himself sometime the previous Friday.

So I call the cops, call the family; the ME comes and fixes time of death, means and method. It's not a *crime* scene, 'cause no crime's been committed; guy just checked out with this big-ass hunting rifle he kept in the closet, and the force of the thing was so heavy his whole skull sort of exploded, shot like ninety per cent of his brain out the top of his head onto the carpet he was lying on and the wall behind. And he stinks. And the family are freaking out, A) 'cause they loved the guy and oh my God how could he *do* a thing like this, we never knew and blah blah blah, but B) 'cause they own the building, and they think they're *never* gonna rent the place out after this.

So I said: 'I could do it.' And they let me. And I did.

—How?

—Dumb fuckin' luck, mainly, 'cause I did *not* know what I was getting into. First off, you got brain dried hard on everything, and when brain dries it's just like epoxy or shit. Didn't have time to find someplace to buy the kind of disposable haz-mat suits we wear now, with a breather and everything, so I did the whole thing in about three layers of clothes – some sweats, a pair of overalls, a big jogging suit over that, plus rubber boots and dishwashing gloves and a big scarf wrapped around my head. Thought I was gonna melt away in the heat, and I had to burn it all afterwards, anyway.

So I went at the brain with a snow scraper I had out in the truck, and I got most of it that way; used a bristle-brush on the rest, and about ten bottles of industrial bleach. I had to sand the floor and varnish it over, but the fact he did it on the rug made it a little better than if he'd done it, say, in bed, or what have you. Bed's a motherfucker to clean if you even can, which most times you just can't.

When I was done, though, it was the craziest thing, 'cause it basically looked exactly like it'd always been supposed to look that way. Like he was never there at all.

—Was that why you kept doing it?

—A hundred to five hundred an hour is why I keep *doing* it. You get me?

—Absolutely. (PAUSE) Pretty high equipment costs, I guess, though.

—Eh. Not when you buy in bulk, so much: suits, chemicals, what have you. Or the brain machine.

—The 'brain machine'?

—Oh yeah, it's cool: this big truck-mounted steam-injector thingie. Whenever we have a job that looks like it's gonna take all day, we bring the brain machine in and it just melts all the crap up and sucks it into a tank, like gettin' dirt out of a rug. And that's a *real* fuckin' life-saver.

No, the all-star pain in the ass is paying for time on the medical waste incinerator, because the guys running that thing make you pay a big extra fee unless you've got at least a hundred pounds of shit to burn, minimum. So these days, we have to keep the waste on ice out at the warehouse 'til we've got enough for a trip – and that can get seriously disgusting. (PAUSE) You're not using my name, right?

—No, just like we discussed. Total anonymity.

—Then I'll tell you this much: first year or so, I used to take it down the dump, torch it myself. To keep us in the black 'til we built up a regular client-base. I remember one time, this *serious* de-comp job – chick was so slimy, she was practically jelly. So I spent about two hours out there throwing plastic bags full of maggots on the fire, and those things, when they go up? They sound just like . . . popcorn.

—Uh-huh. (PAUSE) You started out using bleach – what kind of chemicals do you use now? Special stuff?

—Ancient Chinese Secret, buddy ruff. No, look, seriously – we're selling that information over the website now, in Start Your Own Business FAQ-packs that go fifty bucks a pop. So what do you think: am I gonna give it away to you for free? Please. We're doin' fine; I don't need the PR *that* much.

—Granted.

—It's a going concern, crime-scene clean-up. You know? And there's two reasons for that – well, three. Number one: firepower. Number two: drugs, 'cause drugs'll make you think and do some crazy fuckin' things. And number three . . . people are just a lot more *alone* than they used to be. No family, no friends. Nobody to give a shit. Even in the same building, the people you see every day – you think they're gonna give a shit if you go missing? Most they'll be doing is sitting around going: geez, haven't seen Mrs So-and-so for a while. 'Til the bugs start comin' down through their ceiling. (PAUSE) And then they'll call me.

So. That it?

*

—Um, no ... (PAUSE) What – what would be the weirdest job you ever did, in your opinion?

—You mean messiest?

—I mean weirdest.

—It's *all* weird. (PAUSE) But you're talkin', like ... 'psychic fragments'-type weird. Right?

(PAUSE)

—... well, yes.

(PAUSE)

—... okay.
   So. This guy killed himself while squatting; hung himself from the doorknob. And the house he did it in, it wasn't exactly abandoned, but it hadn't been checked for a pretty long time. Anyway, real estate agent found him. And he didn't want to tell the property-holder, 'cause then the holder calls the cops ...

—Like with the apartment, with that first guy.

—Yeah, just like that. 'Cause it's always the same story with these pricks.
   So the agent calls us. 'S obvious what happened, and there is *not* a lot of the guy left, anyway. It was summer, it was hot; he was probably in there, like ... basically, he melted. Okay? Cranial fluid came out through his face, spinal fluid through his back. Fluid, generally. All this – crud.

—Brain machine time.

—Serious. Except we didn't *have* the machine yet. (PAUSE) But that was why we were gonna do it, right? 'Cause we know if buddy pays us to dispose of a body for him, we're gonna be the people he calls in to do his dirty work for the rest of his life. And I won't lie, man – we *wanted* to be those people, why the fuck not?

*

—And now . . . you are.

—Yeah.

So . . . back then, the whole company was just me and the SO, basically – my 'significant other'. So this was pretty big of a coup for us. And 'cause we're bankin' on this little windfall, him and me decide we're gonna do what we were never able, up 'til now: We hire a third person. This girl, let's call her – Rosa.

I was the one knew Rosa, from my maid days. Sat her down, told her about the company, what the job was gonna be about. But we didn't have the puke book back then, either, and—

—Sorry. 'Puke book'?

—Yeah. It's this book at the office we got now, full of photos from real bad blood scenes, and we run it past everybody who comes in, 'cause if they heave right there then this probably ain't the career they wanna get into.

So I don't know. I don't think she really *got* what she was sayin' 'yes' to, even after we got her all fitted up in the suit, the breather, showed her how to do everything . . . not even then. Not 'til she went in there, and saw it.

But anyway. We get to the house, and just the night before, we'd suddenly figured out how if we bring Rosa along then we're gonna have to fake like it's all been approved already. So the SO sets up a video camera, like we're taping it for the cops, which they like us to do – they want to know what went where, after all the shit's been squared away. In point of fact, it's just in case buddy wants to screw us over, but how's she supposed to know?

I'm humping in the disinfectants, and he's pissin' around with the camera, and Rosa's out there parking the truck, so she comes in last. And because this guy did it from the doorknob on the front door . . . well, I guess it just didn't occur to me. How when you walked in, you were basically walking right over all the – stuff – that used to be *him*.

And that smell. More like a taste than a smell, really. 'Cause you get it worst in your mouth, all the way at the back, even with the breather. Like it's comin' up from inside *you*.

You do get used to that too, believe it or not. Eventually.

But Rosa—

She steps in, hears that sticky sound, looks down. Sees what she's steppin' in. And when I see her face I think for sure she's gonna run right back out the door, but instead, she runs *in* – into the house, away from the camera. Through the doors into what used to be the kitchen.

Well, we gave her about an hour, 'cause it took that long to get the absolute worst of this guy up. And then I go in, like: okay Rosa, c'mon, man.

But.

No Rosa, for one thing. All right. So she's gone upstairs, obviously, or out the back. Or something.

Try to open the door to the back yard, but that sucker's locked – more like nailed shut, maybe ten, maybe twenty years ago. So I yell to the SO, and he goes to check upstairs, and I go down in the basement. And there's . . .

(PAUSE)

. . . at the bottom of the stairs, there's this – I walk into this patch, this sort of – spot. And it's really cold. Really, really . . .

I thought I could sort of hear her, too, just for a second there. Like she was far away. Like she was – yelling.

(LONG PAUSE)

Well, we get the rest of the guy all cleaned up – fast as we fuckin' can – and then we take the camera, and we get the fuck out of there. And we don't tell the agent, and we don't know who the hell else to call about it – her relatives? I don't even know who they are. Cops? Please.

A couple days later, we do an anonymous 911 call to say she was missing. But nothing ever came of that, I know of.

And a week after that, we finally put in the tape and looked at it.

(PAUSE)

Well?

—. . . well, what?

—You wanna know what was on it. Right?

(NO ANSWER)

*

Okay.

First, it's just static. Not even the house, or the guy, or any of us. And then it kind of gives a jump, or a blip, or the light changes or something, and—

—Rosa, right there. But she isn't *there*. I mean . . . she's somewhere, right? But not the house. Not the way we saw it, anyway.

It's like a – construction site, or whatever. Support beams, sky; it's all kind of wet, like it's been raining. Like the place is only half-built, except for the fact that's just fuckin' crazy.

And Rosa wanders around in there, in her haz-mat suit. Takes her breather off, puts it down someplace. And she looks all seriously freaked, which is . . . understandable.

And then she goes off-screen, and she comes back on, and there's that static again. And then—

—she's in a vacant lot, in the middle of nowhere. No house at all. And it's winter. And she's still wearing the suit, but it's all ripped and dirty. And she's – thinner.

More static.

And then it's summer. And . . . she's in a swamp. And most of the suit's gone, 'cause those things – they ain't exactly built to last, 'specially when you get 'em wet.

And . . . she's getting older.

Static, and static, and everything's moving faster. Shit's goin' by like – I don't even know. And Rosa's all dirty and almost naked and her hair is all long, like down to her shoulders. And she looks kinda crazy, now. And she's so *thin*.

Treeline in the background comin' closer and closer, 'til it's really dark 'cause the trees block off the sun. And she's screaming and crying and goin' back and forth, side to side, in those shadows right by the front of the trees. And then—'

—*something*—

—reaches out from the trees, and it pulls her in. By her *head*.

And she's gone.

(LONG PAUSE)

Tape went on a while after that, like it kept goin' 'til we finished up in the house, shut it down and took it home. But there's no more static, and there's no more Rosa.

Thing is, though . . .

Later, we figured out – when I was down in the basement? Standin' in that – whatever the hell? When I was doin' that, it must've been like was standin' exactly where she would have been, at the same time. Right in the same damn spot.

Like I was inside her, or something.

(PAUSE)

There's a 'psychic fragment' for ya.

(VERY LONG PAUSE)

—. . . what was it like?

—Bein' inside her?

—No, Christ. The, uh – that, uh, the . . . thing. You saw grab her.

—Fuck, *that*. Uh—'

(PAUSE)

It was like . . .

(PAUSE)

Kinda like, um – one of those big bugs you see on the Discovery Channel, on those freaky 'freaks of nature' shows. You know? But . . . with skin.

—Skin?

—Shit, I don't know. Like, like a . . . iguana, or something.

—Big enough to pick a grown woman up by her *head* 'iguana'. Are you—
    —are we talking dinosaur, here?

—Look, fuck you, buddy. (PAUSE) I'd know it if I saw it, tell you that much.

*

—And you still have this tape.

—Sure.

—You didn't accidentally erase it, maybe, or—

—Sure. I mean, what'm I gonna do – tape *Wheel of Fortune* over it?

—And – who'd you show it to, exactly?

—Nobody. I saw it, the SO saw it, but aside from him who'm I gonna show it to? Her parents, assuming I ever found out who they were? Tell 'em hey, your daughter slipped sideways in time, got herself eaten by Jurassic fuckin' . . . (PAUSE) Shit, right.

—But you still *have* it.

—Like I said two times already, *sure*. Why?

(VERY LONG PAUSE)

—. . . how much would you want for it?

THE END

Gemma Files was born in London and now lives in Canada. A former freelance movie reviewer, she now teaches screenwriting and Canadian film history at the Toronto branch of the International Academy of Design. In 1999, her short story 'The Emperor's Old Bones' won the Best Short Story award from the International Horror Guild. She has been published in *The Mammoth Book of Best New Horror*, *The Year's Best Fantasy and Horror*, *Queer Fear*, *The Mammoth Book of Vampire Stories by Women*, *Twilight Showcase*, *Grue*, *Transversions*, *Palace Corbie*, *Selective Spectres*, *Demon Sex* and *Northern Frights*. Collections of her fiction are available through Quantum Theology Publications, and four of her stories have been adapted for the anthology TV series *The Hunger*. She is currently working on her first novel. 'The idea for "Job 37" came to me pretty much full-blown,' Files reveals. 'I wanted to write an M. R. James-type ghost story for the quote-quote New Millennium, one which combined brisk, no-nonsense utilitarianism and outright sidelong creep. I could vaguely remember having read an interview somewhere with a crime-scene clean-up expert who claimed their particular morbid area of expertise constituted the fastest-growing new career option in North America – and what do you know? A brief surf of the net proved them absolutely correct. Enlightened and grossed-out in roughly equal measure, I had the first draft written within a week. Enjoy!'

Mother, Personified

YVONNE NAVARRO

Monday, October 23
'I never meant to mistreat you.'

The blinds are tightly drawn, the air stale and cool, washing over him like the damp, foetid rush from an opened basement door. In the gloom, his mother's voice is barely a whisper in his head and Levy Moreless has to lean forward to hear it.

'I'm so sorry, Levy. It was my life – it was so hard, being a single mother back then, homeless. There were drugs, and booze, and I didn't have any money. I couldn't support you, I couldn't . . .'

'It's all right,' he interrupts, trying his best to sound soothing. He nervously pats the bedspread around her shoulders, feeling perspiration gather along the high line of his forehead as he waits for her next words. What she's said so far has made him uncomfortable, but at the same time he feels vindicated and . . . *proud*. He was right all along in his belief that she would have never done what she had to him – left him like that – if she'd been given a choice, had a fair shot at life. All those years of patience on his part, of waiting to hear what she had to say about the past, have finally paid off and now he knows the truth: she isn't a *bad* woman, just underprivileged, like so many others. Misunderstood. It is not an equal world and she was born at the bottom and stayed there, hadn't had the stamina to pull herself up as others were able to do. Sometimes a person has it in them, and sometimes they don't.

She tries to shake her head but the strength isn't there – the best she can do is stare at him with glassy eyes. *'Not all right,'* he hears her rasp. She eats these flowery purple candies and the sweet scent of her mouth caresses his face, the smell of old age and illness, like lavender-scented decay too deep to hide. Despite his embarrassment, Levy leans closer, needing to hear the rest of it, her self-condemnation at her final act of abandonment; perhaps she can feel his want because he hears her struggle to continue. '*I shouldn't have . . . I should have never—*' Her words breaks off and the vacancy of her gaze becomes permanent.

Damn her. All those soft words, but still, at the end, she denies him.

Friday, October 6
'Never seen anything like it,' Sheriff Markhall says. 'Christ on a stick – where's the, uh, rest of her?'

'That would be the middle part,' says Wayne Bailey.

Markhall is amazed at the lack of surprise or emotion, of *anything*, in the other man's voice. He had no doubt that Bailey has seen a lot of things in his career, but this . . . Christ on a stick. Aloud, he only agrees. 'Yeah, the *middle* part.'

'Gone.'

Frustration gets the best of him, if only for a moment. 'Well, hell, Wayne, I'm not blind. I can *see* that.'

Bailey shrugs, then squints around the murder scene. It is autumn and they are standing on a patch of heavily treed land along the banks of Sugar Creek, just at the back of the Quentin farm. The elder Quentin found the body this morning when he let his German Short Hair loose and the dog came trotting back with a skinny, decomposing human arm dangling from its mouth. Last night had given them a steady downpour, shaking free a good portion of what was left of the leaves on the trees; now their branches, nearly clean, reach towards the sky like fingers at the ends of spindly, starving limbs.

'Hard telling in all this muck,' Bailey says. 'I won't be sure how long she's been dead until I get her back to the lab, but if I was to guess I'd say about six or seven days.' He frowns down at the body. 'I will say this though – we're not looking at a youngster here. This woman looks to be in her fifties or sixties.'

Markhall says nothing as his mind turns this over but comes up empty. This is a small town and things like this just don't happen; no one is missing, there have been no domestic calls for at least a month, and as far as he knows, no one even has relatives in from out of town – that said, because while she wasn't looking very attractive right now, he thinks there is enough of the victim's facial structure and features left for him to know she isn't anyone he'd recognise.

How on earth has a nightmare like this fallen in the back pocket of his quiet little town?

SUGAR CREEK HERALD, Monday – October 9

GRUESOME SUGAR CREEK DISCOVERY

The Sheriff's office responded to a call from Leroy Quentin on Friday and discovered the body of a woman on the Quentin property where it ends at the banks of Sugar Creek. The victim's name is being withheld pending notification of family members, and county officials also refused to release the details of the murder other than it was obviously by foul play and the exact cause of the woman's death has not yet been determined. This death is the first murder to occur in Sugar Creek in fourteen years.

Monday, October 23

'Well,' Levy says as he stares at his mother. He can't decide whether he is happy or unhappy. After all this time, perhaps he is only numb, encased in a protective shell carefully constructed over the course of his life. 'That's all there is. I can't do any more than I have for you. I guess it was just your time to go.'

He draws the sheet carefully over the face of the still form on the bed, then goes to the kitchen and gets out the telephone book. He shuffles back and forth through the pages until he finds what he wants, thinking how even the fluttering of the yellow paper seems loud now that she is gone. He finds the numbers he needs and makes a list of who to call first thing in the morning: the newspaper, a casket place about forty miles away, a nice dress shop where he can pick up fitting apparel. No need to call the cemetery because he already owns a family plot, had thought ahead enough to buy that a couple of years ago.

The calls are more difficult than he expects; the grief weighs on him and it is amazing how nosey people are, even when they don't know you. Is it such a crime for a man to want to lay his mother quietly to rest, without all the fuss and muss that usually makes the undertakers rich? He doesn't have several thousand dollars to drop on a fancy wake with accoutrements, and his mother wouldn't have wanted him to waste his money anyway – a trucker's wage is hard to come by when you have to spend a good deal of your time caring for a sick parent.

But finally it's done. His rig is empty and he will pick up the casket in the morning, then stop by the dress shop. In the meantime there are more things to do to ready her for her final resting place, no matter how tired he feels. Week after week, Levy thinks as he gets up and goes back into her bedroom, all that time fighting to keep her going when others would have given up, would have called him crazy for hanging on as long as he did. But a son's love for his mother is unequalled when it's heartfelt, and he can be proud of himself and free of regrets or guilt, especially considering what she did to him. He will not hold the long-ago abandonment against her, though – he will be a better person than that and not turn his back in her time of need as she did to him. Those who forgive will find forgiveness in the eyes of God, and he has striven hard to be worthy of His holy gaze all these years, and to be at peace with himself.

HARMONY DAILY EXAMINER, Tuesday – October 24

> Drannon, Ida, passed away on Monday, October 23, of natural causes. Born February 23, 1945 in Harmony, Georgia, she is survived by son Levy Moreless of 1212 West Central Parkway, Harmony. Services and burial will be private.

Wednesday, October 25
'This is pretty unusual, Mr Moreless. Most people have their undertakers purchase their casket.'

'Well, no one's actually died,' Levy says. He's already decided that a fabrication will be the path of least resistance, so he puts on his most engaging smile. 'What we're doing is putting together this Hallowe'en spookhouse for the kids. We figure on painting this thing black and having a vampire pop out of it.'

The look on the salesman's face relaxes a bit and Levy notices a gold nameplate on the lapel of his suit jacket, a discreet little thing that says *Robert*. 'Ah, I understand.' Robert even grins a bit. 'Then I guess you won't be wanting the lacquer-black one with red satin lining, huh?'

Levy laughs easily, letting the guy think it's all a just a fine, fun joke. In reality, he wants to pop the man in the nose, because there is nothing funny about the death of a loved one and wanting to do things yourself to make sure they get done right. Still, he has to deal with the real-life part – the assholes like this guy – so he puts on another smile and falls into it like it's just another day in the life of a man who doesn't have all these burdens to carry. 'If only we had the budget for that. I guess we'll be sticking with the basic pine, and we'll just use black paint.'

'Too bad.' Robert winks at him, managing in that one facial gesture to take all the class out of his six-hundred-dollar suit and his designer shoes and his suave little name tab. Revealed instead is the true man, the one who probably drinks cheap beer in the roadhouse off Route 26 and tries to grope the barmaid while his girlfriend has gone to the ladies' room. 'Old Drac-baby would've looked awesome popping out of one of our mahogany dead-beds.'

Dead-beds? The term horrifies Levy, but he doesn't dare show it. He stretches his grin a little wider instead, hoping it isn't turning into a rictus. He is getting to the limit of his endurance here and his eyes flick to his watch; that movement and his knowledge of the area and highways – he's in Fort Valley and needs to get back to Harmony – give him the excuse he needs. 'That's really funny,' he says. 'Listen, I hate to rush you but I really need to load up the casket and be on my way. I'm using my eighteen-wheeler to help out with supplies and whatnot, and I don't want to get caught in that stop-and-go traffic coming out of the refinery off the interstate.'

Robert nods sympathetically. 'Yeah, I got you. When I was a kid, before that refinery was built, we didn't have any traffic to speak of out here. Everything was different then. Now the shift whistle blows over there and we get crammed up the ass going in both directions. Unbelievable, isn't it?'

Levy only shrugs and pulls out his chequebook to pay for the casket. 'There are lots of things in this world that are unbelievable,' he says.

And leaves it at that.

HARPERVILLE EXAMINER, Thursday – October 19

MISSING MISSISSIPPI WOMAN FOUND MURDERED

The body of fifty-four-year-old Stella Jackson, a resident of Scott County, Mississippi, was found Tuesday morning in a disused area of the Davidson County Fairgrounds by Tennessee State mainten-ance personnel preparing the fairgrounds for the upcoming Fallfest. The widowed Mrs Jackson was reported missing from her home eight days ago. The Davidson County Sheriff's Department has refused to release the cause of death, but confidential sources inside the Department revealed that identification was made via her driver's license and fingerprints because Mrs Jackson's head had been removed from her body and had not yet been found. The Sheriff's Department has refused to comment.

Sunday October 15

'If you don't behave, the Cannibal Man will come in the night and eat you,' Robin Landers snaps at her eight-year-old son. 'Just like he done to that Stella Jackson woman.'

The temper tantrum that Jimmy is working himself into atop the braided rug on the living room floor stops abruptly, and Robin is proud of herself for thinking so fast on her feet. That pride, however, falters when she sees the look of grim terror that slips over her boy's face. Damn – what was this? She didn't mean it seriously. The story's just a local version of the bogeyman, for God's sake, something started the week after that woman was found out at the fairgrounds with her head cut off. She hadn't thought Jimmy would know about that part, but that was a stupid assumption, wasn't it? He might only be in third grade but the rumours had probably zinged wildly amongst the older boys and no doubt Jimmy had overheard something on the bus. God, now she's probably done some kind of permanent mental damage or something, sometimes the littlest thing—

Jimmy begins to cry. 'Don't let him get me, Mom – don't let him steal my head!'

Hating herself just a little, Robin gathers him in her arms and rocks him. 'Don't worry, honey. Mommy was just kidding – it's just a story, that's all, it's not real. He can't even get in here, you know? Remember that cartoon you saw on the TV this morning? We're just like that – safe and snug as bugs in a rug.' She hugs him tightly and lets her gaze wander to the front door and the big lock above the doorknob, until she is satisfied it's turned the way it should be.

Never hurts to be sure.

Thursday, October 26
It takes him forty minutes to find a place to put his eighteen-wheeler, and Levy thinks again that he should have bought that old pick-up truck from Bobby McNamara a month ago. Should have done a lot of things, he supposes, but that doesn't do him any good now. By the time he gets into the dress shop it's nearly two o'clock and he's starting to worry – what if they don't have anything that will fit her properly, what if he finds something that's okay but has to get it altered? He measured his mother's corpse this morning and thinks he can get the size right with just a little bit of help, but that won't do him any good if they don't have anything appropriate. He wants something in lace, white or cream, the kind of dress his mother would have been married in had she been lucky enough to have that kind of a life.

While her luck hadn't been so good in decades past, his is still holding. When Levy opens the front door to the exclusive little dress shop, his gaze immediately settles on a rack in the back left corner – lots of lace and glitter, all colours and sizes, not a bad selection for a small town like Harmony where the upper-class folks like the Middletons and the Carters had a tendency to do their shopping in Underground Atlanta. The saleslady looks at him warily, taking in everything about him with a quick, sharp eye: his worn but clean jeans, the way the collar of his favourite flannel shirt is frayed on the left side, his ragged trucker's fingernails that are scrubbed clean because he has had to wash his hands so many times over the past week.

Nevertheless she is pleasant; appearances are deceiving and nowadays you never know what the rich will wear in their spare time. Often a person can't tell a society child from trailer trash, a round-bellied trucker from a loyal, loving son who'd do anything for his mother.

'May I help you?' she asks sweetly.

'Sure,' Levy says. 'I'm looking for a dress for my mother. We've got a big family event coming up and she needs something really special.'

'Ah. And do you know what size she wears?'

Rather than answer, Levy hands her the slip of paper with the measurements written on them. She reads what's there but for a moment it doesn't compute, then she gives him a quick, worried frown before returning her gaze to the paper. 'I'm sorry – I meant dress size. I can see the usual bust, waist and hips, but I'm not sure what the rest of these are. We don't generally use these, the woman just comes in—'

'She's bedridden,' Levy puts in quickly, then remembers the extra inches he added. He has sealed the bedroom and cranked the air conditioning up all the way, but his mother's body is still swelling a bit. 'And she's gained a bit of weight.' He nods at the paper, mentally trying on different personae until he finds the one he wants. 'I don't know anything about women's dress sizes,' he says and gives her a sheepish grin. 'That's why I measured her neck and wrists and what all. I guess you don't need that much information?'

The saleswoman smiles. 'No, we usually don't. But let's see what we can come up with – do you see one you like?'

Levy glances again at the rack that first caught his attention. 'Something from there,' he says. 'A light colour. Dark colours don't go well with her complexion.'

'Okay.' He follows the woman over to the rack and waits while she works her way through what's there, checking the tags until she finds a size that satisfies her. 'How about this?'

Levy shakes his head. 'Not pink – she'll say it's too young for her. White, or cream.'

She nods and her fingers brush across the tops of the hangers as she considers the choices. For a moment Levy is fascinated by her fingernails, each of which is painted not one, but *three* colours, in a bright diagonal pattern. The finishing to the fancy manicure is a tiny, fake diamond on each tip and he wonders if, in her youth, his mother ever had a job like that done on her nails. His musing stops when he realises the woman is about to pull a yellow dress from the rack, which will look terrible with his mother's pallor. He has never liked yellow anyway. 'No,' he says. 'White or cream.'

She looks as though she wants to argue, then she shrugs and replaces the dress, finds a different choice and holds it up. 'This?'

He looks at the garment critically, but it's pretty damned good. He would like it to be perfect, but his choices are limited here and time is marching on; his mother's body is beginning to show the effects of death's hand and, as painful as the experience may be, he really needs to put her into her final resting place. The dress has short, bell-shaped sleeves – it's actually out of season – but perhaps that is for the best, since it will make changing her clothes a little easier and lessen the chance that her arms have swollen so much they won't fit inside normal sleeves. The whole thing is plain white lace with a princess collar and tiny pearlised buttons running down the front from neckline to a hem that goes just below the knee, with a nice, white satin underdress. 'This is good,' he says. 'Perfect. I'll pay cash.'

The saleswoman gives him an arch look. 'Just to make things clear, sir, all sales are final. We don't accept returns or exchanges.'

'No problem,' Levy tells her with a smile. 'She won't be bringing it back.'

Each part of this, Levy discovers, is harder than the last.

He'd thought it would get easier as it went on, that the initial loss – that final letting go of spirit from body – would be the worst of it, but bathing his mother for the last time teaches him how wrong he has been. The feel of her papery skin beneath his fingertips, the slow drawing of the soapy washrag along the now-slack flesh of her arms and legs, the way the dry, cool skin of her face drinks in the moisturiser he carefully rubs into it and the rest of her stiffening body . . . it's all like a slow, religious ritual, his own parting of the soul, this time his from hers. Levy is a religious man, but knowing that she's gone on to the Maker and is finally out of pain, which has been substantial for her in the last month, doesn't make it any better. She'd come to him late in life, after years of separation, and now, selfishly, he wants her back, wants her to be here for the next few years so he can get to know her as he should have. Funny how life and fate can alter a person's future just by making the paths of two people intersect.

Finally, Levy is done. Clothed in the white lace dress, his mother's body lies serene and falsely innocent on the bed, like an aged child napping before her first communion. As a closing touch he carefully tucks a lavender-flavoured mint into the dry, toothless cavity of her mouth. The water in the washbowl has cooled quickly in the high air conditioning and Levy's hands are freezing beneath the constant draught from the vents. Despite this, he is sweating from his work; the strain of carefully turning her as he tried not to bruise flesh already discoloured from settling blood – gravity and nature working against him – has reminded him that time is his enemy here.

His back hurts and Levy lets the heat of the shower rinse away the ache and warm his chilled body, wishing it could go deeper and fill the ice-encrusted abyss that surrounds his heart. As he tries to scrub away the smell of decomposition, he thinks about a headstone for his mother's grave, the final thing he wants to do for her but cannot because of the time factor and the money. He wants something in grey stone and carved with her name and life dates, maybe with a rose etched into each corner; perhaps he'll be able to order one for her in a few months, after he makes up the highway hours he's given up during her illness. In the meantime, Levy has made a marker for her grave out of a piece of treated wood, the kind they use to build decks and which will hold up in the weather. The lettering is nothing more than waterproof paint, but he's done it up in careful black letters outlined with white, and since as a sign painter he makes a pretty good trucker, it'll have to do.

Showered and dried, Levy goes to bed and lies in the dark with his eyes open, staring into a blackness that seems eternal and thinking of tomorrow night.

JERUSALEM STAR, Monday – October 16

DEATH COMES TO JERUSALEM

Pope County police discovered the body of Wilma Russell behind the Food Gas 'N' Go at the entrance to Interstate 40 early this morning. Miss Russell, a lifetime resident of Jerusalem, was a waitress in the coffee shop of the Gas 'N' Go and a member of the Jerusalem North Baptist Church. Other employees said they noticed nothing out of the ordinary when she left work the previous night.

Refusing to reveal the details, Sergeant Brendan did say that there were certain acts done to the victim's body which made the crime unique, and that it was clearly not linked to any other in the area. This is the first murder in the Pope County area in more than twenty years and the County Police said that while they have no leads at the present time, they believe forensic evidence will help track and convict the murderer.

'Well?' Jerusalem's medical examiner, Terrence Penn, pulls off his bloody latex gloves and tosses them into the bin marked MEDICAL WASTE, then reluctantly turns to face Sergeant Brendan. The man is well-known for his temper and Penn knows he has to be very careful or he'll find himself on the receiving end of that notable lack of patience. 'Mind you, I haven't finished the full autopsy yet, but cause of death looks to be strangulation.' He nods towards a bloody object in one of the metal bowls next to the table. 'I dug that out from around her neck, tight enough so you can bet the windpipe was crushed, maybe even severed. I doubt you'll get any clue from it though – you're looking at nothing but typical telephone cord, the kind you can buy in a hardware store anywhere.'

The Sergeant waits, fidgeting, and the medical examiner scans the corpse again. It is still dressed and the only areas he's washed so far are the neck and the face, going after the weapon and cleaning her up enough to take a photo for the police. His gaze pauses at shoulder height and the muscle and sinew gaping on both sides. 'I won't be sure until I eyeball some samples under the microscope, but by the angle and edges of the wounds, I'd say her arms were probably removed with some type of saw.'

'Hacksaw?'

'I doubt it,' Penn says. 'Bone is a son-of-a-bitch to cut through. Wood saw's more likely.'

The cop grimaces. 'That same hardware store, huh?'

Penn just shrugs. 'I'll get on the computer and spread this around,' he says. 'Let the other jurisdictions know and see if they can come up with anything.'

'No,' Brendan says sharply. His voice makes Penn jump. 'We don't need a bunch of high-nosed official-types poking around Jerusalem and getting folks more upset than they already are. We'll handle this ourselves and keep things nice and quiet.'

Penn wants to protest, but he knows it's useless. Besides, because of his past, he likes the idea of quiet and inoffensive, of letting vicious things go until, perhaps, they simply roll over and die on their own.

'You ever see anything like this up there in the city?'

'No.' Penn is in his mid-thirties, a refugee from New York and a much more unpleasant first decade in his career. The implication, the *possibility*, of what's lying on the table in front of him represents something he believed he left behind in the tenements and streets of a city filled with hatred and pain. To see it come to roost here, in this peaceful, God-fearing town, makes him feel like a crack has appeared in the edge of his world and revealed an unexpected pocket of poison. 'And I never thought I would, either.'

Friday, October 27
And for Levy, it just gets worse and worse.

At least the weather is good. The earlier weather report of possible showers doesn't carry through and the air stays clear and crisp as the sun sets and the light fades to evening. Levy has taken great pains in the placement of his mother's casket in the back of his rig, making sure that when it bounces or turns she won't jostle around too much and get her nice burial outfit all messed up in this most unconventional of hearses, or – God forbid – her wooden bed upsets and spills her onto the dirty metal surface. When it's full dark he heads towards Peaceful Oakes Cemetery on Highway 240, taking the long way around so he'll come up by the back entrance, the one the kids use at Hallowe'en when they futz around and play spook jokes on one another. This is a good time of the evening – the caretaker's gone home for the weekend and it's early enough so that the sheriff will be more worried about the rednecks spoiling for a Friday night fight at the Magnolia Saloon than he will harmless pranks at the boneyard.

He finds the spot he bought and is pleased to see it's been well cared for. First he carefully cuts the sod and removes it, laying it out in rolls like he's seen groundskeepers do before other funerals. That done, Levy starts to dig, and the work is harder than he expected – do they really dig the holes six feet deep? He can't get the sides as neat and even as they should be, but he does what he can, knowing they have machines for that and he has only his own God-given hands. He gets around four feet down and accepts it as enough; he's been digging for a couple of hours and each hour that passes increases the chance that the sheriff will cruise by on his nightly rounds. Levy doesn't think he's doing anything wrong – his mother, his plot of ground in the cemetery

– but it would just be a whole lot easier to avoid having to explain it. It takes a chunk of struggling but he finally gets the awkward pine casket that will shield his mother's corpse from the surrounding soil into its place within the hole he has dug. Panting a little, he leans over and picks up his shovel, knowing that when he fills in the grave, he will be done with this most painful of tasks.

And then, the worst of it hits home.

He bends double and sobs, feeling suddenly crushed beneath the knowledge that he is here and she is . . . *there*, in that *hole*, he is putting his mother into a dark, cold hole in the ground and covering her with *dirt*. It is the right thing to do, but for a minute or two, an eternal one hundred and twenty seconds, Levy feels like he has never done anything so wrong in his life.

But in the end, as he has always done, Levy grits his teeth and does what he has to.

And at last, after so, *so* long, it is finally over.

INDEPENDENCE REPORTER, Saturday, October 21

BODY DISCOVERED BEHIND RESTAURANT

The Autauga County Sheriff's Department discovered the body of Janet Liding in the dumpster behind a Peter's Chicken restaurant on the north side of Independence this morning. Mrs Liding's husband reported her missing yesterday evening and stated that she did not return home from a shopping trip to the Prattville Mall. Police believe Mrs Liding was killed elsewhere and then moved to the Peter's Chicken location. As yet police have no explanation for the fact that a significant portion of the body is missing, and a full investigation has been mounted. Mrs Liding is survived by her husband, three children, and one grandchild.

'How is she?'

Dr Stackforth doesn't look up from the clipboard until he finishes what he is writing. He has always been proud of the way his penmanship is neat and readable, unlike so many other idiots in his profession who think that the label 'physician' entitles them to fall into a ridiculous stereotype that is nothing but a façade for people too lazy to take the time to control their hands. This afternoon he is especially proud of that control and the way he is able to keep his hands from shaking, despite the condition of the teenaged girl on the hospital bed in front of him, and despite the corpse he had to examine earlier in the morgue. 'She's in shock,' he tells the grey-haired policeman who waits at the entrance to the room. 'Under heavy sedation.'

The cop's name is Davis and he nods in understanding and glances at the bed. He already knows the basic info – Mandy Wallace, age seventeen, high school dropout who likes to party a bit on the wild side, as if that had anything to do with anything. 'Can I talk to her?'

The doctor frowns. 'She probably won't wake up until morning. I doubt you'll get much besides what she's already said, anyway – she's just repeating the same thing over and over about how she took out the morning trash and there the woman was when she lifted the lid on the dumpster. It would've been better all around if whoever did this had at least shoved the body further down so the girl didn't see . . . well you know.'

'Yeah,' Davis agrees, and his thoughts skitter back to that terrible earlier time slot during which he and the morgue attendant had lifted out what remained of Janet Liding and strapped it to the gurney. Afterwards he had gone through the garbage in the oversized trash container piece by piece, but the search had been futile – no clues, and no more body parts. Somewhere out in the world a killer with a hunger for high brutality wanders free, and as much as he wants it, Davis knows he isn't meant to be the man who catches him.

Saturday, October 28
It's a joke, Charlie the groundskeeper thinks as he stares at the freshly turned mound of dirt at the far back corner of Peaceful Oakes. Kids or something, always trying to be smart-asses, and you'd think that Moreless boy had got enough of their shit when he was growing up. There was something down there, all right, but he damned sure isn't going to dig it up without supervision, God a'mighty knew what was waiting in there because *something* sure was – that much dirt just didn't get displaced and leave a mound like that sticking up outta the ground all by itself, thank you very much.

He shakes his head and drives to the maintenance office, dials up the sheriff while he flips through the logbook until he gets to the chart that tells him who owns what plot way back there. He's still on hold when his fingernail skims down the page and stops at the appropriate place, and he almost drops the phone when he sees the name. God a'mighty, he had it right on the nose when he'd said there was no telling how cruel people could be. That damned sheriff still hasn't come on the line so he pulls Tuesday's newspaper out of the pile by the garbage can and checks the obits – hot damn, there it is for everybody and anybody to see.

He's just about to hang up when Tyler Benton's gritty voice finally blasts into his eardrum. 'What's up, Charlie?'

'I'm thinking you better come out to the boneyard, Tyler,' he says slowly. His brain is still trying to accept the signals his eyes are feeding him from the newspaper. 'I'm thinking ... someone got buried out here last night.'

There's a pause on the other end while the sheriff tries to understand him. 'What do you mean "someone"? You telling me you don't know who?'

'Yeah,' old Charlie says. 'That's exactly what I'm saying.'

'There's no record of anyone named Ida Drannon in the Harmony Clerk's Office,' Sheriff Benton says as he scowls at the wooden grave marker. 'Levy Moreless is as orphan as they come – he was found in the women's room at Mercy Hospital when he was two days old. They never was able to track down the mother.'

Charlie shrugs. 'Maybe he finally found her.'

Benton spits a mouthful of tobacco juice off to the side, and while he says nothing, the groundskeeper's inference doesn't pass him by. 'I sent a car to his house but he ain't there. Neighbour says his rig pulled out this morning, probably doing a run. She says he's generally only gone a few days.' He squats and studies the grave marker again, squinting at the letters painted on the piece of wood. 'Pretty meticulous paint job for a prank.'

He glances back but the groundskeeper only shrugs. 'Who knows? My Mabel – God rest her soul – was a teacher at Harmony Grammar and she used to bring home some tales, I tell you. Said the kids tormented the Moreless boy something terrible until he got his growth the summer of his freshman year. After that no one dared – boy shot up to six foot three and turned out to be quite the athlete. Would've been on the basketball team except he threw his knee out in a practice game, so he started driving a truck after school for one of the auto parts places.'

Benton nods. 'Kept on doing the trucker thing, I see.' He jams his hat back on his head and pulls his collar a little closer against the chilly late October wind. It's only mid-afternoon but there's a heavy cloud cover and already it seems dark; he hopes to Christ Moreless knows something about this, because he's going to be pissed as hell if he ends up having to get a back-hoe crew out here to dig up whatever's in this damned hole. 'I'll give the man two days to get back,' he says, wondering if he can stretch the deadline if he has to. Probably not. 'Then we'll see what's what.'

Tuesday, October 30
Levy comes back from his weekend run to West Virginia and finds the biggest nightmare of his life.

It has been a difficult trip, a tough fight to get the overloaded eighteen-wheeler through the mountains in a day-long late fall downpour. At times he was barely able to see the road and more than once it had taken every bit of concentration he possessed to keep from running over the beat-up truck of some miner and his family or the wheezing RV belonging to grandpa and the wife that the old man drove maybe twice a year. There'd hardly been a free second on the road to let his mind relax and think the proper kind of thoughts about his mother, the mourning kind that a man, a *son*, ought to be able to immerse himself into over the week following the righteous burial of a parent. He had planned on heading home and getting a good night's sleep, then coming out to the graveyard in the morning with a big bundle of fresh red roses from the florist over on Gavin Street, but at the last minute he'd turned his rig onto the Perry exit ramp and headed into the Wal-Mart there. It might be only a quick bunch of daisies, but tomorrow was just too far away – he needed to go to the boneyard and do a little private grieving tonight.

And what does he find when he gets there?

This.

Levy doesn't notice the sound of machinery at first; besides the rumbling of the Peterbilt's massive engine, it's chilly outside and he's got the windows rolled up and the heater fan going – he's never much liked the cold temperatures. But the instant he cuts off the engine and reaches for the little bundle of daisies, the uneven revving jumps in to fill what should have been tranquil cemetery silence. Levy looks up in surprise as his hand closes around the plastic-wrapped bouquet, and the high viewpoint from the truck's cab gives him the sight of a back-hoe poised over his mother's grave like a huge praying mantis. He sits there, stunned, as the backward bucket swoops downwards and takes a bite out of the earth, then he registers the other people milling around the growing hole in the soil, all too engrossed in this most heinous of violations to realise he's there.

The flowers fall to the floorboard and are crushed as Levy claws for the handle on the door, stumbling to his knees when he bursts from the truck. For an uncertain moment he scrambles along the ground like some kind of confused beetle, then he's up and rushing forward, arms flailing, mouth and eyes opened wide as the noise of the back-hoe grows in his head until it wipes out the sounds of everyone and everything else around him, a huge black wave that smothers his world. It isn't until the Sheriff slaps him on the side of his head with his blackjack that Levy realises the noise he is hearing isn't the back-hoe at all. It's the sound of his own horrified screams.

'Tell me about the . . .' Sheriff Benton hesitates, not sure how to phrase it. He's never had to deal with this before and for the first time in his career he is in so far over his head that he might as well be sucking water for air. Still, he wants desperately to keep this quiet – no one in Harmony needs a mob of big-city reporters poking their noses and cameras into secrets that are best left alone. Lord knows there were things in Harmony hidden in the darkness of closets and the cellars of old estates, and Benton had a hunch that this was another one destined to be exactly that – best left alone. Still, he'd do what he could without spreading the ugly mess around for outsiders to talk about. 'Tell me about Ida Drannon,' he finally finishes.

'My mother.' Levy Moreless's voice is no more than a monotone, just about a whisper. He sits at the wooden table in the room that serves as an interrogation area, which is really just a storage room that Benton had cleared out last year. The suspect's wrists are handcuffed and his hands are folded serenely together; Benton can't decide if Moreless is praying or just waiting.

Benton chews the inside of his cheek, rolling the moist flesh between his teeth until it becomes painful and he realises what he is doing. 'Well, we got us a problem with that claim, son. We—'

'I'm not your son!'

It is the first sign of emotion from Moreless and Benton's eyebrows rise. 'County records indicate your mother is unknown,' he says. 'What's in that grave isn't your mother. In fact, it isn't any *one* particular woman.' He steps to the table and leans over until he's staring directly into the other man's eyes, but if he hopes to be intimidating, he knows instantly that he's failed. Moreless's gaze is as cold and empty as the sky on a cloudy and moonless January night. 'Who are they?' Benton demands, dropping any pretence of congeniality. 'And where did they come from?'

'I don't know what you're talking about,' Moreless responds in a flat voice. 'The woman in that grave is my mother.'

The Sheriff scowls and thinks about hitting Moreless, then decides it isn't going to do any good. The county had sent over a psychiatrist who'd spent a half-hour with Moreless and used a lot of multi-syllabled words to essentially say the guy was nuts. The reason Moreless is so calm now has a lot to do with heavy sedatives. He probably won't even feel it if Benton beats on him, so why bother?

'She's no more your mother than you're Dr Frankenstein,' Benton says. 'Although I gotta admit you gave it a helluva try.' He bites into his cheek again, stops when he feels the sting of his teeth. 'By my count, I'd say you whacked at least four women. Now I need to know who they were and where you did them.'

'I don't know what you're talking about,' Moreless repeats.

'Mr Moreless, we aren't blind. The body in the casket isn't just one woman. It—'

'Of course it is,' Moreless interrupts. His eyes, formerly so dead, light up and he leans forward on the table. 'It's my mother, can't you tell that? She's old now, sure, but she was blonde like me when she was a young woman. She told me she used to play the piano, and she was a dancer until her back went out on her a few years ago. That's when she started picking up a little weight.' For a moment, Moreless is silent and Benton is afraid to speak, hesitant of stifling the man's sudden urge to talk. 'If she'd been around when I was growing up, she would have been a good mother, you know.'

The Sheriff waits, but Moreless doesn't say anything else. In a bizarre sort of way, the body in the casket fits what this crazy had just described, although proportionately it couldn't have been more screwed up. The dull blonde hair of the toothless skull, the large, slender-fingered hands on the arms, the long, lean legs, all carefully sewn onto a too-pudgy torso.

Benton decides to try a different tactic. 'So where has your . . . mother been all this time?'

'Around.' Moreless gives him a sly look. 'You know. Lots of places.'

The man's answer is the epitome of understated sarcasm, and for a brief, fierce moment Benton wants to punch Moreless. He quells the urge, thinks that it's just too damned bad no one else can see his heroic act of self-control. The lawman will not give the killer the satisfaction of knowing how angry he is, of how well his button has been pushed by that ugly six-word reply; instead, he will allow Moreless the notion that Benton is nothing but a dumbfuck redneck Sheriff and it's all going over his head. Yes, he wants to beat this murderous asshole into a million pieces, but he also wants to find out who the women are that make up his *mother*. Even more than that he wants to do it *quietly*, without turning his little southern town into a media circus. He went through that a couple of years ago when Anisette Middleton disappeared out at the Vinegar Tree Estates; God forbid he be cursed like that again.

'Like where?' Benton keeps his voice bland.

'I-I don't have any idea.'

There is something in the man's tone, a pause, a . . . hint of uncertainty, that makes Benton abruptly realise that in his own twisted way, the killer is actually telling the truth. He knows suddenly that to Moreless, no matter how she started out, now the woman he buried in that grave is just that, *one* woman – a single person rather than the horrid conglomeration of four bodies put together like some B-movie science experiment gone berserk. Levy Moreless will never tell him the truth of where his victims came from because he simply doesn't remember any more.

Sheriff Benton grinds his teeth. If there is any chance of protecting Harmony from the prying eyes of the rest of the country, this means he must take matters into his own hands.

HARMONY DAILY EXAMINER, Tuesday – October 31

DISAPPEARANCE AT THE COUNTY MORGUE

The body of Ida Drannon was reported stolen from the County Morgue sometime yesterday evening. Mrs Drannon had been disinterred from Peaceful Oakes Cemetery yesterday afternoon because of questions raised by the cemetery's groundskeeper regarding possible improper burial procedures. Sheriff Benton speculates the disappearance is a Hallowe'en prank, or possibly a college hazing ritual, but admits that the Sheriff's Department currently has no leads. Mrs Drannon's son, Levy Moreless, could not be reached for comment.

Levy sits quietly on his chair across from the Sheriff's desk and watches the other man watch him.

It takes a long time, but finally the lawman speaks.

'I'm going to let you go,' he says in a gravel-edged voice. 'There's this law that says without a body, it's hard to prove there was a crime. Now I saw the body, and so did a handful of other people, including you. And for the good of this town, we're all going to just keep our mouths shut about that.' Benton angles forward over the desk and fixes his steel-coloured gaze on Levy. 'And so will you.'

'But my mother's body is gone,' Levy says quietly. 'And no one knows where.'

'Well, there is that,' Benton responds, but Levy sees the way his eyes shift up and to the left. He remembers reading somewhere that this is body language, the sure sign of a person telling a lie. He is suddenly sure that the Sheriff knows where his mother's corpse is, but he is equally sure that Benton will never tell him. 'And it's a shame,' Benton continues. 'We'll be looking into it and we'll contact you first thing as soon as we find it.' Another shifting eye movement and he's staring again at Levy. 'But mind you that it's not your place to go looking for her, it's ours. And we're going to handle it, nice and quiet-like, without getting anybody else involved.' The harsh overhead fluorescences make the man's eyes glitter momentarily and the grey irises reflect the light like cold metal. 'Do I make myself perfectly clear?'

Levy considers this for a few seconds, then slowly nods. 'I get it. I don't guess there's anyone I'd ask to help me anyway. I never have.'

Benton nods and looks relieved. He pushes to his feet and gestures at Levy to stand; when he does, the big sheriff pulls a key from his pocket and unlocks the handcuffs around Levy's wrists. The heavy steel falls away with a clank and Levy rubs his skin, lets Benton take him by the elbow and guide him to the door. 'I'm glad we understand each other, s—' He cuts off the word, but Levy knows the bastard was about to call him *son* again. How he hates that; no one but his mother had the right to do that.

Before Levy can think more on it, Benton pulls a shopping bag out of a closet and hands it to him – his personal belongings, wallet, money, jacket and the things that were in his pockets when they took him into custody yesterday. Levy shrugs into the jacket without a word as the Sheriff steers him down the hall and ushers him outside, where the frost-filled October air surrounds him instantly. The sun is bright, but does nothing to warm the coldness within his soul, while across the street a line of laughing children streams into one of the small shops, begging for Hallowe'en treats.

'I don't expect to be hearing from you any more,' the Sheriff says, and his voice is just as frigid as the late autumn air. 'In fact, I reckon it would be best if you headed on out of town in that tractor-trailer of yours and found another place to call home. Yeah, I think that'd be an all-around bonus for everybody involved.'

'But my mother—'

'Well, the truth is,' Benton interrupts, 'that it's likely she won't ever be found. Just figure we've done the best we can and that's all there is to it.'

Levy stares at him for a long moment, then turns and walks away. He feels no hate for Benton or the people of this town, only pity. They don't know how strong a love he had for his mother, they don't *understand*. But he knows, and he can still feel it. If Benton won't find his mother's body, it's only because he won't look. But that doesn't mean Levy won't.

He found her before.

He can do it again.

Yvonne Navarro is a native Chicagoan who has been writing since 1982. She has published thirteen novels (the most recent of which is *Buffy the Vampire Slayer: Tempted Champions*) and more than sixty short stories. She is currently working on more *Buffy* material and a children's book collaboration which she will help write and also illustrate. In addition to maintaining an extensive web site, she is also the owner of a little online bookstore at www.dustyjackets.com. By the time you read this, she should have finally realised her dream of relocating to Arizona. 'This story was a challenge for me,' reveals Navarro. 'The theme is often used in fiction, but I wanted to do something different with it. What was really enjoyable was tying it into Harmony, Georgia, and its "existing" residents. Harmony is a town I first created around 1987, and in which I have occasionally placed characters and events from novels and stories ever since.'

The Receivers

JOEL LANE

People don't talk about it now. They've forgotten, or pretended to forget, just how bad it was. New people have moved in, and new businesses have started up. 'Regeneration' would be putting it a bit strongly, but most of the damage has been repaired. Or at least covered up. As for the madness – well, nothing healed it, so maybe it's still hidden. When you've seen what people are capable of, it's hard to believe that they can change.

To begin with, it was nothing out of the ordinary. The local branch of Safeway reported a sharp increase in the level of shoplifting. No one had been caught. In the same week, a Warwick-based building firm reported the theft of a truckload of bricks. Ordinary items are the hardest to track down. Once they go missing, it's already too late.

At the time, a much more serious theft was concerning us. A former local councillor whom we'd been investigating for corruption had died of blood poisoning at Solihull Hospital – the result of a ruptured bowel, apparently. I don't think we'd ever have got enough on him for a conviction. We'd just closed the case when his body went missing, three days before the funeral. The security guard at the mortuary swore he'd not seen or heard anything. But there was clear evidence of a break-in, in the form of a missing windowpane. Not broken: missing.

I won't tell you the ex-councillor's name. It's all over Birmingham in any case, on plaques set in hotels and shopping arcades and flyovers. He'd have attended the opening of an eyelid. I don't even remember what party he belonged to. It doesn't matter these days. He'd been cosy with the building firm that had some materials nicked. That was the first hint I got of how this might all be connected up.

That October was hazy and overcast, the clouds dropping a veil of warm rain. I remember things were difficult at home. Julia had just turned eighteen, and Eileen was torn between wanting her to stay and wanting her to move in with her boyfriend. It was a kind of territorial thing. Julia was too old to stay in her room when she was at home: she needed the whole house. As usual, I tried to stay out of it, using my awkward working hours as an excuse to keep my distance. I believe in peace and harmony; I've just never been able to accept how much work they need.

It was a while before the police in Tyseley, Acock's Green and Yardley got round to comparing notes on recent theft statistics. What we were dealing with was an epidemic of shoplifting. No one much was getting caught, and the stolen goods weren't turning up anywhere. Most of it was basic household stuff anyway, hardly worth selling on. Shoes, DIY equipment, frozen food, soft-porn magazines, cheap kitch- enware, bottles of beer. If there was an organisation behind all this, what the fuck was it trying to prove? Of course, we had our doubts. Rumours of invisible thieves were a gift to dishonest shop staff – or even owners working a scam. It was happy hour on the black economy.

To start with, we encouraged shop owners to tighten up their security. A lot of younger security staff got sacked and replaced by trained professionals, or by hard cases from the shadows of the hotel and club scene. Suspects were more likely to end up in casualty than the police station. We put more constables on the beat to cut down on burglaries. But stuff still went missing – at night or in broad daylight, it didn't seem to matter. Cash disappeared from pub tills. A couple of empty freezers vanished from an Iceland stockroom. A junk shop lost a shelf of glassware. It made no sense.

Walking out of the Acock's Green station at night became an unsettling experience. There was hardly anyone around. The barking of guard dogs shattered any sense of peace there might have been. Dead leaves were stuck like a torn carpet to the rain-darkened pave- ment. The moon was never visible. Every shop window was heavily barred or shuttered. Slogans began to appear on metal screens and blank walls: HANG THE THEIVES, THIEVING GYPPOS, SEND THE THIEFS HOME. I must admit, I laughed out loud when I saw someone had painted with a brush on the wall of the station car park: WHO STOLE MY SPRAY CAN?

People were being shopped to us all the time, but we never got anywhere. Without the stolen goods, there was no evidence. Some of our informants seemed to feel that evidence was an optional extra when it came to prosecution. Being Asian, black, European, unusually poor or new to the area was enough. As the problem escalated, letters started to appear in the local evening paper accusing the police of protecting criminals, or insisting that the homes of 'suspicious characters' be searched regularly. *If they have nothing to hide, they have nothing to fear.* In truth, we were questioning a lot of people. And getting a lot of search warrants. We were even catching the odd thief. But not as odd as the ones we weren't catching.

Julia really summed it up one evening, during one of our increasingly rare family meals. 'It's like some children's gang,' she said. 'Nicking all the things they see at home. Then hiding somewhere, dressing up, smoking cigarettes. Pretending to be their own parents.' She looked sad. Playfulness was slipping away from her. I wondered if she could be right. Maybe it was some whimsical game, a joke played by kids or the members of some lunatic cult. But the consequences weren't funny. People were getting hurt. Homes were getting broken up.

I remember the day, in late October, when I realised just how serious things had become. I was interviewing some people who'd been involved in a violent incident at the Aldi supermarket on the Warwick Road. A Turkish woman shopping with two young children had been attacked by several other shoppers. She'd suffered a broken hand, and her four-year-old daughter was badly bruised. No stolen goods had been found in her bag or her bloodstained clothes. She told me a young woman had started screaming 'Stop thief!' at her in the toiletries section, near the back of the store. People had crowded round, staring. A man had grabbed her arm and held her while the young woman started throwing jars of hair gel at her. Someone else had knocked her down from behind. She'd woken up in hospital, and it had been a while before she'd found out that her two children were safe.

Then I talked to the young woman who'd thrown the jars. She was only nineteen, a hard-faced AG girl with china-white skin and hair tied back. She chain-smoked throughout the interview, flicking ash over the table between us. Her answers were mostly monosyllables, but a few times she interrupted me with sudden outbursts. 'She wouldn't let go of her little girl. That means she was using her as a human shield.' And later, 'Are you a copper or a fucking social worker? Wake up and join the real world.' I don't think she really heard a word I was saying.

A couple of days later, a tiny padded envelope was sent to the Acock's Green station. It was full of crushed stink bombs. The smell lingered in the building for days. Groups of neo-fascists took to patrolling the streets in combat jackets, led by dogs on steel chains. Meanwhile, the thefts continued. In desperation, all the local police stations joined forces in a massive raid on the homes of suspects. We found next to nothing. But local racists used the operation as a cover for their own little *Kristallnacht*. Asian shops were broken into and smashed up, and a few homes were set on fire. We were caught off balance, too busy hunting for stolen goods to stop the violence. I still wonder if our superiors knew what was going to happen and turned a blind eye.

November was unexpectedly cold. It never seemed to become full daylight. The frost made everything slippery or tacky, difficult to handle. Car fumes made a smoky haze above the streets. I spent the days and nights rushing from one crime scene to another, from thefts to fights to arson attacks, my hands and face numb with cold and depression. It felt like the meaning was being sucked out of everything.

Julia's boyfriend moved to Coventry to start a new job. She started moving her own stuff over there in batches, a suitcase at a time. It was strange to find things missing – pictures, books, ornaments – that I'd come to take for granted as part of the house. Maybe Elaine was letting Julia take some things that weren't strictly hers, just to avoid arguments. I felt too tired to mediate between them; all I wanted to do at home was sleep. Without Julia there, filling the house with her scent and music, I was reminded of how things had been before she was born. When Elaine and I had first set up home together. Maybe we could get some of that back.

It was maudlin retreat into the past that sent me to the allotments in Tyseley, near the street where I'd lived as a child. The allotments occupied a strip of land between an industrial estate and a local railway line that carried only freight trains. There was a patch of waste ground at one end, with some derelict railway shacks and a heap of rusting car bodies. It was overgrown with fireweed and pale, straggly grass. I'd spent a lot of time there at the age of ten or eleven, getting into fights and spying on couples. Somehow I remembered the place as having a kind of mystery about it, a promise that was never fulfilled.

It was my day off – either Monday or Tuesday, I'm not sure. Another chilly, overcast day. I'd been walking around Tyseley all afternoon, trying to make sense of things. How quickly it had all changed, once the fear had taken hold. I wasn't immune either. How easy it was to blame. How hard it was to know. In some way I couldn't understand, the police were being used. Not to find the truth, but to cover it up. There was a time, I thought, before I was caught up in this. There must be a part of me that can stand outside it. The light was draining away through the cracks in the world. By the time I reached the alley at the back of the allotments, a red-tinged moon was staring through the ragged trees.

I was so far up my own arse by then that the first time I saw the child, I thought he was one of my own memories. The light was fading anyway; his face was indistinct. He was reaching through the chain-link fence from the railway side. I remember his fingers were unusually thin and pale; they looked too long for his hands. He glanced at me without making eye contact. His eyes were large and very dark, but his skin was so white it seemed translucent. His brand-new ski jacket made him look bulkier than he probably was. Something about his posture suggested need. I wondered what he was looking for.

A flicker in the half-light distracted me. Another child, ducking behind the derelict shacks. Then a third, somewhere beyond the fence. I realised I was surrounded. But I felt more tired than scared. There was a smell in the air like ash and burnt plastic; probably there'd been a bonfire nearby on the fifth. The evening light felt dry and brittle, like old cellophane. There was no colour anywhere in this world. I could see a double exposure of my own hands as I moved from side to side, trying to catch one of the paper-faced children. The way they jittered and grabbed and hid reminded me of silent films. I wondered how far they'd go to become what they appeared to be.

It was getting too dark to see anything much. I stumbled to the end of the line of shacks, where three old brick garages backed onto an alley. I'd once stood here and watched an Asian kid getting beaten up by skinheads. There was a smell of mould and cat piss. No one was around. I glimpsed two of the film children in a garage doorway, pretending to be a courting couple. I lunged at them, but caught only a rusty metal screen. One of them touched my wrist with soft fingers. It took me a few seconds to realise that he'd taken my watch. My mind kept asking me what was wrong with the garages. I looked around the alley in the unreal glow of city lights reflected off the clouds. Three garages. When I'd been here as a child, there'd only been two.

I hardly said a word at home that evening. Near midnight, I came back with a torch and a spade. The children were gone. The third garage had been clumsily knocked together with bricks of different sizes, mortar slapped on to cover the gaps. It was a *faux* building, made from stolen materials. I prised the metal door loose and stepped inside. The ground was soft under my feet.

Between the uneven walls, every kind of stuff was heaped up: clothes, food, cushions, magazines, all of it beginning to moulder. There was a pane of glass attached to the inside of the brick wall. Beetles stirred in the waning light of my torch. I saw bags of pet food that had been torn open by rats, flesh gleaming from the damp cases of porn videos, soft pizzas rotting in an open freezer that couldn't be plugged in here. My foot slipped on dead leaves, and I put my weight on the spade.

Have you ever dug into a cat litter tray and realised what was buried under the wafer of soil? The blade sank inches into the ground, then lifted a sticky wedge that smelled like a museum of disease. I pushed my left hand against my mouth and bit down. My torch fell and stuck, its light reflecting from pale spots in the exposed slime. Metal glittered. A face swam into view on a scrap of paper, then vanished.

I dug for a while. The ground was full of cash: crumpled fivers and tenners, verdigris-covered coins, all slippery from the layer of nearly liquid excrement they'd been buried in. I gagged and retched any number of times, but I hadn't eaten since lunchtime. Daylight seemed a long time ago. Eventually I got down far enough to reach a number of yellowish, brittle sticks wrapped in dark cloth. There was nothing left of his flesh. I did as much damage as I could with the spade, then covered up the fragments with the strange earth I'd removed from them. The contents of the garage had drained my torch; I doubted it would ever work again. I left it there with the other rubbish.

The moon's small, bloodshot face peered at me as I stood in the allotments, wiping my shoes with dead leaves. I thought about the power of damaged lives. How a corrupt politician might try to come back, feeding on money like a vampire on blood. How he could attract followers desperate for an illusion of normality. No wonder the police couldn't make a difference.

Money talks. But you wouldn't want to hear its accent.

As I walked home, the streets around me were deserted. The sodium light gave the pavement a faint tinge of gold. There were no thieves, no vigilantes, no children, no beggars. If anyone had got in my way, I'd have killed them. I needed someone to blame. We all do. But there was nothing except a smell of shit, and an icy chill in the air.

Joel Lane lives in Birmingham. His tales of horror and the supernatural have appeared in various anthologies and magazines, including *Darklands*, *Fantasy Tales*, *Little Deaths*, *Twists of the Tale*, *The Third Alternative*, *The Ex Files*, *White of the Moon*, *The Mammoth Book of Dracula*, *Swords against the Millennium*, *Hideous Progeny*, *The Museum of Horrors*, *The Mammoth Book of Best New Horror* and *Dark Terrors 4* and *5*. He is the author of a collection of short stories, *The Earth Wire*, a collection of poems, *The Edge of the Screen*, and a novel set in the world of post-punk rock music, *From Blue to Black*. His second novel, *The Blue Mask*, was published by Serpent's Tail in 2002. Lane has also edited *Beneath the Ground*, an anthology of subterranean horror stories from Alchemy Press, and with Steve Bishop he edited *Birmingham Noir*, an anthology of tales of crime and psychological suspense set in the West Midlands, published by Tidal Street Press. '"The Receivers" is one of an ongoing series of supernatural crime stories I've been working on for a while,' explains the author. 'They aim to combine traditional weird elements with modern social and political themes. This story was written last year, and its theme hopefully needs no explanation.'

The Death of Splatter

LISA MORTON

'*Stumpfuckers?*'

Lee Denny looks up from his laptop and has to stop himself from gaping: the woman who has stopped by his coffee shop table and is commenting on his book title isn't really beautiful, but with her dark crimson hair, lean curves and hint-of-husk voice she's certainly striking. She glances from the paperback book beside the laptop and empty coffee cup, up to Lee's face. Lee manages a smile.

'It's a horror novel.'

She picks it up, scanning the cover art which shows a pen-and-ink drawing of a leering hunchback in overalls, and Lee's name in a jagged font.

'You're reading this?'

'I wrote it.'

She cocks her head and arches one eyebrow, then reads his name out loud.

'That's me.'

Her next question surprises him. 'I'd like to read it.'

He's embarrassed to realise that he has simultaneously become hard (thankfully under the table) and has flushed, heat enveloping his face, making him stumble on his words. 'It's . . . uh . . . pretty rough stuff.'

She glances at the book one last time, then sets it down. 'Sounds good. I'll pick one up.'

He tears off a piece of slightly wadded paper napkin, pulls a pen from his laptop case and scribbles down a URL for her. 'You won't find it at your average chain bookstore, but you can buy it online direct from the publisher.'

She takes the bit of napkin and starts to turn to leave. 'Are you here a lot? At this coffee shop?'

'Almost every day,' he acknowledges.

'Good. I'll let you know what I think when I've read it.'

With that she turns and strides off. He watches her go, liking the way her boots clink authoritatively on the asphalt and cause each hip to ride up with her steps, one side to the other. She finally turns a corner and is gone without a look back.

Just then a waitress appears and asks if she can get him anything else. He actually jumps slightly, startled, and from her smirk he's sure the waitress has seen his erection. He tells the waitress he's leaving now, waits a few moments until he can walk upright again, then packs up the laptop and the paperback novel after laying a few ones on the table.

He's quite sure he won't be doing any more writing today.

When Jed Kunkel came down out of the Ozarks, he was twenty-four years old, seven feet tall, 400 pounds and hungry for pussy.

At first he hadn't liked the smell of the city – it smelled like garbage and puke and death. But then he'd gone into a supermarket, and had been surrounded by female odours. Now he'd decided to stay in the city for a while.

He got a job as a bouncer at a trendy nightclub. He knew the owners and other employees and patrons all made fun of 'the hick', but he didn't care, because the nightclub was one big fuck pen. Jed came up with that phrase one night while standing at the door, and was so pleased by it that he smiled for hours.

The nightclub also made trolling easy. Up in the hills, back home, it'd been getting harder and harder to get women. Since the mines had closed, most folks had moved away; the few females left in the area who weren't heavily guarded had long since fallen prey to Jed or some other predator.

But here in the city, at the nightclub, pickings were easy. Jed started one night with a thirty-ish, very drunken woman who'd been thrown out alone at closing. She got in his truck with a giggle and burp. He hoped she wasn't going to barf. He hated that.

He drove her to the abandoned factory. He'd found it earlier that week, in a run-down industrial area. He'd located a side entrance where he could park his truck unseen. He'd sawed through one padlock and was in; he'd set the place up with what he would need.

By the time he arrived at the factory, the woman had passed out. That was fine with him; in fact, it was better. It made it easier to carry her in, strap her down on the table, carefully cut away her clothes . . .

. . . and then saw off her left leg just above the knee. While his nose went crazy with the delicious scents.

Lee finishes out the week in a haze of anticipation mixed with a need to produce, to produce more words, more books. He finishes *Slit Thing*, the sequel to *Stumpfuckers* (although truthfully he'd had the novel sitting on the coffee shop table by his laptop for bait as much as anything else, a ploy that had apparently worked), and begins a new one.

And all the while, the girl is never far from his mind.

He goes to the coffee shop earlier every day, and stays later (to the great irritation of the wait help, but his attitude is fuck 'em). He glances up often, even though he's calculated a minimum of two weeks for her to get the book, read it and report to him. Still, he thinks she might be a fast reader, and the book, after all, is not that long a read.

She's suddenly standing at his table on day eight.

She tosses down her own copy of *Stumpfuckers*, this one with a broken spine (so, Lee thinks, she's one of *those* readers). He waits for her to tell him that it was disgusting, that it was sick, that *he's* sick.

Instead she tells him it was amusing.

'Is that a compliment?' he asks.

She shrugs. 'Good in parts, but too unrealistic.'

'Unrealistic?'

She picks up the book again and thumbs through it. 'Like here, on page thirty-six – you have a man being stabbed through the chest by a dildo. Not possible.'

'Are you sure?' he asks with a slight smile, trying to sound provocative, flirting.

Her answer, without hesitation: 'Yes.'

He feels as if he's somehow losing an important game. He has no idea where to go now, so he falls back on a criticism that has been levelled at him by other women he's known (usually briefly): 'Did you think it was . . . uh . . . misogynistic?'

She's smiling now. 'Of course. So what?'

He's at a loss again, when she adds, 'I bought your other books, too. I've already read most of the sci-fi one . . .'

'*Wire Mistress*?'

'Right.'

A long pause, which he finally breaks. 'Well?'

'*Stumpfuckers* is better. I don't really like science fiction. And what's more is . . . I don't think you do, either.'

'Well, uhhh . . .'

She glances around his table, where a half-empty coffee cup is the only sign of an order once placed. 'Do you ever stop writing long enough to eat?'

'I really just like the coffee here—'

She cuts him off: 'I didn't mean here.'

Goddamn, he thinks, this woman is actually asking me out. 'Oh. Yes, I do that at least once a day, usually at night.'

She leans down over him, so close he can smell the musk of her shampoo. She types an address and a name onto the end of his document. 'Meet me there at eight.'

He glances at the address, and has no idea where it is, but nods vigorously. 'Okay. Yeah.'

She starts to turn to go, then catches herself. 'Oh, by the way – you misspelled "Arkansas".' Then she smirks and exits sidewalk right.

He watches her for a while, then looks down at the name she's typed. Claudia.

His head had never quite healed from the surgery to remove the prohibchip. Of course the operation had been done by a blarket doc, most of whom had probably never even heard of medical school; it had left him with a gaping scar above the right temple, and a large scabby patch where hair would probably never grow again.

Of course the woman he'd had tonight hadn't minded – especially not after he'd slapped the neuropatch on the back of her neck. It had worked just as the doc had promised, and the girl had dumbly followed him to the abandoned tech plant he'd already chosen. Once he'd had her wired to the old steel work bench, he'd removed the neuropatch so she was again aware. It made him even harder to watch her struggle, to hear her shrieks and gasps.

After the first rape, he got hungry, so he put the neuropatch back on her. He reckoned he could have just finished killing her, but he thought he might come back for more later; after all, a man got hungry for more than just food. In fact, maybe he'd start a collection, a whole room full of his fleshtoys. In the meantime, while he was gone it wouldn't do to have anyone who happened to be wandering through this derelict part of the cityburb overhear screaming. So he patched her again, just to be safe. He went through her pockets and found her creddisk, and decided to eat at something better than his usual noodle takeout.

Tonight his wire mistress would provide for him, in so many ways.

Lee returns to his basement, thinking about Claudia, thinking about himself. Thinking about the last date he had, two years ago, with a comic book store clerk. Her name was Vicky; they'd dated twice, then she'd been busy and had stopped taking his calls. They'd never even kissed; worst of all, he couldn't go to that store again.

Lee thinks about the first time he'd been laid, when a college roommate had set him up with the stripper at a party. Fifty bucks had got him fifteen minutes in a hotel linen closet. The stripper had been in her forties, with skin like a worn leather bookbinding and hair like dead leaves; at the time he hadn't minded – he'd finished the instant he slid into her – but later the thought of her made him nauseous.

Now there is Claudia, the first woman who has shown interest in him in a very long time. She doesn't seem to mind that he's slightly paunchy, with rumpled clothes, fraying at the cuffs; that his hair is, at twenty-eight, prematurely receding. She likes him for his work. She's intrigued by him. That makes her sexy.

Lee begins to imagine their relationship going further, and sees potential problems: he doesn't work, and usually has very little extra money. He lives in a friend's basement; although his friend wouldn't mind seeing Lee with a woman (in fact, he'd probably kneel and shout for joy), there's the matter of Lee's pride. He doesn't even have a car.

But maybe Claudia won't care about these things. Maybe she'll be so taken by him that she'll overlook these small shortcomings. Maybe she'll become his muse, exciting both his body and his mind. Maybe she'll think he's great in bed.

He changes into his best shirt and the heavy boots he bought in a garage sale; they're a size too big and usually give him blisters, but he likes the way they look: rugged; slightly menacing.

He takes the bus to the address she's given him. It's not a great section of town; in fact, it looks like an urban war zone. He feels reluctance when the bus pulls away, stranding him in front of a grocery store with signs in a language he doesn't even recognise and rusted bars across the windows. He checks the directions he's printed out from the online map, and sees it's only three blocks or so . . . three blocks down a street where most of the streetlamps have been shot out, and the graffiti is in layers. Half a block ahead of him are two six-foot-tall teenagers with net shirts and tattoos, watching him in amusement. He tries to keep his head down as he passes them, and drops his feet heavily with each step, emphasising the sheer heft of his boots. They ignore him, but he can feel their eyes on his back and he finds himself walking faster.

At last he's at the address, which turns out to be a hole-in-the-wall Thai café. It can't have more than half a dozen tables inside, lit by bare bulbs overhead. In the back is a dusty altar, with food and drink set inside a red alcove. There's a dead fly in one window.

Claudia's inside, waiting for him.

He enters and takes a seat, smiling.

'You're late.'

He smiles a sheepish apology, and tries not to stare. Stare at her leather vest, small and formfitting, with nothing on beneath it.

A middle-aged Asian man in a stained apron mutely hands him a menu. He takes it and glances down the single page that looks as if it was done on a typewriter sometime in the 1970s. He snickers at the name 'Prik King'. Claudia tells him it's the best thing here, if he doesn't mind spicy. He assures her he doesn't, even though he knows that he'll pay for that boast later in the night.

The meal is uneventful, with very little smalltalk exchanged. The food is adequate; Lee's not that familiar with Thai, and thinks it's all too spicy. He's pleased that she offers to pay for herself, since it saves either his wallet or his pathetic explanations. Afterwards, they exit into the asphalt desolation. Lee asks her how she found this place, and she tells him she used to come to this neighbourhood to buy crystal.

'For a friend,' she adds.

They reach her car, an older-model sedan, free of bumper stickers or other unnecessary decorations. She tells him she has to get up early in the morning, so she'll say good night here. He's disappointed, until she hands him a piece of paper with her phone number written on it.

'Call me,' she says, 'and next time I promise it won't be so early.'

He briefly considers asking her for a ride, then decides to maintain *that* illusion for a while longer. He tells her he'll call. He means it, too.

She pulls out, leaving him to find his own way back to the bus stop, his feelings a clash of optimism and anxiety. She expected more, he's sure of it. He should have offered to buy her dinner. He should have tried to get her to talk more. About herself. About his work. He should have tried to kiss her goodnight.

But he hoped she just thought he was mysterious, maybe wary of his own passions. After all, he was the author who *Darkrealm* magazine had once called 'the splatterest and punkest of the splatterpunks'. He'd have to make sure she saw that quote.

Suddenly the neighbourhood didn't scare him any more.

Geek loved the buzz he got off the hunt. In many ways, he preferred the hunt to the actual kill. The final spurt was good, oh yeah, but it didn't last as long as this. He didn't think anything in the world could feel as good as watching the girl from across a street, following her, knowing that she was already his.

In fact, he felt like God.

*

He calls her the next day, in the early evening. He asks what'd be a good night for her, and is pleased when she says tonight – but this time he has to choose what they'll do, and it needs to be good.

He has an idea as soon as he hangs up. His friend is home now, upstairs, and Lee asks to borrow his car. His friend smiles and hands him the keys when Lee tells him he has a date.

He logs onto the web and heads for the local newspaper site, where he soon finds the article he wants. He makes a few notes, straightens up and heads for her place.

She lives in a small duplex in an ordinary, slightly lower-middle-class area. Not nearly as bad as where they ate last night, a fact he's thankful for, especially since the car is not his.

She's waiting outside and as she climbs in she asks where they're going.

'No, no, that'd spoil it.'

She smiles, apparently satisfied with this answer.

He drives to a large shopping mall across town. It's late for the stores by now, so the parking lot is largely empty.

'A mall?' she asks dubiously.

'Not the mall. We'll start in the parking lot, though.'

He drives to the edge of the lot. A few feet away is a small road encircling the mall; beyond that is undeveloped woodland, dark and thick. He parks, grabs a flashlight and gets out; Claudia follows.

He allows a dramatic pause.

'So?' she says.

'Remember that story from about three weeks back? The girl's body they found in those woods?'

Claudia nods.

Lee goes on: 'They found her car right about here. They figure she was forced into the woods, where her assailant raped and then killed her. He really tore her up.'

Claudia looks around. 'How do you know this is where the car was?'

'I have a friend on the force.'

Of course he doesn't; but he figures she'll buy into it. Most people seem to think every writer these days has 'a friend on the force'.

He shines the flashlight towards the woods. 'Want to see where it happened?'

'What do you think?' she says, grinning.

He leads them across the small frontage road and finds what looks like a small, seldom-used trail in the brush. They follow it silently until it opens into a small clearing, surrounded by two fallen and half-rotted logs. It's fall, and the ground is thick with mulchy leaves, damp and springy underfoot. He circles the light around the open space.

'This is where it happened. Where he brought her, raped her and killed her. Right here.'

Claudia follows the light beam forward, examining the area intently, as though hoping to find a missed clue, a drop of blood. When she turns to him, her eyes glitter, caught in the ray of light.

'Did you do it?'

Lee's jaw drops for a second. It didn't occur to him that she might get *that* idea. 'So, what, you think that just because of what I write . . .?'

'Why else would you bring me here?'

'Ahh,' he stumbles for a beat, then, 'I guess we're thinking alike, because I thought if you liked my books you might like something like this.'

It works; she laughs and nods.

'Okay, so you didn't do it.' She almost sounds disappointed, then looks at the brush again. 'So how do you think it happened?'

He considers for a moment, then steps backwards, the way they've just come. He mimics pushing someone before him. 'They figure he had a gun or knife. He made her walk ahead of him, until they came about here. Then he—'

'No,' she cuts him off. 'No more tell – it's time for show. I mean, you don't have to actually kill me.'

Lee utters one nervous bark before he catches himself. 'You want me to . . . ah . . . hurt you.'

'C'mon, that doesn't sound like the Lee Denny who wrote *Slit Thing*.'

'Oh, you've read that one too?'

'I've read all of them.'

Lee begins to think she's lying. She could be trying to trap him. Hell, she could even be with the police. Christ, he thinks to himself, am I suspect?

She picks up a long, mouldering branch, so rotted it can barely support its own weight. 'Do you think she struggled? I do.'

She suddenly swings the branch.

Lee reacts by reflex, turning, drawing back, and the branch impacts on his left shoulder. It disintegrates instantly into a pulpy mess, but the pain is still enough to make both his fear and anger flare.

'Maybe she left her mark on him—'

She raises her hand, with its long plum-coloured and filed nails. The hand comes down, and this time Lee does more than flinch – he catches the hand, stopping her, pushing her back roughly. She stumbles on the mulch underfoot, but doesn't fall.

'What would have happened if she'd screamed, do you think?'

She inhales deeply, opens her mouth – and Lee panics. He scrabbles at her, clumsily, and they both go down, tangled in the thorns and mulch. Lee is as dazed as she is; it takes him a moment to realise that he's on top of her, and that she's laughing at him.

'Gee, Lee,' she begins sarcastically, 'do you think the real rapist was a stumbling idiot too?'

'Fuck—' Lee tries to push away from her.

'You can't leave now, Lee. I haven't even screamed yet.'

This time he clamps his hand over her mouth first. She twists her head and bites him, leaving three red crescents in his fingers. He cries out in pain and shock, then reacts without thinking, striking out. The slap leaves her breathless and dazed.

When she can talk again, she looks at him and tells him, 'I'm still not afraid of you yet.'

Lee understands the game now, and he begins to claw at her. He tears the buttons on her blouse, and nearly apologises.

She stays silent, but goads him on in other ways. Once she bites his ear, hard and painful; once her hand comes up and tears at his hair.

The sex is awkward but quick. When it's over, Claudia picks herself up and silently walks back to his borrowed car. He drives her home; she goes back into her duplex without ever looking at him.

When Lee gets home, he's surprised to see he's got her blood on his shirt. Not a great deal of blood, just a splotch the size of a quarter – but her blood, nonetheless. From when he hit her. When he raped her.

Lee struggles to think the situation through, to understand if this was entrapment or manipulation. But those questions bother him less than the dull, sick sense of disgust which has engulfed him. Disgust so strong it's a physical sensation knotting in his stomach, disgust at both her and himself.

Anxiety, dread, disgust, whenever he thinks about it. And it's all he can think about.

The slit thing had been fun to kill.

Jed had knocked it half out with one punch, then taken it into the woods, down by the river. There he'd torn its clothes off, feeling his long cock harden with each rip. The slit thing had regained consciousness while he was thrusting into it. The look on its face had been priceless; Jed had laughed when he'd seen it. Then he'd had to knock out three teeth when it screamed.

He thought he'd probably near killed it by blowing his wad, but just to be sure, after he'd finished he'd smashed its brains out with a big river rock. Then he'd gone home to a big meal of home-cooked ham and eggs. He'd eaten an entire carton of eggs, washed down with a six-pack of long-necks.

He lay back on his single coy, and stared at the wood ceiling, feeling warm and sated and pleased with himself. Yessiree, he thought, the world seems mighty fine tonight.

Lee doesn't leave the basement for the next two days. He doesn't write, he doesn't drink or listen to music; the television's on, but he doesn't watch it. The sound is turned down so low that it becomes a light babble, a string of noise to keep the silence from completely deafening him.

Instead, he tries to decide what to do. At first he thinks about calling her, but as one day passes, and he's two days past that night, and there are no police at his door, he realises she's not out to see him land in jail. Plus he's terrified to call her. What if she tells him she's been badly hurt, maybe even wants him to pay for her medical bills? What if she tells him she has AIDS? Worst of all, what if she tells him she's had better?

At some point he realises it's now Saturday morning and he's scheduled for a signing at a local science fiction bookstore today. In a few hours he's supposed to smile and chat up fans and sign copies of *Wire Mistress* and play the part of hip envelope-pusher. Instead, he's so unnerved at the idea that she might show that he almost calls and cancels.

A half-hour before the scheduled time he decides to go; maybe it'll be good for him to get out, to see other people, to see readers who will remind him of his passion and vocation.

He shaves, drags a comb through his hair (and winces when he passes over a small spot where a few strands have been yanked out), throws on a leather jacket and walks out the door. He's fifteen minutes late to the store, but they expect that from authors, especially the ones with reputations to maintain.

He scans the line of thirty or so, queasy with anticipation, but she's not there. Relieved, he takes his place at the folding table behind stacks of his books and gets out his favourite signing pen, the one with a little skull face sculpted onto the top.

The third or fourth in line passes Lee a rolled copy of *Stumpfuckers* and asks the dreaded question: 'Where do you get your ideas?'

For the first time, Lee almost tells the truth: that he's really not very good at characters or plots, but as long as he pushes the gore and perversion nobody will notice. Instead, he falls back on the rote answer he uses for interviews, about how he's just reflecting mankind's every-increasing capacity for horror. The fan looks impressed and clutches his signed paperback as if it were a holy relic.

Normally Lee loves signings; in fact, the sense of appreciation, even of adulation, is probably the reason he writes. He knows these people think of him as an iconoclast, an artist, a pathfinder through the fields of feel-good meta-fiction.

But today he notices, for the first time, things about them that annoy him. For one thing they're all young, much younger than him, several even sporting unresolved acne conditions. For another thing, they're all dressed like him, a uniform of black leather and denim. But worst is the way their eyes gleam when they talk about his books. Their voices drop, becoming slightly huskier; some of them sweat or shake. They'd probably like to think the look is feral, but now it just looks somehow needy, like a penniless junkie.

At some point he knows he hates them.

Lee signs the books dutifully, but leaves the instant the allotted time is complete. He knows the store personnel will think him rude, or snobbish, but he doesn't care. He has to escape from these fans, these outsized children who devour impossible paperbound bloodshed in order to call themselves rebels.

He has to escape – but has nowhere to go.

Our interview with Lee Denny was scheduled to last for just one hour during the recent Splatter2001 convention, but actually took three hours because the ever-generous Mr Denny continued to sign books for fans during our poolside chat. Denny has only been writing professionally for four years, but during that time has produced an amazing six novels and a dozen short stories. Fans have bags of books, and invariably mention their favourite Lee Denny-penned scene of death or mutilation (I hear the murder-by-corkscrew scene from Blood Kin *mentioned several times). Lee's relationship with his fans seems a natural place, then, to begin our conversation.*

Q: You seem to have a real connection with your readers.

A: I'm giving them something they don't get anywhere else: release for their rage. Rage is something our society creates, but refuses to acknowledge; if we experience it, we think we must be freaks, there's something wrong with us. Twenty years ago punk music provided an outlet; now it's extremist fiction.

Q: Then do you think of yourself as a horror writer? Or as a writer of 'extremist' fiction?

A: I don't think of myself as anything but a writer. I write what I feel. I'm lucky that a lot of other people feel the same way; I'm also lucky that they can't write!

Q: Aren't there a lot of imitations of your style appearing online now?

A: So I've heard, but I haven't read any of it.

Q: You haven't? Don't you read other horror books?

A: I'm usually too busy writing!

Q: Okay, let's try a tough one: How would you react if one of your books was found in the possessions of a mass murderer?

A: Oh puh-LEASE! We're not going to get into this old question again, are we? Okay, if we are, I'll just say this: if somebody did something really good after reading one of my books, I wouldn't get any credit, so why should I get blame if somebody does something bad? It's ridiculous.

Q: So you wouldn't be just a little flattered?

A: Hey, if it sells a few more books . . . seriously, if I said I was flattered, then that would mean I'm agreeing that my books somehow inspired this nut to kill.

Q: Would you ever consider killing someone in real life?

A: Well, there was this one editor . . . (evil laughter, then) I have considered it – but haven't we all?

He calls her the next day.

He's surprised when she answers on the second ring, even more so when she tells him she wondered what happened to him.

If she wondered, he asks, then why didn't she call him?

'Because,' she replies, 'I didn't have your number.'

The wave of simultaneous relief and disbelief and frustration that passes through Lee ends with him dropping to his couch, his knees to weak to support his weight any longer. 'So you're . . . you know, okay?'

'Christ, Denny, if you'd been any gentler I would've been dressed in diapers. You know, you're not very much like your books.'

He pushes his fingers into his lank hair, pulling. 'They're fiction, Claudia.'

'Oh, now they're just fiction? What happened to the guy who told an interviewer he'd considered killing someone?'

'You've read that too.'

'Yes.'

'I don't understand. Why would you want me to be like Jed, or the Geek, or—'

She cuts him off. 'I don't want you to be like them, Lee. For one thing, you're too smart, and you're not big enough. And I don't think you're from some backwoods place like the Ozarks.'

'I was born in Chicago.'

'Right. I figured.'

A long pause, followed by his question: 'So what is it you want from me?'

'Maybe I'm just trying to figure you out.'

Fair enough, thinks Lee. I'm not exactly Joe Normal.

'Let's go out again.'

Some part of Lee's mind screams *No!*, she can't be trusted, she'll get too close, she's maybe even dangerous. But the thought also excites the reptile brain, and before he can stop it he hears himself anwering, 'Fine.'

She tells him she's busy for the next two nights, but Thursday should work. This time she'll pick him up, about 8 pm. He tells her to pick him up in front the coffee shop, and she laughs at his caution, but agrees.

He hangs up, nervous but excited. He thinks about the conversation, and reassures himself about the upcoming date: *This time I'll control it.*

Then he puts up his feet and jerks off.

Marty's collection is growing – he's got eight of them now, all neatly laid out and trussed up in the second-storey bedrooms. 'Course two of 'em are about done for, so he figures he's really closer to six, but that's not so bad, either.

He thinks about fucking one of 'em, but he's nearly dried up, he's already done so much of that. He wanders into the kitchen, thinking maybe he'll fix himself something to eat when he opens the utility drawer and his eyes happen to fall on Pappy's corkscrew, that big ol' spiral thing he used to open his cheap bottles of red wine with.

Marty gets an idea, and he's so excited about it that he forgets all about food. He takes the corkscrew and rushes up the stairs. He's heard about lobotomies, how they calm down the loudest patients in the state loony-bins, and he's getting mighty tired of having to constantly re-tie that one in the back bedroom, the one with the short brown hair and the small ass.

Sure enough, when he comes into the room she's rolling around, trying to get the ropes loose again. He lays the corkscrew down where she can't see it, then he ties her tighter, enjoying her little whimpers. Then he gets a board and a roll of duct tape; as her terrified eyes roll in her head, he slides the board under her head and duct-tapes her head to it, giving her almost no leeway. Then he holds up the corkscrew triumphantly, and feels positively God-like at the look of stark, over-the-edge-of-sanity horror on her pretty face. He doesn't really know anything about lobotomies, so he just puts the point between her eyes and starts turning.

At first it's hard to get the point in (he remembers Pappy always struggled a little with this part too), then the corkscrew bites down (into the skull, he figures), and the turning becomes easier. Soon she stops struggling. He's surprised at how little blood there is – until he removes the corkscrew. Then it gushes forth, a bubbling spring of red.

And the girl is dead.

He's disappointed, mainly because of the work of burying her now ... but then he remembers he's still got seven more.

And a world of billions outside the house.

When she picks him up, she compliments him for being on time.

'So,' he asks as they speed away from the coffee shop in her car, 'dinner and a movie this time?'

'Oh, I've got something much better in mind. Just wait.'

She turns up the radio, blaring a thrash metal song by a band he doesn't know, and he wonders for the first time how much younger she is. When the song ends, they're entering the downtown area, a bewildering array of one-way streets and towers that block the sky.

'So what is the plan for tonight?'

'It's a surprise.'

He nods, and feels that gnawing uneasiness inside again. He realises he has no chance of controlling this situation – or, probably, of controlling any situation with her. In fact, the truth is: he fears her.

They emerge on the other side of downtown into a desolate industrial district. Even the streetpeople don't cluster here, in these blocks of rusting corrugated metal buildings with broken windows and cracked-pavement yards.

His stomach twists, the unconscious association taking another instant to materialise in his mind: oh Christ. This place looks like something out of my books.

'Claudia, where are we going?'

'I told you, it's a surprise. Something I've been working on the last few days.'

She pulls the car up before a chain-link fence and leaves the engine running while she runs out to take the broken padlock from the chain holding the gate. She swings the gate wide, then returns to the car. She drives down a short way, past one outbuilding to a large, battered warehouse.

There's light coming from one of the dust-laden windows.

He almost decides to tell her he's not leaving the car, or that he's walking out of here. He truthfully is not sure how far it is to a bus stop, or a phone, but at this point a hundred miles through this constructed desert seems preferable to what he's beginning to fear is in that building.

Then she's opening his door, excitedly urging him out of the car.

'Claudia . . .'

'Come on, Lee. I've worked really hard to make this special for you.'

She seems sincere, he thinks. Maybe I'm wrong.

So he allows her to pull him from the car, to take his hand and lead him to an ancient metal door, creaking slightly on rusty hinges. She uses a flashlight to find their way, first through a long-abandoned office, filled with splintered desks and the remains of a 1973 calendar still fluttering on a wall, then through some sort of medical station, with large signs pointing out the location of the eye wash, which looks like a metal drinking fountain with the spout pointed straight up. There's a strong chemical stench pervading the place, even after nearly thirty years of disuse. Lee starts to wonder why it hasn't been torn down, and then realises there's simply no reason to build anything better here.

Then they walk through a last doorway and out onto the main floor of this place, and Claudia turns off the flashlight because there are two propane lanterns spilling light onto a work bench a few feet away.

A work bench where a woman is tied down.

At first he thinks she's dead; she's not moving, and she's so silent that Lee can hear the tiny hiss of the lantern flames. Then, as if reading his thoughts, Claudia dances forward and steps behind the bench.

'She's not dead, Lee, if that's what you're thinking.'

Lee's feet won't carry him closer. 'What is this, Claudia?' he asks, knowing how stupid he sounds.

'You know what it is.' She picks something up from a table behind her, and Lee sees it's covered with small objects: tools, saws, knives. And books.

It's a book she's picked up. She flips it open to a page she obviously knows well.

The book is *Stumpfuckers*.

She begins reading: '"By the time he arrived at the factory, the woman had passed out. That was fine with him; in fact, it was better. It made it easier to carry her in, strap her down on the table, carefully cut away her clothes—"'

Lee cuts her off. 'You don't have to read any more.'

Claudia sets down the book and holds up instead a small knife. 'You can use this. I've got scissors, too, just in case.'

'And then I'm supposed to saw off her leg, I suppose.'

Claudia waves the knife and smiles. 'Not with this, of course.'

Lee finds his legs now, and he walks forward to look from the table to the unconscious woman. 'How did you get her here?'

'Oh c'mon, don't you remember, in *Slit Thing* he uses that tranquilliser on the woman? Your research was good – it worked just like you said it would.'

Lee thinks he might vomit, but he works to hold it back. He thinks absurdly of another line he wrote in *Slit Thing*, a line one victim repeats over and over: *This can't be happening.*

He looks at the proposed victim. She's young, probably about Claudia's age, dressed simply in a blouse and skirt she might have worn to work that day, before she stopped by the bar on her way home, before she let the friendly woman with crimson hair buy her a drink . . .

'Okay, Claudia. This was fun. Now cut her loose and let's go.'

Claudia barks a short, disdainful laugh. 'Cut her loose? I can't cut her loose, Lee. She's seen me.'

Oh God.

'This is not going to happen.'

Claudia looks at him for a moment, then, frustrated, says, 'I don't get you. You write this stuff all the time, but when somebody gives you a chance to experience for real, you shy away. This could take your writing to the next level.'

'I write fiction, Claudia. I don't need to live it to write about.'

'In other words, what you write is all fake. Isn't it, Lee? It's all completely phony, isn't that what you're telling me?'

Before he can answer, the woman on the table moans and rolls her head slightly.

Lee's horror escalates to panic. 'If we cut her loose and drop her off where you found her, she might not even remember you—'

The woman opens her eyes.

'Too late, Lee – she's seen you too, now.'

The woman struggles to focus – and then she begins to scream.

In all the screams he's described in all of his novels, Lee Denny has never imagined anything like this. The scream is impossibly loud, ragged on the edges, as if torn from some part of this woman. Lee wants more than anything to make that sound stop. He bends over the woman, ridiculous in his attempt to calm her. 'It's okay, you'll get out of this—'

He pulls at her wrists and discovers Claudia has bound her with duct tape, yards of the stuff. He looks around and sees the knives on the table behind him. He reaches for one, but the woman screams even louder when he turns back to her. 'No, it's okay, I'm just going to cut you loose—'

And then Claudia is behind the woman, with the small knife held to the woman's jugular. She stops screaming, afraid to move even the smallest part of her throat.

'You see? I know more about how all this stuff works than you do, Lee. You don't really understand people. In fact, I think I could be a much better writer than you. You're not willing to take that final step, are you?'

Lee backs away, his hands shaking so that the knife he held drops to the ground, the small clink sounding like a cannon roar in the echoing stillness of the cavernous space.

'Oh Jesus, Lee, are you really crying?'

He is. He didn't even know until she told him.

'What a loser. No wonder your books suck.'

She bends over the woman with a fresh determination. And Lee runs.

He runs, regardless of door frames he bashes into, of jagged metal that reaches out to tear his clothing, trying to shut out the screams behind him.

He makes it out of the warehouse and down the driveway, out of the fence and down the dark street. He runs, hoping he's heading towards something like a phone or a taxi or even another sign of human habitation. He runs until his out-of-shape body betrays him and he has to double over, gasping for breath. Then he does vomit. When it's done, he falls back for a moment, depleted.

He begins to think now: should he call the police?

And what they'll find: a madwoman, a bloodied victim – and every-where, his books. His fingerprints on a knife. Her testimony that it was his idea, that he was a partner until he chickened out.

He forces himself to move again. After another block he comes to the end of the industrial section and sees what he needs: a bar. The Tender Trap.

He heads for the bar and goes in. It's a dive, regulars with missing teeth and callused hands lined up on the dozen stools, a few more clustered around the tables and the fifteen-year-old pinball game. Lee makes sure his order is memorable – two shots of their best tequila. He spills one on the foul-smelling senior next to him and barely evades a fist fight. He asks what time it is.

After an hour in the bar – all he can stand, and then some – he leaves. On the way out he trips and knocks over a chair, drawing more curses and hoots.

He's sure they'll remember him now. He's got an alibi.

He finds a phone outside and calls his friend. Luckily he's home, and Lee tells him roughly where he thinks he is. His friend manages to find it after forty minutes; Lee tells him only that he got stood up by a date. His friend laughs and sympathises.

Lee doesn't sleep that night; instead, he finds an internet radio channel that monitors police broadcasts. He listens until 2 pm the next day, but there's no mention of a murder in the industrial district. He realises it could be a very long time before the body is found.

Maybe he'll sleep in the meantime . . . but he doubts it.

Lenny was haunted by the ghosts of his own regrets.

At twenty-nine, he thought he was too young to feel this old. The burden he carried felt like a thousand years of life, not the quarter-decade he'd been conscious. It didn't show to the outside world – they saw only a sandy-haired, slightly introverted young man, who spent most of his days painting – but inside Lenny could feel his own spine cracking from the weight. He couldn't imagine going on another fifty or sixty years. He tried to understand how he had come to this, and his mind always came back to one thing:

It had started with her.

Lee's first novel of 'non-extreme fiction' isn't going well.

He started it just yesterday, something to take his mind off that night, now two weeks ago, but his heart's really not in it.

He's read the newspaper every day since, but he's never seen a report on a murder in that area. He guesses it could be weeks, even months before the body is found.

After another frustrating bout with the new book, he decides to check his e-mail. There's an unusually large message from his publisher. Sometimes the publisher passes fan letters on to him; sometimes fans even send him photos or artwork. This e-mail has a file attachment, a graphic; the publisher's brief note says only that this was sent to him, with a note asking that it please be forwarded to Lee Denny. The file attachment reads 'sceneofthecrime.jpg'.

Lee opens the photo.

It shows Claudia, in the warehouse, laughing in the bluewhite glare of a camera flash. And sitting beside her, an arm around her, laughing, is the 'victim'.

Lee stares at the photo on his screen for a moment, then promptly closes and erases the file. He drops a note back to his publisher, asking him to please not forward any more mail to him. Then he takes the last two weeks of the newspaper into the bathroom, places them carefully in the tub and sets fire to them. Inspired by the last few glowing embers, he repeats the action with every copy he owns of every one of his books. He deletes the files from his computer, including the new novel.

Then he grabs a bottle of beer, turns on the television, settles back into the couch and tries desperately not to think about the next fifty or sixty years.

Lisa Morton lives in North Hollywood, California. Her scriptwriting work includes *Meet the Hollowheads* (aka *Life on the Edge*), the Disney Channel's *Adventures in Dinosaur City* (aka *Dinosaurs*), the TV movie *Tornado Watch*, and sixty-five episodes of the cartoon Disney series *Toontown Kids*. For the stage she has adapted and directed Philip K. Dick's *Radio Free Albemuth* and Theodore Sturgeon's *The Graveyard Reader*, and she has also written and directed her own one-act plays. Her short stories have appeared in *Dark Terrors*, *The Museum of Horrors*, *Dead But Dreaming*, *Horrors! 365 Scary Stories*, *Dark Voices 6*, *The Mammoth Book of Frankenstein* and *After Hours*, while an illustrated chapbook entitled *The Free Way* was published by fool's press. More recently, her first non-fiction book, *The Cinema of Tsui Hark*, was published by McFarland & Company, and she is currently working on *The Halloween Encyclopedia*. When asked about the preceding story, Morton replied: 'I think I'd better just keep my mouth shut on this one!'

A Long Walk, for the Last Time

MICHAEL MARSHALL SMITH

As it turned out, the morning was bright and sunny. When she passed the coat she'd put ready in the hallway the night before, May smiled. She wouldn't be needing *that*.

As she waited for the kettle to boil she stood by the kitchen window, looking out over the meadow. Tall grass rolled gently in swathes, rich in the growing light. It was going to be a beautiful day, which was good. She had a long way to walk and the sun was nice for walking in. When the kettle flicked itself off she reached over to the cupboard and rootled around until she found a teabag. After so many years of living in one place, she still hadn't really got used to her new kitchen, and seemed to discover it anew every morning.

She sat in the living room while she drank her cuppa, telling herself she was summoning up the energy to start. But really she was squaring herself mentally to the day's business, readying herself for it. She felt a little apprehensive, as if preparing to attend to something that didn't mean as much as it once had, but which nevertheless needed to be tidied away.

Her tea finished, she padded back into the kitchen, peering sus-piciously down at the floor. Her kitchen in Belden Road had been covered with cheerful lino which she'd kept spotlessly clean. The stone slabs here seemed perpetually on the verge of being dusty, no matter how often she swept them. She had to admit they were nice, though. Very traditional. She knew she'd come to like them as much as she did the rest of the cottage, and in time she'd worry less about keeping them clean. Perhaps.

After swilling her cup with cold water and setting it by the sink to dry, she packed a few things together for lunch. She put a large piece of cheese, a tomato and some bread in a bag, and as an afterthought added a green apple and a knife to cut it with. Chances were she wouldn't need any of it, of course, but would find somewhere to stop along the way. She hadn't explored the area well enough yet, though, and it was better to be safe than sorry.

In the hallway she smiled at her coat once more, this time because of the memories it stirred. Cyril had bought it for her, many years ago. They'd been on holiday by the sea, and the weather had turned so cold after lunch on the first day that they'd gone into the little town to buy some warmer clothes. She'd seen the coat in the window of one of the two tiny shops, and, after some thought, rejected it as too expensive. Then later, as she'd sat drinking tea in the empty teashop by the dark and windy quay, Cyril had run back and bought it for her.

That had been sweet of him, but what she really remembered was when she tried it on. The coat was thick and black, and as soon she had it on they both laughed with the same thought, hooting until Cyril had started to cough wildly and she had to thump him on the back with a cushion. It was a granny coat, the kind old ladies wore, the first such that she'd ever owned. They were laughing because what else was there to do on the day you first realised that you were finally getting old?

Well, there was one other thing – and they'd gone straight back to the boarding house and done it for most of the afternoon. They hadn't felt so very old, that day: but three years later Cyril was dead.

On the doorstep she pulled the door shut behind her. She didn't bother to lock it. After living in London for so long, she forgot that things were different here. She would probably still have locked it if there'd been anything inside worth stealing, but when she'd moved she'd looked at all the things she'd accumulated over the years and realised very few were important enough to bring all this way. Apart from a few sets of clothes and a couple of odds and ends, she'd dispersed everything amongst friends and relatives, which had been nice to do. Her granddaughter Jane, for instance, had always loved looking through the old photographs May kept in a wooden chest. Giving them to her meant she would always have something to remember her by.

That, and their joke, which they'd shared since Jane was small. 'Why do gypsies walk lop-sided?' May would ask, and Jane, though she knew the answer, would always pretend she didn't. 'Because they've got crystal balls,' May would cackle, and the two of them would laugh.

It was a bit of a rude joke, May supposed, but a little bit rudeness never did anyone any harm. If people didn't get a little bit rude with each other every now and then, there'd be no new people, would there?

She hesitated for a moment, looking up her path, and then set off. The road at the bottom turned gradually away across the fields, surrounded by green and waving gold as far as you could see. It was a long road, and May paced herself carefully. There was no hurry.

By late morning she judged she had travelled about three miles – not bad going for an old goat, she thought. It was so easy walking here, listening to the birds in the hedges and banks of trees. It reminded her of other holidays with Cyril, when they used to get out of the smoke and head out for the countryside somewhere, to walk together down lanes and stop at tiny pubs for lunch. It was a shame that he could not be with her now she could walk like this whenever she chose, but it didn't do to regret things like that. Cyril always said that regrets are for people with nothing to look forward to, and he was right.

About half a mile later she rounded a bend to find a little clearing by the side of the road, and saw there was a small pub back up against the trees. Always a believer in signs, May decided that it was time for lunch.

The inside of the pub was cosy, the landlord and his wife as friendly as everybody else seemed to be in these parts, but it was too nice a day to sit inside. May bought a small sherry and a slice of pie to add to the lunch she had brought and took it outside to sit at one of the wooden tables. As she contentedly munched her way through the food she thought of other pubs and other times, thought of them with a calm detachment that had nothing of loss within it. You have what you have, and that's it. There's no point in wishing otherwise. If something was good enough to miss, then you were lucky to have had it in the first place.

After a while she saw a figure walking down the road towards the pub. It was a young man, and he sat at her table to chat and eat his lunch. He was a little glum. He had moved away from his family a year before, and was just back from visiting them. Though most of them were reconciled to his having moved on, his mother was not taking it well. May recognised the feeling she had about today's business, of having to look back and remember things that seemed past, like recalling as an adult what it was like to take exams and tests, so as to be able to sympathise with a child who was only now going through that particular form of hell.

The young man cheered up a little as they talked. After all, he said, he didn't want to go back, and if it took a little time for his mother to get over his leaving, then that was the way it was. This might have sounded harsh to anyone else, but not to May. She knew well enough that nothing would have dragged her back to London now that she was here.

Before she could get too comfortable, she got to her feet and started out again, armed with a recommended spot to look for later from the young man, who was going the other way.

The afternoon was even warmer than the morning, but not too much so, and as she walked May felt her heart lift with happiness. It really was very nice here, as nice as you could want.

By four the quality of the light began to change, and afternoon began to shade towards evening. The landscape either side of the road started to change too, becoming wilder, like a moor. As she kept walking May felt heavy with anticipation, wondering how her business was going to go, and hoping it would be more conclusive than the young man's had been. It wasn't that she minded having to go through it, not at all, but she would feel happier if today could be the end of it.

She kept an eye out for the landmarks the young man had mentioned, looking for the spot he had recommended. She felt that soon it would be time.

Half an hour later she passed a gnarled old tree by the side of the road and knew that she was close. Soon she found the little path which led off the road and followed it as it wound between small bushes and out onto the moor. She stopped once and looked back, across the green, and as far as she could see everything looked the same: a limitless expanse of country under a rich blue sky. How anyone could live anywhere else she couldn't imagine. If anything, she wished she'd come here sooner.

Then the path broadened into a kind of circular grassy patch, and May knew this was the spot the man had mentioned. Not only was it the ideal place to sit, but there was no path out the other side. She lowered herself gently to the warm grass and prepared to wait. The air was slightly cooler now, almost exactly body temperature, and as she sat May felt the first hint of a breeze.

She felt calm, and relaxed, and soon another breeze ran by her, no colder than the air but brisk enough to make the grass bend. Then another breeze came, and another, and soon the grass was swaying in patterns around her, leaning this way and that in lines and shapes that changed into something else as soon as you noticed them. The wind grew stronger, and stronger, until every blade of grass seemed to be moving in a different direction and May's hair was lifted up around her face in a whirl.

Then suddenly all was still.

May had a vague sense that someone was thinking of her. It became stronger, a definite tugging. She let her mind go as quiet as possible, giving herself up to it. Though she could still feel the grass beneath her hands, her mind seemed to go elsewhere, to broaden – and when she opened her eyes the world inside her head seemed as big as the one all around her.

'I'm here,' she said. 'I'm here.'

Immediately she felt warm, and knew that the message had been received.

A moment later a voice came towards her out of the air; at first very weak, then more strongly.

'Who are you here for?' it said.

May's heart leapt. 'Jane,' she said. 'I'm here for Jane.'

She heard the voice ask if there was a Janet, and corrected it, repeating Jane's name, enunciating it clearly.

After a pause she heard the voice again. 'There is a Jane here,' it said, 'Who is speaking?'

'May,' she said strongly, 'It's May.'

The voice addressed the people she could not see. 'Does the name "May" mean anything to you?' it said, and May waited to see if she could hear the answer. She couldn't. It was too far away.

But then the voice spoke to her again. 'Your name seems to mean something,' it said. 'Jane is crying.'

May felt her heart go out to her granddaughter, and wished that she could see her, reach out and touch her. Jane had always been the one who had visited her when her other grandchildren or even children were too busy. Jane had come at the end too, when May had been in the home. Even when May's mind had been confused and dark and she hadn't been very nice to talk to, Jane had always come, and May wanted very much for her to know she remembered her too. Most of all she wanted to show her that the words she'd spoken near the end were not her own, but the random jumbles of a mind that was too old to accurately reflect what was still inside.

'Tell her,' she said, and then cleared he throat and tried again, 'tell her "crystal balls".'

'If you say so,' said the voice, and there was a pause.

Then suddenly May felt warm again, warmer than she ever had before. Her cheeks sparkled as if flushed, and eyes flew wide open, and she felt Jane's life inside her, and she knew that her business was over.

Jane had received the message. She would be able to forgive May for not saying goodbye as herself, and to let her go. She would know that it was all right to move on.

'Did you get that?' asked the medium.

'Yes,' said May, 'I got that. Thank you.'

As suddenly as it had begun, it was over. The connection was broken and May was left sitting on the grass alone.

She stood up and looked towards the path, and wasn't surprised to see that it wasn't there any more. On the other side of the clearing the bushes had cleared, and the way now led in that direction.

She walked into the growing darkness, knowing that there would be light at the end of it. She would miss her little cottage, she thought, but not for long. It had only been a temporary measure, somewhere to stay until she was ready to go.

She was ready now, and she saw in the distance that someone was waiting for her, and she walked more quickly because she wanted very much to see him again. She didn't think he'd mind that she'd left the coat behind. She wouldn't need it again.

If anything could keep her warm for ever, it would be him.

Michael Marshall Smith is a novelist and screenwriter. His debut novel, *Only Forward*, won the Philip K. Dick and August Derleth awards; *Spares* was optioned by Stephen Spielberg's DreamWorks SKG and translated in seventeen countries around the world, and *One of Us* is under option by Warner Brothers. He is a four-time winner of the British Fantasy Award. A collection of his short fiction, *What You Make It*, was published by HarperCollins in the UK; a fourth novel, *The Straw Men*, was published in 2002 (with a very nice cover quote by Stephen King). He lives in north London with his wife Paula and two cats. 'This story came out of a conversation I had quite a few years ago with someone who admitted to having some experience as a medium,' Smith recalls. 'I use the word "admitted" because normally this kind of thing is "claimed", and rather unconvincingly; in this case the woman was keen to play it down, or at least be matter-of-fact about it. This, along with an unusual feeling about her – very calm, relaxed, unassuming – made me take the idea quite seriously. She also mentioned there being some kind of school for mediums somewhere in London, an idea I was fascinated by, though I've never been able to find any information about it: perhaps you can only find the address via a message from the other side, as a kind of entry requirement . . .?'

The Two Sams

GLEN HIRSHBERG

What wakes me isn't a sound. At first, I have no idea what it is, an earthquake, maybe, a vibration in the ground, a 2 am truck shuddering along the switchback road that snakes up from the beach, past the ruins of the Baths, past the Cliff House and the automatons and coin-machines chattering in the Musée Mécanique and our apartment building until it reaches the flatter stretch of the Great Highway, which will return it to the saner neighbourhoods of San Francisco. I lie still, holding my breath without knowing why. With the moon gone, the watery light rippling over the chipping bas-relief curlicues on our wall and the scuffed, tilted hardwood floor makes the room seem insubstantial, a projected reflection from the camera obscura perched on the cliffs a quarter-mile away.

Then I feel it again, and I realise it's in the bed, not the ground. Right beside me. Instantly, I'm smiling. I can't help it. You're playing on your own, aren't you? That's what I'm thinking. Our first game. He sticks up a tiny fist, a twitching foot, a butt cheek, pressing against the soft roof and walls of his world, and I lay my palm against him, and he shoots off across the womb, curls in a far corner, waits. Sticks out a foot again.

The game terrified me at first. I kept thinking about signs in aquariums warning against tapping on glass, giving fish heart attacks. But he kept playing. And tonight, the thrum of his life is like magic fingers in the mattress, shooting straight up my spine into my shoulders, settling me, squeezing the terror out. Shifting the sheets softly, wanting Lizzie to sleep, I lean closer, and know, all at once, that this isn't what woke me.

For a split second, I'm frozen. I want to whip my arms around my head, ward them off like mosquitoes or bees, but I can't hear anything, not this time. There's just that creeping damp, the heaviness in the air, like a fogbank forming. Abruptly, I dive forward, drop my head against the hot, round dome of Lizzie's stomach. Maybe I'm wrong, I think. I could be wrong. I press my ear against her skin, hold my breath, and for one horrible moment, I hear nothing at all, a sea of silent, amniotic fluid. I'm thinking about that couple, the Super Jews from our Bradley class who started coming when they were already seven months along. They came five straight weeks, and the woman would reach out, sometimes, tug her husband's prayer-curls, and we all smiled, imagining their daughter doing that, and then they weren't there any more. The woman woke up one day and felt strange, empty; she walked around for hours that way and finally just got in her car and drove to the hospital and had her child, knowing it was dead.

But under my ear, something is moving now. I can hear it inside my wife. Faint, unconcerned, unmistakable. Beat. Beat.

'"*Get out Tom's old records . . .*"' I sing, so softly, into Lizzie's skin. It isn't the song I used to use. Before, I mean. It's a new song. We do everything new, now. '"*And he'll come dance around.*"' It occurs to me that this song might not be the best choice, either. There are lines in it that could come back to haunt me, just the way the others have, the ones I never want to hear again, never even used to notice when I sang that song. They come creeping into my ears now, as though they're playing very quietly in a neighbour's room, '"*I dreamed I held you. In my arms. When I awoke dear. I was mistaken. And so I hung my head and I cried.*"' But then, I've found, that's the first great lesson of pregnancy: it all comes back to haunt you.

I haven't thought of this song, though, since the last time, I realise. Maybe they bring it with them.

Amidst the riot of thoughts in my head, a new one spins to the surface. Was it there the very first time? Did I feel the damp then? Hear the song? Because if I did, and I'm wrong . . .

I can't remember. I remember Lizzie screaming. The bathtub, and Lizzie screaming.

Sliding slowly back, I ease away towards my edge of the bed, then sit up, holding my breath. Lizzie doesn't stir, just lies there like the gutshot creature she is, arms wrapped tight and low around her stomach, as though she could hold this one in, hold herself in, just a few days more. Her chin is tucked tight to her chest, dark hair wild on the pillow, bloated legs clamped around the giant, blue pillow between them. Tip her upright, I think, and she'd look like a little girl on a hoppity horse. Then her kindergarten students would laugh at her again, clap and laugh when they saw her, the way they used to. Before.

For the thousandth time in the past few weeks, I have to squash an urge to lift her black-framed, square glasses from around her ears. She has insisted on sleeping with them since March, since the day the life inside her became – in the words of Dr Seger, the woman Lizzie believes will save us – 'viable', and the ridge in her nose is red and deep, now, and her eyes, always strangely small, seem to have slipped back in their sockets, as though cringing away from the unaccustomed closeness of the world, its unblurred edges. 'The second I'm awake,' Lizzie tells me, savagely, the way she says everything these days, 'I want to see.'

'Sleep,' I mouth, and it comes out a prayer.

Gingerly, I put my bare feet on the cold ground and stand. Always, it takes just a moment to adjust to the room. Because of the tilt of the floor – caused by the earthquake in '89 – and the play of light over the walls and the sound of the surf and, sometimes, the seals out on Seal Rock and the litter of woodscraps and sawdust and half-built toys and menorahs and disembowelled clocks on every tabletop, walking through our apartment at night is like floating through a shipwreck.

Where are you? I think to the room, the shadows, turning in multiple directions as though my thoughts were a lighthouse beam. If they are, I need to switch them off. The last thing I want to provide, at this moment, for them, is a lure. Sweat breaks out on my back, my legs, as though I've been wrung. I don't want to breathe, don't want this infected air in my lungs, but I force myself. I'm ready. I have prepared, this time. I'll do what I must, if it's not too late, and I get the chance.

'Where are you?' I whisper aloud, and something happens in the hall, in the doorway. Not movement. Not anything I can explain. But I start over there, fast. It's much better if they're out there. 'I'm coming,' I say, and I'm out of the bedroom, pulling the door closed behind me as if that will help, and when I reach the living room, I consider snapping on the light, but don't.

On the wall over the square, dark couch – we bought it dark, we were anticipating stains – the Pinocchio clock, first one I ever built, at age fourteen, makes its steady, hollow tock. It's all nose, that clock, which seems like such a bad idea, in retrospect. What was I saying, and to whom? *The hour is a lie. The room is a lie. Time is a lie.* 'Gepetto,' Lizzie used to call me before we were married, then after we were married, for a while, back when I used to show up outside her classroom door to watch her weaving between desks, balancing hamsters and construction paper and graham crackers and half-pint milk cartons in her arms while kindergartners nipped between and around her legs like ducklings.

Gepetto. Who tried so hard to make a living boy.

Tock.

'Stop,' I snap to myself, to the leaning walls. There is less damp here. They're somewhere else.

The first tremble comes as I return to the hall. I clench my knees. my shoulders, willing myself still. As always, the worst thing about the trembling and the sweating is the confusion that causes them. I can never decide if I'm terrified or elated. Even before I realised what was happening, there was a kind of elation.

Five steps down the hall, I stop at the door to what was once our workshop, housing my building area and Lizzie's cut-and-paste table for classroom decorations. It has not been a workshop for almost four years now. For four years, it has been nothing at all. The knob is just a little wet when I slide my hand around it, the hinges silent as I push open the door.

'Okay,' I half-think, half-say, trembling, sliding into the room and shutting the door behind me. 'It's okay.' Tears leap out of my lashes as though they've been hiding there. It doesn't feel like I actually cried them. I sit down on the bare floor, breathe, stare around the walls, also bare. One week more. Two weeks, tops. Then, just maybe, the crib, fully assembled, will burst from the closet, the dog-cat carpet will unroll itself like a torah scroll over the hardwood, the mobiles Lizzie and I made together will spring from the ceiling like streamers. *Surprise!*

The tears feel cold on my face, uncomfortable, but I don't wipe them. What would be the point? I try to smile. There's a part of me, a small sad part that feels like smiling. 'Should I tell you a bedtime story?'

I could tell about the possum. We'd lost just the one, then, and more than a year had gone by, and Lizzie still had moments, seizures, almost, where she ripped her glasses off her face in the middle of dinner and hurled them across the apartment and jammed herself into the kitchen corner behind the stacked washer-dryer unit. I'd stand over her and say, 'Lizzie, no,' and try to fight what I was feeling, because I didn't like that I was feeling it. But the more often this happened, and it happened a lot, the angrier I got. Which made me feel like such a shit.

'Come on,' I'd say, extra-gentle, to compensate, but of course I didn't fool her. That's the thing about Lizzie. I knew it when I married her, even loved it in her: she recognises the worst in people. She can't help it. And she's never wrong about it.

'You don't even care,' she'd hiss, her hands snarled in her twisting brown hair as though she was going to rip it out like weeds.

'Fuck you, of course I care.'

'It doesn't mean anything to you.'

'It means what it means. It means we tried, and it didn't work, and it's awful, and the doctors say it happens all the time, and we need to try again. It's awful but we have to deal with it, we have no choice if we want—'

'It means we lost a child. It means our child died. You asshole.'

Once – one time – I handled that moment right. I looked down at my wife, my playmate since junior high, the perpetually sad person I made happy, sometimes, and who made everyone around her happy even though she was sad, and I saw her hands twist harder in her hair, and I saw her shoulders cave in towards her knees, and I just blurted it out.

'You look like a lint ball,' I told her.

Her face flew off her chest, and she glared at me. Then she threw her arms out, not smiling, not free of anything, but wanting me with her. Down I came. We were lint balls together.

Every single other time, I blew it. I stalked away. Or I started to cry. Or I fought back.

'Let's say that's true,' I'd say. 'We lost a child. I'll admit it, I can see how one could choose to see it that way. But I don't feel that. By the grace of God, it doesn't quite feel like that to me.'

'That's because it wasn't inside you.'

'That's such . . .' I'd start, then stop, because I didn't really think it was. And it wasn't what I was trying to say, anyway. 'Lizzie. God. I'm just . . . I'm trying to do this well. I'm trying to get us to the place where we can try again. Where we can have a child. One that lives. Because that's the point, isn't it? That's the ultimate goal?'

'*Honey, this one just wasn't meant to be,*' Lizzie would sneer, imitating her mom, or maybe my mom, or any one of a dozen people we knew. 'Is that what you want to say next?'

'You know it isn't.'

'How about, "*The body knows. Something just wasn't right. These things do happen for a reason.*"'

'Lizzie, stop.'

'Or, *Years from now, you'll look at your child, your living, breathing, beautiful child, and you'll realise that you wouldn't have had him or her if the first one had survived. There'd be a completely different creature there.* How about that one?'

'Lizzie, goddamnit. Just shut up. I'm saying none of those things, and you know it. I'm saying I wish this had never happened. And now that it has happened, I want it to be something that happened in the past. Because I still want to have a baby with you.'

Usually, most nights, she'd sit up then. I'd hand her her glasses and she'd fix them on her face, and her small, green-grey eyes would blink as the world rushed forward. She'd look at me, not unkindly. More than once, I'd thought she was going to touch my face, my hand.

Instead, what she said was, 'Jake. You have to understand.' Looking through her lenses at those moments was like peering through a storm window, something I would never again get open, and through it I could see the shadows of everything Lizzie carried with her and could not bury, didn't seem to want to. 'Of all the things that have happened to me. All of them. You're probably the best. And this is the worst.'

Then she'd get up, step around me and go to bed. And I'd go out to walk, past the Cliff House, past the Musée, sometimes all the way down to the ruins of the Baths, where I'd stroll along the crumbling concrete walls which once had framed the largest public bathing pool in the United States, and now framed nothing, marsh-grass and drain-water and echo. Sometimes the fog would roll over me, a long, grey ghost-tide, and I'd float off on it, in it, just another trail of living vapour combing the earth in search of a world we'd all got the idea was here somewhere. Where, I wonder, had that idea come from, and how did so many of us get it?

'But that isn't what you want to hear,' I say suddenly to the not-quite-empty workroom, the cribless floor. 'Is it?' For a second, I panic, fight down the urge to leap to my feet and race for Lizzie. If they've gone back in there, then I'm too late anyway. And if they haven't, my leaping about just might scare them in that direction. In my head, I'm casting around for something to say that will hold them while I swing my gaze back and forth, up to the ceiling and down again. I feel like a carnival barker. Hold on, there, kiddies. Step right up.

'I was going to tell you about the possum, right? One night, maybe eight months or so after you were . . .' The word curls on my tongue like a dead caterpillar. I say it anyway. 'Born.' Nothing screams in my face or flies at me, and my voice doesn't break. And I think something might have fluttered across the room from me, something other than the curtains. I have to believe it did. And the damp is still in here.

'It was pretty amazing,' I say, fast, staring at where the flutter was as though I could pin it there. 'Lizzie kicked me and woke me up. "You hear that" she asked. And of course, I did. Fast, hard scrabbling, click-click-click. From right in here. We came running and saw a tail disappear behind the dresser. There was a dresser, then, I made it myself, the drawers came out sideways and the handles formed kind of a pumpkin-face, just for fun, you know? Anyway, I got down on my hands and knees and found this huge, white possum staring right at me. I didn't even know there were possums here. This one took a single look at me and keeled over with its feet in the air. Playing dead.'

I throw myself on the ground with my feet in the air. It's like a memory, a dream, a memory of a dream, but I half-believe I feel a weight on the soles of my feet, as though something has climbed onto them. For a ride, maybe. Tears, again.

'I got a broom. Your . . . Lizzie got a trashcan. And for the next, I don't know, three hours, probably, we chased this thing around and around the room. We had the windows wide open, all it had to do was hop up and out. Instead, it just hid behind the dresser, playing dead, until I poked it with the broom, and then it would race along the baseboard or into the middle of the room and flip on its back again, as if to say, okay, now I'm really dead, and we couldn't get it to go up and out. We couldn't get it to do anything but die. Over and over and over. And . . .'

I stop, lower my legs abruptly, sit up. I don't say the rest. How, at 3:45 in the morning, Lizzie dropped the trashcan to the floor, looked at me and burst out crying. Threw her glasses at the wall and broke one of the lenses and wept while I just stood there, so tired, with this possum belly-up at my feet and the sea air flooding the room. I'd loved the laughing. I could hardly stand up for exhaustion, and I'd loved laughing with Lizzie so goddamn much.

'Lizzie,' I'd said. 'I mean, fuck. Not everything has to relate to that. Does it? Does everything we ever think or do, for the rest of our lives . . .' But of course, it does. I think I even knew that then. And that was after only one.

'Would you like to go for a walk?' I say carefully. Clearly. Because this is it. The only thing I can think of, and therefore the only chance we have. How does one get a child to listen, really? I wouldn't know. 'We'll go for a stroll, okay? Get nice and sleepy?' I still can't see anything. Most of the other times, I've caught half a glimpse, at some point, a trail of shadow. Turning, leaving the door cracked open behind me, I head for the living room. I slide my trenchcoat over my boxers and Green Apple T-shirt, slip my tennis shoes onto my bare feet. My ankles will be freezing. In the pocket of my coat, I feel the matchbook I left there, the single, tiny, silver key. It has been two months, at least, since the last time they came, or at least since they let me know it. But I have stayed ready.

As I step onto our stoop, wait a few seconds, pull the door closed, I am flooded with sensory memory – it's like being dunked – of the day

I first became aware. Over two years ago, now. Over a year after the first one. That woody, tarry taste of echinacea-tea in the back of my throat, because I had a cold. Tiny strip-bandage in the webbing between my second and third fingers where I'd carved the latest six-inch splinter out of my skin the night before with the sterilised sewing needles I kept in a cup on my work bench. Smell of varnish, and seals, and salt-water. Halfway to dreaming, all but asleep, I was overcome by an overwhelming urge to put my ear to Lizzie's womb, to sing to the new tenant in there. Almost six weeks old, at that point. I imagined seeing through my wife's skin, watching toe- and finger-shapes forming in the red, waving wet like lines on an etch-a-sketch.

'*You are my sun—*' I started, and knew, just like that, that something else was with me. There was the damp, for one thing. And an extra soundlessness in the room, right beside me. I can't explain it. The sound of someone else listening.

I reacted on instinct, shot upright and accidentally yanked all the blankets off Lizzie and shoved out my arms at where the presence seemed to be, and Lizzie blinked awake and narrowed her spectacle-less eyes at the shape of me, the covers twisted on the bed.

'There's something here,' I babbled, pushing with both hands at the empty air.

Lizzie just squinted, coolly. Finally, after a few seconds, she snatched one of my waving hands out of the air and dropped it against her belly. Her skin felt smooth, warm. My forefinger slipped into her bellybutton, felt the familiar knot of it, and I found myself aroused. Terrified, confused, ridiculous, and aroused.

'It's just Sam,' she said, stunning me. It seemed impossible that she was going to let me win that fight. Then she smiled, pressed my hand to the second creature we had created together. 'You and me and Sam.' She pushed harder on my hand, slid it down her belly towards the centre of her.

We made love, held each other, sang to her stomach. Not until long after Lizzie had fallen asleep, just as I was dropping off at last, did it occur to me that she could have been more right than she knew. Maybe it was just us, and Sam. The first Sam, the one we lost, returning to greet his successor with us.

Of course, he hadn't come just to listen, or to watch. But how could I have known that, then? And how did I know that that was what the presence was, anyway? I didn't. And when it came back late the next night, with Lizzie this time sound asleep and me less startled, I slid aside to make room for it, so we could both hear. Both whisper.

Are both of you with me now, I wonder? I'm standing on my stoop and listening, feeling, as hard as I can. Please, God, let them be with me. Not with Lizzie. Not with the new one. That's the only name we have allowed ourselves this time. The new one.

'Come on,' I say to my own front door, the filigrees of fog that float forever on the air of Sutro Heights, as though the atmosphere itself has gone Art Deco. 'Please. I'll tell you a story about the day you were born.'

I start down the warped, wooden steps towards our garage. Inside my pocket, the little silver key darts between my fingers, slippery and cool as a minnow, and I remember a story my father told me once. over a campfire, about young Hiawatha and his first trip into the forest, hunting a bear. He killed the bear with the help of a little talking silver fish he'd originally planned to eat. When the bear had been felled, Hiawatha leapt up, and he was so excited that he forgot his arrow, his bow, and the fish, which slipped silently into the shallows and was not seen or heard of again. My father, the cantor, and his Indian folktales. Coyote stories, especially. Trickster stories. I don't know why I'm thinking of this now.

In my mouth I taste the fog, and the perpetual garlic smell from the latest building to perch at the jut of the cliffs and call itself the Cliff House – the preceding three all collapsed, or burned to the ground – and something else, too. I realise, finally, what it is, and the tears come flooding back.

What I'm remembering, this time, is Washington DC, the grass brown and dying in the blazing August sun as we raced down the Mall, from museum to museum, in a desperate, headlong hunt for cheese. We were in the ninth day of the ten-day tetracyclene programme Dr Seger had prescribed, and Lizzie just seemed tired, but I swear I could feel the walls of my intestines, raw and sharp and scraped clean, the way teeth feel after a particularly vicious visit to the dentist. I craved milk, and got nauseous just thinking about it. Drained of its germs, its soft, comforting skin of use, my body felt skeletal, a shell without me in it.

That was the point, as Dr Seger explained it to us. We'd done our Tay-Sachs, tested for lead, endured endless blood screenings to check on things like prolactin, lupus anticoagulant, TSH. We would have done more tests, but the doctors didn't recommend them, and our insurance wouldn't pay. 'A couple of miscarriages, it's really not worth intensive investigation.' Three different doctors told us that. 'If it happens a couple more times, we'll know something's really wrong.'

Dr Seger had a theory, at least, involving old bacteria lingering in the body for years, decades, tucked up in the fallopian tubes or hidden in the testicles or just adrift in the blood, riding the heart-current in an endless, mindless, circle. 'The mechanism of creation is so delicate,' she told us. 'So efficiently, masterfully created. If anything gets in there that shouldn't be, well, it's like a bird in a jet engine. Everything just explodes.'

How comforting, I thought, but didn't say at that first consultation, because when I glanced at Lizzie, she looked more than comforted. She looked hungry, perched on the edge of her chair with her head half over Dr Seger's desk, so pale, thin, and hard, like a starved pigeon being teased with crumbs. I wanted to grab her hand. I wanted to weep.

As it turns out, Dr Seger may have been right. Or maybe we got lucky this time. Because that's the thing about miscarriage: three thousand years of human medical science, and no one knows any fucking thing at all. It just happens, people say, like a bruise, or a cold. And it does, I suppose. Just happen, I mean. But not like a cold. Like dying. Because that's what it is.

So for ten days, Dr Seger had us drop tetracyclene tablets down our throats like depth-charges, blasting everything living inside us out. And on that day in DC – we were visiting my cousin, the first time I'd managed to coax Lizzie anywhere near extended family since all this started – we'd gone to the Holocaust Museum, searching for anything strong enough to take our minds off our hunger, our desperate hope that we were scoured, healthy, clean. But it didn't work. So we went to the Smithsonian. And three people from the front of the ticket line, Lizzie suddenly grabbed my hand and I looked at her, and it was the old Lizzie, or the ghost of her, eyes flashing under their black rims, smile instantaneous, shockingly bright.

'Dairy,' she said. 'Right this second.'

It took me a breath to adjust. I hadn't seen my wife this way in a long, long while and as I stared, the smile slipped on her face. With a visible effort, she pinned it back in place. 'Jake. Come on.'

We paid admission, went racing past sculptures and animal dioramas and parchment documents to the cafés, where we stared at yoghurt in plastic containers – but we didn't dare eat yoghurt – and cups of tapioca that winked, in our fevered state, like the iced-over surfaces of Canadian lakes. But none of that was what we wanted. We needed a cheddar wheel, a lasagna we could scrape free of pasta and tomatoes so we could drape our tongues in strings of crusted mozzarella. What we settled for, finally, was four giant bags of generic cheese puffs from a 7-11. We sat together on the edge of a fountain and stuffed each other's mouths like babies, like lovers.

It wasn't enough. The hunger didn't abate in either of us. Sometimes I think it hasn't since.

God, it was glorious, though. Lizzie's lips around my orange-stained fingers, that soft, gorgeous crunch as each individual puff popped apart in our mouths, dusting our teeth and throats while spray from the fountain brushed our faces and we dreamed separate, still-hopeful dreams of children.

And that, in the end, is why I have to, you see. My two Sams. My lost, loved ones. Because maybe it's true. It doesn't seem like it could be, but maybe it is. Maybe, mostly, it just happens. And then, for most couples, it just stops happening one day. And afterwards – if only because there isn't time – you start to forget. Not what happened. Not what was lost. But what the loss meant, or at least what it felt like. I've come to believe that time alone will not swallow grief or heal a marriage. But perhaps filled time . . .

In my pocket, my fingers close over the silver key and I take a deep breath of the damp in the air, which is mostly just Sutro Heights damp now that we're outside. We have always loved it here, Lizzie and I. In spite of everything, we can't bring ourselves to flee. 'Let me show you,' I say, trying not to plead. I've taken too long, I think. They've got bored. They'll go back in the house. I lift the ancient, rusted padlock on our garage door, tilt it so I can see the slot in the moonlight and slide the key home.

It has been months since I've been out here – we use the garage for storage, not for our old Nova – and I've forgotten how heavy the salt-saturated wooden door is. It comes up with a creak, slides over my head and rocks unsteadily in its runners. How, I'm thinking, did I first realise that the presence in my room was my first, unborn child? The smell, I guess, like an unripe lemon, fresh and sour all at once. Lizzie's smell. Or maybe it was the song springing unbidden, over and over, to my lips. '*When I awoke dear. I was mistaken.*' Those things, and the fact that now, these last times, there seem to be two of them.

The first thing I see, once my eyes adjust, is my grandfather glaring out of his portrait at me. I can even remember the man who painted it; he lived next door to my family when I was little and Lizzie lived down the block. My grandfather called him 'Dolly', I don't know why. Or maybe Dali. I don't think so, though.

Certainly, there's nothing surreal about the portrait. Just my grand-father, his hair thread-thin and wild on his head like a spiderweb swinging free, his lips flat, crushed together, his ridiculous lumpy potato of a body under his perpetually half-zipped judge's robes. And there are his eyes, one blue, one green, which he once told me allowed him to see 3-D, before I knew that everyone could. A children's rights activist before there was a name for such things, a three-time candidate for a state bench seat and three-time loser, he'd made an enemy of his daughter, my mother, by wanting a son so badly. And he'd made a disciple out of me by saving Lizzie's life: turning her father in to the cops, then making sure that he got thrown in jail, then forcing both him and his whole family into counselling, getting him work when he got out, checking in on him every single night, no matter what, for six years, until Lizzie was away and free. Until eight months ago, on the day Dr Seger confirmed that we were pregnant for the third time, his portrait hung beside the Pinocchio clock on the living room wall. Now it lives here. One more casualty.

'Your namesake,' I say to the air, my two ghosts. But I can't take my eyes off my grandfather. Tonight is the end for him, too, I realise. The real end, where the ripples his life created in the world glide silently to stillness. Could you have seen them, I want to ask, with those 3-D eyes that saw so much? Could you have saved them? Could you have thought of another, better way? Because mine is going to hurt. 'His name was Nathan, really. But he called us "Sam". Your mother and me, we were both "Sam". That's why . . .'

That's why Lizzie let me win that argument, I realise. Not because she'd let go of the idea that the first one had to have a name, was a specific, living creature, a child of ours. But because she'd rationalised. Sam was to be the name, male or female. So whatever the first child had been, the second would be the other. Would have been. You see, Lizzie, I think to the air, wanting to punch the walls of the garage, scream to the cliffs, break down in tears. You think I don't know. But I do.

If we survive this night, and our baby is still with us in the morning, and we get to meet him someday soon, he will not be named Sam. He will not be Nathan, either. My grandfather would have wanted Sam.

'Goodbye, Grandpa,' I whisper, and force myself towards the back of the garage. There's no point in drawing this out, surely. Nothing to be gained. But at the door to the meat-freezer, the one the game-hunter who rented our place before us used to store wax-paper packets of venison and elk, I suddenly stop.

I can feel them. They're still here. They have not gone back to

Lizzie. They are not hunched near her navel, whispering their terrible, soundless whispers. That's how I imagine it happening, only it doesn't feel like imagining. And it isn't all terrible. I swear I heard it happen to the second Sam. The first Sam would wait, watching me, hovering near the new life in Lizzie like a hummingbird near nectar, then darting forward when I was through singing, or in between breaths, and singing a different sort of song, of a whole other world, parallel to ours, free of terrors or at least this terror, the one that just plain living breeds in everything alive. Maybe that world we're all born dreaming really does exist, but the only way to it is through a trapdoor in the womb. Maybe it's better where my children are. God, I want it to be better.

'You're by the notebooks,' I say, and I almost smile, and my hand slides volitionlessly from the handle of the freezer door, and I stagger towards the boxes stacked up, haphazard, along the back wall. The top one on the nearest stack is open slightly, its cardboard damp and reeking when I peel the flaps all the way back.

There they are. The plain, perfect-bound school composition note-books Lizzie bought as diaries, to chronicle the lives of her first two children in the 270 or so days before we were to know them. 'I can't look in those,' I say aloud, but I can't help myself. I lift the top one from the box, place it on my lap, sit down. It's my imagination, surely, that weight on my knees, as though something else has just slid down against me. Like a child, to look at a photo album. Tell me, Daddy, about the world without me in it. Suddenly, I'm embarrassed. I want to explain. That first notebook, the other one, is almost half my writing, not just Lizzie's. But this one . . . I was away, Sam, on a selling trip, for almost a month. And when I came back . . . I couldn't. Not right away. I couldn't even watch your mom doing it. And two weeks later . . .

'The day you were born,' I murmur, as though it was a lullaby. *Goodnight moon.* 'We went to the redwoods, with the Giraffes.' What-ever it is, that weight on me, shifts a little. Settles. 'That isn't really their name, Sam. Their name is Girard. Giraffe is what you would have called them, though. They would have made you. They're so tall. So funny. They would have put you on their shoulders to touch EXIT signs and ceiling tiles. They would have dropped you upside down from way up high and made you scream.' *Goodnight nobody.* That terrifying, stupid, blank page near the end of that book. What's it doing there, anyway?

'This was December, freezing cold, but the sun was out. We stopped at a gas station on our way to the woods, and I went to get Bugles, because that's what Giraffes eat, the ones we know, anyway. Your mom went to the restroom. She was in there a long time. And when she came out, she just looked at me. And I knew.'

My fingers have pushed the notebook open, pulled the pages apart. They're damp, too. Half of them are ruined, the words, in multi-coloured inks, like pressed flowers on the pages, smeared out of shape, though their meaning remains clear.

'I waited. I stared at your mother. She stared at me. Joseph – Mr Giraffe – came in to see what was taking so long. Your mom just kept on staring. So I said, "Couldn't find the Bugles." Then I grabbed two bags of them, turned away, and paid. And your mom got in the van beside me, and the Giraffes put on their bouncy, happy, Giraffe music, and we kept going.

'When we got to the woods, we found them practically empty, and there was this smell, even though the trees were dead. It wasn't like spring. You couldn't smell pollen, or see buds, just sunlight and bare branches and this mist floating up, catching on the branches and forming shapes like the ghosts of leaves. I tried to hold your mother's hand, and she let me at first, and then she didn't. She disappeared into the mist. The Giraffes had to go find her in the end, when it was time to go home. It was almost dark as we got in the van, and none of us were speaking. I was the last one in. And all I could think, as I took my last breath of that air, was, *Can you see this? Did you see the trees, my sweet son, daughter or son, on your way out of the world?*

Helpless, now, I drop my head, bury it in the wet air as though there were a child's hair there, and my mouth is moving, chanting the words in the notebook on my lap. I only read them once, on the night Lizzie wrote them, when she finally rolled over, with no tantrum, no more tears, nothing left, closed the book against her chest and went to sleep. But I remember them, still. There's a sketch, first, what looks like an acorn with a dent in the top. Next to it Lizzie has scrawled, 'You. Little rice-bean.' On the day before it died. Then there's the list, like a rosary: 'I'm so sorry. I'm so sorry I don't get to know you. I'm so sorry for wishing this was over, now, for wanting the bleeding to stop. I'm so sorry that I will never have the chance to be your mother. I'm so sorry you will never have the chance to be in our family. I'm so sorry that you are gone.'

I recite the next page, too, without even turning to it. The I-don't-wants: 'a D & C; a phone call from someone who doesn't know, to ask how I'm feeling; a phone call from someone who does, to ask how I am; to forget this, ever; to forget you.'

And then, at the bottom of the page: 'I love fog. I love seals. I love the ghosts of Sutro Heights. I love my mother, even though. I love Jake. I love having known you. I love having known you. I love having known you.'

With one long, shuddering breath, as though I'm trying to slip out from under a sleeping cat, I straighten my legs, lay the notebook to sleep in its box, tuck the flaps around it and stand. It's time. Not past time, just time. I return to the freezer, flip the heavy white lid.

The thing is, even after I looked in here, the same day I brought my grandfather out and wound up poking around the garage, lifting boxtops, touching old, unused bicycles and cross-country skis, I would never have realised. If she'd done the wrapping in wax paper, laid it in the bottom of the freezer, I would have assumed it was meat, and I would have left it there. But Lizzie is Lizzie, and instead of wax paper, she'd used red and blue construction paper from her classroom, folded the paper into perfect squares with perfect corners, and put a single star on each of them. So I lifted them out, just as I'm doing now.

They're so cold, cradled against me. The red package. The blue one. So light. The most astounding thing about the wrapping, really, is that she managed it all. How do you get paper and tape around nothing and get it to hold its shape? From another nearby box, I lift a gold and green blanket. I had it on my bottom bunk when I was a kid. The first time Lizzie lay on my bed – without me in it, she was just lying there – she wrapped herself in this. I spread it on the cold cement floor, and gently lay the packages down.

In Hebrew, the word for miscarriage translates, literally, as something dropped. It's no more accurate a term than any of the others humans have generated for the whole, apparently incomprehensible, process of reproduction, right down to 'conception'. Is that what we do? Conceive? Do we literally dream our children? Is it possible that miscarriage, finally, is just waking up to the reality of the world a few months too soon?

Gently, with the tip of my thumbnail, I slit the top of the red package, fold it open. It comes apart like origami, so perfect, arching back against the blanket. I slit the blue package, pull back its flaps. Widening the opening. One last parody of birth.

How did she do it, I wonder? The first time, we were home, she was in the bathroom. She had me bring Ziplock baggies, ice. For testing, she said. They'll need it for testing. But they'd taken it for testing. How had she got it back? And the second one had happened – finished happening – in a gas station bathroom somewhere between the Golden

Gate Bridge and the Muir Woods. And she'd said nothing, asked for nothing. 'Where did she keep you?' I murmur, staring down at the formless, red-grey spatters, the bunched-up tissue that might have been tendon one day, skin one day. Sam, one day. In the red package, there is more, a hump of frozen something with strings of red spiralling out from it, sticking to the paper, like the rays of an imploding sun. In the blue package, there are some red dots, a few strands of filament. Virtually nothing at all.

The song comes, and the tears with them. *You'll never know. Dear. How much I love you. Please don't take. Please don't take.* I think of my wife upstairs in our life, sleeping with her arms around her child. The one that won't be Sam, but just might live.

The matches slide from my pocket. Pulling one out of the little book is like ripping a blade of grass from the ground. I scrape it to life, and its tiny light warms my hand, floods the room, flickering as it sucks the oxygen out of the damp. Will this work? How do I know? For all I know, I am imagining it all. The miscarriages were bad luck, hormone deficiencies, a virus in the blood, and the grief that got in me was at least as awful as what got in Lizzie, it just lay dormant longer. And now it has made me crazy.

But if it is better where you are, my Sams. And if you're here to tell the new one about it, to call him out . . .

'The other night, dear,' I find myself saying, and then I'm singing it, like a Shabbat blessing, a Hanukkah song, something you offer to the emptiness of a darkened house to keep the dark and the emptiness back one more week, one more day. 'As I lay sleeping. I dreamed I held you. In my arms.'

I lower the match to the red paper, to the blue, and as my children melt, become dream, once more, I swear I hear them sing to me.

for both of you

Glen Hirshberg lives in Los Angeles with his wife and son. His novelette, 'Mr Dark's Carnival', which was first printed in Ash-Tree Press's *Shadows and Silence* and later appeared in *The Year's Best Fantasy and Horror: Fourteenth Annual Collection*, was nominated for both the International Horror Guild Award and the World Fantasy Award. A second novelette, 'Struwwelpeter', appeared originally on SciFi.Com and has been selected for both *The Year's Best Fantasy and Horror: Fifteenth Annual Collection* and *The Mammoth Book of Best New Horror Volume Thirteen*. His latest novelette, 'Dancing Men', will appear in Tor's 2003 anthology, *The Dark*, and his

first novel, *The Snowman's Children*, is published in the United States by Carroll &
Graf. Currently he is putting the final touches to a collection of ghost stories and
working on a new novel. About 'The Two Sams', he admits: 'This is probably the
most personal story I have put to paper, and therefore, hopefully, the most self-
explanatory. Most of my ghost stories originally were conceived to be told to my
students, but I have only tried reading this aloud once. Never again . . .'

In the Hours after Death

JEFF VANDERMEER

I

In the first hour after death, the room is so still that every sound holds a terrible clarity, like the tap of a knife against glass. The soft pad of shoes as someone walks away and closes the door is profoundly solid – each short footstep weighted, distinct. The body lies against the floor, the sightless eyes staring down into the wood as if some answer has been buried in the grain. The back of the head is mottled by the shadows of the trees that sway outside the open window. The trickle of red from the scalp that winds its way down the cheek, to puddle next to the clenched hand, is as harmless now, leached of threat, as if it were coloured water. The man's features have become slack, his mouth parted slightly, his expression surprised. The wrinkles on his forehead form ridges of superfluous worry. His trumpet lies a few feet away . . . From outside the window, the coolness of the day brings the green-gold scent of lilacs and crawling vines. The rustle of leaves. The deepening of light. A hint of blue through the trees. After a time, a mouse, fur ragged and one eye milky-white, sidles across the floor, sits on its haunches in front of the body and sniffs the air. The mouse circles the man. It explores the hidden pockets of the man's grey suit, trembles atop the shoes, nibbles at the laces, sticks its nose into a pant cuff. A metallic sound, faint and chaotic, rises through the window. The mouse stands unsteadily on its hind legs and sniffs the air again, then scurries back to its hole underneath the table. The sound intensifies, as of many instruments lurching together in drunken surprise. Perhaps the noise startled the mouse, or perhaps the mouse was frightened by some changed aspect of the man himself. The man's chin has begun to sprout tendrils of dark green fungi that mimic the texture of hair, curling and twisting across the man's face while the music comes ever closer. The tendrils move in concert. The clash of sounds has more unity than raw cacophony, yet no coherence. It seems as if several people tuning their instruments have begun to play their own separate, unsynchronised melodies. Somewhere in the welter of pompous horns and trumpets, a violin whines dimly. The tendrils of fungi wander in lazy attempts to colonise the blood. The music rollicks along, by turns melancholy and defiant. The man hears nothing, of course; the blood has begun to crust across his forehead. The smell of the room has become foetid, damp. The shadows have grown darker. The table in the corner – upon which lies a half-eaten sandwich – casts an ominous shade of purple. Eventually the music reaches a crescendo beneath the window. It has a questioning nature, as if the people playing the instruments are looking at one another, asking each other what to do next. The man's face moves a little from the vibration. His fungi beard is smiling. In a different light, he might almost look alive, intently staring at the floorboards, into the apartments below. Bells toll dimly from the Religious Quarter, announcing dinner prayers. The afternoon is almost gone. The room feels colder as the light begins to leave it. The music becomes less hesitant. Within minutes, the music is clanking up the stairs, towards the apartment. The music sounds as if it is running. It *is* running. The tendrils, in a race with the music, have spread further, faster, covering all of the man's face with a dark green mask. As if misinterpreting their success, they do not spread out over the rest of his body, but instead build on the mask, until it juts hideously from the face. The door begins to buckle before a blaring of horns, a torrid stitching of violins. Someone puts a key into the lock and turns the doorknob. The door opens. The music enters in all its chaotic glory. The man lies perfectly still on the floor beside the almost dry puddle of blood. A forest of legs and shoes surround him. The music becomes a dirge, haunted by the ghost of some strange fluted instrument. The musicians circle the body, their distress flowing through their music, their long straight shadows playing across the man's body. But for a tinge of green, the man's face has regained its form. The fungus has disappeared. Who could have known this would happen? Only the dead man, who had been looking into the grain as if some mystery lay there. The dead man lurches to his feet and picks up his trumpet. Smiles. Takes his hat from the table and places it on his head, over the blood. Wets his lips. He puts the trumpet to his mouth as all the other instruments become silent. He begins to blow, the tone clear yet discordant, his own music but not in tune. The faces of his friends come into focus, surround him, buzzing with words. His friends laugh. They hug him, tell him how glad they are it was all a joke; they had heard the most terrible things; please, do not scare them that way again. They did not know whether to play for a funeral or a rumourless resurrection. Unable to decide, they had played for both at once. He laughs, pats the nearest on the back. Play, he says. But he is not part of them. Play, he implores. But he is not one of them. And they play – marching out the door with him, they play. He is no longer one of them. When the door closes, the room is as empty as before, although the stairs echo with music. Over time, the sound fades. It fades until it is not even the memory of a sound, and then not even that. Nothing moves in the room. The man has been returned to himself. This is the first hour of death in the city of Ambergris. You may not rest for long. You may, in a sense, become yourself again. Worst of all, you may remember every detail, but be unable to do anything about it.

II

In the second hour after death, the man finds himself with his musician friends playing a concert in a public park. A crowd has gathered, some standing, others kneeling or sitting on benches. The trumpet is hot and golden in the man's hands. With each breath he blows into his trumpet, he feels the surge of an unidentifiable emotion and a detail from his past appears in his mind. The man feels as if he were filling up with Life, each breath enhancing him rather than maintaining him. He remembers his name – the round, generous vowels of it – but resists the urge to shout it out. A name is a good foundation on which to build. The members of the audience are cheerful smudges compared to the clear, sharp lines of his friends as they move in time-honoured synchronicity with their instruments. Their names, too, pop into his head – each a tiny explosion of pleasure. Soon, he swims in a sea of names: mother, father, brother, daughter, postman, baker, bartender, butcher, shopkeeper ... he smiles the radiant smile of a man who has recalled his life and found it good. This is the pinnacle of the second hour, although not all are so lucky. To some, the knowledge of identity seems to be escaping through their pores, each exhaled thought just another casualty of the emptying. The man, however, is not so truthful with himself. He smells the honeysuckle, tastes the pipe smoke from a passer-by, hears the tiny bells of an anklet tinkling through a pause in the music and does not wonder why these sensations are dull, muffled. His friends' faces are so near and sharp. Why should he worry about the rest? The blur of the world shouldn't be his concern. The instru-

ments that seem so cruel, all honed edges, the metal reflecting at odd
angles to create horrible disfigurements of his face? Why, it is just a
trick of the shadows. The quickness of his breath? Why, it is just the
aftermath of musical epiphany. The fluttering of his eyelids. The
sudden pallor. The smudge of green that he wipes with irritation from
his cheek . . . When the concert ends and the crowds disperse under
the threat of night, the man is quick to nod and laugh and join in one
last ragged musical salute. An invitation down narrow streets to a café
for a drink elicits a desperate gratitude – he slaps the backs of his
friends, nods furiously, already beginning to lose the names again:
pennies fallen through a hole in a shirt pocket. On the way to the café,
he notices how strangely the city now speaks to him, in the voices of
innuendo and suggestion, all surfaces unknown, all buildings crooked
or deformed or worse. The sidewalk vendors are ciphers. The passers-
by count for less than shadows; he cannot look at them directly, his
gaze a repulsing magnet. He clutches his trumpet, knuckles white. He
would like to play it, bring the jovial wide vowels of his name once
more into focus, but he cannot. The names of his friends fast receding,
his laughter becomes by turns forced, nervous, sad, and then brittle.
When they reach the café, the man looks around the beer-strewn table
at his friends and wonders how he fell in with such amiable strangers.
They call him by a name he barely remembers. The sky fills with a
darkness that consists of the weight of all the thoughts that have left
him. The man wraps his jacket tight. The streetlamps are cold yellow
eyes peering in through the window. The conversations at the table
tighten around the man in layers, each sentence less and less to do with
him. Now he cannot look at them. Now they run away to the edge of
his vision like a trickle of blood from a wound. The man's last image of
his dead wife leaves him, his daughter's memory lost in the same
moment. Even the dead do not want to die. Stricken, face animated by
fear, he stands and announces that he must leave, he must depart, he
must go home, although thoughts of the grainy apartment floor leave a
dread like ice in his bowels . . . this, then, is the last defiant act of the
second hour: to state a determination to take action, even though you
will never take that action. The world has become a mere construct – a
hollow reed created that you might breathe. You may hear echoes of a
strange and sibilant music, coursing like an undercurrent through
inanimate objects. This music may bring tears to your eyes. It may not.
Regardless, you are now entering the third hour of death.

III

In the third hour after death, all other memories having been emptied and extinguished, the repressed memory of lifelessness returns, although the man denies the truth of it. Denies the sting of splinters against his face, the taste of sawdust, the comfort of the cool floorboards. He thinks it is a bad dream and mutters to himself that he will just walk a little longer to clear up the headaches pulsing through his head. The man still holds his trumpet. Every few steps, he stops to look at it. He is trying to remember what he once used it for. The third hour can last for a very long time. After a while, staring at his trumpet, an unquenchable sadness rises over him until he is engulfed in a sorrow so deep it must be borne because nothing better lies beyond it. It is the sorrow of lost details; the darkness of it hints at the echoes of memories now gone. Indirectly, the man can sense what grieves him, but the very glittering reflection of its passage is enough to blind him. To him, it feels as if the natural world has made him sad, for he has wandered into a park and the sky far above through the branches seethes with the light of a restless moon. If the man could only see his way to the centre of a single memory and hold it in his mind, he might understand what has happened to him. Instead, from the edge of his attention, the absence of mother, father, wife, daughter, leaves only outlines. It is too much to bear. It must be borne . . . In some cases, recognition may take the form of violent acts – one last convulsion against the inevitable. But not in the man's case. In him, the sorrow only deepens, for he has begun to suspect the truth. The man wanders through gardens and courtyards, through tree-lined neighbourhoods and along city-tamed streams, all touched equally by the blank expanse of night. He is without thought except to avoid thought, without purpose except to avoid purpose. He does not tire – nothing without will can ever tire – and as he walks, he begins to touch what he passes. He runs his hands through the scruffy tops of bushes. He rubs his face against the trunk of a tree. He follows the line of a sidewalk crack with his finger. As the night progresses, a tightness enters his face, a self-aware phosphorescence. When he leans down to float his hand through a fountain pool, his face wavers in the water like a green-tinged second moon. Passers-by run away or cross the street at his approach. He has no opinion on this; it does not upset or amuse him. He is rapidly becoming Other: Otherwhere, Otherflesh. His trumpet? Long ago fallen from a distracted grasp . . . Eventually, the trailing hand will find something of more than usual interest. For the man, this occurs when he sits down on a wooden bench and the touch of the grain on his palm brings a familiarity welling up through his fingertips. He runs his arms across the wood. He strokes the wood, trying to form a memory from before the sorrow. He lies down on the bench and presses his face against the grain . . . until he sees his apartment room and the blood pooling in the foreground of his vision and knows that he is dead. Then the man sits up, his receding sorrow replaced by nothing. Tendrils of fungi rise from their hiding places inside his body. The man waits as they curl across his face, his torso, his arms, his legs. And he sees the night for possibly the first time ever. And he sees *them* coming out from the holes in the night. But he does not flinch. He does not run. He no longer even tries to breathe. He no longer tries to be anything other than what he is. For this is the last phase of the third hour of death. After the third hour, you will never be unhappy again. You will never know pain. You will never have to endure the sting of an unkind word. Every muscle, every sinew, every bone, every blood vessel in your body will relax to let in the darkness. When they come for you, as they surely will, you will finally understand, under the cool weavings of the tendrils, what a good thing this can be. You will finally understand that there is no fourth hour after death. And you will marvel that the world could be so still, so silent, so *clear*.

Jeff VanderMeer has had work appear in ten languages in seventeen countries, in such anthologies and magazines as *Dark Voices 5*, *Dark Terrors*, *The Mammoth Book of Best New Horror Volume Seven*, *Nebula Awards 30*, *Infinity Plus: The Anthology*, *Asimov's SF Magazine*, *Amazing Stories*, *Weird Tales*, *Interzone* and *The Third Alternative*. His book, *City of Saints & Madmen*, garnered praise from many critics and ranked fourth on SF Site's list of the Top 10 Books of 2001. It was also a *Locus* recommended collection. Other recent volumes from the World Fantasy Award-winning author include the mass-market paperback *Veniss Underground*, also from Prime, and the non-fiction collection *Why Should I Cut Your Throat?* from Cosmos. He has also completed work as co-editor on two new projects: *Leviathan 3* (Ministry of Whimsy/Prime) and *The Thackery T. Lambshead Pocket Guide to Eccentric & Discredited Diseases* (Chimeric), both released in 2002. VanderMeer also recently placed seventh on *Locus Online*'s controversial list of the top ten writers of fantasy/SF short fiction. Seven just happens to be his lucky number. '"In the Hours after Death" is marginally set in Ambergris,' he explains, 'the imaginary city that I have written about for the last ten years. I wrote it after completing another Ambergris story, "The Cage", which is very much about death. So, thinking about death late one night, as one sometimes does, I came across a story in an old Dedalus fiction collection – Austrian decadents, I think it was – that had the line "In the hour after death" in the first paragraph. I immediately closed the book without finishing the story and wrote the first draft of "In the Hours after Death". In it I was, I suppose, creating a wake for "The Cage" and getting my mood and thoughts down on paper. Luckily, my story in no way resembles the decadent story that provided the starting point for it.'

Under My Skin

LES DANIELS

I

The six apes sat around the conference table while they waited for their meeting to be called to order. One of them began to scratch and grunt, but he slipped back into silence when the others stared him down. This was no time for clowning: there was money at stake. It was quiet in the boardroom – almost too quiet. Finally the tallest, sleekest and handsomest of the great primates shuffled to his feet and cleared his throat. He handed each of the others a thick sheaf of white paper as he began to speak.

'This is the first meeting of The Gorilla Gang,' he said, 'but if we work together it will not be the last. You have been chosen because each one of you is an expert in his field. You are the best of your breed, gentlemen, and you deserve to be congratulated. I applaud you!' He pounded his gigantic hands together as he looked around the room. His fur, with its beautiful tints of red and gold, seemed almost afire where it was touched by bars of sunlight streaming through the Venetian blinds. The boss looked like a leader, Jack admitted to himself, but that was probably nothing but the skin.

'Gentlemen, I suggest we remove our heads.' The boss reached for his massive, hairy cranium and yanked it upwards; his five followers acted in imitation. 'Monkey see, monkey do,' thought Jack with just a trace of rancour.

'I appreciate the gesture of solidarity you made when you all agreed to arrive in full costume, and it's good publicity too. The press boys got some swell photos,' the group's leader continued. 'But now we're on our own and these heads are just too darned hot. I'm sure I'm not the only one who's passed out from wearing one, especially when I had a dumb director who was trying to be a tough guy.' There was laughter all around the table. 'You've got to be able to breathe, am I right? Sure, smoke 'em if you've got 'em.'

With his head off, the boss was just an ordinary guy named Bill Wilson. His hair was blond and his eyes were blue, and he probably thought he was good-looking enough to be an actor, Jack suspected, but not the kind of actor he had turned out to be. Like the rest of them, he was just a monkey man, with only the suit he owned standing between him and the unemployment line. Wilson had been lucky, though. When the war came he'd been rated 4-F, because of an old hip injury that he said helped him with his ape walk, and so while others like Jack were sweating in real jungles, actually fighting for their lives, Bill Wilson waltzed right into the best role any of them was ever likely to see.

The Gorilla Girl was what they call a sleeper, a picture that didn't cost much but took in a lot at the box office. Some of the critics even liked it, because it wasn't about the female monster they had expected, but about a beautiful girl who used the brute beast she'd raised from a chimp (people thought it worked that way) to take revenge on the men who'd killed her lover. It had been an easy performance for Wilson, Jack surmised. After all, how tough could it be to show affection for his co-star, an imported beauty with a fake name, fabulous hermans and a sultry style? Yet there had even been talk of an Oscar nomination for Wilson, although Jack suspected that was just a press agent's dream. Still, when Wilson and What's-Her-Name had died in each other's arms, their bodies riddled with vigilante bullets, there wasn't a dry seat in the house. *The Gorilla Girl* had made Bill Wilson the King of the Monkey Men, and that was that.

Unfortunately, there wasn't much of a kingdom left any more, and that's what this meeting was all about. Jack thumbed through his script while Wilson talked, wondering what sort of part he might get. A monkey, sure, but what kind of a monkey? They were all fucking monkeys, but Jack would probably be the one at the bottom of the cast list. That's how things generally went. Japan had surrendered, the war was over, and it was supposed to be a new world, but his monkey suit still stank.

The suit stank because it was made of old hair and glue and leather, marinated for years in human sweat, but it stank most of all, Jack thought, because it was out of work. *Gorilla Girl*, in 1944, had come at the peak of the cycle for horror pictures, and jungle pictures too. Now people wanted 'realism', whatever that was, and times were tough on guys who played gorillas. Ray Corrigan, the big, rugged-looking fellow sitting at the far end of the table, had somehow finagled a second career playing cowboys. Talk said that he was planning to sell his suit to the first comer who could meet his price, but Jack didn't believe it. The suit was a lifeline, a meal ticket, a union card, a faithful friend. Without it, a man would be nobody. A day labourer, like Jack had been too often in the last few years. Jack turned to his left and bummed a Lucky Strike from Charlie Gemora, the tough little Filipino who had been employed as a simian thespian since movies were silent. Then he realised that Wilson was talking again.

'And now they think they can play us off against each other,' the blond man said. 'If there is a job, they pay peanuts. If it wasn't for Monogram, we'd all be starving. Art Miles here got a feature there a while ago, right, Art?'

'Right. *Spook Busters*. But that was almost two years back. With those goddam Bowery Boys. They must be thirty years old, easy, but they still act like juvenile delinquents.'

'Yeah, but it was a job,' rasped grey-haired Emil Van Horn as he ground the stub of a Kool into a glass ashtray. 'I worked with the best. Abbott and Costello. Bela Lugosi. W. C. Fields. And now I can't get arrested.'

'Lugosi's not doing much better himself,' drawled Ray Corrigan, 'and Fields is juggling for God now. People don't want entertainment any more anyway, just social justice pictures and all that stuff.'

'Which brings us to you, Jack,' said Bill Wilson, transfixing his colleague with a bright blue gaze. 'You're the only one here who's worked the suit at a major studio in the last year. Columbia, wasn't it?'

'Yeah, right,' said Jack, suddenly in the spotlight. 'Two days, playing stooge for the Three Stooges.' He got a little chuckle, and hated himself for liking it.

'So it's not going great for any of us,' continued Wilson. 'And now I hear Willis O'Brien has cut himself a deal over at RKO.' Everybody groaned. O'Brien had worked on the greatest monkey movie ever made, and nobody would ever dare deny it. *King Kong*. It had come out fourteen years ago, in 1933, but it was a show nobody had ever forgotten. The only problem was that it used some kind of trick photography instead of a man in a suit. If O'Brien scored again, every other monkey in Hollywood would be a dead duck. 'That's why I decided to write this script,' said Wilson, tapping with one fuzzy finger at the pile of pages in front of him. '*The Gorilla Gang*. This is our way out, gentleman. Instead of waiting for jobs and then fighting each other for 'em, we should be working as a team. You know, we should all hang together, or swing on the same vine, or something.'

'We're all bananas on the same bunch,' muttered Jack. 'No difference between us.'

'That's right, Jack!' grinned Wilson, his white teeth flashing. 'And that's what this script is about. A bunch of apes get hit by some of this atomic stuff, you know, and suddenly they're smart! They evolve! So they form a gang and they fight for money and power, and there's some laughs and some tears and some scary parts, and we all end up as lovable as King Kong or Frankenstein. I tell ya, it's a winner.'

'I don't know about this evolving stuff,' rumbled Corrigan.

'Jesus, Ray, it's only a movie! Don't make a federal case out of it!'

'Who's gonna put up the money?' demanded little Charlie Gemora, vocal for the first time. 'Us?'

'Don't worry,' Wilson reassured him. 'I know there's not enough cash in this room to pay for the credits, much less the movie. But if we can get all the top ape actors in town to come in on this project, then we've got a little clout. Maybe even a money magnet. Come on, you know what we've got that they haven't got. We've got the suits.'

'They could make their own,' suggested Van Horn as he squinted at the cover of Baker's screenplay.

'They couldn't afford to make six suits. Not for a low-budget picture. Not like our skins. They're special. Each one of these suits has a story. You all know that, even if you don't want anyone else to know what it is.'

'So you sell the show to Poverty Row, and we all get through the year,' sighed Arthur Miles. 'That's not bad, but what happens in 1948?'

'We're not going to sell it to the studios,' Wilson insisted. 'At least not the way you mean. Hollywood's changing, and the government's going to take the studios apart. Gentlemen, we're going independent. You've heard of United Artists, and Liberty Pictures. People are producing their own movies. Alfred Hitchcock. Frank Capra. And there are people ready to distribute them. We get financing, and then we each own part of the action. Maybe we'll get to make some sequels. What if we hit it big, like the Mummy, or even the Bowery Boys? How would you like a piece of that?'

'Who did you say was gonna pay for all this?' asked Emil Van Horn.

'Don't worry! The script will bring in the financing,' said Wilson. 'And anyway, we're not accountants, we're actors. And right now, we're having a party!' He pulled a battered briefcase from under the table and extracted from its interior a cellophane package of paper Dixie Cups, and a bottle of Old Crow to fill them. Jack looked around the table, populated by six simians sitting in the afternoon sun, their hirsute bodies surmounted by the heads of six worried, middle-aged men. Some of them looked hopeful, the others only thirsty. Jack reached for his shot of whiskey and downed it in one gulp.

II

Jack let the script fall into his lap, leaned back in his ragged easy chair, pulled the chain on the lamp beside him and sat thinking in the dark. With his eyes shut, he hardly noticed the intermittent blue flashes of the neon drugstore sign two floors below his rented room. On the inside of his eyelids, he was replaying scenes from the pages he'd just finished reading, and he had to admit a lot of it looked pretty good. The script was bullshit, really, and he knew there were things wrong with it. He was even pretty sure some of the words weren't spelled right. Yet a few of those scenes were just about foolproof. The gorilla lurking in the shadows near the uranium dig, who suddenly understands the words that men are saying and answers back. The gang forming in the jungle, shouting slogans and waving torches as they anticipate their attack on civilisation. Their savage conquest of a small South African town. The Gorilla Gang on the rampage as bank robbers, wearing zoot suits and fedoras, driving cars and brandishing machine-guns. Their daring foray on a diamond mine, which takes a shocking twist when they discover a cave that serves as the hideout for a group of fugitive Nazi officers. Among them is Hitler himself. After a wild, triumphant battle against a greater evil, the beasts are hailed as heroes, pardoned, and appointed international agents to fight tyranny around the world. The end.

The story was corny, Jack knew that, but it could work. Obviously Wilson had written the star part for himself, but they all had good scenes. *The Gorilla Gang* could save everybody's ass. There was just one problem.

During the fight in the cave, one of the monkeys was going to die. The funny guy, the one who kept slipping back into his jungle ways, the one everybody liked. His death scene was a real tearjerker, guaranteed to make everyone remember Pearl Harbor and all that, but at the end the character would be dead. If there were more movies, he wouldn't be in them, and the man playing him wouldn't be making any more money. As soon as he saw the words on the page, Jack felt his guts turn into a bag full of ice cubes. He knew, as surely as if God had whispered it into his ear, that he would be asked to play the monkey who didn't make it.

He picked up his towel and his bar of Lifebuoy, walked down the hallway to the communal bathroom, made sure it was unoccupied, then did what he had to. Afterwards he washed his hands and face, then looked at himself in the mirror for a long, long time. Water trickled down his face; he looked like a crying child. Was this the look of a loser? Why did everybody think as soon as they saw him that they could walk right over him? The mirror might have known the answer, but it didn't say, and after a while he got tired of waiting.

Back in his room, Jack fished in his pants pocket for the shred of paper with Bill Wilson's number on it. He put on his last clean shirt, checked in the closet to make sure his monkey suit hadn't walked away, and headed downstairs to the drugstore to make his call.

Jack hurried past the blue and orange Rexall sign, pushed through the revolving door and into the pale glow of fluorescent light that bathed the store. Funny how it made everything look like it did on the big screen. Light was a big part of the magic, whether you were selling apes or aspirin. The store looked just about as big and fancy as a movie house too, and the phone booths were way at the back. As he approached them, passing row after row of toothpaste, tampons and razor blades, Jack began to feel like he was walking the last mile. Maybe he should wait for a minute, do something to build up his strength. He took a left turn towards the lunch counter and planted the seat of his pleated tan pants on the red leather seat of a shiny chrome stool. A punk with pimples and a paper hat asked him what he'd have, but didn't really seem to care. Jack ordered a burger and a Dr Pepper, and was soon left alone with his thoughts. Not enjoying the company too much, he spun around on his stool and spied a little coloured kid hunkered down in front of the magazine stand. The kid was surrounded by row upon row of comic books, their covers fanned out like some deck of cards that held the secrets to mankind's dreams and delusions. *Action Comics. Marvel Mystery. Smash. Crack. Whiz.* The kid had the latest *Jumbo Comics* in his clutches, and he was poring over it like he was studying for a test, his black and white sneakers rubbing together as he turned each page.

Jack understood the feeling. Way too old for comics himself, he nevertheless picked up a copy of *Jumbo* once in a while anyway, always shamefacedly telling the newsie it was for a son he didn't have. The reason for the sale was right on the cover, of course: Sheena, the Queen of the Jungle. Even the way it sounded was like poetry: Shee Nada, Quee Nada. Jungle. Still, it was the pictures that counted, drawings of the impossibly gorgeous blonde in her leopard-skin swimsuit, striding through the jungle and meting out bloody justice to humans and animals alike. Sometimes she wrestled apes, sometimes she stabbed the wicked priestesses of forgotten tribes, but she never let anybody get away with anything. She knew the good apes from the bad apes, just like she knew the good tribes from the bad tribes. She was never wrong. She had a sort of a boyfriend named Bob, and sometimes he carried her spear, but mostly she was there for every guy who had a dime to share with her. A lot of them were soldiers not too long ago, just like Jack was, but he had an even better reason to remember her.

Maybe the sweetest job he ever had, just after he got out of the service, came about when he hooked up with a blonde who ran a hoochie-coochie show called 'Rita Wilson's Jungle Rhythms'. Unless they caught a good gig with a house band, the rhythm was just an old Gene Krupa record with an extended drum solo, but Rita looked pretty fine in that leopard-skin outfit she'd sewn herself, and she didn't seem to mind where the monkey touched her when they danced, even if he couldn't feel much through the paws. Jack could never quite figure out if she really liked it or just thought it was good for the act. Maybe she didn't know either, but it didn't matter much after the cops in Burbank raided a performance of 'The Angel and the Ape'. Rita and Jack were charged with 'lewd and lascivious behaviour', and somehow he never forgot how splendid that sounded, no matter what it meant. Rita was a tough cookie; she just paid her fine and moved on, but Jack got a month of room and board from the county, which turned out to be more than he could get when he got out. He never saw Rita again.

A white plate clattered on the black marble counter. 'Here's your burger, bud,' said the punk in the paper hat. Jack looked down at a dry disk of meat between two halves of a stale bun, and at a pale section of pickle about the size of a quarter. He wondered why he kept coming here, but deep down inside he knew. It was easier.

'Hey, boy! This ain't a liberry!' bawled the soda jerk. 'You gonna buy something?' The kid at the magazine stand jumped like he'd been caught stealing, but actually he was guilty of a much worse crime: caught dreaming. He dropped the comic book and backed towards the door.

'Wait a second,' said Jack. The kid froze, trying to figure his odds. 'Come back here, man, and take your book,' said Jack. 'I'm gonna buy it for you.'

'What do I have to do for it?' asked the kid, suddenly all angry and street smart.

'You just have to read the whole thing,' said Jack. 'Now pick it up and take a hike.'

Summoning up all the dignity he could muster, the kid retrieved the comic book and walked away; he didn't start to run until he was out the door. 'It's only a goddam dime,' Jack said to nobody in particular. He tossed a small silver circle on the gleaming black counter. He felt better than he had all day, but the burger soon changed that.

Jack killed his soda, dug up another dime and headed for the phone booths. He had to set up a private meeting with Bill Wilson while there was still time, before everything went wrong again.

III

Jack's pre-war Plymouth would have been grey if he'd had the money to get it painted. As things stood, however, the old rattletrap not only looked like a leper, it was one of the walking wounded. Jack hated to take it out, even when he had gas money, because he never knew when it might break down. And then there was the muffler, or rather the lack of one. The heap sounded like a strafing Stuka, complete with high-pitched whine, and the black smoke pouring out of the exhaust pipe combined with the ungodly noise to make the car a certified cop magnet. The missing headlight didn't help either. So it wasn't really a surprise when Jack got a ticket on his way to Bill Wilson's, but it didn't do much to cheer him up. If he couldn't afford to pay a mechanic, then how was he supposed to pay the fucking fine? And why was he living in this shithole city, anyway? New York, nobody had a car. Nobody needed one. But no, they had to make movies out in goddam Los Angeles, where every stinking thing was twenty miles away. He jacked up the blare of brass on the radio and screamed along with it. Phil Harris and the boys built to a wild crescendo and gave out one last big blast of big-band jazz. Then the speaker popped, and the music died too.

Jack was grinding his teeth and punching the steering wheel, lost in the canyons for almost an hour, before he finally found what he was looking for. Wilson's house was small, dark logs and warm windows. Not much more than a cabin, really, but the man owned his own place, and the car parked beside it was a white Pontiac that looked almost new. There was nothing else around but the inky shadows of rocks and trees, and the big black sky spattered with small white stars. That's something else wrong with the City of Angels, thought Jack: it's a jungle out there.

He climbed out of the car and shut the door slowly, almost afraid to make a sound. It just seemed rude, somehow, out here in the middle of nowhere. A spinning cloud of bugs surrounded his head as he approached the cabin, and as he swatted at them he heard a screen door screech open. In front of him stood a man silhouetted against a rectangle of yellow light. It was Bill Wilson, dressed in a loud Hawaiian shirt and dungarees. 'That you, Jack?' he asked. 'You find the place okay?'

'Okay,' muttered Jack, not even knowing why he lied. He followed Wilson inside. The whole ground floor was one big room, its walls as homey and rough-hewn as the cabin's exterior. A stove and a refrigerator and a kitchen sink stood at the back, but the space was dominated by heavy, unfinished furniture which Jack took to be redwood. A big table, some sturdy chairs, too many bookcases. Straw matting on the floors in place of carpeting. An open staircase led up to a bedroom and, as Jack learned after a few drinks, the bathroom too. 'Nice,' said Jack as he looked around. There were several framed glossy photographs, and Jack recognised faces almost at once: Dorothy Lamour, Hedy Lamarr, Maria Montez, Hollywood jungle queens all over the place. Wilson was a fan too, thought Jack, then realised that all the pictures were personally inscribed. How well had Wilson known these women? 'Really nice,' said Jack. Just how big had *The Gorilla Girl* actually been? He stepped back from the shiny, black and white visions of lipstick and mascara, and then he turned around. On the opposite wall was something equally striking but not so pretty: a huge, crudely carved mask, a simple, snarling visage painted in shades of black, white, and brown.

'That one I didn't know personally,' admitted Wilson, 'but I went a long way to get it.'

'Africa, huh? You really been there?'

'I've been everywhere, Jack. Worked on filthy stinking ships in all the seven seas. Always wanted to see the world, so I just went out and did. Ended up seeing a lot of things I wished I hadn't.' He walked towards the kitchen, and Jack noticed his peculiar limp again. 'Drink,

Jack? Bourbon all right with you? The boys finished off that bottle this afternoon, but I've got another one here. Gotta watch out for yourself, you know. Have a seat, Jack. Ice?'

Sitting across the redwood table from Bill Wilson, three fingers of Old Crow in his hand, Jack felt like he was back in that meeting with the other monkey men, but this time he had the undivided attention of the only one who mattered. The time was right for him to stake his claim, but instead he asked something that made no sense at all. He gulped down half his drink. 'You get that skin in Africa?' he asked.

'Why, Jack! You know better than to ask that! Nobody ever asks where a skin comes from!' Wilson's protests were a parody of indignation; his blue eyes were bright with mockery. 'These things aren't easy to come by. I dare say some of them are illegal. And all of them have secrets.'

'No secret about mine,' said Jack. 'I got it from my uncle. He was in vaudeville. I used to love watching him when I was a kid, and he left it to me when he died.' Jack killed his drink. 'The only thing anybody ever gave me. So I took it and made a living from it. But it's like going around the world, I guess. You see some stuff you don't like.'

'And you might not like knowing about your skin, if that's all you've bothered to find out. Have another drink. What do you think it's made of?'

'Leather and hair, mostly.'

'But where did the leather and hair come from, Jack? What died so you could be in show business? Is it pig skin and yak hair, like Van Horn's? I think he made it himself, but there's something strange about that, too, if you stop and think about it. Don't you know who made yours? Don't you care? I think you've got a real skin there, Jack, know what I mean?'

Wilson's grin was maniacal, but Jack just sat and stared. He'd never really thought about stuff like this for long, even though he couldn't always stop the dreams.

'The audience never worries about it, do they, Jack? They probably think all the skins are real. Like that Boris Karloff picture, *The Ape*. You know, you just take a dead monkey and spoon out the stuffing, and then you climb inside. They don't know it's more like a mummy, do they? A dried-out old corpse you wrap around yourself till nothing shows of you except your eyes. And the worst thing is you wanted to do it. You wanted to be it. Like something called out to you from a hundred thousand years ago. It's bred in the bone, Jack, and that scares even a big cowboy like Ray Corrigan. Doesn't it scare you?'

Wilson paced across the room, his whiskey glass waving in the air, his hip lurching weirdly. He tapped the wall beside a neatly framed eight by ten. 'And the women love it, too. It's in the blood. It's some kind of magic. Without the skin, I'm just an old merchant seaman who walks funny. With it, somehow, I'm somebody. Do you think I'd ever have met any of these pin-ups if I didn't have the skin? It's all any of us have, Jack. Take away the suit and there's not a Barrymore in the bunch.'

Jack was getting nervous, but he was still too interested and too angry to get up and leave. Maybe he was earning himself some leverage here. 'You've got the best monkey suit I've ever seen,' he said.

Wilson stopped moving and stared at a wall as if he could see something on the other side. 'It was just about the same as murder,' he said. 'And they made me do it, too. Wouldn't just sell it to me. They made me earn it, Jack. Something sacred, they said. A sacrifice. Like it was their god, but still they wanted to get rid of it. And maybe they were right. I feel like I've been working for the damned thing ever since, trying to please it, but it's never been enough. I should have left it alone. I wish to God I had.'

'What kind of an animal did you say it was?' asked Jack.

Wilson sat down again. He poured another drink and downed it in one continuous motion. 'Funny about that, you know? People don't care. Gorilla, ape, orang-utan, they don't give damn, as long as it's big and strong and hairy. Some of these suits don't look like anything that ever walked the earth. Ever see Charlie Gemora with Lugosi in *Murders in the Rue Morgue*? No? Well, it was years ago. Charlie had his suit on, whatever it's supposed to be, and the goddam director kept cutting back and forth between Charlie and some close-ups of a live monkey half his size. And nobody even noticed!'

'But what about . . .?'

'You know, Charlie's not the only one who worked with Bela Lugosi. And did you hear Van Horn carrying on this afternoon? Well, I worked with Lugosi too, you know. Say what you like, he can really control the camera, the poor old bastard. He really fills the screen. Let me tell you a story. No, really. You'll like this. I was with old Bela on a picture for PRC. The worst. They made Monogram look like MGM. Bela used to hide in his dressing room when we weren't shooting, so nobody got to talk with him much. But we had one day on location – Bronson Caverns, natch – and there was nowhere for him to go, so I got next to him when we broke for chow. It was just a lousy box-lunch, an orange that cost a nickel and a dried-up old sandwich. So he picked that up and looked at it, gave it the eye, you know how he was. And then he said to me, "Vot's dis?" So I took a big bite out of mine, looked straight back at him, and said "Baloney". And Bela looked at me, and he looked at the sandwich, and he pulled back the bread and looked inside, and then he said what he said. You know what he said? He said: "Baloney? Perhaps not."'

Wilson threw back his head and laughed like a hyena. His face swelled up and fumed red, his eyes were wet, and he pounded on the redwood table till the bourbon bottle jumped and rattled against the silver Ronson table lighter, but Jack just sat and stared.

'I don't get it,' said Jack.

'What? You never saw that show? *The Black Cat?*'

'The one you made with Lugosi?'

'No, Jack. The one Lugosi made with Karloff. He had that line in there, you know. Great, great line. "Supernatural, perhaps. Baloney, perhaps not."'

'I never saw it,' said Jack, suddenly realising that Wilson was dead drunk, then noticing that he wasn't much better off himself. Wilson had stopped laughing, as if someone had turned off a phonograph. 'I gotta go to the can,' said Jack.

'Upstairs,' Wilson advised him. 'You'll see it. And when you come back, we'll talk about about *The Gorilla Gang*. After all, that's why you're here, isn't it? Top of the stairs. And you never saw that movie? You're a funny guy, Jack.'

His stomach sinking as he pulled himself upright, Jack took in the words that sealed his fate. 'Funny,' he mumbled. He staggered towards the stairs. 'What kind of skin did you say that was again?'

'You know,' said Wilson, opening up a silver cigarette box to reach for a cork-tipped Herbert Tareyton. 'The best kind. No kind. Not a monkey, not a man. The kind of skin that scares a guy like Corrigan. The kind that says there might not be a God, Jack. You know. The missing one. Just call him Mr In-Between.'

Swaying at the top of the steps, Jack looked down at Wilson, who was bent over the table so that his blond hair fell across his face. His shoulders were shaking, but Jack wasn't sure why. Smoke shot out of Wilson's mouth and formed clouds around his head.

Jack turned away and into Wilson's bedroom. It was big and almost empty, containing next to nothing but a bed and the bamboo chest at its foot. There were more African masks and Hollywood photos on the dimly lit walls, but Jack didn't care about those now. He knew as if he had X-ray eyes what was hidden at the foot of the bed, and he tiptoed towards it across straw mats, desperate to go unheard by the man below. He held his breath as if he thought that might help, and was emboldened by a fusillade of coughing from below. He reached for the chest with trembling fingers, convinced that the hinges would betray him with some ungodly squeal, but the lid opened as smoothly as a banana skin.

Still not breathing, Jack reached inside and pulled out Bill Wilson's skin. It was as smooth as smoke, as heavy as the night. Jack took a breath as he embraced it, and when his lungs were full to bursting he exhaled, then drew in the scent of the skin almost against his will. For a second he missed the stench he had expected, but then he was overwhelmed by the aromas of sunshine and tall grass, of cool pools and shadows, of ripe fruit and flowers hanging in the trees. It was a primitive perfume, and Jack was dizzy inhaling it for a moment, but then he remembered where he was. He stuffed the skin back where it belonged, barely remembering to hurry into the bathroom and flush the toilet before he headed back downstairs.

'Find everything okay?' asked Wilson. 'Have a smoke.'

'Okay,' said Jack. He sat down opposite his host.

'So you read the script. Great. You know, you're the first guy to get back to me. You'd think they'd be more interested.'

'Maybe they don't read so fast,' muttered Jack.

'You think you're joking? Half the people in this town don't read. Even the big producers. Their wives or secretaries read the scripts, then tell these self-styled masterminds what they're all about.'

Jack grunted.

'Well?' asked Wilson. 'You wanted to talk. What did you think?'

'Never mind what I thought.' Jack reached for a cigarette and tapped it on the silver box. 'Just tell me about the casting.'

Wilson actually gave him a light, hefting the big silver Ronson while he looked Jack square in the eye. 'You must have liked it,' Wilson said, 'or you wouldn't be worried about your part.' He poured two more drinks out of the half-empty bottle. 'Don't worry, Jack. You've got the plum. Stuck in your thumb and pulled out a plum, Jack. You've got laughs, tears, everything. It's a star-maker.'

'I knew it,' said Jack. 'You want me to play Koko.'

'That's right, Jack, Koko. You're Koko.' Wilson rubbed his hands together in a simulacrum of glee.

'You son of a bitch,' snarled Jack. 'You go to hell.' He took an angry drag on his Herbert Tareyton, then snuffed it out on the silver ashtray.

'But Jack! What's wrong? You've got the best part!'

'Except for yours. Aw, I expected that. But you're making me the guy that gets killed. You get all the monkey men in Hollywood together, then you shoot me, and you cut me out of the sequels. Out of the money. Me. Why me?'

'Jesus, Jack, you didn't believe all that crap about the sequels, did you? That was just to get the boys worked up. We've got one chance in a hundred of getting a sequel. I don't even have financing for the first one yet, probably won't unless everyone gets on board. But it could be a payday, Jack, and if it happens you've got the scene-stealer. Believe me.'

Jack thought it over for as long as it took to swallow another ounce of bourbon. 'I won't be the one who dies,' he said.

'Don't be like that, Jack. Look, if we get lucky we can always finagle it. You know, we'll bring Koko back as a vampire or something. No, I've got it. *Gorilla Zombie*! That's it! Can't you just see it? *Gorilla Zombie*!' Wilson swept his hand in an arc in front of his face, envisioning a title fourteen feet high. Jack grabbed that hand and smashed it down on the table so that the bourbon bottle and the silver box and the silver lighter and the silver ashtray all jumped and rattled and dropped down on the redwood table once again. The bottle fell on its side and Old Crow leaked onto the floor. 'Are you shitting me?' demanded Jack.

Jack clutched the collar of Wilson's Hawaiian shirt and pulled their faces close together. 'Why don't you give that part to Corrigan? He's trying to sell his suit anyway, get out of the monkey business . . .'

'The cowboy?' said Wilson, not even bothering to pull his head away. 'You heard him today. No sense of humour.'

'Get Gemora to do it.'

'He's no comedian, Jack. I don't even know if he can read lines.'

'Look, just because I worked with the Stooges doesn't mean I can't be scary too. You should have seen me at Corregidor. I killed three men, you know, two of them with my hands. And I didn't fight my way back here to be treated like some kind of clown!'

Wilson finally pushed Jack away, then pulled himself upright and swayed over the table. He spoke slowly and deliberately. 'If you don't want the part, you don't have to take it. I can get somebody else if I have to. I thought you'd be grateful.'

'Grateful for a hand out, you mean?' screamed Jack. 'Grateful to be standing at the end of the line again?' He picked up the bourbon bottle, looked at it for a moment, then brought it down on Wilson's head in an explosion of glittering glass and purple blood.

Wilson sat down clumsily. 'Jack,' he said. He'd been saying it all night long. Jack hit him with the jagged stub of the broken bottle and it did something bad to his right ear. 'You stupid, ugly, fucking...' muttered Wilson, but before he got the last word out, Jack cut him off with a wild swing that opened Wilson's throat like a ripe watermelon. Wilson didn't even seem to care about it; he just slumped down and died. Right away, there was lots of his blood on the table.

Jack had gone ape. What had possessed him? He stood in the middle of the room with dripping hands and wondered what he'd done. He wanted Wilson to sit up again and pretend everything was still all right, but knew without even looking that that would never happen. Then he realised with a shiver that he really didn't want anything of the kind. He wanted all the dead things in the world to stay dead, especially the one sprawled on the table in front of him. Instead, it slithered down to the floor with a sound like a load of wet laundry. Jack jumped; he couldn't help it. Then he swore.

Every primitive instinct in the back of his brain told Jack to run and run like hell. There wasn't going to be any movie, and there wasn't going to be any sequel, but there could still be some sort of life for him if he didn't get caught. It wasn't his fault. A man could take only so much, and Jack had taken enough. Now he had to save himself, and that meant he couldn't hit the road before he covered his trail. He had to think fast: the longer his car stayed parked outside, the bigger the chance that someone would spot it. But what had he left inside that might lead back to him? He was trying to figure out how to get rid of his whiskey glass (wash it? break it? take it home?) when he realised what was on it. Fingerprints.

Jack was dead. How many things had he touched in this damned house? Come to think of it, was there anything he hadn't touched? The doors, the walls, the pictures, the bookcases, the stairs, the chest, the toilet, the bottle, the cigarette case, the ashtray, the lighter. The skin. Bill Wilson. There was no way he could ever wipe it all clean in time to make his getaway. Shit! He kicked the table and that fancy silver lighter clattered to the floor. Jack just looked at it for a moment, and then he grinned. The lighter. If he couldn't get his fingerprints off everything in the house, he would just have to get rid of the house instead.

He fumbled with the big silver lighter, got it open, and spilled a few ounces of fluid on the lump of wet wash that been Bill Wilson. It didn't seem like quite enough fuel. He went into the kitchen to rinse his hands, noted the gas stove with some satisfaction, and actually whooped with glee when an angel led him to a drawer which contained a flat blue and yellow can of lighter fuel. Like an animal marking its territory, he squirted the stuff all over the straw matting, the walls, the furniture, the bookcases, the pictures of the women he would never meet.

Jack backed towards the exit, pulled a book of drugstore matches out of his pocket and set them aflame in a deft, one-handed motion. He turned the doorknob and pulled, making sure there was open air behind him before he tossed the burning square of cardboard into the room. No sense in being a damned fool. When the flame hit the fluid, the house belched like a Titan eating tacos, and a blast of hot air pushed Jack out the door, just where he wanted to be. He stood suspended in time for an instant, ready to keep moving towards his car, then turned and walked back into Bill Wilson's burning house.

He had to have that skin. He wasn't sure why – he could hardly use it on the job, and it was evidence against him – but suddenly that beautiful red-gold monkey suit cried out to him to be rescued. He felt like he would be saving a baby and robbing a safe in the same gesture, but he knew the way he knew his own name that he had to get that skin if he ever hoped to live with the memory of what he'd done. It could make everything worthwhile. He was moving faster than he was thinking, but there was no doubt in his mind that he had time to get in and out before the fire caught him. He needed only a few seconds, and the stairs weren't even burning yet. And that skin was some sort of miracle. He could almost hear it calling to him. Yet at the same time he saw the red and yellow flowers of flame blossoming from floor to ceiling, and acknowledged that he was living out the conflagration cliché of every cheap monster movie ever made. Scrambling up the steps on all fours, he ran towards the chest at the foot of Bill Wilson's bed. He heaved open the lid.

The wonderful skin leaped out and wrapped itself around Jack's head. In a heartbeat he was blind and deaf, his mouth full of hair and the scent of dead animals in his nostrils. He was hot and he couldn't breathe. Jack fell to the floor as he scrambled and clawed at the thing that tormented him, his brain a molten ball of panic, and then suddenly he pulled himself free. Had he gone crazy? No matter. Screw the skin, it was time to leave. He rushed for the stairs, now full of billowing smoke and flickering light.

Something stood at the top step. Dead black against the orange glow behind it, the empty skin tottered between Jack and freedom, waving its arms like an angry ape. He saw to his horror how hollow it was, then it was upon him once again. He knew why it had called him back into the house when it wrestled him around and sent him tumbling down the stairway head over heels, each step striking him like a baseball bat in the hands of some simian slugger.

Jack landed on his back, looking up at the bedroom. He could see the skin capering above him, then watched as it danced away and threw itself through an upstairs window to the safety of the lawn below. Jack had broken something, maybe a lot of things. He couldn't raise his head. He couldn't move. He was beginning to realise now why so many horror films ended in fire: it hurt like hell. But why was he being punished? Was it really all his fault? Why were his eyeballs boiling in their sockets? Why was his skin sizzling in his fat and falling from his face? Why, when he was finally found, would he look like nobody at all?

IV

From *Variety*, October 27, 1947.

ACTOR FOUND DEAD

Bill Wilson, the actor who gained critical acclaim for his role in the indie hit *Gorilla Girl*, was discovered dead yesterday in the smoking wreckage of his home outside of Hollywood. Widely acknowledged as the leader of that strange breed whose profession is portraying primitive primates, at the time of his death Wilson was preparing production of an all-star ape production to be called *The Gorilla Gang*. His previous films include *The Jungle Juggernaut*, *Human Sacrifice*, *The Sinister Scientist*, and *The Saint at the Circus*. Apparently his final act was to throw his monkey suit, considered the best in the business, to safety just outside his burning house. The cause of his death is under investigation.

Also dead at the scene was John 'Jack' Jackson, a small-timer whose only notable screen appearance came in Universal's musical *Campus Cuties of 1938*. He was seen cavorting behind bandleader Paul Whiteman in the novelty number 'Monkey Man'. Jackson is said to have been the only Negro in Hollywood who made his living acting in an ape-skin.

Les Daniels has been a freelance writer, composer, film buff and musician. He has performed with such groups as Soop, Snake and The Snatch, The Swamp Steppers and The Local Yokels. A CD of his 1960s group with actor Martin Mull, The Double Standard String Band, was recently released. His first book was *Comix: A History of Comic Books in America*, since when he has written the non-fiction studies *Living in Fear: A History of Horror, Marvel: Five Fabulous Decades of the World's Greatest Comics* and *DC Comics: Sixty Years of the World's Favorite Comic Book Heroes*. More recently, he is the author of *The Complete History* volumes of *Superman: The Life and Times of The Man of Steel, Batman: The Life and Times of the Dark Knight* and *Wonder Woman: The Life and Times of the Amazon Princess*. His 1978 novel *The Black Castle* introduced his enigmatic vampire-hero Don Sebastian de Villanueva, whose exploits he continued in *The Silver Skull, Citizen Vampire, Yellow Fog, No Blood Spilled* and *White Demon*. His occasional short fiction has appeared in a number of anthologies and he has edited *Thirteen Tales of Terror* (with Diane Thompson) and *Dying of Fright: Masterpieces of the Macabre*. About the preceding story, Daniels explains: 'Several of the minor characters are real people, actors who eked out a living decades ago by impersonating apes. I read an anecdote about one of them whose costume was stolen, reducing him to penury, homelessness and eventual death, and thought it might make a good background for a story of supernatural revenge. However the tale took an entirely different turn from what I had first intended, and in fact no theft occurs. Such departures from the original plot don't happen often in my work, but I was pleasantly surprised by the result.'

Sweetness and Light

JOE MURPHY

Jo Jo grinned big for the officers. His cheeks tightened, drawing back until his teeth showed clearly, and his eyes squinted in the harsh jail-cell fluorescence.

'Jeez,' said Officer Ben, who was really Officer Benjamin Clark and new to the force. In dumbing down his name, Jo Jo knew, Clark was trying to be kind to a poor little retard. Jo Jo wasn't retarded. He simply knew how to use his looks.

'What'd I tell you?' Officer Dayton nodded, staring from Jo Jo's mouth to his fellow officer. Dayton, a fat, bottom-feeding rube, dumbed things down for no one. 'Ever see a mouth like that? Fifty says he can do it.'

'You got a bet.' Officer Ben reached for his wallet.

Dayton glanced down the row of cells to be sure no one was watching. After a broad smile, he nodded encouragingly. 'Go on, Jo Jo.'

Jo Jo held out his hand.

'Yeah, okay.' Dayton pulled out his wallet, took a bill and slipped it between the bars.

A lousy ten. But Jo Jo smiled and tucked the bill into his worn jeans.

To command the rube you had to obey the rube; that was the rule Sweetness had taught him. The payment demanded their respect.

Unimportant as these two were, he needed their goodwill. He was in enough trouble already; Sweetness would be here soon.

Jo Jo walked over to the cell toilet, a stump of dirty porcelain set against the cinder block wall. He stopped to study the yellow and brown-stained rim, then got down on his knees.

Dayton chuckled; Officer Ben did not, but the dark-skinned man's eyes met Jo Jo's. Jo Jo turned back to the toilet. He opened his mouth as wide as he possibly could, pausing when his jaws began to ache, in the true spirit of showmanship.

Jo Jo lowered his head and bit down. His teeth ground against the thick stains of the toilet rim. He tasted urine, bleach, and just a hint of faeces. His jaws tightened. The porcelain cracked.

He clamped down harder. A grinding sound filled his ears, magnified through the bone conduction of his massive jaws.

The porcelain crumbled, filling his mouth like a bunch of stones as Jo Jo's teeth came together. He looked up at the officers; his cheeks bulged.

'Shit!' Officer Ben gasped.

Dayton grinned at his buddy and held out a hand. Officer Ben dropped a crumpled fifty into it without ever taking his eyes off Jo Jo. The guy had turned pale.

'Here comes the good part.' Dayton winked at Jo Jo.

Jo Jo tilted his head back to open his throat. Keeping his lips closed, he munched the porcelain into smaller chunks that slid down easily. When his mouth was empty he stood and grinned.

He turned his back on the officers. The sound as he unzipped his jeans seemed like a shriek in the quiet. Jo Jo urinated into the toilet, zipped, flushed, and ambled over to the bars.

'Never seen anything like that,' Officer Ben breathed.

'Carnies. At least they used to be. I saw their act three times!' Dayton laughed. 'Got a nice little place over on Fifth. His mom tells me they're retired now. Wait'll you get a load of her.'

Jo Jo grinned big. Not showmanship this time, but anger, though they'd never know. Sweetness was anything but his mother. Dayton, like most rubes, assumed it from appearances.

Jo Jo's spindly little body looked more like a child's than a thirty-seven-year-old man's. When he was two the doctors had diagnosed him as microcephalic, but that was only because the rest of his head seemed tiny next to his jaws.

By the time Jo Jo realised that he really wasn't retarded, it was too late to change things. He'd ducked school to hide in the public library. He'd given up Tolkien and Dunsany for the more realistic Charles Fort and Kafka.

When a teacher who actually seemed to care, if only for a year, almost discovered the truth, Jo Jo fled deeper into the inner city, his last refuge a nameless bookstore.

There, an old man eager for the touch of anyone, no matter how deformed, had traded favours. Magazines of glossy nymphs mounting magnificently endowed men gave way to yellowed, pictureless volumes of Sacher-Masoch, and then de Sade.

Finally, the old man's gnarled arthritic hands had done things even Jo Jo's body couldn't forgive. Street life was hell until he'd found the carnival.

The cellblock door buzzed and clanked; the officers turned.

'Dayton!' a voice called. 'The boy's been cleared.'

'No shit?' Dayton shook his head.

'Yeah, the old lady found her ring under the counter. His mother's here now. Bring him up.'

Officer Dayton shrugged and pulled out some keys. He unlocked the cell. 'Let's go, little man.'

Jo Jo nodded eagerly although this wasn't entirely the case. Officer Ben, the idiot, offered his hand. Smiling, Jo Jo took it and let them lead him from the cell. Finally, he was through with these worthless rubes. Sweetness would take him home.

They pulled into the spotless driveway of the little bungalow: a white frame house with a dark mansard roof, as unremarkable as any of its neighbours, but the best Jo Jo had ever lived in.

Oleanders lining the front yard scented the air, and small, neatly cut grass squares extended from them to meet the well-washed sidewalk. Jo Jo kept the shrubs carefully pruned, the grass perfectly clipped, but saved his real efforts for the back yard.

Sweetness killed the engine of their battered Volkswagen. Jo Jo climbed out. He hurried around the car and opened her door.

Sweetness neither looked at him nor spoke as she stepped into a twilight still heavy with summer heat. Her large sunglasses turned towards the front door. The low hem of her blue long-sleeved smock swished against leather boots when she limped directly towards him.

He got out of her way by trotting to the front door, had it open by the time she arrived. Cool air brushed his face. The hum of the central air unit flowed around the click of Sweetness's right boot, and the thunk of the left with its built-up heel.

She said nothing. Deep in Jo Jo's throat an ache began. He closed the door that kept out the rubes and came to her in the plainly furnished living room.

Sweetness reached with blue-gloved fingers to remove her shades. A curl of long black hair that framed her face tangled and clung to one earpiece, releasing only at the last moment. Eyes dark as the brown mansard roof stared down at him.

Her head shook slightly, a tremble of disapproval in her soft voice. 'Jo Jo, what did you take?'

He trotted across the room and retrieved a beige wastebasket lined with a black plastic bag. Getting down on his knees, Jo Jo looked up at her and tried to plead with his smile.

His voice box had long since been scraped, worn and cut away; he could not speak except in the scratchiest of whispers. With Sweetness this angry, he dared not speak at all.

Opening his throat, Jo Jo retched into the wastebasket. Pain spasmed up his stomach, through his throat and into his jaws. Up came the porcelain.

As the last chunk dropped past his lips, Jo Jo retched again. It hurt more this time; it always did. His hand moved below his mouth. A diamond ring, wet with bile, dropped into his palm. He held it up for her.

'You were careful?' Sweetness asked casually. She reached down, took the ring and studied it. 'You replaced it with one of the good cubic zirconiums? No one saw?'

Jo Jo nodded and rasped, 'For you. Not for the house. Just this once?'

Tiny, almost imperceptible scars around Sweetness's thin lips softened into a smile. Her eyes turned from the ring to gaze down at him. Dropping the ring into a pocket, she opened her arms. 'That's so sweet, baby. Come here.'

Jo Jo hurried to her embrace. His cheek nuzzled the soft cotton of her smock over the knot of scar tissue where her breast had once been. Her arms closed around him.

'What am I going to do with you, baby?' Sweetness whispered and held him fast. 'We're close enough to losing the house as it is. Insurance money doesn't last for ever. And how many times have I told you: we don't bait and switch where we live. We go into Detroit now, or someone will catch on.'

Tears leaked from Jo Jo's eyes, blotted by Sweetness's smock as her arms tightened. He whimpered softly.

'You know what has to happen.' Her arms fell away.

He clung to her, holding this last moment. Her hands took his shoulders, then tightened, increasingly, until he wanted to howl. Finally, he could stand no more and let go.

'Bring me a can,' Sweetness told him.

Jo Jo looked up at her and tried to hold back a sob. His head shook.

'You have to bring it, Jo Jo.' Her voice grew harsh and then softened. 'You *have* to.'

By her cold caring eyes, he knew this was true. Jo Jo slumped into the yellow-tiled kitchen, to the paper sack by the fridge. Hands trembling, he took out a single tin can, the label gone, leaving only scabs of glue and paper. When he returned she sat upon the armless velvet divan before the big sliding-glass doors that looked out into his back yard.

Because of his quick obedience, she allowed him to gaze into the darkening twilight. He dared not look too long; but when he turned back to her, she too stared into that same evening dusk.

'Come here, baby.'

Jo Jo came to her, bowed his head and offered the can. Her arm slipped around his neck, squeezing him into a headlock. With her other hand, Sweetness snatched the can from his fingers.

Jo Jo gasped, prelude to a sob. Sweetness used that moment, as he'd known she would, to ram the can between his teeth. His jaws closed upon the metal, gnashing though it, until the sharp edges of each rending cut into his gums.

The can twisted in her grip, ripping apart. Jagged edges lacerated his tongue and the insides of his cheeks. A sharp prong slashed down his throat and there was nothing he could do to keep from choking – except swallow.

Mewling, bubbling up blood, Jo Jo doubled over, falling to the floor. Agony tore through his throat and twisted his gut. He lay there, coughing, wheezing and fighting to breathe around the pain.

Sweetness waited until he looked up, her face blurred through his tears.

'You don't learn any other way, baby.' Sweetness shook her head and rose. 'You know the rule. Do my will or eat a can.' She stooped and a blue-fingered glove, spotted now with blood, stroked his cheek.

'Take the wastebasket and go to your room. But because you did what you did out of love . . . I forgive you.'

She didn't wait to see if he obeyed: there was no need. He listened to the swish of her smock as she crossed the carpet, then to the clack and thud of her boots on kitchen tile. The door to her room squeaked closed.

Anything but tin. In his career Jo Jo had eaten almost everything: wood, iron, bricks, cinder blocks, anything Sweetness had used in their act, or that the rubes could carry into the tent with their callused, sweaty paws. Just not tin.

Jo Jo lay on the thick red carpet until the worst of the pain subsided. He managed to turn his head and gazed out at the back yard. The evening darkness reminded him of the last fading glimmer of a spotlight just before things turned black.

He wanted to shudder, knowing Sweetness had yet to discover the real evil he'd begun here in their home. That would hurt too much. Instead, grimacing, he climbed to his feet, fetched the wastebasket and crept into his room, closing the door.

Jo Jo remembered little of the night. A small mercy, because of the terrible struggle to work the can out of him. Only part of it would come up his throat again. The rest, of course, he would gradually push out the other end.

The worst was over; but he wasn't done. His body would not forgive him until it began to heal. Curled upon his sleeping-bag, he didn't really mind so much. He had everything that mattered.

In the quiet of their bungalow, he listened to the sounds of her morning. The thud and thump of bare feet as she entered their adjoining bathroom made him smile until he looked at the bathroom door and remembered the evil.

She hadn't noticed last night when she'd showered. Jo Jo prayed she wouldn't now. He held his breath, listening to the toilet flush, and followed her with his mind, sighing when her footsteps took her to the kitchen. He was safe.

From the kitchen, he heard her enter the hall. It hurt, but he grinned at the clink of the tray she set outside his door.

Sweetness was bound by her own rules; she would not enter his room.

When she finally left for physical therapy, he crawled to the door, reached up, grunting, to turn the knob. He pulled the black plastic tray inside and dragged it with him back to his sleeping-bag. A folded paper square lay next to a green pitcher.

I love you.

She was magnificent! Jo Jo shivered with painful pleasure at her spidery print. He settled down on his sleeping-bag, curling happily around the tray and the note. He tilted the pitcher to his lips and warm sugary water filled his mouth. Now he had all day to rest, to heal, and to look at their poster.

The two-feet-by-three rectangle shimmered in its glass frame, catching the early sunlight from the window. Centred on the wall before him, the poster was the only other object in the room.

Tarkinton's Grand Carnival Presents
Sweetness Barnette, The World's Strongest Woman
With Jo Jo Light, The Human Vacuum Cleaner.
See Them And Be Amazed!

Truly, Sweetness was amazing. In those days, she would stride out at the beginning of their act in her chain-mail bikini. Her six feet, six inches of size, her rippling, weightlifter's muscles, put all the rubes to shame.

Bricks crumbled in her slender fingers. She ripped phone books in half. She even lifted the Volkswagen Beetle, their road car, completely off the ground. The stupid rubes never caught on to that trick.

The day wore into darkness as he gazed at the poster.

When he could see it no more, Jo Jo turned to the window, to his wonderful back yard.

Putting down the Volkswagen, Sweetness would pull him from the back seat. Stiff, encased in his silver lamé costume, hands and feet bound, Jo Jo really did look like a human vacuum cleaner.

Sweetness would stride around the ring, holding him by the silver handle centred in the small of his back. He sucked in the crumbled bricks, pieces of iron bars, halves of telephone books, and whatever the rubes would throw – everything except tin cans.

When their act ended to the applause, whistles and jeers of the idiots, the stagehands killed the spotlight. In that split second of privacy, the light too dim for the rubes to see, too black for the stagehands to rush out, she would pull him against her.

The soft skin of her wondrous breast upon his cheek, bound and helpless in her arms, he would nuzzle her, grinning. And always she would say, 'Great job, baby.'

Jo Jo sighed and gazed at his marvellous yard. Perhaps it was the way the high charcoal fence blended with the emerald-lustred lawn; maybe it was caused by the distant merging shadows of houses and evergreens. Not since the carnival had he found such a darkness.

'I could have saved you,' he whispered.

If only he had been with her in place of that idiot rube, with his big bankroll and horny hands. Or in a car behind them when the accident happened. Jo Jo would have dashed down the embankment to rip through metal and flames, to pull her from the car. Instead, the fire had destroyed her superb flesh, her divine muscles, and killed, for all time, their amazing act.

Instead of the note, the next day, stood a muffin, along with the water pitcher on the tray. By noon, his body had forgiven him enough that Jo Jo was capable of leaving his room and cooking some oatmeal.

He rested again until 4.30 pm. Then he rose and fixed chicken Madeira on herbed biscuits, leaving it hot and ready on the table because Sweetness would be home at six. No sooner had he shut the door, returning to his sleeping-bag, then he heard her come in.

Jo Jo shifted restlessly. His body, the amazing thing that it was, had forgiven him truly now in favour of its own demands. Sweetness had needs of her own that he must fill.

In his dark room, he inched closer to the great evil of the bathroom door. A narrow yellow rectangle of light glowed beneath it. *Almost* a rectangle, certainly the mark of Jo Jo's wickedness.

In his need, in lust forbidden, he had to see her. It didn't matter what she looked like now. The scars meant nothing. But as she had burned, now he burned, scorched by the glimpse of her bare feet, all he could view as she towelled herself dry.

Day by day, whenever guilt did not overwhelm him, Jo Jo had gradually filed the corner of the door, just a tiny bit that came off easily when he scraped his great teeth across it. He lay there now, eye to this place, breathless as she moved about.

An ankle, nothing more. Its ruined flesh twisted as she moved. Bristling hairs thrust up through scarred peaks and valleys too remote for a razor to reach.

His breathing stopped as she neared his door; wood creased his forehead, the floor hard against his cheek as he strained to see. Fear cut into him with the thought of discovery.

The door lock clicked and he wanted to shriek. The door remained still. The light went out. Jo Jo rolled onto his back, teeth tight lest the sigh escape. He smiled. As the offered dinner was his signal, so that click was hers.

Hurriedly he showered and cleaned the bathroom. Turning out the light, he stepped naked into the shadowed living room. Reclined upon the armless sofa, lit only by the softer darkness of his back yard through sliding-glass doors, she waited.

In a silence as deafening as the carnival's roar he came to her. He knelt and only then looked up. Sweetness gazed at him, a soft smile curling the ends of her lips. The moonlight did things to her eyes he couldn't begin to describe, but would hold in his mind till his mind was no more.

Without ever turning his gaze, he listened to the soft slide of her pink pyjamas as first one slippered foot, and then the other, shifted from the couch. Her toes touched the floor. Her gloved hand whispered down the length of her terrycloth robe and slowly drew up the hem.

She had slit the fabric where pyjama legs joined. White thread hemmed each side of the material. It gleamed in the darkness, contrasting with her tight satin curls. Here alone the scars did not reach.

With all the discipline at his command, Jo Jo's fingers clenched into knots behind his back. Their touch was forbidden, an act of betrayal Sweetness would not allow. His head bowed.

Her smell entered him and he breathed in until his chest burned. His tongue touched her, parting the perfect musky lips. She gasped. His lips pursed and kissed the soft curls.

Deeper his tongue probed, until it found a nubbly jewel. Her hand touched the nape of his neck; he gave himself over to her guidance. He heard the couch shift, her low moan that came with the arch of her back. Finally, silence. Her thighs tightened upon his ears.

Nothing was said in the bungalow that night. Its mansard roof and white wood walls held the mocking rumble of the rubes at bay. Jo Jo smiled at the breathy sigh of the air-conditioner, the click of its relays when he finally rose and studied Sweetness's sleeping form.

The sliding-glass door squeaked quietly as he closed it behind him. Naked, he lay face down upon his wonderful lawn.

In the vast expanse of its caress, he found the terrifying freedom to release his need. In the darkness, that so mirrored the moment of a fading spotlight, he let it go.

The next day, he'd just finished trimming the borders around the back-yard fence when the phone rang. Jo Jo dashed into the bungalow. Even when she was away, Sweetness didn't allow him to answer the phone, but if it were her, she might tell him to pick up.

'You've reached the Barnette residence,' the answering machine said in Sweetness's voice. 'Please leave a message.'

Jo Jo frowned at the man's voice. His shoulders sagged and he glared at the machine.

'I'm sorry, Ms Barnette, I know you didn't want us to call you at home. This is Jim Thorton of Greater Lansing Realty. A developer who's interested in constructing an apartment complex has contacted us. They're making an extremely generous offer. I know you weren't interested in selling when we talked before. But please call. Again, sorry to pester you at home. Bye.'

Jo Jo squeezed his eyes shut, legs folding him down on the floor. When he looked again, the machine still sat on the end table. His hand trembled; he reached for the erase button.

No! There was no need! To command her completely he would

obey her abjectly. By her own rules, Sweetness would make the right decision. Tonight he would come to her on his belly. This time he would save them both.

Early that evening, Jo Jo opened the bathroom door and got down on the floor. His body ached, twitching at times, a churning inside him as if he'd drunk a dozen cups of coffee. He couldn't stand it any more.

His cheek pressed against the cold tile of the bathroom floor. With the greatest of disciplined movements, he scraped away a small piece of the wicked corner, savouring the taste of sawdust.

Quickly he scooted into his room and closed the door. Then he inspected his work. It looked a bit wider, but not too much so. He smoothed the edge with his thumb. Her mind would be on the shower anyway. His cheek flattened against the polished wood floor. He could see the toilet and even the towel rack. Perfect!

He heard the front door open. Jo Jo closed his eyes, savouring the scent of duck with black bean sauce and tamarind jus, asparagus with red pepper sauce, and fresh rolls. The whole house smelled of it by now.

His fingers tapped his knee with the thud and thump of her footfalls as she crossed the living room. His eyes opened only with the muted voice of the answering machine.

The hateful message ended abruptly; Sweetness must have pressed the erase button before it was through. Nothing moved in the bungalow for a long time.

Jo Jo gazed out the window at the darkening lawn. Relays clicked, the air-conditioner huffed on. As if this were some secret signal between her and the house, Sweetness began to move. He grinned when she entered the kitchen. Again she paused, but finally continued to her room. His ears strained. Was that the whisper of her clothing as she changed?

She returned to the kitchen and he touched himself, wanting to groan, but not allowing it. It must have taken her hours to eat. By the time he heard the shower come on, Jo Jo was crouched, rocking back and forth on his sleeping-bag.

On hands and knees, he crawled to the bathroom door. Lowering himself, he jammed his face to the floor, eye pressed to the hole. The pink and yellow flowers of the shower curtain rippled. He breathed steam fragrant with strawberry soap.

Sweetness stepped out. Her arm, webbed with thick strands of scars, reached for a towel. The webbing grew to ridges that spread over her chest, forming mashed mountains of pallid lumps in place of breasts. The towel rose to her bald head, to the twisted bits of flesh that were once ears.

Jo Jo's body squeezed into a single slash of need. His forehead creased into the door causing a sharp tick of noise from the wood itself. Sweetness flinched and stared at the door. She looked into his eye.

Her wail rose up and down, like the harsh, twisted screaming one hears beneath a roller coaster. She surged forward, splintering the door. Jo Jo flung himself backwards, head reeling from the blow.

Outlined in the bathroom light, Sweetness glared down at him, one fist knotted, the other clutching a wad of towel. The scars on her chest writhed as twisted shadows with her rapid breathing.

'Rube!' Her shout hit him like an onrushing truck. Jo Jo cringed and opened his mouth. Sweetness flung the towel, knocking the poster off the wall. The glass shattered, pieces scattering across the floor.

Sweetness lunged at him. Naked, fused fingers wrapped around his head. She jerked him up, her arm wrapping around him, scars rough against his cheek. The floor shuddered as she stomped through the house.

He could hear them both crying; his hands clutched her arm. In the bright yellow kitchen she jammed him against the fridge, reached down and snatched up a can.

She dragged him into the dark living room. He stumbled, peeling skin from the backs of his toes. She slammed down upon the armless divan; the rug burned his knees.

Her ragged sobs filled the bungalow. Sweetness crushed the can against his lips. He would never make her believe he was sorry. Jo Jo opened his mouth.

The can crumpled hard enough to force a front tooth from its socket. Sweetness twisted the can and skinned flesh from his palate. Again she twisted, then jerked it back. A torn edge flayed his tongue.

Once more, she forced it in until her knuckles filled his mouth, two more teeth lurching from their places. Somehow, he managed to swallow. Twisted metal slashed down his throat.

'Take one last look, little man.' Jerking his head back, she held him by the neck so that he could view the terrible thing his wickedness had made of her. 'One last look and one last taste.'

Spreading her legs, she forced him down between her. The last thing he heard before the naked scars of her thighs covered his ears was a harsh, sobbing whisper. 'I'm selling the house.'

Bloody lips and gums pressed against her labia. What had he done?

Even as he tried to stop it, the fear rushed through him, knotting his gut, spasming his legs and then pistoning them out again, forcing Sweetness down on the divan.

Up came the can. Rage clasped his hands to her scar-ridged buttocks, the loss of everything that mattered opened his throat, and the need for a last moment of vengeance forced the metal from his lips and deep, deep into the one place the scars had never reached.

Jewels of agony scattered through his mind with the breaking of his pain-hinged jaw. Sweetness arched her torso; the force of her legs snapped his back. Her bladder and bowels released. Blood splashed over his face.

They lay together in the blackness of the bungalow. They lay in a silence more deafening than the roar of any carnival. For a long time nothing moved. Nothing could move, bound by the rules of their love.

Pat . . . Pat . . . Pat. A soft wet sound began below him. Some time later, Jo Jo realised it was her blood, dripping from the divan to the carpet. This final secret signal brought him from his daze. Body numb and useless from the neck down, he discovered an unexpected smoothness upon his cheek. He might still save them both.

With an agony no different, no greater than the life Fate had demanded, Jo Jo Light managed to turn his head. His lips brushed a small space of clear skin upon her inner thigh – a miracle that had somehow escaped the scars. He kissed her.

Would Sweetness accept this small offering? Was she even alive?

Her leg relaxed its grip to whisper over the naked skin of his back before falling to the floor. Her hair rustled; a spring in the divan creaked, marking the turn of her head; he knew where she gazed now, what the moonlight would do to her eyes. He realised her hand lay upon his hair when it moved, turning his head only a little, but just enough.

Together, they looked out into a darkness that held the moment of a dying spotlight. By her grace, he stared out at his wonderful lawn.

Joe Murphy lives with his wife, up-and-coming watercolour artist Veleta, in Fairbanks, Alaska. He has been writing seriously for nine years, whenever their dogs – Lovecraft, Dickens and Lafferty – and their cats – Plato, Kafka and Sagan – allow him to get near the keyboard. His fiction has appeared in magazines and anthologies including *Horrors! 365 Scary Stories*, *Bones of the World*, *Book of All Flesh*, *Chiaroscuro*, *Crafty Cat Crimes*, *Cthulhu's Heirs*, *Demon Sex*, *Gothic.net*, *Legends of the Pendragon*, *Marion Zimmer Bradley's Fantasy Magazine*, *On Spec*, *Silver Web*, *Space and Time*,

Strange Horizons, Talebones and *TransVersions*. Twelve previously published stories are now on the Internet at Alexandria Digital Literature and he is a graduate of the writer's workshops Clarion West 1995 and Clarion East 2000. 'I was attending Clarion 2000 in Michigan when I wrote "Sweetness and Light",' recalls Murphy. 'I was rather nervous about the piece. What would the other writers think of me? Was I some kind of pervert? I talked the idea over with Suzy McKee Charnas and she encouraged me to go ahead. Once done, I was still uncertain about the piece, however with still more encouragement from Samuel Delany, Maureen McHugh, and even more encouragement from Gregory Frost, I cleaned it up and submitted it. I grew a lot as a writer thanks to Clarion.'

Haifisch

CONRAD WILLIAMS

I first saw Jens Korff on the hottest day of the year. I had been delayed on the journey into work because the tube train had ground to a halt mid-tunnel when a passenger tried to lever open one of the doors. We were stuck down there, between Warren Street and Oxford Circus, for forty minutes. Some people fainted. One woman tried to get undressed. A fight broke out when a man refused to share his water with his fellow passengers. Nobody told us what the problem was. In the end, we started moving again, but six people from our carriage had to go to hospital to be treated for heat exhaustion. I arrived at the office cursing London Underground with the kind of hardcore swear words unheard of outside a comprehensive school play-ground. I felt like a sponge with all of its moisture crushed out of it. I felt like shit.

And then I saw him. Maybe it was because nobody had shown any shred of courtesy for anybody else down in that hell-hole that was the Victoria Line. Maybe it was because he just looked so miserable, so beaten, that I went to help him. I was late anyway, what could another few minutes matter?

He was trying to get his wheelchair up the kerb and onto the pavement. He used the camber to generate some speed, but it wasn't enough to get off the road. A woman walked straight past him. A man slowed, gave him a sympathetic look, but continued on his way. By the time I reached him, he had managed to flip the wheels of the chair on to the pavement but the slope up to the surface proper was proving too steep for him. The wheelchair kept slithering back towards the road. He was a game bastard; he didn't give up.

'Here you go,' I said, and pushed him into a position where he could comfortably take over. He turned around in his seat, looking up at me from beneath the hunch of his shoulder. Though he was squinting into the sun, I could see enough of his eyes to tell they were black, like dull, little buttons. The crinkles around them deepened, as if he were smiling, but his mouth remained a flat line.

'Thank you,' he said, his voice lispy and quiet, almost shy. *Sank you.* It sounded foreign, German perhaps. 'I make this journey once a day now, for the past two weeks. You're the first person to help me.'

'It's nothing,' I said, stepping away. My mind was on the the meeting that had started without me. They'd be checking their watches and rolling their eyes now.

He closed his eyes. Shrugged. 'Maybe it is. To me.'

A blanket, the tartan pattern of which had been completely reworked by daubings of egg, soup, curry and coffee, was a stiffening comforter for his legs. His shirt was bedraggled and missing buttons, but his tie was crisply knotted and his hair neatly shorn and oiled. He smelled mealy. He smelled of death, the kind that doesn't realise what it is yet. Death was tasting him, I thought. And death always likes the flavour, in the end.

He nodded curtly and spun away from me, working the wheels with arms that were densely packed with muscle, at odds with the frailty of the rest of his body. I caught sight of a tattoo on his forearm, of faded blue lettering: *alice.*

I work in the tape library of a film production company, doing a job that a monkey could do; a not particularly clever monkey at that. But it was all there was when I went for it and I have a car and the rent to pay. It's better than digging holes in the road and the people I work with are friendly. They pay me more than the job deserves and there's a fair pension. So I'm not moaning. I spent more time chasing girls than I did A-grades so I got what I deserve.

I had a bad day at the office, that day. All the envelopes I stuffed had to be re-stuffed because I forgot to include an important piece of paper with the mailing. And then, when I put them through the franking machine, they were all upside down. Which doesn't really matter in terms of getting them to where they need to be, but in terms of pro-fessionalism, it's up there with domestic airport security in the States. I wish I could blame it on the nightmare journey in, or the relentless fist of heat, but it was the old man in the wheelchair who was putting me off my stroke. I couldn't stop thinking about him. And then Barney came in from the loading bay with a million parcels that needed sorting and delivering to the various departments before 5:00 pm and old men in wheelchairs became about as relevant to me as Nicaraguan coffee yields.

*

The next day was a Saturday. I spent it as I spent most of my Saturdays, hanging around outside the local cinema, trying to summon the nerve to ask the girl at the ticket booth if she'd like to go out for a drink with me. She wasn't what I would call beautiful; I always think of beautiful women as being aloof and knowing. Natalie was pretty. Meaning: innocence and openness. She had a clear complexion and apple-green eyes. Her mouth was perky, as though primed for a kiss. I was just absolutely sold on her and I knew that if I didn't get in there fast, someone would beat me to it, if they hadn't already.

I went in, strode up to the booth and said: 'Do you want to *Spider-man*?'

'I'm sorry?'

'I mean, would you like to come to see a film with me?'

'I'm working.'

'Well, I don't mean now, obviously.'

'I've seen everything.'

'Everything?'

'Pretty much. I work in a cinema.'

'A drink then?'

'Okay.'

'Why not?'

'I said okay.'

'Oh, all right. Great.'

I was out of practice. She smiled and I was so astonished by the openness of her face, the sheer accessibility of her nature, that it was impossible not to smile back. I caught sight of my reflection in the mirror wall and I was grinning like I'd won first prize in a Live For Ever competition.

That evening I picked her up from the flat she shared with her sister in Archway. She left me standing in the hallway, a damp smell rising from the worn carpet, while she went to get her coat and handbag. There was a picture on the wall of a coast seemingly hunkered down beneath a squall. Wallpaper tongues lolled at me. When she returned, I saw she had put a little colour on her lips. I thought that was a good sign. I drove her up to Alexandra Palace, where we bought drinks at the Phoenix Bar and took them outside. It was a little chilly but we were both wearing plenty of clothing and the dribble of sunlight soaking into the horizon bore enough warmth for ten minutes' staring out over north London. We wandered around the funfair by the boating lake and then I suggested we head back to town, maybe get a bite to eat before I dropped her off. I don't really remember us talking about a great deal, but I felt comfortable and she made me feel good. I suppose that's about as much as anybody can hope for.

'I had a good time,' she said, at her door. Darkness had sucked the colour from her face, but she still looked good, like something sculpted from marble. Her skin was flawless. Her eyes gleamed, soaking me up.

'Me too,' I said. She was what? Twenty-four? Twenty-five? Her youth came off in waves from her like the perfume from flowers that makes bees dizzy. When she smiled, a little crease dug in right above her lip. I tell you, I've never fainted in my life, but when she smiled . . . it was like some Pavlovian response: drooling almost, I smiled back.

She leaned in and pressed her mouth against mine. A beat. Then away. Her mouth maybe was like all the other mouths that have landed on mine over the years, but it was so different right at the same time. I don't remember the journey home, but I'm certain it was the best drive of my life.

I do remember my dream, though.

I was running across a terrible landscape of detonated buildings and acres of bloodied soil scarred with twists of barbed wire. Some of the barbs sported medallions of flesh. I was running as fast as I could, but the squeak of wheels behind me was unswerving in its determination. It didn't matter to me what I was sprinting through – thick mud, glass and concrete, the liquefied shell of a human body – as long as it meant it got me further away from the monster that was tracking me. That rhythmic squeak, squeak, squeak . . . it followed me out of sleep with the certainty of my heartbeat. I was so scared, I didn't have the energy to cry out.

'Too bad it won't last,' he said.

'What?'

I was a million miles away, my lips tingling at the remembered thrill of another's touch. Horseferry Road was nose-to-tail. Taxi drivers shouted at lorry drivers, 'Wind your neck in and *do* one, wanker!'

He was in his wheelchair, in a recess of an abandoned sandwich shop called Sloppy Joe's. A hand followed the curve of a wheel as though deriving succour from its touch. Or perhaps in order to calm the steel, I thought crazily, remembering my dreams.

'Your girlfriend. Your new woman. It's over, whether it lasts two years or ten. Like me, your relationship with her doesn't have legs.'

'How do you know? What are you talking about?' I started walking away, eager to be away from the snarl of traffic and this wheelchair freak, but he slithered after me, his twisted feet in his slippers scuffing on the pavement.

'I used to have a sweetheart, like you,' he said. I didn't look at him. His words were accompanied by an awful scuffing as he strove to keep up with me. One of the wheels, I noticed, squeaked rhythmically, like some strange, mechanical heartbeat. 'It's not time that destroys us, you know. It's circumstance. Things change, just a little, on that rocky path of life, and the pebbles we dislodge cause landslides.'

I hurried across a road, knowing the kerbs would hinder him.

Imogen, one of the Reception girls, was approaching work from my left. I hailed her and she smiled, came over to walk with me, but she had noticed the old man, and eyed him nervously as he heckled me.

'What's your dad doing out today?' she asked.

'Funny,' I said. 'I thought he was the person you slept with last night. I don't know. He's giving me grief for some reason. Maybe because I helped him yesterday.'

'Helped him how?'

'Just got him over the road.'

'I think he's pissed.'

I looked back at him. There was indeed a bottle protruding from the blanket across his knees. 'Well, that's a relief,' I said. 'I thought he was plain nuts.'

The old man shouted, 'Even if you get to stick your pee-pee inside her, even then, it's just a matter of time before it's finished.'

'Who's he talking about?' Imogen asked.

I shrugged. 'My mother,' I said, and hurried her, shrieking, inside.

He was still there at lunchtime. I had called Natalie mid-morning to ask her if she wanted to share a sandwich in St James's Park. On my way out, I saw him huddled beneath an awning, the empty bottle hanging from his fingers. He had wet himself. I looked at my watch. I was impatient; I didn't need to be at the park for another twenty minutes. I stood there for a while, grinding my teeth, wishing I had never clapped eyes on the old bastard, and then I went over and shook him awake.

'Where do you live?' I said.

He looked up at me with pained curiosity, like a child who has just been distracted from his rattle. He dropped his bottle and mumbled something.

'Elverton Street?' I knew Elverton Street, it was a matter of minutes away. 'Which number?'

I dragged the brake off with my toe and trundled him over the road. He was protesting, trying to jam his hands down on the wheels, but I was whipping him along at a fair lick and his palms just skidded off the arches. Once outside his house, I felt in his pockets for his keys and let us in. A high smell of polish hit me as I struggled to get the wheelchair over the threshold. On the walls flanking the hallway hung maybe two dozen black and white photographs, old pictures of men in uniform, standing in harbours, faces white and gaunt, hungry lean men with their collars up, lips pinched thin around cigarettes, eyes dark with forgotten knowledge. The weather in all of the pictures looked oppressive, bitter.

'Friends of the family?' I asked, and received a mouthful of German, none of which sounded like an offer to make myself at home.

I parked him next to the fire – there were a pair of grooves well worn into the carpet, so it looked like his favourite position – and made to go, impressed by the cleanliness and order of his flat. Clearly he wasn't in as bad a situation as I had anticipated.

'Wait!' he said, very clearly, and I turned around.

'Okay, okay,' I said, pretty calm, all things considered. Bang went my lunch hour with Natalie. 'At least let me make a phone call,' I said. And then I said, 'What kind of gun is that?'

It was a Mauser, apparently. A Mauser HSC. Standard issue, according to Korff, for all German naval officers. He waggled and waved it in my direction as he talked and the sweat in the crook of my knees gathered and dribbled down my calves as I sat on the sofa, listening to him, staring at the snub-nosed muzzle. I thought of Natalie checking her watch, sighing, making her way out of the park, scribbling *666* and *bastard* next to my name in her Filofax.

Focus was gradually coming back into his eyes. He started to gain control over the spit that was leaking out of his mouth. He said, 'I met Günther Meikle once, in the May of 1944, just a month before he died. He told me that he would not survive the war. He knew he would die, but that was all right. I think he spoke to me because I had served under a great friend of his, the Kapitänleutnant on the *Edelweissboot*. You know, Werner Rathke. Meikle shook my hand and a month later he was dead. Shot while trying to escape the interrogation centre at Fort Worth, Virginia. He was my idol. He sank twenty-five ships.'

I said, 'Are you going to shoot me?'

He looked at me as if surprised to see me in his living room. 'Don't worry,' he said, finally, the words coming out of him in a long sigh. 'The gun is not loaded. It hasn't been loaded since the end of the war.' He stared into his lap, his head hanging so low on his neck that it seemed it must snap off. He said, 'You can go.'

I stood up, never taking my eyes off the gun in his hand. I edged out of the living room and into the hall, past the photographs on the wall. The door catch in my hand felt ice cold. 'Shit,' I said. And then I said it again, loud.

Back in the living room, Korff had dropped the pistol and was crying tearlessly. His mouth was open, but no noise was coming out of it. I picked up the pistol and set it on the table out of his reach. Then I sat down again.

'Is there something I can do?' I said. 'Something to help you? Do you have any family? I could get in touch with them for you.'

'I left the German navy feeling like a dead man,' he said. 'I had spent five years fighting for my country, and for most of those years I was stuck in a steel tube in the water. *Unterseeboot*, we called them. The U-boat. Most of my friends were lost. Most of them are still in the Atlantic, sunk to the bottom, swaying like weed in the currents. You know . . . do you know . . . he first things the fish take are your eyes. I imagine the chances are high of eating a fish from the Atlantic that has feasted on the eyes of a man . . .'

I sat back in the sofa. My hands felt clammy against each other: I had been grinding the palms against each other for minutes. I said, 'Well, I don't know—' but he was moving on. I gained the impression that what he was saying, or gearing up to say, had been on his mind a long time. It sounded rehearsed, as if he had said it many times with only this immaculate, empty room for an audience. But at the same time I knew that I was the first to hear this. Every shred of me strained to leave, to get out before it was too late, but he had started and I was finished.

'Are you all right?'

I smiled back at her, but my mouth must have looked like the edge of a piece of corrugated cardboard. 'I'm fine. Anyway, it's you who I should be asking after. I'm sorry about lunch.'

'Forget it.' And she showed me how a smile ought to happen. She could have been playing with dog dirt or telling me how she agreed with everything Pol Pot ever did and I wouldn't have cared less as long as I could have been left alone to stare at her mouth for a while.

We finished our drinks and walked back to the Tube. I left her at Camden and she kissed me, gave me a hug, said she'd talk to me the following day – all the kinds of things you want to happen with a girl you're so deeply into you could burn up. I wandered back down the High Road, happy that she was happy with me and that things could go along as slow as she liked because I was enjoying the pace of things too. I thought I might catch a night bus home, but the prospect of walking to Tufnell Park was also attractive. It was pretty late now; the pubs had long emptied and the traffic was thinning, the number of figures on the pavements bleeding away into the sidestreets, back to their homes. I reached the end of the road and felt my legs give way. I put out my hand and it was grazed badly by the brick wall as I went down. I sat amongst the empty KFC boxes and Prêt à Manger coffee cups, breathing hard and feeling the cold concrete seep through my jeans. The things he'd said. The fucking things he'd said.

I got home somehow, falling through the door at around 3.00 am. My face in the mirror was the colour of drying cement. I ignored Toby and Roz, two of my flatmates, who were smoking weed around a table littered with wine glasses and a pack of cards, and went upstairs. Penny was in bed.

'Can I borrow your iMac?' I asked.

She moaned and pointed at her desk. It wasn't a yes or a no, but I went over, unplugged the machine and lugged the computer by the handle back to my room. Once everything was arranged on my desk, I booted up the iMac, plugged in the phoneline and logged on. I called up Google and, for want of a better, fed in the word 'unterseeboot'. I trawled around the first few pages of search results and then returned to the search engine where I tried 'Jens Korff'. Nil. Then I tried 'U-boat strategy', 'U-boat defence against depth-charge attack', 'U-boat unorthodox crew duties'.

I tried: *Who was responsible for removing the bodies from battlefields?*

No joy, beyond a couple of ghoulish sites that delighted in presenting pictures of dead bodies.

Then I remembered something Korff had said about his superior. What was his name? Something *Rathke*? And his boat. The name of his boat. Something to do with Christopher Plummer, I had thought at the time.

I went downstairs and made some coffee, endured Toby's dope-fuelled recounting of that night's card-playing in excruciating hand-by-hand detail and finally escaped, wishing that I'd never stopped to help

Jens Korff on the pavement. Wishing I'd left him at the kerb to grow
older and die. Wishing I'd pushed him in front of a fucking delivery
van.

Back upstairs I typed in *Edelweiss* with, for good measure, *Rathke*.
There was one reference. One was enough.

At work the next day, I read through the list of names – German naval
recruits who had served under Werner Rathke on the *Edelweissboot* –
that I had printed off Penny's iMac. There was no Jens Korff. But there
was a Jens Müller. And a Marcus Korff. And many other names besides.
All of them were accompanied by birthdates that fell more often than
not between the years 1915 and 1925. It wasn't so far-fetched an idea
that he had made up his name. Old men now, those that had survived.
Those that had died during the war would have been frighteningly
young, too young. I imagined how they might have felt, sinking beneath
the freezing, black waters of the Atlantic as they set off to attack Allied
Forces ships. I tried to imagine Jens as one of those wolfish young men
in the photographs, eyes dark with a knowledge that no young adult
should ever be allowed. When I looked back at the list of names, I had
screwed it into a ball beneath my fist.

Shortly before lunchtime I saw Korff dragging himself past the
window on the main street, excruciatingly intent on reaching his usual
destination, his blankets bunched on his lap like a disfigured pet. I
watched him go, and grabbed my jacket.

Elverton Street was quiet but for a man in a paint-spattered track-
suit trying to get impacted insects off the windscreen of his car with a
dish scourer. He paid me no attention as I walked past him and stopped
in front of Korff's door. It was locked, as was the front window. I
strolled around to the back street, resisting the urge to run and draw
attention to myself. Korff was going to be a while.

Korff was not as fastidious about security at the rear of his flat. A
flaking wooden gate collapsed in on a back yard strewn with rubble,
swollen bin-bags, nests of takeaway cartons and empty bottles of Bell's
whisky. Bastard cabbage pushed through the cracks in the paving
stones; a raft of nettles was anchored to the foot of a garden shed that
looked as solid as drenched cardboard. Inside, on top of an ancient
chest freezer mottled with rust, I found a claw hammer that I used on
the back door to the kitchen and ground my teeth against the noise of
splitting wood. I shut the door quickly behind me and peered out, but
nobody had watched me break in. I pressed the heel of my hand against

my chest, trying to calm the thud of my heart. No sounds inside the flat. I almost wished there were.

I returned to the hallway and checked the photographs on the wall: men shaking hands in the bitter cold, stiff in uniform, whitened by the brittle weather. They stood before the dark hulks of U-boats in black harbours. Some of the men were made indistinct by the primitive photographic equipment, or drizzle, a caul that would not improve the fortunes of these sailors. One picture showed a pair of men laughing in the foreground while another two, blurred by lack of focus, were caught in the act of transporting a crate onto the U-boat. Even distance could not conceal the skull that had been stencilled on to the wooden slats.

Three feet from me, through the frosted window of Korff's front door, an arm reached up and its shadow fell through the glass, snaking across the carpet to cling to my shoes. I backed away and was in the kitchen by the time Korff was able to manoeuvre himself across the threshold. He pushed a cloud of booze before him. I was about to ghost out of the back door when I heard him weeping. He was heading my way. I moved behind the edge of wall that contained an ironing board and held my breath, noticing too late that my footprints on the lino betrayed my passage through Korff's flat.

I needn't have worried; he was interested only in loading up on more liquor. His trembling hands tore at the screw-top of the bottle. I almost said something. I almost did. But I have to admit that I wanted him to drink long and hard. I wanted him to find oblivion one way or another, because I knew that I wasn't too far away from finding it for him. I don't suppose I realised how close to the edge of my own reason I had ventured.

And while we spent those seconds together in the kitchen, me watching the back of his head and him watching the end of his bottle as it tilted towards and away from him, I thought of his hands scrabbling on the frost-scarred earth, his breath coming in fast rounds, like the machine-guns that had destroyed the silence a few hours before . . .

He keeps his breath coming quickly because it mists before his eyes, and that makes what he's looking at more manageable, the detail milky, ill-formed; to focus on this is to know what madness means. And it's not the clay in the soil turning the ground this colour. And these things he's picking up and putting in a hessian sack, they aren't branches torn down from trees by stormy weather. He removes the rings and puts them in his pockets. He has to use a knife to separate these intestines from the body they've spilled from. He doesn't look up, he refuses to look up, as the dying owner of the guts feebly protests. It all goes in his bag, as much as he can carry. Did he volunteer for this job? He doesn't think so but he can't remember. Does he love the Reich enough to converse with what ought to be unspeakable? Arbeit macht frei, he thinks as he lifts a detached face up by the eye sockets. Into the bag. Arbeit macht frei.

Three weeks later and he's in the engine room of U-293. It's night, and they're ploughing across the surface five miles off Long Island, USA, on a special patrol. By day they submerge and the engine room grows unbearably hot. He's convinced he can smell the body parts, but his colleagues tell him to stop being so grisly, to go and shower properly if he can smell stuff. The refrigeration is working fine, they tell him. Dummkopf. Dummkorff.

They drop off the sabotage team at midnight and return to deep waters. Three hours later, he hears Rathke's sharp voice stabbing the thick air inside the submarine. A cutter has picked up U-293 on its radar and is in pursuit. Rathke orders that the engines are killed. The propeller slows. The sub begins to sink. There is a slight jarring as the snout of the craft lands in the soft sand on the Atlantic seabed. Korff is no longer worried because he's into the drill, the routine that was hammered into him during weeks of hard training in the Baltic Sea. At the precise moment he anticipated that he would be immersed in fear, fear didn't come into it. He had no time to be scared. His brothers were depending on him and he must not let them down.

Now the call for silence. All systems dead. The sonar's ghostly calling is all they can hear. Death is in the water.

'It's only a patrol craft,' whispers Rathke. 'We wait. If the captain is inexperienced, we might try climbing to periscope depth and use torpedoes. If not, then we are still prepared. Yes?' His eyes scour every one of his men, searching for steel.

Korff has dreamed of this moment a thousand times. At such times, he imagines the hull of the U-boat to be invisible and the black, woven silk of the sea presses against him. There is a shark in the water and Jens knows that it has his smell in its blood. The shark has been seeking him for many years, as many years as Korff has been alive. He imagines that he and the shark came into being at the same point in time.

An explosion. The waves from the blast gently rock the U-boat. Werner Rathke's face swings into him, heavily shaded by the reluctant emergency lighting. His lips have vanished, spittle clings like invisible limpets to his teeth. 'Remember,' he says, and his voice is sour with adrenalin, 'not on the first charge. We have to risk a few explosions.'

Before Korff can nod his head, the captain is creeping back to his station. The reek of men who know that a hull breach will end their lives in an unimaginably terrible way pervades the craft. The chambers might be pressurised, but Korff has a headache that squeezes the tender meat behind his eyes until black motes swim across his vision. He stands by the ballast-tank release valves and though the sweat stings his eyes, he does not blink. He watches his captain as though he were a spirit that his gaze codifies.

Another three depth charges detonate each one closer than the last. The fifth explosion sends men sprawling.

'Now!' Rathke calls and Korff yanks the valve open and sends the soup of bodies, the limbs and guts of men who had dismembered each other on a Caen battlefield, streaming to the surface.

No more depth charges fall. Soon, they hear the engines of the cutter diminishing. When they can hear the ship no more, Rathke orders their return to Brest.

Once he had fought with his wheelchair and taken it over the threshold into the garden (in one crazed moment, I actually felt myself instinctively reach out to help him) I hurried from the flat but once again paused by the photographs, drawn by the power of their history and the benign smiles that flirted with insanity.

One photograph in particular struck me as odd and it took me a few seconds to understand why. Jens Korff was standing next to an older man, their body language making it obvious that they disliked each other. Both were bleakly regarding the camera. I say that, though only one of them, Korff, had eyes. The other's had been scratched from the print with a sharp instrument. I quickly slid the photograph from its frame and stuffed it in my pocket. It wasn't on Korff's sightline; presumably it would be a while before he missed it. On the back of the photograph, written in pencil, was the name I had expected to see: *Werner Rathke*.

Natalie brought me back from the brink. All we did was sit by the river and eat bagels and cream cheese, read a couple of magazines, hold hands – but it was enough. Later I drove her home and she held on to me at the front door as if I was going away for a long time. I fought it, but I couldn't help thinking of Korff, of whether he had a sweetheart in some German port who had kissed him goodbye and hugged him tightly before he went into the water with his comrades.

'Come in,' she said, finally. She was warm and she smelled of apples. Under the streetlamp, her pulse trapped and released shadow in the hollow of her throat.

'I'd love to,' I said. 'But I've got stuff I need to do tonight.'

'Stuff?' she said, smiling, but there was a stiffness to her voice that wasn't there before.

'Yeah. I promised I'd design a new letterhead template for a guy at work. It's no big deal – it'll only take me half an hour – but I've never been asked to do anything like that before and it might be good for me. The guy who asked me doesn't know a computer from a box of crackers.' I was amazed at the fluency of the lie, and disgusted at myself at the way she took it in. She smiled, more naturally, and kissed me for a long time on the mouth.

I said, 'Look, I'll talk to you tomorrow, okay?' And a wave and another smile and she was gone, the door snicking shut behind her. I waited till I saw the hall light go off before moving away. My guts felt as though they'd been packed with ice.

I couldn't have gone through with it, as much as I yearned for her spread out before me, wanting me. She was in my head all the way home, her naked body reaching up from a blanket, her skin bathed in pale fire from the bleached streetlamps outside her window. But I couldn't have done it when Korff was so deeply embedded in my thoughts.

There are no roses on a sailor's grave.

I woke up with those words in my mind and recoiled from them in the dark. I could hear voices in the living room: Roz and a stranger, laughing, chinking glasses. I could hear Toby snoring next door. Penny would still be out, working at the hospital. I wasn't particularly close to my flatmates, but they were all I had. Natalie was on my side too, that was beyond question, yet I felt more alone than at any other point in my life. I pulled the duvet up around my face and tried to gauge how much night was left by staring at the square of dark in the window. I had not gone directly home the previous night. I had caught a late Tube to St James's Park and walked through the sleeping cobbled street market of Strutton Ground, past the Channel 4 TV building on Horseferry Road, lit up like a glass sculpture, and into Elverton Street, not knowing what I intended to do until I reached the front door. There was a light on in the living room and I could hear the television, see its subtle flicker of colour and light against the ceiling through the crack in the curtains. I could hear something else too. A banging noise, like a chef flattening cuts of veal with a rolling pin, coming deeper from within the flat. I raised my fist three times to knock on the door and failed three times to go through with it.

I was about to run back to the Underground, see if I could catch the last Tube, when he lifted the letterbox flap and said: 'I knew you were here today, Seth.'

I froze. Night shifted above the rooftops like the twist of currents in deep water.

'Won't you come in?' he asked. A thick, yeasty smell accompanied his words into the street.

'I really shouldn't—' I began, as the door opened. I felt the flat's interior heat envelop me.

'No,' he said, and I heard the creak of his wheelchair as he moved back inside, leaving me to lock up behind him. 'You really shouldn't.'

'I want you to tell me about her,' he said. The Mauser was on the table by his chair, its barrel pointing my way. It hadn't been loaded before, so maybe it wasn't now. But why have it out if it wasn't loaded? I hated the way he thought he could control me so easily. I hated even more the fact that I didn't have any fight in me, perhaps because he was so old, a loose bundle of bones thrown in a chair. How did you fight against that?

'There's nothing to tell,' I said.

'Of course there is,' he said, leaning forward in his chair and licking his lips. When he smiled, heavy ivory-coloured teeth sloped back from his mouth. It was a smile the complete opposite of Natalie's. I didn't want to return it. I wanted it in a box, buried in six feet of soil. 'She's a real looker. She has a nice . . . smile. A smile that reminds me of my own sweetheart. Astonishing, the similarities. A smile you could fall into. A smile to make you believe in God.'

'How would you know that?'

'I get around,' he said, rubbing his hands over the top of his wheels. 'Vroom, vroom.' He looked at the gun and then looked at me. 'So tell me about her. What's she like, to talk to, I mean?'

'She's fine,' I said, as icily as I could manage. 'We get on well.'

'It won't last, you know.'

I shrugged. 'Maybe not. But I'm having fun in the meantime. Can I go now?'

'What were you doing here today? Why were you hiding in my kitchen?'

I opened my mouth and nothing came out. 'I was concerned,' I said, at last, knowing that the colour in my face would tell him I was lying, but he was touched.

'I could give you a key,' he said. 'After tomorrow, well, then you can come and go as you please. I could do with a little help around the home. And I'd pay you. After tomorrow.'

'What's happening tomorrow?' I asked.

He said, 'I'm saying goodbye to an old friend.'

He let me go after that. If he noticed the photograph on his wall was missing, he didn't mention it. At the door, he stopped me.

'I had someone, once. Alice, her name was.'

'I know,' I said, pointing at his tattoo.

His hand went to it, covering the blue letters as if I had somehow intruded on his privacy, or hers.

'She died while I was at sea,' he said. 'I found out later that my superior on that ship – I told you about him – he had been having an affair with my girl. I say affair . . . but he brutalised her. Raped her. She never said a word to me. She was scared I would be banished to some concentration camp or other if I confronted him. She killed herself, hanged herself from the rafters in the attic with the lacing from a corset she wore when she first went with him. In her letter to me she explained everything.'

I was closing the door behind me when he said something that tightened my chest, as if I'd tried to squeeze into a jacket that was two sizes too small for me.

'He lives around here, Rathke. How's that for a coincidence?'

I must have dropped off staring at the night through that window with its peeling paint and condensation, even though I believed I might never sleep again, because I woke up with a headache, and a need to find Werner Rathke that consumed me like the keenest hunger. I considered calling the police, but I could imagine how they'd react when I told them about a geriatric invalid trundling off to mete out some justice after fifty years.

He lives around here.

When I got into the office I hit the phone books and found him pretty much immediately, but when I called there was no answer. He lived a matter of a few minutes' walk away. I had to go.

Perkin's Rents was a little road connecting Great Peter Street to Victoria Street. The windows of countless apartments were studded into its walls. I found the right door and rang the bell – a scrap of paper with the initials WR pencilled on to it had been Sellotaped above the corresponding number of Rathke's flat – and when there was no response I rang Rathke's neighbour, who buzzed me in without asking what it was I wanted. There was a small lift, but it didn't work when I jabbed the call button. Instead I pushed the timer switch for the stairwell lights and trudged up, trying to ignore the smell of piss and overcooked vegetables. Meals-on-Wheels cartons were piled up outside many of the doors. On one landing I had to step over an unopened bag of mush that was rotted lettuce leaves and a splintered bicycle pump. I got to Rathke's flat just as the light clicked off. The timer switch up here didn't work so I knocked at the door, wondering how many clues I would need before I realised he wasn't in, or was in but very dead.

'Go away.' The voice was almost too low to detect, but I heard it. I heard the fear that drove it too.

'Mr Rathke?' I called, bending to push in the flaps of the letterbox.

'Leave me alone. Just go. Go to hell.'

'Herr Rathke,' I persisted. 'I need to speak to you. I know someone you know. I think you're in danger.'

I was expecting anything: curses, more requests to get out, a demand to know who I was and what danger I thought he was in. I didn't expect him to start laughing.

'*I'm* in danger?' he said. 'Me? *Me?*'

'Yes,' I said. 'Were you aware that Jens Korff—'

The door swung open. It was open long enough for me to tell that here was a man close to death, older than Jens Korff, more frail too, although he could manage to walk. The flat behind him was like a smeared palette of browns. The door was open just long enough for him to say, 'It's my wife who is, who was, in danger. He has no interest in killing me. He understands the true meaning of pain. Pain isn't physical.' He leaned into me, his face in shadow, his white hair like ice on fire. 'Pain like this, it lasts a lifetime.'

Then I was alone on the landing. I heard a squeak, and the sound of wood splintering. From above, the lift doors clunked shut and the gears began to grind into action. The lift proper sank into view, its opaque windows concealing something stunted and pink, like an organ suspended in milky preservation fluid. It turned its face to me, but I couldn't make out any features, beyond the shadow of deep creases scoring it all over.

I hurried down the darkened stairwell, but slipped on the bag of salad and landed heavily on my back. For a minute or so I lay there, pain ricocheting around my spine and legs, the wind knocked from me. It would be the ultimate irony, I thought, if I were to end up an invalid. But gradually movement came back to my numb legs and I was able to lever myself upright. The door downstairs had long since slammed shut. There was nobody on the street when I glanced out of the window. At street level I checked the lift entrance. Two grooves had split the frame, at around the height that a couple of wheels on a wheelchair might be.

I didn't go back to work. I mooched about the street market on Strutton Ground, looking at the cut-price toiletries and CDs and the demonstration of a magic sponge that could clean any stain, 'Guaran-bleedin-teed, ladies and gentlemen!' At the end of the cobbled thoroughfare a flash of sunlight on a steel rim jerked my head upright, but it was just the wheel arch of a taxi as it performed a tight U-turn in the road. I wandered up to the main drag anyway and crossed the road. I thought I might head up to the pub on Dartmouth Street for a pint because I certainly didn't want to go back to the office. I passed New Scotland Yard and was aiming to nip over Tothill Street when I saw the puddle. Or rather, the tracks made by the thin wheels that had passed through it.

I followed them. And when they ran out, on Birdcage Walk, I didn't need to follow them any more, because I could see him, struggling to get on to the pavement. I didn't help him this time. I waited until he'd done it himself and then sauntered into St James's Park, keeping thirty or forty yards behind him.

He crossed the footbridge and steered left. And stopped. I waited on the bridge to see what he was going to do next, but he just sat there, next to the fence surrounding the lake, while the geese and the ducks tried to work out whether he was there to feed them or just take in the view.

After ten minutes, he checked the walkways around him, but there was nobody in sight. Then he removed his blanket and stood up.

I had been expecting something like that for so long, it wasn't a shock to me. I just shook my head at his temerity. He was carrying something in a clear polythene bag. Stepping gingerly over the fence, he approached the lake and knelt by its edge. My view was obscured by a clump of reeds, but I could see that he'd dumped the bag there when he stood up again. Then back over the fence and into his wheelchair, rearranging that tired old Tartan blanket over his knees. He was about to carry on along the path, in the direction of Buckingham Palace, but he remained for a moment, looking back at the reeds. Eventually he trundled away.

There were thirty or forty bags, I found, nestled in the water, deep into the reeds where the birds couldn't get at them. The first one I pulled out contained a hank of hair still attached to a portion of greenish scalp. The second one was filled with bloody teeth. The third was a hard knot of meat I tried not to recognise. I didn't look at any more. I went back to the office to call the police.

But I didn't make it back. I know I should have gone straight to a phone, but I needed a drink so I went to the pub and sank a Hofmeister and a double Jack. When I came out I knew I had to hear his version first, before it ended up in the newspapers. When I got to Elverton Street, his door was open.

He was lying on the floor of his flat, the pristine cream of his carpet turned into a Pollock by however many litres of blood had sprayed out of his head. I couldn't believe he was still alive, not with the top of his skull sheared off like a boiled egg. A cushion next to him was smouldering where he had used it to muffle the explosion. His leg was twitching; piss had darkened his beige slacks with a strip that ran from his crotch to his calf. His eyes were all over the place, thank God, because I don't know what I would have done if he'd focused on me. I leaned over him and he gripped my wrist with appalling strength.

'You killed Rathke's wife,' I said. 'After all this time, you had to have revenge? How does that work? How can you feel good about that? You've stewed in your sad little juices all this time and forgotten to live your life because of it.'

He couldn't hear a word.

'I did her too,' he slurred. In the blood that streamed from his mouth were splinters of bone. 'The bitch. All that time she thought she got away with it. Well I got her too. This . . .' he thrust the tattoo under my nose, but it was obscured by blood. 'This was a reminder to me over the years. I got her too. I got her too.'

'But she killed herself,' I said. He didn't hear that either.

He died at the moment his strength seemed at its greatest. He was gripping me so hard that he was lifting himself off the floor.

Me. Korff. The gun.

Sunlight streaming through the front window. No sounds. Not even traffic. Or maybe there was, but I couldn't hear it. The vibrant colours that had flooded my senses a few minutes before had been bleached. I was fading everything out. Soon it was just me and Korff. And then a little while later it was just me.

And the manila envelope sticking out of Korff's pocket.

I was hoping that the blood on the corner had been splashed there just now, rather than seeping through from inside. I stared at it until I wasn't sure that I was in the room any more.

I did her too.

I picked up the envelope and tore it open, shook it to dislodge its contents, which slithered on to the table. And as I reared away, shock swelling in my heart to the point where I was sure it must burst, my first reflex, as always, was to smile back.

Conrad Williams's debut novel *Head Injuries* was published to widespread acclaim in 1998 by The Do-Not Press and was optioned by Revolution Films. A novella, *Nearly People*, with an introduction by Michael Marshall Smith, was published in 2001 and has subsequently been nominated for the International Horror Guild Award. Over the past fifteen years, Williams's work has appeared in numerous magazines and anthologies, most recently *The Mammoth Book of Best New Horror*, *Phantoms of Venice*, *The Museum of Horrors*, *Cemetery Dance* and *The Spook*. He has also been published in three other volumes of *Dark Terrors* and is a past winner of the British Fantasy Award. 'This story popped into my head one day while I was at work,' the author remembers. 'I looked out of the window and saw this poor old man in a wheelchair, trying to get up the kerb on to the footpath. Nobody stopped to help. I suddenly imagined this frail soul as a refugee from history, someone who had once been strong, ambitious, dangerous, and who might still possess the capacity to commit terrible acts. That idea dovetailed sweetly with a website I stumbled upon that detailed a novel way in which the German U-boat crews put off their Allied pursuers. I haven't been able to find the website since, so maybe it's been pulled. Or perhaps I'm kidding myself, and it never existed outside my own head . . .'

The Road of Pins

CAITLÍN R. KIERNAN

I

May

Without a doubt, Mr Perrault's paintings are some of the most hideous things that Alex has ever seen and if her head didn't hurt so much, if it hadn't been hurting all day long, she might have kept her opinions to herself, might have made it all the way through the evening without pissing Margot off again. The first Thursday of the month so another opening night at ARTIFICE, another long evening of forced smiles for the aesthete zombies, the shaking of hands and digging about for dusty scraps of congeniality when all she wants is to be home soaking in a hot, soapy bath or lying facedown on the cool, hardwood floor of their bedroom while Margot massages her neck. Maybe something quiet playing on the stereo, something soothing, and the volume so low there's almost no sound at all, and then her headache would slowly begin to pull its steelburr fingers out of the soft places behind her eyes and she could breathe again.

'You shouldn't have even come tonight,' Margot whispers, sips cheap white wine from a plastic cup and stares glumly at the floor. 'If you were going to be like this, I wish you'd gone home instead.'

'You and me both, baby,' and Alex frowns and looks past her lover at the smartly dressed crowd milling about the little gallery like a wary flock of pigeons.

'So why don't you leave? I can get a taxi home, or Paul will be happy to give me a ride,' and now Alex thinks that Margot's starting to sound even more impatient with her than usual, probably afraid that someone might have overheard the things she said about the paintings.

'I'm here now,' Alex says. 'I suppose I might as well stick it out,' and she rubs roughly at the aching space between her eyebrows, squints across the room at the high, white walls decorated with Perrault's canvases, the track lights to fix each murky scene in its own warm, incandescent pool.

'Then will you please try to stop sulking. Talk to someone. I have to get back to work.'

Alex shrugs noncommittally and Margot turns and walks away, threading herself effortlessly into the murmuring crowd. Almost at once, a man in a banana-yellow turtleneck sweater and tight black jeans stops her and he points at one of the paintings. Margot nods her head and smiles for him, already wearing her pleasant face again, annoyance tucked safe behind the mask, and the man smiles back at her and nods his head too.

Five minutes later and Alex has made her way across the gallery, another cup of the dry, slightly bitter Chardonnay in her hand, her fourth in half an hour, but it hasn't helped her head at all and she wishes she had a gin and tonic instead. She's been eavesdropping, listening in on an elderly German couple, even though she doesn't speak a word of German. The man and woman are standing close together before one of the larger paintings, the same sooty blur of oils as all the rest, at least a thousand shades of grey, faint rumours of green and alabaster, and a single crimson smudge floating near the centre. The small, printed card on the wall beside the canvas reads *Fecunda ratis*, no date, no price, and Alex wonders if the old man and woman understand Latin any better than she understands German.

The man takes a sudden, deep breath then, hitching breath almost like the space between sobs, and holds one hand out, as if he intends to touch the canvas, to press his thick fingertips to the whirling chaos of charcoal brush strokes. But the woman stops him, her nervous hand at his elbow, hushed words passed between them, and in a moment they've wandered away and Alex is left standing alone in front of the painting.

She takes a swallow of wine, grimaces at the taste and tries to concentrate on the painting, tries to *see* whatever all the others seem to see; the red smudge for a still point, nexus or fulcrum, and she thinks maybe it's supposed to be a cap or a hat, crimson wool cap stuck on the head of the nude girl down on her hands and knees, head bowed so that her face is hidden, only a wild snarl of hair and the cruel, incongruent red cap. There are dark, hulking forms surrounding the girl and at first glance Alex thought they were only stones, some crude, megalithic ring, standing stones, but now she sees that they're meant to be beasts of some sort. Great, shaggy things squatting on their haunches, watching the girl, protective or imprisoning captors and perhaps this is the final, lingering moment before the kill.

'Amazing, isn't it,' and Alex hadn't realised that the girl was standing there beside her until she spoke. Pretty black girl with four silver rings in each earlobe and she has blue eyes.

'No, actually,' Alex says. 'I think it's horrible,' never mind what Margot would *want* her to say because her head hurts too much to lie and she doesn't like the way the painting is making her feel. Her stomach is sour from the migraine and the bitter Chardonnay.

'Yes, it is, isn't it,' the black girl says, undaunted, and she leans closer to the canvas. 'We saw this one in San Francisco last year. Sometimes I dream about it. I've written two poems about this piece.'

'No kidding,' Alex replies, not trying very hard to hide her sarcasm, and she scans the room, but there's no sign of Margot anywhere. She catches a glimpse of the artist, though, a tall, scarecrow-thin and rumpled man in a shiny black suit that looks too big for him. He's talking with the German couple. Or he's only listening to them talk to him, or pretending to, standing with his long arms crossed and no particular expression on his sallow face. Then the crowd shifts and she can't see him any more.

'You're Alex Marlowe, aren't you? Margot's girlfriend?' the black girl asks and 'Yeah,' Alex says. 'That's me,' and the girl smiles and laughs a musical, calculated sort of a laugh.

'I liked your novel a lot,' she says. 'Aren't you ever going to write another one?'

'Well, my agent doesn't think so,' and maybe the girl can see how much Alex would rather talk about almost anything else in the world and she laughs again.

'I'm Jude Sinclair. I'm writing a review of the show for *Artforum*. You don't care very much for Perrault's work, I take it.'

'I'm pretty sure I'm not supposed to have opinions about painting, Jude. That's strictly Margot's department—'

'But you *don't* like it, do you?' Jude says, pressing the point and her voice lower now and there's something almost conspiratorial in the tone. A wry edge to her smile and she glances back at *Fecunda ratis*.

'No,' Alex says. 'I'm sorry. I don't.'

'I'm not sure I did either, not at first. But he gets in your head. The first time I saw a Perrault I thought it was contrived, too self-consciously retro. I thought, this guy wants to be Edvard Munch and Van Gogh and Albert Pinkham Ryder all rolled into one. I thought he was way too hung up on Romanticism.'

'So are those things supposed to be bears?' Alex asks, pointing at one of the looming objects that isn't a megalith, and Jude Sinclair shakes her head. 'No,' she says. 'They're wolves.'

'Well, they don't look like wolves to me,' and then Jude takes her hand and leads Alex to the next painting, this one barely half the size of the last. A sky the sickly colour of sage and olives, ochre and cheese draped above a withered landscape, a few stunted trees in the foreground and their bare and crooked branches claw vainly at an irrevocable Heaven. Between their trunks the figure of a woman is visible in the middle distance, lean and twisted as the blighted limbs of the trees and she's looking apprehensively over her shoulder at something the artist has only hinted at, shadows of shadows crouched menacingly at the lower edges of the canvas. The card on the wall next to the painting is blank except for a date – 1893. Jude points out a yellowed strip of paper pasted an inch or so above the woman's head, narrow strip not much larger than a fortune-cookie prognostication.

'Read it,' she says and Alex has to bend close because the words are very small and she isn't wearing her glasses.

'No. Read it out loud.'

Alex sighs, growing tired of this, but ' "A woman in a field",' she says. ' "Something grabbed her",' and then she reads it over again to herself, just in case she missed the sense of it the first time. 'What the hell is that supposed to mean?'

'It's from a book by a man named Charles Fort. Have you ever heard of him?'

'No,' Alex says, 'I haven't.' She looks back down at the woman standing in the wide and barren field beyond the trees, and the longer she stares the more frightened the woman seems to be. Not merely apprehensive, no, genuinely terrified, and she would run, Alex thinks, she would run away as fast as she could, but she's too afraid to even move. Too afraid of whatever she sees waiting there in the shadows beneath the trees and the painter has trapped her in this moment for ever.

'I hadn't either, before Perrault. There are passages from Fort in most of these paintings. Sometimes they're hard to find.'

Alex takes a step back from the wall, her mouth gone dry as dust and wishing she had more of the wine, wishing she had a cigarette, wondering if Judith Sinclair smokes.

'His genius – Perrault's, I mean – lies in what he *suggests*,' the black girl says and her blue eyes sparkle like gems. 'What he doesn't have to *show* us. He understands that our worst fears come from the pictures that we make in our heads, not from anything he could ever paint.'

'I'm sorry,' Alex says, not exactly sure what she's apologising for this time but it's the only thing she can think to say, her head suddenly too full of the frightened woman and the writhing, threatful trees, the pain behind her eyes swelling, and she only knows for certain that she doesn't want to look at any more of these ridiculous paintings. That they make her feel unclean, almost as if by simply seeing them she's played some unwitting part in their creation.

'There's nothing to be sorry for,' Jude says. 'It's pretty heady stuff. My boyfriend can't stand Perrault, won't even let me *talk* about him.'

And Alex says something polite then, nice to meet you, good luck with the review, see you around, something she doesn't mean and won't remember later, and she leaves the girl still gazing at the painting labelled *1893*. On the far side of the gallery, Margot is busy smiling for the scarecrow in his baggy, black suit and Alex slips unnoticed through the crowd, past another dozen of Albert Perrault's carefully hung grotesques, the ones she hasn't examined and doesn't ever want to; she keeps her eyes straight ahead until she's made it through the front door and is finally standing alone on the sidewalk outside ARTIFICE, breathing in the safe and stagnant city smells of the warm Atlanta night.

II

June
The stuffy little screening room on Peachtree Street reeks of ancient cigarette smoke and the sticky, fermenting ghosts of candy and spilled sodas, stale popcorn and the fainter, musky scent of human sweat. Probably worse things, too, this place a porn theatre for more than a decade before new management and the unprofitable transition from skin flicks to art-house cinema. Alex sits alone in the back row and there are only eleven or twelve other people in the theatre, pitiful Saturday night turn-out for a Bergman double-feature. She's stopped wondering if Margot's ever going to show, stopped wondering that halfway through the third reel of *Wild Strawberries*, and she knows that if she goes to the pay phone outside the lobby, if she stands in the rain and calls their apartment, she'll only get the answering machine.

Later, of course, Margot will apologise for standing her up, will explain how she couldn't get away from the gallery because the carpenters tore out a wall when they were only supposed to mark studs, or the security system is on the fritz again and she had to wait two hours for a service tech to show. Nothing that could possibly be helped, but she's sorry anyway, and these things wouldn't happen, she'll say, if Alex would carry a cell phone, or a least a pager.

Wild Strawberries has ended and after a ten- or fifteen-minute intermission, the house lights have gone down again, a long moment of darkness marred only by the bottle-green glow of an exit sign before the screen is washed in a flood of light so brilliant it hurts Alex's eyes. She blinks at the countdown leader, five, four, three, the staccato beep at two, one, and then the grainy black-and-white picture. No front titles – a man carrying a wooden staff walks slowly across a scrubby, rock-strewn pasture and a dog trails close behind him. The man is dressed in peasant clothes, at least the way that European peasants dress in old Hollywood movies, and when he reaches the crest of a hill he stops and looks down at something out of frame, something hidden from the audience. His lips part and his eyes grow wide, an expression that is anger and surprise, disgust and horror all at the same time. There's no sound but his dog barking and the wind.

'Hey, what is *this* shit?' someone shouts near the front of the theatre, a fat man, and he stands and glares up at the projection booth. Some of the others have started mumbling, confused or annoyed whispers, and Alex has no idea what the film is, only that it isn't *The Seventh Seal*. On-screen, the camera cuts away from the peasant and now there's a close-up of a dead animal instead, a ragged, woolly mass streaked with gore the colour of molasses; it takes her a second or two to realise that it's a sheep. Its throat has been ripped out and its tongue lolls from its mouth. The camera pulls back as the man kneels beside the dead animal, then cuts to a close-up of the dog. It's stopped barking and licks at its lips.

'Jesus fucking *Christ*,' the fat man growls and then he storms up the aisle, past Alex and out the swinging doors to the lobby. No one else leaves their seat, though a few heads have turned to watch the fat man's exit. Someone laughs nervously and on-screen the peasant man has lifted the dead sheep in his arms, is walking quickly away from the camera and his dog follows close behind. The camera lingers as the man grows smaller and smaller in the distance, and the ground where the sheep lay glistens wetly.

A woman sitting a couple of seats in front of Alex turns around and 'Do *you* have any idea at all what this is?' she asks.

'No,' Alex replies. 'No, I don't.'

The woman frowns and sighs loudly. 'The projectionist must have made a mistake,' she says and turns back towards the screen before Alex can say anything else.

When the man and the dog have shrunk to bobbing specks, the camera finally cuts away, trades the stony pasture, the blood-soaked patch of grass, for a close-up of a church steeple and the cacophony of tolling bells spills out through tinny stereo speakers and fills the theatre.

'Well, this isn't what I paid six dollars to see,' the woman two seats in front of Alex grumbles.

The fat man doesn't come back and if the projectionist *has* made a mistake, no one seems to be in much of a hurry to correct it. The audience has grown quiet again, apparently more curious than per-turbed, and the film moves from scene to scene, flickering progression of images and story, dialogue pared to little more than whispers and occasional, furtive glances between the actors. A mountain village and a wolf killing sheep somewhere that might be France or Italy, but impossible to tell because everyone speaks with British accents. The peasant man from the opening scene (if that truly *was* the opening scene) has a blind daughter who spends her days inside their little house gazing out of a window, as though she could see the mountains in the distance.

'Ingmar Bergman didn't make this film,' the woman sitting in front of Alex says conclusively. 'I don't know who made this film,' and then someone turns and asks her to stop talking, please.

Finally a young boy is found dead and a frantic hunt for the wolf ensues, night and wrathful villagers with torches, hounds and antique rifles wandering through a mist-shrouded forest. It's obvious that this scene was shot on a soundstage, the contorted, nightmare trees too bizarre to possibly be real, nothing but plywood and chicken wire and papier-mâché. Some of the trunks, the tortuous limbs, are undoubtedly meant to suggest random scraps of human anatomy – the arch of a spine, a pair of arms ending in gnarled roots, a female torso sprouting half-formed from the bole of an oak.

And Alex thinks that maybe there's something big skulking along through the gloom just beyond the wavering light of the torches, insinuation of spiderlong legs and sometimes it seems to move a little ahead of the hunters, other times it trails behind.

The woman seated two rows in front of Alex makes a disgusted, exasperated sound and stands up, her silhouette momentarily eclipsing the screen. 'This is absurd,' she says. 'I'm asking for my money back right now,' speaking to no one or to everyone who might be listening. She leaves the theatre and someone down front laughs and 'Good fucking riddance,' a husky, male voice whispers.

On-screen, a shout, the bone-wet snap of living wood, and one of the villagers raises his gun, extreme close-up of his finger around the trigger before the boom and flash of gunpowder. The tinny speakers blare rifle-fire and the furious barking of dogs, so loud that Alex puts her hands over her ears. A man screams and the scene dissolves, then fades away to daylight and a high-angle view of a dirt road winding across the fields towards the village. The camera zooms slowly in on a small gathering of peasant women waiting at the end of the road; silent despair in their weathered faces, loss, resignation, fear, and one by one they turn and walk back towards their homes.

Alex squints down at her watch, leans forward in her seat and angles her wrist towards the screen, the greysilver light off the scratched crystal so she can read the black hour and minute hands. Only half an hour since the film began, though it seems like it's been much longer, and she wonders if Margot is home yet. She thinks again about the pay-phone outside the theatre, about the gallery and the answering machine.

She glances back at the screen and now there's a close-up of a skull, a sheep's, perhaps, but Alex isn't sure; bone bleached dry and stark as chalk, a leathery patch of hide still clinging to its muzzle, the empty sockets for eyes that have rotted away or been eaten by insects and crows. The lonely sound of the wind and the film cuts to the peasant's blind daughter, a music box playing *Swan Lake* softly in the background and she stares out the window of her dead father's house. She's neither smiling nor does she look unhappy, her hands folded neatly in her lap, and then a man is speaking from somewhere behind her. The cold, guttural voice so entirely unexpected that Alex jumps, startled, and she misses the first part of it, whatever was said before the girl turns her head towards the unseen speaker, raises a hand and places one index finger to the centre of her forehead.

'I saw the light again last night,' she says, the milky, colourless cataracts to prove that she's a liar or insane, and then the girl's hand returns to her lap.

'Floating across the meadow,' she says.

The music box stops abruptly and now there's the small, hard sound of a dog barking far, far away.

'Who are you? Your hand is cold—'

'Which road will you take?' the guttural voice asks, interrupting her. 'That of the needles, or that of the pins?'

She turns to the window again, imperfect, transparent mirror for her plain face, and for an instant there seems to be another reflection there, a lean and hungry shadow crouched close behind the blind girl's chair. And then a popping, fluttering racket from the projection booth and the world is swallowed in pure, white light and Alex knows that the film hasn't ended, it's merely *stopped*, as inexplicably as it began.

The house lights come up and she keeps her seat, sits waiting for her eyes to adjust as the handful of people remaining in the theatre stand and begin to drift towards the lobby doors, confused and thoughtful faces, overheard bits of conjecture and undisguised bewilderment.

'It could've been Robert Florey,' a man who looks like a college professor says to a blonde girl in a KMFDM T-shirt, slender girl young enough to be his daughter, and 'Do you know, Florey, dear?' he asks. 'I've always heard there was a lost Florey out there somewhere.'

'Well, they might have told us they didn't have *The Seventh Seal*,' another man complains. 'They could have said *something*.'

And when they've all gone and Alex is alone with the matte-black walls and the sugar-and-vinegar theatre smells, she sits and stares at the blank screen for another minute, trying to be certain what she saw, or didn't see, at the end.

III

July

Margot away for the entire week, a lecture series in Montreal – 'Formalism, Expressionism, and the Post-Modernist Denial', according to the flier stuck to the refrigerator with a magnet shaped like an apple core – and Alex left alone in the Midtown condo paid for with the advance money from *The Boats of Morning*. Four days now since she's gone any further than the row of mailboxes in the building's lobby. Too hot to go out if she doesn't absolutely have to, eggs frying on sidewalks out there, so she stays half-drunk on Absolut and grapefruit juice, smokes too much and watches black-and-white movies on television. Whatever it takes not to think about the typewriter in her office down the hall from their bedroom, the desk drawer full of blank paper. Margot called on Wednesday night and they talked for twenty minutes about nothing in particular, which is almost all they ever talk about these days.

'You'd like it here,' Margot said. 'You'd like the sky here. It's very big and blue.'

Late Thursday afternoon and Alex comes back upstairs with the day's mail, the usual assortment of bills and glossy catalogues, a new *Rolling Stone*, an offer for a platinum Visa card at twenty-one and one-half per cent interest. And a large padded envelope the colour of a grocery bag.

Her name and address are printed neatly on the front in tall, blocky letters – MS ALEX MARLOWE – and there's no return address, only the initials J. S. written very small in the upper left-hand corner. She leaves everything else on the dining table, a small mountain of unopened mail accumulated there already, debts and distractions for Margot to deal with when she gets home; Alex pours herself a drink, takes the big brown envelope to the sofa in front of the television and opens it with the pull tab on the back. Inside there's a videocassette, along with a couple of pages of lavender stationery, some newspaper and magazine clippings held together with a lavender paper clip.

Alex sips her drink, the vodka too strong, so she stirs it absently with an index finger and looks down at the top sheet of stationery. It takes her a moment to place the name there – Jude Sinclair – a moment before she remembers the pretty girl from the gallery, dark-skinned, blue-eyed girl who'd tried ardently to explain Albert Perrault's work to her. Alex leans back against the sofa cushions, glances at the TV screen (an old gangster film she doesn't recognise), and takes another sip from her glass. 'Dear Alex,' the letter begins, and she notices that it was typed on a typewriter that drops its 't's.

Dear Alex,

I'm sure ₜhaₜ you won'ₜ remember me. We ₜalked briefly aₜ ₜhe gallery in May. I was ₜhe chick wiₜh a serious hard-on for M. Perraulₜ. I ₜhink I ₜold you ₜhaₜ I'd wriₜₜen poems abouₜ ₜhe 'Secunda raₜis,' do you remember thaₜ? I suspecₜ you may have ₜhoughₜ I was a flake. Did you know about P.'s accidenₜ?? ₜerrible. I was aₜ ₜhe funeral in Paris. I ₜhoughₜ you mighₜ wanₜ ₜo read one of ₜhe poems (I have burned ₜhe oₜher one). Hope you are well. My love ₜo Margoₜ.

    Jude S.

Alex pulls the pages free of the lavender paper clip, places the first page on the bottom and the second is the poem, the one Jude Sinclair didn't burn; she looks at the black videocassette, considers stuffing it all back into the envelope and tossing the whole mess into the garbage can in the kitchen. Perrault one of the last things she's in the mood to think about right now; she'd almost managed to forget him and his paintings, although Margot talked about him for weeks after the show. They heard about the accident, of course, a motorcycle wreck somewhere in France, and finally, that seemed to close the subject.

Alex takes a long swallow of her drink and scans the first few lines of the short poem, a copy obviously produced on the same typewriter as the letter, the same telltale dropped 't's and a few inky smudges and fingerprints on the lavender stationery.

'Jesus, who the hell still uses carbon paper,' she wonders aloud, setting her drink down on the coffee table, and Alex starts over and reads the poem through from the beginning. 'The Night We Found Red Cap' and then a forced and clumsy attempt at Italian sonnet form, eight-line stanza, six-line stanza, Jude Sinclair's slightly stilted, perfectly unremarkable impressions of the painting.

Alex glances quickly through the clippings, then: the *Artforum* review of the show at Artifice, review of another Perrault exhibit last summer in Manhattan, *Le Monde*'s account of his motorcycle accident and a short French obituary. And at the bottom of the stack, a photocopy of a very old lithograph; she sets the rest aside and stares at it, a pastoral scene centred around some strange animal that resembles a huge wolf more than anything else she can think of, though it's reared up on its hind limbs and its long, sinuous tail makes her think of a big cat, a lion or a panther, maybe. The creature is attacking a young woman and there are other mutilated bodies scattered about on the ground. In the distance are men wearing tricorne hats on horseback and the creature has raised its head, is gazing fearlessly over one shoulder towards them. Beneath the scene is the legend, 'La Bête du Gévaudan'. On the back, someone, presumably Jude Sinclair, has scribbled a date in pencil – 1767.

Alex lays the small bundle of paper down on the coffee table and picks up her drink. The glass has left a ring of condensation on the dark wood, the finish already beginning to turn pale and opaque underneath. An heirloom from Margot's grandmother or a great-aunt or some such and she'll have a cow when she sees it, so Alex wipes the water away with the hem of her T-shirt. But the ring stays put, defiant, accusing, condemning tattoo and she sighs, sits back and takes another swallow of the vodka and grapefruit juice.

'What are you supposed to be, anyway?' she asks the videotape; no label of any sort on it for an answer, but almost certainly more Perraultiana, an interview, possibly, or maybe something a bit more exotic, more morbid, a news report of his accident taped off TF1 or even footage shot during the funeral. Alex wouldn't be surprised, has seen and heard of worse things being done by art groupies like Jude Sinclair. She decides to save the video for later, a few moments' diversion before bed, leaves it on the couch and goes to fix herself a fresh drink.

*

Something from the freezer for dinner, prepackaged Chinese that came out of the microwave looking nothing at all like the photograph on the cardboard box, Kung Pao pencil erasers and a bottle of beer, and Alex sits on the living room floor, watching *Scooby Doo* on the Cartoon Network. The end of another day that might as well not have happened, more of yesterday and the day before that, the weeks and months since she's finished anything at all piling up so fast that soon it'll have been a year. Today she stood in the doorway to her office for fifteen minutes and stared uselessly at her typewriter, vintage Royal she inherited from her father and she's never been able to write on anything else, the rough clack-clack-clack of steel keys, all the mechanical clicks and clatters and pings to mark her progress down a page, through a scene, the inharmonious chapter to chapter symphony towards conclusion and THE END.

When the beer's gone and she's swallowed enough of the stuff from the freezer to be convinced that she's better off not finishing it, Alex slides her plate beneath the coffee table and retrieves Jude Sinclair's videocassette from the couch. She puts it into the VCR, hits the play button, and in a moment Scooby and Shaggy are replaced by a loud flurry of static. Alex starts to turn down the volume, but the snow and white noise have already been replaced by a silent, black screen. She sits watching it, half-curious, impatient, waiting for whatever it is to begin, whatever the blue-eyed girl from the gallery wants her to see.

In the kitchen, the phone rings and Alex looks away from the television screen, not particularly interested in talking to anyone and so she thinks she'll let the machine pick up. Third ring and she turns back to the TV, but it's still just as dark as before and she checks to be sure that she doesn't have it on pause by mistake. The soft, green glow of digital letters, PLAY and a flashing arrow to let her know that she doesn't, that either the tape's blank or the recording hasn't begun yet, or maybe Jude Sinclair's filmed a perfectly dark room as a tribute or eulogy to Perrault.

'This is bullshit,' Alex mutters and she presses fast forward. Now the blackness flickers past as the counter tallies the minutes of nothing stored on the tape. In the kitchen, the telephone rings once more and then the answering machine switches on, Margot's voice reciting their number, politely informing the caller that no one can come to the phone right now but if you'll please leave your name and number, the date and time, someone will get back to you as soon as possible.

And then Margot answers herself, her voice sounding small and distant, sounding upset, and 'Alex?' she says. 'Alex, if you're there please pick up, okay? I need to talk to you.'

Alex sighs and rubs at her temples. A bright burst of pain behind her left eye, maybe the beginnings of a migraine, and she's really not up to one of Margot's long-distance crises, the two of them yelling at each other with half a continent in between. She glances back to the television screen, presses play and the nothing stops flickering.

'Hello? Alex? Come *on*. I know you're at home. Pick up the damned phone, *please*.'

It really is blank, she thinks. *The crazy bitch sent me a fucking blank videotape.*

'Alex! I'm not kidding, okay? Please answer the goddamn telephone!'

'All right! Jesus, I'm *coming*!' she shouts at the kitchen, gets up too fast and one foot knocks over the empty beer bottle; it rolls noisily away towards a bookshelf, leaves behind a glistening, semi-circular trickle of liquid as it goes. By the time Alex lifts the receiver, Margot has started crying.

'What? What's wrong?'

'Christ, Alex. Why can't you just answer the fucking phone? Why do I have to get fucking hysterical to get you to answer the phone?'

And for a second Alex considers the simple efficacy of a lie, the harmless convenience of *I was on the toilet* or *I just walked in the front door*. Any plausible excuse to cover her ass.

'I'm sorry,' she says, instead. 'I've been in a funk all day long. I'm getting a headache. I just didn't want to talk to anyone.'

'For fuck's sake, Alex,' and then she coughs and Alex can tell that Margot's trying to stop crying.

'Margot, what's wrong?' Alex asks again. 'Has something happened?' She wants a cigarette but she left them in the living room, left her lighter, too, and she settles for chewing on a ragged thumbnail.

'I saw something today,' Margot says, speaking very quietly. Alex hears her draw a deep breath, the pause as she holds it in a moment, then the long, uneven exhalation and 'I saw something terrible today,' she says.

'So what was it? What did you see?'

'A dog attack,' and she's almost whispering now. 'I saw a little girl attacked by a dog.'

For a moment, neither of them says anything and Alex stares out the window above the kitchen sink at the final indigo and violet dregs of sunset beyond the Atlanta skyline. The pain behind her left eye is back, more persistent than before, keeping time with her heartbeat. She has no idea what to say next, is about to tell Margot that she's sorry, default sentiment better than nothing, better than standing here as the pain in her head gets bigger, listening to the faint, electric buzz and crackle coming through the telephone line.

'I was walking in the park,' Margot says. 'Lafontaine, it's not far from my hotel. This poor little girl, she couldn't have been more than five and she must have wandered away from her mother—'

And now Alex realises that she can hear the faint, metallic notes of a music box playing from the next room, something on the video after all, and she turns and looks through the doorway at the television screen.

'—she was dead before anyone could get it off her.'

Grainy blacks and whites, light and shadow, and at first Alex isn't sure what she's seeing, unable to force all those shades of grey into a coherent whole. Movement, chiaroscuro, the swarm of pixels pulled from a magnetised strip of plastic and then the picture resolves and a young woman's face stares back at Alex from the screen. Pupilless eyes like the whites of hard-boiled eggs, a strand of hair across her cheek, and the music box stops playing. A dog barks.

'Who are you? Your hand is cold—'

'I never saw anything so horrible in my life,' Margot says. 'The damned thing was *eating* her, Alex.'

'Which road will you take?' a guttural voice from the videotape asks the young woman. 'That of the needles, or that of the pins?'

The pain in Alex's head suddenly doubling, trebling, and she shuts her eyes tight, grips the edge of the counter and waits for the dizziness and nausea to pass, the disorientation that has nothing whatsoever to do with the migraine. The entire world tilting drunkenly around her and 'I have to go,' she says. 'I'm sorry, Margot. I'll call you back, but I have to go right now.'

'Alex, no. *Wait*, please—'

'I promise. I'll call you back as soon as I can,' and she opens her eyes, hangs up the phone quickly so she doesn't have to hear the confusion in Margot's voice, the anger, and the young woman on the television gazes at her blind reflection in the window of her father's house. Her reflection and the less certain reflection of the hunched, dark figure crouched close behind her.

'The road of pins,' she says. 'Isn't it much easier to fasten things with pins, than to have to sew them together with needles—'

Then the film cuts to a shot of the door of the house – unpainted, weathered boards, the bent and rusted heads of nails, a cross painted on the wood with something white; slow pan left and now the window is in frame, the clean glint of morning sunlight off glass and the round face of the peasant's daughter, the indistinct shape bending over her, and the camera zooms out until the house is very small, a lonely, run-down speck in a desolate, windswept valley.

Alex hits the stop button and the VCR whirs and thunks and is silent, the screen filled with nothing now but shoddy, Saturday-morning animation, four hippie teenagers and a Great Dane bouncing along a swampy back road in their psychedelic van, the cartoon sliver moon hung high in the painted sky, and she sits down on the floor in front of the television. When she presses eject, the tape slides smoothly, obediently out of the cassette compartment and Alex reaches for it, holds it in trembling, sweatslick hands while her heart races and the pain behind her eyes fades to a dull, bearable ache.

A few minutes more and the phone begins to ring again and this time she doesn't wait for the answering machine.

> Incommensurable, impalpable,
> Yet latent in it are forms;
> Impalpable, incommensurable,
> Yet within it are entities.
> Shadowy it is and dim.
>   Lao-tzu, *Tao Teh Ching*

Caitlin R. Kiernan's short fiction has been collected in *Candles for Elizabeth, Tales of Pain and Wonder, From Weird and Distant Shores* and *Wrong Times* (the latter with Poppy Z. Brite), and has been selected for both *The Mammoth Book of Best New Horror* and *The Year's Best Fantasy and Horror*. Her first novel, *Silk*, received the Barnes & Noble Maiden Voyage and International Horror Guild awards, and her second, *Threshold*, appeared in 2001. More recent publications include *In the Garden of Poisonous Flowers*, a novella illustrated by Dame Darcy, and *Trilobite: The Writing of Threshold*, both from Subterranean Press. She divides her time unevenly between writing and her work as a vertebrate palaeontologist, with the lion's share going to the former. She has not yet been to Greece. 'In early 2001,' recalls Kiernan, 'I experienced the first true bout of writer's block in my career. I was a hundred pages into a novel, a sequel to *Silk* called *Murder of Angels*, and, suddenly, a few pages into Chapter Three, the words just stopped coming. From late January to mid-April I wrote almost nothing, and certainly nothing of any merit. It was terrifying. Finally, I shelved *Murder of Angels* and wrote this story, "The Road of Pins", which is, at least in part, about writer's block. The novel remains shelved to this day, a reminder of those awful two and a half months; I think I'm actually afraid of that manuscript at this point, as though it somehow *caused* the writer's block. Anyway, "The Road of Pins" has a number of other inspirations: Charles Fort, "Little Red Riding Hood", and the Beast of Gévaudan. It also draws on my fascination with "lost" films, a subject that I'd explored earlier in the stories "Salmagundi" and ". . . Between the Gargoyle Trees".'

Black

TIM LEBBON

She only screams for the first two minutes. Some of the screams may be words in her own language, but if so, they are a curse. She still makes noises after that but they are unconscious and dead, not echoes of life. He hears the knife going in, whispering through skin and flesh, grating on bone, its serrated edge sucking like a jelly shaken from its mould as he pulls it out. He is changing this mould radically. She sighs, but it is gas escaping her rent body. She coughs, but it may be blood bubbling in her throat. Still he stabs, slashes and gouges, just to make sure. He tries to concentrate on the white-hot anger and rage he feels, propagating them in the hope that they might camouflage the worrying excitement. The pleasure. He's enjoying this. She begins to drip from the edges of the table, more solid scraps of her following soon after, and a steady rain of fluid patters down onto the flagstone floor. He closes his eyes and listens, trying to distinguish the cleansing rain outside from that within. He's still shaking with fury, fear and dread, and even though he knows that what he's doing is so wrong, he cannot take it back. He will not take it back. It's her fault, it's the fault of her kin and kind, and this is his release. At least he can smell the truth of that.

Ed carved another niche into the damp plasterboard wall. As the knife penetrated and pink plaster squeezed out he expected blood to well from within, the wall to quiver and scream and smell of insides. He expected this every time, and every time it did not happen. Yet the fear was always just as fresh. Sometimes he believed that every memory he had was made up, pulled together hurriedly by his still-waking mind before he could become fully conscious and realise that he was actually no one at all.

The only real memory he could never doubt was of the murder that had changed his life.

'Thousands,' he said, standing back from the wall and surveying the damage he had wrought. The bare painted partition was scarred across its surface with a mark for every day he had been here. They started in the left bottom corner as inch-high, delicately cut indicators, the tender slices of a surgeon operating on his own child. But now, the latest was the hacking of a murderer. Tracing them from left to right did not tell his story, because at some point he had decided to mix in the marks, make them disordered and confused. Not his story, no, but perhaps his state of mind.

'Thousands of days.' He'd counted to begin with. Each mark added to the number he kept in his head, the length of time he'd been here, and because back then his memory still was not too bad he would wake in the morning and remember the number from the night before. Then he'd started to forget, and it had become necessary to re-count the marks several times each week. This he did not mind, essentially – he had nothing better to do – but it was tedious and, as the violence of the knife strokes grew, all but impossible.

So now he left it at this: thousands. With what he could remember of his life, that was as good as for ever.

The flat was sparse and dirty. He ate take-out food mostly, and old boxes and bags and sachets were piled on the kitchen surfaces, plates in the sink waiting to be washed when all the clean ones were used. The bin stank of mould and rotting meat. Ed liked that. It reminded him of what he had done, and he only wished he had the conscience to view it as a punishment rather than simply an annoying smell. He paid for his food with a debit card from a bank account that seemed always to honour the transaction. He had an idea that he'd had a good job once. Perhaps he was still being paid. He didn't deserve it – he felt that he was deserving of very little, and he knew the dead woman would agree – but it was there, and he needed to eat, and his scruples hardly went that deep. If he'd once had morals, they'd been slaughtered by that knife as well.

The same knife he now used to mark the passing of his own life.

He'd have laughed at the irony if he hadn't sickened himself so much.

Ed put down the knife and went for a walk. He did this most days, wandering past the greasy take-away food bars, the tacky cheap jewellery shops, money lenders and video emporiums and dingy pubs, their closed doors and smoky interiors almost begging potential customers not to enter. Passing faces he did not know, he acknowledged no one and, in turn, was ignored. He was certain that sometimes they did not even see him. He'd read somewhere that the human mind filters out everything not required from its surroundings, otherwise the information input would be far too massive. He liked not being a part of anybody else's life.

Ed preferred living in the city because he could be just another mystery, even to himself. He deserved no less. As happened every day, flashes of what he had done haunted him; tastes, sounds, feelings, smells of his crime assailed him at every step, either reflected in shop windows, carried on the air or manufactured inside his head. Trying to ignore them was like trying not to breathe. Accepting them, suffering, was all he could do to make amends.

He certainly did not deserve to meet Queenie.

On that hot July afternoon when he first saw her, he simply watched. He hadn't had sex since the war, rarely even masturbated, but seeing the woman in the park stirred feelings that surprised him with their intensity. He wanted her, yes, but he was also interested by her. The strange things she did went some way to explaining that, but also the way she moved, the clothes she wore, the way she flicked her long hair back over her shoulder quickly and impatiently, as if it were merely an annoyance.

Ed sat on a bench by the pond and tried to blend into the background. He hated being noticed at the best of times, but now, watching this woman, he craved invisibility. The more fascinated he became with her and her actions, the less he wanted to meet her.

She must be planning something, he thought. Scouting the area for a filming. Or perhaps she was an artist. She was lurking beneath a clump of trees at the edge of the park, holding something up to the sky – a light meter, Ed guessed – taking photographs, scratching around at the foot of the trees with a small trowel as if looking for buried treasure. She kept out of the sun. If she did emerge from beneath one group of trees, she would quickly cross the sunlit grass to another area of shadow. Her skin was dark and weathered – she obviously spent a lot of time outdoors – but she seemed to much prefer the comfort of shadows to the hot caress of the sun. Ed could relate to that. He wondered what crime she was trying to hide from.

It took over an hour for her to notice him. In that time he sat motionless on the bench, the sun slowly burning his bald pate, hardly even twitching as a group of teenagers cycled by so close that one of them touched his shoe with his wheels. He watched her set a camera on a tripod and take one photograph every five minutes, fix small boxes to several trees with nails, sweep leaves away from the bole of a lightning-struck tree as if to reveal its skeletal underside. She finally sat down and took a bottle of water from a rucksack . . . and that was when she saw him.

Ed held his breath, startled, as she froze and stared across at him. She was too far away for him to see her expression clearly, but she put her bottle down and stood without looking away from him.

His heart began to race, sweat popped out on his skin, his sunburned scalp tightened. She was not only standing, she was walking, coming out into the sun and seemingly oblivious of it for the first time, striding across the grass and glancing away now and then, though infrequently and not for long.

He felt her attention upon him, like fresh sunbeams cooking his skin.

Ed stood, turned his back on the woman and walked quickly away. He aimed through the kids' playground, dodging toddlers as they darted around his legs and hoping that he could lose her through there if she chose to follow. But when he looked back over his shoulder he saw her standing by his bench, hands on hips, staring after him. She shielded her eyes as he looked and he thought perhaps she smiled. But it could have been a shadow pulling at her lips, making him see something that was not really there.

He left the park without looking back again.

He has smelled insides before, of course, but never like this. In the war he has seen more dead bodies than anyone ever should, two of them – the rebel unwilling to give up his guns, the government soldier angry and aggressive at his intrusion – the results of his own actions. He hates every single corpse because they remind him of why he is here, what these people are doing to each other, and each shot, shattered or gutted body seems to be one more mocking taunt aimed directly at him: we're doing this, *they say,* and you can't stop us. *So he has smelled insides . . . but never this close up. Never this fresh. Blood mists the air as he strikes, copper tints overlying the rich tang of burning from outside, strong and vital as he breathes it in, sticking inside his nostrils, embedding itself to remind him of this moment for ever. The smells change as his stabbing arm becomes heavier and the knife impact further down his victim's body: sickly-sweet as the heart is punctured; acidic as the stomach is torn open; and shit. Underlying it all is the cloying stench of cheap perfume. It's intended to remind him of roses and honey, he supposes, but in reality it's the aroma of desperation. Any idea that a clean and scented body can superimpose itself over the horrors happening here must be desperate, and he wonders when she found the time or inclination to buy this. He imagines what he is doing as some sort of alternative perfume advert for TV and almost smiles ... almost ... because then the mouthwatering smell of roasting human hits his nose from outside. He wonders what he will eat tonight. He swallows a mouthful of saliva and tastes death.*

He didn't know he was going back until he opened the door of his flat and ventured out into the twilight.

The park closed at eight o'clock, but he knew plenty of ways in. He spent a lot of his time wandering, day and night, and the park was always a convenient and innocuous venue. No one would see him in there, if he so chose, and he could hide and watch and wonder just what he was missing. Sometimes he saw someone walking on their own, but their expression was always happier than his own. On other occasions he spotted couples sitting or strolling hand in hand, and they reminded him that he had forgotten so much. Once he'd seen two people making love on a park bench, trying to be secretive about it, but the woman's increasingly frantic movements and gasps revealing their passion. He had stayed and watched until the end. The movements and sounds reminded him of the woman he had murdered, even though their cause had been much different. Perhaps he knew why it was called the little death.

They had all made him mad, every single one of them. Every word and gesture and smile that marked what they were doing to their country and kin as normal drove him into a frenzy. He'd been sent there to protect them from themselves – he'd killed for them – and yet they willingly went about their continuous self-destruction.

Sent there to protect them. Ironic.

He walked along darkened streets, moving quicker through pools of light thrown by streetlamps. He'd been here for a long time, the marks on his wall testified to that, but still he found his surroundings unfamiliar. It was as if the scenery was frequently rebuilt and reordered, mostly to resemble its former self but with a few vital differences that prevented him from recognising it totally. Stopped it from ever feeling like home.

He reached the park and climbed the wall at one of its lower stretches. He could hear kids playing around near the bandstand, glass smashing as they lobbed bottles down the concrete steps, so he turned the other way. The pond was just around the corner, and next to it the trees, and within their deeper evening shadows perhaps he would find the secret of why the woman had been there.

Ed looked up and saw the full moon, stars quivering with atmospheric distortion. He tried to appreciate the beauty of the view but, as ever, he could not realise any sense of wonder. It was long gone. The shadows pooled around the bench he'd sat on earlier seemed deeper than normal, thicker, untouched by moon- or starlight. He wondered whether someone had spilled something, but he had no wish to venture close enough to find out. The shadows seemed . . . *there*. Something, not nothing. A definite presence rather than an absence of light.

Ed moved his head to get a full view with his peripheral vision. He did not like what he saw, but then he rarely did. Someone – perhaps it was his mother, although she was swallowed up along with most of his early memories – had once told him that if he was stressed or wound-up he should see the beauty in things. The movement of a tree, each leaf performing its own independent dance to create a wondrously pure choreography. Or the way light fell on a puddle, a reflection of the world in there, a whole universe in a splash of water. Roses swaying in the breeze, waves of that same breeze rippling across a field of long grass, a flock of birds twisting and turning like one organism, not a thousand. All things of beauty, none of which Ed could see. Now he would see only a stump blown apart by shellfire, a porridge of blood and oil in a landmine crater, a hand clawed in the still air . . . and his knife stealing what little beauty he'd managed to find in that foreign country.

Before they sent him there, he'd never even heard of the place.

'Look just to the side of what you want to see,' a voice said. It was deep but evidently female, husky and knowledgeable.

Ed spun around, fearing an attack by the teenagers but knowing straight away that he'd found her. Or rather, she'd found him. He wished he'd stayed at home. 'Who's there?' He was not used to talking with people, and the quaver in his voice embarrassed him. Scared of the dark, she'd think. Maybe she was right. Ed liked to exist in shadows, but perhaps it was his fear of them holding him there, a guilt-induced masochism.

'You saw me earlier.' She came from the night beneath the trees, stopped a few steps from him and switched on a torch. His vision was stolen for long seconds. 'Come back for another look?'

'I was wondering what you were doing.' Ed could see the woman silhouetted before him. She pointed the torch at the ground behind her, throwing her face into deep shadow. He wondered whether she had two eyes, a nose, a mouth, or something wholly different.

'Why?'

It was not a question he had expected, although he'd been asking it for hours. He was not used to interacting, and to find something of interest like this was a surprise. Anything of pleasure would be mocking the life he had taken. Sometimes, on the worst of days, even breathing felt bad.

Everything went back to that. His life began in a foreign country when he was a murderous twenty-two.

'Well, you seemed so . . . intent. What is it? Animal research? You filming squirrels, or something?'

'I'm waiting for a murder.'

'Murder.' Ed felt cold, his balls shrivelled and an icy, accusing finger drew a line down his back, nail cutting to the bone. *Murder*. One day he feared they'd come visiting, the fellow soldiers who'd brought him back and let him go, letting the incident fade into the shadows of war, honour amongst thieves, that sort of thing. There's always been that fear . . . but it was a yearning as well. He could not bring himself to account for what he had done because he was a coward. It would take someone else to do it for him. *Murder*.

'There'll be one here soon. That's why I'm here. I'm . . . sort of an early warning system, I suppose. Dark, isn't it?'

'Yes.' He'd noticed. The woman turned the torch off and for a moment, an instant, it was pitch black. Then his night vision moved in and he could see the shadows forming around them. The woman seemed nearer than she had been. And when she spoke again he was sure he could smell her breath.

'They call me Queenie.'

'Why?'

'Avoidance Queen. I avoid most of the important things in my life.'

'Like what?' Ed saw her shadow shrug but she offered no response. 'So what's your real name?'

'You can call me Queenie, too.'

'So what are you avoiding here? Searching for a murderer, you say?'

'That's not what I said. I'm looking for a murder, not a murderer.'

Ed felt that she was playing games, but perhaps it was simply that most of his conversations were with himself. He stepped back a couple of paces, shoes whispering across the soft carpet of pine needles. The air felt thick. Movement was difficult 'You can't have one without the other.'

'Well . . .' She giggled quietly, little more than a heavy breath through her nose. 'Sometimes a murder is just a death brought on too soon.'

This was too close. Ed felt memories tapping the inside of his skull like little insects, flying around and seeking escape, trying to force themselves upon him once again. They often used devious means, these memories . . . jumping out of doorways and the TV screen, emerging fully-fledged from single phrases, smells and sounds and sights inspiring their own dark memory cousins. He lived that time enough without actively bringing it on.

'I have to go,' he said. The instant he spoke everything went quiet, a deathly silence, the air swallowing movement and sound and seemingly solidifying around him. Even the shadow of the woman became solid and still, from living to statue in an instant. He turned to leave. She touched him.

'Don't go,' she said. Her fingers bit into his arm, but in desperation rather than anger. 'Please . . . I don't get to talk about this much. It'll go dark, it always goes dark, and in the blackness there's murder. Please! People just don't listen, they say I'm mad and walk away. Don't walk away.'

'What are you *doing*?' Ed said. Was she playing with him again?

'I've put light meters on the trees. And time-lapse cameras. I hope they aren't stolen. I'm waiting for it to go dark.'

Ed almost stayed. She'd piqued his interest, demanded his attention. Some of those things she was saying . . . *Sometimes a murder is just a death brought on too soon* . . . He wanted to become involved.

But he could not allow that. He was nothing, no one, and he did not deserve anything like this.

'It *is* dark,' he said. And as he walked away, trying not to hear her muttering behind him, he whispered to himself: 'It's *always* dark.'

She offered for him to taste her. Maybe that's why he's killing her, but he thinks not. Her underwear is still tangled around her ankles, and as if to taunt him the taste of women comes out from behind his teeth, dripping from the roof of his mouth like ghost memories burrowing down from his brain, laying tangy caresses on his tongue. Perhaps if he'd accepted her invitation his rage would have been subsumed. Maybe she would still be alive. But time could not be reversed. Drowning out that sweet taste of love is the bloody taste of death. Her blood is in the air, misting when the knife comes out and permeating the dank atmosphere of the alley, more spilled blood in this bloody land, soon the air itself will taste of blood if the killing goes on, the hate and murder born of the differences passed down from father to daughter, mother to son. He wonders whether their respective gods find it all amusing. And he tastes a bitter, furious anger swimming there in the blood, black spots of rage camouflaged in the very physical taint of the woman's death. He swallows, rubs his tongue against the roof of his mouth in an effort to distil the taste . . .

because it scares him. It scares him because he knows it cannot be his own, his anger is false because he does not truly know what these people are going through, why, what they really feel ... his is a tourist's rage at something that offends him, and it could never taste this bad. He spits and it lands on the woman. The taste grows worse. Hands lay on his shoulders, heavy and invisible, but for now they do little but help him thrust the knife in again. There is no one else here but him and the woman, but those hands have the feel of him, and the bitter tang of dread floods his mouth as blood arcs across his chin and teeth.

This time, he knows the dread is his own.

And he sees what he has done

Ed woke up from dark-soaked dreams to a dawn barely any lighter. He glanced at the clock blinking beside his bed. Must be wrong. It should have been daylight by now. Even through the hangover, the searing pain behind his eyes and in his throat that was testament to his binge the previous night, he knew he should be seeing more than this.

He rubbed his eyes but it did not help.

Queenie. She sprang into his mind and ambushed his thoughts, turning them away from the urge to vomit and then drink some more. If he went back to the park today she'd still be there. Sitting beneath the trees perhaps, or adjusting the equipment she'd placed around the little copse, replacing batteries, examining film and data tapes. *Light meters?* Strange.

Ed managed to haul himself upright without puking, but then he stood and swayed as his senses spun and swapped places, and he vomited down the wall. Standing there, leaning against the woodchip wallpaper as he heaved gushes of liquid poison from his guts, he noticed how each splinter of wood in the wallpaper had its own definite shadow. Most of them were small, little more than smudges, but one or two of them seemed far too large. As he gasped in air and tasted foulness, he picked at one of these wood chippings and felt it crumble between his fingernails like a desiccated fly. He dropped the dust to land on the puddle of puke, and seconds later the shadows faded away.

Ed rubbed his eyes and sat heavily onto his bed. He was used to waking like this, even welcomed it sometimes, but it often lowered whatever defences he'd managed to erect against the memories plaguing him. Trying to rub the ache from his eyes he saw her face as she realised what he was about to do, her eyes widening and filling with something that would have scared him had he not had the upper hand. Pinching his nose and snorting to force out the damp remnants of vomit, he smelled insides other than his own, parts of her that should never have been touched by daylight. And the ringing in his ears, the rapid pumping of his heart as it struggled to purify his system, both could have belonged to her, a fearful whine and her heart galloping with fear.

It'll go dark, it always goes dark, and in the blackness there's murder.

Ed tried to revive himself because he needed to think, and like this it hurt. He drank a pint of water and washed down three aspirins, opened the windows to his dank flat and leaned out to let the fresh air do its worst. He could just about make out the park from here, its oldest and tallest trees peering over rooftops. The sky was clear, but the streets were shaded, not shadowed but unclear nonetheless. The brightness of the day had been turned down. Some cars had their sidelights on. A young couple were standing on the street corner, whispering like lovers, but Ed thought not.

There was a knock at the flat door.

He spun around and leaned back against the window sill to steady himself. The knock came again and he nodded, yes, he hadn't imagined it. No one had come to his front door for years other than to collect monies due. He usually had it to give them, but still he resented their intrusion into his own private world. They looked at him like voyeurs, their eyes cameras to record and incriminate . . . or perhaps he just imagined it.

'Who is it?'

'It's happening,' a voice said. Queenie. So much mystery in that one statement, so many possibilities (*you're caught, they know, you're a murderer, time to run, run again*).

'What's happening?'

'It's growing dark. The light's losing out, no one has noticed yet but all the readings hold up. Let me in. The landing light's bust.'

Ed stepped to the door, drew the bolts and swung it open. Queenie entered without an invite, wafting cheap perfume and the smell of cleaned clothes. If she *had* slept in the park, she'd made an effort to be presentable before coming here this morning.

'Nice place,' she said, looking around at the scarred walls and the refuse littering the floor and tables, and Ed hated the sarcasm, really hated it, his resentment running deep.

'I live like I live.'

Queenie's eyes widened

her eyes widened and filled with something fearful, frightening

and she started talking excitedly. 'The murder's soon, it has to be, the darkness is here and soon it'll be black, black as night without stars or moon, blacker than last night, but in the day.' It sounded like she was looking forward to it.

'Eclipse?'

She shook her head. 'No, not eclipses. Every time it's happened before it's been localised and has gone unreported, even from the authorities. I've followed the places it's happened, always got there after the event, been trying to narrow down future locations ... find a pattern.' She looked pensive for a moment, glanced around his flat at the mess of Ed's life, then back at him. 'Maybe I've found it,' she whispered. Then she became animated once more, excited. 'There's been no film of it, little talk about it in the media. Well, *Fortean Times* picks it up sometimes, of course, and other folks like that.' She looked at him and, as if knowing how all but his worst memories were lost, she smiled. 'Blackouts.'

Ed frowned at this strange woman who seemed to have some sort of claim to him. He'd seen her twice but already she was confiding in him, passing on something she was obviously passionate about, letting him in. 'I really don't want any part of this,' he said, and even as he spoke it was a lie.

She looked at him, eyebrows raised and lips pressed together. 'You'll see it soon enough,' she said. and still he could not read her.

'Why should I see blackouts?'

'Why shouldn't you? You live here and this is where it's going to—'

'But why do you think I of all people should see it? Why ... pick on me?'

Queenie was silent for a while. She seemed confused. 'Well, I didn't. You came looking for me.'

Ed could only stare at her, standing in the middle of the room he had yet to invite her into. And suddenly, amazingly, there was a stirring in his groin, a hardening so uncommon in all the years since his time in Eastern Europe, another use for the blood he now thought of as impure and tainted with the murder, the murderous attack it had fuelled.

That made up his mind. 'Out.' he said.

'But I have to tell you. Don't you want to know? Don't you understand what I'm saying here?'

'No I don't, it's a load of shit you're trying to feed me, I don't know what's wrong with you and I really, really don't want to know. Out!' *He* did *want to know* ...

'But I've been told I can give you a chance.'

Ed shook his head, loosening those strange words from where they had stuck. Denying them. It was just too complicated. 'Get out of my flat!' he hissed.

Queenie made to move towards him, faltered, took a step forwards. Ed really thought that she was coming for him, her hands would come up and she would hold him or hit him or something equally inexplicable. But after standing there for a few seconds, glancing out the window over Ed's shoulder, looking into his eyes and searching for something in there, she turned and left.

The door snicked shut and Ed looked at the clock. Not even midday.

He picked up his knife from the bedside table, looked for an unmarked spread of wall and carved in his mark for today.

And kept carving. Silent, his breathing even, his eyes open but unseeing, hands clenched around the haft but unfeeling, the *scratch, scratch, scratch* going unheard, Ed carved days that never were into his wall, spanning midnights and middays without blinking, weeks passing with only a spot of blood where he'd nicked his finger, the wall filling faster and faster as months sliced by.

Fooling himself, an ironic deception, with cuts.

By one o'clock, when he opened his first bottle of wine and stared at the sun hanging weakly in the clear blue sky and the shadows hunkering unreasonably around doorways and beneath cars in the street down below, Ed had been in the flat for another six months.

Four o'clock came. Ed had consumed two bottles of wine and was slowly working his way into a third. Bad Hungarian red. There'd been a scare a while back about anti-freeze in the wine, poisonous, bad for you, and Ed had been concerned and worried. That was before he'd been sent to Eastern Europe. Now he wished it were true. Not brave enough to take his own life, he often thought that a freak death like that would be rather poetic.

As usual when he got drunk it was not the shimmering loss-of-control felt by most other people. His limbs went numb, yes, and his voice would undoubtedly slur had he cause to use it, but the main effects were more insidious. He felt the light leaving him. Both metaphorically and literally his light was fleeing, bleeding from organs pickled and ruined by bad alcohol: metaphorically, because he was losing the last dregs of hope, decency and guilt that still held out against the dark cancer of his soul; and literally, because on occasion he saw the dark.

He could never have mentioned that to Queenie. He rarely even remembered because it happened so infrequently.

He saw the dark.

Shades of grey where there should be colour. Light bulbs fading and flickering as if gauze was being waved before them, the black gauze of mourning, not wedding-white. Shadows sitting in the sun. And just as soon as he became sober the next day he forgot about it, cast it back into the depths of his mind where other memories dwelt like monstrous sea creatures, cruising the darkness and rising only occasionally to assault the small barren island his life had become.

Strangely enough, he did not feel under siege. Sometimes it was the exact opposite; sometimes, he thought he was a threat to everyone else.

He can see her. Obviously he can, he's murdering her after all, but he can really see her. Not the composite image of a human being our brains usually perceive – that face, those grey-green eyes, two arms, birthmark on the neck . . . all go together to make someone we know and whom we never really see – but the actuality of her as a person made up of many, many things. He's destroying those things, slicing them asunder as if working on an item in a biology class, and perhaps this is why he sees her as she really is. Because her eyes are wide open and filled with something he hates, hates and fears, while she is still alive they are filled with anger and rage and something that can only be curse, a horrible look that he wants to slice out, the look of someone who has won, someone who knows that victory is not hers now but will be in the future. So he slashes at her eyes and it takes several stabs before they both go. Her right arm begins to twitch, jumping on the concrete paving slabs, blood is pulsing from several cuts down near her hand where she'd initially tried fending him off, and every now and then her limbs enter his peripheral vision like curious ghosts watching over his shoulder. He feels the rage rising, something so basic and pure that he fears it more than he can understand, because it is not his own. He can almost see it. Black spots dance before his eyes, speckling in and out of existence like flies popping in and out of the dying woman's flesh. At first he thinks they are in his eyes, because he's in a white-hot panic as he keeps stabbing, slashing, gouging. But then he blinks and wipes blood from his face with his left hand, and the spots are still there. He moves his head from side to side and they do not move with him. They are separate from him, more of the woman than him, and her rage must be far, far more powerful than his own. He realises then how pathetic and self-obsessed his murdering this woman is. As if he could possibly solve anything by taking one more life, a life he had come here to protect at that. But he sees the knife rise and fall, rise and fall, sees flesh opening up, sees parts of the woman that should never have been seen, ever. When he was young he'd peel a banana and think I'm the first and last human to ever lay eyes on this piece of fruit flesh. *Now he is the first and last to see a different flesh. He feels the warm dampness of it on his skin. And the rage rages on.*

Ed surfaced slowly from another drunken, dream-filled slumber to find that it was early evening. And at the window in his flat's messy living room, something was fluttering against the glass.

He sat up quickly, trying to shake the fuzziness from his eyes, and he listened for the scraping across the glass. There was nothing. He stood, pulled the net curtain aside and thought he saw a bird. It took a few seconds to realise that whatever was out there was not solid. It was like a breeze given form, physical yet with nothing firm enough to be seen, stalking across the glass, trying to gain access.

'Get lost,' Ed said, opening the window. The thing dissipated when there was no longer glass between them. Perhaps it had been a shadow cast from somewhere far off.

The street was quiet and still, but Ed saw that things were wrong. The dark, he thought, it's the dark come before the murder, but he was thinking in Queenie's voice.

He needed to go and find her. He needed to know what she knew of the dark. The dark, and the rage he sensed was drawing near again.

He left his flat as he had so many times before – without hope.

Outside, night was forcing daylight into hiding. House windows no longer reflected the cloud-smeared sky, the cars and people travelling through the streets or the façades of buildings standing opposite. Now they were black, as if the light had already been sucked from the buildings' innards, leaving only a void to press against the glass on the inside. Ed sensed a pressure behind these windows – he could almost see the glass bowing outwards – and he walked closer to them. Moving away from the road towards a more noticeable danger felt good. Once or twice he thought he saw himself reflected in there, but the light was fading fast now and he could just have been a shadow. Perhaps it was even someone walking behind him, keeping step, but when he glanced over his shoulder he was alone.

The animals knew that something was amiss. Pigeons huddled together on window sills, heads tucked beneath wings but looking up frequently, unable to sleep. Occasionally some of them would take flight, as if touched by nothing that could be seen. Cats sat behind several windows observing the street, watching the pigeons roost and panic, their heads turning here and there, none of them licking their paws, none outside in the street. There were no dogs sniffing along the gutter or pissing against garden walls, no magpies or crows or sparrows fighting over the remains of burgers trodden into pavements, no bees buzzing between gardens. no flies aiming for nostrils or eyes.

Another flock of pigeons lifted from a garage roof, their wings applauding the strange silence that had fallen over the streets. Even though cars travelled back and forth and people walked the pavements, sounds did not seem to echo, and Ed constantly brushed at his ears as if expecting some deadening material to be draped there. A car passed ten feet away, but its motor could have been coming from the next street. He coughed and felt it thrum through his head and chest, but its sound was dull and muted. He saw other people acting in the same bemused manner: rubbing their ears; watching cars drift quietly by; stamping feet or making some other noise to test their perceived deafness. It was as if the air was thickening, damping sound and diluting echoes into dull mumbles of what they should have been.

Cars approaching from the direction of the park had their headlights on full. Those moving the other way soon turned theirs on as well. The traffic was moving even slower than the usual rush-hour crawl.

Ed left the residential street and walked past the first of the shops. A man was busy pulling down a shutter and padlocking it into place, glancing warily over his shoulder as Ed approached.

'Who are you?' the man asked.

'No one.'

'Something's going to happen,' the man said, eyes dancing in their sockets like loose ball-bearings. He couldn't keep his gaze in one place. 'Something soon, and something bad. Maybe there'll be a riot. Do you think there's going to be a riot?'

Ed looked along the shopping street at the cars wending their way home, the people minding their own business even more than usual as they hurried, heads down, inexplicably trying not to bring attention to themselves. 'I quite doubt it,' he said, but the man was already hurrying away.

A motorcycle passed by accompanied by an explosion of shadows. They buzzed the bike like the dregs of a bad dream, black butterflies, negative snow, but totally without form. The motorcyclist was waving his left hand around his head, flicking his hand at the air as if trying to sign to someone behind him. Ed watched his hand and wondered what he meant.

The shards of shadow darted at the rider's helmet ... and disappeared.

Ed saw what was about to happen, but he could do nothing to help it. He tried to draw breath but it was like breathing in the middle of a thick fog. His lungs felt heavy and full, but not with air. And then the bike flipped sideways, the rider left his mount, the machine hurtled up onto the pavement and through a shop window – the smashing of glass sounding like wind-chimes in the distance – and the street came to a standstill.

At last, Ed could shout. 'Watch out!' he croaked, realising how foolish it sounded now. Realising too that he had allowed someone else to die. If only he had shouted ... if only he had been able to warn ... The man lay half-beneath a parked car, his helmet askew on his head, the car body dented where he had impacted. Someone was kneeling beside him and reaching for the helmet and lifting the visor, tugging, taking it off ...

Ed ran across the street, not wanting to see what gushed out when the man's head was released. He dodged between the stalled cars and the drivers staring in blatant fascination at the scene unfolding in the gutter behind him. He did not look at any of them. He knew what they were feeling because he felt it himself sometimes, a revelling in the pain of others that helped him live with his own agonies. It was necessary, he supposed, and it kept him going however much he had no desire to carry on. They were shocked and excited, and pleased that their own troubles had been unloaded – for however long – on someone else. Something strange was happening right here and now, but a man was dying in the road. For a while, that would obsess these people and give them an escape.

Looking down, Ed saw shadows writhing across his legs as he ran through the beams of car headlights. They seemed to be stitched into his trousers, swathes of dark fluttering behind him like loose cloth. He ran on without looking down again.

'Oh God!' he thought he heard from behind him, but it might as well have been a cry from hidden memory.

He had to find Queenie. Night was falling too early. And try as he might, Ed could not shake the ever-increasing certainty that he had seen it all before.

He can feel blood on his hands. The hard haft of the knife in his right hand counterpoints the warm wet thing he holds in his left, his palm pressed flat to the body's chest to hold it against the wall as he drives the blade home, again and again. A few moments ago he could still feel its heart beating, but that gave out with a spasm, as if the big muscle was trying to force the knife back out with its own violence. The blood from there seemed warmer than the rest, more sticky, like sweet treacle instead of runny syrup. The body is sliding down the wall so he pushes harder, trying to keep it upright, his blows striking its shoulders and neck as it moves down, then its chin and face. His finger slips inside a cut as he pushes and he turns it around in there. He can't help comparing the feeling with one more loving and sensuous. Something scratches his finger – a bone splintered by the heavy knife – and he moves away, letting the body slump to the ground. His face is dripping with sweat, cool where sprayed blood dries there, soon to be a crust, cracking and flaking away like red autumn leaves. Something else settles around him. Heavy and dark and intimate, it reaches out formless hands to steady him, or perhaps to push him down. It enters his throat and makes it hard to breathe. For a second he feels a sudden, total rush of antagonism, fear and hate . . . unbridled hate . . . and then he is running. His feet slap on the pavement, rain taps patient fingers on his forehead and scalp, there's plenty of time, it says, and his clothes catch and scrape where he is sweating. He is running. Again.

As he reached the park the dark had already won.

The streetlamps were still on but their light was weak. Car headlights struggled to part the air, their beams all but ineffectual now. Since running from the crashed motorcycle Ed had seen two cars hugging lampposts, and another one burning where it had come to rest on its roof. Burning, blazing, the stench of roasting meat bringing back dreadful memories, the sight of flames . . . but the flames looked weak and far away, as if he was viewing them on a videotape, a copy of a copy of a copy. They appeared weaker than they should, too. Perhaps the fuel was trying its best not to burn today.

The normal had changed. People were not coping.

And then he wondered why he was running. He was searching for Queenie because she'd told him about this, and deep inside beneath those noxious memories he thought he knew much more than he'd like to believe. But he'd just seen someone die, smelled more people burning in their crashed car, and even then he could hear the muffled sound of smashing glass and a scream, penetrating the darkness as effectively as a sigh into a pillow. He sought danger, felt more comfortable in its presence, so why was he running? Why not stand still and let it come? He would not fight. He would accept whatever the darkness had chosen for him because he knew it, he had seen it

(and smelled it and tasted it)

and although he could not accurately recall when and where, he knew it must have been at the murder. When he was killing that woman, subsumed by his own rage and impotence and anger, the darkness must have touched him.

But a greater rage had been with him as well, something far beyond his own.

And that curse in her eyes.

He climbed the wall. The park was much darker than he had ever seen it. No stars peered through the cloud cover, no streetlight bled through the railings, but Ed knew where to go. He'd been there before and she would be there now. He would find his way in the dark.

'Can you feel it?' Queenie said as he neared the copse of trees. 'Can you feel the rage?'

Ed stopped and tried to locate the voice. It had come from his left, he thought, over where the trees gave way to the shrubbery bordering the stream. He paused, held his breath and waited for her to talk again.

She whispered in his right ear, 'I've never known it so powerful.' She touched his shoulder and walked behind him, drawing her hand across the back of his neck and scratching him with her nails. It was not sexual, he knew that right away, because it hurt. She was trying to hurt him and he didn't know why.

'What's happening?' he asked. If felt like a foolish thing to say. He should know. But right now, standing here in total darkness, a strange woman threatening him and turning him on, he was more confused than ever.

'I've always arrived afterwards.' He could smell her breath, garlic and staleness, no vanity there. 'After the event, watched them clean up the bodies and take them away, seen them put it down to just another murder.' Her voice sounded stronger than it had before, and the more excited she became the heavier the accent. He'd not noticed it before now, perhaps because it brought back way too many memories. She was foreign, but her grasp of English was perfect. Ed wondered if she knew that she was letting it slip. 'But with each one the blackouts lasted longer, because they were searching . . . searching for you, Ed.'

'Me?' He could taste her hate. '*Me?*' He felt her breath caress his ear and neck. She was standing so close that her heat touched him in waves.

'You fuck.' She spoke quietly, but her voice was loud with venom and anger and rage. And her accent, far from distorting her words, made them all the more clear to him.

'You've tracked me down,' he said, wondering if Queenie was a daughter or a niece to the woman he had killed. In a way, he was glad. He waited for the attack.

'I didn't. They did. My mother and the other dead. You're not as invisible as you think. Every time you kill she sees, and she knows your mark, and together . . . they track you again. It takes time. But they find you.'

They?

'Their hate for you blocks out the sun.'

Ed stared up into the blackness and wondered just what he was looking at. 'I don't understand.'

'Murderer.'

'Yes . . . But I still don't understand. Was she your mother? I can't see you. I'm so sorry, whoever she was I'm so sorry, but I've lived with it . . . really, it's destroyed me, you don't know how much.' He should have been crying, but he felt nothing, no sympathy or regret. He thought of all the things that could have been, but he could not remember any of them.

'Destroyed you?' Her voice was breaking now, rage giving way to tears and perhaps increasing because of that. 'Destroyed *you*? I identified . . . I named my mother by looking at her jewellery. That's why we knew it wasn't just another ethnic killing in that bloody war: she still had her jewellery. Anyone else would have taken it. Destroyed? She was *ruined*. I couldn't even look her in the face to say goodbye.' She sobbed as a memory came back. 'It was gone.'

Ed opened his mouth, but there was nothing he could say. Darkness flooded in and sent searing pain into his teeth, dried his tongue. Why was she Queenie, the Avoidance Queen? Her life? *All* of it? Maybe she'd shunned her future just to do this, track him.

'So now you've found me—'

'*They've* found you. My greatest desire – my fantasy, my dream – is to see you in pain caused by me. It's what I've given up everything to achieve. But I dare not argue with them. They have much more reason.'

They, they, they?

She touched him again, a callused hand coming around his throat to hurt but not kill – there were others ready to do that, more in the dark than Queenie – and Ed reacted quickly. He grabbed her wrist and twisted, brought his other arm around to strike out at where he thought she should be. His fist connected with something, he didn't know if it was hair or her woollen sweater, and then he was running through the park, the ground invisible but still there for now, and behind him he heard Queenie shouting something after him but, thankfully, her voice was lost.

He had to get home. Back to the flat, to relative safety, before she found him again. Before *they* found him . . . whoever *they* were. Already he could sense faces pressing against his mind, demanding entrance, requiring acknowledgement. They were still too far away to recognise.

Still running, he came to the park wall. The level of the ground was raised almost to the wall coping, but on the other side there was a five-foot drop into the street. Ed tripped over the head of the wall and fell out into space, arms pinwheeling, a frantic squeal escaping him for a second before he struck the pavement below. His head met with the kerb, and it was only as he faded into a stunned daze that light seemed to offer itself, a flash of white pain from inside. In that light, as if born of it, memories swam and enlarged, vicious memories of that time years ago when he had changed and destroyed his own life by taking someone else's.

But they were all wrong . . .

The woman lying on the compacted mud floor, yes, the smell of burning outside, her eyes cursing him as the knife came down again—

And the woman, already a corpse, pressed against a wall with one hand while the other carves in, her blood running down his arm beneath his sleeve, coating his teeth as it sprays—

And blood staining the clean white sheets beneath her as it rains outside, the stink of the city rising up as the violent storm washes them from the gutters—

And the knife grates as it slips from her outstretched hand and calls sparks from the pavement down by the river—

And in the back of the car, thinking she was there for something else, his shoulder and head pressed awkwardly against the roof as he tries to swing his arm back and forth, back again . . .

And others.

One tastes of cinnamon, another smells of vanilla; one feels cool and calm even under his attack, another is hot and fevered; one goes quietly, another sounds like a steam-engine whistle as she screams . . .

Others. Many others.

And with all of them, the fury and rage.

Ed came around, dizzy with the shock of memory and the impact of his skull on the pavement.

What was he? What kind of animal, monster . . . he should stay where he was, wait for the sad heart of this darkness to find him and exact the revenge it had been seeking for years. Growing all the time, expanding, because every time it drew near he repeated his crime, fed it a fresh rage to find him with next time, more anger, and in a way he supposed he *was* providing for his own punishment.

So he should wait and submit . . .

But there was still time. It was looking for him, a deeper shadow in this blackness, even now he could hear a scream as someone was picked up and tossed away when the dark realised it had the wrong person.

I should submit . . . I'm an animal . . . all those people, all that life . . . there's still time . . . I should die . . . I can escape . . . I'll let her, let *them* kill me . . . I can find light again.

Confused, crying, terrified, wretched, Ed felt his way along the boundary wall of the park, knowing he was going the right way. Cowardice and an instinct for survival – really for Ed they had become one and the same – drove him on. If Queenie was following, he did not hear her or sense her, and she would be as blind as him. He wondered what time it was and whether anyone was even doing anything about this, this weird darkness that had fallen, no stars no moon no lights, artificial light swallowed and beaten back like clouds of leaves before a hurricane. And he realised that he did not care. Because no one could do anything.

This was all for him.

He ran, letting go of the wall and launching himself into space. He tried to steer by sound and touch alone, but every mutter he heard became the scream of one of his victims, every thud of his foot on the road was a knife driving home. He ran through the landscape of his murders, remembering more than he ever thought he could have forgotten. And there were always more memories to come.

Ed found his way home, read the house number by touch, kicked open the front door, ran up to his flat. He had no idea how. He wondered, as he fumbled the handle, how many times he had done this before.

He flicked on his light, expecting nothing, and seeing only a ghost before him.

'Mother!' Queenie shouted, screamed. 'Mother, he's here, get him, get him!'

'Shush!' Ed hissed, almost laughing at how ridiculous that sounded.

'Mother!' She screamed again and again, the drastically weakened effect of the ceiling lights making her seem almost transparent, a smudge on his vision, nothing more.

'Just stop!' Ed shouted. He could hardly hear himself. Maybe the dark was eating at his ears, burrowing in to reach his brain because she, and *they*, had found him already. He wondered how many . . .

'How many?' he asked, but Queenie was screaming louder now, her own voice and rage seemingly able to penetrate the damping effects of this blackness, rattling the windows and setting his hair on end.

'Mother, mother, mother!'

He scrambled around, looking for the doorway and escape, hand alighting on something else entirely.

'Mother, mother . . .'

He lunged at her, the knife an extension of his fear.

'Mother . . .' And then Queenie was quiet.

He worked for five minutes, reminded of all the smells and tastes and sounds that haunted his memory, and taking in some new ones. Once or twice, as Queenie slid further down, the knife went straight through to the wall, marking a few more bloody days in his life.

He left the flat, feeling his way through the dark, feeling it thicker around his neck and heavier on his eyes, wondering just when it would become too hard to push through, too *there*. But it never did.

He felt the rage, old angers rising and a fresh, new hatred giving the blackness an electric edge. 'Sorry Queenie,' he whispered, but really he wasn't sorry at all.

Perhaps soon, when the memories were lost again, he'd imagine that he was.

He found his way to the back door of the block of flats. It was rarely used and he had to kick it open, but outside he ran straight into a car. He could barely breathe now, they were coming, and pure instinct drove him on even though he knew he was finished. Like a man putting his hands over his head to save himself from a falling building, Ed continued to fight and struggle on. To pause, to wait for the inevitable, was too much for him to do. He was too scared.

He opened the car door, reached in and found a torch. And it was only when he clicked it on – shining it around the car at the other torches, batteries, gas lamps, flares, fireworks, cans of petrol – that he realised it was his own.

Ed carved another niche in the timber panelling above his bed. There were over two thousand scratches there already. It still didn't feel like home.

He waited for the timber to bleed red sap, but there was none, it was dry. He expected this every time, and every time it did not happen. Yet the fear was always just as fresh. Sometimes he believed that every memory he had was made up, a whole lifetime manufactured in his sleep and given vent in his waking hours.

The only real memory, the one he could taste and smell and feel, was of the murder that had changed his life.

Tim Lebbon's books include *Mesmer*, *Faith in the Flesh*, *Hush* (with Gavin Williams), *As the Sun Goes Down*, *Face*, *The Nature of Balance*, *Until She Sleeps* and *White and Other Tales of Ruin*. His novellas *White* and *Naming of Parts* were both awarded British Fantasy Awards for best short fiction as well as being nominated for International Horror Guild Awards. His short fiction has been published in many magazines and anthologies, including *The Mammoth Book of Best New Horror*, *The Year's Best Fantasy and Horror*, *Night Visions 11*, *Keep Out the Night*, *Foreboding*, *The Darker Side*, *Dark Arts*, *October Dreams*, *The Children of Cthulhu*, *Phantoms of Venice*, *The Mammoth Book of Sword and Honour* and *The Third Alternative*, while a serial novella will run in *Cemetery Dance* magazine. Future books include *Dusk* and *Dawn*, a fantasy duology from Night Shade Books; *Into the Wild Green Yonder*, a collaboration with Peter Crowther from Cemetery Dance Publications, and a novella collaboration with Simon Clark for Earthling Publications. 'I've always been interested in guilt, how people handle it and how it affects them,' explains Lebbon. 'Everyone's guilty of something and we all cope in different ways. Some people can bury it, however bad it may be. Others are destroyed by it, however minor the transgression. And some, like the main character in "Black", are in denial. But however it's handled, guilt is tenacious. It gets you in the end.'

A Drug on the Market

KIM NEWMAN

Had my first London enterprise met with a lesser success, Leo Dare would not have invited me to join the *consortium*; and had it met with a greater, I should not have accepted his invitation.

However, response to the patent Galvanic Girdle, an electrical aid to weight reduction, merely shaded towards the positive end of indifference. After the craze for such sparking yet health-giving devices in my own native United States, this came as a disappointment. My British partners in the endeavour preferred to make known the virtues of the marvellous modern invention through public demonstration, with testimonials from newly slender 'Yankee' worthies, rather than incur the apparent expense of taking advertising space by the yard in the illustrated press. This was a sorry mistake: our initial penuriousness served to alienate the proprietors of those organs. The 'papers took to running news items about the nasty shocks suffered by galvanised ladies of a certain age through overuse or misapplication of our battery-belt. In brief, the Fourth Estate was set against us rather than in our corner. The grand adventure of 'slenderness – through electrocution!' – the slogan was my own contribution to the enterprise – was frankly sluggish and slowing to a halt. I foresaw a lengthy struggle towards profitability, with the prospect of a smash always a shadow to the promise of rich dividends. I was not looking to get out – the example of New York proved that the trick could be done, and the odd singed spinster would be easy to set aside with a proper advertising campaign – but when the third post of a Tuesday brought a card from Leo Dare, requesting my presence at the birth of a *consortium*, my interest was pricked.

The public does not know his name, but Leo Dare is an Alexander of the market-place, a hero and an example among the enterprising. Unlike many of his apparent peers, he endows no museums or galleries, seeks no title or honour and erects no statues to himself. He is not caricatured in *Punch*, quoted in sermons or travestied in the works of lady novelists. He has simply made, risked, lost and regained fortunes beyond human understanding. In '82, Leo Dare cornered quap – an unpleasantly textured, slightly luminescent, West African mud which is the world's major source of elements vital to the manufacture of filaments essential in the (then-uninvented) incandescent lamp. Great quantities of the radioactive stuff sat in warehouse bins for years, as rivals joked that the sharp fellow had been blunted at last. A succession of night-watchmen succumbed to mystery ailments, giving rise to legends of 'the curse of the voo-doo' and of witch-doctors conjuring doom for those who stole 'the sacred dirt'. Then, thanks to Mr Thomas Alva Edison, control of quap became very desirable indeed and Leo Dare, clearly the reverse of cursed, cashed out in style. In '91, he introduced pneumatic bicycle tyres and obliterated overnight the market for solid rubber. Not only do pneumatic tyres offer a more pleasant, less guts-scrambling bicycling experience but they are prone to puncture and wearing-out, necessitating frequent purchase of replacements and creating an ancillary demand for repair equipment, patches and pumps – in all of which our Alexander naturally took an interest.

The particular genius of Leo Dare, that quality which those 'in the know' aptly call 'Dare-ing', is not in discovery or invention – for canny minds are at his beck and call to handle those tasks – but in the conversion through enterprise of intellect into affluence. The old saw has it that if 'you build a better mouse-trap, the world will beat a path to your door'. In these distracting times, the world has other things on its mind than keeping apace with the latest rodent-apprehension patents, and any major advance in the field has to be brought forcibly to its attention. Even then, Better Mouse Trap must compete with inferior snares that have an established following, or lobby successfully for a Royal Seal of Approval, or are simply blessed with a more 'catching' name. Better Mouse Trap, Ltd. will find itself in the care of the receivers if its finely manufactured products are placed in stores beside a less worthy effort retailing at 2d cheaper under the name of Best Mouse Trap. Leo Dare could make a fine old go of Better Mouse Trap, but if he had the rights to Worse Mouse Trap, he would represent it as Best Mouse Trap of All, emblazon the box with a two-coloured illustration of an evil-looking mouse surprised by a guillotine, undercut Best Mouse Trap by ½d and put both his competitors out of business within the year. Snap! Snap! Snap! That is Leo Dare.

'This is Mr William Quinn,' said Leo Dare, introducing me to the three gentlemen and one lady cosied in armchairs and on a sofa in a private room above a fashionable restaurant in Piccadilly. 'As you can tell from the stripe of Billy's suit, he's one of our transatlantic cousins. A veritable wild Red Indian among us. He'll be looking after our advertising.'

From the looks on the faces of those assembled, I did not impress them overmuch. As a member of a comparatively new-fangled profession, I was accustomed to glances of suspicion from those whose business forefathers had managed perfectly well in a slower, smaller world without stooping to plaster their names on the sides of London omnibuses. Come to that, they had managed quite well enough without omnibuses. Our host, who had no such delusions, spoke as if I was already aboard the *consortium*.

It is a peculiarity of Leo Dare that he has no premises of his own. Concerns in which he takes a controlling interest might lease or purchase offices, factories, yards, warehouses, firms of carters and distributors, even railroad trains and cars. He himself resides in hotel suites and has, as the courts would say, no fixed address. It is his practice to engage rooms temporarily for specific purposes. This well-appointed salon, with waiters and attendants firmly shut outside, was the destined birthplace of our fresh venture.

Leo Dare is one of those fellows you can't help looking at, but would be hard-put to describe. In middle years, trim, of average stature, clean-shaven, sly-eyed, impeccably dressed but not ostentatious, he has that sense of command one finds in the best, if least-decorated, generals and statesmen. He alone was standing, back to a fireplace in which a genial blaze burned, one hand behind him, one holding a small glass of what I took to be port.

'Quinn, meet the rest of the *consortium*,' said Leo Dare. 'This is Enid, Lady Knowe, the philanthropist. You'll have heard of her many charitable activities, and of course be familiar with her family name. Her late father was Knowe's Black Biscuits.'

'"An Ounce of Charcoal is a Pound of Comfort",' I quoted.

Lady Knowe, a thin-faced young woman dressed like an eighty-year-old widow, winced. I tumbled at once that she didn't care to be reminded that the funds for her philanthropy came from a species of peaty-looking (and -tasting) edible brick. Knowe's Blacks were dreaded by children entrusted to nannies who believed (or maliciously pretended to believe) their consumption was good for digestion.

'Sir Marmaduke Collynge, the distinguished Parliamentarian . . .'

A beef-checked man in clothes too small for him, Sir Marmaduke seemed to be swelling all through our meeting, indeed all through our acquaintance, as if the room were far too hot for him and he had just enjoyed an enormous meal unaugmented by Knowe's Black Biscuits. He grunted a cheery greeting.

'Hugo Varrable, our research chemist . . .'

A young fellow of about my age, with long hair, a horse face and stained hands, Dr Varrable sat with a leather satchel on his lap. The chemist prized his satchel, which was stuffed to bulging with what I assumed were formulae and vials of experimental compounds.

'And Richard Enfield, administrator of the estate of the late lawyer, Gabriel Utterson.'

A well-dressed gadabout, no longer young, Mr Enfield had the high colour of a man who has spent as little time in his rainy, foggy homeland as possible. He gave a noncommittal, very English wave.

'Does the name "Utterson" mean anything to you, Quinn?' Leo Dare asked.

I confessed that it did not. Leo Dare seemed pleased.

'What about the name of Jekyll? Dr Henry Jekyll?'

'Or Hyde?' suggested Varrable, glumly.

Of course I knew the story. A few seasons back, even the New York 'papers were full of little else.

'Dr Jekyll was the scientifical fellow who brewed the potion that turned him into another man entirely,' I said. 'The dreadful murderer, Edward Hyde.'

'Capital. You did follow the story.'

I shrugged.

'But, Quinn, did you *believe*? Do you credit that a dried-out elderly stick might, by the consumption of a chemical elixir, be transmogrified into a thriving young buck? That he might undergo a radical metamor-phosis of mind and body, shucking off the respectable front of Jekyll to indulge in the licentiousness of Hyde?'

I laughed, a little nervously. My humour was not shared by anyone in the room.

'Well, Quinn. Speak up.'

'Mr Dare, I read the published accounts of the strange case of Dr Jekyll and Mr Hyde. I even saw the Mansfield company's stage drama-tisation in New York, with startling theatre trickery. Knowing some-thing of the workings of the newspaper business, I have assumed the matter blown up out of all proportion. Surely, this Jekyll simply took a drug that unseated his wits and used disguise to live a double life. He cheated the gallows by suicide, I believe.'

'They were two men,' said Mr Enfield. 'I knew them both.'

'I bow to personal experience,' I said, still not fathoming the import of all this.

'Do you not see the opportunity created by our control of the Jekyll estate and by the notoriety of his case?'

'You know that I do not. But I have a strong suspicion that you do. You, after all, are Leo Dare and I am someone else. It's your business to see overlooked opportunities.'

'Spoken like a true ad man, Quinn. Just the right tone of flattery and familiarity. You'll "fit" in all right, I can avow to that.'

I was still no wiser.

'How would you react if I were to tell you that we had, working from the fragmentary papers left behind by the late Dr Jekyll, reconstructed the formula of his potion? That our clever Dr Varrable has reproduced the impurity of salts that was the key, one might also say *secret*, ingredient of Jekyll's elixir of transformation and is at present applying his talents to a system whereby we might compound that miraculous brew in bulk? That our *consortium* has sole licence for the manufacture, distribution and sale of the "Jekyll Tonic"?'

Quiet hung in the room. I was aware of the crackling of the fire.

'Surely,' I ventured, 'Britain has a surfeit of murderers as it is? The *Police Gazette* is full of 'em.'

Leo Dare looked a little disappointed. 'The murderousness of Hyde did not emerge for some months, remember. Initially, the experiment was a remarkable success. Jekyll became a new man, a younger, fitter, more *vital* man. Can you not see the possibilities?'

I began to smile. 'In bottles,' I said. 'Lined up on a druggist's shelf. What do you call them here? Chemist's shops. Little blue bottles, with bright yellow labels.'

'I see you understand well enough,' said Leo Dare, approving.

'The formula must be highly diluted,' said Varrable. 'Maybe one-tenth the strength of that Jekyll used, with water . . .'

'*Coloured* water,' I put in.

'. . . added to minimise the unpleasant side-effects. I say, Quinn, why *coloured*?'

'So it doesn't *look* like water. Otherwise, suspicious folk think that's all it is. I served a rough apprenticeship in a medicine show out West. The marks, ah, the *customers*, ignore the testimonials and the kootch dances. They open their wallets for the stuff that has the prettiest colour.'

'Well, I never.'

'Look to your own medicine cabinet at home. You're an educated man, and I'll wager you purchased your salves and cure-alls on the same basis.'

'We've decided to call it a "tonic",' said Leo Dare.

I thought for a moment, then agreed with him. 'The biggest hurdle will be the public perception of our product as the stuff of melodrama and murder. The name should not have associations with magic or alchemy, as would be the case with "miracle elixir" or "potion" A "tonic" is something we all might have at home without becoming bloodthirsty monsters.'

'From henceforth, the word "monster" is barred among us,' decreed Leo Dare.

Mr Enfield looked down into his empty glass. 'I concur. Though, for a tiny fraction of our customership, the attraction will all be wrapped up in the business of Jekyll and Hyde. Some souls have a temptation to sample the dark depths. We should be aware of that and fashion strategies to pull in that segment without alienating the greater public, whose interest will be chiefly, ah, cosmetic. Everyone above a certain age wishes to look younger, to feel younger.'

'Indeed. And we offer a tonic that will let them *be* younger.'

'We should be cautious, Mr Dare,' said Varrable. 'The formula must be carefully tested. Its effects are, as yet, unpredictable.'

'Indeed. Indeed. But it is also vital, Dr Varrable, that we consider the practicalities. I have asked Quinn to apply his wits to matters outside your laboratory. Many considerations must be made before Jekyll Tonic can be presented to the public.'

'What of the legalities?' I asked. 'Aren't there stringent rules and regulations? Government boards about medicines and poisons?'

'There certainly are, and Sir Marmaduke sits on them all.'

Sir Marmaduke grunted again and made a speech.

'It is not the place of this House to stand in the way of progress, sirrah. The law should not interpose itself between a thing that is desired and the people who desire it. That has always been my philosophy and it should be ever the philosophy of this government. If Jekyll Tonic, this wondrous boon to all humanity, were to be denied us because of the sorry fate of one researcher, where would frivolous, anti-medicinal legislation cease? Would sufferers from toothache be prevented from seeking the solace of such perfectly harmless, widely used balms as laudanum, cocaine and heroin? I pity anyone who persists in needless pain because the dusty senior fatheads of the medical profession, who earned their doctorates in the days of body-snatching and leeches, insist on tying every new discovery up in committees of enquiry, of over-regulating and hamstringing our valiant and clear-sighted experimental pioneers.

'The present manufacturers have taken to heart the lesson of Dr Jekyll, and have gone to great lengths to remove from his formula the impurities that robbed him of his mind even as it gave him strength of body and constitution. Jekyll Tonic is a different matter now that it has been improved and perfected. Its effects are purely beneficial, purely physical. I myself shall ensure that all the members of my household take one tablespoonful of Jekyll Tonic daily and am confident that there will be no ill-effects. This Parliament must declare for Jekyll Tonic, and *decisively*, lest the health of the nation be sapped, and our overseas competitors draw ahead.'

Mr Enfield clapped satirically. Sir Marmaduke bowed gravely to him.

'Think of the enormous benefit it will be for the poor,' said Lady Knowe. 'Always think of the poor.'

'Jekyll Tonic will retail at threepence, but we intend to put out an *extremely* diluted version in a smaller bottle at a halfpenny a bottle,' said Leo Dare.

'For paupers and children,' explained Sir Marmaduke.

I began to do summations in my head. Leo Dare gave figures.

'A farthing for the bottle, the cork and the gummed label; a quarter-farthing for the tonic itself . . .'

'That little?'

'In bulk, yes. I have cornered the uncommon elements. The rest is just water and sugar for the taste.'

'More than twopence halfpenny sheer profit?'

'We expect demand to be enormous, Quinn. Especially after you have worked your own brand of alchemy.'

This put galvanic girdles in the ashcan.

'One thing,' I said. 'What does the tonic actually *do*?'

'I suppose someone had to ask that question, Quinn. What does the Jekyll Tonic actually *do*? Let us try an experiment.'

He raised the glass of what I had taken for port, looked at the clear pink-orange fluid, touched the rim to his lower lip, then inclined his head backwards. He took in the glassful at a gulp and swallowed it at once.

Shadows crept across his face.

But it was only the firelight.

'Most refreshing. I can assure you, as I'll be willing to attest before lawyers, that I feel enormously invigorated and that my senses are sharper by several degrees of magnitude. The outward effect made famous by Dr Jekyll is only notable after a *course* of tonics, and then only in the cases of those who most desire a change of appearance. I myself am happy with the way I look.'

I understood perfectly. I had been in the snake-oil business before.

But never with the Jekyll name.

I foresaw rooms full of gold, profits pouring in like cataracts, fortunes made for all of us.

Varrable's 'laboratory' was a former stables in Shoreditch. Leo Dare had lately purchased Mercury Carriages, a hansom cab concern, not in order to run the operation (whose slogan was an uninspiring 'Fleet and Economical') but to close it down. A sudden surge in demand for quality horsemeat in Northern France made it more profitable to despatch Dobbin to the knackers than to retain the nag in harness.

Leo Dare had come to an arrangement with several long-established businesses with a combined interest in the hackney carriage trade (their more pleasing slogan, 'Hansom is as Hansom Does!'), pledging to eliminate a rogue firm given to undercutting the fares of bigger rivals in return for a substantial honorarium and a percentage of increased profits over a period of five years. Had the cab combine turned him away, he would doubtless have reduced Mercury fares to a laughable minimum and brought about a complete catastrophe in the carriage business, taking his profit from subsidiary concerns. The Mercury premises were at his disposal, and now served as a convenient head-quarters for the developmental work of the Jekyll Tonic *consortium*.

Our research was carried out in such secrecy that no sign outside the works marked our presence. On this first visit, I found the address only by the sheerest chance. I noticed a thin crowd of shifty-looking fellows in heavy coats and scarves loitering on a corner. From the long buggy-whips several of them were toting, I gathered that these were freshly unemployed cabbies, mindlessly haunting their former base of oper-ations. Mercury Carriages had tended to draw their drivers from a pool of swarthy immigrants from the Mediterranean countries, and so I noted not a few fezzes among the traditional flat caps. A couple of big bruisers in billycock hats guarded the stable doors, with cudgels to hand, as a precaution against an invasion of these disgruntled cast-offs.

My own carriage, a sleek four-horse job retained permanently at my disposal by Leo Dare through another clause in his agreement with the cab trust, drew up outside the stables, exciting mutters of discontent from the corner louts. I got out, told the liveried coachman to await my convenience, and presented my credentials to the bruiser who looked most capable of coherent thought.

'Yer on the list, Mr Quinn,' I was told.

A regular-sized door cut into the large stable doors was hauled open and I stepped into a doubly-malodorous place. Doubly, for its former usage was memorialised by the trodden-in dung of equines (currently gracing the plates of provincial French gourmands, I trusted), while its current occupation was most pungently signalled by the stench of chemical processes. I wrapped a handkerchief around my nose and mouth, which gave me the look of a desperado robbing a stage-coach. My eyes still watered.

If you think of a laboratory, you doubtless form a mental picture of tables supporting contraptions of glass tubes, beakers and retorts, with flames at strategic places. Coloured liquids bubble and ferment, while strange heavy smoke pours from funnel-shaped tube-mouths. Perhaps one wall is given over to cages for the animals – rats, rabbits, monkeys – used in experimentation, and in a corner is an arrangement of galvanic batteries, bottles of acid, switches, levers and metallic spheres a-crackle with the blueish light of harnessed lightning.

This was a former stables. With open barrels of smelly gloop.

Hugo Varrable, in a much-stained apron and shirtsleeves, stirred a vat with a long stick. He wore a canvas bucket on his head. It looked like a giant dirty thumb stuck out of his collar, with an isinglass faceplate for a nail.

'It's all done, Billy,' said Varrable, voice a mumble inside the bucket. He turned from the vat to pick up a stoppered flask of the now-familiar fluid. 'Come on through.'

He led me out of the stables into a courtyard where the fleet of Mercury cabs, stripped of brass fittings and iron wheelrims, sat decaying slowly to firewood. Leo Dare would profit from that come winter.

'Have our volunteers appeared?' I asked.

Varrable took off his bucket and coughed. 'Some of them.'

'Only some?'

Varrable shrugged. 'The Jekyll name may have given one or two second thoughts about participating in the experiment.'

'Indeed.'

Awaiting us in what had once been the common-room of the cabbies were three lank-haired, languid individuals, students who fancied them-selves ornaments to the aesthetic movement. One of the species was a young woman, though she wore the same cut of velvet breeches and jacket as her fellows. They had been exchanging bored, nasal witticisms. At our entrance, they perked up. Beneath their habitual posing, they were skittish. All considered, apprehension was understandable.

'This won't do, Doc,' I said, alarming our volunteers. 'The effect of the Tonic we want to push the most is rejuvenation. These exquisites are sickeningly youthful enough as it is.'

'There are other effects, measurable upon all subjects.'

'Yes, yes. But our "selling point" is the youth angle. Are you telling me you could find no elderly or infirm person willing to take part in the testing of our medical miracle?'

'We put the word out at an art school. All the patent medicine concerns do the same.'

'There's your problem, Doc. However, it's easily set right. If you'll excuse me for a moment.'

I stepped out of the common-room and went round to the main gates. The bruisers let me pass and I crossed the road. The loitering ex-cabbies edged away from me with suspicion. Among the Turkish brigands and Greek cutthroats, I found several English individuals of advanced age, faces weathered from exposure to the elements, backs and limbs bent by years spent hunched at the top of a cab, breath wheezy from breathing in gallons of London pea-soup.

'Who among you would care to earn a shilling?' I asked.

Varrable worked the results up into a learned paper no one actually read. Leo Dare arranged for its publication in an academic journal whose name eventually lent weight to our campaign. When *The Lancet*, alarmed by the spectres of Jekyll and Hyde, ran an editorial against us, thunderous voices among the medical profession – not to mention Sir Marmaduke Collynge – were raised against the brand of irresponsible trade journalism that inveighs against a perfectly legal product which has yet to be judged either way by the final arbiters of such matters. 'The public shall make up its own mind,' said Sir Marmaduke, at every opportunity, 'for it always does, the average fellow being far more astute than your addle-brained quack, consumed with envy of the achievements of younger, more free-thinking men.'

As the brewing and refining continued in Shoreditch, Leo Dare took the elementary precaution of establishing, through Lady Knowe, a philanthropic trust to dispense grants supporting avenues of medical enquiry whose pursuit was blocked by the hidebound bodies responsible for the allocation of funds at the country's major universities, medical schools and teaching hospitals. This enabled many a hobby-horse to be ridden and pet project to be nurtured, doubtless contributing (in the long run) to the health of the nation and the wealth of scientific knowledge. A correlation of this generosity was that researchers who benefited from the foundation's beneficence were predisposed to uphold the reputation of the late Dr Henry Jekyll on the public podium and give testimony that his work, though unfortunately applied in the first instance, was perfectly sound. These worthies tended to have passionate beliefs in the benefits of naturism, monkey glands, cosmetic amputation, the consumption of one's own water, phrenology, galvanic stimulation (our old friend), vegetarianism and other medical tangentia. However, their MDs were every jot as legit. as those of the head surgeon at Barts or the Queen's own physician, and the public (perhaps regrettably) tends to think one doctor as good as another when reading a testimonial.

Having observed the experiment first-hand, I did not quite become a fanatic believer in Jekyll Tonic. However, I had to concede that it was a very superior species of snake oil.

For a start, its effects were immediate and visible.

Our would-be poets and unemployed cabbies did not transform into a pack of Neanderthal men and take to battering their fellows with makeshift clubs, but several evinced genuine transformations of feature and form. A very bald fellow instantly sprouted flowing locks that were the envy of the decadents in the room, suggesting we could market the Tonic as a hair restorer (always a popular line). Arthritic fists, all knuckles from a lifetime of gripping reins, opened into strong, young hands. A shy stammerer among the students was suddenly able to pour forth a flood of impromptu rhyming and would not shut up for two days, when the effect suddenly (and mercifully, for his circle) wore off. Another poet, an avowed anarchist and shamer of convention, rushed from the stables, eluding our guards, hacking at his hair with a pen-knife. He was later found to have taken a position as a junior clerk with a respectable firm of solicitors, which he quit suddenly as his old personality resurfaced.

Varrable remained concerned that the effects of the tonic were essentially unpredictable, as proved by further experimentation with a range of volunteers from wider strata of society. We thought we should have to pay substantial 'hush money' to a curate who sampled Jekyll Tonic and passed through a bizarre hermaphrodite stage to emerge (briefly) as a woman of exceedingly low character with an unhealthy interest in the gallants of Britannia's Navy. Leo Dare overruled our request for cash, predicting (correctly) that the cleric in question would rather bribe *us* to keep from his Bishop any word of the Portsmouth adventures of his female alter ego.

None of our volunteers killed anyone, which was a great relief.

Only the anarchist and the curate vowed never to repeat the experience. I had a sense that the cleric came reluctantly to the decision and would eventually alter it, perhaps making surreptitious purchase of the Tonic once it was generally available and indulging in its use only after taking precautions in the name of discretion. The others returned, bringing with them sundry family-members and friends. They all clamoured for the Tonic in a manner that suggested Leo Dare had another 'winner' on his hands.

The Hon. Hilary Belligo, the stammering aesthete, splutteringly conveyed to us that he would be prepared to forgo the shilling remuneration we offered for participation in the experiment and would meet any price we suggested if an inexhaustible supply of the Tonic were made available to him.

Varrable and I independently liquidated all our other holdings and ploughed our money into the *consortium* stock issue. The next day, before any public announcement had been made, the value of our shares tripled.

I drew the line at sampling the formula myself. If called, I was only too happy to swallow a few ounces of coloured water – doubtless the same recipe Leo Dare had theatrically quaffed at our first meeting – and declare myself satisfyingly rejuvenated.

Varrable formed a theory that the effect of the Tonic was to reshape each individual into the person they secretly wanted to be. The ageing, stuffy Jekyll had become the young libertine Hyde; but, as the name suggests, the violent thug had always been 'hiding' inside the respectable man. Sometimes, as perhaps with Jekyll and certainly with our anarchist and our curate, the transformations proved a shock to the subjects because the Tonic was no respecter of hypocrisy. It acted on *secret* wishes, some concealed even from those who harboured them. Many were unaware of the fierceness that burned in their breasts, the *need* to be somebody else. My own reluctance to take the Tonic came from an unanswered question: I thought that I was perfectly happy to be myself, but what if I were wrong? What if some notion I couldn't consciously recall was stuck there? As a lad, I wanted to be a pirate when I grew up. Would a course of Jekyll Tonic have made me grow an eye-patch and a pegleg? Might I not have come to myself, like that sore curate in a Portsmouth grog-house, to find I had taken the Queen's shilling and was miles out to sea on a ship of the line?

'Our stock issue is closed,' announced Leo Dare. 'Those not aboard by now have missed the omnibus.'

The *consortium* was dining out, no longer in a private room.

Now part of the game was to be seen, to be envied and admired, to cut a dash before those who mattered. We had taken a table at Kettner's and were very visible. Leo Dare had insisted Varrable and myself be taken to Sir Marmaduke's tailor and outfitted in a manner befitting 'men on the rise'. Suits of American cut would not do.

Envious glances were tossed at us. The *maitre d'hôtel* presented a succession of inscribed cards from plutocrats and captains of industry. Leo Dare glanced at any message before smiling noncommittally across the room and not extending invitations to our table. The cards from journalists and editors were handed to me, those from churchmen and society leaders to Lady Knowe, those from scientists (who would a month ago not have cared to recognise his name) to Varrable. Between us, we had enough cards for a deck – we could have played whist with them, to show our indifference to those outside the *consortium*.

'I'm no longer at home to fools clamouring for an inside chance at a few shares,' chuckled Sir Marmaduke, mouth full of well-chewed beefsteak. 'Barely a month past, I offered the bunch of 'em a chance to buy in. To a man, they said I was cracked, sirrah, cracked.'

We all laughed, heartily. Even Lady Knowe, whose mode of dress dropped a decade each time we convened. She still wore black, but her gown was less widow's weed than dark blossom.

Leo Dare, whom no one had ever seen eat, oversaw our gustatory indulgences and, begging permission from Lady Knowe, lit up a black *Cubano* cigar. He exhaled clouds that seemed to take sculptural shape before dissipating.

'Our conquest of the market has been so complete,' he said, 'that the "smart money" has stayed away. Some call us a "bubble", you know. They predict a "smash"! Soon, they'll learn that the old certainties have gone. In the coming age, men – and women, Lady Enid – such as we shall set the pace, make the decisions, reap the profits. The Twentieth Century shall belong to us.'

When Nietzsche writes of an 'Overman', the philosopher means Leo Dare.

'So we are smarter than "the smart money",' I said.

In my mind, I held the picture of Hilary Belligo, trying to get out the words, the light of inspiration dying in his eyes, to be rekindled as a physical and mental *need* far stronger than any poetic impulse would ever be.

'There'll be no limit to the demand for the Tonic,' said Varrable. 'We could ask five pounds a thimble, and some would pay it.'

I thought of the Hon. Hilary. Varrable was right.

'Let us not be over-greedy,' said Leo Dare, which made Mr Enfield giggle. As usual, the controller of the Utterson-Jekyll estate was slightly soused.

'Think of the poor,' said Lady Knowe, sipping champagne. 'The *poor* poor.'

A card was delivered to her, not from a churchman, but from a golden-haired Guardsman. She giggled at the inscription and placed it separately from the others. I wondered if she'd been at the Jekyll. Samples were already in circulation among the *consortium*.

'I have been reconsidering the matter of price,' said Leo Dare. 'I don't think sixpence a bottle is unreasonable. Any objections?'

Heads shaken all around the table.

'Passed,' said the entrepreneur. 'Now, let us drink to the memory of the late Dr Henry Jekyll, without whom, *et cetera et cetera* . . .'

'*Et cetera et cetera*,' we chanted, raising glasses.

Varrable and newly hired assistants continued the course of volunteer tests, making slight refinements to the formula, and the *consortium* stock continued to gain value by the proverbial leaps and bounds. Shore-ditch's first telephonic lines were strung, with matching sets of the apparatus installed in my sanctum, once the snug nest of the proprietor of Mercury Carriages, and Varrable's command post above the factory floor. Varrable became addicted to the gadget, 'ringing up' on it several times a day to pass trivial messages, though a perfectly adequate speaking tube between our offices was left over from the Mercury days.

As my role in the enterprise became paramount, I closeted myself with secretaries to take dictation, commercial artists to work up sketches and a few trusted experts to bounce ideas against. For weeks, we 'brain-stormed'.

A Marvel of the Modern Age!

Ladies – Make of Yourself What You Will!!!

Release the Young Man inside You!

A Kitten Can Be a Tiger!

Transformed and Improved!! Transmogrified and Reborn!!

It has always been a credo of mine that an advertisement cannot have too many exclamation points.

We bought space on public hoardings and in the press, and sent sandwich-men out onto the streets. We put up posters on the platforms of the London Underground Railway and inside the trains themselves, where passengers had no choice but to look at them. We were plastered on the sides of 'buses, in the windows of chemists' shops and on any walls that happened to be bare before our trusty regiment of boys with paste-pots passed by. Striking illustrations, engraved by the best men in the business, were augmented by 'unsolicited' testimony from our volunteers, much the best of it genuinely unsolicited. I decided to keep the Hon. Hilary in the background, for he was now almost permanently in his secondary personality and the quality of his rhyming, while undoubtedly visionary, was of a nature to prove alarming rather than reassuring. Varrable insisted we keep supplying our initial volunteers with the Tonic so he could study the effects of repeated use. He also asked for more bruisers at the laboratory, to guard against possible riots from the much-swelled cabbie crowd. It seemed our people couldn't get enough of the Jekyll. Varrable tried to water the formula down, to make its effects less immediate and lasting.

Some use could be made of the statements of cabbies and longhairs, but willing participants were also found among the better classes. We prominently displayed sworn testimonials from gracious ladies, leading churchmen, military officers and, inevitably, Sir Marmaduke Collynge. I interviewed all manner of folk who had sampled the Tonic, helping them set down in appropriate words the benefits they genuinely felt had accrued to them. Major General Cogstaff-Blyth, 'the Hector of Maiwand', was quoted as saying 'with this spiffing stuff in him, your British soldier shall never lose another battle!' I had the Maj.-Gen. put on his best medals and troop down to Speakers' Corner to harangue passers-by with the merits of Jekyll Tonic, and lobby for a bulk purchase of the wonder fluid by the War Office.

In any enterprise, only so much can be done by buying space to hawk your wares. True success can be achieved only if the press find themselves so harried by the interest of their readership that they are obliged – nay, *forced* – to augment paid advertising by running stories that pass as unbiased journalism but which essentially serve to boost your reputation. To reach this point, you have to worm your way into the public mind by fair means or foul. Firstly, I provided the lyrics for an entire song-book of ditties which were set to tunes by a couple of tame music students willing to work in lucrative anonymity. The theory was that one at least of our songs was bound to catch the nation's fancy. Certainly, for a time, 'Changing for the Better (through a Course of Jekyll Tonic)' was heard on every street-corner – Leo Dare magnani-mously promised me a fifty per cent cut of the song-sheet income – and hardly less success was met by 'An Inspirational Transformational Super-Sensational Stuff' and 'You've Got to Be a Jekyll Tonic Girl (to Get the Boy You want)'.

The greatest success of this campaign was, I venture to say, the affair of the Jekyll Joke.

It took no little negotiation and expense to arrange for the 'patter comic', Harry 'Brass' Button to conclude his turn at the Tivoli Music Hall with an apparent ad. lib. remark of my own coinage. 'With Jekyll Tonic I feel like a New Man,' said Button, then adding with an indescribable leer, '. . . luckily, the wife does too!' The results were as startling to the performer as anyone else. Not only was Button's 'punch-line' greeted nightly with gales of laughter but also applause that lasted for minutes, delaying the first-act curtain. The audience could only be quieted if he agreed to give the 'Jekyll Joke' over again, as much as seven times. Attendances were up and expectant patrons turned away in crowds. A sticker across the posters outside the hall announced 'the "Jekyll Joke" *will* be told'. Eventually, new posters were put up claiming the Tivoli as 'home of the hilarious "Jekyll Joke"'.

Harry Button, whose check suit and mobile eyebrows had been rather falling from favour, was precipitously elevated to the top of the bill, displacing an entire family of acrobatical contortionists and an opera singer who had conducted a famous *amour* with a Ruthenian Prince. Button only sampled the Tonic once that I heard of. He wept for six hours, then swore off it for life. But he told and retold the Jekyll Joke. I don't doubt that, though his top-of-the-bill days are now but a memory, he still tells it at the drop of a hat. Certainly, he truly believes his was the brain that conceived the marvellous line and he'll try to thrash anyone who says different.

Some fellows entirely unconnected with the *consortium* whipped up a song that Button refused to include in his act on the grounds that it was an affront to the dignity of what had now become a much-loved, therefore *respectable*, music hall institution. However, every other comic in London sang 'Have You Heard the Jekyll Joke?/It'll make you laugh until you choke!/Have You Heard the Jekyll Joke?/Old Brass Button is the funniest bloke!' In the Strand, whenever Harry Button was about, children chanted the chorus, especially the repeated refrain 'now tell us another one, Brass!'

With the departure of Mr Richard Mansfield from the London stage, we commissioned our own dramatisation of *The Strange Case of Dr Jekyll and Mr Hyde*, emphasising the positive aspects of the transformation and omitting any mention of the late Sir Danvers Carewe. After all, Edward Hyde never came to trial and so was not proved a murderer in any court of law. Our lawyers sent reminders of this fact to any who tried to publish or stage the hitherto-accepted version of the story. On behalf of the Jekyll Estate, Mr Enfield accepted a great many grudging retractions and apologies. Several times in the play, our Dr Jekyll took a swig of his formula and approvingly exclaimed, 'It's a tonic!'

All this, it should be remembered, was well before the Tonic was available in stores. By the time we were ready to begin manufacture and distribution, the *consortium* had gathered again and concluded that 6d was far too meagre a price to ask for such a highly demanded and beneficial commodity. Lady Knowe bleated a little about pricing the Tonic out of the reach of the poor, but we decided that – though the Jekyll Tonic was of such incalculable good to the public that it must in effect be declared price*less* – we would settle upon the trivial sum of 1s a bottle, in order to effect the greatest possible distribution of the wondrous blessing we were about to grant humankind in general.

'A shilling is little enough to pay,' said Leo Dare.

I was mentally formulating an alliterative sentence employing the words 'modern', 'marvel' and 'miracle' in some fresh order when a discreet rap at the door disturbed my process of thought.

'Go away,' I shouted at the Porlockian person. 'It can wait.'

The office door opened a crack and an unfamiliar individual peeked around, holding up something shiny.

'Generally, that's not the case, sir.'

The newcomer was a shabby little man with a London accent. I pegged his section of the market at once – clerk or undermanager, with a little education but no elocution, the son of someone who worked with his hands, the father of someone who'd 'do better'. He would be most susceptible to advertisements that linked the product with easy living, good breeding and 'class'. A life lived with unformed needs and aspirations, and thus an ideal customer. He'd be looking for something but not know what it was. Enter: the Jekyll Tonic.

'Inspector Mist, sir,' he announced, 'from Scotland Yard.'

I gave him another look. He had a bloodhound's big wet nose and a drooping moustache that covered his mouth entirely. His hat was a year or so past style and his topcoat was too heavy for him, as if the pockets were full of handcuffs for felons, packets of plaster of Paris for footprints and magnifying lenses for clues.

'Come in, Inspector. You're Sheriff of these parts?'

'You would be the American, sir. Mister . . .'

'Quinn.'

'That's the name.'

'How can I help you?'

'Rather delicate matter, sir. Are you acquainted with . . .' he consulted a note-pad . . . 'a Mr Belligo?'

'What has the Hon. Hilary been up to now? Subversive publications with obscene illustrations?'

'Misappropriation of stock is mentioned, sir. In short, theft.'

'I was under the impression that he was of independent means.'

'Ran through 'em, sir. Looked around. Found another source of readies. Only it wasn't exactly his to tap.'

'Lock the villain away, then. I imagine he'll find an eager audience for his verses in one of your excellent prisons.'

'Have to catch him first, sir.'

'He's not around here.'

'Didn't say he was. Only, it seems you have something the absconder needs. A tonic, I believe. Likely he'll come nosing about.'

The policeman picked up a bottle from my desk.

'Is this it? Jekyll Tonic?'

'No,' I said. 'Just a sample of the bottle. The bottle is important, you know. The comforting size, the colour, the quality of the wax around the stopper, the adhesive label.'

'Looks like a bottle to me.'

'Very perceptive, Inspector.'

'That's as well, then. If Mr Belligo pops up . . .'

'I'll send a lad to the Yard.'

'We'd be grateful, Mr Quinn.'

'There is a flaw to your trap, though. At the moment, Jekyll Tonic is a *rara avis*, obtainable only from our experimental laboratories, downstairs in this very building. As of,' I consulted my new gold watch, 'as of eight o'clock tomorrow morning, it will be on sale all across London, then the country. You might have to post a man at every chemist's shop in the nation.'

The bloodhound face drooped.

My first thought upon arriving fresh and early in Shoreditch to see a line of policemen outside the factory was that one of our devoted test-subjects had done himself or someone else injury while in the grips of Jekyll Tonic fever. The fellow who would now have to be known as the Dis. Hon. Hilary Belligo sprang naturally to mind. It turned out that Leo Dare had merely suggested it would be sensible to take precautions against rioters. I looked about for the dogged Inspector Mist. If present, he was in one of those impenetrable Scotland Yard disguises.

We understood that the chemists' shops and apothecaries' dispensaries which would be our main retail outlets would abide by no decree we might make that the Tonic should be withheld from sale until a certain standardised time. I knew enough about storekeepers to guess they would agree to all our terms and then sell the stuff as soon as they got it, probably knocking a penny off the shilling to undercut the fellow across the street.

So, it was to be a free-for-all.

At eight o'clock, the old stable gates opened and carts trundled out, laden with straw-packed crates of clinking bottles. Each cart was manned by a former Mercury cabbie (retained at a generous two-thirds of his previous wage) and a bare-knuckles boxer with a handy shillelagh. The purpose of the latter individuals was not so much to prevent any attempts at seizure of the Tonic supply as to suggest to the world at large that the product was so desirable that such attempts were highly likely.

Because it seemed expected of us, we put up a stall outside the laboratory, manned by several smart young women recruited from the chorus of the Tivoli, all neat in abbreviated sailor-suits and hats with pom-poms. Harry Button had asked an outrageous fee to act as shill at the stall, so we had declined his services. I noticed that the comic had turned up for the historic moment anyway, a little surprised that the eager public were clamouring not for his Joke but for the inspiration of same, the Tonic itself. The first Jekyll Tonic offered for sale direct from the factory was available at an introductory price of 9d. Our shutters went up simultaneous with the emergence of the carts.

We were all there. Leo Dare hung rather in the background, calmly puffing one of his cigars. In press photographs taken that morning, as so often in Kodaks of the *entrepreneur* and Overman, Leo Dare's face is indistinct, masked by frozen shrouds of smoke. Sir Marmaduke and Lady Knowe made speeches, drowned out by the Babel of eager customers beseeching the attention of our becoming sales assistants. Varrable, emerged again from his bucket, still fussed about the vats, already concerned with brewing up tomorrow's batch of Tonic.

I found myself in a corner of the stableyard with Mr Enfield.

He drew a draught from a hip-flask and offered it to me.

'Is that . . .?'

'Not on your nellie,' he said.

I took a swallow. Strong whisky.

'I saw Hyde trample the little girl,' he said. 'Worst thing I ever did see. The look on his face.'

'Monstrous? Evil?'

'No. It was like he was walking over more pavement. As if no one else mattered at all. He was scared all right, when the mob had his collar, scared for himself. A shirty little bastard he was, whining and indignant, with clothes too big for him. That was what was inside Jekyll.'

The first customers were swigging from their own bottles. On labels they hadn't read, we had printed a warning advising that the daily dose should not exceed a spoonful taken in a mug of water. It was not our fault some patrons were too excited to read and regard these instructions.

'The formula was lost,' I said to Mr Enfield. 'Even Jekyll couldn't recreate it. You could have kept it that way. If you were really worried, you could have suppressed the Tonic, stopped this even before it started.'

Mr Enfield looked at me. He took another drink.

'You really don't know Leo Dare, do you?'

At that moment, I was distracted.

In the street, ten or fifteen new devotees of the Jekyll Tonic were changing. It was like a Court of Miracles from *Notre Dame de Paris* crossed with the news of the Relief of Mafeking. Crutches thrown away! Speaking in tongues! Vigorous embraces! Cries for more, more, more! Supply at the stall was exhausted, and the sales girls apologised. Banknotes were waved in fists. Coins were thrown. One girl nearly had her eye put out by a flung florin.

The police moved in, augmenting our bare-knuckle men.

I saw the most beautiful woman I ever beheld in my life, a slim blonde angel wrapped in the voluminous garments of a much, much larger lady. She threw away a veiled hat to unloose a stream of glamorous golden hair. She took my arm and looked at me with unutterably lovely eyes.

'The children call me "pig-face",' she said, wondering.

I did not understand.

'A mirror,' she said. 'Have you a mirror?'

I patted my pockets though I knew I did not have a glass about me. At my shrug of apology, she left me – a slave to her memory – to ask another bystander.

Beyond the crowd, I saw Varrable having heated words with Leo Dare. The chemist listened, arms folded, as Leo Dare stabbed the air with a cigar to emphasise points.

The transformed angel found a mirror and was stunned by her new face, a female Narcissus absolutely smitten with herself.

The mirror was passed around. Our customers beheld their fresh selves. I heard a scream from one, who covered his head with his jacket and plunged alarmingly through the crowd. He was soon forgotten. Others danced on the cobbles, leapt up and down with abandon, shouted 'look at me!', performed feats of strength such as lifting a grown man up in each hand, turning cartwheels. A ragged choir lit into 'An Inspirational Transformational Super-Sensational Stuff'.

Word escaped that I was connected with the *consortium* and I was hugged and kissed. I trapped light-fingers reaching for my wallet and watch and kicked away a junior ruffian who scurried off with good humour to ply his trade elsewhere.

Leo Dare and Varrable caught the ear of Sir Marmaduke. He stood up on a platform by the stall.

'Friends, friends,' announced Sir Marmaduke, booming at the crowd with a voice proved in Parliamentary debate. 'Owing to the unprecedented demand, a fresh batch of the wonder Tonic is being brewed up even as we speak. It will take some hours for the complex scientifical processes necessary in its manufacture to be brought to complete fruition, but on behalf of the Jekyll Tonic *consortium* we pledge that the demand shall be met even if it means working our factory round the clock. The Jekyll will be on sale again by twelve noon, this we guarantee.'

'Maybe they still got some at Filkins the Chemist, down the road,' suggested someone.

Half the crowd dashed off.

They soon came back. It had been the same at Filkins the Chemist, and at shops all over London.

The Jekyll Tonic had not so much arrived as exploded.

The 'papers were full of it. Questions were asked in the House (and answered at length by a personage familiar to us all). More vats were bought and more fellows engaged to stir the compounds. Our credit was accepted by suppliers of equipment and chemicals. Carts continued to trundle out three times a day, laden with cases of the Jekyll Tonic. The former stables grew more crowded and we had to lease larger premises adjoining the original site. In addition to the vat-stirrers, we had (after unfortunate incidents) to engage more bruisers to watch that the workers didn't siphon off or sample the raw Tonic. Then we had to take on ex-soldiers and former policemen to crack down on the bruisers.

It turned out that there had been a deal of pilferage, and 'super-strength' Jekyll Tonic was being made available to the criminal classes of Whitechapel, Limehouse and Wapping. Inspector Mist snuffled around again, with reports of running battles in the streets between Irish and Hebrew bully-boys with illicit Jekyll interests and the Chinese tongs who found patronage of their opium dens drastically reduced. Leo Dare was not overly concerned, assuring us all that this had been accounted for in his calculations. It would serve only to sharpen the appetite for our legitimate Tonic. All considered, that a street brawler of previously average reputation could see off a dozen Chinamen though one of the celestials had embedded a hatchet in his skull was as fine a testimony for us as any recommendation from a Bishop or Baronet. We did, however, bring swift and merciless court actions against competitors who ventured to sell coloured tincture of laudanum as 'Jeckell Tonik' or 'Jickle Juice'. I made sure to add to all our posters the rubric 'accept no imitations, swallow no substitute . . . there is only one original Jekyll Tonic!'

Borrowing against my stock, I removed myself from lodgings in Lewisham to a house in Kensington. Suddenly equipped with (or weighed down by) the trappings of a man of stature, I had to beseech from Sir Marmaduke and Lady Knowe information about how best to employ a household's worth of bowers and scrapers. It took me a disastrous week to learn that the finest servants were not necessarily the most unctuously deferential butlers or the prettiest, cheekiest maids, but rather the faintly drab individuals who actually took the bother to do the work they were paid for. I received so many invitations that I had to engage a secretary with a type-writer to respond to them all. I did not let it go to my head. It was all very well to be popular and sought-after, but it was what was on deposit at Coutt's that counted.

Varrable, the last man I should have thought likely to gain a reputation as a rakehell, was seen about town with, in succession, a chorus girl with a dimple, a Drury Lane ornament whose beauty had prompted several duels in Paris, the wealthy young widow of a lately-deceased African millionaire and the youngest daughter of a Duke. Sir Marmaduke was offered a Cabinet position, but declined on the grounds that his business interests engaged too much of his time for him to be concerned with the minutiae of canals and waterways. Lady Knowe took tea with the Prince and Princess of Wales, dressed in white for the first time in her life in honour of the occasion. Her philanthropic concerns became extremely fashionable, and many distinguished names were added to her roster of charitable souls. Mr Enfield sold all his stock (mostly, through third parties, to me) and departed for the South Seas, still muttering doom under his breath. He was fleeing from a fortune, but would not be reasoned with and if profit was to be had from his squeamishness I saw no reason why I should not be the one to scoop it.

For me personally, Jekyll Tonic was Inspirational, Transformational and Super-Sensational. And I did not even taste the stuff.

At some point in any venture, my job changes from 'starting up' to 'looking after'. Once the train is up to full steam, it needs a steady hand on the throttle and a good eye on the track ahead. There is no time to relax, to sit back and let the coffers fill. Each day brought a thousand questions from the press, from tradesmen, from the factory. My secretary wore out her type-writer and a new, improved model had to be purchased. I arranged tours of inspection, interviews with various members of the *consortium* (never Leo Dare, of course), supervised the design of new and improved labels for the bottles. I no longer had a fresh canvas: the name of Jekyll Tonic was known, and had to be protected rather than bruited about. That was the chief reason for seeing off the Jickle and Jeckell jokesters.

All at once, we were the *only* Tonic. Bovril was forgotten, even when advertised by an admirable image of a cow being strapped into an electric chair. Carter's little liver pills piled up unsold in the stores. Dentists reported that even heroin, miracle drug of the decade, was sorely out of fashion. Sufferers from all maladies and pains demanded to go 'on the Jekyll' and would accept no substitutes.

*

By now, a week into the reign of the Tonic, I was surprised by nothing. Approaching Varrable's office early in the morning, I passed a lady who had just emerged from our chemist's sanctum. Though her hair and costume were in disarray, I recognised Mrs Mary Biddlesham, a supporter of Lady Knowe's latest endeavour, to ship supplies of the Jekyll overseas to missionaries in order to coax out the decent Christian lurking within every benighted heathen. Mrs Biddlesham repaired her clothing in a manner that led me to form a conclusion as to the activities with which she had been engaged overnight. She did not meet my eye or answer my good-day.

I found Varrable fussing with his cravat, admiring himself in the cheval glass, and in good spirits.

'You are a wonder,' I said.

Varrable smiled and paraphrased one of my slogans. 'Inside every kitten, there's a tiger!'

I shrugged.

'With claws, Billy,' he assured me. 'I have the scratches to prove it.'

A divan had been installed in Varrable's office, as an aid to abstract thought. Its cushions were on the floor and I gathered that little in the abstract had transpired on the previous evening.

The remains of a late supper stood on a side-table.

I picked up an empty glass, and sniffed the dregs.

Varrable raised a decanter.

'It looks like port, remember,' he said.

'Doc, you've become a blackguard.'

'Have I not? I don't know about the average advertising man, but the average research chemist isn't thought of as a "catch" by the ladies. It's something to do with the penury and long hours, of course, but the reason most often given is the *smell*. At school, they call chemistry "stinks". It stays with you for life. Not so stinky now, of course.'

He sniffed his newly manicured nails.

'I don't go near the vats any more,' he said. 'We have low people for that.'

'So this is your secret?'

'It's all our secret, isn't it? I confess I've been conducting my own course of private experiments. I should write it up, I suppose. "The Effects of Dr Henry Jekyll's Transformational Formula upon the Fairer Sex, as Observed First-Hand by Dr Hugo Varrable, with Fifteen Water-Colour Plates and Extensive Footnotes". At first, I propose a toast and we both "take a Jekyll", only mine is coloured water. An observer has to be distanced. I admit that I do tend to intervene, possibly affecting the outcome of the experiments. A certain, ah, *class* of female is excited by the prospect, and will probably deliver the desired results with a placebo of coloured water. But my interests in that sort ran dry some time ago. Their inner selves are too close to the skin. No, to demonstrate the truly miraculous effects of the Tonic, I have to seek not Rosie O'Grady but the Colonel's Lady. In this case, the Commodore's Lady.'

'What if they're like us, Doc? What if they don't want to find out what's inside or know already? A lot of people are still afraid of the Jekyll.'

Varrable laughed.

'Don't I know it, Billy! Mrs Biddlesham, for one. In her case, I simply gave her an *aperitif* with the compliments of your Hibernian friend, Mr Michael Finn.'

'The results?'

'Most satisfactory. I'm not the only researcher in this field. A great many gentlemen have been purchasing the Tonic not for themselves, but for ladies of their glancing acquaintance. Sir Marmaduke insists his household take a tablespoon a day. He lines up his maidservants like sailors being given the rum ration. And he's been rejuvenating himself with regular doses. I understand a few women of dubious character or attractions have ventured their own experiments along these lines. I couldn't approve of that, of course.'

I was not, of course, shocked. But I did perceive a flutter of danger.

'When your, ah, lady-friends, come to themselves, how do they feel?'

'Delighted and rotten all at the same time, I should imagine. I've never really asked. Do you think I should make enquiries? Do a "follow-up" study?'

I thought a moment. There would be complaints. It was but a matter of time before some soiled dove took the matter to the police. No lady of good name would want this to come out in the courts, but eventually some tart with nothing to lose would try it on. And I would not have wanted to be in Varrable's expensive new shoes if word of last night's experiment were to reach Commodore Biddlesham, whose expertise with both cutlass and revolver could be attested to by not a few deceased Shanghai river pirates.

'You still don't use the Jekyll?' I asked. 'I mean, Doc, this is *you*?'

He looked surprised at the question, but insisted he'd never touched a drop.

Still, even without drinking it, the Tonic had brought out something inside him that would never go back in hiding.

'Tonight, a fresh direction,' he said, sliding on his smart new jacket. 'I am entertaining the Flavering Sisters, Flora and Belinda. Their father, the Earl of Roscommon, sits on the board of the University of . . . well, you know who he is. A year ago, Billy, I was discharged from the faculty. Merely for pursuing a line of enquiry involving the effects of caustic solutions upon the mammalian eye. A petition was got up about vivisection and a to-do burst in the 'papers. My name was "Mudd", like your countryman, Dr Samuel Mudd. Now, it might as well be "Rose", for it seems that with the Jekyll Tonic millions pouring in I smell a lot sweeter. This is the Strange Case of Dr Varrable . . . and Mr Rose.'

'Flora and Belinda,' I mused. 'With which delightful young lady do you intend to experiment?'

Varrable fixed a fresh-cut rose to his lapel and sniffed it.

'You misjudge me. Why choose only one?'

'You've complicated our lives at the Yard, sir, and no mistake.'

Inspector Mist had become a frequent visitor to Shoreditch.

Given that, with the Jekyll craze, all I saw were smiling faces, hungry eyes, beautiful women, happy bankers, deferential servants and ecstatic *consortium* comrades, the presence of the Inspector, who trudged about under a perpetual black cloud, was almost a refreshing change. In a world of sunshine and champagne, he brought his own little patch of gloom and weak tea.

'One swig and you change face, body, height, everything. Don't match a description. Don't look like your picture in the *Police Gazette*.'

'You mean the Threadneedle Street bandits?'

'Indeed. A touch of your "Wild Wicked West" in staid old foggy London. There were heart attacks, you know.'

'So I read.'

A small band of habitual crooks, minor rogues who had never done anything worse than lift a purse or knock over a coster-monger, had staged a raid on the Bank of England after the manner of Jesse James. They careened up Threadneedle Street on horses and in a carriage, discharged revolvers at random over the heads of shocked crowds and dashed into that august financial establishment, demanding that cash and bullion be handed over. Before setting out on this exploit, each of the gang had drained a bottle of Jekyll to become another person entirely. It was popularly supposed that the transformed criminals were ape-faced, spider-fingered, devil-horned, cyclops-eyed sub-human fiends. The *Pall Mall Gazette*, perhaps inevitably, had referred to the miscreants as 'a pack of Hydes'. I had already dashed off a telegram to the editor threatening withdrawal of advertising unless a balanced retraction appeared within the week.

'Suppose it's a mercy your average villain is so thick-headed,' said the Inspector. 'This mob had spent all their lives dreaming about robbing the Bank of England. It was the Land of Cockaigne to them, sir. They thought of a golden temple. Heaps of bank-notes and piles of silver sovereigns lying around for the taking. Then they crashed in and discovered it was a bank like any other, only snootier. Vaults and strong-boxes, inaccessible to the raiders. When we caught up with them, they had less loot to hand than you'd expect from a provincial post office job. All themselves again, they were, blinking and surprised. Hadn't taken elementary precautions. Got 'em by the mud on their boots. And the blood on their coats.'

Two bank employees had been 'pistol-whipped'. One seemed likely to die.

'Still, a question is answered. One left over from the Hyde business.'

'What question, Inspector?'

'It's like this, sir. We knew what happened when Jekyll drank. He became Hyde. But, even without the potion, there are Hydes in the world. See 'em every day. Not a few on the Force, in fact. Now we know what happens when Hyde drinks. It doesn't make him cleverer, which is a terror and yet a mercy, a terror because all trace of scruple, even that which rises from fear of being caught, evaporates like dew in the morning. But a mercy because your Hyde is a stupid crook. And stupid crooks are easy to catch. But not all villains are idiots, Mr Quinn. Jekyll was a villain, after all. He was different from Hyde, not separate. What mightn't happen if a clever villain drinks your Tonic? What then, sir?'

I had the uncomfortable sensation that I was being judged.

'It's just patent medicine, Inspector,' I said. 'It doesn't really *do* anything, except in the imagination. Oh, it's dramatic, all right. Makes people pull faces. But it wears off in a tick, and you're back for another bottle. There's nothing inherently Evil about the stuff. Have you tried it?'

'Yes sir. Have you?'

Not loitering for an answer, Mist left.

Jekyll Tonic had been on sale for two weeks. I was returning to Kensington just after dawn. The sun was up, but the thin fog had yet to dissipate. This was not the fabled pea-souper I'd heard about back in the States, just wispy yellowish stuff that hung in the air like the colour-swirls in a glass marble. I trailed my stylish new cane through some strands, setting them in motion like phantom streamers.

I was still a little 'tight' from last night's celebration, hosted after the show at the Tivoli by Harry 'Brass' Button, in honour of the success of our venture. The entire company of the music hall had been in attendance, and most of the finest, most fashionable in the city. Not to mention the Flavering Sisters – quite the Jekyll Fiends these days, with happy results for Varrable that he was generous enough to share with his comrades in the *consortium*. Even Lady Knowe's besotted Guards-man-intended took notice. Of our principals, only Leo Dare – who never appeared at parties of any kind – was absent. I took this up with Sir Marmaduke, who mused that our colossus of finance must be at bottom 'a sad, lonely sort of chap', allowing that he was enviably single-minded in the pursuit of cold wealth, but that he lived the life of a monk, in his cell-like hotel suites, reading only ledgers, measuring his life's worth only in bank deposits. 'What's the point of it all if you can't drown yourself in it, sirrah?' Sir Marmaduke then took his tablespoon-ful of Tonic and joined with the ladies of the chorus and several ladies of distinction, including Lady Knowe and Mrs Biddlesham, in an enthusiastic performance of the can-can, lately the sensation of Paris.

I rounded the corner and observed an orderly commotion.

A crowd was gathered outside my house. Not a mob, but men in black coats and bowler hats, celluloid collars shiny, paper clutched in their hands. My first thought was that they were newspaper reporters. Was the Threadneedle Street Gang at large again?

'It's 'im,' someone shouted, and they all turned.

They rushed at me, thrusting out wax-sealed envelopes, ribbon-tied scrolls and telegrams. I was briefly in fear for my person, but to a man they handed over documents, raised hats politely, bade me good-morning and departed. I was left alone outside my house, hands full of paper. I stuffed as much as I could into my pockets.

My front door opened and my butler emerged, silverware stuck out of his coat-pockets and a crystal punchbowl (full of pocket-watches, snuff-boxes and other portable items of value) in his embrace. He was followed by Cook and two maids, hefting between them a polished mahogany dining table with the linen still on, bumping alarmingly against the door-frame and scraping spiked railings as they came down my front steps.

The butler saw me and did his best to bow without dropping anything.

366   KIM NEWMAN

'In lieu of wages, Mr Quinn. Please accept my regret that we are unable to continue in your employ.'

Lucy, the 'tweeny', sniffled a bit.

I was too astonished to say anything.

'If you would stand aside, sir,' said my former butler. 'So we might pass.'

I did as he suggested and found myself holding the door open to effect the removal of my former dining table. Lucy, eyes downcast, muttered something about it being 'a dreadful shame, sir'. I watched my entire staff struggle down the road, like a Whitechapel family doing a midnight flit.

I did not have time to examine all the papers in my pockets before the bailiffs showed up.

Within the hour, I realised that I did not have so much as a Knowe's Black Biscuit to my name.

The Shoreditch facilities were besieged, but not by customers. That would come later. Creditors barred the gates so that we could not even supply our own stall with the Tonic, let alone distribute as normal. I saw my secretary sprinting off into the fog, cased type-writer on her back like a snail's shell.

Varrable was on the 'phone, needlessly cranking the handle faster as his sentences sped up, hair awry. I gathered that he was talking with his stockbroker. A Flavering girl was perched on the divan, dead flowers in her hair like Ophelia, shivering as if in a rainstorm. Her colour was off, as if she were coming down with the influenza.

Windows smashed somewhere.

'Sell some *consortium* stock,' Varrable shouted. 'Use the funds to cover . . . what funds? Why, that stock is worth fifty times what we ploughed into it. A hundred.'

Varrable went white. He replaced the telephonic apparatus in its cradle.

'Billy,' he said, voice hollow. 'I could do with a tonic.'

The Flavering girl obediently sorted through empty bottles.

'Not *that* tonic,' Varrable said, with utter disgust. 'There's brandy around somewhere.'

I found the decanter and poured a generous measure. Varrable snatched the glass from me and raised it to his mouth. Then he gasped in horror and set the glass down.

'Billy, you nearly . . . No, the real brandy. It's in the desk.'

I found a bottle and filled two more glasses.

Varrable and I both shocked ourselves with drink. The brandy hit the last of the Tivoli champagne, but did no good.

'Just before close of trade yesterday,' Varrable explained, 'a vast amount of *consortium* stock went on sale. It went in small lots, to dozens, *hundreds* of buyers. There's been clamour for the issue for months, but it's simply not been available. When it was "up for grabs", there was what my man called a "feeding frenzy". A share worth fifty pounds yesterday isn't worth five shillings this morning. And won't be worth fivepence tomorrow.'

'Dare-ing,' I said.

Varrable nodded, swallowing more brandy. 'He sold at fifty pounds, Billy. Without telling us. We're all ruined, you know. Except *him*.'

I could not quite conceive of it.

'There's still the business,' I said, 'the Tonic. Money is pouring in. Buck up, Doc. We can cover debts in a day, costs in a week, and be in profit again by the end of the month.'

Varrable shook his head.

'Jekyll Tonic sells at a loss. Even at a shilling.'

This was news.

'Oh, in the long run, costs would have come down,' said Varrable, bitterly. 'But there is not going to be a "long run". There were unforeseen expenses in development, you see. The original estimates were optimistic. We were moving too swiftly to revise them.'

I understood. A harvest had been reaped, profit had been made. Leo Dare had taken his money out and moved on.

'I borrowed against the stock,' I admitted.

'So did I,' said Varrable.

My pockets were still stuffed with writs of foreclosure, bills suddenly come due, summonses to court, notices of lien, announcements of garnishee and other such waste paper.

A quiet knock came at the door. A doggy head poked around.

'I realise this is an inconvenient time for you both,' said Inspector Mist, 'but I am afraid I must ask you to accompany me to the Yard.'

The thing of it is that if Jekyll Tonic had not worked, Leo Dare would have stayed in it longer. If it were just the coloured water he himself was prepared to drink, the horse might have been ridden for years. Then there might have been gravy enough to keep us all fat. But, as Varrable had always said, the effects were dramatic but unpredictable, and that made the venture a long-term risk.

The Threadneedle Street raiders inspired similar crimes, no more successful but equally spectacular. Veiled ladies brought suit against the likes of Dr Hugo Varrable for artificial exploitation of affections, which had in more than one case led to Consequences. Every murderer and knock-down man in the land was purported to be under the influence of the Jekyll, though it is my belief that as many heroic rescues from burning buildings or sinking barges were carried out by persons temporarily not themselves as were homicidal rampages or outrages to the public decency. All manner of folk disclaimed responsibility for reprehensible actions by blaming the Tonic. Sermons were preached against Jekyll Tonic, and Editorials – in the very same 'papers that had boosted us – were written in thunderous condemnation. Lawsuits beyond number were laid against the *consortium*, which no longer included Leo Dare. The simple duns for unpaid bills took precedence, driving us to bankruptcy. The criminal and frivolous matters dragged on, though many were dropped when it became apparent that the coffers were empty and that no financial settlement would be arrived at. A tearful Harry Button was booed off stage before he could give his infamous Joke, and shortly thereafter found himself bought out of his contract and booted into the street by the Management. Temperance organisations shifted the focus of their attention from the demon alcohol to the impious Jekyll Tonic.

Sir Marmaduke and Lady Knowe made numberless attempts to get in touch with Leo Dare, but I recalled those cards he had made a pack of and ignored in Kettner's and did not waste my efforts. A man with no fixed address finds it easy not to be at home to the most persistent callers. At length, both worthies departed from the stage in no more dignified a manner than 'Brass' Button. Sir Marmaduke, sadly, retained a gold-thread curtain cord from the fixtures transported away by the bailiffs and hanged himself in his empty Belgravia town house. Lady Knowe, perhaps surprisingly, married her Guardsman. The couple decamped for a posting in Calcutta, where she devoted her energies to improving the moral health of Her Majesty's troops by campaigning against boy-brothels.

The formula remained ours alone, our sole asset, but many competitors were working to reproduce its effects. A Royal Commission was established and, with uncharacteristic swiftness, made all such research illegal unless conducted under Government supervision. I suspected some in Pall Mall still maintained Major General Cogstaff-Blyth's notions of a Regiment of Hydes trampling over the Kaiser's borders, chewing through *pickelhaubes* with apelike fangs and rending Uhlans limb from limb. Regulations closed around the Jekyll. An amendment to the Dangerous Drugs Acts insisted that the Tonic now could not be sold unless a customer signed the Poisons Book and waited until the signature was verified. By that time, it was a moot point since there was no Jekyll to be had anywhere. Our Shoreditch factory ceased manufacture when the stock crashed, and supplies dried up within the morning.

Varrable and I spent some nights enjoying the hospitality of one of Her Majesty's police stations, mostly through the good graces of Inspector Mist, who realised we had nowhere else to go and no funds to procure lodgings. A great many lines of enquiry were being pursued and we were told not to leave London. Questions would doubtless be asked of us on a great many matters, but no criminal charges were forthcoming as yet.

We trudged, cabless, to Shoreditch.

The factory, thoroughly looted, was abandoned. Our bruisers, our pretty sales-girls, our secretaries, our vat-stirrers, were all flown. And the fittings and furnishings with them. Even the prized telephones.

'What if he didn't drink coloured water that time?' said Varrable, with his now-habitual look of wide-eyed frenzy. 'I'd brewed up the first test batch. It could have been the real Tonic. He could have *changed*?'

'Leo Dare has no Hyde side,' I said. 'He was always himself.'

Varrable admitted it, smashing a beaker too cracked to steal.

We were in the stables, where vats stood overturned and empty, the flagstones stained with chemicals. The stinks still clung to the place. The gates had been torn down and taken away.

'Look,' said Varrable, 'the cabbies are back.'

Opposite the factory was a knot of loitering fellows, despondent and jittery, as I remembered them.

'I imagine not a few of our employees will be joining them,' I said. 'It was all over too swiftly for them to draw more than a week's wages.'

'It's breathtaking, Billy. He sucked all the money out, like you'd suck the juice from an orange, then tossed away the pith and peel. No one else saw anything from the Jekyll bubble.'

The loiterers formed a deputation and crossed the road. They marched into the factory.

'This might be it, Doc. Prepare to repel boarders.'

'They don't look angry.'

'Looks can be deceiving.'

In the gloom, we were surrounded. I made out fallen faces, worn clothing, postures of desolation and resentment.

'D-d-d-d-octor V-V-V-Varr . . .' stammered one of the louts.

From his shabby clothes and battered face, it would have been impossible to recognise the exquisite aesthete, but the voice was unmistakable. The Hon. Hilary Belligo.

'Is there anything left over?' asked one of Hilary's fellows.

I shook my head. 'We are at a financial embarrassment,' I said. 'All in the same boat.'

'N-n-n-not m-*money!*'

'Tonic.'

I remembered a happier day and Varrable's declaration that the likes of Hilary Belligo would be happy to pay five pounds a thimble for the Jekyll. I wished I had a crate of Tonic in a safe store somewhere, but it was all gone, shipped out and drunk. There wasn't a bottle left on a shelf in London. When supplies stopped coming from the factory, devotees haunted the most out-of-the-way shops and tracked down every last drop. There had been fearful brawls before the counters to get hold of it, as devotees paid whatever canny chemists asked. Even Jickle Juice and Jeckell Tonik, supposedly withdrawn from sale, were snapped up and drunk down. Fools had forked over ten guineas for empty Tonic bottles refilled with Thameswater.

I shrugged, showing empty hands.

'I might know where some Tonic remains,' said Varrable, smoothing his hair with stained hands. 'But we'll need to see, ah, *expenses* up front.'

The desperate souls all had money about them. Not much, and not in good condition – torn bank-notes, filthy coins, bloody sovereigns. I cupped my hands and they were filled.

'Be here tomorrow, at ten,' said Varrable. 'And keep it quiet.'

They scurried away, possessed with a strange excitement, a promise that took the edge off sufferings.

'*Have* we a secret reserve, Doc?'

Varrable shook his head, disarranging his hair again. 'No, but I still have the formula,' tapping his temple. 'Some of the ingredients must remain here. Few would want to loot chemicals. I can brew up Jekyll in the laboratory, rougher than the stuff we bottled, but stronger as well.'

'The demand is still there.'

I knew Hilary Belligo's crew would ignore Varrable's order to keep quiet. By tomorrow, word would be out. In two short weeks, a great many people had become used to a spoonful of Jekyll every day. The business was gone, the *consortium* collapsed, but that didn't mean the *need* had evaporated.

'It'll be illegal,' I ventured. 'Under the Dangerous Drugs Act.'

'All the better,' Varrable snorted. 'We can ask for a higher price.

That lot'll slit their grannies' throats for a drop of the Jekyll. And we're sole suppliers, Billy. Do you understand?'

Varrable was as possessed as the Hon. Hilary. With another kind of need.

Leo Dare had passed from the story. He left us all with new needs, but also new opportunities.

'I understand. You're the chemist, I'm the salesman. We'll need a place to work. Several, to keep on the move. Mist won't just forget us, and he's no fool. We can no longer afford fixed addresses. We'll need folk for the distribution, lads to stand on street-corners, fellows to sit in taverns. Servants, perhaps, to get to the customers with the folding money. We'll need places to hide the profits. Not under mattresses, in investments. Respectable, above-board. We'll have to see off the opium tongs. Maybe those East End roughs are still interested in the Jekyll trade. We could pitch in with them. The law of the land will not be with us, just the law of the market. We'll need new names.'

'I have mine. Harold Rose.'

'And I'm Billy Brass. Do you know, ah, Harold, I think that this way we shall wind up richer than before.'

I had the strangest impression that Leo Dare was smiling down upon me.

And so your friends Dr Rose and Mr Brass embarked upon a new venture.

Kim Newman has won the Bram Stoker Award, the British Fantasy Award, the British Science Fiction Award, the Children of the Night Award, the Fiction Award of the Lord Ruthven Assembly and the International Horror Critics Guild Award. A film journalist and broadcaster, his novels include *The Night Mayor*, *Bad Dreams*, *Jago*, *The Quorum*, *Back in the USSR* (with Eugene Byrne), *Life's Lottery* and the *Anno Dracula* sequence, comprising the title novel and its sequels *The Bloody Red Baron*, *Judgment of Tears* (aka *Dracula Cha Cha Cha*) and the forthcoming *Johnny Alucard*. Also upcoming are *An English Ghost Story* (currently being developed as a movie from a script by the author) and *The Matter of Britain* (again with Byrne). Newman's short fiction has been collected in *The Original Dr Shade and Other Stories*, *Famous Monsters*, *Seven Stars*, *Unforgivable Stories* and *Where the Bodies Are Buried*, while his story 'Week Woman' was adapted for the Canadian TV series *The Hunger*. In 2001, Newman directed a 100-second short film, *Missing Girl*, for cable TV channel The Studio. 'This is my second stab at a sequel to Robert Louis Stevenson's *Strange Case of Dr Jekyll and Mr Hyde*,' admits the author. 'The first was "Further Developments in the Strange Case of Dr Jekyll and Mr Hyde", published in Maxim Jakubowski's *Chronicles of Crime* and also found in my collection *Unforgivable Stories*. That took a very different tack in imagining what might have happened after the events of

Stevenson's story than "A Drug on the Market". Dr Jekyll appears briefly in my novel *Anno Dracula*, and there's a return visit to his house in the forthcoming *Johnny Alucard*. Obviously, the original lingers in the memory, sparking ideas that need to be written up. I even liked the film of Valerie Martin's brilliant novel *Mary Reilly*, though I think Eddie Murphy should be prohibited by law from making another *Nutty Professor* sequel. Of all the founding texts of the horror/monster/Gothic genre, Stevenson's novella strikes me as being the best all-round piece of writing. While *Frankenstein* and *Dracula* are big, sprawling books full of flaws and hasty patches, careless of characterisation, choked by plot, *Strange Case* is put together, as Stephen King once noted, like a Swiss watch, without a wasted word, cliché character or dull paragraph. Mr Hyde is one of the genre's most vividly imagined monsters: not the lusty caveman of most film versions but a shrunken, frightened, bullying, vicious little man who never picks on anyone his own size. In this piece, I was also influenced by H. G. Wells' *Tono-Bungay*, which has a terrific section about a voyage to corner quap (a wonderful word Wells seems to have invented and which I hope comes back into circulation) and is an early fulmination against the advertising industry. Though it doesn't play with the original text in the way *Anno Dracula* does, "A Drug on the Market" does take a similar line: extrapolating from a story about individual monstrousness to imagine its effects if spread to a wider society that is Victorian London but also our own world a century on.'

Slaves of Nowhere

RICHARD CHRISTIAN MATHESON

'I am you.
Your jagged dream.
Your child.
Yourself.
I hold you, soothe you.
Suckle and destroy you.
I am no one.
Everyone.
I have been gone so long.'

The entry was handwritten; a delicate pain.

JoJo stared at it. Glanced at the clock, death by fragments circling its void face.

The next one would be here soon.

'I hear my insides,
Bloodless and swallowed.
I am an eclipse.
A funeral.
An unsoothed blank.'

JoJo sipped cognac, stared at Manhattan as if it were a sad child, watched near buildings where the unloved sat alone; interred in night windows.

The Spanish mirror reflected dark tresses, full lips. Eyes long past dread. Fingers slender, resting in silver rings; elegant, bandaged. Walls, emptied of family; meaning. Too many years ago. Decades ... centuries.

Always.

'Please take me away
from me.
Bring the perfect
sorrows
of sleep.
My hand in yours.
For an hour, I would die.
For a minute, I die forever.
Reborn in nowhere.'

Mouths and hands, kissing, licking.
Reaching, tearing JoJo open.
Sperm; pearl graffiti.
Looking into a hundred eyes, a thousand needs.
The pen inched and curved, ink a helpless pathway.

'My eyes are your shame.
Look in the mirror.
I am there.
I am you.'

The man would be here soon.
The woman.
The couple.
Then, the man who wanted to rape his daughter. And the woman who wanted to be held by herself, allow tracing tongue to wander her own mouth, lick her coral pussy, taste secretions; dead nectars.
And the other man who . . .

'I am nowhere.
I have no colours.
No sound.
I am tired.
Invisible.
I need to be held.
I need to die.'

JoJo placed down pen, finished the cognac.
Grasped the razor, sat on velvet chair, slid sharp blade over wrist like a stroke of perfume. Listened to the drowsy slippage of blood deserting veins. Rain crawling windows. The clock slowing, dying.

The doorbell; *the appointment.*

JoJo slowly rose, walked to the door, fingertips a red seepage. Peered through the eyehole. The man was slight, short. Would want to feel big, be within something tight, childlike. Hear his own daughter, screaming for Daddy as he thrust inside her. JoJo saw the little girl's photograph in his hand: freckled smile, trusting eyes.

JoJo went empty inside, as icy bleach spread and all was a dead nausea. Then, it began: the agonies of detail.

The expression eased, now shy, unsure. Wrists quietly re-sealed. JoJo's hair slowly became blonde, body pale, young. No longer tall, bearded. Breasts retreated, nipples withdrew to pink simplicity, pubic hair lightened, vanished, revealing vestal softness. Sweet blue eyes looked afraid; a rapist's ethereal doll.

It would hurt.

Some did.

Others wanted pain.

To be filled; controlled. Bloodied by lust, indifference. Every day, the same hungers; desperate, broken. An hour or two to lose themselves, find themselves, pretend it never happened.

JoJo held pen to the book of ten thousand poems. Aside countless handwriting styles, another page filled, in child's naïve script, trusting letters, dotted with hearts.

> *'I am a song*
> *I may have heard.*
> *Such a sad song.*
> *I am you.*
> *Your jagged dream.*
> *I hold you, soothe you.*
> *Suckle and destroy you.*
> *My eyes are your need,*
> *my flesh your shame.*
> *I am lost in elsewhere.*
> *A slave of nowhere.*
> *I have been gone so long.'*

It was time to open the door.

Richard Christian Matheson is the son of veteran science fiction and fantasy author Richard Matheson. A novelist, short story writer and screenwriter/producer, he has scripted and executive-produced more than five hundred episodes of prime-time network TV and was the youngest writer ever put under contract by Universal Studios. His début novel *Created By* was published to great acclaim in 1993, and his short fiction has been collected in *Scars and Other Distinguishing Marks* and *Dystopia*. Matheson recently scripted four feature films, at various studios, which he will executive-produce. He has also completed a pilot script for a one-hour series about avarice and mysticism, he will adapt Roger Zelazny's *The Chronicles of Amber* as a four hour mini-series, and has just sold a thriller spec screenplay. A horror screenplay R.C. and his father wrote for Ivan Reitman was scheduled to go into production in 2002 and is rumoured to be a huge project for Universal Studios. He has also completed his second novel and is writing a third. Matheson continues to play drums for the blues/rock band Smash-Cut, in which he performs along with Craig Spector and Preston Sturges, Jr. The band is currently at work on its début album and plays clubs in Los Angeles. 'For a time, betrayal was the season,' reveals the author about his story. 'It seemed many friends had been hurt by some deceit; a falsity perfectly presented, a lie veiled as care. Few saw it coming, wanted to admit they did, could face it. They capsized, bled, retreated; hearts torn, faith poisoned. I also began to note those who refused to adapt to the reasonable needs of others, triumphant in a pretended armour; slain hopes grieving through detachment, wounds guised as autonomy. At either extreme were broken selves. In adapting to life and love, some do better than others, though paradox intrudes. Often those who do it most brilliantly dwell in voids. Somewhere in this elusive algebra of authenticity and adaptation, I considered those who are condemned to it, not by choice but curse.'

The Prospect Cards

DON TUMASONIS

Dear Mr Cathcart,

We are happy to provide, enclosed with this letter, our complete description of item no. 839 from our recent catalogue *Twixt Hammam and Minaret: 19th and Some Early 20th Century Travel in the Middle East, Anatolia, Nubia, etc.*, as requested by yourself.

You are lucky in that our former cataloguer, Mr Mokley, had, in what he thought were his spare moments, worked to achieve an extremely full description of this interesting group of what are probably unique items. Certainly no others to whom we have shown these have seen any similar, nor have been able to provide any clew as to their ultimate provenance.

They were purchased by one of our buyers on a trip to Paris, where, unusually – since everyone thinks the *bouquinistes* were mined out long ago – they were found in a stall on the Left Bank. Once having examined his buy later that evening, he determined to return the following day to the vendor in search of any related items. Alas, there were no others, and the grizzled old veteran running the boxes had no memory of when or where he purchased these, saying only that he had them for years, perhaps since the days of Marmier, actually having forgotten their existence until they were unearthed through the diligence of our employee. Given the circumstance of their discovery (covered with dust, stuffed in a sealed envelope tucked away in a far corner of a green tin box clamped onto a quay of the Seine, with volumes of grimy tomes in front concealing their being), we are lucky to have even these.

Bear in mind, that as an old and valued customer, you may

have this lot at 10% off the catalogue price, postfree, with
insurance additional, if desired.

  Remaining, with very best wishes indeed,

  Yours most faithfully,

    Basil Barnet
BARNET AND KORT,
ANTIQUARIAN TRAVEL BOOKS AND EPHEMERA

No. 839

Postal view cards, commercially produced, various manufacturers,
together with a few photographs mounted on card, comprising a group
of 74. Mostly sepia and black-and-white, with a few contemporary
tinted, showing scenes from either Balkans, or Near or Middle East,
ca. 1920–30. The untranslated captions, when they occur, are bilingual,
with one script resembling Kyrillic, but not in Russian or Bulgarian;
the other using the Arabic alphabet, in some language perhaps related
to Turco-Uighuric.

  Unusual views of as yet unidentified places and situations, with public
and private buildings, baths, squares, harbours, minarets, markets, etc.
Many of the prospects show crowds and individuals in the performance
of divers actions and work, sometimes exotic. Several of the cards
contain scenes of an erotic or disturbing nature. A number are typical
touristic souvenir cards, generic products picturing exhibits from some
obscure museum or collection. In spite of much expended effort, we
have been unable to identify the locales shown.

  Entirely unfranked, and without address, about a third of these have
on their verso a holographic ink text, in a fine hand by an unidentified
individual, evidently a travel diary or journal (non-continuous, with
many evident lacunæ). Expert analysis would seem to indicate 1930 or
slightly later as the date of writing.

  Those cards with handwriting have been arranged in rough order by
us, based on internal evidence, although the chronology is often unclear
and the order therefore arbitrary. Only these cards – with a single
exception – are described, each with a following transcription of the
verso holograph text; the others, about 50 cards blank on verso, show
similar scenes and objects. Our hypothetical reconstruction of the
original sequence is indicated through lightly pencilled numbers at the
upper right verso corner of each card.

Condition: Waterstain across top edges, obscuring all of the few details of date and place of composition. Wear along edges and particularly at corners. A couple of cards rubbed; the others, aside from the faults already noted, mostly quite fresh and untouched.

Very Rare. In our considered opinion, the cards in themselves are likely to be unique, no others having been recorded to now; together with the unusual document they contain, they are certainly so.

Price: £1,650

Card No. 1

Description: A dock, in some Levantine port. A number of men and animals, mostly mules, are congregated around a moored boat with sails, from which large *tonnes*, evidently containing wine, labelled as such in Greek, are being either loaded or unshipped.

Text: not sculling, but rather rowing, the Regatta of '12, for which his brother coxswained. Those credentials were good enough for Harrison and myself, our credulity seen in retrospect as being somewhat naïve, and ourselves as rather gullible; such, however, is all hindsight. For the time being, we were very happy at having met fellow countrymen – of the right sort, mind you – in this godforsaken backwater at a time when our fortunes, bluntly put, had taken a turn for much the worse. When Forsythe, looking to his partner Calquon, asked 'George, we need the extra hands – what say I tell Jack and Charles about our plans?' To that Calquon only raised an eyebrow, as if to say it's your show, go and do as you think fit. Forsythe, taking that as approval, ordered another round, and launched into a little speech, which, when I think back on the events of the past weeks, had perhaps less of an unstudied quality than his seemingly impromptu delivery would have implied. Leaning forward, he drew from his breast pocket a postal view card, and placed it on the table, saying in a lowered voice, as if we were fellow conspirators being drawn in, 'What would you think if I told you, that from here, in less than one day's sail and a following week's march, there is to be found something of such value, which if the knowledge of it became common, would

Card no. 2

Description: A view of a mountain massif, clearly quite high and rugged, seen from below at an angle, with consequent foreshortening. A fair amount of snow is sprinkled over the upper heights. A thick broken line in white, retouch work, coming from behind and around one of several summits, continues downward along and below the ridge-line before disappearing. This evidently indicates a route.

Text:—ania and Zog. Perfidious folk! Perfidious people. Luckily, our packet steamer had arrived and was ready to take us off. A night's sailing, and the better part of the next day took us to our destination, or rather, to the start of our journey. After some difficulty in finding animals and muleteers, we loaded our supplies, hired guides, and after two difficult days, arrived at the foothills of the mountains depicted on the obverse of this card. Our lengthy and labourious route took us ultimately up these, where we followed the voie normale, the same as shown by the white hatched line. Although extremely steep and exposed, the slope was not quite sheer and we lost only one mule and no men during the 1500-yard descent. Customs – if such a name can be properly applied to such outright thieves – were rapacious, and confiscated much of what we had, including my diary and notes. Thus the continuation on these cards, which represent the only form of paper allowed for sale to the

Card no. 3

Description: A panorama view of a Levantine or perhaps Balkan town of moderate to large size, ringed about by snow-covered mountains in the distance. Minarets and domes are visible, as is a very large public building with columns, possibly Greco-Roman, modified to accommodate some function other than its original religious one, so that the earlier elements appear draped about with other stylistic intrusions.

Text: vista. With the sun setting, and accommodation for the men and food for the animals arranged, we were able to finally relax momentarily and give justice, if only for a short while, to the magnificence of the setting in which the old city was imbedded, like a pearl in a filigreed ring. I've seen a lot of landscapes, 'round the world, and believe me, this was second to none. The intoxicating beauty of it all made it almost easy to believe the preposterous tales that inspired Calquon, and particularly Forsythe, to persuade us to join them on this tossed-together expedition. I frankly doubt that anything will come of it except our forcing another chink in the isolation which has kept this fascinating place inviolate to such a degree that few Westerners have penetrated its secrets over the many centuries since the rumoured group of Crusaders forced their

Card no. 4

<u>Description</u>: A costume photograph, half-length, of a young woman in ethnic or tribal costume, veiled. The décolletage is such that her breasts are completely exposed. Some of the embroidery and jewellery would indicate Cypriote or Anatolian influence; it is clear that she is wearing her dowry in the form of coins, filigreed earrings, necklaces, medallions, and rings. Although she is handsome, her expression is very stiff. [Not reproduced in the catalogue]

<u>Text</u>: Evans, who should have stuck to Bosnia and Illyria. I never thought his snake goddesses to be anything other than some Bronze Age fantast's wild dream, if indeed the reconstructions are at all accurate. Harrison, however, has told me that this shocking – i.e. for a white woman (the locals are distinctively Caucasian: red hair, blue eyes and fair skin appearing frequently, together with traces of slight Mediterranean admixture) – déshabillé was common throughout the Eastern Ægean and Middle East until a very short while ago, when European mores got the better of the local folk, except, it seems, those here. I first encountered such dress (or <u>undress</u>) a week ago, the day after our late evening arrival, when out early to see the market and get my bearings, and totally engaged in examining some trays of spices in front of me, I felt suddenly bare flesh against my exposed arm, stretched out to test the quality of some turmeric. It was a woman at my side who, having come up unnoticed, had bent in front of me to obtain some root or herb. When she straightened, I realised at once that the contact had been with her bare bosom, which, I might add, was quite shapely, with nipples rouged. She was unconcerned; I must have blushed at least as much

Card no. 5

Description: A naos or church, on a large stepped platform, in an almost impossible mélange of styles, with elements of a Greek temple of the Corinthian order mixed in with Byzantine features and other heterogeneous effects to combine in an unusual, if not harmonious, whole. The picture, a frontal view, has been taken most probably at early morning light, since the temple steps and surrounding square are devoid of people.

Text: light and darkness, darkness and light' Forsythe said. 'With this form of dualism, and its rejection of the body, paradoxically, until the sacrament is administered, the believers are in fact encouraged to excess of the flesh, which is viewed as essentially evil, and ultimately, an illusion. The thought is that by indulging mightily, disdain is expressed for the ephemeral, thus granting the candidate power over the material, which is seen as standing in his or her way to salvation.' 'What does that have to do with your little trip of this morning?' I remonstrated. We had agreed to meet at ten o'clock to see if we could buy manuscripts in the street of the scribes, for the collection. Paul reddened and replied 'D'you know the large structure on the square between us and the market? I was on my way to meet you, when I happened to pass through there. It seems' – and here he went florid again – 'that in an effort to gain sanctity more quickly, parents, as required by the priests, are by law for two years to give over those of their daughters on the verge of womanhood to the temple each day between 10 and noon, in a ploy to quicken the transition to holiness. Any passer-by, during that time, who sees on the steps under the large parasols (set up like tents, there to protect exposed flesh) any maiden suiting his fancy, is urged to drop a coin in the bowls nearest and

Card no. 6

Description: A quite imperfect and puzzling picture, with mist and fog, or perhaps steam, obscuring almost all detail. What is visible are the dim outlines of two rows of faces, some veiled, others bearded.

Text: poured more water on the coals. By now it was quite hot, and I could no longer see Forsythe, but only hear his voice. The lack of visibility made it easier to concentrate on his words, with my eyes no longer focused on <u>details</u> I had found so distracting. 'The incongruity of it all makes my head reel – how could they have maintained all this in the face of the changes around them? After all, a major invasion route of the past three millennia lies two valleys to the west...' Nodding in unseen agreement, my attention was momentarily diverted by the sound of a new arrival entering the room, and seconds later, a smooth leg brushed for a second against mine; I assumed it was a woman, and durst not stir. 'Not that they've rejected the modern at all costs – they've got electric generators and some lighting, a fair amount of modern goods and weaponry find their way in, there's the museum, that Turkish photography shop, the printing press, and – oh, all the rest. But they pick and choose. And that religion of theirs! All the Jews and Muslims and Christians here are cowed completely! Why hasn't a holy war been declared by their neighbours?' With Paul ranting on in the obscuring darkness, I grunted in agreement, and then, shockingly, felt a small foot rub against

Card no. 7

<u>Description</u>: Costumed official, perhaps a religious leader or judge, sitting on the floor facing the camera. He is bearded, greying, with a grim set to his mouth. One hand points gracefully towards a smallish, thick codex held by the other hand. From the man's breast depends a tall rectangular enamelled pendant of simple design, divided vertically into equal fields of black and white.

<u>Text</u>: Sorbonne, three years of which, I suppose, could explain a lot, as for example, his overpowering use of garlic. 'Pseudo-Manicheeism' he continued, 'is solely a weak term used by the uncomprehending for what can only be described as perfection, the last word itself being a watered-out expression merely, for that which cannot be comprehended through the feeble tool of rational and sceptical thinking, which closes all doors it does not understand. Oh, I know that some of you' – and here he eyed me suspiciously, as if I was running muckin' Cambridge! – 'have tried to classify our belief, using the Monophysites as opposed to the Miaphysites of your religion in an analogy that neither comprehends nor grasps the subtlety of our divinely inspired thought! As if It could be explained in Eutychian terms! Our truth is self-evident and is so clear that we allow, with certain inconsequential restrictions and provisos, those of your tribe who wish, to expound their falsehoods in

the marketplace, assuming they have survived the rigours of the journey here. You were better to perceive indirectly, thinking of flashing light; the colours green, and gold; the hundred instead of the one; segmentation, instead of smoothness, as metaphors that enable one

Card no. 8

Description: Another museum card, with several large tokens or coins depicted, which in style and shape resemble some of the dekadrachm issues of 5th century Syracuse. The motifs of the largest one shown, are, however, previously unrecorded, with a temple (see card 5) on the obverse. The reverse, with a young girl and three men, is quite frankly obscene. [Not reproduced in the catalogue]

Text: tea. I was quite struck with the wholesome appearance and modest demeanour of Mrs Fortesque, who was plainly, if neatly dressed in the style of ten years ago – evidently, they had been out of contact with Society in London since arrival! The Rev Fortesque was holding forth on how they were, as a family, compelled by local circumstance, and frankly, the threat of force, to adhere strictly to the native code of behaviour and mores when out in public, the children not being exempt from the rituals of their fellows of like age. Calquon frowned at this, and asked, 'In every way, Reverend?' to which the missionary sighed, 'Unfortunately, yes – otherwise, we would not be allowed to preach at all.' There was a small silence while we pondered the metaphysical implications of this when a young and angelically beautiful girl of about twelve entered the room. 'Gentlemen, this is my daughter, Alicia . . .' smiled Mrs Fortesque proudly, only to be interrupted in the most embarrassing fashion by the sudden sputtering and spraying of Forsythe, whom we thought had choked on his crumpet. Thwacking him on the back, until his redness of face receded and normal breathing resumed, I thought I saw an untoward smirk lightly pass over the face of the young girl. 'What is it, old man?' I solicitously enquired. Paul, after having swallowed several times, with the attention of the others diverted, whispered sotto voce, breathlessly, so that only I could hear 'Yesterday – the temple

Card no. 9

<u>Description</u>: An odd view, taken at mid-distance, of a low-angled pyramidal or cone-shaped pile of stones, most fist-sized or slightly smaller, standing about one to two feet high. A number of grimacing urchins and women, the last in their distinctive public costume, stand gesticulating and grinning to either side, many of them holding stones in their hands. Given the reflection of light on the pool of dark liquid that has seeped from the pile's front, it must be – midday.

<u>Text</u>: brave intervention, with dire consequence. 'For God's sake, Fortesque, don't . . .' shouted Forsythe, as I well remember, before his arms were pinned behind him, and with a callused paw like a bear's clamped over his mouth, in much the same situation as myself, was forced helplessly to watch the inexorable and horrific grind of events. Eager hands, unaided by any tool – such is the depth of fanaticism that prevails in these parts – quickly scooped out a deep enough hole from the loose soil of the market square. The man of the cloth, who had persevered in the face of so much pagan indifference and outright hostility for over a decade, was for his troubles and valiant intervention unceremoniously divested of his clothing and dumped in the hole, which was quickly filled – there was no lack of volunteers – immobilising him in the same manner as Harrison, who was buried with his arms and upper breast free. They were just far enough apart so that their fingers could not touch, depriving them in fiendish fashion of that small consolation. I remember the odd detail that Fortesque was half-shaven – he had dropped everything when informed of Harrison's situation. Knowing full well what was in store, he began singing 'Onward, Christian Soldiers' in a manly, booming voice that brought tears to my eyes, whilst Harrison, I am ashamed to say, did

Card no. 10

<u>Description</u>: Group portrait, of nine men. Six stand, wearing bandoliers, pistols with chased and engraved handles protruding from the sashes round their waists, decorative daggers, etc. The edges of their vests are heavily embroidered with metallic thread in arabesque patterns. All are heavily moustachioed. A seventh companion stands, almost ceremoniously, to their right, holding like a circus tent peg

driver a wooden mallet with a large head a foot or so off the ground; a position somewhat like that of a croquet player. The eighth man, wearing a long shift or kaftan, is on all fours in the centre foreground, head to the left, but facing the camera like the others. A wooden saddle of primitive type is on his back. A ninth man, dressed like the first seven, is in the saddle, as if riding the victim, who, we see, has protruding from his fundament, although discreetly draped in part by the long shift, a pole the thickness of a muscular man's forearm.

Text: no idea, being sure that all this was misunderstanding, and could easily be cleared up with a liberal application of baksheesh. This was our mistake, as Calquon was led from the judge's compartments, arms bound, to a small square outside, where there was a carved fountain missed by the iconoclasts of long ago (of whom there had been several waves), with crudely sculptured and rather battered lions from whose mouths water streamed into the large circular limestone basin. We followed, of course, vehemently protesting his innocence all the while, and were studiously ignored. Poor Calquon was untied, and forced onto his knees and hands in a most undignified and ludicrous position. A crowd of people had already gathered under the hot midday sun, including many women and children. Hawkers walked through the throng that gathered, offering cold water from tin tanks on their backs, each with a single glass fitted into a decorated silver holder with a handle, tied onto the vessel by a cord. I saw, lying off to the side, on the steps of the fountain, a wooden stake, bark removed from its narrow end, smoothed and sharpened to a nasty point. A fat greasy balding man wearing the red cummerbund of officialdom came out of the crowd, with a bright knife in

Card no. 11

Description: A market with various stalls and their owners. A wandering musician is off to the left, and a perambulating vendor of kebabs, with long brass skewers, is on the right.

Text: painful for everyone concerned, particularly George. A guard in crimson livery, decorated with gold thread, was sitting smoking his hubble-bubble a short distance away from our gloomy group, every now and then looking up from his reverie to make sure things were as they should be. Perhaps it was the smoke from the pipe, or sheer bravado – I have never known, to this day – but Calquon, poor George, asked for a cigarette, which Forsythe immediately rolled and put on his lips, lighting it, since this was impossible for our fellow, whose arms were bound. He took a puff, as cool as if he were walking down Regent Street to Piccadilly, and then, for the first time noticing the women and children seated at his feet, asked us in a parched voice what they might possibly be doing there. I shuffled my feet and looked away, while Paul told him in so many words that they were waiting for his imminent departure, for the same purpose that women in the Middle Ages would gather around criminals about to be executed, in hope of obtaining a good luck charm that was powerful magic, after the fact of summary punishment was accomplished. This, as we were afraid, enraged our unfortunate en brochette companion, who became livid as we tried to calm him. Writhing in his stationary upright position, would after all do him no good, given that out of his shoulder (from whence I noticed a tiny tendril of smoke ascending), there was already protruding

Card no. 12

Description: A public square, photo taken from above at a slant angle, from a considerable distance. Some sort of framework or door, detached from any structure, has been set up in one corner. A couple of dark objects, one larger than the other, appear in the middle of that door or frame which faces the viewer, obscuring what is going on behind. A large agitated crowd of men of all ages – from quite young boys to bent, aged patriarchs, all wearing the truncated local version of the *fez*, are milling around the rear of the upright construction. A number of local police, uniformed, are in the thick of it, evidently to maintain order.

Text: wondering what the commotion was about. I was therefore shocked to see in one tight opening the immobilised head of a young woman of about twenty-five, and in the other her right hand. Instead of the ubiquitous veil, she had some sort of black silk bandage that performed the same function, closely wrapped around her mouth and nose. She was plainly emitting a sullen glare – easily understood, given the circumstance. There was no join or seam; for the life of me, I still do not understand the construction. Every now and then the frame and the woman contained by it would violently shake and judder. The expression under her shock of unruly red hair remained stoic and unperturbed. Walking to the other side (<u>make sure that Mildred doesn't</u> <u>read this</u>!!) I saw the crowd of men – there were about 80 to 100, including about twenty or so of the few negro slaves found in these parts – with more pouring into the square – jostling in the attempt to be next: those nearest had partially disrobed, and had taken 'matters' in hand, fondling themselves to arousal, for taking her in the fashion preferred here, which is of that between men and boys, from behind. Despondent as I was, I had no intention other than to continue, when I was suddenly shoved forward into the midst

Card no. 13

<u>Description</u>: A view down a narrow street, with the high tenements and their overhanging wooden balconies blocking out much of the light. The photographer has done well to obtain as much detail as is shown here. A cupola or dome, and what is perhaps a minaret behind it, are just visible at the end of the lane. Three young (from the look of their figures as revealed by the traditional dress, cf card 2) women in black, each with a necklace from which hangs a single bright large pendant, stand in the middle of the way, at mid-distance. They appear to be approaching the camera. Surprisingly, for all that they are bare-headed, etc., they are wearing veils that conceal their features utterly. There are no others in the street.

<u>Text</u>: said to Forsythe that there was no point to it, that we would have to, at some moment, accept our losses and the futility of going any further. With the others gone, I argued, it was extremely unlikely that we could continue on our own; we should swallow our pride, and admit that we had come greatly unprepared for what we had in mind. It was best, in other words, that we make our run as soon as backs were turned. Forsythe disagreed vehemently, and meant that on the contrary, we were obliged by the sacred memory of our companions to carry on, an odd turn of phrase, considering what we had hoped to accomplish and obtain, by any means. And then he said cryptically, 'It doesn't matter in any case – the deed is done.' I immediately took this as admission that the object of our expedition had been somehow achieved without my knowledge; <u>that</u> was the likely cause of the troubles we had experienced, and the growing agitation of the populace I had uneasily witnessed the past few days. As we discussed our dilemma outside the carpet shop, one of many lining the street, I became aware of a silence,

a hush that had descended. People turned to face the wall, in fear, I thought, as I saw three females approaching. These

Card no. 14

Description: A poor reproduction of the second state of plate VII of Piranesi's *Carceri*. In fact, the ascription is given on the verso of the card, the artist's name (G. B. PIRANESI) appearing in Latin capitals inserted amongst the Arabic and Kyrillic letters.

Text: less than the Carceri! What everyone had once thought the malarial fever dreams of a stunted, perverse genius, I saw now only to be honest reporting. I was absolutely astounded, once the dragoman, smelling of garlic and anisette, had removed the blindfold from my eyes. A lump came to my throat, and tears threatened to engulf me, when I thought of the others done away with through treachery, foul ignorance and intolerance. I suppose rumours regarding the disappearance of the sacred entity of the valley had much to do with the situation, too. Controlling my emotions – here, for a man to weep is a sign of weakness, with all the consequences such a perception entails – I saw around me. A number of individuals, male and female, nude or partly so, were being ushered along the spiral staircase wrapped around an enormous stone column down which I myself must have descended only a few minutes before. Natural light played through a number of cleverly placed oculi in the invisible ceiling, concealed by the complex bends and angles of the place. Turning,

Card no. 15

Description: Another crude reproduction of a Piranesi 'Prisons' plate, this number VIII, ascribed as above.

Text: I saw yet another vista of the Italian artist before me, and began to understand, for the first time, that the plan of all his mad, insane engravings was a coherent whole, either taken from the actuality before me, or perhaps plotted out from his prints, and converted to reality, by some unsung architectonic genius. The Venetians had been here, I knew, during the mid-1700s, when things had settled down. Perhaps one of their workmen was given the book, and told to produce, or . . . With my glance following the staircase from its beginning, flanked by gigantic military trophies, with plumed helmets much larger than any human head, I traced the turn upwards to the left, and saw, between two enormous wooden doors opening on an arch, a large rack. A series of ropes hung down from the supporting wall, and I could see the faint glow of a brazier and hear the distant screams of the poor women and men, white bodies glistening with the sweat of fear, who hung

Card no. 16

Description: tinted, clearly a display of gemstones, perhaps from a museum of natural history or local geology. One of the larger groups, arranged separately from the others, with green colouring obviously meant to indicate emeralds, appears to be the fragments, longitudinally shattered, of what must have been a single enormous stone.

Text: subincision being the technical expression. As you can imagine, I was wildly straining against my bonds, in fact, you could say I was struggling to the point of extreme violence, to, as it turned out, no avail. In spite of all my agitated effort, I was clamped to some sort of heavy metal framework or stand that immobilised me more or less completely. Naked, helpless, dreading whatever was in store, I saw the same three young women approach into the torchlight from the encircling darkness. Without a word, my gaolers and the others left and I was alone with the unholy trio. As if at a signal, they simultaneously removed their veils and I was momentarily stunned, almost drugged, by the sight of their incredible beauty. Remember, this was the first time I had ever seen one of the local women unmasqued – if these were representative of the rest, it would easily explain any number of puzzling local rituals and customs. In spite of my extreme situation, I could not help myself – the ravishing faces, the fulsome breasts with their shapely crimsoned nipples, the long black glistening hair

Card no. 17

Description: A market place, with many and various stands and displays. An ironmonger, a merchant of brass teapots, a seller of cured leather are all easily discerned. In the centre, arms like a Saint Andrew's cross before his chest, holding a large knife in the one hand, a two-pronged fork in the other, is a seller of grilled and roasted meats. On the small portable gridiron in front of him, a number of sizable sausages are warming, split neatly lengthwise.

Text: darted out with the tip of her tongue, and then slowly extended it again. To my horror, I saw it was no tongue: it was a long razor-sharp dagger or splinter of green glass or stone; a smaragd dirk that was somehow attached or glued to the root of what remained of her tongue. The other two, kneeling close on either side of her, each reverentially held, both with two hands, the one heavy breast nearest them of their chief colleague, as if ritually weighing and supporting these at the same time. This observation was made on the abstract, detachedly, as if I were outside my own body. More mundanely, I was screaming and thrashing – or attempting uselessly to thrash. Praise to the gods that be, I passed out completely, and awoke with the foul deed done, blood running down me and pooling on the cold flagging, and the three dark sisters gone. Looking down, as my original captors re-entered the chamber, I saw that the operation had been carried out, just as had been described to me by the temple priest, and I fainted once more. When

Card no. 18

Description: Not a postal card, but rather a half-length portrait photograph mounted on thick pasteboard, of a family group from about the 1920s. The two parents are quite young, and formally dressed: the father in a dark suit, to which is pinned an unidentified order or medal. He holds a small Bible clasped to his breast. The woman is handsome, in a white lacy blouse buttoned to the top of her graceful neck, with masses of hair piled high on her head. The young daughter is quite simply beautiful, an angel.

Text: would not have recognised, but for the signal distinctive wedding ring on her finger. 'Mrs Fortesque,' I blurted out, as we stood amongst the milling crowd in the shade of the souk. 'I had no idea—' but stopped when I saw the blush originating from beneath the missionary wife's veil spread to her ample and attractive sun-browned bosom (a pendant black enamelled cross its sole decoration), with the attendant rush of blood turning the aureoles – modestly without cinnabar – to the precise same shade of red so favoured by the local women. I saw, at the same time, the fleshy peaks slowly stiffen and stand, that motion drawing forth a corresponding response on my part, something I hardly had conceived feasible, after the trauma of the operation of four days ago, with the insertion of the papyrus strips to prevent rejoining of the separated parts while the healing occurred. 'I should perhaps explain myself,' she said, regaining her composure. 'The local rules are very strict; were I not, when attending to my public tasks and duties outside the house, to attire myself with what we consider wanton and promiscuous display, it would be here viewed as flagrant immodesty, and punishable, before the crowd, by the

Card no. 19

Description: An ossuary chapel, where the style of the classic Romanesque interior is partly obscured by the encrustation of thousands of skulls and skeletal parts, that form, or cover, the interior architecture. This photograph taken at the crossing, facing the nearby altar, where, instead of a crucifix or a monstrance, an enamelled or painted rectangular metal plaque stands upright, its left side white, its right black.

Text: that the crucifix was now exchanged for a small pendant medallion, half black, half white, the symbol of the local cult. The thought of Mrs Fortesque having gone, so to speak, over to the other side was shocking, and at the same time extremely piquant and arousing, with my recently acquired knowledge of what that fully entailed for the woman involved. Having just come to the rendezvous from my daily session with the local doctor, who was treating me with that disgusting metallic green and gold powder, the source of which I was loath to ponder on, I scarcely thought myself physically capable of what was to follow, given my general and peculiar state. Nonetheless, when the missionary's widow, after furtively glancing about only to find the chapel empty – no surprise, since it was midday and most families were at home, doors shuttered for the day's largest repast – reached for and embraced me, the last thing I had awaited, I found myself responding in a most unexpected fashion. 'But the children – your late husband—' I stammered, as she pushed me back against a column, so the decorative knobs of tibiæ and the like bruised my spine, with her bare breasts crushed against my chest and her hot searching lips

Card no. 20

Description: A statue, whose dimensions are given as 13 by 5 by 5 [in, it is assumed], these last representing the base. A female goddess, in flowing robes, very much gravid, standing in a bronze boat formed like the body of a duck, whose head is the prow. Within its open beak it holds a cube.

Text: certain? It's only been a month . . .' I lingered at these, my own words, astonished at the assertion. 'Of course I am,' she snapped back, then containing herself with difficulty, lowered her tone, and continued, 'I've not been with anyone, before or since,' she said, bitterly smiling. She was very much enceinte, astoundingly so, in a way that would have been impossible had I been responsible for her state. I kept on looking at her in bewilderment. My first thought was 'propulsive force – perhaps; generative principle – never!!' Still holding my hand lightly, she followed up, saying, 'It does seem impossible, doesn't it? Not just the time – I mean, given what had happened to you, in addition. Think, though, was anything odd done to you then, or about that time? I mean . . .' At that, the thought of the daily calls to the doctor snapped into mind. Once I had found out the disgusting source of the gold and green powders, I had ceased from visiting him again. Had our meeting in the ossuary been before or after the 'treatment's' short course? I could not remember, for the life of

Card no. 21

Description: Another souvenir card assumed to be from the local natural history collection, exhibiting a quite large centipede of unknown type, with several interesting and anomalous features. The scale beside it a quarter-inch stick, since inches would make the creature ridiculously large.

Text: smooth and horrendously distended vulva with a disgusting plop. The three witches – I cannot think of them as being other than that – hurried to the trestle immediately, clicking the emerald daggers they had for tongues excitedly against their teeth. The multitudinous onlookers and priests held their distance. Mrs F seemed to be in a state of shock, but was still breathing with eyes closed. Horrified, I cast a look at Alicia, who stood imperturbed in her youthful nakedness, motionless, still holding the thick black candle cool as you like, as if she were in Westminster Abbey. The bloody caul and afterbirth were snipped at and cut with glassy tongues, and I saw, when the three stepped back, a foul, thick, twitching, segmented thing, snaky, glinting green and gold, thick as a moray eel, writhing between the poor woman's bloody legs. The chief witch nodded to Alicia, who slowly moved forward, setting her candle carefully at her mother's feet. At another signal, she picked up the glistening demonic shape, which unwound itself into a heavy, broad, segmented centipede-like beast of dimensions that left me gasping. Alicia uncoiled the slimy monster, gleaming with ichor, and draped the hellspawn 'round her shoulders, just as if it was a feather boa. Pausing only for a moment, she turned to me with a thin leer, and asked 'Want to hold it? It's yours too!' Revulsed, I turned, while she shrugged and set off on the ceremonial way, the crowd bowing to her and her half-brother, sister, or whatever, the belt of hollow birds' eggs – her only adornment – clicking around her slim hips, brown from hours on the temple steps – as she swayed, during

Card no. 22

Description: A shining centipede probably of gold, coiled upon a dais of ebony, or some other dark wood, this last encrusted with bejewelled precious metal of arabesque form. The central object's size may be inferred from the various items imbedded in it: Roman cameos, Egyptian scarabs, coins from crushed empires and forgotten kingdoms, some thousands of years old, the votive offerings of worshippers over the millennia we infer the sculpture to have existed. The object is fabulous: an utter masterwork of the goldsmith's art rivalled only by the Cellini salt cellar and one or two other pieces. It almost seems alive.

Text: almost worth it. Calquon and Harrison are dead, what has become of Paul, who thought up all this, I have no idea. I have been subjected to the most hideous torture, and seen the most awful sights, that few can have experienced without losing their sanity. It is deeply ironic after all I have been through, that I by chance only yesterday discovered the object, hidden away in my belongings. What remains to be seen is whether I can bring it back to civilisation with myself intact. I cannot trust Alicia, who has clearly let her elevation to high priestess and chief insect-keeper go to her head. During my last interview with her, whilst she dangled her shapely foot provocatively over the arm of her golden throne, I, in a vain effort to play upon her familial bonds and old self, reminded her of her younger brother, who had not been seen for days. At that she casually let drop that he had been sold on to Zanzibar (where there is, I believe, an active slave market) to ultimately disappear into one of the harems of the Arabian peninsula (Philby may be able to inform more fully). 'I never could stand the little pest,' was her remark, so it would be foolish to hope for any sympathy from her quarter. I am being watched quite closely, with great suspicion. Can it be they <u>know</u>? If I ever leave here alive, it will be an absolute sensation. Biding my time, I cannot do anything now, but I can at least try to smuggle these surreptitiously scribbled notes out to the French vice-consul in the city where we bought the mules. He is a good fellow, though he drinks to excess at

An additional 52 cards remain (see photo-copies), which although of great interest, bear no hand-written notes, and therefore are not described here, with the following single exception:

Card: not in sequence, i.e. unnumbered by us

<u>Description</u>: A photographic postal card of a large exterior wall of a stone building of enormous size. The impressive dimensions become apparent once one realises that the small specks and dots on the stereobate of the vaguely classical structure are in fact people – some alone, others in groups, these last for the most part sheltered under awnings set up on the steps. What most catches the eye, however, is the magnificent low relief work covering most of the wall, depicting, it would seem, some mythological scene whose iconographic meaning is not apparent. It is in character a harmonious mixture of several ancient traditions: one sees hints of the Hellenistic, Indo-Grecian, and traces even of South-East Asian styles. The contrasts of tone make clear that the bare stone has been brightly painted.

<u>The relief itself</u>: It appears a judgement is being carried out. In the background, solemn ringlet-bearded men draped in graceful robes, all in the same pose, all copies of the other. All hold a square object, somewhat in form like a hand-mirror divided into one field black and one field white, and watch with blank eyes the man before them who is strapped to a plank, while a large fabulous beast, part man, part insect, with elements of the order Scolopendra predominating, tears at him in

the fashion of the Promethean eagles, and worse. To the right, a young priestess or goddess, nude but for a chain of beads or eggs around her waist, stands contrapposto, with one arm embraced about an obscene creature, a centipedal monstrosity of roughly her own height, leaning tightly upright against her. She is pointing with her free hand towards the tortured man. The expression on her empty face has affinities with several known Khmer royal portrait sculptures. She faintly smiles, as if in ecstasy.

Don Tumasonis, after a largely picaresque and misspent youth, settled down, he thought, to a quiet life on the outskirts of a Scandinavian capital, with a charming, if Norwegian wife; lively, if rambunctious cats; and interesting, if space-consuming books. Little did he anticipate the chain of events awaiting, forcing him into the mendicant life of a writer with little more than a bronze parachute to protect him. He has since published stories in *Ghosts & Scholars*, *All Hallows*, *Supernatural Tales* and the Ash-Tree Press anthology *Shadows and Silence*. As he explains: ' "The Prospect Cards" draws its inspiration from many sources: stuffy booksellers' catalogues, volumes of 18th and 19th century Levantine travel, a walk along the Seine, Kipling, Rider Haggard in his usual more perverse mode, and anthropological literature. Its mood was influenced by the books of George MacDonald Fraser, Glen Baxter and the character of John Cleese. It was meant to be humorous, but seems to have got out of hand.'

Handwriting of the God

CHICO KIDD

'I have made my way, I know you, and I know thy name, and I know the name of her who is within thee: Invoker of thy Two Lands, destroyer of those who come to thee by fire, lady of spirits, obeyer of the word of thy Lord is thy name.'

The Book of the Dead

He couldn't resist another look at the papyrus before he put it away. Not in over forty years of scratching for treasures (but usually finding no more than detritus) in the white sands and stony cliffs of Egypt had he seen anything quite so beautiful.

With infinite and meticulous care, he unrolled a tiny section and drank in the delicate painting like a fine wine. His fear of damaging the frail thing was not quite enough to prevent one final greedy sight of the painted figures in their vibrant colours, clear and bright as if they had been drawn the day before, stylised yet wonderfully lifelike.

In the flickering lamplight, raven-haired girls moved through a stately dance, their lithe bodies plain beneath their diaphanous skirts. A crowned woman offered a blue lotus flower to a pharaonic figure. Musicians – a flautist, a drummer, a blind harper – played to guests at a feast. Men with the heads of beasts and birds marched in stately procession. Here was Thoth, the scribe; there, crocodile-headed Ammut, eater of the damned.

His lips moved silently as he read some of the hieroglyphs: *Thoth, great god, Lord of the holy words, place-taker of Re, ibis-headed, god of truth and wisdom, five times very great,* and his hand crept almost of its own accord to stroke the small golden statue which stood on the table beside him.

And at first they had assumed this to be a run-of-the-mill funerary papyrus of no particular importance.

Valentim Ruivo smiled once more in sheer delight at his prize and smoothed its ancient surface more gently than, in years gone by, he had caressed the soft hair of a lover, remembering and savouring the delicious moment when he had first seen it.

Just an ordinary wooden funerary statuette, a little more time-damaged than some, its painted inscription illegible; finding it hollow, as such things often were, they had been unsurprised to discover a roll of papyrus inside. Indeed they had laid it on one side, preoccupied as they were with the golden Thoth statuette and the small but exciting hoard of other artefacts they had unearthed earlier.

Finally, though, Ruivo had come back to the papyrus, laid it on this very table after setting the remains of his lunch on the floor to be out of the way. Taking his pocket-knife, he raised the outer fold of the roll with some care, but not the delicacy he now used. And what a sight had met his eyes. He sighed with pleasure at the recollection. Such moments were not very often granted. One had to grub in the dirt for forty years to find such a reward. Although the ultimate prize, an unplundered tomb, was yet to be discovered, every Egyptologist worth his salt was convinced that it was out there: an Eldorado of the desert, a treasure trove of wonderful things.

The shaft had seemed so unprepossessing, too. It had smelled so foul that none of the locals would dig there, claiming that the vile stink was a sign that it was infested by *afrits*, evil spirits. So Ruivo, who did not believe in such things any more than he credited stories of cursed tombs and crumbling bandaged mummies three thousand years dead stalking the night, had wrapped a cloth over his mouth and nose and descended.

Ship of the desert, my arse, thought Luís Da Silva irritably for the hundredth time as he braced his thighs around the camel's singularly uncomfortable saddle. I might have known it would be about as enjoyable as being keelhauled.

Torn between an urgent need for a smoke and a desire to wipe the sweat running down his face, and able to do neither – nothing on earth would have induced him to release his grip on the wooden handhold – he wondered again how he had let himself be persuaded to visit an archaeological dig in the dusty middle of Egypt. It was about as far from the sea as it was possible to be without actually being *in* the Sahara Desert. And therefore not the native element for a Portuguese ship's captain, or even a remotely suitable environment. He found that he was uncomfortable this far away from water. His ship, the barque *Isabella*, was hundreds of miles away in Alexandria.

He squeezed his right eye shut, disorienting himself completely, and attempted to lean his head far enough sideways to wipe it on his sleeve, but succeeded only in reaching his unshaven cheek. It rasped along his sleeve. Should have shaved, too, he thought in annoyance, opening his eye hastily before he overbalanced.

The eyepatch he wore on the other side was now so unbearably damp and gritty he'd tried to give up even thinking about it. I wish I'd taken the damned thing off before I got up on this wretched beast, he thought. Normally he wore the patch to avoid subjecting people to the sight of the scar that ran from eyebrow to cheekbone, souvenir of an encounter with a demon which had cost him his left eye. But the snaggle-toothed guide who accompanied him boasted not only a horribly puckered crease down half his face but also seemed to be missing part of his nose, so Da Silva didn't think he would have objected.

However, the speculation was academic. Thirty-odd years spent at sea meant he could keep his balance without even thinking about it on a bucking deck in the teeth of a force nine gale or a fifty-foot sea, but rocking on top of a camel had deprived him of all stability. And illogical as he knew it was, the handhold was the only thing that gave him any sense of security above the creature's ungainly gait.

I just hope Senhor Ruivo appreciates this, he thought, otherwise I'm going to go straight back to London and personally strangle Jorge Coelho. This was the shipping agent who had persuaded him into this folly: an old friend who had presumed rather too much on friendship this time.

The dry wind, which did nothing at all to alleviate the heat, tugged at the cloth over his head, and he was glad at least that he had taken his guide's advice and relinquished his hat. Otherwise it would have been long gone into the sands of Egypt. He rather envied the native's loose robes, as well, although he was dressed as sensibly as a European could, even to the extent of omitting collar and tie; even so, everything had become moist and most of it was itching. The majority of people wore far too many clothes, in his opinion. Especially, he thought with an inward smile, women.

Ahead, he saw his first ghost since they had left the outskirts of Luxor, and brought his attention back to the present, wondering if that meant they were nearly at their destination.

It was a very ancient ghost, this one, faded almost to nothingness, little more than a heat-haze shimmering over the desert. For a moment, he doubted his perception, and then more phantoms came into view, drifting aimlessly over the pallid scorching sands.

This ability to see the dead was the other legacy of his encounter with the demon, and it had taken some getting used to, until he realised that all he had to do was ignore them, and he had just about trained himself to do that. It had taken nearly five years, though. Getting used to missing an eye had been a lot easier, and, of necessity, a lot quicker, too.

'How far?' he asked his guide, who, as before, refused to reply to Arabic in the same tongue and answered in English, which annoyed Da Silva considerably, even though his English was almost as good as his Portuguese.

'Ten minute,' the guide replied, spreading his hand three times, and thus confusing Da Silva completely. I wish I hadn't asked, he thought crossly, and returned to observing the ghosts.

In fact, since the camels' lurching stride was deceptive, Ruivo's camp came into view not much more than five minutes later. Da Silva, whose temper had begun to fray, gave silent thanks, and scanned the scene in front of him.

He picked out the archaeologist with ease, for the simple reason that everyone else in sight was obviously Egyptian. Ruivo, bustling towards them, put him in mind of a stork wearing a straw hat, lanky and stooped, with a birdlike gait.

The guide induced the camels to kneel, and Da Silva leant hastily backwards, just in time to avoid a forward dive over his mount's head which would have been a dramatic, if a little over-flamboyant, introduction to his client. Terra firma had never felt so welcoming, although he was surprised and annoyed to find his knees were shaking. He handed the guide a handful of piastres – less than he would normally have done, but he was irritated by the man's insistence on speaking English – and turned his attention to alleviating his various discomforts.

By the time Ruivo drew near, he had put the headcloth to good secondary use in mopping his face, especially under his eyepatch, and was standing bareheaded, squinting in the brightness, and smoking a small black cheroot. All I need now is something to drink, he decided, looking at the sky and estimating the time to be around eleven, before I melt away completely. His mouth, like everything else, felt full of sand.

'*Capitão* Da Silva,' the archaeologist said effusively, a smile splitting his beard, which, being pure white from jaw-level, gave the rather startling impression that he had just dipped his chin in a bowl of milk. 'So good of you to come all this way.'

Yes, I think so too, thought Da Silva, shaking the proffered large, bony hand and finding it curiously strengthless as well as unpleasantly clammy. 'Senhor Ruivo,' he replied. 'I'm sure it will be a pleasure once I find out what I'm doing here.'

Ruivo looked taken aback, Da Silva was mordantly amused to see, and he smiled to himself, his ill humour forgotten. You don't get away with it that easily, he told the older man silently.

'Well, er, we don't quite have all the comforts of home,' said Ruivo, 'but I expect you wouldn't refuse a drink.'

Da Silva, who knew prevarication when he saw it, but was in need of replacing some of the liquid he had sweated off, raised his eyebrows, feeling the familiar pull of the scar at the left one. 'That would be very welcome.'

The archaeologist blinked owlishly, as if not quite sure how to react. The captain spoke like an educated man, but looked like a ruffian. He looked him up and down, taking in his vaguely piratical air, single, incongruously blue eye, crumpled suit of unbleached cloth and collar-less shirt – Ruivo himself wore not only a neatly knotted tie but a coat and waistcoat as well, even if they were of lightweight fabric – and suggested, 'The local beer is quite refreshing, especially after a dusty ride.' Dusty, yes, that was one way of describing it.

'Fine,' said Da Silva, ignoring the other man's scrutiny, though beer was not normally his first choice. He knew better than to ask for water. Ruivo, who did not seem overly affected by the blistering heat, gestured for him to take a seat under a canvas canopy and he ducked under the flap. The captain was not a tall man, but it was the sort of thing that you instinctively think is going to be too low. Having once met a doorway that smacked him on the forehead, he was prepared to err on the side of caution.

'Allow me to introduce you to my colleague,' the archaeologist said from behind him as a dapper Egyptian in a suit almost as creased as Da Silva's, but of infinitely better cut, half-rose to his feet and gave a small bow. 'Senhor Doutor Hassan El-Aqman, of the University of Cairo. El-Aqman,' he switched to English, 'this is Captain Da Silva.'

'*Sabáhil khayr,*' Da Silva said, and shook hands, noticing as he did so that the Egyptian was missing the top of his middle finger. El-Aqman smiled broadly, showing a mouthful of extremely white teeth. He had delicate features, almost like a girl's, but his voice, when he spoke, was exceptionally deep.

'You speak Arabic, Captain; how pleasant to meet a European so cosmopolitan.'

Da Silva, who spoke a number of languages, returned the smile –

somewhat less expansively – and was endeavouring to think up some pleasantry when he was interrupted by Ruivo. The archaeologist had relinquished his hat, revealing a bald scalp fringed with white hair like a monk's tonsure.

'And here is my other colleague,' he announced, adding to someone unseen, 'do come and meet Captain Da Silva.'

On the point of sitting down, Da Silva resumed the vertical as a dark-haired young woman bent her head to come under the awning, and he wished once more that he had bothered to shave earlier. He wiped his sweaty palm hastily on his trousers.

'May I present Miss Phoebe Hardy,' said Ruivo. Miss Hardy had straight black brows and a strong face, and was clad in a man's shirt, waistcoat and trousers. The sight was sufficiently arresting for Da Silva to picture his wife similarly dressed, and enjoy the image. She held out a tanned hand, and proved to have a firm grip.

'Hello, Captain,' she said in a strong American accent.

'Delighted to make your acquaintance,' he replied. 'You're from Boston, I think?'

'Why, yes,' she said, a little surprised. 'You have a very good ear, Captain.' Helped by a second mate from that city, he thought, but merely smiled.

Miss Hardy sat down, thus giving everyone else leave to do the same, and Da Silva took off his jacket and bundled it under his chair. He rather wished he could take off the damp shirt as well, an idea that amused him. People were still remarkably straight-laced, though there had at least been some improvement in that since the turn of the century. Spending most of his life at sea gave a slightly different perspective on the purpose of clothing. He decided to roll up his sleeves instead, and unfastened his cuffs without looking down.

The introductions complete, Ruivo called for refreshments and beamed round at everyone, clasping his bony hands around one knee. His air of bonhomie was not nearly sufficient to mask the tension under the canopy, and Da Silva wondered exactly what was going on. He decided to let them tell him in their own time, however, since the heat was like an oven now, and he contemplated what remained of his cheroot. There didn't seem to be another drag left in it, so he ground it out on his boot-sole.

'So,' he said, raising an eyebrow at Ruivo, 'what does everyone do here?' And looked round at the others.

'Miss Hardy is our resident artist,' the archaeologist explained, still beaming, 'and Dr El-Aqman lends his expertise and makes sure that no artefacts find their ways into places they shouldn't.' His smile became rather forced as he said this, a fact which was not lost on Da Silva. Ah, he thought, so that's it. I'm to be asked to do a spot of smuggling. Now he could sit back and enjoy the show. He rubbed at the scar on his cheekbone and crossed his legs, only to uncross them a moment later due to accumulated humidity.

Drinks arrived on a tray carried by an urchin with one arm in a grubby plaster cast, some species of fruit juice or sherbet for El-Aqman and beer for the other three. The glasses were all cold enough to come beaded with moisture, Da Silva noticed. Not quite all the comforts of home, he observed, but a few of them, all the same. He took a long drink of the beer, which proved a little watery but thirst-quenching, perhaps because of that. After this the Egyptian doctor pulled out a gold cigarette-case and offered it round. Miss Hardy took one, but Ruivo declined, as did Da Silva, preferring his own smokes. Cigarettes, even Egyptian ones, were pretty tasteless in comparison. He accepted a light from El-Aqman, though.

He would quite happily have sat there for the rest of the day, but apparently was not to be allowed to do this. The company, having consumed its refreshments and made small talk, broke up, leaving only Ruivo sitting with him.

The archaeologist, showing the first sign of being affected by the furnace heat, took out a limp handkerchief and wiped his face, which reminded Da Silva of his own discomfort. As if I need reminding, he thought damply, sticking a finger under his eyepatch to try and let some air in.

'Why am I here, Senhor Ruivo?' he asked.

Ruivo laughed nervously, the humourless reflex of embarrassment, and fixed his gaze on Da Silva's eyepatch. 'Because you can see ghosts.'

Well, that's the last thing I expected, the Captain thought in surprise. 'I suppose you got that from Jorge Coelho?' he asked, scratching his eyebrow. Who I will definitely strangle now.

'Yes,' said Ruivo. 'Is it true?' He looked at Da Silva curiously, perhaps looking for some sign of feyness. The captain laughed shortly.

'If that's what you want, I'd look a damn fool coming all this way if it weren't,' he retorted. 'Though if you have some idea of getting me to locate tombs for you, I'm afraid you're out of luck. It doesn't work that way.'

'Oh, er, no,' the older man said, looking thunderstruck, as if he wished he *had* thought of that. He dropped his gaze to his hands, twining and untwining in his lap. 'It's just that a . . . colleague of mine, ah, borrowed some artefacts we unearthed, and then had a heart attack before he could return them.'

Borrowed. And there was I thinking you wanted me to do some smuggling, thought Da Silva, taking hold of a handful of damp shirt from over his ribs and flapping it ineffectually. I do apologise. 'And what do you want me to do?' he asked aloud, simply for the rather malicious enjoyment of watching Ruivo squirm.

'Well, we, er, I, wondered if there was any way you could, you know, ask him what he did with them.'

Da Silva had known it was coming, and liked the idea no better for that. Seeing the dead was one thing. He did it all the time. Summoning them to ask them questions, however, he found distasteful. It meant not only commanding them, but literally binding them to his will. And that smacked too much of slavery for him to be comfortable with it. He had had too much first-hand experience of slavery for that. Nineteen years of it. And though the man was five years dead now, it was a legacy he couldn't easily shake off.

'You do realise I would have to be at your colleague's grave to do that?' he asked. half-hoping to hear that the deceased had been shipped home for burial.

But the archaeologist gave another of his nervous laughs and said, 'Actually I have his ashes here, will that do?'

Good God, thought Da Silva, raising his eyebrows; these people aren't just grave-robbers, they're ghouls. 'Yes, that would do,' he said, trying for nonchalance, but unsure how far he succeeded. 'How is it you happen to have his ashes?'

'He was my brother,' Ruivo explained hastily, a little intimidated by the captain's expression. 'He wanted them scattered out here, so I, er, postponed the scattering for a while.'

'Pragmatic,' remarked Da Silva, amused, taking out another cheroot and contemplating it. 'Is that it?'

'Well, I'd also like you to supervise our small shipment to Lisbon, of course, after all, we did charter your vessel. I want it packed properly for the voyage – I don't trust these river pirates to do that.'

'Of course,' agreed the captain gravely. Why else would I trek all this way down the damned Nile, if not for that? Unable, for the moment, to find a light, he snapped his fingers at the hovering boy and said, '*Kabrít.*' The urchin grinned hugely, and instead of matches produced an enormous American cigarette lighter. He flipped it open with a flourish and produced a flame big enough to roast an ox. Da Silva smiled back, allowed the lad to light his cheroot, and handed him another in return.

Ruivo watched disapprovingly as the boy stowed it in his robes. 'You really shouldn't encourage these children to smoke,' he said sternly. Da Silva shrugged.

'I don't think he needs any encouragement from me.'

'No, I suppose not,' Ruivo agreed, adding in a surprisingly tolerant tone, 'Different ways, that's all.' He fell silent, staring out at the shimmering desert. It was the hottest part of the day, and nothing was stirring. The heat was a nearly tangible thing: it even had its own scent, the smell of roasted dust. It was almost difficult to breathe. Da Silva, looking out as well, found now that he really couldn't tell the difference between ghosts and heat-haze, shuddering over the sand. The desert stretched away into the distance, clean as a bleached skeleton, inhospitable and totally alien.

'Nothing at all from here clear to the Atlantic,' he remarked, clearing sweat out of his eyebrows with a finger, 'except sand.'

'It's not your first visit to Egypt, I presume?' the archaeologist enquired lazily. Even he looked hot now, and seemed content to sit in the sweltering airless shade.

'My first down this far,' Da Silva replied. And my last, I hope. 'Put into Alexandria and Port Said a few times. Visited the Pyramids, of course, years ago now, gawked like a tourist.'

'Well, they are, of course, eminently gawkable,' Ruivo agreed. '*Soldats, songez que, du haut de ces pyramides, quarante siècles vous contemplent.*''

'Forty centuries look down on you,' repeated Da Silva, the words running cold down his back despite the day's heat. 'Who are you quoting?'

'Napoleon,' said Ruivo. 'A man who was actually so sensitive to history that he had his soldiers use the Sphinx for target practice.'

Da Silva laughed, amused. 'And our own countrymen have shown consideration and sensitivity in the colonies, I suppose?' He exhaled deeply, and, to his surprise, achieved a spontaneous smoke-ring. This feat was sufficiently startling to engage his attention for a minute.

'About talking to Valentim—' the archaeologist ventured, running a finger inside his collar. His face glistened moistly.

'Valentim being your brother?'

'Just so. When – what would be a good time?'

'Any time you like,' said Da Silva, and laughed at the other's expression. 'Truly. I'm not a spiritualist, Senhor Ruivo. I don't need any props; it doesn't even need to be dark. All I need to know is, did your brother dabble in magic at all, as far as you know?'

There was a pause. 'Well, I'm not actually sure,' Ruivo said at last. 'I would have said yes. It's the sort of thing he would try, although he was very much the sceptic in many ways. Why do you ask?'

Because in that case I'll need some of your blood, thought Da Silva, reluctant to spring that information on the other man out of the blue. He could have used his own, of course, but the damned ghost was Ruivo's brother. And blood calls to blood. That never changes.

His mouth was dry from smoking, and tasted of dust. 'Is there any more of that beer?' he asked, and Ruivo waved the boy to fetch some. He wasn't accustomed to drinking much during the day, but it wasn't as if the beer was very high in alcohol. Tasted like cat's piss anyway. A nice Portuguese red, though . . . would have sent him straight to sleep, he knew.

The urchin hurried off with alacrity, probably hoping to be rewarded with another cheroot – he had, Da Silva observed, already smoked the one he'd given him earlier.

'Wait here,' said Ruivo suddenly, and got to his feet. And where would I go? the captain thought, rubbing his unshaven chin, which felt decidedly grubby. The archaeologist clapped his battered straw hat back on his head and stooped to go out into the scorching sun. Da Silva fidgeted in the canvas chair, trying to shift his damp clothes from his sweaty skin, and watched his progress, struck again by his oddly avian gait, remembering pictures he had seen of bird-headed ancient Egyptian gods. He lifted his eyepatch and tried to blow air upwards. Nothing seemed to work. Everything was sticky, sandy, slick with perspiration. The dusty wind stirred the sand in little whorls without cooling the air.

No flies, he thought suddenly. Not even mosquitoes. Too damned hot for them, I suppose. He frowned at the idea of mosquitoes. In all his years of voyaging to tropical coasts he had somehow managed to avoid malaria, and at forty-four he did not want to start now. Oh well. There wasn't much he could do if he did get bitten when evening came, and he scratched pensively at his right ankle in reflex.

Ruivo reappeared, carrying a wooden box which presumably held his brother's ashes, and Da Silva sighed at the idea of moving. On the other hand, though, perhaps he could get this over and done with and return to the comparative comfort of Luxor. Although even that, unfortunately, would involve getting on a camel again. Perhaps he could hire a horse instead, or even a mule.

Exhaling explosively, he picked up his discarded headcloth and mopped his face and neck again, annoyed to think that he hadn't taken advantage of the other man's absence to remove his eyepatch entirely, even if temporarily. At that moment, the urchin materialised at his elbow with a fresh glass, and Da Silva passed him a cheroot.

'*Shokran*,' the boy said, and made to resume his squatting position in the shade just outside, but the captain chased him away. He did not want him to witness a ghost being raised. God knew what sort of a to-do that might cause. Then he picked up the glass and drank most of the beer in one long draught. That was a little better. Not much, but a little.

'Here,' Ruivo's voice made him turn as the archaeologist ducked under the canvas – he actually needed to – and placed the box he was carrying carefully on the table. 'Now, do I need to open it?'

'No,' said Da Silva, still reluctant, and ran his fingers through his damp hair. 'You want to do this now, then?'

'Why not? You said we didn't need to wait until evening.'

Da Silva nodded, fiddling with his eyepatch. 'Yes, I did, didn't I?' As he got to his feet he realised he had never raised a ghost in front of witnesses before. It made him a little apprehensive. 'Do you want your colleagues here?'

'Oh, I don't think so,' said Ruivo hastily. So he hadn't told them, then. 'Now, do you need anything else?'

'A drop of your blood, I'm afraid,' Da Silva answered, remembering occasions when he had had to slice into his own arm with his knife, and winced. 'Do you think you can stab your finger, or something?'

The archaeologist looked alarmed, and stared down at his hands. 'I – don't know.' He took out a pocket-knife and opened the blade, then shook his head. 'Here, you'd better do it, if that's what you need.'

'Put your hand flat on the table.' Ruivo complied. 'What was your brother's full name?'

'His full name? Valentim João – ouch!' The archaeologist jerked back as Da Silva stabbed his thumb with the small blade. Both men watched the blood welling out for a second, then Ruivo lifted his hand from the table and squeezed the small wound.

A drop of blood fell on the box, and then another. 'Valentim João Ruivo,' said Da Silva softly, remembering other times, other ghosts, and something unidentifiable made him shiver. From the startled expression in the other man's eyes, he felt it too.

In front of the table, in the breathless desert heat, a shadowy figure began to form, at first indistinguishable from a heat-haze, but then taking shape rapidly and beginning to solidify – no, not exactly solidify, thought Da Silva, wiping a hand over his face, that was the wrong word. It steadied, wavered less, but failed to gain plasticity. It faded in and out of existence, now almost substantial, now spectral.

'Valentim—' began Ruivo. The ghost turned to him, reaching out a semi-transparent hand, and his brother held out his own, blood still oozing from the thumb. Ghosts and living people could not touch, but as phantom hand met real one and passed through it, through the blood of his brother, there was a sound like soft thunder, and Valentim Ruivo's ghost took on the semblance of reality, like a photograph in a developing tray. He looked entirely real, except for an almost imperceptible haziness round the edges.

'Manoel?' he said. There was nothing spectral about his voice. It sounded remarkably like his brother's.

'Where's the papyrus?' Ruivo asked, before Da Silva could speak. The ghost shook his head, seeming distressed.

'You cannot refuse to answer me, Valentim João Ruivo,' Da Silva interrupted, and at the sound of the name, the ghost's head snapped round to face him.

'Don't make me answer,' he said. 'It's better you don't find it again,' and an expression of pain passed across the phantom face.

'What do you mean?' his brother demanded.

'Disaster,' whispered the ghost. 'Disaster all round. I can't say any more.' A cold fist seemed to squeeze Da Silva's heart.

'Tell me,' he said, wishing Ruivo would shut up. I should have told him to keep quiet before we started, he thought, though I don't suppose that would have worked. Damned man can't keep his mouth closed. Sweat trickled into his eye and he knuckled it away.

The ghost turned an anguished face to him. 'I can't,' he said. 'You know there are some things I can't tell.'

'Then where's this papyrus your brother wants?'

'Please,' the ghost implored. Da Silva raised an eyebrow at Ruivo.

'We have to know,' said the archaeologist. 'Or that confounded El-Aqman will take away our permit. He thinks we stole it.'

'Tell him,' Da Silva ordered. The ghost shook his head, fighting the compulsion, but unable to resist.

'I put it back where we found it!' he spat, strain making his voice shrill. 'But it didn't do any good.'

Ruivo frowned. 'What do you mean, it didn't do any good? What were you thinking of?' Be *quiet*, damn you, thought Da Silva angrily, or I'll knock you cold, I swear it. He wiped his damp palms futilely down his trousers.

'Didn't do any good because I'm dead, you fool.'

'Mother of God,' exclaimed Ruivo, 'how did you die?'

'Shut up, Ruivo,' Da Silva snapped. 'He can't tell you that.' He turned to the ghost. 'What *can* you tell us?'

'Nothing more.' Shaking his head from side to side, seemingly in pain. 'I wish I could. I wish I could. Believe me.'

'Scatter his ashes, Ruivo,' said Da Silva, sickened by the ghost's anguish; by the whole business.

'But what if—'

'You've got what you wanted, now do what *he* wanted. Or I will.' Ruivo stared at him, then nodded abruptly and picked up the box. His brother's ghost watched. Da Silva turned to him. 'I'm sorry,' he said.

The archaeologist said quietly, 'Goodbye, Valentim,' and took the box outside.

'Goodbye, Manoel,' whispered the ghost, a little wistfully, and dissolved as his brother let the desert wind take his ashes.

'*Obrigado*, Valentim João Ruivo,' said Da Silva into the sudden silence.

Outside, Ruivo stood still for some time, staring out into the great emptiness. Da Silva sat and watched him, waiting for his heart to stop racing. He finished his beer, wondering what had distressed the ghost so much. Speculation was pretty useless, but he could no more stop himself from speculating than he could from – well, from seeing ghosts.

He wiped his face again, lit another cheroot, and waited for Ruivo to rejoin him.

At last the archaeologist, with an audible sigh, turned and came back into the shade. His face had grown haggard and Da Silva realised, startled, that the man was probably pushing sixty. How long has he been grubbing in the desert, pursuing dreams? he wondered. Thirty years, forty? Ruivo pinched the bridge of his nose and closed his eyes wearily, then slowly opened them again and stared tiredly at the captain.

'I suppose I owe you an explanation,' he said. Da Silva shrugged. He had worked some of it out already, but was still intensely curious. And he had no intention of going back to Luxor until he found out the full story.

Raising an eyebrow, he said, 'You'll have to tell me something before my brain overheats with wild guesses. What's this papyrus that has the pair of you so excited?'

'Why, it's the most amazing thing,' said Ruivo, becoming animated all at once. 'Beautiful colours, perfectly preserved, quite unique. Popped inside a funerary statue just like any old scroll – they often contain papyri,' he added, apparently just then remembering he was speaking to a layman. 'But I should begin at the beginning. Do you want another drink? Where's that wretched boy? Ahmed! Ahmed!'

'I sent him away,' Da Silva explained, blowing smoke out and wondering vaguely whether the day could possibly get any hotter.

'Oh. Of course. Yes. I'm, er, glad you thought of that.' Ruivo raised his voice and called again. 'Ahmed! Where are you?' The boy came trotting up, bare feet apparently impervious to the burning sand.

Having made the domestic arrangements to his satisfaction, and at the same time, Da Silva noted, successfully postponed the promised explanation, Ruivo resumed his seat. His clothes were looking rather the worse for wear now, his collar decidedly limp. Beads of sweat were running down his nose. They had made dark spots on his linen trousers.

'You were going to tell me about this papyrus of yours,' Da Silva prompted him, fed up with waiting.

'Do you have children?' the older man asked, with apparent irrelevance.

'Yes,' replied Da Silva, his wife's face coming clearly into his mind, and missing her strongly. 'A son and a daughter. Why?'

'My son and my brother brought out that papyrus. And now my brother's dead, and my son's in hospital in a coma.'

'What happened to him?'

'We don't know. The morning before Valentim died, he simply never woke up. Brain fever, the doctor called it. Which means he has no idea, either.'

Da Silva digested this. He did not believe in coincidences. 'Did anything happen to anyone else who handled the papyrus? Who else did?'

'Just the three of us – Miss Hardy, Dr El-Aqman, and myself.'

The boy Ahmed brought more drinks. Ruivo turned to tip him, and Da Silva surreptitiously lifted his eyepatch and mopped beneath it. Something was going on, and if past experience was anything to go on, things would start getting unpleasant very soon. He sighed. It was almost too hot to think.

'You'd better tell me everything. From the beginning.'

Ruivo looked at him with a slight frown. 'You're not what I expected, you know.'

And you're prevaricating again, Da Silva thought in exasperation.

What the hell *did* you expect, Madame Blavatsky? He settled on a more diplomatic, noncommittal, raised eyebrow. 'Go on,' he said, mildly.

The archaeologist took a sip of his drink. 'Well. There was a shaft that looked promising. You understand we play hunches a lot.' Da Silva nodded. He himself never underestimated the power of a hunch. 'It had been marked but not excavated. When we enquired we found the workmen wouldn't go near it. They said it had *afrits* in it – that's a kind of evil spirit. Apparently you can tell when these things are about by their terrible smell.'

'Most of Cairo must be infested, then,' observed Da Silva, drily, and Ruivo laughed, a high-pitched, strangely girlish giggle.

'Just so,' he agreed, and went on with his narrative. 'So, anyway, Valentim decided to dig into it himself, with Julião – my son, that is. I mean, Valentim took a pick and started swinging at the rubble. He was sixty-one! No wonder he had a heart attack! We eventually managed to get a few of the younger men to dig. They either didn't believe in these spirits or the bonus we offered them spoke louder. That happens a lot. So we covered up our faces, because it really did smell vile, and got to work.' He paused to take a drink.

Da Silva, caught up in the story, wiped sweat away automatically and wondered why, after getting on for three glasses of beer, his bladder wasn't complaining.

'Not far down,' Ruivo went on, 'we found a side passage, loosely blocked by rubble, and at the end of that, a burial chamber. Of course it had been plundered. The grave-robbers hadn't even left the mummy. It was full of rubbish, stones, broken wood. There was a stone sarcophagus – the lid was smashed to bits – but they had missed a few small items, including a battered wooden statue which held the scroll.

'As I said, we thought it a common funerary papyrus. We didn't even bother to look at it until we'd cleared out all the artefacts.' He smiled in pleasure at the recollection.

'Where are the other artefacts?' Da Silva asked, rubbing thoughtfully at his cheekbone, trying without much success to ignore the sweat trickling down his ribs. He had been, despite himself, almost mesmerised by Ruivo's tale: the change which had come over the archaeologist as he related it was quite remarkable. He was reliving it. The dark shaft, the rubble-strewn passage, the smashed sarcophagus, the detritus on the floor which hid the few treasures overlooked by the thieves, all were very real to him.

'Under lock and key. I'll show them to you later. You'll be interested, I'm sure.'

'Yes.' Da Silva nodded. 'And the papyrus? What was it?'

'It was astonishing,' said Ruivo. 'Quite unique, as I said. Nothing like it has ever been recorded. What it was – well, my brother was the linguist. He said it was sacred poetry. Praising the gods. Hymns, perhaps, or prayers.'

'Prayers,' repeated Da Silva, thoughtfully, lighting another cheroot and staring at the white-hot sand outside. There must be more to it than that. Why would he want to get rid of prayers? 'Did your brother write down any of his translations?'

'Yes, he did,' Ruivo said, 'but he knocked a lamp over in his tent the night before he died, and his notebook got burned. He was really upset – or he seemed to be. Now I'm not so sure. We should have asked him.'

'He wouldn't have been able to tell us,' Da Silva told him. 'You heard what he said. Ghosts have to follow rules, too, you know.' He ran a hand through his sweaty hair. 'Are you going to retrieve the scroll?'

'I have to. El-Aqman wants it for the Cairo Museum.'

'You should tell him what your brother said.'

Ruivo stared at him. 'Are you mad? The man's a complete materialist. He wouldn't believe in a ghost if it appeared in front of him and shook his hand.'

'As you wish,' said the captain, with a shrug. 'What exactly did you tell the good doctor – and Miss Hardy – about me?' He sat back in the chair and eased his trousers away from his thighs in a futile attempt to let some air in. Ruivo coloured.

'Er, just that you could find missing items.'

Won't tell them I talk to ghosts, but makes me out to be some kind of dowser, thought Da Silva, torn between annoyance and amusement. 'I see,' he said, and got to his feet. 'Shall we go and find a missing item, then?' The idea of going out into that heat was daunting, but it was preferable to ferreting about in pitch darkness when evening came.

'Now?' the archaeologist exclaimed.

'Yes, why not? Perhaps whatever your brother was afraid of will be less of a threat while the sun's up.' He tossed the butt of his cheroot out into the sands and squatted down to rummage in the pack he had brought until he found the long knife he normally wore concealed down his back. The silver in the blade's alloy was remarkably effective against things that were not human, and its fourteen-inch length equally so against those that were. Holding the sheath loosely in his right hand, he turned towards Ruivo. 'Shall we go?'

The older man stared at the knife, apparently taken aback by this assumption of control, and said in a bemused tone, 'You'll need a hat.'

'Right,' said Da Silva, fishing a squashed fedora out of the pack and clapping it on his head, 'lead on.'

'This way,' the archaeologist said, putting on his own hat and setting off in the merciless heat across the sand. It was not easy to walk on, being soft and powdery, and quantities of it soon found their way into Da Silva's boots. Everyone in their right mind was under cover, having a siesta if they had any sense, and in minutes he was regretting the impulse which had led him to suggest this. The sun beat down like a great bronze hammer, and sweat was pouring off him. The gritty wind blew in his face, threatening to remove his hat. He shoved the knife through his belt and held the hat down instead. Ahead of him, Ruivo's jacket flapped like a cloak.

They had not gone very far when Phoebe Hardy's voice called out, 'Hey, you fellows, where are you going?' and the lady herself came striding towards them. She may have preferred the comforts of masculine garb, but she was keeping the sun off with an equally practical, if somewhat incongruous, parasol.

'I'm taking the captain to see where we found our little hoard,' Ruivo explained, tipping his hat to her. 'Don't stay out in the sun too long, dear Miss Hardy.'

'I'll tag along,' she said, blithely ignoring this rather feeble attempt to get rid of her. 'Hot enough for you, Captain?'

Da Silva took his own hat off and wiped his brow. The sweatband inside the hat was living up to its name. 'I've encountered climates I like better, Miss Hardy,' he replied, replacing it hastily on his head as the sun battered at him with renewed ferocity. 'But you look very cool. How long have you been in Egypt?'

'Four years,' she replied with a smile, acknowledging the compliment. 'You do get used to the weather, if that's any help.'

'I don't intend to stay long enough to do that,' he said drily.

It was really too hot even to carry on a conversation. The heat got into the throat and made breathing difficult, and the burning dry wind was intensely annoying. He removed grit from his eye, and wished he could do the same for the other side. I really wish I hadn't suggested this, he thought. Charging off across the desert like a bloody camel. I must be mad.

'Not far now,' said Ruivo encouragingly, if a little breathlessly, gesturing at the low cliff-face which rose ahead of them.

Miss Hardy moved to walk beside him. 'It'll be better out of the sun,' she said.

That's the understatement of the year, thought Da Silva, but enjoyed her back view in her trousers. She had long legs and a trim figure, and there was no harm at all in looking.

'Here we are,' Ruivo said, and stood to one side to let Miss Hardy precede him into what looked like a crack in the cliff. Following them, Da Silva found it widened immediately into a narrow defile full of welcome shade and the faintest of ghosts, fluttering almost invisibly in the dark-shadowed interior. The sun did not reach the bottom, even at its highest. Its absence was an infinite relief. He took off his hat, flapped it briefly in front of his face, and sat down on the cool ground. When he pulled off his boots, he found he could tip about half a pound of sand out of each one. Miss Hardy laughed at his expression.

'There must be a knack to walking on sand,' he said, looking at her feet.

'I suppose there is,' she said. 'I don't even think about it now.'

A faint reek reached him then, something undeniably foul but without any immediately recognisable provenance. You wouldn't say drains. Or latrines. Or dead cat. But you certainly didn't want it to get any stronger.

He got to his feet. 'Do you smell that?' he asked, remembering Ruivo's story of evil-smelling *afrits*.

'Yes, that's the famous stink,' the archaeologist replied. 'That's why we couldn't get anyone to dig.'

'I'm afraid it gets worse,' said Miss Hardy, who was tying a handkerchief bandit-fashion over her nose and mouth. 'Ready?'

'Lead on,' said Da Silva. A prickle of unease went across his back, and he frowned. He never ignored such feelings, not since he gained the ability to see ghosts. At the same time he thought he heard music. Surely *that* had to be imagination, unless someone had a phonograph in the desert. Still, stranger things had happened.

Ruivo and Miss Hardy were already ten feet away, and he hurried after them, his sense of disquiet deepening with the growing foetor. He took the knife from his belt, drew it, and dropped the sheath on the sand.

Now the stench was all around them, thick enough to cut, strong and unclean and meaty but not quite like decaying matter, yet not entirely like anything living, either, though there was something feral about it, something predatory and tigerish. And now the music was unmistakable, although the others showed no sign of being able to hear it. Now why am I not surprised at *that*? he thought sourly. Strange, plangent music, full of unfamiliar chords and curious harmonies. Sweat ran into his eye, and he wiped it away with his sleeve.

'There's the shaft,' said Ruivo. '—*Mother of God!*'

Da Silva didn't see where they came from, but suddenly two frightful figures hopped out of nowhere and swooped towards the archaeologist, who fell back, eyes wide with terror.

They were not the stuff of nightmares. They were worse than that. Wrapped in fluttering rags, the flesh beneath looked flayed, suppurating, bones glinting yellowly through in places. They were not even remotely human. A little less than man-sized, their faces had long muzzles, improbably fanged, and their mouths gaped open, jaws lolling brokenly as their heads wagged on their shoulders. They had no eyes, just blazing sockets like searchlights. Their taloned feet were birdlike, their limbs were hinged wrongly, and in their hands they held curved swords. A weirdly debilitating keening noise issued from their lipless maws, an intensely horrible counterpoint to the odd music which still sounded. Their very presence was terrifying.

Yelling, Da Silva charged them. It was pure reflex: he was too scared to swear, too angry to retreat, and he had no time at all to think. His mind registered only armed creatures attacking an old man, and did not stop to think about odds. His instincts yammered at him to turn and run. He ignored them.

He ducked under a whistling slash from a scimitar, and pushed the paralysed Ruivo out of the way, pivoting to parry the long curved blade in a flurry of sparks, and disengaging instantly. It was longer than his knife, but his reach was greater. That made a change. On the other hand, there were two of them. And he only had one eye.

Then the other came screeching at him. It was inhumanly fast. He skipped back rapidly, flailing his knife in long parries, the thing seemingly a little confused at his left-handedness. Noting this he went on the offensive, blocking its swordthrust and slashing downwards like an executioner with his knife, just missing severing its neck. He dodged the scimitar, but the thing kicked forward impossibly with its taloned foot, ripping his leg from shin to knee, and the strange ululating music reached a crescendo.

The pain was breathtaking for a split second, and he drew in a grating sob, bringing the knife up again to split the creature open from belly to chest. Its shriek abruptly cut off, and it crumpled, thick ichor spilling from it. Da Silva felt blood running down his leg into his boot.

Terrified that he couldn't see its companion, he spun away on his unwounded leg before the creature hit the ground, to see Phoebe Hardy fencing with the other, using her sadly battered parasol and cursing with impressive fluency. Her handkerchief had slipped down around her neck.

'Get it, Captain,' she panted, and he went for the creature, thoroughly enraged now. Pick on women and old men, will you, he thought. It gave way at first, wary of the blade, but quickly pressed back. It was more skilful than the other one, or maybe just not confused by a left-handed opponent. The curved blade slashed out in a lightning cut, narrowly missing his belly as he knocked it aside, and he felt his gut clench. He knew to watch for the razor-clawed feet, now, and dodged a kick deftly, but landed on his wounded leg and staggered as it nearly give way under him.

The thing darted inside his guard, scimitar raised, and he yelled and punched it in the face with his right fist. It skittered back with a surprised-sounding bleat, and he followed it up with a knife-thrust that ought to have gutted the creature, but thanks to its wrong-jointed legs merely dealt it a flesh-wound. He muttered an imprecation, and then had to parry another fierce jab from its blade.

I'd better finish this bloody thing off, he thought. Now, preferably. He was panting heavily, sweat was running into his eye, his leg was a long agony, and he knew he was tiring. On the other hand his adversary seemed indefatigable. Then the flailing scimitar tip caught him on the upper arm, slicing open a shallow stinging cut. He swore again and backed off rapidly, swinging his knife at arm's length as the music filled the air with its weird chords once more.

Screeching, the creature followed him, and then Phoebe Hardy flung its dead companion's scimitar at its legs, tripping it. Da Silva ducked under a sword-swipe gone awry and severed the thing's hand, which thumped to the ground, the curved blade flying out of its grip. The creature squealed like a stuck pig, turning to a dying gurgle as Da Silva cut its throat open with a blow that nearly took its head off. It slumped at his feet and he had to jump back to avoid it.

There was silence, sudden and abrupt. The two dead creatures seeped into the ground, liquefying as he watched. In a moment, the sand had absorbed them, not even leaving a stain. And the foul smell was also gone. All he could hear was the sound of his own breathing, harsh and ragged. He wiped his eye with his shirt-sleeve, the knife suddenly weighing a ton, and looked at the shallow cut on his arm. It was already inflamed.

'And those, I presume,' he said when he had got his breath back, 'were *afrits*.'

He pushed the blade into the sand to clean it, and looked up to see Phoebe Hardy, very white in the face, kneeling beside Ruivo, who seemed to have fainted. She was rubbing her right hand on her thigh.

'C-captain, I—' Her voice sounded strained.

Da Silva limped over to them, his torn trouser-leg flapping against his bleeding shin. 'What's the matter?' Don't tell me the other brother's keeled over as well, he thought disgustedly.

She looked at her palm, grimacing. 'That sword, it felt repulsive. I could hardly bear to touch it. Now my hand—' she turned it to show him. The palm was swollen and red, like a bad rash. Miss Hardy bit her lip. 'It hurts,' she said. She was shaking, he saw.

What a good thing I came prepared, he thought, and took a hip-flask out of his pocket. Sweat ran down his face, and his leg was throbbing fiercely, but first things first. 'May I borrow your handkerchief?'

'Surely.' As she unknotted it, he lowered himself to sit beside her. She handed him the cloth and he soaked it with holy water from the flask and tied it around her hand. Her skin was very soft and smooth.

'Oh, that's better,' she said, surprised. 'That can't be plain water; what is it?'

'Holy water,' he told her with a smile, and wet his own handkerchief to clean the inflamed cut on his arm. The swelling vanished as she watched. 'These . . . things always get infected. I don't think our flesh can endure the touch. But this always seems to do the trick.'

He hitched up his torn trouser-leg to look at the gash on his shin and winced. It had begun to suppurate, and the skin around was hot and shiny. Blood still welled out from the wound. His sock was red and sodden. The pain came in waves, making him lightheaded, and he wondered if he would pass out.

'Let me do it,' said Miss Hardy suddenly, unwrapping her hand and holding out the handkerchief to him for fresh water.

As she sponged the long slash, Ruivo opened his eyes. They were still shadowed with horror. 'Is that what killed my brother?' he whispered hoarsely.

Miss Hardy didn't even look up. Da Silva rubbed a hand over his face. 'We'll never know,' he said tightly. The holy water was beginning to take effect, but the wound was bad enough in itself to hurt like hell.

'Blessed Virgin,' said Ruivo, and crossed himself. A fat lot of good that does now, thought Da Silva, not that he had ever, himself, found prayer to be particularly effective.

'This is going to need stitching,' said Miss Hardy. 'But I can cover it up for now, so it won't get too dirty. Can you walk back to the camp?'

Da Silva exchanged a glance with Ruivo, but the archaeologist still seemed unwilling to speak. Damn the man! Exasperated, Da Silva scowled at him, and said to Miss Hardy, 'First I'd like to see where you found the papyrus.'

'We can do that any time,' she said.

'No, I don't think so. We should go now. There might be more of those ... things around.' He found a cheroot – he was nearly out of them – and lit up, drawing in the smoke gratefully. There were plenty more in his pack, anyway. I'm glad I'm still able to worry about things like that, he thought, and the memory of the *afrits* made him suddenly cold. He laughed at himself. Getting old, Da Silva.

Ruivo shuddered, and struggled into a sitting position. 'Dear God, do you suppose there are?' He looked around wildly, as if expecting another attack.

'I think we'd smell them, don't you?' Da Silva said, and stood up, wincing, trying to ignore the throbbing from his leg. Miss Hardy took his offered hand and he pulled her to her feet. 'Can you stand, Senhor Ruivo?'

Trying to smile, the archaeologist nodded, and got up slowly. His face was grey, and for a moment Da Silva was afraid the older man *was* going to have a heart attack. Miss Hardy appeared to have had the same idea.

'I think you'd better stay here and rest, Mister Ruivo,' she told him, briskly, not unkindly. 'I can take the captain inside.' Ruivo looked as if he wanted to object, but felt too ill to do so. He leant against the wall of the gully, mopping his face. 'Come along, Captain,' she went on. 'This won't take long.'

The entrance to the shaft was shored up with timber, and piled rubble in the vicinity had evidently been excavated from it. A pair of lanterns stood just outside and Miss Hardy picked one up and shook it. It sloshed reassuringly and she pulled a cigarette-lighter from her pocket and lit it. I feel superfluous, Da Silva thought, amused, and scratched his shoulder, just above the shallow cut on his arm.

Eyeing the dark entrance, he asked, 'Shall I bring the other lantern?'

'No, it's not far,' she replied, obviously too polite to suggest that he might need both hands free. 'Steep slope to start with, and low – don't bang your head.' She bent down, and disappeared into the opening.

With a grimace, he threw away the butt of his cheroot and followed her. The lantern threw odd shadows, but he could see that the shaft led steeply downwards. Someone had made a makeshift handrail from a piece of rope, and wooden slats nailed to the floor at intervals prevented the headlong slither threatened by the loose stones and sand covering it. He caught hold of the rope gratefully, and began to descend.

Bent almost double and hanging onto the rope in Miss Hardy's shadow, he still felt his feet wanting to slip. The shaft was claustrophobically stuffy, the sense of rock all around quite oppressive. Its choking airlessness made it hot as the antechamber of Hell. Da Silva had cooled down a little, but now the sweat was running off him worse than ever.

'How far?' he asked, and his voice boomed and echoed. He had the irrational feeling that the air was going to run out.

'Just here,' said Miss Hardy, reassuringly, indicating a dark opening to the left. This passage was just as low as the first, but at least ran level. After about twelve feet it opened into a square chamber, and Da Silva straightened with a sigh of relief. Both his legs were protesting, not just the injured one. He wiped sweat from his face with one hand, and wiped the hand on his trousers. I never knew I was claustrophobic, he thought.

Miss Hardy put the lantern down on the stone sarcophagus, which was the only thing in the chamber, and turned to him with a smile made grotesque by shadows. Da Silva looked around, struck by how perfectly square the chamber was. The walls were quite unadorned, which disappointed him obscurely.

'No paintings,' he said, constrained to whisper, as though that would conserve the air.

'No,' she agreed. 'But still—!' And he realised that she was just as excited about the find as Ruivo. For himself, he would be glad to get out of this dry, suffocating, dusty, underground place of the dead. The sooner the better.

First, though, there was something he had to do. It had better be there, he thought, and wondered what the hell he would do if it wasn't. That would destroy his credibility, all right. He reached into the sarcophagus, which reminded him of nothing so much as a great stone bath, and picked up the scroll which lay in there, hidden by shadows.

'All right, Miss Hardy,' he said, 'we can go now.'

She clapped a hand to her mouth. 'Omigod,' she exclaimed, eyes wide with surprise, 'how did you know that would be in there?'

'I'll tell you later,' he said. 'Now let's get out of here.'

*

Back in Ruivo's camp, people were stirring. The worst of the noon heat was over now, and the wind was actually managing to bring a little relief. Phoebe Hardy, who turned out to be resident medic as well as the dig's artist, stitched up Da Silva's leg and dusted the wound with sulphur. Ruivo provided clothes of his son's, which proved a reasonable fit, to replace his ruined shirt and trousers. He even managed to have a sort of a wash, though he had to miss out on shaving. There was not enough water for luxuries.

Now he sat under the canopy, leg propped on a stool, smoking and feeling reasonably comfortable for the first time that day, and watching El-Aqman cooing over the papyrus like a mother with a new baby. Beside him, Ruivo hovered like the anxious father, while Miss Hardy showed the captain some of her sketches. There were views of the camp and of people working, as well as detailed drawings of statues, jars and pots. Da Silva looked at her at least as much as he looked at her pictures. From time to time, he noticed, she rubbed her right palm gently. He didn't think she knew she was doing it.

Finishing his cheroot, he tossed the butt out to join the others in the sand. 'I don't think I thanked you for what you did back there,' he said quietly. 'That was very brave of you.' We might not have made it out of there otherwise, he thought.

'It was pathetic,' she said. 'I wanted to pick that sword up and stab that thing, and all I could manage to do was throw it like a silly girl.'

Da Silva took her hand. He was reassuring her, so that was all right. 'You picked it up,' he said. 'Not everyone could have done that. *I* certainly wouldn't want to.'

'Really?'

'Yes, really. Listen, Miss Hardy. These things are . . . inimical. We can't endure their touch. You saw what it did to your hand. Just picking it up was a remarkable thing.'

She let her hand lie in his. 'I think you could call me Phoebe, you know. Since we both—' Saved each other's life, she didn't say. 'Or am I being too forward for you? American women are notorious for that, I'm told.'

'I see,' he said, gravely. 'All *Americanas* are forward, and all sailors are superstitious. Phoebe,' he added at her quizzical expression. I need to stop this, now, he thought, uncomfortably, and scratched the scar on his cheekbone.

'And?' she prompted, raising her dark eyebrows. 'Your name is?'

'I'm sorry. It's Luís.'

'Luís, were those things guarding the papyrus, do you suppose?' He shook his head, frowning thoughtfully.

'I don't think so. Otherwise they would have tried to stop you digging in the first place. I think your workmen were exactly right. That place was their home.' But you don't believe in coincidences, his mind insisted.

'Do you know what they were?' she asked.

'Just what we were told, I suppose,' he replied, grinning without much humour. 'You don't need to know their names to kill them. You know their nature. That's enough. You only have to know a name if you want power over something.'

'How do you know all this?'

Too strongly tempted to kiss her, and knowing she wouldn't object, he looked away. 'I've met this sort of thing before.' He touched his eyepatch. 'That's how this happened.'

Ruivo interrupted them. 'Come and see the scroll, Captain Da Silva.'

He raised an eyebrow at Phoebe and pushed himself to his feet. His leg throbbed angrily, but two steps took him to the table.

Looking over El-Aqman's shoulder, he was struck by the brilliant colours of the papyrus. He had only the sketchiest knowledge of Egyptology. But, like most people, he had seen representations of tomb paintings. To that extent, they were familiar: the stylised stance of the figures, their leaf-shaped eyes. The men with heads of hounds, vultures, snakes, the odd little pictures that were hieroglyphic writing.

'What am I looking at?' he asked.

'*The Book of the Dead*,' Ruivo said. 'Or perhaps not.'

'Perhaps more than that,' El-Aqman supplemented, his deep voice almost preposterous coming from his slight frame. 'Do you know anything at all about ancient Egyptian burial practices, Captain?'

'Only what most people do, I suppose,' Da Silva said, trying to put all his weight on one leg without overbalancing. 'Mummies and so on. Preparing the body for the afterlife.' He remembered something else. 'Pots and food and stuff they thought the dead person would need.' He stuck a finger under his eyepatch and tackled an itch since no one was looking at him. The Egyptian was nodding, but still had his attention fixed on the papyrus.

'Well, Captain, apart from all those grave-goods, every mummy was entombed with a copy of part of the *Book of the Dead*,' he explained, adding with a scholar's pedantic precision, 'That's a misnomer, by the way. Its proper title, *pert em rhu*, means 'coming forth by day' or 'manifested in the light'. It's a guide to the afterlife, spells to help the dead person on his way to paradise. He would have to pass many trials and be judged first.'

A kind of Baedeker Guide for the dead. Da Silva looked down at the papyrus again, as if by staring at it he could decipher the contents. He did not entirely understand the others' fierce fascination with the scroll. 'And that's what this is?'

'That's what we thought it was,' said Ruivo. 'But apart from the content, there's something extremely odd about it.'

'Yes,' El-Aqman agreed, and lifted his head, his dark eyes glinting. 'Despite its very beautiful state of preservation, gentlemen and lady, it is about a thousand years older than the statue in which it was found.'

'What!' exclaimed Phoebe Hardy, getting to her feet and coming to join them. 'That's impossible. Isn't it?'

'In that it ought to have fallen to pieces as soon as Valentim tried to unroll it, yes,' said Ruivo. 'As to what it is, we'll have to wait for Dr El-Aqman to translate it for us.'

'Well, not all of it,' said the Egyptian with a smile. 'That will take weeks. But I should be able to give you some idea of the content by the morning.'

Da Silva slept uneasily in Julião Ruivo's tent, disturbed by dreams of a vaguely crocodilian thing gnawing at his leg, which was not particularly surprising, considering the way the damned thing felt when he woke up. I forget it always feels worse the second day, he thought, fingering the neat bandage gingerly. There was no trace of heat from the wound. He decided this was a good sign. It still took him a while to get himself up from the camp-bed. Getting too old to be gallivanting about in the desert.

Still, the service was better than some *pensãos* he had stayed in. There was a jug of hot water, enough to shave. Someone had mended his shirt. There was even something that passed for coffee. He drank it sitting outside in the tent's shade.

And then all hell broke loose.

He didn't see how it began because he had ducked back inside to finish dressing. But suddenly there was pandemonium in the camp, people rushing to and fro and shouting at the tops of their voices. If that had happened two minutes ago, he thought, buttoning his shirt, I'd have cut myself. As it was, he hadn't even spilt his coffee.

Ruivo, clad in a robe, emerged from his tent like a turtle's head from its shell, blinking, his white tonsure disordered, and grabbed at a passing arm. They were too far away for Da Silva to hear what was said, but at the man's reply, Ruivo swiftly crossed himself. The captain's eyebrows rose. A moment later Phoebe Hardy ran out into the still-cool morning and conferred briefly with the archaeologist. Then both of them turned to look at Da Silva.

I suppose I'd better go and see what's up, he thought, and began to limp towards them. Phoebe met him halfway. 'Dr El-Aqman's dead!' she blurted out.

'Dead?' he repeated stupidly. Get a grip on yourself, he told himself. 'How?'

'We don't know . . . Luís, the papyrus—?' He didn't know whether she was asking him whether it was safe, or whether it was responsible. She turned towards El-Aqman's tent. Ruivo was staring at it, apparently rooted to the spot.

As they watched, an Egyptian whom Da Silva recognised as the doctor's manservant emerged from it and halted abruptly when he came level with the three of them.

'What happened?' Da Silva asked him, in Arabic. The man rolled his eyes.

'Allah knows,' he said. 'You are the *moghrebi*?'

The word, as far as he knew, meant a person who talks to demons. How did *that* get started? he wondered, never surprised at the power of rumour.

'Never mind that,' he said. 'You're sure he's dead?'

Looking at him a bit pityingly, the man drew a finger across his throat. 'Scared to death,' he said, in case Da Silva hadn't got the message. The captain raised an eyebrow and pushed past him into the tent.

Scattered pages of notes met his eye. The papyrus lay on the table. El-Aqman lay on the ground. Flies crawled on his delicate features, which were set in a rictus. Seeing the dead man's expression, he understood the servant's comment. The Egyptian's eyes were wide open, his mouth gaping in a silent scream. His fists were clenched tightly, his body rigid.

Above the corpse, El-Aqman's ghost boiled. There was no other way to describe it. It was a writhing mist as thick as molasses and its surface seethed, as if unable to settle into a coherent form. Half-fascinated, half-appalled, Da Silva touched the man's dead face and found it still warm. He had never encountered such a new ghost before, he realised. A shudder ran down his back and he turned around quickly. There was nothing there, of course.

His leg throbbed fiercely at him as he squatted to gather the fallen papers. He could not read Arabic as well as he spoke it, and the scrawled words meant nothing to him.

Papyrus of Setna. Book/books of Thoth. Tomb of Nefer-ka-Ptah son of Mer-neb-ptah (unknown). In Hermopolis? And again: *Books of Thoth. All-powerful.*

He stared at the scroll on the table as if it were a scorpion, scratching his cheekbone thoughtfully. Then he picked it up as well and ducked under the tent-flap into the strengthening sun.

'Well?' Ruivo said, and Da Silva heard desperation in his voice.

'I think he probably had a seizure,' he said. 'No, don't go in. Here, these are his notes.' He held out the papers.

Ruivo took them from him reluctantly, and began to read. '*Papyrus of Setna.* Very ancient text. Surely—? *Books of Thoth.* Yes. *Tomb of,* yes, where Setna found the magic book. Oh . . . my . . . God.' His mouth dropped open.

'*Books of Thoth?*' Phoebe whispered. They exchanged glances in some kind of mystic communion, which annoyed Da Silva greatly.

'He's implying the papyrus is one of the *Books of Thoth,*' Ruivo explained. 'The spell to control the whole world and gain power over life and death. Supposedly written by the god himself. Thoth. That must be why it's preserved so well.'

'How old is the scroll?' asked Da Silva.

'Four thousand years,' Phoebe replied.

'Wait a minute,' Da Silva said. 'Let's put things in perspective here.' He lit a cheroot. They helped him think. 'Do you believe in the gods of ancient Egypt?'

Do you believe in God? something said to him. He still did, he supposed, though not in the strictly Catholic way he had been brought up. The power of prayer, for one thing, was greatly overrated. And the power of priests too great. Well, some priests, anyway. The one who supplied him with holy water was a good and humble man.

'Not as objects of worship,' said Ruivo irritably. 'What do you take me for? But if demons and evil spirits are real, I'm sure good and benevolent spirits exist. Other than angels, that is. And those may be what the ancient Egyptians worshipped. Akhnaton realised this—'

'And you think one of these "good and benevolent" beings wrote this . . . magic spell?'

With an impatient glance, Ruivo snapped back, 'Why do you find that so hard to believe? What you do is magic.'

'I suppose it is,' Da Silva admitted. 'But you're asking me to believe something a lot more profound than talking to ghosts.'

'Speaking of which,' said the archaeologist, looking slyly from El-Aqman's tent to Da Silva and back again.

Oh no.

'Talking to ghosts?' Phoebe asked in a puzzled voice.

Da Silva rubbed the scar on his eyebrow again. 'That's how I knew where to find the papyrus yesterday.'

'My God,' she said, staring at him as if, he thought crossly, I've grown an extra head. It's not as if nothing unusual happened yesterday! He turned to Ruivo, and expelled smoke.

'And what would you ask the doctor? I can't ask him how he died.'

The archaeologist looked taken aback. 'Well – er—'

'Ask him what he found out?' suggested Phoebe.

'We know that.' Da Silva pointed at El-Aqman's notes.

'These may not be complete,' Ruivo said. '—Yes, what is it?' This to El-Aqman's manservant, who was hovering close by. Nervously, the man gestured towards the tent.

'You have some bureaucracy to deal with,' said Da Silva, glad to deflect Ruivo's determination, even if temporarily.

He walked slowly towards his tent. His leg was aching and he needed to sit down for a while. In addition, the sun was gathering strength rapidly, and he had left his hat inside. Damned desert, he thought wearily, not relishing the thought of a repeat performance of the previous day's furnace heat. As far as he was concerned, the proper place for sand was on the sea-bed.

Finding the patch of shadow in front of the tent had shrunk away, he carried on until he reached the communal canopy. The boy Ahmed was sweeping its canvas floor, and grinned widely when he saw Da Silva.

'Is there any more of that coffee?' the captain asked him.

'Yes, boss. For both?'

Looking round, he saw that Phoebe had followed him. He mimed drinking coffee at her, and she called, 'Sure.' Ahmed, correctly interpreting her tone if not the expression, scuttled off.

'Tell me about the *Book of Thoth*,' Da Silva said, sitting down gratefully.

She didn't reply at once, but sat down herself and drew a few deep breaths. A tear leaked out of her eye and she brushed it away impatiently.

Damning himself for his insensitivity, Da Silva stood up again.

Winced as pain shot along his leg. Went and put a hand on her shoulder.

Phoebe came awkwardly into his arms, chokingly trying not to cry. He held her, regretfully, for a long minute, smelling the clean scent of her hair, and then she disengaged with an attempt at a smile.

'Thanks,' she said. 'Sorry to get all weepy on you.'

'*De nada*,' he said absently, remembering her wielding her flimsy parasol like a rapier, flinging the *afrit*'s unclean sword at it. Coming out of that calm as if she'd been at a tea party. He would never understand women. Come to that, a lot of men did incomprehensible things as well.

'I didn't even like him very much,' she confided, blowing her nose. 'He was too – smarmy, if you know what I mean. A lot of Egyptian men get that way over women. The ones that don't think I'm a brazen harlot for wearing trousers, that is,' she added, her smile less forced this time.

At that moment, Ahmed came back with the coffee. Da Silva passed him a cheroot and found the boy looking at him curiously. He raised an eyebrow at him.

'Is it true you killed an *afrit* yesterday, boss?' he asked.

With difficulty, Da Silva restrained himself from laughing. 'Two,' he said. 'Now shove off.'

The urchin laughed in delight, and scampered away. Da Silva resumed his seat and picked up his coffee. It tasted a bit like ground mud, but it was preferable to beer at eight in the morning.

'Cigarette?' Phoebe asked, offering him her case. 'Or do you always smoke those awful things?' Oh, why not, he thought. I wonder how many years it is since I smoked a cigarette? Her lighter flared, and he sat back, carefully stretching out his injured leg.

'The papyrus?' he reminded her.

'Yes. Of course,' she said. 'Well, there are several references to *Books of Thoth*. Dr El-Aqman seems to think this is one called the papyrus of Setna. He was the son of the pharaoh Rameses the Second, and he was a magician. He was said to have found this book in a tomb in the necropolis at Memphis. The book had two very powerful spells in it. Now, the man who told him where to find it warned him that taking it away would be a bad idea, but old Setna did it anyhow. And he got the power he wanted, but he had such a miserable life that he eventually decided to put the book back where he found it and seal up the tomb again.'

Tasteless. He knew it would be. But he went on smoking it. 'Memphis is near Cairo, isn't it?' he said. Six hundred miles away.

'Yes, that's true. But the pharaoh whose tomb it was in hasn't been identified. But if it was found once, it could be found again. Maybe whoever found it next just didn't have Setna's scruples.'

Like Ruivo, she became more animated when talking about her favourite topic. 'Do you know whose tomb it was you found?' he asked her.

'We think her name was *Meryt-ankh*,' she replied. Pausing to extinguish her half-smoked cigarette, she looked up at him speculatively. 'Luís.'

'Yes?'

'Can you really speak to ghosts?'

He nodded, his face expressionless. 'It's a talent I could live without.'

'Could you speak to hers? Meryt-ankh's? In the tomb?'

Oh, God, yes, I suppose I could, he thought, remembering the claustrophobic chamber with distaste.

'She's been dead a very long time,' he pointed out. 'It might not be possible. And we can't speak her language.'

'Dr El-Aqman could,' Phoebe said.

Cigarette halfway to his mouth, he stared at her, a dozen thoughts warring in his mind. Eventually he said bleakly, 'You're a single-minded bunch of people, aren't you?' and stubbed out the cigarette in the tin ashtray.

Da Silva, fortified if not mollified by a shot of arrack provided by Ruivo, sighed deeply and lit a cheroot to take the taste away. It had been more like drinking turpentine than anything potable. I'm fated to drink bad brandy all over the world, he thought. Looking around cautiously, trying to avoid the strong, sandy breeze, he slipped into the doctor's tent. Phoebe and Ruivo hovered outside, supposedly standing guard but looking, he decided mordantly, more like the comic henchmen of a villain in a melodrama.

El-Aqman's body had been transferred to the camp-bed. It was still clenched in rigor. The Egyptian's ghost, now a calm drift of transparent mist in the air, also lingered. In fact it would linger there for the rest of time, growing fainter as the years went by. It, like all the shades which were Da Silva's near-constant companions, was merely an echo. An image. No more than a flickering nickelodeon film. The ghosts he summoned were another matter entirely.

He would have to be quick, he knew. But calling ghosts – necromancy was a term he didn't care for – wasn't exactly the sort of thing that came with an instruction book. Well, maybe it did, but he had no intention of consulting that kind of text. Ever. He had also never tried to summon the recent dead before.

His long knife was resting in its usual place, a sheath down his back, though not concealed. But he wanted to try something else before drawing blood, feeling, not unreasonably, that he had already shed enough.

Unsure as to whether it would work, he put his hand on El-Aqman's dead forehead. It felt like cold stone.

'Dr Hassan El-Aqman,' he said softly. The name echoed strangely in the tent. How could canvas echo? A shock ran up his arm, and he jerked his hand away, suspiciously eyeing the corpse.

Which sat up and stared at him.

He choked on smoke, and El-Aqman spoke. 'So, Captain, now I know why they call you *moghrebi*.' His voice was much like it had been in life, but somehow hollower, without substance.

'Only if you style yourself a demon,' he said. The ghost, he now saw, had come to a sitting position *out* of the Egyptian's body. It looked like an ill-defined pair of Siamese twins.

El-Aqman's ghost looked amused and freed himself from his corpse, swinging his feet over the side of the cot and standing in one fluid movement. 'Come now, Captain. You summon ghosts, and you slay *afrits*. And more, I sense. What are you but a sorcerer?' Da Silva blinked, unable to think of a good retort to this, and wiped a drop of sweat from his cheek. 'So why have you summoned me?'

You don't know everything, then, do you? Da Silva said silently. 'They want you to talk to someone named Meryt-ankh.'

This time the ghost laughed. 'You think you can summon a shade so old? Well, Captain, maybe you can. And maybe I can speak with her. But will she answer?'

'Will you?' asked Da Silva, and El-Aqman winced.

'If I can,' he said. 'I am yours to command.' Now it was Da Silva's turn to grimace. 'Ah, you have little liking for that notion, I see. Perhaps you are a man of the light after all.'

Intrigued as he was by this definition, Da Silva felt the pressure of passing time. 'Tell me, then,' he said, 'is the papyrus the *Book of Thoth*?'

'It is *a* Book of Thoth,' replied the ghost, looking amused again.

'Da Silva!' came Ruivo's voice, urgent and petulant. 'Hurry up, man.'

'Ah, the impatient Mister Ruivo,' El-Aqman said. 'Is this your command also?'

Glaring at him, Da Silva said, 'Yes, come on, let's go.'

Outside, the sun hammered down. Waves of scorching air rolled off the sand, and the light was as intense as the heat, bright as a phosphorus flame. There was no one around the camp. Apart from Ruivo and Phoebe, it could have been a city of the dead.

Shading his brow and feeling sweat break out along his hairline, Da Silva put on his hat. Phoebe, having lost her parasol, had resorted to a headcloth.

El-Aqman looked down at his spectral body curiously. 'I never imagined a ghost would look so solid,' he remarked in a conversational tone. 'But then, I never believed ghosts existed in the first place.'

By the time they reached the gully again, Da Silva's clothes were soaked. His knife chafed. Sweat was running off him, not to mention collecting under his eyepatch. His leg ached fiercely, and the cut on his arm was stinging. Cursing under his breath, he sat down in the shade and repeated his boot-excavation. Phoebe borrowed his hat and fanned herself.

'I am impressed, Captain,' El-Aqman's ghost said. 'Not a trace of *afrits*. Not that I credited such things when I was alive, of course.'

Da Silva put his boots back on and wiped his face with his sleeve. 'Let's get on with it,' he said grimly. *Before I change my mind and tell the whole pack of you to go to hell.*

He sent the ghost down the shaft first, followed it with knife in hand, because he felt safer that way. Phoebe, holding one of the lanterns, came third, and Ruivo brought up the rear, carrying the other. Their shadows, caught by the light, waxed and waned as they descended.

The sultry, airless chamber was no more bearable on second acquaintance, even though Da Silva knew what to expect this time. He scratched his scar, supposing that it was logical for a seaman to find confined spaces oppressive. And especially confined spaces hundreds of miles from the nearest ocean. Suddenly he desired, very strongly, the sea's clean smell, a fresh clear wind. The sounds of ropes and canvas.

Two living people and one dead one watched as he placed his knife on the empty sarcophagus and rolled up his shirt-sleeves. It was the ghost who spoke.

'That's a formidable weapon, Captain,' he said. 'What do you use it for?'

'Killing *afrits*,' said Da Silva shortly. 'Amongst other things.' He wanted a smoke, and wished he had taken the opportunity to light up before charging down here. Too late now. 'Well,' he said. 'Better get on with it. Are you ready, El-Aqman?' The ghost nodded.

Picking up the knife again, he held his right arm over the gaping tomb and nicked the wrist, almost catching a small white scar. He was better at it this time. Just a couple of drops of blood fell into the sarcophagus.

'Meryt-ankh,' he said.

And knew instantly that he had summoned a magician. They did not come easily. They resented being bound to his will. Which was understandable. The underground chamber shuddered and dust cascaded from the ceiling. His heart thumped at the sudden dread of entombment. A wave travelled across the stone floor, sending Ruivo reeling. Phoebe grabbed at the wall, Da Silva the edge of the shivering tomb . . .

. . . Out of which came a roaring sandstorm, filling the chamber, obstructing sight, deafeningly loud. It roiled above the sarcophagus, dark as a thundercloud, howling. The air itself was fighting him. Sweat poured off his face, but he couldn't pause to wipe it away. He shouted her name again, and the pressure seemed to ease a little, the wind to calm, to take shape. And so he said it a third time, and stilled the storm.

Standing on the other side of the sarcophagus from Da Silva was a woman's figure. She was tall, and quite plump. Having subconsciously expected her to look like the slim figures of the papyrus, he was oddly disappointed. Her robe was white, severely plain, but cut to display a generous amount of cleavage. The cloth was thin enough that her nipples showed through. Round her neck was a wide collar of beads and gold.

El-Aqman spoke and she turned towards him, her face distorted like a Fury. Meryt-ankh's voice thundered in Da Silva's mind, battering at him. Her lips did not move. Her voice intruded on him, a trespasser in his head.

I am the sorceress Meryt-ankh. I do not need shades of men. Begone. She made a brief gesture, and El-Aqman's ghost turned into a pillar of white flame. From behind him, Phoebe gasped. He hardly heard her. Controlling this ghost was like trying to steer a ship in a hurricane. *All my old servants are gone. I have had to seek new ones. Only Am-mut, devourer of souls, still waits. Where are my guardians?*

'Your guardians are dead,' he said hoarsely, and lifted his knife with an effort. The ancient ghost eyed it warily.

By your hand. What do you want, necromancer?

'What is the papyrus?' he asked.

'Is it the *Book of Thoth*?' Ruivo added, having apparently still not learnt to keep his mouth shut around ghosts.

The sorceress laughed, and it was terrible to hear, like the tolling of monstrous iron bells. *You think to use the spells of the god, mortal? They will rebound on you, seventy times seven. Return me the papyrus.*

Da Silva's arm ached with the effort of holding the knife. Sweat ran into his eye, down his temples, dripped off his nose. The air was becoming foul. His leg throbbed. His entire body hurt with the strain of mastering Meryt-ankh. And his soul, too, he thought. 'You can threaten,' he forced out the words, 'but what can you do? Nothing.'

She opened her mouth and white-hot flame roared out, bright as the sun, too fierce to look at. He looked down, away from it, and brought the knife up. It took both hands to lift it. The flame broke against the blade, and died. But he staggered back with the force of it, and would have fallen to his knees but for Phoebe grabbing him. The sorceress's ghost watched. *Very good, little man,* came her voice in his head.

'I think,' he said breathlessly to Phoebe, 'you should put the papyrus back and seal up this tomb.'

'No,' said Ruivo.

She rounded on him. 'What about Julião? What about your son?' she asked. 'Luís, ask her if—'

I know the woman's thoughts. I am not unmerciful. Return me the papyrus, and her lover will recover.

'I'm not—' said Phoebe indignantly.

The dead shall not live again, but all else shall be as it was.

Breathing was getting difficult now. The sorceress's power pushed him back until he reached the wall. He rather wished he could burrow into it. The knife weighed as much as a man. His arms were trembling with the strain of holding it.

Out of the corner of his eye he saw Phoebe make her way towards Ruivo, moving slowly, as if walking into a gale. She tried to wrest the scroll from his hand. He resisted her. 'I won't let you,' he shouted. His voice seemed to come from a long distance away.

Da Silva strained against the power. It had stuck him to the wall like a butterfly on a pin. His only lifeline was the knife he held out in front of him, which the sorceress's ghost could not pass. His sight was fuzzing from exhaustion.

Phoebe finally succeeded in wrenching the papyrus from Ruivo and started to struggle towards the sarcophagus. Da Silva, transfixed, saw the archaeologist pull a revolver from his pocket and slowly raise it. He opened his mouth to warn her, but no sound came out.

Let it be, necromancer. Meryt-ankh raised her hand again and turned towards Ruivo. Da Silva slid down the wall into a crouch, and braced his shaking elbows on his knees to maintain his knife's upright position. Pain flared up his leg and he let out an involuntary grunt.

Ruivo fired the gun. Echoes bounced off the walls until it sounded like an artillery barrage. At the same moment Meryt-ankh made a throwing motion towards him. The bullet exploded in mid-air.

And then Ruivo exploded as well, something bursting out of his chest in a confusion of blood and bone. Phoebe staggered to the sarcophagus and dropped the papyrus inside and Meryt-ankh smiled.

The lanterns went out. In their after-image Da Silva thought he saw a beast, something like a crocodile, snap up whatever had erupted from Ruivo. And then in the sudden blackness he fancied he heard something feeding.

Darkness. Blind, utter, complete. Night could not be called dark in comparison. He fought down panic, searched for matches, found none. The blackness pressed on him, like a heavy, suffocating blanket.

'Phoebe?' He could hear her breathing shallowly.

'Yes,' came her shaky voice. Was there anything else there?

'Cigarette-lighter.'

'Oh . . . of course.' It clicked, then clicked again. 'Come on.' Then flared, showing her pale face. She re-lit one of the lanterns. It burned dimly, reminding Da Silva there was little air left, as if he needed reminding. Staring around wildly, he saw only Ruivo's crumpled body. He went to wipe sweat from his face, found he was still clutching his knife. The handle had dug grooves into his palm. Blood from his other wrist made it sticky.

Unsteady, he pulled himself to his feet and limped across to examine the archaeologist. He turned the body over with his foot, dreading what he might find. And found no mark on it.

'What was it? That came out of him?' Phoebe whispered.

'I think it was his soul,' said Da Silva. 'Come on, we have to get out of here.' Something was tugging urgently at him. He didn't ignore such warnings.

She stood her ground, still staring at the archaeologist's dead body. 'But – what about Mister Ruivo?'

'He's dead, Phoebe, now come on!' He grabbed her hand, but she stooped, obstinately, feeling for a pulse in Ruivo's neck.

'He's cold!' she exclaimed. And then looked up at the ceiling, her eyes widening as a tremor shook the chamber.

The next minute they were running down the passage, gasping for breath, the lantern swaying wildly in Phoebe's hand, as stones and dust rained down. His leg erupted with pain at every step. There was a rumbling, like thunder yet somehow unlike. Thunder is a thing of the air. This was a noise of stone, of earth, of magma's slow seethe in the planet's core. It was almost too deep to hear, but its resonance was chilling.

As Da Silva followed Phoebe's headlong rush into the sloping shaft, and the relief of fresher air, the tunnel collapsed with a roar, spewing out a billowing cloud to engulf them. They scrambled up the shaking conduit, slipping and slithering on the loose stones and debris, and he blessed whoever had put in the climbing aids. Debris and stone fragments shook loose around them, and Phoebe cried out as a chunk of rock hit her on the head. She hung onto the rope, but the lantern plummeted past Da Silva, narrowly missing him, and shattered on the tumbled stone below. The oil ignited in a brief flare, and died.

But they were nearly at the top. Phoebe flung herself out into the daylight and he followed a split second later. They staggered a few steps down the gully, and then his leg gave way. He collapsed in the cool sand, sucking in great breaths of air, and sensed Phoebe on her knees beside him, doing the same.

The earth convulsed again, like a huge beast shaking a troublesome insect off its skin. This was followed by a deep rumble, and dust puffed out of the entrance to the shaft. The timber baulks shoring it up cracked and fell, and a few stones and a small cascade of earth rattled down the cliff-face. Then everything was still.

Blood streamed down Phoebe's face from a shallow cut on her brow, splitting a swelling bruise in half. Da Silva mopped it with her headcloth.

'I'll do yours if you do mine,' she said, putting her hand on his knee.

The following day, the walking wounded – as Da Silva thought of them – visited Julião Ruivo in his hospital bed to break the news of his father's death.

Julião was a cheerful-looking young man of around thirty who presumably favoured his mother, since there seemed to be no paternal resemblance at all. Da Silva watched the two younger people somewhat indulgently. Phoebe may have denied the sorceress's insight, but he thought it might turn out to be a prophecy.

'I'm so sorry about your father,' Phoebe was saying to Julião, holding his hand. Like the forward *Americana* she called herself, he thought with an inward smile. 'That they should both die so close to each other . . .'

'We were never very close,' said Ruivo's son. 'Still, it is strange . . . and Dr El-Aqbar as well . . .' His voice trailed off. He was still weak from his illness.

'Call it the curse of Meryt-ankh,' said Da Silva, from the window.

'Description of the beast Am-mut: Her forepart is like that of a crocodile, the middle of her body is like that of a lion, her hindquarters are like those of a hippopotamus.'

                                                                    The Book of the Dead

Chico Kidd has been writing ghost stories since 1979 under the name of A. F. Kidd, a choice influenced by classic writers such as M. R. James, E. F. Benson and others. Her fiction has been published in such small-press magazines as *Ghosts & Scholars*, *Dark Dreams*, *Peeping Tom*, *Enigmatic Tales*, *All Hallows*, and the anthologies *The Mammoth Book of Best New Horror*, *The Mammoth Book of Ghost Stories 2*, *Vampire Stories*, three volumes of Karl Edward Wagner's *The Year's Best Horror Stories* and the hardcover volume of *Ghosts & Scholars*. Almost all the short stories were finally collected together in one volume by Ash-Tree Press as *Summoning Knells and Other Inventions*. Her first novel *The Printer's Devil* was published in 1995 by Baen Books (under the name of Chico Kidd rather than A. F.), and a volume of collaborations with Rick Kennett, featuring William Hope Hodgson's character Carnacki the Ghost-Finder, were recently collected by Ash-Tree as *Number 472 Cheyne Walk*. In September 2000, a Portuguese sea-captain called Luís Da Silva barged into a story called 'Cats and Architecture' (published in *Supernatural Tales 2*) and demanded to have his story told. Since then he has appeared in nine more short stories and two and a half novels which are currently under consideration. 'This story came into being because I wanted to see if I could write an Egyptian archaeology tale without featuring mummies at all,' admits the author. 'There are no special anecdotes about this particular story but there is a curious coincidence apropos the Da Silva stories as a whole. When I found I was going to be writing a lot about the Captain, I thought it would be a good idea to learn Portuguese. In the course of this I discovered the wonderful (and Nobel Prize-winning) author José Saramago. His first novel, *Manual de Pintura e Caligrifia* (*Manual of Painting & Calligraphy*) features a character called Chico who also works in advertising, and also mentions a writer named Luís da Silva. Make of that what you will.'

Midday People

TANITH LEE

I

The Ancient Romans had called noon the Ghost Hour. She had been told this, or read it, but could not remember why. The Italian light perhaps, she thought, staring out across the square. It took away the shadows, it bleached and turned the buildings to flat gold, and any people walking there, they were golden too, and without physical depth.

Unlike Chrissie, sitting under the dark pink umbrella of the café table. She could never tan; she even found it quite hard to *burn*.

'It's fucking hot,' observed Craig.

Chrissie turned to him attentively. 'Yes, it is.'

'And that food. Too heavy. Oily. I'm going in for a lie-down. Or a throw-up. Whatever comes first.'

She thought probably it was the *amount* of food he had consumed, rather than its type (surely even Craig had known that Italy meant pastas and cheeses and olive oil). Also the two bottles of red wine they had drunk between them. Although he did not like wine.

'Oh, I'm sorry,' she brightly said. 'Yes, of course. Let's go in. It's almost siesta time, isn't it?'

'God, get your facts straight. Not yet.'

'Oh, I see.' He could be right or wrong, but was right of course. And she, stupid.

As they rose, she imagined the few people around them might think the English couple were going in so soon because they were eager for fervent holiday sex. This was not at all the case. Craig would indeed go straight to sleep, lumpen on his bed, his thick short sweaty hair plastered to the pillow. She would lie on the bed next to his, and look up at the curious patterns of pale stains in the white ceiling. She was, after three days at the little hotel, getting to know these stains. She tried to make them into something interesting (childishly attempting to enjoy even this). Then, adult, she would try to go to sleep instead. But she was always awake, wide, wide awake.

At about five, Craig would himself wake, lumber into the bathroom and piss, grumbling, angry at his leaden head. At the room. At the hotel for something – some noise that had irritated him, a fly that might have got in, Italy, Italians. Her.

As they crossed the square, Chrissie looked longingly over at the church, with its biscuity façade and carved doorway. She wanted to go to the church, look inside, maybe attend a service even, decorous, with a scarf respectfully tied over her hair. She was not religious, yet she would like to do that, here. And she would like to walk round the town, go out into the countryside, admire the olive trees and the vineyards in the dust-haze, the round hills with villas tucked up on them under old red roofs—

So far, they had not done much. They had seen more of the hotel than anything else.

Why had he wanted to come, she wondered? Oh, that was easy really, he had been showing off to a colleague when he produced the idea of the trip. More to the point, why had Craig wanted Chrissie to come with him?

They were only in their thirties. They had only been together, that is lived together, for two years. It had never been much good. They both worked, but he considered what she did with her group of decorators to be 'fey' and useless. 'Tarting up the houses of rich cunts,' was Craig's term for it. Meanwhile his high-powered job kept him out a lot, drinking and eating with his clients. Coming back, he had no time for her, yet expected, as a man much older might have done, the flat cleaned and, if he had not had a meal, one ready. If this meal was then not to his taste, he told her so. Usually it was not.

She had tried, blaming herself, making excuses for him.

But by now she wondered why they stayed together. Fear she supposed, on her side. She was in looks thin and ordinary, and before Craig, had had very little interest taken in her by men. As for him, probably she was convenient. One day some other woman would appear on the scene and sweep him off. And Chrissie dreaded the inevitable shame. But then, it might not happen, because Craig was no catch himself. Not very tall, heavy and thickset and now, from all the wining and dining, getting extra chins and quite a belly, his small-eyed, discontented face had no compensatory attractions, his voice grated, and his personality was – well, what?

Void, she thought.

And, humiliated as he pushed rudely in front of her into the side street, almost shoving her out of the way, she pretended instead to have stopped on purpose to look at something. And she cursed herself. All this should end. He loathed her. Surely there might be one man in the world, someone with low enough standards, who might care for her, actually like her, find her talented and appealing despite her 32 B bra-size and her limp dull hair? And even if there was no one – could she truly not manage on her own? Probably, if she suggested they part, he would shout for joy. Only it was all so complicated now – the flat in both their names, the joint account and – coward, coward, she thought.

And—

saw that, pretending to look at something, she *was* actually looking. *Staring*. Back across the square. At two people, there by the fountain. Two golden people, glittering in the middle-of-the-day light bright as the scattering water.

Oh, typical Italian young, gorgeously clad in their shining youth. *Am I jealous or simply having a religious experience?*

She could not take her eyes off them. And they, in their perfect new-minted world would never notice, so it was quite all right.

They wore jet-black shades. His hair was as black, and the girl's was corn-blonde, like the bars of sunlight. Their clothes, smart, white, or simply whitened by the glare – the bare arms strong and graceful, the long throats and mouths that had not lost, like fruits, their juice—

She was in love with both of them. And really, they were not so young. No. They did not wear the fashions one saw the young put on everywhere – yet wealthy they must be. They glowed with health and money, as with light.

Something made Chrissie glance along the side street after Craig. Walking away, he had either not noticed he had lost her, or else he was entirely indifferent. Either way, it meant much the same. In the shadow that did not fall from anything, but simply amassed in the channel of the narrow street because the sun had not got into it, Craig looked extremely thick. Physically, that was. Too solid, as if he were trying to prove his existence, his importance; opaque as a block of stone.

Chrissie looked back towards her beautiful ones. They were still there, not speaking, leaning at the fountain's rim, oblivious of the water spotting their flawless garments and skin. Lizards, she thought, golden lizards from another planet.

And then both their heads turned, and *they* looked, each of them, right at her, through their inky shades.

Chrissie felt herself colour. ''*Scusi*,' she muttered. Her Italian was hopeless and virtually non-existent – and anyway, they could not hear her from this distance.

She turned herself, quickly, and walked after Craig into the thunder-shade of the street.

By the time she reached the hotel, Craig was nowhere to be seen.

'Has my husband gone up?' she asked the man hovering at reception. She said it happily, as if this loving 'husband' and she had been separated by unavoidable circumstance, and arranged to meet again, lover-like, in the erotic seclusion above.

The man agreed the *signore* had taken the key and gone upstairs.

Chrissie began to walk towards the stairs. They would take longer, and also provide a little exercise. She had nearly reached them when she hesitated. She fumbled in her bag, pretending to search for something without which she could not go up. She could not face it. Not again, lying so close to Craig and a hundred miles from him, divided by wine, sleep and his utter antipathy.

She would not cry. *God, don't let me cry.*

Oh the hell with it, cry if you want, she thought, this is Italy not bloody Cheltenham.

Oddly, the urge to cry at once receded.

Across from her she noticed the bar, open and airy, the now-one-thirty light streaming in over small marble tables and rococo chairs. Above the counter, every bottle had become a lamp with a flame of sun blazing inside, green lamps and scarlet ones, indigo and apricot.

Should she, after the wine?

Apparently she should. She was *in* the bar, and now another, smiling man approached, with coal-black curls, and she ordered her drink from him, a large vodka, not especially Italian at all, but when it came, dressed in its glass, it was an Italian vodka, with Italian ice.

The room was empty, save for herself and the barman. She sat drinking slowly, looking out into the street to which the sun had now miraculously soaked through. She wondered how that was. In the light, everything sprang alive out there, the burnt sienna of walls, the terracotta roofs, the red and rose geraniums—

Chrissie put down her glass and shrank back into the little chair. Caught in a window, there on the street, *They*. They idled by the bar, past the hotel, framed in sun and geraniums. Her Beings from the fountain.

She named them abruptly, she did not know why, Arrigo and Gina. Arrigo and Gina moved over the windows, one window after another, making each window wonderful a moment. Then they were beyond the last window. Where were they going?

It was the vodka of course which made Chrissie get up. She walked hurriedly from the bar now, back across the hotel lobby, out into the street – as if to an appointment. Not with an unmarried husband in a loveless bedroom, but to something – strange, inexplicable, crazy, *terrible*.

What was she doing? This was stupid. She stood in the street, looking along it, the way they must have gone. The sun scorched now directly down on her – and yet, shadows were beginning to come back, yes, creeping like spilled darkness from the edges of things.

Chrissie started to walk rather fast along the street. A merry dog ran by. Some children were laughing in a doorway. In a yard a fair young man perched on a stationary Lambretta, and a fair girl, hand on hip, hair streaming. But these were not They.

When she reached the street's end, a huddle of buildings stood around a space with a tall tree, perhaps a plane, and the shadows were coming – but nothing else. She had lost them, lost Arrigo and Gina. And that was just as well. What would they have said to her, *done* to her, with those slimly muscled bronze arms, those cruel serpentine-fruited tongues – some torrent of abuse and a calling of *polizia*? What was she, some stalker?

She braced herself to retreat. Precisely then she became aware of them once more.

It was almost as if they had not been there until she made the (mental) move to give up, which was absurd.

And they waited – were they *waiting*? – at the mouth of an alleyway, where a bunting of gaudy washing hung, doubtless deceptive to the eyes. But they – once more they were staring back at her. Chrissie felt a wave of fright and dismay, and next second – they were sliding away from her, as if they stood on a platform with wheels – how could that be? And the washing and the alley were all she could see.

Astonished, she found she bolted forward, she also on wheels attached to *their* wheels . . . And running across the space, under the deep metallic flags of the plane tree, right up to the alley mouth, and there, only there, she stopped, as if – ended. For they were not to be seen any more. Finally they had eluded her and slipped away.

Lovers, she thought. Let them alone.

I must be mad, she thought.

She felt sick, but it went off. Then she only felt ludicrous and shaken, as if she had fallen over on the cobbled street and made a fool of herself. By that time it was just after two o'clock, and in the square the church bell was ringing.

II

By the evening Craig was very hungry and needed, he said, a stiff drink. So they went out, but only back to the small restaurant in the street the other side of the square, which they had visited every night so far. Craig ate voluminously, but without enjoyment. It was Chrissie who complimented the waiter on the very good food. They – Craig – drank a lot of alcohol. Chrissie watched the bottles and the brandies mount up. She was unable herself to eat or drink much.

When they came out, the evening had arrived and filled the street and square with soft blue ashes, lit by the gentle globes of old-fashioned wrought-iron lamp-standards. People were there who strolled arm in arm, gladly together – plump matrons with young dark eyes, benevolent men in shirtsleeves, and many Romeos with their Juliets.

'Isn't it a lovely evening – shall we—'

'You do what you want. I have to see to some work.'

'Work.' Her voice sounded flat and childishly silly.

'You don't think I can just laze about like you, do you? Where do you think the money came from for this jaunt? Not your pathetic little rich-cunt-pleasing rubbish. No way.' Craig explained/told her that now he would go up to their room and make some international calls on the firm's mobile. He would also, she knew, order a bottle of brandy or whisky to go with this, and smoke a pack of Marlborough. If she stayed with him then, in the cramped bedroom, that was it: a desert storm of smoke and fumes and his important voice talking loud across continents. She knew, because this was how it went at home.

'Okay,' she said. Neutral. 'I'll just—'

'Get on with it then. Do something on your own for a change.' And he left her, standing there.

She poised in the square, pretending they had planned all this beforehand. She watched the couples going round and round her, talking to other couples or groups seated at outside tables, all under the great wild-eyed stars that were swarming in the sky and the coloured lightbulbs that were coming on. Music sounded, a horn, a mandolin, then an accordion, perhaps from a radio, or from some unseen orchestra. And the carousel of loving couples were dancing, some of them, though not the younger ones, who strutted to and fro like warriors who will always win their war. Or some swayed into the shadows, and two became one.

Chrissie thought abruptly of Arrigo and Gina. But that was not true. She had been thinking of them all the time.

She walked to the lunch café and found a little table going spare, just inside. She ordered an espresso to bring her round.

Of course, she had been looking out for them, even if she had not admitted as much. At the restaurant, out of the restaurant windows, in the square and streets both going and coming back.

Other men and girls were by the fountain now, splashing each other with its spray, amused, and drinking cola.

Had she ever done that? Ever, ever? On frigid English nights?

There had been summers, so perhaps. But always it was done in disappointment, sadness, alone, then as now.

Stop it. Have some coffee. Forget all that.

Chrissie drank her coffee.

Outside, the darkness grew darker. There was absolutely no sign of Arrigo or Gina. Obviously they had only been passing through and were now gone, in a slim white car, back to some extraordinary other place, some sparkling city, some villa on the navy blue hills, strung with lights, a vivacious party, or a deep bed.

Not until it was ten o'clock did Chrissie return to the hotel. She idled even then, and in the street, not at all dark now with its ornamental streetlamps, wondered if she might be mugged, an unattractive woman loitering by herself in the night. But the night was not dangerous, not here.

When she got back to their room, Craig had annexed the bath. She took the opportunity to open windows. Moths would fly in and he would shout at her, but that was better than the stench he had created.

She thought about throwing his mobile phone from the window and down on the cobbled courtyard below, between the pots of roses and lavender. But she did not.

All she did was undress and get into the twin bed which he had told her, on the first night, was hers.

She thought she would take a long while to get to sleep, especially after the espresso, but her encoffeed heart drummed her excitedly fast from wakefulness.

She regained consciousness, surprised, in the centre of the night, and saw Craig's bulk, like some mountain she could never get over.

The windows were once more shut. Yet when she went to clean her teeth, some silvery thing sang. Was it a nightingale?

She had been dreaming – of what? She wanted to recall. Then she remembered a man in the dream, an old man, who had emerged from the carousel of dance in the square, and said to her, 'Why do you think we take luncheon, and make siesta, at those hours? To keep us safe off the streets and the squares.'

How puzzling. What a peculiar dream – but dreams were *dreams*.

Craig rumbled in his slumber like a train, or an approaching earthquake, and then was silent again, as if even to snore would be to offer her too much companionship.

The next day she asked if they might go to the city. She had always wanted to see the cathedral. Also, could they not browse in the shops, visit the museum – the Roman ruins of a circus? 'Well, go,' he said. 'Why do I have to hold your hand?'

'But I thought you wanted—'

'This jaunt was your idea. I'm just the one paying for it.'

I am paying for it too, she thought.

And then, *is* it my fault? Have I dragged him here against everything he wanted? He can, after all, drink brandy and whisky and make calls at home. I'm inadequate. Should I have come on my own? But then he would have complained because the flat was dirty and no one did the shopping . . . And he's told me I can't cope, not on my own. Yes, I'm a fool. I do see that. I make a mess of things.

She recollected how Craig had criticised her choice in music. He only liked classical music – 'What else is there? That? That's not music.' But then too, only certain classics were all right. Bach, and Mozart. Rachmaninov, apparently, was a load of 'soapy crap', and Bartók and Prokofiev 'certifiably insane'. Sometimes Craig played Wagner at top volume, and the flat shook, and twice a neighbour had come to remonstrate, and Chrissie, trembling, had had to deal with this, before the neighbour gave up on reason, and began instead to retaliate with the most appallingly bad loud pop music at all hours of the day and night.

After recalling all that, Chrissie shook herself and went out into the street and meandered towards the square. She had tried to talk herself into hiring a cab to take her to the city, but her Italian was so poor – *he* spoke it quite fluently, though his accent was not good, so sometimes people would seem bemused: 'Fucking cretins,' deduced Craig. Even so, he could usually make them understand, could understand *them*. He had told her on her own she would be a laughing-stock, monetarily cheated, perhaps physically attacked, in the city. Told her all that before he told her to go alone.

Chrissie sat at the table under the dark pink umbrella.

She had drunk two glasses of rough white wine and was thinking, if the city cathedral was out of bounds, she might try to see the church across the square.

But she kept glancing at her watch. As if she were waiting for someone. Who?

She knew who exactly.

And now the watch said 12:00 am.

No one much was in the square. Like yesterday, and the days before.

A stooped man scurried over it, darting from one side to the other, as if evading enemy surveillance. A woman went by with baskets, walking fast, disappearing into a doorway.

Those that were here seemed to cling to the square's edges, the outdoor tables closest to the three cafés, the steps of the church. It was completely relaxed, reasonable. Sensible to avoid the midday sun, the blare of trumpets in heaven that continued from noon until two—

Chrissie finished the last of her wine. As she put down her glass, she saw, through the base, the stem, the globe of it—

They were there. Her Beings. Arrigo, Gina.

By the fountain, as before.

She had not seen them enter the square, missed it, as she had the going-away of the boys who had been sitting smoking on the church steps, and the people from nearby tables.

How very odd. It had not been this way yesterday, had it? She – and They – were alone in the square.

Alone in the light, the glistening, glistering gold.

Golden Arrigo, with his crow-wing of hair, golden Gina, with her lemon, Botticelli Venus hair, and herself, Chrissie, a small nothingness taking up (and wasting) a tiny bit of space.

Don't stare. For God's sake.

She lowered her eyes.

In the side of the wine glass, however, she saw them still. They were moving now, out of the square. She felt a pang of loss. Where were they going? The same destination as yesterday? *Stay put. Don't get up.*

Chrissie found she had got to her feet, and tried to discover an excuse for this. While she was doing that, again she glimpsed them, how they paused. And then – it was irresistible – she looked at them again.

Made of spun crystal, coloured like Murano glass.

Perfect.

They were gazing back at her through their sunglasses. *At Chrissie.*

And then, infinitesimal, perhaps imagined, the slight motion of their two heads, the flicker of light on hair. *Come on then*, the movement seemed to say. *Come with us.*

Chrissie, rooted in earth. Heart in mouth, palms wet—

While they stood. Waiting.

A kind of sound that had no sound—

She too moved, quickly. She ran, forgetting she had not paid for her drinks, towards them. And now they ebbed away, so she must *really* run—

She did not think what this must look like, as normally she would have done. Her thoughts seemed absent now, as under great pleasure, horror or agony, sometimes they are.

Which was *this*, anyway? What were they doing, calling her, summoning her, yet never letting her catch up? Ah, she was thinking again now.

She saw she had reached that open area between buildings, the spot with the curious, metal-leafed tree, and she had not seen the street she ran through before that, or anything.

They were under the tree.

Under the tree, and in front of her. And

she had reached them.

Chrissie stopped running. She was panting. It did not matter, not really.

They were only three or four feet away.

Oh God, how splendid they were. Not like anything as human as a film star or a statue – they were like fabulous insects made of ivory, gold leaf and gems. And somehow, through the black shades, she could make out – the blue of his eyes, aquamarine, and hers, like platinum over pearl – but it was guesswork, maybe. She could not truly see.

'I'm sorry, I thought—'

Chrissie heard herself blurt that, but this was all.

And then he, Arrigo, beckoned with his hand.

Although like jewels, they wore no jewellery. Not even the expensive watches she would have expected. And their clothes, so seamless, elegant and simple, were of a material that reminded her of Egyptian linen. Not only their flesh then, translucent and shining.

Now they were walking on. The three of them. Not too far. Just to this corner, where this rose-brown masonry craned into a half-shade, and there, between the plaster and the cobbles underfoot, Gina bending, brushing with her fingers, a sort of green frond which grew from the stone.

Is it a weed? Chrissie did not ask. Not necessary. She was meant to pick it, that was all. Why? Oh, but she knew. She knew everything.

She knew who they were.

All in that moment.

And an internal singing, like the nightingale's, rushed through her, music gold not silver, sharp not sweet.

She bent also to the frond, and watched her thin hand with no nail varnish or rings, and the hand snapped off the frond.

Chrissie raised the weed to her face and sniffed at it. It smelled pungent, like a herb. Neither appetising nor un.

It would be a little bitter, she thought, like paracetamol. And tingle on the tongue, like aspirin.

At that instant too, suddenly, essentially, she could smell *them*. They had a scent like honey, and the clean fur of cats. But also they smelled of dry heat, like sand.

She twirled the frond of weed-herb between her fingers, admiring the green suppleness of it, which had forced its way, spinelessly, through the hard plaster and adamant cobbles. She was happy. Then, all she could smell was the afternoon.

She flung round – there was no one else there. That is, They were not.

Children were playing under the plane tree. Women called across from upper windows in a mellifluous Italian Chrissie could not fathom. Gusts of a rich spaghetti sauce hovered through the air. The town was awake. It was noisy, and five past two.

III

She did nothing. Nothing at all. Days passed – how many? – two, three – probably only one – and she did nothing.

The frond-weed-herb, whatever it was, wilted in the glass of water in the bathroom.

He never mentioned it. Never *noticed*?

Was that bizarre?

Yes, it was bizarre.

Chrissie, however, looked at the frond as it shrivelled. And at lunch-time, when they went down to the café with pink sunshades, she looked
– she looked—

For them.

But they were not there.

No, they *were* there, but she could not *see* them.

Campari with ice. Red wine. Antipasto. Fresh peaches in a basket. The brandy bottle (his).

A green lizard (not gold) spangling across the baked earth. Cyclamen in pots on a wall.

Today I'll walk out and see the vineyards.

She did not.

She sat, long after Craig had gone back to the hotel. She sat looking, looking. Not seeing them. Seeing their *absence*.

Those nights, or that night, Craig and she ate their dinner in the usual restaurant.

The priest who emerged from a little side door by the church, at a quarter past twelve, listened to Chrissie's stammering request. He spoke enough English, and did not seem to mind her lack of anything but the most basic Italian, which mostly consisted of exclaiming *Bella!* and endlessly apologising to or thanking him.

She had thought the church was locked, but it was not.

He let her go in, and in a panic of courtesy, Chrissie pulled off her sleeveless cardigan, and draped it over her head.

When she did this, he glanced at her, and she thought his face was sorry, sorry for her. She noted he had seen she was not a Catholic. So then she stood there, ashamed to have let him down.

And how graceful it was, when he genuflected before the altar and the Idea of God. Yes, she wished she had been a Catholic, and able to do it, not just for his sake, but her own, to offer this, and receive the undoubted blessing of an inner response.

It was a powerful church, dark amber out of the sun, the windows hanging in space, brass gleams cast at random, as in some cunning ancient painting. The stone floor and pillars induced a sense of heavy depth, as if under water. There was a triptych above the altar, birth, ministry, death and resurrection.

Chrissie went round and gazed at the few ornaments, the windows and paintings. Then she sat on a wooden seat for half an hour. She felt she was an impostor and should not be there. Part of her wanted to throw itself howling at the naked, nail-pierced feet of the Christ. But why? What could she ask for?

She had never been religious. This was ridiculous now. *She* was ridiculous (as Craig had again told her, when she protested at today's policy of having a sandwich lunch in the hotel bar). She did not have the effrontery to go running to Jesus.

In the end, she had to face the fact the church could not help her. She got up and went out by the other little side door the priest had taken when he left her. She did this, she believed, quite innocently.

Outside was the narrowest, dimmest alley.

For a moment, she might have been anywhere in Italy, even in time. The encroaching walls were cracked and high and somehow black even in the shadowed daylight. Chrissie thought that she must go left, to return herself to the square. But the alley looked twisted that way, almost deformed – impassable, and it stank of urine and some sort of trouble – she did not know what that was, but vaguely she heard, or thought she did, angry male voices. Her independence, which was so pathetic, had maybe been stated enough when she left Craig at the hotel. So she went the other way along the alley. The wrong way. And here the light came, a topaz flood, and then she walked out into a place that seemed to have formed between two cliffs of sunstruck primrose plaster. High above, a delicate iron balcony let loose a torrent of violet flowers all down the wall.

And under these, they were waiting for her.

There came a wash of terror. But adventure, joy, always made Chrissie afraid. She laughed, and Arrigo and Gina laughed back at her, soundlessly, their teeth like summer-resistant snow.

And then – they were—

They were touching

her—

caressing her . . . they were covering her like a silk blanket.

Chrissie had not often been deliberately touched. In love-making, even then, the explorations of her flesh were (she surmised) unimpressed and, accordingly, swift and desultory.

But no one anyway ever could have touched her – like this. *Their* hands, sliding over her, *their* arms encircling her, *their* lips – their *tongues* – moving across her face, her neck, her skin – They pressed firmly against her. Every surface of her felt them on itself. And she could not particularly notice which was Arrigo, which Gina – it did not matter – they were, all three of them, One.

So warm, so electric. It was like sex, yet not like sex. It was another *kind* of sex? Perhaps, maybe – for it had its own glorious momentum, its own rising to summit after summit—

Don't let it ever stop.

She lay back on the wall, in their arms, holding them, feeling them against her (part of them) these hot, satiny-smooth bodies, that were scented of fur and sand and honey and – Was she conscious? Yes – No—

Her eyes were shut. She could not open them. She spun upward, mile after mile, swimming with Arrigo and Gina in a sea of sun, desire and flame.

They did not kiss her. They did not seek to probe her body in any way. She was not penetrated. No, she was *permeated*. It was – *osmosis*.

Oh – God—

What *were* they? In her swimming blind delight, the questions darted round her, swimming too, like tiny pretty fish. Arrigo and Gina were not ghosts – for they were solid, she could feel and grasp them, as they her.

There had been another dream. Forgotten, now – with the questioning fish – it surfaced too. What had the dream shown her? Something visual – she had seen the square, and a banner floating there, as if in some renaissance festival. White, with golden words written over it, and what had the words said? Something spelled out in her own faulty Italian – what? What?

Who cared? Only this, with them. Only they – They—

Never let me go.

Never stop.

Don't leave me—

Take me with you—

On the banner, seen now over hills of the mind, through hazes of unthought, the words, hardening. She read them from the drowning sea.

Popolo di Mezzogiorno.

A cloud must have swallowed the sun. She tried to ignore how abruptly cold she was, chilled and shivering.

But the wall, reality, pushed hard into her back, and the purple flowers so near her face gave off a tang that all at once she did not like, a cat's-piss smell – and she was alone.

Chrissie opened her eyes. A sob wrenched convulsively as sick out of her mouth. She coughed and swore. She raised her wrist, visibly shaking, and stared at her shaking watch. One minute after 2.00 pm.

She drew the withered weed out of the glass that afternoon as Craig slept like an exhausted rhinoceros. The stem was rotten, the rest of it parched and blackened. The scent, if anything, was slightly stronger.

The latest bottle, whisky this time, still two-thirds full as only brought up here this afternoon, stood on the little desk between the windows.

Craig slept, but carefully she kept her back to him. She undid the whisky and crumbled into it the frond, which swirled in the clear brown liquid, for a moment like flakes from a fire, then melted, disappeared.

Chrissie did not know what the frond was, its exact nature or name. Only that it had fragilely forced its way through stone. She did know what it would do, approximately. It was no use making out she did not. So she would fail to be at all astounded at following developments and would need to take extra care, be cautious, and, in the theatrical sense, act. As she had acted for years with Craig, pretending to a light-hearted tolerance and respect that had long since died. And instead of a thick grey rhinoceros hide, like his own, that she had also tried to pretend she had, she must become soft and startled, emotional and desperate. Just those very things she had always had to keep inside, from about the age of thirteen.

After she had seen to the whisky, Chrissie took another shower. (He cursed and grumbled at her when she came out, for waking him, then went back to sleep.)

Having dressed, she went down and had an espresso in the bar. There were a few people there by now; it was about four-thirty, and the light deepening, thickening, the lamp-like bottles turned to chunks of green and tawny shadow.

She engaged the barman in a little touristy banter. He flirted at her, kindly, nicely, seeing she would know enough not to push her luck, but would appreciate the civility.

'My husband's been getting so tired,' she added sadly. 'We so want to go to the city, see the red and white cathedral. But he just can't face it. And I'm afraid the food isn't agreeing with him. Such a shame. I *love* the food.'

When she had finished the espresso, she went out for a stroll. In the lobby, an oldish, blond man was standing talking to the reception clerk. She heard the blond man say, 'They won't listen, never will, won't believe what you tell them. About the streets, the square. Especially the square.'

Chrissie thought he spoke in an accented English; how else could she understand? An American, perhaps.

As she crossed into the spotlight of levelling sun at the threshold, as if into a red-gold box, isolated, she heard the man say, 'Only a couple of hours. Does it hurt to watch out, to take precautions, just from twelve till two? Little enough. Doctors say you should keep out of the midday sun now, anyway. For the skin. Too many bad rays getting through.'

Chrissie found she had hesitated. Pretending now to examine the strap of her sandal.

'*Popolo*,' said the man. 'Citizens of noon,' the man said. '*Mezzogiorno*.'

And then she realized he spoke in Italian, not English, and suddenly she could not understand him.

She stepped out into the street, where cats were lying on balconies and in doorways, and a woman was selling bunches of flowers from the hills.

The bell sounded in the square. Five o'clock.

Inside, upstairs, behind her, Chrissie visualised Craig rolling off the bed, pouring himself two or three stiff drinks before taking his shower.

Craig did not want dinner, he said (he told her why not; the disgusting food), but she, being a wimp, would make a fuss if they did not go out.

They walked down to the restaurant, through the square. (The families were strolling. Two handsome young men on Lambrettas entertained a batch of beautiful girls – *bella! bella!* Stars had appeared.) Craig's colour was not good. He looked a little older.

In the restaurant he pushed most of the food far from him across the plates.

'Filthy fucking muck,' he said, too loudly. Around the room, faces glanced and away. The other diners looked almost fearful. But not precisely of Craig. Of something.

Although he did not eat, Craig drank copiously. He had the brandy, all the bottle.

His speech was slurred.

His little bluish pinkish eyes peered at Chrissie.

'What are you staring at me for? Eh? Fuck you, you stupid cunt bitch.'

If he had made a public scene like this previously, and now and then it had come close, Chrissie would have curled together, shrivelled with embarrassment and terror. Tonight, she sat looking obediently away from Craig, her face stamped with a sort of compassion.

The other people in the restaurant would see how much he drank, how he behaved, his violence, the purple-red and porridge-sludge tones that alternated in his face. And they would observe how sorrowful Chrissie was, how meek, how she did her best, stayed quiet and unruffled. And yet so concerned – she had often pretended to solicitous concern before.

When Craig smashed his brandy glass – part accident, part dislocated rage – the manager came out with his son, a tanned and muscular youth in jeans and a white shirt.

'I regret, *signore*, I must ask you to—'

'Leave? My fucking pleasure, you nonce.'

At the door, she slipped back.

'I'm so sorry. He's not himself. He's been feeling ill. He works too hard.'

'*É ben difficile, signora*. But – it is nothing. Yourself, you are always welcome, while you remain.'

But in his face, as well, even in the face of the burly and competent son, a shifting of unease, a *carefulness*.

Outside, suddenly Craig swung sideways and vomited raucously on to the cobbles.

This went on some while, during which Chrissie stood, a picture of anxious helplessness, wide-eyed, clutching her hands together. Calm, and unmoved.

Raising his now mozzarella-coloured face, wiping his mouth. 'There's the advert for this crap joint,' croaked Craig at the empty street. 'That's what their food's good for, in that shithole.'

But then he had to lean over and commence puking again, and for some time, his sounds were restricted by and to this activity.

IV

All night Craig vomited. At first he made it to the bathroom, returning, staggering, to crash on his bed. Later he told her to bring him the

waste-paper basket, and presently he told her to empty it. This became
the routine. The colours changed, however. Black appeared, and
crimson.

Between the bouts of his sickness, Chrissie slept a little, lying on her
bed. There was an awful smell in the room, but this time he did not
object when she opened both windows.

Above her, in the faintly luminous night, she saw the stains in the
ceiling were quite different after dark, yet still she could make nothing
of them. And then she believed she had, and she followed the map of
stains and came into a place of nothingness, crowded with unseen,
incredibly tall trees, but then a fearsome noise began and she woke up
and it was Craig being sick again.

(The sounds he made now were so alarming, she was half-surprised
no one had come to knock on their door. If they did, she was primed
and had her performance all ready.)

When first light began, Craig spoke to Chrissie, in what was left of
his voice. 'Get me a doctor.' So she got off the bed and went out of the
room, closing the door behind her. She had kept on her clothes from
the previous evening, and now she ran her fingers through her hair
which never, anyway, looked like anything, so why bother. Then she
turned the sign round on the door handle, so that it read, in Italian,
French and English, *Do not disturb*.

There was already movement in the hotel. Spectral maids pattered
through the corridors with armfuls of linen. In the lobby, the doors
stood open to a cool nacreous dawn and they were watering the flowers
in tubs by the doors.

Outside, birds sang.

Chrissie went straight to the square and sat at one of the tables left
out, but its umbrella folded to a pencil, the doors of the café shut.

It was very early. She would have to wait.

She could smell the dew, the morning. She might never ever smell
that again, or see a dawn or a night. She understood this quite well,
and what she had renounced.

Each day, there would only be two hours of life. But a life of gold
and crystal, a life of perfection. Spent – with Them.

All this they had promised her when they showed her the venomous
frond. If only she would be brave enough. They had really wanted her.
They had made that so obvious. Why did not matter. And armed with
that she had been brave. Although, in fact, it had needed no bravery at
all. Which was as well, since her courage had been entirely used up by

the years of staying with him. To kill him – that had only been, ultimately, common sense.

Chrissie sat calmly, almost mindlessly, at her table, and when the café opened just after eight, various people came and put up her umbrella, and wiped the table, and brought her coffee and an orange.

She enjoyed them so much, the black bitter drink with its caffeine zing, the tart fruit – the last foods she would eat in this world.

She knew They did not eat, and when she became one of them, neither would she.

Were there others? Other *people of the noon* – perhaps. Possibly, when no longer visible to the susceptible human eye, they assumed, or returned to, some other form. Which was—? – diamanté lizards – gleaming smokes – that glitter which sometimes came, when glancing away from something bright, and was thought to be some reflex of the optic nerve—

Was she excited at the prospect before her? Oh, she was radiant. She thought of how she would change, her skin turning to copper and her straw hair to spun gold. She thought of their embrace. Their love.

She had never been loved. Had she ever, herself, loved? No. Not until now.

'Arrigo,' she murmured, 'and Gina. And . . . Chrissie . . .'

Men and women came and went around her and about the square. A cart rumbled by, a lorry. Mopeds. A girl who shouted. Children tumbling. A striding man with striding dogs. Her table was no longer approached; the waiters did not come to chivvy her, ask her what else she would have. They left her in her thrumming peace. As if they could see the shining cloud which contained her, as she waited for her lovers in the sunlight's unfolding sunflower.

At about ten to twelve, Chrissie rose. When she did so, a curtain seemed to hang down from the burning sky, which drew itself all round her. Beyond the curtain, the quietness throbbed faintly with the undertones of other things, separate existences. The square had emptied entirely; no one was there any more, but for herself. All around, barricaded inside the glass windows of the cafés, she saw them, these others, at the tables, eating and drinking, playing cards. And in windows above the square, high up, she saw them too, their backs turned, their shutters closed. Already she had left them all.

Chrissie stood by the fountain. Its spray leapt up and over, over and up. She had brought nothing with her. She would need nothing ever again.

She knew, this time, she would see them arrive. The midday sun would bring them out, like flowers, like blisters in paint, like creatures from under a rock.

The bell rang from the church, cracked and irreversible.

They came up out of the rim of the fountain's bowl and up from the ground. It was the way something might squeeze out of a tube, except that the tube was invisible. They were ectoplasmic, yet liquidly glassy. She thought of the wings of insects which, emerging from the chrysalis, must harden in the sun.

And then they were really there.

The light flared off them, through them, out of them, and heat radiated from them.

Chrissie smiled, and Arrigo and Gina smiled. Chrissie stretched out her hands, and as she did so, the sun flamed on her skin, the harmfully *bad rays* of twelve o'clock till two. And her skin was altered. It was peachy and translucent – Already, it began.

'I did it,' Chrissie said to Arrigo and Gina. 'I poisoned him with the plant.' They smiled. 'He'll probably be dead by now.'

Chrissie thought abruptly, perhaps not everyone uses the poison that way. Maybe they swallow it themselves. Or even sometimes it isn't poison, that isn't appropriate – a knife concealed in a wall, a razor-blade in a dustbin – we are all their potential victims, we susceptible ones. We won't heed the warnings. They can do their work through us, one way or another way—

But she was not scared, no, not at all. For the first and last time in her life, Chrissie was exalted.

And then – what was it? Some new sound, some other awareness – Chrissie felt that after all, she and they were not quite alone in the noon square. And although she did not care, she looked over her shoulder. This was when she saw the two policemen, in their dark uniforms, with their spouting guns, standing across from her, at the entry of the street which led to the hotel.

Like Arrigo and Gina, the policemen wore sunglasses, very black, and as she had infallibly known it with Arrigo and Gina, Chrissie now knew that the policemen were staring directly at her. She turned again, away from them.

Arrigo and Gina smiled.

'Well,' Chrissie said. 'They must have found him – I thought it would happen in the night, someone coming in – I was all ready to act upset, frantic – but then it was morning and – oh, I forgot, didn't I, to empty out the last of the whisky – I thought it wouldn't matter. It can't now, can it? It's too late. See my hands – my hands are almost transparent, aren't they—' But no, she thought then, something in her stumbling, the motion-sickness of the fall, no, her hands – were just as always. Bony, opaque, white, thin and *thick*.

Chrissie began to feel the new feeling, which was of utter darkness, there in the sun. Darkness and a wild flash of anger. For the town had known, this nice Italian town, most of them. They had seen, and warned, and stood aside, protecting themselves, knowing that Chrissie was the dupe – was the one – who would be lost—

She thought how lions stalked a herd of deer, and how one deer would become hypnotised, or was singled out because it was already in some way impaired and slow. How the lions brought the deer down. And then the rest of the herd settled, and began again to feed innocently on the grass, alongside the lions feeding on the meat of the dead deer.

Arrigo and Gina still smiled, but they did not touch her. No need for it now. Instead they took off their own sunglasses, as if to see her better.

Their eyes were not as she had imagined. They were small and round and brilliant blood-red beads, without pupil or white, set in swivelling scaly portholes. The eyes of lizards. And their strawberry tongues (lizardlike) flicked in and out two or three times. *Tasting*.

'Oh,' Chrissie said, blankly.

Arrigo and Gina dissolved. They shimmered away, they and their horrible radioactive beauty and their reptile eyes and their satisfaction.

And Chrissie once more looked back towards the policemen, who remained exactly where they were. Waiting, perhaps, as Chrissie did, to see whether or not she too could impossibly grow transparent and vanish, or if she was only a human English woman, who had premeditatedly and viciously murdered a man in the hotel, her motives clear as day, and who was too fucking stupid to have covered up her tracks.

Tanith Lee began writing at the age of nine and became a full-time writer in 1975 when DAW Books published her novel *The Birthgrave*. Since then she has written and published around sixty novels, nine collections and over two hundred short stories. She also had four radio plays broadcast during the late 1970s, and early '80s, and scripted two episodes of the cult BBC-TV series *Blakes 7*. She has twice won the World Fantasy Award for short fiction and was awarded the British Fantasy Society's August Derleth Award in 1980 for her novel *Death's Master*. In 1998 she was shortlisted for the Guardian Award for Children's Fiction for her novel *Law of the Wolf Tower*, the first volume in the 'Claidi Journal' series. More recently, Tor

Books has published *White as Snow*, the author's retelling of the Snow White story, while Overlook Press has issued *A Bed of Earth* and *Venus Preserved*, the third and fourth volumes, respectively, in the 'Secret Books of Paradys' series. She is currently working on a sequel to her novel *The Silver Metal Lover* for Bantam Books. 'Two of the hours of day that fascinate me the most are sunset and noon,' reveals the author. 'But there has always been something sinister, perhaps, about the departure of light, while midday is dangerous, not only now, but always. It is the time of sunstroke, of accident, when eyes are blinded a moment, even fatally, by the raw presence of the sun. Added to this now, the warnings of apparently no longer shielded UV rays. Only mad dogs and Englishmen are stupid enough to dare it. All over the Mediterranean, they resort to the siesta. Is there something more to all this? Some instinct valid as the uneasy alertness encountered in the early hours of morning, or in the 'tweenlight of dusk? Bright light conceals maybe even better than shadows . . .'

The Boy behind the Gate

JAMES VAN PELT

As you are now,
So once was I.
As I am now,
So you shall be.
Prepare for death and follow me.
from a tombstone in the Central City Cemetery

Central City: Today

Pine tree tops creaked overhead, but the air didn't move in the granite-strewn gully as Ron hiked up the steep gulch. He consulted his compass then rechecked the map. Another hundred yards above him should be the Golden Ingot #9, and if the rusted mining equipment he'd been climbing over and around for the last ten minutes were any indication, the map was right. He scanned the ground, his eyes aching from sun and dust. The backpack, heavy with a powerful flashlight, rope and bolt-cutters, thumped against his kidneys. Was anything out of the ordinary? Was there any sign? A patch of cloth? A child's shoe? Could Levi have walked this far? Ron imagined the eight-year-old being towed up the mountain, hand in hand with the stranger who'd taken him. Would Levi have been crying, aware in his little-boy way of the danger he was in?

Ron closed his eyes. He wanted to imagine Levi scared. He hoped he was scared to death because the alternative . . . Maybe he'd been wrapped in a blanket or a plastic sheet slung over the man's shoulder. They knew who the man was, Jared Sims, but Levi wouldn't have known. Ron shivered and continued climbing.

A jumble of cable, thick as his wrist and so rusted that wherever the metal crossed itself it had corroded into one piece, blocked his path. Ron scrambled partly up the gully's slope around it. Piles of yellow and white mine tailings humped up above him, and soon he topped out to the relative flatness of the claim. The old map he'd photocopied in Central City had shown him where the mine was; it wasn't marked on the USGS maps. Most of the abandoned mines and shafts had been filled in: too much chance of some tourist wandering around old mining property, snapping pictures of busted-down mills and what was left of miners' cabins, and then stepping on some rotten boards covering a shaft a hundred feet deep. So over the last twenty years, the state and park service had been closing the properties. Still, the Gilpin County mining district had been huge and thousands of claims had been made. There were hundreds of openings even now for someone to find if he knew where to look: perfect, mysterious holes blasted into the mountain, timeless monuments to long-dead miners' hopes. Perfect places to hide a little boy you didn't want found. Here, at the Golden Ingot #9, except for the rust, it could be 1880 again. He half expected to surprise a dozen miners waiting for their turn in the bucket and the long ride down the shaft.

Ron kept his eyes down. Little chance that there'd be a footprint in the yellow gravel, but it didn't hurt. Maybe Levi would have dropped something for him to find. It seemed years ago, but it was only last winter that Ron had read him *The Lord of the Rings*. The hobbit, Pippin, had broken from the Orcs and dropped a sign that he was still alive, a beautiful beech-tree-leaf brooch. Levi had said, in his little man's voice, 'That was very clever of him, Daddy, wasn't it?' Ron remembered Levi's head resting on his arm while he read. He could almost feel the weight of his little boy leaning against him until they got to the end of the chapter. 'Read some more, Daddy. Read some more,' he'd said sleepily.

A pile of boards lying almost flat looked hopeful. Ron lifted the end of one. It creaked as it rose slowly, pulling a dozen nails from the rotted plank beside it. Dust slapped into the air after Ron moved it aside and dropped it. The next one showed a shaft's edge. A minute later, he'd cleared most of the boards. The pile looked like it hadn't stirred since Grover Cleveland held office, but since he was here, he was going to check.

The afternoon sun showed only six feet of shaft wall, while the rest was black. Was the bottom only a dozen feet away, or was this one of those deep, deep holes reaching hundreds of yards down?

As always, as he had scores of times since the police gave up looking ten days before, he crouched at the shaft's edge, cupped his hands around his mouth and called into the darkness, 'Levi! Levi! Are you there, son?'

Wind stirred sand behind him, blowing a little over the edge where it glittered in the sunlight, then disappeared. Only the breeze's sibilant hiss answered him.

Central City: 1879

Images flitted in Charles's mind as he stayed motionless in his bed, listening to the boy's even breathing on the floor beside him. It was the small hours of the morning, when time came unanchored, and memories piled willy-nilly atop one another. Charles could see them all: his wife dying, the Laughlins, the McGaritys, the bloody hands in the mine. The fireplace coals had long since died, and the moon's thin line outside the window cast almost no light through the muslin drape. He'd light a candle if he dared, but if he did, the boy's eyes might be open; he might look at him through the flickering light and know that he knew.

He couldn't sleep. No, not that. Charles would dream, and in his dreams he'd see the Laughlin children burning up, their red skin baking from within. 'Scarlet fever,' the nurse from Idaho Springs had said. 'Poor things.'

Charles had stood at the Laughlins' door that morning, a basket of bread and clean sheets hanging from one hand, blinking at the darkness in the room. Only the sun behind him provided light. They'd covered the one window, and the cabin smelled close and moist and sweaty-sick. The nurse sat by three-year-old Lisa to his left. Against the back wall lay Evelyn with her mother sitting beside her. The baby's crib rested in the opposite corner. William Laughlin sat at the rough-hewn table in the room's middle, resting his forehead in his hand.

The boy crept around Charles, even though he'd told him to stay with the mule. His arm wrapped around the back of Charles's leg, and he leaned into the room. Charles put his hand down to push him back, but he didn't. He didn't like touching his son, the stranger who lived with him every day. Lisa panted under the blankets, blonde hair plastered to the side of her face. Four-year-old Evelyn turned to the wall, her chest still for a moment before she drew her next wheezing breath. Her mom, a hint of the scarlet flush across her own cheeks visible in the sunlight, pressed a wet cloth to Evelyn's forehead.

'The little one?' Charles said.

William Laughlin shook his head without moving his hand. 'She went during the night.' He coughed. It sounded wet and pathetic.

'I brung some things,' Charles said. He stepped deeper into the room and the atmosphere pushed back. Outside the sun shone bright and men filled the valley, moving surely from mine to mill, loading ore wagons or carrying supplies. Blasting echoed off cliff walls above and Clear Creek murmured like watery wind. But here, the air felt dead with fever.

William draped a hand over the basket's edge. 'You're a right Christian, Charles.'

'You going to your shift?' Charles moved back. The heat in the room oppressed and he didn't want to breathe so close to the sick girls.

'I'll be along.'

Charles retreated to the porch. The boy leaned over Lisa, his legs bright in the sun pouring through the door, while his upper torso faded in the room's shadows. He drew a finger across the little girl's forehead, through her fevered sweat. He stood, facing his father, his finger up as if he'd erased chalk off a blackboard. For a moment he looked at Charles as if surprised to see him still waiting for him, then he put his finger in his mouth.

When they crossed the footbridge over the creek, Charles said, 'Why'd you do that, boy? I told you to stay out.'

The boy held onto the mule's bridle, his head not even coming up to the mule's chin. 'They'll burn, Papa.'

Charles nearly stumbled, then glanced at the boy. He wore an old flannel shirt too big for him with the sleeves rolled up. Pale, skinny arms. Dark hair cut above his eyebrows. Dark eyes. He was given to long, unblinking looks. A serious mouth, like his mother who died bringing him into the world eight years before.

'I'm glad he's out of me,' she'd said in the moment before she died screaming.

'What do you mean, boy?'

'I put the death in them.' He held up his finger that had touched the girl as if in proof. 'Just like the other lambs.'

'Don't talk like that.' Charles pulled the bridle from the boy's hand, his own hand shaking. 'You go on home, and I don't want to see a mess in the cabin when I get back. Sweep the floor.'

'I can smell the fire,' the boy said before turning towards their cabin.

Charles thought about his son all day, deep in the mine, as he worked the single jack, bent low in the tunnel only three-quarters of his height, placing the steel bit against the stone, pounding it a bit deeper with each blow, rotating it each time to clear the bit, pausing just before he drove the hammer home. The angle had to be perfect. The placement, perfect. He had to judge before he struck. Striking without looking could shatter the drill. There was always the pause before the hammer came down to be sure he was doing the right thing. So there could be no mistake. It was a feeling of good or bad in the way the drill stood. Charles considered his judgement with the hammer to be his only genius. He never struck wrongly. *Clang!* The hammer would fall against the rod. Rock dust crumbled from the hole. *Clang!* He'd hit it again, his strong right arm driving the blow home. Numbing work to create a hole for the charge. He could raise the hammer all day with that arm; the work had made it larger than the other one, a giant's arm, but he couldn't shape the boy with it. He couldn't even hold him.

The boy had been bad from the beginning. His wet-nurse took sick and died. After that, no one would help Charles, so he fed the child himself with goat's milk, certain that the first winter would kill him, having no mother to care for him, but as winter filled the mountains with snow and cutting wind, even as influenza swept through the camp taking many babies, the boy thrived. He was walking by the next summer and Charles would leave him locked in the cabin when he worked his shift, half expecting to find the toddler dead on his return. But every day the boy met him, a little taller, a little stronger, and never smiling.

Setting the powder took a half-hour. Each hole had to be filled with the proper amount. Then the fuse cord had to be measured. Charles worked methodically. This deep in the mine, the stale air hurt his lungs and gritty rock coated his eyes and tongue. He checked the candle burning brightly in its shadowgee stuck in the wall. When he set the last charge, he retreated to the bucket lift, covering his nose and mouth with a soaked bandana to protect against the dust. After the blast, he stood with head bowed, breathing through the wet cloth.

Charles wanted to love him. He tried. The weather in the boy's heart was cold, though, and hugs meant nothing to him. He never played. He never cried. And always, around him, children died. Diphtheria. The grippe. Typhoid. The croup. Pneumonia. Whooping cough. Small-pox. Lingering diseases. Wasting illnesses. The cemetery filled with tiny corpses.

The ore cart rattled on the rails as Charles pushed it towards the broken ore. For the rest of his shift he'd fill the cart, take it back to the lift, empty it and return for another load. No candles lit the path, but that didn't matter. Charles didn't mind the dark most days, but today he couldn't stop thinking about the boy. What does the boy do while I'm at work? What does he daydream about? Charles imagined him wandering through the camp, looking for children.

In the spring he'd taken the boy to a funeral. Seamus McGarity had lost both his boys and his wife to dysentery three days apart. Mc-Garity, his kin and friends circled the coffins, two tiny wood boxes and a long one. During the prayer, Charles looked down at his boy dressed in mourning black. The corners of the boy's mouth turned up and his eyes were shining. At the ceremony's end, the boy dropped dirt in each grave. Surreptitiously, he also put a handful of grave soil in his pocket.

'Lucky your kid's doing good,' McGarity said to him the next day as they waited for the bucket to take them down the shaft. His lunch pail dangled from his hand and the miner looked exhausted, as if he hadn't slept for a month. 'He came by a week ago. Found him sitting by the door.'

'What did he want?' Charles wished he could pat McGarity on the shoulder. How would it be to lose your whole family? There'd been other men whose children died who drank themselves to death. The other miners stood away from them. People died in the camps all the time, but it wasn't easy to be next to the bereft, not at first.

McGarity didn't answer for a while. He stared out over the valley, but he didn't appear to be looking at anything. Finally he said, 'Caleb used to sing his little brother to sleep. I don't think he knew I was listening. "Amazing Grace" it was. Learned it from his mom. He had a nice voice for a ten-year-old.'

They found McGarity at the bottom of a shaft a week later. Was he drunk and fell in, or did he jump?

At the blasting site the dust still hung in the air, surrounding the candle in a pale globe. Charles hefted ore into the cart. My boy's not human, he thought, as each rock crashed against the metal. Methodically he bent and lifted, bent and lifted. Not human. Not human. Charles pictured the boy with his finger in his mouth, salty-bitter from the Laughlin girl's scarlet-fever sweat.

After a while Charles stopped loading. His hands stung. He stepped next to the candle's feeble light and held them up. Blood ran down his wrists from his ragged fingertips. Dully he realised he'd not worn his gloves. And a certainty came to him, a gravestone-solid conviction: my boy's a monster!

Charles lay in his bed, motionless. The boy breathed evenly on the floor below him. Only the sliver-moonlit window floated in the dark. Charles kept his eyes wide open. If he shut them, even for a second, the boy might stand. He might lean his unsmiling face close. The boy might run his finger across Charles's forehead.

'I see you burning, Papa,' the boy would say. He always called him Papa, like it was a curse.

And dawn was hours away.

Ron sat in his van on the abandoned mining road near the boulders the park service had used to block the path, his map spread out on the seat beside him marked with Xs for mining claims. From Central City there were so many. The historical marker at the town limits proclaimed THE RICHEST SQUARE MILE ON EARTH. He shook his head. If only it were that small.

Starting at Black Hawk at one end of the valley to the other end of Central City was a couple of miles. Mine tailings spotted the slopes on both sides. Then there were the gulches: Chase, Eureka, Russell, Lake, Pecks, Fourmile and others the map didn't name with mines of their own, and the road went on to the ghost towns of Yankee Hill, Ninety Four, Alice and Kingston. Nevadaville was only a stone's throw to the west. He could almost see the honeycomb of tunnels.

Ron smoothed the map, but his attention shifted. On the floor, barely visible in the blue dusk of sunset, a red plastic building brick lay canted on its side. He stretched around the steering wheel, crinkling the map with his elbow, and picked it up. The brick had almost no weight sitting on his palm. He straightened, put the brick on the dashboard.

They didn't have building bricks when he was a boy. His dad had given him Lincoln logs, and over the years, Ron's dad had added to the set until they filled a box almost too big to fit under his bed. Ron made forts and villages and fences and barns. Two short logs crossed over each other served as cannon. His dad came into his room one night and they built a tower together, half as tall as Ron.

Years later, when Levi was six, Ron had said to his dad, 'You never told me how much fun being a father would be.'

'I didn't think of it at the time,' his dad said.

Ron fingered the building brick. He'd never made a tower with Levi.

The sky grew dark and Ron didn't move. He thought about putting Levi to bed. 'Have good dreams,' he'd say. For forty nights now, Levi had not had Ron to wish him a bedtime without nightmares. He thought about throwing a baseball back and forth. He remembered reading to him, book after book, Levi's head resting against Ron's arm as they sat on the couch.

Ten days ago the Denver detective in charge of the investigation said, 'We're giving up the search, Ron. You're going to have to face the possibility your son is dead. Sims killed his victims. We know that.'

They sat in the detective's temporary office in the Gilpin County court house. Ron struggled to remain calm. The detective didn't look over twenty, and it was clear Ron made him uncomfortable.

'He didn't kill them right away,' Ron insisted. 'The Perez girl he kept in his basement for a week. In Colorado Springs he kept that baby in a storage garage for four days. His house was in Central City. My boy is in a mine somewhere. It's logical.' Ron held a crumpled flyer. HAVE YOU SEEN THIS CHILD? Levi smiled from the page, a strand of his black hair across his forehead, his dark eyes turned towards his cake before he blew out the candles.

With the detective, Ron had walked through Sims's house, a restored turn-of-the-century Victorian gingerbread with no closets. Posters covered the livingroom walls, all children. Except for the kitchen, blocked with yellow crime-scene tape and the outline of Sims's body on the floor, the rooms were meticulously tidy. Magazines on the coffee table were fanned out perfectly, the same half-inch overlap on each. On Sims's dresser in the bedroom, a line of brass padlocks stood like sentinels in a military row. They were the only decoration. Ron wondered what could make a man like Sims. Couldn't love have saved him? Love, pure love, might have kept Sims from hating, just as pure love would find his son. The police didn't love Levi enough to find him.

The detective shook his head. 'If he hadn't shot himself, we could ask him. But he did. We've had crews up and down the area. If your son were there, we would have found him. He might have lasted a week without food. Only a couple days without water. It's been a month. Sims buried his victims. I'm sorry to have to say it this way, but I'd guess your boy is in a shallow grave.'

Ron gripped the arms of the chair to keep from leaping at the man. 'There's bonds between a father and his son. I'd know if he had died.'

'The department can arrange counselling, if you request it,' the detective said.

'You're not a father, are you?' Ron looked past the detective. Black-and-white photographs hung on the wall behind him: men standing before a wagon, holding shovels and lunch boxes; a long shot of Central City down main street when it was still dirt; the front of a school, forty or fifty children sitting on the steps, their severe-looking teacher standing behind them with her arms crossed.

Ron touched the hard edge of the plastic building brick sitting on the dashboard and thought about the kids in the school a hundred years ago no different than his own boy, all dead by now for sure, and Levi, who might not be. Razor-edged stars filled the sky through his windshield. The air had cooled, caressing his face through the open windows. This far up the rutted road he couldn't hear traffc from the highway or crowd noise from the casinos that filled Central City. He canted his head to hear better. Something clicked repetitively in the distance, maybe a night bird or a locust. He wondered if locusts lived this high. For a long time he rested his finger on the brick and listened. The night vibrated with its own muttering. Unidentifiable sounds that he guessed might be the breeze sliding over rocks and through the scrubby grasses. A high squeak that might be a bat. He couldn't tell. The mountain was perfectly black and the cloudless sky danced with stars that provided no illumination.

He turned on the ceiling light to read the map. If someone saw him from a distance, he thought, he'd look like a time traveller in his craft, light glowing through the windows, unattached to the Earth.

Eventually he turned the light out and fell asleep sitting up, his head pillowed on a jacket against the door, windows still open so he could hear if Levi should call.

Charles slipped out of the cabin before dawn, the eastern sky just barely lighter than the west.

The wind came up the valley, and in it he could hear the stamp mills thrumming as they crushed ore.

He trudged up the switch-back trail towards the mine, his hands heavy; his head heavy. Had any child the boy met lived? There weren't that many children in the camps. The school in Nevadaville had one hundred and fifty students last year, he'd heard, but there were ten thousand miners in the district. Central City had a small school, and so did Blackhawk. Charles had never sent the boy, but he was supposed to go in the fall. The town was growing. More families came in every day. They were building churches.

At the top of the hill, he paused. From here in the pre-sunrise grimness, most of the town was visible in purples and blues. He couldn't find his own cabin, though. Then he gasped. A black aura like a cloud hid it from him, and for a moment it seemed as if it grew tentacles that flowed down the dirt roads, over the wooden sidewalks, sniffing at each door. The wind rippled the cloud's top, then blew in his face, carrying the smell of a crypt and the fevered dampness from the Laughlin cabin.

Charles shook his head. There was his cabin! There was no black cloud. He held his hands over his pounding heart. Am I going mad? A hallucination! But the question echoed hollowly. This was not madness.

He'd seen the cloud as a vision, a sign. He backed up the trail, afraid to take his gaze away from the cabin.

When a man's dog goes wild, he shoots him. It's his responsibility. What was his responsibility as a father of a monster?

When Charles worked the mine that day, he stuffed his pockets with candles, and he kept one lit no matter where he was. The shadows beyond the weak candle light were like the shadow creeping from his own house.

If Sims had locked Levi in a mine, it would have to have several qualities, Ron thought as he shouldered his pack. Pine lining the mountain top glowed in the morning light, but the sun wouldn't touch the valley's bottom for another hour. Ron checked his map and began the long hike up the old road. It had to be both close enough for him to get to, but far enough off the beaten track that it was unlikely anyone would find it. It had to be far enough back that even if Levi screamed for help, no one would hear him. There would be food and water. The question was, how much food and water? Sims wouldn't have planned on leaving Levi with over a month's supply.

Each step up the road felt like the ticking of an immense clock counting down. How much time was left? Was Levi even now crouched against a locked gate, light leaking around the edges, on the brink of death by thirst or starvation? If he ran out of water, might there be water in the mine itself that he had been drinking to keep himself alive? Ron thought about *Tom Sawyer*, not the high jinks of the little boy, but the awful image of Injun Joe trapped in McDougal's cave. After Ron's dad had read him that part, Ron had nightmares for months about eating bats while trying to carve through a thick wooden door with a broken knife.

Ron quickened his pace, his calves burning, keeping his eyes open for evidence of tunnels not on his map. He'd followed dozens of faint trails to dead-end mines in the last ten days, peered down scores of open shafts, rattled the locks on handfuls of metal gates, always looking for a sign, always listening for Levi's voice. He crossed from the valley's shadow into the sunlight, and even this early in the morning the rays heated his shirt. It would be a hot one today.

The road ended at the tumbled remains of a small mill. Busted beams pointed skywards, a skirt of rotten wood at their feet. Ron rested for a moment, his hand against a grey post. Splinters flaked onto his skin. Behind the ruin a narrow path vanished over a ridge. Weeds grew into

the twin grooves that were too narrow for an automobile. He imagined
steel-rimmed wagon wheels and a cart of ore making its way down the
road behind a team of horses. Time seemed irrelevant here. It could be
1880 again, or 2080; the mountains wouldn't know the difference. But
he wasn't timeless, and the clock counted; every minute passed was
another minute that Levi suffered alone. Could an eight-year-old die of
fright? What if he believed his daddy had forgotten him? Ron whimpered at the thought.

His photocopied map called this the Sunderson Mill. Above it were
several mines: West Yellow Dog, New Baltimore and Crossroad. Ron
spread the map over his knee. Small Xs indicating digs crowded the
gulch. There could be ventilation shafts, drainage tunnels, powder
storage crypts, false starts, dead ends and full-bore excavations that
needed checking.

It would take all day.

'Come with me, boy,' said Charles, his hands shaking. It had taken him
several minutes to push open the cabin door. He couldn't shake the
impression of the cloud he'd seen around his house in the morning. It
seemed to hover still, insubstantial, but present just the same. The sun
shone mutedly through it, and the air felt cooler than it did ten feet
away.

'It won't work,' said the boy. He sat on the edge of his bed, his dark
hair dishevelled, his gaze steady and challenging.

Charles swallowed hard. 'What won't work?'

'What you are planning.' The boy came towards him, across the
cabin's single room.

Charles backed away into the sunlight, gripping the hammer hanging
from his belt. The weight of his satchel tugged at his shoulder. For a
second he envisioned beating the boy down where he stood, before he
could get away. He forced his fingers from the hammer.

'We are taking a walk.'

'I know.' The boy strode past him and up the road out of town.

Charles watched him, his breath caught in his throat. Suddenly the
air seemed to clear and the sun pressed against him. Had it always been
this way around the boy? Had he been in a daze from the moment the
child was born?

It was as if the boy followed a trail traced for him in the dirt. He
walked in the road's middle, barely giving way when a wagon came
towards him. The horse's nostrils flared at his smell.

Charles caught up to him when they turned onto the Sunderson Mill
Road. The mines above it had gone bad the year before, and the mill
was closed.

'The mountains hold things, Papa.' The boy's hands hung straight at
his side, as if he were standing at attention, not hiking a steep road.

He had no words to say to him. Am I the monster? thought Charles.
The boy's mother wouldn't want this. Have I done something to
deserve a curse? Every step hurt. Part of him wanted to run away. He
could do it: leave the boy on the road, catch the new train out of town
and be in Denver before anyone knew. His family lived back east.

Another part denied that anything was wrong. Charles thought, what
if I'm insane? My boy is strange, for sure, but he's not evil. What child
growing in the mountains with a dead mother and a father who worked
the mines wouldn't mature differently?

And a third part wanted to fall on the boy like a bear and rend him,
bloody bone from bloody bone.

'Keep going,' Charles said when the boy slowed at the mill. The
windows were already broken and its door hung askew.

'Don't you love me, Papa?' he said. The boy looked at him sardoni-
cally. 'A Papa should love his son.'

The trail climbed as quickly as stairs for a hundred yards, while the
afternoon sun touched the mountaintop before them. Charles choked
on the words, 'Of course, I love you.' And he knew that he did. He
loved him even as he wanted to kill him, even as he was afraid. Was
this right? He thought of sick children sweating in their fevers, dead
children. 'They'll burn, Papa,' the boy had said.

At the ridge's top, the trail flattened and split. Winding to the right,
it led to West Yellow Dog, a fifty-foot drift that started with a yard-
wide vein of quartz and wire gold but petered into low-grade ore that
wasn't worth the cost of the powder to extract it. The middle trail
ended at the New Baltimore, a failed attempt to find West Yellow
Dog's wire gold by coming at it laterally. Charles had worked the New
Baltimore for six months before the owners shut it down.

He'd never been in the Crossroad on the left trail, but, as the hard
rock Cornishman who told him about it said, 'The claim was snakebit
from the beginning.' The rumour was that the first prospector had
been drilling into the rock to set a charge, and when he hit the drill for
the last time, it disappeared into the rock. There was a tunnel already
there. A silly story, but the claim didn't pay out, and there had been
accidents.

They took the turn to the left, around a granite wall, out of the sun and into the stone bowl that held the mine. Rock surrounded them on three sides, like a small arena. The sound of Charles's hard-soled boots echoed. At the far side, a metal gate held closed by a clasp lock marked the mine's entrance.

'You're going to be staying here, boy,' Charles removed a chisel from his satchel, set its edge against the lock, raised the hammer, then paused. Always he judged before he struck. Was the chisel set correctly? Would the hammer do its job? There could never be a strike without the pause for judgement, where a mistake could be saved. The metal's sharp report reverberated off the rocks. Another blow broke it, then Charles pulled the door open; it screeched against the stiffness in its hinges. He'd never seen a mine entrance like the Crossroad's. The floor looked worn smooth, as if thousands of feet had marched on it through the years. How had the miners done that?

'Don't you love me, Papa?' the boy said again.

Charles didn't look at him. From his satchel he removed a blanket, candles, a small bundle of food and a water bottle. 'I'll be back tomorrow.'

'You must not be my Papa.' He didn't sound insincere this time. 'My Papa loves me. He'll find me, my Papa.'

'Just get in!'

Charles could barely see the new lock he put on the door through the tears.

Behind the iron gate, he heard the boy move, a large sound, as if what stirred in the tunnel had suddenly grown huge. He fell back. Impossibly, the door stirred in its iron frame, and for a second Charles thought the inch-thick bolts might pull from the rock. He scuttled away. Even at the edge of the granite arena, when Charles looked at the mine entrance, he could hear the boy behind the gate, breathing loud, his heart throbbing. The sky grew dark and the air thick. A noxious cloud seeped around the door's edges, filled the stone chamber, its tendrils crawling on the floor towards Charles. The boy said, his voice full of old mining timbers and cold, wet stone a thousand feet deep, 'Papa?'

Charles fled.

West Yellow Dog had been dynamited. All that remained of its entrance was twisted ore cart track. Ron searched the cliff base to both sides. A niche three hundred yards to the right might have been where they stored powder, but it was only ten feet deep and didn't have a door. Below the mine, partially hidden behind scrubby pine growing between the rocks, he found a small tunnel barely tall enough for him to enter on his hands and knees, but twigs and dirt blocked the way a few feet in and it smelled of marmot. Ron sat on his haunches outside the hole and closed his eyes against the sun.

He'd know if Levi had died, wouldn't he? A father and son had a bond, he'd told the detective.

Within his view, visible only because the sun cast long shadows, several foundations rose from the grass in the clearing below the slope. There must have been a small community here, or they might have been part of the mining operation. At the Gilpin County Courthouse, Ron had looked at pictures of the town from the 1880s, and beside them were modern shots taken from the same spot. The buildings changed. Trees changed. But the rocks and mountains stayed the same. He trembled. To the mountain, time didn't exist; all times were interchangeable. He glanced at his watch. To a little boy dying in a mine, every second stretched like skin on fire.

He pushed himself upright.

The New Baltimore had a park-service gate on it. Ron slowed as he approached. Covered in dust, the remains of a broken lock lay on the ground. He rubbed the scratches in the metal. No rust. Someone had been here this summer.

'Levi!' His voice sounded hollow and out of place.

The gate gave reluctantly, its base dragging over the rock as he pulled it open. Moisture seeped from the walls a few feet in. Resting one hand on the black-slime ceiling just above his head, he shone his flashlight on indistinct footprints on the muddy floor. Back in the depths, a watery *plink-plink-plink* broke the silence. The tunnel split. To the right, a pile of rock and broken timbers blocked the way. To the left, the passage sloped downwards for another twenty feet before ending at a pool of water. The footprints led here. Ron played the quivering light across the surface, penetrating to the bottom. Rocks. More timber. Metal so heavily rusted he couldn't tell what its original shape had been. No wrapped bundle. No horror-story patch of white that resolved itself into a face.

He released a pent-up breath. Why had someone broken into the mine? Turning, he studied the walls and ceiling. A slippery, unhealthy-looking fungus covered the surfaces, and the stagnant air smelled rotted and mildewed. Near the ceiling to the left of the pool, a patch of rock peered through the growth, as if it had been brushed clean, and above it, a crack wider than his fist swallowed the light. Ron reached in, touched plastic. He found four bags in the crack, about a pound each. A whiff of the first one showed he'd uncovered someone's stash.

Ron left the bags on the floor. Ten minutes wasted.

According to his map, all that remained was the Crossroad. It took a half-hour of backtracking across the gulch's east side before he found a faint trail that led to a gap around a rock wall.

He spotted the lock on the door on the other side of the stone arena as soon as he rounded the corner, a brand-new brass padlock, like the row of them on top of Sims's dresser. He ran without thinking about it. Old metal door, not park-service. Ron ripped off his backpack, fumbled for the bolt-cutter, gripped the handles and squeezed. The lock snapped.

Was now the moment when he would know? Ron had dreamed of finding Levi in a thousand ways. Bad dreams, in some, where Levi was dead. Either dead over a month, or, even worse, dead a few days. He'd be starved or dead from thirst or exposure. In some dreams he was alive but sick, damaged from exposure or the time alone. In one dream Levi didn't know him, his mind gone. What could be worse than an eight-year-old driven insane by abuse and fear? In that dream, Ron loved his son back to sanity. No evil could be so bad that love could not change it to something good.

Ron tore the lock from the hasp, jammed his fingertips into the gap between the door and the frame. Pulled.

In the good dreams, Levi waited. 'Daddy!' he would cry. He always called Ron 'Daddy', like it was a blessing.

The door swung open.

Charles didn't even try to get to sleep. Sitting at the table in his cabin, the tiny slice of moon providing the only light again, he thought about the locked gate and the boy behind it. His intention was to never return.

He thought, what's the greater evil? Every time he closed his eyes, he saw dead children, a fingerprint on their foreheads; he also saw the boy at the Crossroad, staring at a candle, maybe, or sleeping. What kind of dreams would a bringer of death like him have? But Charles was evil too. The boy, no matter what else he was, was his son. A father should take care of his own. One time when Charles was young he locked a storage shed on his father's farm. A week later his father sent him to fetch some tools. The storage shed stank, a solid wall of putridness rolling out when Charles opened the door. A cat had been

locked in, its mouth gaping open, dry as dust; the stomach burst. If he
had known, wouldn't it have been merciful to have killed the cat a week
earlier?

Charles looked through the darkness to his own bed. He couldn't
imagine sleeping again. The boy behind the gate moved in his mind.
The room was so black, Charles could almost see the boy without
closing his eyes. Like the cat, the boy was locked in. But the cat wasn't
the devil. No, not by a long shot. Maybe a creature like the boy thrived
on the black air behind the gate. Could such a thing be killed by an act
as simple as being shut into a mine? What if it could do some magic to
save itself?

In a sudden vision, Charles saw himself as an older man walking
down a street. A beautiful carriage clattered by, the horses' hooves loud
on the bricks. In the vision, Charles glanced up. Sitting in the carriage
was his son, grown now, and the look he gave from the carriage was
full of hate.

Charles made a fist on the table, alone in his cabin in the midst of
the night, and moaned. The boy was behind the gate. 'I'm cursed,'
Charles said to the four walls. Already he felt the guilt like a blood-
soaked blanket settling over his head, suffocating him.

He's a boy dying slowly, my son, Charles thought. He's a monster
who can save himself in some evil way.

Like the New Baltimore, the Crossroad was wet. Footprints showed
clearly in the mud. Little prints. A child's shoes.

'Levi!' Ron's eyes strained to see into the mine, pulse throbbing huge
in his chest. 'Are you there, son?'

He took a few steps down the tunnel. Where was Levi? Ron turned
on his flashlight. The powerful beam cut into the air showing the path
curving away before him. His feet slipped on the muddy floor as slick
as polished marble and suddenly he felt scared, as scared as he'd ever
been in his life. His breath puffed out in a plume before him. Every
instinct told him to run. The mine didn't feel right. The air clung to
his arms like icy cockleburs, and he had to brace himself with a hand
against the wall. Then the floor shook, but it wasn't just the floor;
everything jolted or quivered. Every cell in his body flinched. He wasn't
sure if he had turned around and was heading out. He thought, the
world has shifted.

He stepped forward again. Where am I? Where am I going?

A voice came from the tunnel before him, a little boy's voice.

'Papa?' it called.

Ron rushed forward, his fear forgotten. He would greet him with love like he'd never known.

'Papa?'

His son was coming home.

Charles stood at the Crossroad gate. He'd pulled it open, but he wouldn't step inside. No, he was too frightened for that. He couldn't *see* the boy, or all would be lost. He had one chance to make it right, and only one.

'Boy?' he yelled into the mine.

For a long time there was no sound, then Charles felt a peculiar twitch, like the mountain had shrugged. The air itself contracted, and his ears popped.

He shook his head. Whatever else was going on, he could not be swayed.

'Boy?' he shouted again.

A voice came from far back in the mine. 'Daddy?' it cried. 'Is that you, Daddy?'

Small feet splashed through the mud, growing louder.

'I knew you'd come, Daddy,' the voice exclaimed, very close now.

Charles stood by the door out of sight, his hammer raised high, paused above him. When the boy stepped out, he would bring it down. Oh, yes he would. He would end it here.

And all would be right.

James Van Pelt lives in western Colorado with his wife and three sons. One of the 1999 finalists for the John W. Campbell Award for Best New Writer, he teaches high school and college English. His fiction has appeared in, amongst others, *Dark Terrors 5*, *Asimov's*, *Analog*, *Realms of Fantasy*, *Talebones*, *The Third Alternative*, *Weird Tales* and *Alfred Hitchcock's Mystery Magazine*. His first collection of stories, *Strangers and Beggars*, was published in 2002. 'The genesis of "The Boy behind the Gate" occurred long before I became a father,' recalls the author. 'During the summers, I often explored the old mills and ghost towns in the mountains west of Denver. Every once in a while there would come a report of a body found at the bottom of a deep shaft, and, of course, kids always turned up missing. It didn't take much imagination to picture a child locked in the mines. But Mark Twain and Injun Joe went there first. For the longest time the story was entitled "Two Dads", and I still think of the story with that emphasis. Those two poor, tortured dads. Is the one's love strong enough to overcome evil? Will the other pause just long enough before he strikes to change his mind? As a dad, I hope so.'

A Hollywood Ending

MICK GARRIS

Lady Hollywood is such a tease.

Every time I have given her up for a lack of interest, she tells me how beautiful and talented I am, kisses me with a playful lick of the ear, and rests her perfectly lipsticked head in my lap, her chestnut hair spilling over my thighs. But when I reach for a little handful of tit, she pulls away with a laugh.

It's always been frustrating, but it used to be cute. It was cute when I was an Artist, and fought to slay dragons with my Art. It was cute when I bounced through one after another of her silicone-implanted minions in my quest for her throne, each time climbing another Everest to be the Everlast. I wore tights and a cape back then, if only in my mind. I was invincible.

But I've since been vinced.

A steady diet of the Lady's fare led me to believe in the world of Happy Endings. Everything will always work out, she told me. And I believed her. We share the misfortune of those who suffer around us, but we are certain that their grief can never grip us personally in its thrall. Irreversibly bad things happen to other people. When my little sister crashed through the sliding glass door and her face bloomed in a welling red roadmap, I knew we could rush her to the hospital, stitch her up, and she'd be good as new in a couple of weeks. I knew that when my brother contracted AIDS, a cure would be found as he nobly fought off the spectre of death, and I would have him back to go laugh at the latest preposterous piece of crank-'em-out crap at the Chinese with me. There was no doubt that the experimental drugs my father took in the medical tests would save his life from the ravages of four decades of smoking that attacked his heart like Apaches around the wagon train. When my dog disappeared after the side gate was left open by the gardener, I knew he'd show up shivering on the porch late that night. And without question, when I got the opportunity to write and direct a Major Hollywood Studio Feature Film, Lady Hollywood herself would swoon in delight and beg me to make her mine. I might say yes, but I might play independent and hard to get.

We fear the worst, but expect the best. We have learned to expect the Happy Ending.

But Daria died in a pool of her own blood, staring up at me with wide, confused, Keane-painting eyes. Jerry wasted away horribly, angry and bitter and in pain, and died without a trace of the noble grace of Tom Hanks in *Philadelphia*. Dad responded wonderfully to the wonder drug, but when the tests were done, they would no longer supply it to him and he shuffled quietly off the mortal coil. I found Chewbacca in the back yard brush a week after his little heart gave out struggling to untangle himself from the fence. And when the Big Screen curled its mighty index finger my way, I answered the beckon with a masterpiece that crashed and burned mightily, and tossed me into a world of indifference. I was the crumpled Kleenex dropped into the toilet after being used to wipe away the secretions.

And yet, until now, I continued to believe in Happy Endings. I was the puppy who'd had its face rubbed into its own shit until it learned to poop outside, the beaten wife who kept coming back for more, because the pummelling blows showed I was loved; I was Sybil, filled with water and chained to the piano by a mad mother's crazy act of devotion; the Child of God who was robbed of those I loved and who loved me by a God who chose strange ways to display his love for me. And I continued to kneel in prayer.

After climbing and falling repeatedly in the morass of Lady Holly-wood's theme park of tough love, I soon felt only pain or nothing. At USC I burned with excitement and the thrill of discovery. I pondered the profound, was brave and inventive; creativity sparked from my fingertips. All of my waking hours – and many of my sleeping – were spent exploring, inventing, creating. Or hustling hook-ups, but that's another story.

Of course, I had no idea that my knowledge and my insights were puddle-deep; it didn't matter. It was all about expression, even if what was expressed was bullshit. And, admittedly, a lot of it was.

When did I stop caring?

I remember passion. It was passion that brought me into this unforgiving, fickle land of pick-me!-pick-me! It was passion that fuelled the twenty-hour days on the student films and the first feature. But when the feature tanked, I was scorned by Lady Hollywood, and not for the last time. It took time and a baby – a mutant, mewling beast I'd discovered on a downtown LA street corner – to get another date. Oh, she kissed me deep during production, but when the project fell off its rails and went down in flames, she sought out newer, more virile playmates.

I went inert, creatively and physically impotent, flushed of drive and thrown off my game. I went looking for work, not inspiration. Dragged through the dregs of series TV and even pornography, being behind a camera was all about pay cheques, not passion.

There was rediscovery, however. Through a tryst with a late movie star – a story I really hope I never have to tell again – I discovered that Lady Hollywood had a glorious past, one that shimmered and sparkled and breathed heavy. There were images that lit the screen in a way the Modern Masters of CGI never imagined. It's funny to think that my discoveries with her, with the fickle bitch of the silver screen, actually deepened me. Well, maybe it just seemed like it. But for a while, anyway, I held space warps and DTS explosions and computer-generated mummies and sequels that were really remakes and music-video film-making in disdain. I went on a quest for peace, a monk seeking salvation, a hermit drenched in the balm of celluloid archaeology.

I wished the world were viewed in black and white.

But a guy has to eat or be eaten. especially at Lady Hollywood's table.

It was time again to be reborn, to burst out of the placental sac and shower myself clean of the corruption of my cinematic sins, which were many. Time to void myself of the love of the old Hollywood made flesh turned repulsive, leaving in its wake a cyclopean corpse ready to submit to her next debased customer. I had to leave behind the world of mutant babies and Jean Harlow. I had to dust myself anew with baby powder, spread my Phoenix wings in resurrection, and learn from a past of my own, if you'll allow me to mix the occasional metaphor. It was time to live a life rather than watch one.

It was time to work.

The writing had again opened the door a crack. Charlie Band offered me a ten-day shoot at his studio in Romania. Canada isn't cheap enough for Full Moon, oh, no. Australia? Sure, that's even cheaper, but come on. New Zealand? Cheaper still, but still too stiff. How about Mexico? Nice and close, even if English is the second language. *Really* cheap there. Nah. Have you seen the exchange rate in Romania lately? You could buy a castle for the price of a Double Double with Cheese there. Just think how far you could stretch a production budget. Okay, so nobody speaks English, there are no film facilities or experienced workers, and they're only now discovering the joys of electricity. That's perfect for Full Moon. We rolled it, it rolled us, and the *Puppet Freaks III* DVD came out in the fall, complete with my first commentary track, as well as an exclusive behind-the-scenes documentary. Rent it, don't buy it.

PFIII didn't open any doors, but it did pay a couple of bills. The good news is that nobody notices a film like that except for the very youngest of *Fangoria* subscribers. I did a couple of convention appearances to promote it and sat at the back of the hall, ostensibly to sign autographs. The only takers were a handful of seventeen-year-olds who wanted me to read their scripts.

Through Band, I did meet some financing guys, the characters with Cannes tans, Italian cars, English suits, Israeli accents and Swiss bank accounts. And I managed to talk them into putting up a couple of hundred grand for my can't-miss digital video masterpiece. Believe it or not, *Edible* actually got picked up by Lions Gate and, fuelled by a really go-for-the-throat website, got a pretty credible limited theatrical release. It became a bit of a cult classic and a *cause célèbre* amongst the midnight movie crowd. I didn't know they even existed any more, frankly. Never underestimate the touching tale of lesbian cannibals living and dining in the Seattle underground.

Though my status on the *Fangoria* convention circuit was elevated, the Lady I most loved just wouldn't love me back. What could I do to get her to notice me? Just what did I have to do? Couldn't I put the lessons I had learned to work? Couldn't I create a masterpiece of wit, intelligence, sophistication, originality, surprise and suspense, dig deep into my psyche and explore the very heart of man? Was I up to the task, not only of self-exploration, but also of telling a tale that could enrich, enlighten and entertain? If not me, who? If not now, when?

So I wrote and discarded and wrote and wrote and discarded and wrote and wrote and wrote and discarded, and finally wrote some more. And one summer day, I emerged from my condo at the Marina, the bright mauve sunlight digging its fingers into my CRT-glazed eyeballs, and took a deep breath of the air that smelled as brown as it looked. I had completed a new script, and I knew it was my masterpiece. A little long, perhaps, at 146 pages, *Happy Endings* was everything I'd learned about life, love and relationships in all my twenty-six years. It was funny, it was tender, it was shocking, it was surprising. It even had a happy ending. I slid it into an envelope and called Metzler at

Immaculate Artists to have it picked up. Metzler was delighted to have a spec script to sling, and I was energised. It was a box of Valentine chocolates, offered up to the Goddess of Love.

To celebrate, I decided to take myself out to a movie. Let's see, what'll it be? Which masterwork would I choose? *Planet of the Apes? America's Sweethearts? Final Fantasy? Swordfish? Rush Hour 2? American Pie 2? Dr Dolittle 2? Jurassic Park III? Osmosis Jones? Original Sin? Cats and Dogs? Ghosts of Mars?*

I knew one thing with dead certainty as I perused the listings in the *LA Times Calendar*: nobody was going to buy *Happy Endings*.

So when Metzler called me back in a couple of weeks, it had nothing to do with my masterwork. But it was an offer. *An offer!*

'UPN has an MOW about a cheerleader whose botched breast enhancement surgery left her disfigured and suffering from lupus and a virulent case of lawyeritis. It's a true story, shoots on an eighteen-day schedule in Manitoba, they got one of the girls from *Lucky Charms*, two directors have already left the project, the nineteen-year-old UPN VP is a lifelong *Fangoria* subscriber who loves your work and it starts shooting Monday. Can you get on a plane today?'

Not only could I and would I . . . *I was glad to get it!*

How far the mighty have fallen.

Being on a set energised me. I was making decisions, calling the shots, and charming Miss *Lucky Charms* in her trailer. I'd heard she was a bitch, but not to me. Maybe it was because she was from series and I was from features. We coupled mightily and profoundly between set-ups. I'd thought my experience with the monster baby and Jean Harlow and the porn work would have forever deadened my drive, but the bodily investigations we undertook in her Winnie were frequent and creative, as you might expect from artists such as ourselves. Princess Charming claimed not to have been entered since before her rehab stay, and was primed and juicy, igniting sleeping fires within my deprived male flesh. When she unsheathed, revealing creamy and alarmingly realistically augmented breasts, graced with swollen, extended nipples with silver skull piercings that dangled in grinning, shining tinkles from their proud pink hostesses, my heart swelled and every part of me stood up to salute their glory.

Though her pubis was Naired clean of any trace of hair, her labia were pierced and protected by a tiny gold padlock. It caught a beam of sunlight and my eye. She smiled when she saw me discover the tiny gold key on the spider-web-fine gold chain around her neck. She lifted her sheaf of hair to grant me access, her buoyant breasts reaching high, and I lifted the award necklace over her head. I took the little key to Nirvana in my teeth and leaned deep down into Candyland, unlocked the Gates of Hell, and climbed her Stairway to Heaven. There I go mixing metaphors again.

We explored orifices I never knew existed in the human body with such energy and invention that I was rubbed raw and swollen for weeks.

The movie was a piece of shit – how could it be otherwise on an eighteen-day cookie-cutter schedule? – but it was a union piece of shit, and I got paid and laid and rolled some film. It got a seven rating, which for any other place is Tank City but for UPN is phenomenal, and put me on their A-list. Of course, the A-list at UPN is like the X, Y, or Z at a real network, but Guild minimum is Guild minimum.

Lady Hollywood was spreading her legs again.

But hadn't I learned? How could I not see the hollowness of this existence, the artistic and moral and downright cynical bankruptcy of my life? Because I was getting lots of money and pin-up pussy, that's how. The Princess got respectable reviews for the first time in her life, and insisted that I direct any movies-of-the-week that she starred in.

So now I had sort-of-famous cathode candy on my arm at screenings, offers from the networks to direct really shitty TV movies in Canada with even shittier TV actors, and a glimmer of access to the Lady I truly hoped to make mine again. But nobody in the big leagues of features notices what you're doing in the world of television. I know that when I had my brief stab at the Big Time, I didn't.

I mean, who can watch that shit? Seventeen minutes out of every hour is spent yelling at you to buy some piece of crap you don't want, don't need, and would make you sick if you put it in your mouth. It's the same old stories, the same old rhythms, the same old laugh track, the same old caricatures, the same old shit. But the big cathode eye sits in every room in the house, daring you not to watch it. The programming is just the agar that supports the bloom of mouldy commercials, sticking you in the eye with a hypodermic filled with buy-me poison, drilling products into your pod-person brain so that you cannot resist the urge to purchase them when they present themselves so noisily at your friendly neighbourhood supermarket.

Following the path of least resistance, I said yes to television, the only club that would have me as a member. I made another MOW with Princess Charming, this one the totally true – no kidding! – story of a feckless young lady lawyer who discovers a ring of body-part harvesters, selling livers and kidneys and eyeballs to high-rolling, incomplete buyers over the Internet. This one we shot in New Zealand, somehow substituting Wellington for Baltimore, and the Princess for an educated, intelligent, progressive lady lawyer. Well, the Princess, for all her charms, is sweet and beautiful and really good company, but her SATs would surely have stood in the way of a legal career.

We mated madly in her trailer (though I'd worked my way up to a contractual full single trailer of my own, hers was more divinely sized and appointed), and the unlocking and entering was performed with increasing frequency. We tried to keep it to lunch breaks and after wrap, but it was hard to keep it under wraps when the trailer rocked noisily to our samba. It was a set visit from *Entertainment Tonight* that spilled the beans of our relationship to the national television-viewing audience. Not that it hurt to be publicly outed as the poster-girl-for-nipple-rings' studly boy toy, but it pissed off her muscular tennis pro/ underwear model husband. It could have got ugly, had the *Smoking Gun* online tabloid not discovered Mr Thirty Love's proclivities for hired shemale encounters in the bungalow where John Belushi died at the Château Marmont.

Jesus, is there no morality in Hollywood?

I continued to be buffeted about by the broken winds of Lady Hollywood, passive and mindless as I fielded offers of one lame MOW after another. I took whatever was offered, knowing at least that I was directing, that I was making movies, that I had not sunk to the depths of series television. Hiatus was over and the Princess was back at her own series, Reno-divorced from Mr Fruit-of-the-Loom, begging me to shoot episodes, but was very understanding when I told her that I could be intractably reversing the course of my career if I did. I kept after Metzler to get me feature meetings at the studio, but he was finally earning some kind of an income off of my television work and was not so motivated. He was, however, able to get me a meeting on a new Jacqueline Smith pilot.

To this I said no.

I was working, earning a living, punching a clock, fucking a desirable TV débutante, and leaving my brain empty and sodden. If I allowed any personal reflection, I'd have been so filled with self-loathing that I'd have jumped off the Hollywood sign. So instead, I shaved my already thinning scalp, grew a soul patch and a paunch and dove headfirst into a personal study of alcoholism. It took me a six-pack to even sit through our cast-and-crew screening of *Speaking Parts* at the TV Academy in North Hollywood. Oh, it was all very chichi, with the finest catering – braised organ meats and the most cunning little cookies shaped like body parts – and an open bar. Everyone was very taken with the Importance of the Film, congratulating one another on its Theme and Performances, high on its Emmy shots, when in truth this masterwork of disposable cinema would be forgotten the day after it aired. They all are. They are the cornstarch binder that holds the advertising cocaine. We try to make movies, but they are just delivery systems for the bleating of commercials.

When I looked at the sea of agents and actors and journalists and hangers-on milling about, freeloading on ritzy-titzy comestibles in the regal lobby, broadcasting too-loud conversations on their eensy cell phones, and I saw how many of them had gleaming shaved skulls, soul patches and a paunch, I realised in a stomach-dropping moment of truth . . .

I had become One of Them!

I was an interchangeable film-rolling robot, dipped in screenings at the Academy and catered desserts, draped in Hugo Boss and Julius the Monkey, nightclub-hopping at all the right places, memorising the LA-to-Toronto flight schedules on Air Canada, talking about Nielsen shares and ad rates, turning my nose up at series and basic cable movies while wallowing in the lowest headline graveyard true-story pieces of shit. I was just another anonymous first name on Lady Hollywood's dance card . . . a name she would never get to by the end of the night. I spoke in terms of act breaks and TVQ and Broadcast Standards and hot series stars and their availability, no matter how wrong they were for the parts. I realised that I hadn't thought with my imagination since the days before Harlow. I had been embraced, imprisoned and embalmed: a POW of the MOW.

Just when I was awakening from my pod-guy stupor, just when the pennies started to fall off my eyes, just when I was ready to remind the rest of the world that I was an artist, by God, in other words, just when I was about to fix my world . . . they stopped making TV movies.

It wasn't a subtle shift, either. In the wake of *Who Wants to Be a Millionaire*, *Survivor*, *Big Brother*, *Temptation Island*, *Boot Camp*, *Lost*, *The Mole*, *Murder in Small Town X*, *The Amazing Race* and all the other so-called 'reality shows' – in other words, shows where you don't have to pay members of the Screen Actors Guild, the Writers Guild of America or the Directors Guild of America, where there are no residual payments for rerun and syndication play – there was no room for my meat and potatoes. Even if the Reality Ratings were not great, com-pared to their low cost they were extremely profitable. So with a legacy of audience expectations lowered by a diet of cheap-shit, Canadian-cranked dime-a-dozen woman-in-jeopardy TV movies that featured one star from a familiar series and a supporting cast of anonymous Canadian thespians, the networks gleefully jumped to the next lower rung on the ladder of commercial delivery.

And I was out of work.

No longer the boy wonder, I was going to turn twenty-seven on my next birthday. The prospects were not bright. My résumé reeked of mediocrity, the shooting star of my youth gone dark, the fire extinguished by assembly line crap, without a signature or a personality.

The passion long gone, it took the return of unemployment to realise I had no friends. None. Oh, it's all kissy-face and love-ya-hon' on the set, where you are thrown together with a new group of cast and crew on each new project. But when those twenty-some days of prepping and shooting are over, so are your relationships. Princess Charming, of course, was drenched in friends, her little Nokia constantly tweeting with one ass-kiss or another wrapping her in love. But when I wasn't working, a condition that by now I should have been well-equipped to deal with, I was all alone: just me and my DVDs.

I was loved by Princess Charming; she told me so repeatedly. But hers was a lalaland love, tuned by the eye of *Access Hollywood* and *E!* While she worked on her series (and frankly, I don't know anyone who has ever seen it), I went to the movies, watched movies at home, sat by myself in the most popular restaurants and wondered what to do with myself. Masturbation was an option, but since that was my career, I just was not so motivated. It started to take more than a couple of shots of Jack Daniel's to numb me to sleep.

I stared out of the Marina condo, bored out of my skull, and unable to imagine. I wanted to write, but nothing came out. Not even bad ideas. Nothing. I was used up at twenty-six. Lady Hollywood had sapped me of my vital fluids without even taking me within her most private of parts. Ever teasing, never pleasing. The semen of my imagination was locked within my testicles, and I was getting creative blue balls. So I just opened bottles and emptied them. I felt more creative, but nothing ever got on paper. Or that which did was no better than what I'd sicked up in the toilet.

Finally, I relented. The Princess was so sweet, her eyes so dewy, the halo of her hair so perfectly framed when she suggested one last time that I could make her show something special, that I agreed to direct the season finale. It was a two-hour special, so I could at least make believe it was something special, and not *really* an episode: more like an MOW. *Exactly* like an MOW, at least in the eyes of DGA scale. Eighty-eight minutes of movie sandwiched between thirty-two minutes of bellowing buy-me and network promos flogging their latest 'unscripted' monstrosities.

But this was the new me. Again. No, really. This was my chance to dazzle Lady Hollywood, to grab this homely little piffle of a series by the neck and shake it until it cried uncle. I was a plastic surgeon, and by God, I would carve a beautiful countenance out of its dowdy visage or I didn't deserve a date with the Lady. I took the script and marked it up with diagrams and designs and ideas. My imagination, unbridled by the ninety pages of soulless, mindless blather, embroidered fabrics of visual splendour. It doesn't have to cost a fortune to make something look wonderful. The independents do it all the time. So let's shake things up a little here. I came on like a preacher and managed to get the lazy, tubby IA crew to catch fire, getting everybody on the bus taking us to the best damned *Lucky Charms* episode ever. And it worked: for once, the crew felt liberated, encouraged to go beyond the beyond. The sets were actually wild and kind of wonderful. It became a sort of acid-dream playground, where we broke all the rules and created a phantasmagoric colour wheel of a movie. I got the actors to really stretch, re-imagine their characters and ground them in what passed for real emotion. It was weird and funny and ... well, let's not get carried away here, but at least it was not like any of the other episodes of *Lucky Charms*.

The Princess couldn't have been more delighted. She loved me, she loved the show, and even the other girls on the show, who hated anything she loved, got into it. And both of them offered me space in their trailers when the Princess wasn't in earshot. Okay, I did one of them, but not the other. I do have standards ... at least when I'm working.

The brass at the WB were delighted with the dailies, if at first a bit confused. But hell, they'd lost *Buffy* and *Roswell* to UPN, and this was all they had left. I had taken to drinking only Fiji water to keep my head clear, and though we shot a few eighteen-hour days, managed to come in on time and only slightly over budget. I actually took pride in this, this *episode*, and made it something that I actually cared about. Maybe I'd even do one of these again.

Then it aired. As cast and crew gathered at Residuals and hooted and cheered it around the bar's big screen, the rest of the nation was oblivious. This very-best-ever episode of *Lucky Charms* was its lowest-rated. Ever. It was opposite *Millionaire* on ABC, a *Big Brother* rerun on CBS, *Weakest Link* on NBC, a 'When Bad Drivers Attack!' special on Fox, and *Buffy* on UPN. But we weren't just killed by the big boys;

even basic cable got better ratings: USA, Fox Family, PAX, TBS, TNT and even TNN all got better numbers than we did. And our Very Special Episode never even got reviewed . . . not even by the trades.

No more offers.

In a life of crashing and burning, this might have been the nadir. At least my popular Princess still loved me. But I was not prepared for what she had to say the next time we coupled. It was a typically sweaty, liquid liaison, an acrobatic, aerobic performance of breathtaking quality. The vast picture window of her bedroom looked out over the San Fernando Valley from our perch on the hillside overlooking Studio City. The rain was Biblical, beating against the glass as we pounded against each other. I had bite marks from those little skulls all over my body, and I reciprocated in kind. Ours was a pretzel logic that knew no convention: every orifice was fed and satisfied, no appendage left wanting as we melted together like rubber and road. I was depleted, sucked dry by a vampire that drew pearly white blood and clear sweat from my body. Lying on our backs in a cooling pool of those vital fluids, we stared up at one another in the ceiling mirror that looked down on us. Her meaty breasts jiggled with the pounding of her heart. Our faces were flushed and sheened with perspiration.

'I love you,' she told me.

'Mmmmm.'

'Do you love me?'

'Sure.' I supposed I did. Why not? She was great.

'What do you mean, "sure"?'

'I mean sure, as in of course.'

'"Sure" you love me?'

'That's what I said.'

'Then tell me.'

'I just did.'

'No, you said "sure". I want to hear the words.'

Why not? I mean, it was no big deal. I loved her. What's not to love? Okay: 'I love you.'

'Can't you tell me without me asking?'

'Okay. I love you. I'll tell you more often. I'll bring it up on my own. I love you, Princess.'

She smiled. She did have the sweetest smile. But I sensed this was leading somewhere. A shadow of dread started creeping across the room towards me.

'Should we think about getting married?'

Bombshell. 'Sure; we can think about it all you want. Why?'

''Cause I love you. And you love me. And 'cause I'm pregnant.'

Inside, I screamed. I have a major problem with the whole baby thing. I mean, it's not like I have a whole lot of experience with babies, but the experience I had with little Asta was all I ever wanted ... hell, much *more* then I ever wanted. No babies. Not for me. No drooling, screaming, sucking, shitting, constantly feeding little squirming pink creatures for me.

'Pregnant?'

'You know, gonna have a baby.'

Okay, it's been confirmed. I was terrified. As I think about it now, at least I was feeling *something*. That was new. But better to be the Hollywood Zombie I had become than confront fatherhood. I didn't know what to do. I didn't know where to turn. I longed to be an ostrich and jam my head into the sand. Babies are bad enough, but Hollywood babies! She wouldn't let me look away, her face niacin-rosy, freshly fucked and shining with satisfaction. Truthfully: irresistible.

'How pregnant are you?' I asked.

'All the way.'

'I mean how long?'

'About eight weeks.'

'So it's not too late for an abortion.'

She just stared at me, those lovely eyes taking on a glinting wetness, filling and spilling as she trapped me in her sight. I couldn't have spoken a less welcome sentence. I tried to reach for her, to take back the ill-timed, if perfectly logical, statement. But she broke. Her body was given over to wracking wails and snuffling.

When the sobs subsided and she was able to speak, she spoke. 'With you or without you, I'm having our baby. I thought you'd be happy.'

I can't stand crying. I melt, I give way, I die. I tried to tell her that it just wasn't the right time. Her career was on the line here. And so was mine. There's some momentum going here, and a baby would stop everything short. She didn't care about her career; she had enough money and investments to see her through whatever happened, and Hollywood was shallow and hollow and merely a means to an end. There was life after *Lucky Charms*. Well, I'm glad she thought so. I'd never considered that there was any other life than the one we'd chosen. But, hey, it was her body. If she wanted a baby, she would have her baby. Still, the thought of a squalling, bawling infant spitting up and shitting up filled me with dread. Not enough dread to give up the Princess and all her charms and career opportunities, but dread. I couldn't think of myself as Daddy – didn't even want to – but I couldn't stop her from becoming a mother, no matter how foolish the notion. As was my wont, I was picked up by the winds of circumstance and blown into the gutter of Hollywood nuptials.

The wedding at Hollywood Presbyterian was enormous and star-studded. Well, *TV*-star studded, but that counts on *Access Hollywood*. The rest of her coven was there, as well as low-level WB and UPN celebrities and dignitaries. Press agents called to get their *Survivor* loser clients on the guest list, Sam Rubin had an exclusive KTLA wedding party interview, and the swarms of bottom-feeding entertainment media piddled in our pool and drank our champagne. A couple of members of O Town kind of sang, and teenage girls thronged the perimeter of the church, hoping to grope – or at least glimpse – a Fifteen-Minute-Famer. It was noisy and cheerful, and nothing really went wrong. The Princess's mother beamed, at forty-two a wonderfully prescient reflec-tion of how beautifully the Princess herself would ripen. When she hugged me after the ceremony, I felt her visibly sizable peek-a-boo nipples harden under the braless silk blouse, and she actually sneaked me a little tongue. I couldn't keep from getting an erection, but I gave her nothing back. I mean, I'm a happily married man. Not that I expected to remain so, Hollywood marriages being what they are, but this was new, fresh and respectable.

The Princess herself, however, never was more glorious. Her face glowed, luminous in the lightest application of very natural make-up. Even swollen with child, her beauty was almost ethereal, resplendent in a custom-made Rei Kawakubo gown that allowed her protruding baby belly to be seen, even highlighted. Somehow, her pregnancy made her even more desirable. She was due to pop the pup in a month or so, so there was no secret about her condition. Most of the wedding presents were really baby presents, which pissed me off a little, but I got over it.

Our honeymoon was spent at the Four Seasons Sayan in Bali, a gift from Aaron Spelling, the generous producer who owned the Princess. The night we arrived, despite the jetlag and exhaustion, the spectacular sunset views of the Ayung River from our outdoor rock bathtub lit a fire within us. I had been afraid of pregnant sex since the swell of the baby's presence had become overt. I mean, I didn't want to put out its little eye or anything, though I knew I was being foolish. But then she stood over me, dripping wet and blissfully bare, her belly swollen with baby and her breasts with milk, and a curtain lifted. She'd long ago removed the nipple-skulls so that there would be minimal milk leakage, and stood completely naked, mind and body, her flesh like French vanilla ice cream, her butterfat skin shining and hairless. The new heft of her breasts was irresistible, so I reached up and slid my hands up her body to them. My face followed, and soon I was tasting warm mother's milk as I nursed it from her. It was my favourite meal of the trip.

She gripped my hairless head in her hands and eased it lower. I slid my face along the tight, round tummy and found succour in the smooth valley below, where she had celebrated the marriage with a ritual casting-away of lock and key. I dined on her physical magnificence for a while before she eased my head back up to her stomach. She wanted to rest it there, wanted me to listen to our child. I could hear its little heart beating from her womb, a tiny tattoo nearly drowned out by the tom-tom beat of her own. And then, a surprisingly brisk little kick tapped my face through her belly. She held my head there, and something happened. For a moment, I went blind.

Everything went black, but the sounds got louder: new and different sounds, not of Balinese monkeys and birds, but of a thudding, rushing heartbeat. It was a deafening, repeating, 5.1 surround whoosh. As my eyes got used to the darkness, I saw that there was colour forming in the black: red, of course. Blood-red, with a sparkle of gold. I could see inside through my baby's eyes. Tiny, incomplete fingers flexed clumsily before my face in the placental sac. Peering through the dim light, I could make out perfect little baby toes, even down to their little toenails. In the dim glow through the amniotic fluid, I could make out a pretty good-sized little pecker for a kid his age. We'd had all the tests done, of course, and knew it was a boy, but I was proud that my son was well-endowed.

Then the veil of darkness lifted and I was back on our private stone balcony overlooking the cliffside jungles and rice terraces, a glamorous and beautifully voluptuous young starlet dripping wet and breathing hard as she held my head against her bare skin. I climbed from the pool, lifted her up in my arms and laid her on her side on the bed, ignoring the water. I spooned against her back, hands pressed tight to her stomach and entered her from behind. As I pounded into her uncontrollably, animal instinct ruling the rooster, she threw her arms behind and gripped my ass, pulling me in deeper and faster.

And then, again, that same something happened. I left my head and entered junior's . . . while I was entering and re-entering his mother. I could see the length of my erection stretching and penetrating the Princess from within, the repeated plunging rhythm hypnotic in the dim, red-gold-black light. As the Princess was caught up in spasmic paroxysms of what I hoped was delight and fulfilment, I helplessly spat my seed into her and watched its milky mist creep slowly into the baby's amniotic bath. As I withdrew from her hallowed cave, I also withdrew from this link to an unformed mind and back into the monkey chants and damp, purpling sky of the Balinese evening.

Stunned, I stared at my beautiful wife (*wife!*), stupored by what had just happened. She saw immediately that something was up.

'What's the matter?'

What could I say? What did I *know*? I'd seen through the eyes of my unborn son while I was fucking his mother? That's exactly what I told her. And bless her little tattooed heart, she thought that was beautiful.

Well, it scared the shit out of me. And it kept happening, at unexpected and disorienting times. We'd be sitting in an ancient Ubud temple, watching the villagers monkey-chant for tourists, when suddenly I'd be pre-born, the sound outside muffled and drowned out by the Princess's pounding heartbeat. It was a sensation of floating in space, of womb scuba-diving, staring through the cloudy, not yet fully formed eyes of a pre-infant. Tiny fingers weakly flexed and explored, reaching out and touching the womb, the toes, the little baby weenie. Everything else in my brain evaporated as I slid back into sensory prehistory, brain activity sliding to a nearly complete halt, running on instinct, not intellect, resting, easing myself free of the world outside. I was at peace.

Peace.

My mind had not been at rest . . . well, *ever*. Until now. It was like letting go. Being free. Cutting the cord. Free fall.

And then I woke up.

The loud, rhythmic, atonal chatter of the chanters drove spikes into my newly sensitive ears, jangled me, threw me violently back into my own body in the real world. I hated it, and ran outside for some semblance of quiet.

As I stood smoking out in the sultry Indonesian night, the chanting a distant dissonance, the far-off wailing of priests curling through the night sky like smoke, I tried to catch my breath. The rushing of the Ayung River calmed me, took me back to the womb. Suddenly it occurred to me that I was more than ten thousand miles away from Hollywood. I had moved to another planet.

On this planet, there were no avaricious agents, no numbskull network executives, no call sheets, no rush-hour freeway parking lots, no tap-dance meetings on movies you wouldn't even *watch*, no Monday box-office reports, no cheering the failure of another over-budget creatively bankrupt celluloid stinker, no lunches at gilt-priced snooty see-me emporia where everyone is watching the mirrors out of the corners of their eyes, no taking it up the ass from ferocious ego monsters driving huge Jaguars to mask the incapacity of their penises, no style-monster *fashionistas* dictating what must be worn and how, no unavoidable advertising spoiling every vista, no hip-hop pounding mercilessly in your head, no seven-act structure, no broadcast standards, no MPM, no Tom Shales, no artifice, no knife-in-teeth competition, no keeping up with the Joneses. Hell, no Joneses at all.

No, on this planet there was earth, sky and water. There was the Princess. There was our son. And I was with them. We had been reduced to the Elements. My heart swelled as it dawned on me that I truly loved them. They filled me, they expanded me. They were a part of me. We were linked, chemically and spiritually. Someone once described love as caring more about the one you love than about yourself. I had never imagined that plausible, even possible. Not until now. My marriage, fatherhood: they had seemed so abstract, so distant until now. But I woke up. My love had sprouted, grown wings, lifted me. The Princess and my son opened up a brand new chamber in my heart. This chamber was not protected by a wall of cynicism, was lacking in irony, was startlingly open and sincere. It's a chamber open to pain . . . but worth the pain. To my amazement, I was truly in love.

I turned to see the Princess, following her tight, round tummy out of the temple and into the fragrant night, and I smiled at her. She approached me, asked me if I was okay, and I pulled her into my arms and enveloped her. I held her head in my hands and kissed her softly, all over her face. When I told her 'I love you' over and over, it made her laugh and cry at the same time.

So this is that feeling that everybody writes about, sings about, makes movies about. The Princess had reached out to me from within, and I had never even been aware. As I looked into and past her eyes, I was in her thrall. Being reduced to the beginning of life, she and our son became meaningful; I'd been chasing the Bitch Hollywood, when what was important was here, right here in the jungle. Right here in my arms. Our connection had been made on a corporeal, carnal level, but existed beyond that somehow. I felt older, deeper, wiser. And it kind of hurt.

We silently held hands as we peered out over the vast valley of rice terraces, a jewel-box of diamonds strewn across the coal-black sky. Curls of smoke rose like thoughts from the farms. And we kissed like Brad and Jennifer. No. Like us. Nobody else has ever kissed like us.

We left the villa wide open to the night sky as we coupled that night. It was as carnal as ever, but deeper, meaningful, evocative as body met body and minds melted away into instinct. Butterflies fluttered into the room, floating over us and lighting on our wet, sticky bodies as we linked, rocked, plundered in abandonment. She fiercely grabbed me by the scalp and pulled my head back so our eyes would be locked when we both erupted into a violent, mutual orgasm that wouldn't end. She exploded in repeated shuddering waves of almost frightening fulfilment as I kept spurting and spurting into her.

We fell asleep linked, uncovered, pretzelled. It was the first night I had fallen asleep without Scotch or Ambien or even a Tylenol PM in a couple of years.

What a great honeymoon.

On the flight home, I spent most of my time in the womb, my adult face sleeping against the curve of mother's belly, floating mindlessly, wordlessly in the balm of amniotic fluid, a sensory deprivation tank that worked internally as well as on the other senses. I was unborn, gearing up for Independence Day, but in no hurry. I could feel everything tuning up, completing, making ready. I could feel the baby's hand stroke curiously and calmingly against the wall that separated him from me. He let me know he loved me in his silent, unborn-baby way.

As we approached LAX, I woke to find the Princess sound asleep, her head on my shoulder, drooling, her eyes rolled back in her head. I thought she looked adorable, and couldn't keep from gently kissing her forehead. I was relaxed and comfortable in my own body, rested and happy. I looked out the window as we made our way through the crust of muddy smog that covered the basin like a flu, the ant farm of freeways choked to stagnation. It looked brown and dry and uninviting, a corpse laid out on its pyre, ready to be ignited to set its spirit free. Princess Charming awoke with a kiss as the 747 dropped to enter the dead body of Los Angeles.

Home.

Studio City had changed in the two weeks since we left: noisier, more crowded, browner, drier, smellier, brighter, less polite, meaner, more selfish. The answering machine was flashing '99' over and over; it was full. The cleaning lady had left the mail piled on the dining room table, a tower of babble that meant nothing. You could throw it all out and never notice the difference. After all, the business manager got all the cheques. We were home, but we didn't feel we belonged there. It had changed too much.

The truth, of course, was that we had changed. In Bali, we had become a family.

We cocooned. Spinning a web of solitude around us, we turned inwards indulging ourselves in each other. Yeah, we linked sexually, but it went way beyond that. It was hypnosis, infatuation, adoration, obsession. And I couldn't keep from kissing the mound of her stomach, silently and psychically communing with my offspring. It was a disgustingly Hollywood idyll, ordering out from Chin Chin and Mexicali and filling the new nursery with all the finest from Baby Town Online while we waited for Junior to be born. We were too focused to miss Bali's dissipating hold on us, too wrapped in anticipation to notice that California began to take us over again. Everything changes; everything wears off. And you don't even notice as it happens to you.

The baby was due on May 25th. I was born on May 25th, 1977, the same day *Star Wars* opened. In fact, my mother went into labour as she waited in line at the Chinese Theatre for the first show. It practically killed my father that he had to take her to the hospital and miss the movie after waiting in line for over two hours. He came back for the midnight show that night. To this day, my mother has never seen *Star Wars* or any of its sequels, won't even have the videos in the house. It's her own private little protest, and perhaps fuelled my fire to make movies in the first place. Nothing like a little repression to provoke a little rebellion.

Baby Day drew nearer. The Princess's belly looked like an over-ripe peach about to burst from its skin. Every night after we made love, I drifted into the mind of the little boy in her womb, floating and forming, the rest of the planet at bay, moving more, seeing more. We were getting ready to break water, hit the lights, roll sound and camera, and call for action.

May 25th. 3:20 am. I woke screaming, my eyes wide but blind, wrapped in blackness, a spike of pain shattering my skull from within, detached, terrified, in a sudden jolt of agony that I could not cast off. I could feel the Princess's hand gripping my own, but I couldn't see her. Her nails dug painfully into my hand, surely drawing blood, but I was inside her, blind, screaming.

Dying.

Just as quickly, the pain ended. I opened my eyes, and there was my wife, eyes rolled back in her head, panting, pale, perspiring. She clutched me tightly, and now it hurt. She managed to look at me with red-laced eyes, speaking between agonised breaths: 'Something's wrong. Call 911.'

I broke out in a sweat of terror, fumbled for the phone in the predawn moonlight, and managed to hit 911. I held her close, whispering over and over how everything was going to be okay, how I loved her so much, as we waited for the cavalry.

The ambulance raced us to Cedars Sinai, where her obstetrician screeched up in his Testarossa at precisely the same moment. He called all the shots, taking charge and rushing her into emergency. But despite his handsome, Robert Redford strength, the hustle of the best medical technicians and facilities money can buy, it was to no avail. Here, in this town, at this price, we were as hopeless as the homeless on Skid Row.

Our baby was born dead.

In the movies, your baby doesn't die. You laugh together and make home movies and go to Disneyland and Yosemite and keep a family album and mark his growth on the kitchen wall and save for his college and cry at his wedding. In the movies, love is enough. In the movies, faith saves the day.

No, in the movies your baby doesn't die. Neither does your baby sister, or your brother, or your father. But especially not your baby.

That only happens in real life.

Movies are better.

I had linked with our little boy in a connection no other parent has ever shared with his child, actually lived in his little head. But I had no idea that his head was so malformed, that the brain extruded through the open spot at the top of his little skull. By the time he was ready for his close-up, it was too late. After a brief flash of intolerable agony, he was gone.

And so was the Princess. When she was awake, she was crying, deep, racking sobs, wailing that ripped through the house with grief. When she wasn't crying, she was unconscious, knocked out by sedatives, sleeping pills, anti-depressants and vodka. I cried with her, held onto her, tried to ease her grief, but I was grieving too deeply to be of any help. I tried to be strong for her, but she didn't want my strength, and pushed me away. All I could do was sit on the balcony, tears coursing down my cheeks as I listened to her anguished, jungle wail behind the closed bedroom door, throwing and shattering things and screaming at God.

I held onto her, tight, not letting her pull away. She beat on my chest with her fists, but I wouldn't let her go. She collapsed into me, exhausted, then fell asleep in my arms.

My pain was deadened by hers. She was in such excruciating agony, draped in a smothering cowl of death, that I felt useless, responsible.

For three solid months, she cried and I drank and cried. Her mother came by, but the Princess wouldn't come out of her room to see her. Friends from the show came to see her, to try to bring some light into her darkness, but the door remained locked. The rest of the coven tried to pull her out for lunch, but she didn't do food any more.

Without wearing her celebrity, her face clean of make-up, dressed only in sweats, eyes red and swollen, her face under a constant river of tears, she looked like a miserable little girl, an orphan in the storm, a helpless, hopeless little fawn abandoned in the forest. Bambi after the fire had killed her mother.

She surely blamed me, as she couldn't bear to look at me. I could see the immolating look in her eyes before she turned away, and I couldn't blame her. It had to have been my fault. She was right. After three months of this life of the living dead, she asked me to move out so that her mother could come and be with her. I had finally experienced the revelation of love, and it chewed me up and spit me out. Love is pain. I tried to fight her, to hold her, to keep us together, but all I reminded her of was the baby we lost. She lost. The baby I didn't want in the first place. But the baby only I had shared a psychic link with. She had never been in his brain, and resented me for it. And for everything else. The baby made me real, and the real hurt.

So I moved back to a faceless, transitional condo at the Marina City Club, just me and my pain and my DVDs.

I wanted to hold the Princess, feed her strength, kiss her, be the reason for her to climb back into her life. I wanted to be her hero. But now she hated me. She probably always would.

Is this what everyone wants? Is all of this horror worth the moments of bliss? Is it better to feel than to be oblivious? The choice between fantasy and reality is being made throughout the basin, every minute of every day. And for most, the choice is easy. For me, there was no choice. Yes. For me, the flash of fire was worth it.

But now, as the graduated filter of browning sky began to drop, I yearned for the release I had found in my baby's mind, that sense of freedom, the extraterrestrial departure from real life, the rejection of all that was earthbound. For me, all that was earthbound was awful. Everything hurt. This was a life not worth living. I didn't want to start over again. There was no more Phoenix left within me. My nine lives had just about been used up. I just wanted it all to stop.

I stood on the twenty-first-floor balcony and realised how easy it could all be if I just jumped. A bungee jump without the bungee. Ten seconds of gut-punching terror, and then freedom. Release. Peace.

Peace.

I stared out into the ocean, its effluent-brown fingers lapping at the hulls of multi-million-dollar ego yachts, and my mind drifted back to the monkey forests and winding rivers of Bali. The twenty-four-hour rush hour clotted the Marina, but my brain was lifted to the better planet that lay beyond this one.

Acrophobic, I tiptoed to the edge of the balcony. All it would take is a single step, and I could fly. The pain would stop.

The phone rang.

Should I answer? What difference could it make? Why didn't I just make that simple leap? The phone rang again, daring me. Another glance over the balcony. Another ring. No, this was not the time. I stepped inside and answered the phone.

It was Metzler. Spelling wanted to know if I had any series ideas to pitch for pilot season. Lady Hollywood calling.

It always happens. Just when you're ready to give that bitch a shove, just when you're ready to tell her to fuck off, she calls and asks for a date. Well, I was no longer interested. She was getting old, anyway, losing teeth, gaining weight, and her hair was going grey. I had only thought I had loved her. The Princess was much more my type, even now.

'Listen to me,' he said. 'They love you there. You come up with a series, write and direct the pilot, you don't have to run the show. It's a big chunk of change, and if the fucker's a hit, you're talking hundreds of millions of dollars.'

Well, I didn't care about hundreds of millions of dollars any more. However . . . however . . .

Maybe I did have an idea. The cogs turned.

'I'm sure you've got something better than the shit they're running,' he said. 'Think about it.'

I thought about it.

'You know . . . I do have something I've been working on. Something . . . *special*.' Something they deserve. I could hear the saliva forming in his mouth.

'Tell me.'

'No,' I told him. 'Not over the phone. I've got something that's just what network television is looking for. I promise. Get me a meeting in the agency boardroom with the mucky-mucks. The highest flyers at each of the networks. This is going to be an auction.'

'An auction!' His hands scraped together. 'This sounds delectable!'

'It's better than that. Can you set it up?'

'I'm on the phone. I don't know if I can get everybody there at the same time, though. We might have to do separate meetings.'

'No. I'm pitching this once. If they can't make it, fuck 'em. Twenty-four hours to bid, and that's it. And if it doesn't sell, it doesn't sell. I don't really give a shit. And keep business affairs away for now.'

He was panting. 'You're making my job easy. I'll call you back.'

Immaculate Artists has a gorgeous Scandinavian modern conference room, with soft, calming indirect lighting, plush leather seats that roll with a whisper on the walnut flooring, de Kooning originals spotted in warm, pleasing light, and a vast array of fresh fruits, whatever you wanted to drink, and fresh, still-warm baked goods from Belwood. Iger and Kellner sent underlings, but Sassa and Moonves and Valentine and most of the other jumbo jets were there. Sceptical, resentful of the secrecy and of my station in the network TV universe, but present and accounted for. Had I been David Kelly or Chris Carter or John Wells or even the Endemol guy, they'd have fawned and cooed and kissed me on both cheeks, adding zeroes to their chequebook offers.

But it was just me, the guy who directed the lowest-rated episode of *Lucky Charms* ever. But even losers like me can become big winners with the right idea at the right time. It's possible. And that possibility, especially when pumped up by Metzler and Immaculate and thrown up for bid, was worth missing one session with the personal trainer.

When they finally settled in for the 11:00 am appointment at 11:35, Metzler turned it over to me. I didn't even stand; it was better this way. I looked at each of them in turn, cleared my throat, took a gulp of Fiji water, and began:

'If your legal team is squeamish, you might as well leave the room now. However, if you're bold, adventurous enough to take a chance on something that could change the course of network television, then hear me out. It's taking unscripted television to its cutting edge. It doesn't rely on stars or writers or directors. It is inexpensive, but powerful. I dare anybody not to watch this show.'

No one left the room. No one moved. No one even fidgeted. But no one betrayed any interest, either.

I went on. 'This show might dance at the edge of legality, but I've got ways around that. There are always ways around that. This show travels around the world, is universal in appeal, and faces a life- and death-issue every single week. It's called *Suicide!* With an exclamation point.'

The room relaxed. Some of the mucky-mucks looked at one another and smiled.

'We solicit viewers with the most heart-rending tales of woe, and choose the most telegenic, document their horrible lives, do "dramatic recreations", interview all those around them who have made their lives so miserable, and have the audience vote who deserves the most elaborate and spectacular suicide. At the end of the show each week . . . a magnificently staged death. It's probably illegal in the States, but that's the international angle. We go to exotic places all over the world to document these deaths, sell it world-wide, tie in with all these Death with Dignity groups, and tell Regis to go fuck himself.'

Throats cleared in the room. They had to make it physically evident that it disgusted them without them actually saying so.

'Think about it,' I continued. 'It's got romance and heartbreak, the triumph over adversity, life and death, good guys and bad guys, far-reaching, exotic locations all around the world. I'm telling you, it's universal.'

Metzler grinned like the Cheshire Cat. He knew these guys a lot better than me. It seemed to me like they found the whole thing distasteful, that they were ready to walk out in an offended huff.

'Nobody's hands get dirty. We shoot in secrecy in a different location every week. All legal responsibility is held by the producers, not the networks. And all legal issues will be assumed by me and the production.'

Still no reaction.

'There will be no pilot, although I will tell you I'm halfway through production of the first episode.'

Surprised looks around the room, though they quickly tried to hide them behind slack masks of disinterest.

'In the first episode, there is no voting anyone off the planet. We have our star, and we have our commitment. I will be the first person to take his own life on international television. I am going to commit suicide, whether you buy this show or not, and it will all be recorded and edited to better than network-quality standards. All proceeds from the show will go to my wife, and you can assign any showrunner you want to continue the production, though I have all approvals. I've got a commitment from Chuck Woolery to host and Bill Conti to score. The mastered show will be delivered to the winning bidder, along with a show bible and all the attendant shit you'll need.

'Thanks for your time.'

Metzler took over with a single sentence. 'You have twenty-four hours to make your offers.'

I stood up and walked out before they could.

I went home and edited the footage I'd been shooting on digital video for the last week on the Mac. I didn't get far before the phone rang again. You and I both know it was Metzler. The suits were squirting zeroes all over their bids. Every network but NBC made offers, incredible offers, groundbreaking offers. I think NBC wanted to stand as a beacon of higher standards, but in truth, they just didn't want to pony up the big bucks. I'd made the biggest deal of my life, and it was dependent on my death. Which was exactly what I wanted.

Predictably, Fox made the winning bid.

The Garuda flight to the Balinese capital of Denpassar was quiet, uneventful, save for documenting it with my video equipment. I tried to look as pensive as possible for the camera. The pain made it easy. I just wanted all of this to end, to let me go. But I tapped away on my iBook, writing Woolery's narration and editing my self-interview as we bisected the sky.

The Malaysian video crew I'd hired from Kuala Lumpur met me in a limo at the airport, and became my constant companions. The camera guy didn't speak a word of English, but the soundman spoke enough for us to communicate. The industrial ugliness of Denpassar photographed beautifully: gnarled, smoky traffic, scraggy dogs and cattle in the streets, the frenzy of motor scooters and trishaws through the clusters of pre-fab, smog-stained concrete towers and garish signs made for exciting, exotic video, and great counterpoint for the lush, quiet beauty inland.

We left the snarling city in our wake as we dug deep into the heart of the island. Roadside shops gave way to breathtaking greenery, and vast stretches of palms and brilliant tropical flowers and emerald hillside rice terraces. The simple, natural beauty of the thick, ropy vegetation that reached its fingers everywhere calmed my heart. The scent of incense burning was ubiquitous, and ropes of its smoke lifted from the offerings of gorgeous, fragrant flowers at every doorway.

Finally, we reached the resplendent Amandari. It's a luxurious retreat, the perfect place for a Hollywood castaway to hide in splendiferous comfort for his last night on earth. Outrageously expensive, but not when it's part of the production budget. This entire hour of programming would cost maybe a quarter of what they were paying one of the stars of *Friends* for an episode. The staff at the Amandari had no idea what we were doing with all the lights and cameras, but were extremely solicitous, happy to have such high-flying clients in the thick of such a very low season. My last supper, recorded in loving close-ups and soft, magenta light, was elegant and delicious, if a bit fussy for my taste. But it made for good television, framed by the burbling artificial brook and the vast jungle reaching up into the pink clouds of the purple sky. Jungle birds cawed obligingly and a gentle, humid breeze caressed me.

I missed the Princess. I missed my son.

I sent the crew off to their less luxurious digs in Ubud and went to bed. Alone. The bed was soft and welcoming, the setting perfect, but I couldn't notice. I wanted the Princess with me. I wanted my son. I wanted a life that mattered. And all I got was this lousy T-shirt.

The next morning was kissed by a quick wash of rain, leaving a damp scent of plumeria in its wake. The sun grinned and the jungle around me stretched and yawned awake with me. It was time. I bathed, shampooed, shaved to look my best for my performance. I couldn't eat breakfast.

The crew met me at the hotel and drove me down a deep chasm to a lonely, overgrown location at the bank of the Ayung. Moored to the shore was an intricately carved teak boat, the faces of Hanuman and the other Balinese gods mocking me with their smiles and goggle-eyes. A small coterie of locals was there with the boat, covering it in dried palm fronds and straw. The river emptied out into the brown, uninviting sea just a hundred or so yards away, as my crew set everything up.

Clouds scudded dutifully across the sky, perfecting the landscape for video. I helped the crew set up four cameras at the best possible angles and took one with me as I climbed onto the bed of palms at the centre of the craft. Each of the crewmembers shook my hand and waded back to their positions. The cameras got their final focus marks, the recorders started rolling and I took a can of gasoline from one of the locals and stood, pouring the acrid fluid all over the fronds. I had written a speech, but it seemed anti-climactic. Show it, don't tell it, Hitchcock said. Did I really have to put the bullshit in words? It all boiled down to two simple sentences, and that's what I said before I flicked my Bic:

'It all just hurts too much. I love you, Princess.'

Ignition. Lift off.

The flames erupted around me and licked me like hungry devils. The heat seared me and my first breaths of the sudden fire scorched my lungs. Though I could not breathe, I watched as the flames devoured my flesh, blistering and melting it in a stench of cooked meat. My body hair burned off in an acrid stink. My skin bubbled and blistered, expanding before it contracted, dripping fat on a fire that grew with each spatter. My meat went red before it charred black, and though my eyes burst, I could still see. I drifted high above the inferno with its